Circle of Ash

Sterling Magleby

News and more of the author's work at:

SterlingMagleby.com

reddit.com/r/Magleby

Contact the Author:

Sterlingktb@gmail.com

Cover Art By

Stephanie Brown

offbeatworlds.com

ISBN: 9798652350178

Para Carolina

Por creer y amar a través de toda la locura de escribir

ACKNOWLEDGEMENTS

This novel took the better part of five years to conceive, write, and finish. I had a lot of help along the way, from the critiques I received on the Scribophile website to the camaraderie of friends from a Salt Lake City writer's group to my wife Carolina's patience with my never-ending obsession. It's impossible with a book this size to credit every single person who helped me along the way, but there are a few to whom I'd like to extend special thanks, in no particular order:

Brandon Barrus, for his feedback on one of the earliest manuscripts;
Tracy Hickman, for his advice in navigating the modern literary world;
My brother and sister, Austin and Clarissa, for critiquing a number of early drafts and helping shape the book in its infancy;
Caroline Thaung, for insightfully critiquing the whole damn thing *twice;*
My mother Stephanie, for teaching me to read and write and then encouraging my love of both literally as long as I can remember;
Chet Sandberg, for his extensive critiques and in-person discussion;
My father Spencer, for teaching me how to work even at times it would be much easier not to;
Evan Kaiser, for feedback and exceptional encouragement;
All of the kind and excellent readers who have followed and encouraged my work on Reddit;
David Harr, for his tireless, prompt, and intelligent reviews
Nelson Lau, for encouragement, suggestions, and linguistic help
Judy Lynn, Heather Hayden, Nick Eli, Elle Turpitt, Becca Bell, Deirdre Huesmann, Vermilion Wilde, Ava Jones, Joseph Isaacs, and Hanna Day, for being exceptional critique partners who stuck with the story when it was a much more muddled creature;
Joshua Salois, for his early encouragement and feedback;
Kristin of the SLC Writer's group Just Write, for putting together a great community and the conditions for some of my best writing sessions;
and
You, for reading. None of this would be worth it without you.

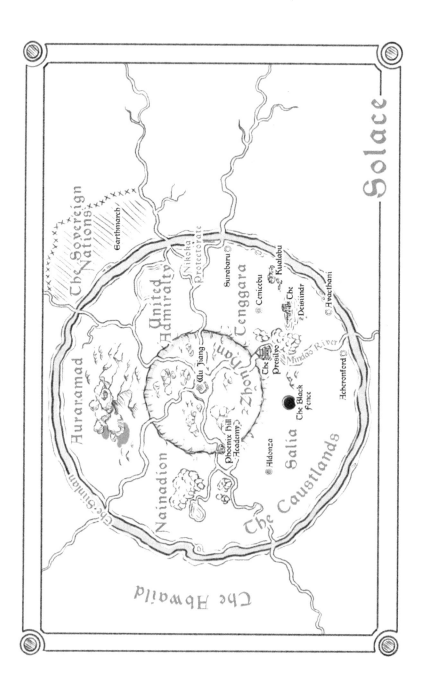

Solace

The Sovereign Nations

Earthmarch

United Admiralty

Nihoka Protectorate

Surabaru

Tenggara

Cemicebu

Kualabu

Che Deusindr

Avathani

Huraramad

Wu Jiang

ZhouJian

Che Presilpe

Mindoo River

Achronford

The Simlan

Phoenix Hill Academy?

The Black Fence

Nainadion

Hildonza

Salia

The Caustlands

The Abworld

Aftermath

She stood with her feet bathed in ashes. Her shoes were gone, gone somewhere, her clothing ragged. Embers bit at the air around her, flashing orange and grey and luminous green. Green. Wrong color, but why not, nothing else was right.

She knelt to lay him down, let him sink into the soft embrace of the cinder-bed that blanketed everything as far as she could see. He was heavier now that he was dead. She didn't look at him; she had seen enough already.

Instead she remained on her knees, and watched the newborn sea of ashes that stretched from the shore out to the darkened distance. It rippled with the motions of the strange sludge beneath: slow, heavy, moving with no wind, long sloshing sounds in the still air of aftermath. Here and there the cindergrey surface parted for a glimpse of pallid green light.

"No," she said, but the word was useless, already worn down to nothing. She weathered the crashing wave of despair, then rose to her feet and walked forward until the ground gave way to greasy muck which slushed between her toes. A deep breath led to a fit of coughing that doubled her over, and her long grey hair hung down as she bent, blackening the ends with soot.

She spat blood into the ash, and kept on walking until she was hip-deep and felt something seize her ankle. "No," she said again, and terror hurled all other feeling aside as she was dragged under. Not like this.

Chapter 1

Solace is a world full of strange things, but the Siinlan lies apart even so. Immense, impressive, deadly dangerous, bleakly beautiful. We understand very little about the Siinlan, even though in some sense it defines our world, encircling the whole of the Caustlands like a grey-green penumbra. With the notable (and, in this writer's opinion, regrettable) exception of the Sovereign Nations, every one of the Fallen live within its bounds. It is our bulwark, albeit a volatile one, against the endless unwelcome of the Abwaild beyond.

Yet its mysteries elude us. What throws the silver shimmer of its Veil so far up into the sky? What stirs the mire-sludge of its inner and outer rings? What drives the flow of the Gyring Ash through between them?

What sustains the things that drown undying beneath the surface of it all?

Perhaps these are things we are not yet meant to know. The Caustlands are a Divine gift to we the Fallen, after all, and the Divine must have Their reasons for this most emphatic of borders. True, the Caustlands can themselves be a place of perils, a mortal proving-ground, but Solace is a treacherous world and we must give thanks for this formidable boundary carved into her face.

- Elena Taishi, *And Solace Turned Toward Day*, 57 SE

Kualabu, Tenggara, The Caustlands, 341 SE

Dayang settled back into the covers as her mother turned the lantern flame from soft daytime white to warm bedtime orange. She tugged the sheets up to cover her small silk-clad shoulders, and looked round at the bedroom's familiar features, letting them calm the little knots of chaos in her mind:

Shelves full of well-loved books and echoplays.

Nurul's bed, neat and empty, bringing a pang of jealousy for her sister's later bedtime.

Her bamboo practice shield, given pride of place on the wall above her nightstand.

A pair of jeans half-flopped into the laundry basket.

She frowned as a thought crept into her settling mind and sat up, tall for an eight-year-old but still small against the big carved headboard.

"Can I stay up until Father gets back?"

Mother paused, then fiddled with the lantern knob for a few more moments without glancing Dayang's way. Her long black hair, still half-coiffed from the day, spilled over the fine silk of her nightgown.

"We don't know what time he'll be back. He might not even make it tonight."

"Why don't we know?" Dayang demanded. He was supposed to be back today, Mother had been saying so for days. And he'd been gone leading this caravan for weeks.

Mother's back stiffened. "It's too dangerous to send word ahead right now."

"Why?" she asked again.

A long pause. Dayang began to worry she'd asked a wrong question.

"Because of the attack, Dayang." Mother's voice was smaller than usual, drawn away.

That made no sense. The attack was over, had ended this morning. And the ashwights hadn't even gotten past the walls; that hadn't happened since Dayang was really little, when Grandmother and Grandfather had died. Dayang didn't remember it very well, just a few impressions and feelings. Grown-ups telling her not to be afraid. Mother crying in Father's arms. Prayers and strange distant noises.

Mother half-turned, seemed about to finally say something, when the distinct sound of a heavy door opening and thudding shut came from downstairs.

Dayang threw back the covers and sprang out of bed, halfway out the door before Mother could really react.

"Dayang! Come—"

But Dayang wasn't listening, and maybe Mother knew it because she cut off her own words with something like a sigh.

The hallway flew by, and then the stairs, leapt down two-at-a-time. She could hear Father's voice up ahead.

"...can't be a coincidence that they'd raid our caravan so soon after the attack on Kualabu." There was a worried urgency to his voice she couldn't remember hearing there before.

Dayang rounded a corner, very nearly barreled into the opposite wall, and stopped. Father was there in the parlor, looking dusty and tired against the room's spotless finery. His guard captain stood beside him, tall and stoic in her dull-scaled armor.

Father showed a moment's surprise at her sudden entrance, and then his big dark eyes crinkled at the edges and some of the weariness drew back from his face.

"Dayang!" A hint of restrained laughter in his voice. "What are you doing down here in your nightclothes?"

"I heard you come in and came down to see you." She thought this answer was pretty obvious, even though some bit at the back of her mind knew what he really meant. That didn't matter right now anyway. He was home!

"Well, I'm very happy to see you," Father answered. "But I need to finish talking to Aashni." His guard captain inclined her head but did not otherwise move or speak. Dayang heard her mother's footsteps going back up the stairs, but only spared a fleeting moment to wonder why.

"Something important?" Dayang asked. "About your caravan?"

Father raised his chin as if to nod, then stopped himself. "Sort of. But it's also about the town. About Kualabu."

"Okay," she said.

Father fixed her with an expectant gaze. Dayang gazed right back.

"Okay," Dayang said again. "You can talk."

Father laughed, and even Aashni's stern face showed a twitch of amusement.

"I wasn't asking for your permission, Dayang."

"I meant I could wait. While you talk. I'm good at waiting."

"That's good," Father said, and there was a sort of attempted sternness in his voice Dayang felt she could safely ignore. "I meant we need to finish talking alone. That's what people usually mean. It's implied. You'll have to learn this sort of thing as you get older."

"What's 'implied' mean?"

"Something that isn't said in exact words, but you still know it's there."

"Oh." Dayang frowned. "Like when you asked what I was doing down here."

Now Aashni did smile, and Father gave a small laugh.

"I'm glad to hear you admit it. Yes. Like that."

Dayang huffed, short and sharp, making her small shoulders sag before squaring again on the next breath. "Why can't I hear? I want to know." Unease crept up her chest to settle in her throat. What about the town could be so serious that they didn't want her to hear? The attack was over. Kualabu was fine. Mother had even been talking to a friend about how the town was "cleaning up" after, though they'd both looked a little ill discussing it. But everything was fine, it had to be okay. Father was home.

Father and Aashni exchanged glances. Father opened his mouth as if to speak, put on his giving-orders expression. But something else crept in and chased it off his face, something thoughtful.

Dayang narrowed her eyes. "I could've just listened where you can't see me, like Nurul does. Like she's probably doing right now. But I didn't."

Aashni turned away at that, and Dayang saw the pauldrons of her armor shaking along with the broad shoulders they covered.

Father sighed. "You shouldn't tell on your sister, Dayang."

"I'm not!" A stab of indignation struck deep, and she barely kept herself from stamping her foot on the intricate rug. "I just know how she is! You know too!"

Aashni was still facing away, slightly hunched, and Father hid his face in his hand for a moment.

"Sometimes politeness means not saying the things you know."

"Oh." Dayang dropped her gaze to the rug. "Sorry for being impolite." In truth she was still annoyed by what she thought was kind of a stupid rule, but she didn't want to shame Father in front of Aashni.

He looked at her for a long moment. "I suppose ignorance doesn't do much to protect you, does it?"

Dayang wasn't sure what he meant, or if he was even talking to her.

"You can stay, Dayang, but you have to be quiet until we're done."

She nodded, feeling the solemn weight of the concession, and tucked herself down onto the floor by the sofa.

Aashni glanced her way, then gave the slightest of shrugs before turning back toward Father. "I'd just gotten word back from Tunku when I caught up with you here, he says they managed to chase down and, ah," she flicked her gaze Dayang's direction, "*defeat* one of the Pelo bandits from the caravan raid. Only he wasn't a Pelo at all, just some Salían lowlife with facepaint and shoddy costuming."

Pelos. The strange people who lived on the other side of the Siinlan, out in the Abwaild. Not Fallen, like regular people. Weird silver markings over their skin, spoken of as if they weren't quite human. Which meant this story was getting exciting, maybe.

Father tapped his fingers against the carved wood of a corner-column. "So their scout was telling the truth. Which makes sense, why in Hell would Pelos risk crossing the Gyring Ash *and* the Mire on both sides of the Siinlan just to raid a caravan?"

Both grownups fell silent at this. Dayang tried to picture it in her head. A group of strange people in even stranger clothing, wading into the deep grey-green sludge of the Ashlit Mire from the yet stranger landscape of the Abwaild. Making it through the endless embertrees, finding a way across the slow goopy flow of the Gyring Ash before having to cross the Mire all over again on the Caustlands side. It was sort of thrilling, but her imagination wasn't quite up to the task; she'd only ever seen either the Abwaild or the Gyring Ash in pictures.

"It also begs the question," Father continued at last, "of why they'd bother with the disguise?"

"I really don't know," Aashni replied.

Silence again. Aashni took a long swig from the vacuum flask at her belt. Coffee, strong enough that the scent wafted across the parlor.

Dayang stirred with questions unasked, tugging her knees against her chest and rocking back against the wallpaper until finally it became too much and one of her questions escaped restraint.

"The caravan got attacked by Salíans pretending to be Pelos? I thought Salíans were friendly." She'd seen Salíans in town before. Adventurers, mostly, Mother had said. You couldn't really tell by looking, they came in all sorts of colors, including exotic pale shades of hair and eye. Dayang had liked to run up and talk to them when she was younger, but had stopped after enough scoldings on the risks and rudeness of pestering strangers.

Her question earned her a frown from Father, but a brief one, and his voice dropped into a familiar lecturing groove. Lesson time, then, which was good because it meant she wouldn't get in trouble for talking. "A pause doesn't mean we're done talking, Dayang, but no, Salíans aren't always friendly, just like Tenggarans aren't always friendly. Most of the bandits we deal with are from right here in Tenggara. Every country will have all kinds of people in it. Salía's no different. You can't judge people solely by where they're from."

Dayang considered this, and the way Mother sometimes talked about foreigners, then set that aside and furrowed her brow. "How did you know he was Salían? They all look different."

"So do the Pelos, actually," Father said. "Different groups in different parts of the Abwaild. The Abwaild is immense, it covers all of Solace apart from the Caustlands where we and the Salíans and almost all the other Fallen live."

"All of Solace? The whole world?" Dayang asked. It was hard to imagine, but she tried, picturing the grey-green expanse of the Siinlan right outside the town walls, then strange endless wilderness stretching out beyond.

Aashni cut in with a slight smile. "Yes, the whole world, except for the Caustlands. And we knew the bandit was Salían because he was carrying some papers written in Ambérico and Gentic."

"What's Ambérico?" Gentic was easy, she was learning it in school. They spoke it all over the Caustlands, her teachers said, and so she should know it too.

"A language mostly just spoken in Salía," Father said. He paused, frowned, gazed down at his gloved hand. "And parts of the Sovereign Nations, but they're a long way off."

"Oh," Dayang said. She opened her mouth, decided she'd pushed her luck enough, and closed it again.

"Anyway," Aashni said, "these bandits-playing-Pelo—or whatever the Hell they really were—seemed to think our caravan would be a quick hit-

and-run. On their way somewhere else." She glanced at Dayang, then at Father, and raised an eyebrow. He nodded, his face tight.

Aashni let out a deep breath and continued. "We think they were on their way here. They must have heard about the ashwight attack and figured Kualabu would have all its guards—and any mercenary help scrounged from adventurers—concentrated on the walls nearest the Siinlan, watching the Ashlit Mire in case of another wave. We warned the town immediately, of course. Probably the bandits intercepted our warning and so never attacked. Only interested in an easy raid."

Aashni glanced her way again, and Dayang wondered. *She's explaining a lot for me, because Father wants me to learn and so she's doing it even though it also makes Father look sad.*

Father nodded. "Climb an undefended wall, hit a few locations they've scouted in advance, and leave."

Dayang jumped to her feet. "Bandits can't just get over the wall! Why do we have them all around the town if that can happen?"

"Usually," Aashni said, "they're patrolled by guards." She glanced a question at Father, who nodded and continued for her.

"And humans aren't really the reason we have the walls."

Dayang suppressed a shudder. She thought about the Ashlit Mire, and nightmares, and things that didn't need to breathe. Thought about Mother crying in Father's arms, and a casket that was nailed shut. The feel of a sparring-stick gripped in her hand. "Oh," she said in a small voice.

Father's smile was warm, reassuring, still a little sad. He walked over and scooped her up into his arms, and she went willingly.

"I think it's time for bed." He carried her up to her bedroom, tucked her in. Dayang stayed silent; her head was full of thoughts even as Father walked away from the bed and shut off the lamp.

He paused in the doorway, a shadow in the meager light from the hall. "How's your training? Have you been practicing?" There was a mix of emotions in his voice she wasn't really sure she wanted to pick apart.

Dayang nodded, feeling a small surge of pride. "I can hold the shield up for twice as long now! And do my practice-forms all the way through with the special weights!" It had been a goal she'd looked toward to what felt like forever, a constant small hunger, a tiny itch. Those practices had been hard, too, full of pain and bewilderment, but she had never asked to quit.

Father smiled, inclined his head, his big dark eyes searching her, then flicking aside to empty air as his smile faded.

"That's good, Dayang."

Chapter 2

Seven months and seven days
Wisdom guide you in her ways
Fortune touch the life that grows
Father share from all he knows

- Traditional chant for expectant mothers

Presilyo Monastery, Inoue Island, The Caustlands, 340s SE

The rosary was the first clear thing Sanyago could remember. The rosary, and the monk. Before, there had been a man, and sadness, and unfamiliar places. These were wisps in a haze, but the monk and the rosary were clear. Exceptionally so, as Sanyago must have been very young, old enough to walk and understand but speak only simply. Still, he remembered the monk and the rosary. He saw them sometimes in dreams.

Like this one. He stirred on his bunk, turned over, stretching his legs and then pulling them in close.

The rosary was red, paint spread over the fine grain of big wooden beads, swinging carelessly from the thick short neck of the monk who held him. Sanyago grabbed at it, catching it after a couple of tries, tugging.

The big man laughed, gently uncurling small chubby hands with his own large, gnarled fingers. "So ready to say your prayers, little one?" He slid one bead back and forth along its string as Sanyago watched. "We will get you your own." The Ambérico he spoke came accented, its tone and rhythms strange.

Sanyago stared up at the big kind face, all laugh lines and jowls and dark, knowing eyes. His dreaming self recalled the rustle of sky-blue robes as the monk shifted Sanyago's small weight against his own expansive torso, the feel of hard strength under a cushion of fat. The scent of incense, of sweat, a hint of last meal's spices on the man's breath. The wide, almost impish smile, set against skin like weathered copper; the rocking motion caused by the man's limp as he carried Sanyago over long shadows cast by a low sun.

"Come then, little one. Let us meet your new brothers."

The dream shifted, broke into fragments which slipped his mind's grasp when examined too closely:

Blue-clad monks, coaxing movements, playing games, giving graceful demonstration.

Other children, faces and eyes of every color.

Seven boys, all older, all larger, jostling and chattering and laughing and fighting.

Being shoved and mocked and ignored.

A great babble of languages uncomprehended—

Now there was a monk, staggering along the pathways of the monastery. His left arm ended in a raw but bloodless stump. He cried out in a ragged voice, something about Outside, something about Below. The words made Sanyago's mind feel bloated and smeared...

He shuddered hard against his thin mattress, murmuring half-formed words through half-open lips. Other sleepers stirred around him, answering with murmurs of their own, pained and confused. A few low moans. One boy cried out and woke panting just as Sanyago fell back into deepest sleep.

... and the monk was tackled by others, silenced, dragged away. Sanyago was pretty sure he was not supposed to see this. The memory cut into his dream-flow like a glass knife, clear and sharp. It shattered when dropped. Sanyago could not bear to look at it, and the stream of fragments continued as though it had never broken off.

—music, sung in great soaring chorus.

Bits of scripture and prayer, talk about the Triune Path he would now follow.

Endless distinctions between forbidden Ragado and permitted Silado.

11

The smell of old wood and damp stone.

The sharp, lingering odors of eight boys in close quarters.

Four double bunks in a small room; low ceilings and dim, flickering hedgeflame lamps.

These memories were nearly as hazy as the shadows cast by those cheap, torn-paper lanterns, but their emotions threaded clear and strong through his sleeping mind:

The loneliness of being an outcast in his own room.

The frustration of language, struggling to master the Gentic that everyone used when they had no other tongue in common.

The happiness he felt when he found an adult he could chatter with, or at, in his native Ambérico. He heard other boys speak it too, sometimes, but never the ones from his room with whom he lived, ate, and learned. He would approach them, smiling and eager, and their faces would push him away even when their hands did not.

Alone, with never a moment of solitude.

Sanyago woke, becoming slowly aware of the wooden lattice that supported the empty bunk above, barely there in the deep late dark. He sat up, memories still piling through his mind, shaking his head as he tried to sort them into some sort of waking sense.

He remembered all the times he'd sat here with his thoughts, wishing there was someone he could talk to without being scoffed at for his awkward forays into Gentic, thinking how his one attempt at imitating the rising, falling, swooping singsong of Common with two of the boys from Zhon Han hadn't gone any better. They had laughed at him, sent rapid mocking words back and forth among themselves. He had recoiled from their laughter, retreated into himself.

Sanyago leaned forward, wincing at the small creak of metal and wood, pausing to make sure it didn't interrupt any of the even breaths and erratic snores around him. There was a hint of moonlight through the window facing his bunk, just enough to leave traces of blue and silver in the darkness of the room. Both moons must be out on the same side of the sky.

He leaned back again, remembering better things. Chores were not so bad. Song was wonderful, etching words in the air with his voice, feeling them drawn into converging choral focus. But learning was best of all. After some frustration he'd begun to pick up Gentic more quickly, and had learned to read, Gentic and Ambérico both in their shared alphabet:

Sanyago found the books to be a welcome distraction from the crowded seclusion of his room; they never rebuked him for his curiosity. He found a fascination with maps, too, poring over them, imagining other places and how to get there.

He was an apt pupil in these book-studies, but it was in his other training that he really excelled. Bright, his teachers called him. Promising. Graceful. He mastered ways to stand, ways to move, ways to think about moving. Mastered them quickly, felt them in his bones, kept them tumbling through his head. He took pleasure in this, but his pleasure hid a sharp edge. The monks would glance his way when speaking to each other, gesture, exchange stone-faced nods. They expected something of him, something heavy, and he did not know what it was.

Sanyago went back to sleep, and dreamed of practice-sets performed within a circle of shadowed faces.

The next day four of the oldest boys left his room, and only three came in to replace them. Vasili, long and lanky, perhaps the palest person Sanyago had ever seen. Andhlib, compact and gruff, with skin the color of freshly-turned earth from the monastery gardens. Mauricio, an olive-skinned, wiry boy who spoke Ambérico, though his accent was strange. The shared language gave him a moment's hope, but Mauricio replied to his questions with clipped answers, and turned away. It wasn't hard to guess why; Sanyago was still a favorite target for the other boys, small and strange and too closely watched by the teachers.

Weeks went by. Sanyago threw himself into his learning, distracted himself from his loneliness, his place outside. But he held on to a small reserve of hope, and it surged when he learned a new boy was coming to their room. A transfer from another group, the teachers said. He had come to the Presilyo at a later age than most, and they were to be kind to him. A Salían, they were told. Sanyago was excited; he knew that many Salíans spoke Ambérico. Sanyago thought he had probably come from Salía himself, though this was not a permitted question and so he could not know for sure.

The new boy came the next day. Just a little older than Sanyago and tall for his age of perhaps six, Staafaen was nearly as big as the four senior boys still bunking in the room. His skin was a deep, even black, much darker even than Sanyago's sun-baked brown, and his ash-grey eyes made for an almost startling contrast. He stood a moment in the center of the

13

little room after being herded in, looked round, caught Sanyago's gaze.

"Hello," he said quietly. "My name is Staafaen."

The name sounded Gentic too, though the accent had a hint of Ambérico to it. Sanyago smiled.

"Staff-ehn," he repeated, carefully sounding out each syllable. He still had a little trouble with the nasal Gentic 'aa' and breathy 'eh'.

"It's very Gentic, I know." Staafaen said. "People just call me 'Laris' most of the time. I used to be a lot skinnier before I came here."

Sanyago thought about that, then grinned as he got it. Laris, short for "Larguío," an Ambérico word meaning tall and thin. "Mine is Sanyago," he said in Ambérico. "Pleasure meeting you, Laris." The teachers had been very insistent on teaching formal manners of late.

Laris flashed him a wide, brilliant smile; it split the steady solemnity of his carved-onyx features, genuine and rare. "You speak Ambérico?" he answered in that same language. "I thought you might." His accent had a strange flavor to it, but was clearly native. "My Gentic is good but I don't want to speak it *all* the time." His face went solemn again. "My parents spoke Gentic sometimes, before they... died. But they mostly spoke Ambérico. I remember..." His face contracted into silence.

Sanyago nodded, looked around a bit uneasily. The topic of parents was taboo among the boys, none of whom wanted to contemplate what they'd never had or dearly missed. But Mauricio wasn't listening and no one else spoke Ambérico, so he went on. "I don't remember my parents. I think maybe they were Salían, like you."

Laris returned the nod, and they both fell into silence for a time, regarding each other, a little awkward in the shadow of broken taboo. Sanyago thought about some of the things the monks liked to say about attachments, and went over the Litany of Letting Go in his mind, as he'd been taught. *I release the grasp of my desire. Attachment falls away. My want drifts on by.* He wasn't sure it worked, he never was.

Laris broke the silence, eyes gone wide in sudden excitement.

"I heard your name from Movements Master Castillo, when he was talking with another teacher. He said you'd almost mastered the Seventh Quickened Chaos." Laris pronounced each word of the practice-set's Gentic name in careful cadence.

Sanyago grinned wide, bouncing up and down on the balls of his feet.

"Yeah! I think so, anyway. It's my favorite one. I like at the end how

14

you can feel it just behind and around your arms and legs, kind of guiding them for you. You want me to show you sometime?" He felt intensely pleased that a teacher had taken enough notice of his achievements to mention them to someone else.

Laris nodded slowly, eyes full of bright energy even as he maintained his steady stillness.

"I'm looking forward to sparring, but I want to be ready. I want all the help I can get." His voice held none of the resentment Sanyago sometimes heard from other students, just matter-of-fact determination.

"Next time we have free-play, I'll show you."

Laris bowed, one hand curled over his closed fist. "Good, thank you. The Chaos sets aren't my best but I want to learn them as well as I can. Foundations Master Yeong says it's almost as important to know your opponent's moves as your own."

Sanyago ran his forefinger thoughtfully along the socket of one dark brown eye, glancing at the other boys. A few seemed annoyed at not being able to understand the conversation. Laris hadn't seemed to notice, still talking excitedly about his training. Sanyago leaned forward, raising his voice so the rest of the room would hear.

"You're excited to be in our class, then?" he asked in Gentic, looking Laris in the eye before shifting his gaze meaningfully toward the other boys.

The flow of enthusiastic Ambérico halted. Laris looked at him a moment, then bowed toward the other boys.

"My apologies, brothers," Laris said in his precise, deliberate Gentic. "I'm excited to join you. I was just...just happy to speak my...parents' language." He winced at the last two words, acknowledging that he'd broken the taboo, but the other boys simply inclined their heads; this was clearly a painful admission. They glanced at each other, then back at Laris. Sanyago thought he could read their faces. *Strange little Sanyago making friends with the new boy, this Staafaen, so tall and serious*? they seemed to ask, and then answered; *Better be careful now.*

For the first time he could remember, Sanyago's hopes did not recede. Maybe this would be an end to feeling alone.

Their new brother settled in, and time marched on. Practice, chores, meals, sleep, prayers, lectures, lessons, sermons. Sometimes snow, sometimes fallen leaves, sometimes sun, often heat, often cold. Laris was there through it all, he and Sanyago together in the easy, open way of very young friendship, any storms passing quickly and without much fuss.

Laris was serene during meditations where Sanyago was antsy, questioning in lessons where Sanyago was accepting, often listening and watching when Sanyago wanted to be speaking and doing. He was always much taller than Sanyago as they grew, always quieter, though he was by no means shy. They both got along well enough with the other boys, here a game, there an argument, here a crude joke shared in low voices, but for Sanyago, Laris was the one constant.

The year came when they had all turned eight, or as close as anyone could tell, since most of them had only guesses for birthdays, including Sanyago himself. They all gathered together for Foundation Master Yeong's training, the first of the day. It was a brightening morning in early spring, and they were doing their best to stay warm, standing in line under orders to keep still. Sanyago's muscles tensed and twitched, moving just enough to eke out a little heat but not invite a grown-up's wrath.

Master Yeong arrived precisely on time, as always, fifteen minutes after they had formed themselves into a line, as always. He walked up and down the row of students, the hint of a smile on his round and weathered features.

"You have reached a most significant marker in the long course of your training, Novices," he said in his warm, even voice. "Today, we put what you have learned together. All the movements, the balance, the quick reactions, the awareness. Today take your first real steps toward walking the Triune Path as true fighting Somonei."

Chapter 3

I once asked a man along the side of the road where he was going. It was a sad little road, thin on the ground and undernourished by a famine of travelers.

"I am going to the highway between Cenicebu and Surabaru," he said. "This path does not lead anywhere else, and I do not intend to leave it."

I pointed out that the road also led back to the unremarkable village behind us. This was pedantic, but I was bored, as it really was a very lonely road. My pack mule was not a very excellent conversationalist. Also he smelled.

"There is no need to be pedantic," the man replied. "Obviously I am not going that way."

This was true, though in fact he was not going any way very quickly. My mule was an almost maliciously slow animal, but we still had caught up easily. In fact the cussed creature actually seemed annoyed as we slowed to converse, so sluggish was the man's pace.

"Are you going to Cenicebu, then, or to Surabaru?" I asked, pulling on the halter of my burdensome burden-bearer. "Continuing on into Salia or Nikoka? Heading toward Zhon Han, perhaps?"

"Right now I am not going to any of those places. I am going to the highway between Cenicebu and Surabaru." His tone was infuriatingly sure of itself.

"Surely now you are the one being pedantic."

"I am not. I am going to the highway between Cenicebu and Surabaru."

"You are meeting someone at the crossroads?"

Calling the spot where this anemic little road met the Migiro Highway a "Crossroads" was maybe laying it on a little thick. I could not imagine it as a place where anything momentous could ever occur. Certainly neither god nor demon would show up there to purchase a soul like they do in Salian legends.

"Perhaps I will meet someone there," he said, "but I have made no such arrangements. I do not intend to linger once I reach the highway."

I was feeling exasperated, of course I was. Even so, I tried not to show it. I hadn't talked to anyone in more than a day. Finding inventive new profanity to hurl at a mule does not count.

"Well, I for my part am going to Surabaru, to avail myself of the excellent market there."

"No," he said, almost off-hand. "You are not going to Surabaru. You are going to the Migiro Highway, same as I am. Where you are going and where you plan to be are not the same thing."

I fumbled for a few moments before finally finding a response. The words I flung at this insufferable traveler were not quite as creative as the ones I had come up with for my smelly companion on the endless road, but time does limit us all. I then took my leave of this irritating dispenser of wisdom. I think I actually managed to get a trot out of my mule.

And speaking of that damned beast, he was snake-bit and died before we even got to the highway. I had to go back to the village for help.

- Qailah Percaya, *Journeys and What-the-Hells,* 327 SE

Kualabu, Tenggara, The Caustlands, 345 SE

"Your shield is not an afterthought, Dayang."

Dayang Marchadesch looked up at her teacher. He towered over his twelve-year-old student, looming even more than usual as she lay sprawled amongst the fragments of her training-shield.

Dayang shook her head, still half-rubbing, half-cradling her bruised forearm while doing her best not to cry. She pulled her legs in, knowing she should attempt to get back up. Fortunately, her muscles had remembered enough of their training to keep her from falling directly onto her tailbone. Unfortunately, all the sinew and bone between her calves and lower back seemed to have taken the shock instead. None of it wanted to cooperate, but she insisted, pressing her jaw in against itself.

She clambered up onto one knee, trying to stand. *It hurts*, she thought but did not say. Saying would mean trouble.

"Yes, Guru Hang," she said at last, tasting the coppery roughness in her throat from breathing too hard for too long.

"Stand faster," he said. His voice was soft—but soft, she knew, did not mean gentle. He was absolutely not above hitting her when she was down. *A real opponent will see a fall as an opportunity, not an occasion for pity*, he'd say.

Watching his sparring-sticks warily, Dayang scrambled quickly to her feet, pushing through the hurt.

"No," he said. "You do not watch your opponent's weapons. He will use them to deceive you. Do not watch his eyes either. A wise enemy will misdirect you with his gaze. And if there is another attack..."

Then the enemy won't be human anyway. She nodded, shifting her attention to the movements of his frame, doing her best to read his body language. Hang Che was deft and quick for such a big man; broad as well as tall, the dark-bronze skin exposed by his sleeveless vest showing heavy muscle. A few scars crisscrossed over slightly aging flesh, souvenirs from his long adventuring career.

They circled each other, sketching a small ring within the airy expanse of the training-hall. Dayang kept her gaze on his hips, his shoulders, flicking her attention upwards every so often, just in case his lined and weathered face happened to give anything away. She didn't know how old he was, but guessed he must be passing through early middle age, perhaps in his seventies or eighties; his shoulder-length black hair was only just starting to show streaks of grey. Age had certainly not begun to impede him in any way she could see.

"Better," he said. "Perhaps in a few more years you'll be ready to at least be useful, if the walls are breached again."

Dayang kept her feet moving carefully, center of gravity held lower, all reaction to the idea of another attack tamped down.

"You must take care not to focus too fully on that particular threat," Hang Che continued. "Even those parts of the Caustlands that are far away from the Siinlan can be dangerous." He smiled, a stone-wolf thing that didn't reach his eyes. "They are often full of people, just to start with. Now pick up your shield again."

"It is broken, Guru Hang." She dared not glance away to look at the bamboo remnants.

"So? Things break. They are still usually better than nothing."

She kept her eyes on him, scuttling over to the two largest chunks and crouching to scoop them up. She managed to get her arm through both straps and grip one, though each strap now belonged to a separate piece and they flopped about her hand and forearm.

"Your shield is broken because you paid more attention to your weapon. Your arm is hurting because you neglected it in favor of the other." He stepped in and jabbed at her with one of his sparring-sticks.

She attempted to deflect, but was unable to get the angle exactly right given the bamboo shard's unsteady independence. The blow bounced off in an unpredictable upward direction, making her duck and flinch. The delicate bones of her hand smarted and immediately began to ache.

Hang Che's other sparring-stick whipped around, coming to rest just short of thumping into her neck. "And now you have neglected your weapon-arm in favor of your shield, and you are dead."

Dayang bit down to keep from swearing, then nodded. "Could I not also jump back, or duck under, or step in?"

He smiled thinly, tapped her on the clavicle with his stick. "Good. You are considering options. You could, but in this situation, would these have been ideal moves?"

She thought a moment, then shook her head. "No, Guru Hang. But 'ideal moves are not always possible'," she said, reciting one of his favorite sayings back to him. "Especially with a broken shield," she finished, letting just a hint of frustration touch her voice.

He tilted his head to one side, then the other, his smile compressing a bit more. "Again good, but also misleading. A parry would still have been better there, and you know it. You must extend your awareness to all aspects of the fight at all times. Soon, when you begin to train with armor, you will have to learn to keep it positioned, use it to deflect. And always you must be training to accept a blow correctly when it is inevitable."

She stood stock-still, considering her stance, his stance, their previous movements and momentum, their likely course, letting them run back and forth through her mind. She nodded again. "Yes, Guru Hang. I should have parried down and to the side…" she demonstrated with the sparring-stick in her right hand, "…and then stepped forward on the left to attack with the broken shield."

He allowed his smile to spread, just a little, and stepped back. "Not too bad. But talk is easy. Tomorrow, you will have a new shield, and you will have to show as well as tell."

She winced, rubbing at the almost unbearable ache that had settled into her arm.

He waved the injury off. "Practice what you've been taught, and it will be better by then, or at least well enough to train with. You don't want to be one of those highborn dilettantes with lots of expensive training and no idea how to deal with the realities of an actual fight. You should be fervently grateful for every bruise, scrape, and cut you have to push past."

"Yes, Guru Hang," she said reflexively. She had just enough time to raise her sundered shield when he slid forward to strike, but she was not fast enough, and only managed to deflect the attack on her left. His other stick caught her sharply on the bony ridge of her weapon-arm.

Smack.

She cried out, as much in frustration as in pain.

He must have seen anger in her eyes, because he scowled in return and rested the smoothly-sanded end of his stick against the tip of her nose.

Her sparring stick lay in the dust, fallen from nerveless fingers.

"Do not say 'yes' if you do not mean it. Do not say 'yes' if you have not really heard."

Dayang let her breath out, shoulders falling then quickly squaring again. She twisted her forearm, flexed her hand, resisting the urge to rub at the spot the blow had landed.

"I understand, Guru Hang," she replied, this time looking him square in the eye.

"Good." He glanced over her shoulder, lifting his chin. "Ah. Your little friend is here." His smile was cool. Amused.

She followed his gaze, turning herself round completely so he wouldn't be able to read the spike of annoyance on her face at his condescension. Dayang knew without looking that it was Sara. She supposed the "little" description did fit; at eleven, Sara was much smaller than she, still awaiting the beginnings of adolescent growth while at twelve Dayang was well into her own.

And even when they were younger, Sara had been tiny and delicate next to Dayang's sturdy, athletic frame, her calm careful temperament contrasting Dayang's headstrong brashness. Still, they had been close friends since starting school together at the ages of five and six, and any slight toward her made Dayang bristle.

Not that Sara had noticed; she was too busy staring at the nasty welt Dayang had received, eyes gone wide and one curled hand held halfway over her mouth.

She really does look small, Dayang thought, noticing how the elaborately-carved beams of the training hall arched high over her friend's head. *But that doesn't mean she's a "little girl."*

"Your friend will be fine, girl," Hang Che said coolly. His smile was sardonic, his eyes dismissive. "She's almost finished with her training session and has a great deal to practice and ponder. Don't you, Dayang?"

Dayang turned back to face him and bowed. "Yes, Guru Hang."

"Very good. You are dismissed, Miss Marchadesch. Clean up your shield before you go." He turned on his heel and strode out of the hall, brushing past Sara without so much as a glance.

Dayang set her jaw as she crouched to collect the long jagged shards.

After finishing the mind-numbing hunt for every tiny piece, Dayang dumped a small armful of bamboo debris into the rubbish heap. She stood there in thought for a moment, then walked back round the corner to the training hall's carved-lattice double doors where Sara stood waiting.

"Sorry about Guru Hang," Dayang said, crossing her arms over each other to rub hands over battered flesh and bone.

"Sorry for what? You're the one he hit with sticks for two hours." Sara's teasing tone and wry crooked smile failed to mask a touch of concern.

Dayang cocked her head, stopped and stretched experimentally to see just how many of her muscles complained. It was a full chorus. She winced. "I'm used to that, but at least he doesn't talk down to me. The way he—"

Sara laughed, putting a hand gently on Dayang's sore but sound upper arm. "I don't care. I'm just some girl and he's a town legend."

Dayang sighed, and let her back slump for just an instant before straightening it again. The second part was certainly true; Hang Che and a handful of old comrades had decided to retire here in Kualabu when their adventuring days were done. She wasn't sure how much truth there was in the endless stories that circulated about their exploits, but she did know they'd saved countless lives the last time ashwights had breached the walls.

"Hmmmph." Dayang could still hear the cool near-contempt in her teacher's voice, see that insufferable little smile on his face.

Sara snorted, kicking a small smooth stone back and forth between her feet as they sauntered down Kualabu's narrow, hilly streets toward home. It was a day off school, and younger children playing on the pavement stopped their games to glance at the two girls. Grown-ups sitting out on porches offered lazy afternoon greetings, raising glasses of tea or water.

Tired as she was, Dayang let Sara lead the way, and watched her black, perfectly-straight hair swing back and forth over the small of her back. Straight black hair was a feature shared by most of Kualabu's native residents—the human ones, anyway—but Dayang had always envied Sara's in particular. It was glossy and fine, always seeming to flow just right down her back. Dayang's own charcoal hair was quite thick, and while straight it never wanted to go all in the same direction. She generally had to braid it back behind her ears, as she'd done today.

Not that hair was the only difference, not by a long way. Sara had the sort of fine-boned features you saw in illustrations of Old World legends, while Dayang's were best described as "strong." And Dayang had her father's large dark eyes; Sara's were smaller, thinner, colored a striking golden-brown. Sara was still too young to draw attention from boys—young enough to be dismissed off-hand by the likes of Hang Che—but Dayang had heard people talk about how Sara would be a great beauty as she grew into womanhood.

They didn't say that about Dayang. But she loved her friend, and jealousy would only get in the way of things that really mattered. Sara had an easy, soft-spoken way with people Dayang lacked, was capable of a sort of deep kindness that sometimes made Dayang ashamed of her own somewhat prickly nature.

After the long silence, Sara stopped and turned. "It's nice of you to care so much about what he said, but really, I don't. If it annoys you that much I can just stay away from your training sessions."

Dayang frowned. "I don't want you to think you're not welcome. Best friends, right?"

Sara flashed her a bright smile and hugged her. Dayang groaned theatrically.

"Yeah, I know, you're sore." Sara pulled away, giggling.

They spent the rest of the walk to Dayang's house chattering about school, games, parents, siblings, favorite books and least favorite people—

23

and, of course, the echoplay Dayang had received for her twelfth birthday, a Wuxia adventure story she wanted Sara to watch with her. "It's awesome!" Dayang told her. "The combat is really, really well done, and they had a really good cast for this one. Father picked it up on his last trip to Zhon Han."

Sara nodded eagerly. Dayang knew her friend didn't quite match her own level of enthusiasm when it came to well-choreographed martial arts, but the chance to watch something new that didn't come from Kualabu's somewhat sparsely-stocked public library was exciting on its own, and Sara had a boundless interest in anything new and current. She even, she'd once confessed with a shrug and a smile, read the newspapers every day. Front to back, even the boring parts. Since then Dayang would listen to her news summaries, and she'd listen to Dayang wax enthusiastic about training and techniques.

As they neared the Marchadesch residence's expansive front porch, Dayang spotted her older brother Pandikar sitting out on a big bamboo chair. He was whittling, the fine bladed carving-knife looking absurdly delicate in his large hand.

"Hey, Dayadesch," he called out in a singsong voice before looking back down at his work. His tongue stuck out the corner of his mouth a little as he worked his knife over some of the piece's finer details.

"Hey, Pandimarch," she replied amiably, climbing the short stairs with Sara. "Whatcha carvin'?"

"Saw-handle. Trying to get the runes just right. Isra says the form itself isn't what's important as long as people can read them, but I don't want it to look sloppy." He paused, flicking a tiny curl of wood from the tip of his knife.

"She still gives you a swat every time you push the knife too far?" Dayang asked, and Pandikar laughed, nodding without looking up.

"Yep." He made a series of delicate scraping motions with his blade before lifting the oak handle almost to his nose to squint at it. "But I don't make that mistake very often anymore, so these days it's mostly just annoyed looks. She's good at those."

Isra Shinawatra was Pandikar's artisan-master. This, to Dayang's mind, made her basically his Hang Che, as they'd both been hired by Father. She doubted her brother had any bruises from his Lingmao mentor, though. Isra was a very small person, and Pandikar, at the age of fifteen, already stood taller than Father. Dayang knew that Pandikar had some training along more martial lines from when he was younger, but he didn't really have the disposition for it and Father hadn't pushed him to continue.

"It's so pretty." Sara leaned over to examine the piece more carefully. This was true enough, as Pandikar was a talented artist with his carving tools, but Dayang thought it was also true that Sara had a harmless crush on her brother. Sara hadn't mentioned it, so neither would she, and of course he was clueless.

Pandikar's broad smile at the compliment brightened his big-boned features, and he turned the halfway-finished handle round so his admirer could see it from every angle. "Thanks, Sara." He looked up at Dayang and frowned, dark eyes taking her in with a slight arch of his thick black eyebrows.

"Daaaaamn, Dayadesch," he said, cocking his head. "Hang Che really put you to the test today, huh?"

"I held my own," Dayang replied, a little tetchily.

"I'm sure you did." Pandikar was maybe the only older person she knew who could say something like that with absolutely no hint of condescension. When he wanted to, anyway, and wasn't upholding his sacred older-brother duty to tease.

She smiled, shrugged, suddenly feeling a lot younger than twelve in the pure pleasure of praise.

Enjoy the feeling while it lasts, a sardonic piece of her mind advised. *You'll almost certainly see your sister later.*

"Anyway," she said, gesturing toward the front door with her chin. "Who's home?"

"Father is meeting the head of a caravan that came into town late. Our illustrious elder sister is out seeing people and places more interesting than ordinary minds like ours could even *begin* to understand."

Sara snickered, and Pandikar flashed her a lopsided smile Dayang was sure would haunt her poor friend's dreams for weeks.

"Mother is here, though." He waved the saw handle in the direction of Dayang's forearms. "Might wanna cover those up, Dayadesch, or she and Father are probably gonna have, uh, words."

Dayang grimaced and nodded. She didn't relish the thought of trying to sleep through a parental shouting match. "It's too warm for me to have any reason for wearing a jacket, though. Can't just grab something from the entry closet and pretend I was wearing it the whole time."

Pandikar considered this, scraping long, delicate ribbons of wood off one side of the handle, creating a small, untidy nest on the lap of his faded blue jeans. "Hmmm. You'll have to go in through the back way. Stick your training clothes in the laundry bin and change, then tell Mother you didn't want to come in the front all filthy."

Dayang glanced down at her clothes, which weren't actually due for a cleaning yet, then gave her brother a quizzical look. She'd sweat some, sure, but that's what her undershirt and shorts were there for, and of course she'd be washing *those*.

Pandikar laughed, shaking his head, and flicked some of the wood shavings in her direction. They landed in the unbraided part of her shoulder-length black hair, still a bit tangled and sweaty from her training session. "Aw, come on, Dayadesch, think. Of course they're not dirty enough, so what? You think Mother will know what you've put in the bin?"

Dayang wrinkled her nose at him as she picked the tiny flecks of wood out one-by-one, then nodded. Mother was not going to know; Mother had never washed a garment in her entire life and was unlikely to start now. That's what the help was for.

"Yeah, okay. I think I can get the bruises to fade by morning if I really concentrate on my meditations tonight. Save us all some grief." She turned to leave, then sighed and turned round again. "Thanks, Pandimarch."

"Thanks, Pandikar!" Sara echoed, and followed Dayang round the spiral-carved corner pillar to the back porch. Mother must have been in the parlor; they made it up the back stairs without seeing her. Dayang felt a tiny knot of tension loosen and slip away as she opened the door to the spacious bedroom she shared with her sister Nurul.

It only took Dayang a few moments to change, toss her not-very-dirty outer practice clothing into the laundry basket, and make a half-hearted effort to cover it with two pairs of jeans and a panoply of socks excavated from the bottom. She'd dig them out later, before the housekeeper could complain to mother about Dayang trying to make her wash clean clothing.

Her undershirt and shorts she left on, deciding she'd wear a long house-robe over them. No point changing until she had the chance to take a proper bath. She *had* washed her face at least, and taken a few great uncivilized gulps of water directly from the bathroom sink's faucet.

"You should put some salve on that." Sara frowned at the swelling forearm bruise as Dayang slipped her hands through her robe's long arms. "Doesn't it hurt? It looks like it seriously hurts."

Dayang winced at the mention, feeling a small pulse of remembered pain, and reminded herself not to let the sleeves slip past her wrists while Mother was present. "Yeah, it hurts. I'm not supposed to put anything on it, though. Hang Che has me practicing Fathom-meditations to speed healing. I'll go through them tonight before bed."

"Wish I could learn Sihir-stuff like that," Sara said. Her fine-boned features held a wistful expression, light brown eyes looking off into some imagined middle distance.

"Well," Dayang winced again as she bent to put on her house-slippers. "I could teach you some, but you basically have to get hurt first, or it's hard to really practice."

Sara considered that, then made a face. "Yeah, okay, no. Maybe if I hurt myself accidentally I'll ask."

"Sure," Dayang replied, knowing she never would. That's what physicians were for, and she doubted Sara would ever take on any kind of a martial bent. "You're learning stuff too though, right? At your mom's shop? She sells some really interesting stuff."

"Yeah. Course, mostly she has me sweep floors and move merchandise around, that kinda thing. But I do learn a lot." Sara smiled and mimed tidying up Dayang's cluttered shelves. "Seriously, though, Mom makes sure I get chances to watch when she haggles, and she's started letting me help with some of the bookkeeping. And I'm learning a lot about the items we stock. I guess maybe in the end I'm okay with just learning to *sell* Sihir-stuff instead of doing it, especially after seeing what it puts you through."

Dayang smiled back as they walked to the stairs, and shook her head. "Hang Che mostly has me doing the same drills over and over and over. Or exercises. Maybe I'll trade you sometime." There were days when the training was especially hard that Dayang wished fleetingly that she could trade lives with Sara, do nothing more strenuous than lift or scrub a few things here and there, but then she'd remember the boredom and hastily repent.

Sara giggled and shook her head as they walked down the richly-appointed hall. "Nope, I think I'll stick with broomsticks. No one ever tries to hit me with them."

No, Dayang thought, Sara's family just sold things to people who did the hitting. Or hired them for security. Kualabu's steady flow of adventurers in the market for expensive Sihir-goods had made Sara's mother one of the wealthiest women in town.

Dayang found herself wondering whether Sara's mother ever pondered whether all that wealth and hired muscle could have saved her husband, back during the last breach of the walls. *No, I hope not.* She turned away from the line of thought with an internal shudder.

Mother sat in the parlor just as Dayang had expected, drinking coffee and reading a book with a fancy embossed cover. This was also expected. Mother was almost never without a book unless she was out or had company, and sometimes not even then.

She was an elegant woman, fairly tall by Tenggaran standards, imperious and sharp of feature— though 'dignified' and 'defined' would be kinder words, Dayang thought. Even in her house robe, she looked as though she would be right at home in some grand hall, gliding down a polished floor with a flock of servants trailing along. Dayang supposed this was the result of her late grandparents' intensive training of their only child, but she would never ask. Mother didn't talk about her parents, not ever.

Some wounds don't ever heal, Dayang, Father had told her. *And sometimes grief stays fresh forever.* She glanced around at the parlor's many echoframes, noting bodies and faces in their illusory depth behind treated crystal, catching her grandfather's light brown eyes above the gentle dignity of his smile.

"Good evening, Mak Cik," Sara said, bowing slightly with the elder-woman honorific.

Mother looked up from her book, giving the girl a gracious patrician smile. "Good evening, Sara. Dayang. How was your practice?"

"It went well, Emak," Dayang replied, using the formal title Mother always insisted on when it wasn't just family present. She wasn't really sure if "went well" was a lie or not—which immediately reminded her of the bruises, and she glanced down to make sure her sleeves still reached her wrists.

"Glad to hear it, Dayang," Mother said, taking a long slow sip from her coffee cup. As always, Dayang noted a deep well of reserve in her mother's voice when she spoke of her daughter's training. As always, Dayang ignored it. "And how is Guru Hang?"

Dayang grimaced a little despite herself. Mother raised her carefully-plucked eyebrows.

"He was kind of rude to Sara," Dayang said grumpily. "Like she was barely even there. I got kind of mad, but I don't think he noticed."

Mother sighed. "You need to learn some deference, child. Guru Hang does not need to stop to acknowledge every girl who crosses his path. He is a highly-honored Wira, a respected warrior."

"And a town lady's man, from what I hear," came Pandikar's voice from down the hall. He'd finished his work on the saw-handle for the evening and was tossing it back and forth in his hands as he ambled in.

Mother frowned at him. "Pandikar! Show some respect! What kind of example are you setting?"

"A realistic one, I hope," Pandikar said as he settled onto the parlor's only overstuffed chair. Dayang and Sara sat down carefully on one of the small sofas. Dayang envied Pandikar's plush seat, as it was the only piece of furniture in the room made more for comfort than appearance.

"I'm not saying he's not a great trainer, and everyone says he's never gotten involved with one of his own students. That's something not all teachers can say, even over at the civil school." He wrinkled his nose as he spoke, flicking at one of his earrings.

"Pandikar..." Mother warned.

"Father says respect doesn't mean being blind," he replied.

This appeal to authority did not have the effect he was looking for.

"Your father," she said acidly, "is a highly respected merchant all through Tenggara, and you are a boy with no more than fifteen years under his belt. You will speak—" she raised her chin, fixing her son with a down-the-nose glare, "—with respect when talking about your elders."

"Yes, Emak," he said, not a trace of resentment in his voice.

Dayang envied this ability; she'd learned to hide her motives and feelings in physical conflict, but never in argument or conversation. It had earned her countless reprimands by parents and teachers alike. Even so, she decided to try a little diplomacy.

"Pandikar is right—" she said, and as her mother's glare turned toward her she hurried to finish, "—that he's never bothered me that way, I mean."

Nope, she thought, seeing her mother's eyes widen and her eyebrows try to reach her hairline. *That didn't work.*

"Dayang! I should hope not! Why would you even bring such a thing up? Both of you, go up to your rooms. I'll send your father to have a word with the pair of you."

"Yes, Emak," they said in near unison. Dayang felt a swift sinking of her hopes for the afternoon, and fought to keep her expression afloat. Mother glanced over at Sara, who looked deeply uncomfortable, and smiled apologetically. Dayang took advantage of her diverted attention to give Pandikar a rueful look. He grimaced and shrugged helplessly.

"Sara, my dear, I do apologize for my children's lack of decorum. You know, of course, you are always welcome in our home." Mother drained the last of her coffee and put on a carefully cultured smile.

"Thank you, Mak Cik," Sara said. "It's no problem."

"Please go ahead and ask the housekeeper for a snack on your way if you're hungry."

Sara nodded, bowed, and left with a sympathetic smile in both Dayang and Pandikar's directions. Dayang did her best to put up a stoic face in return, but it was pulled back down by the sheer weight of her anger and disappointment.

Dayang slowly climbed the stairs up to her room, then sat and glowered at her shelf for several long moments before pulling one of the many crystal slates off it. She ran her finger over the Common ideographs that formed the title along one side, which was about as long as her arm from elbow to fingertip. Her fluency in Common wasn't great yet, especially when it was actors yelling things across a stage, but for a Wuxia story it didn't really need to be. She was fighting back tears, which she knew was stupid and made her angry but there it was; she had really wanted to watch this echoplay with Sara.

The feeling was strong enough that she could barely pay any real attention to the tiny, slightly translucent figures performing their dutiful recreation of the play in the space above the tablet. Mostly, she just stared dully through the stage at the smooth crystal plane beneath. She couldn't summon the focus to decipher much of the Common in the actors' echoed voices.

She sat and half-watched anyway. The play was nearly over when her father came home. Dayang could hear him laughing in the other room at his wife's low, scandalized voice, though she could not make out any words through her door. When he did come to see her, he simply kissed her goodnight and told her to be more careful about what she said around her mother. It must have been obvious she had been crying, but he said nothing about it.

He had also brought her a new practice shield; Hang Che must have sent a messenger as soon as she'd left. Dayang thanked him, then sat and stared at it, felt her muscles twitch, felt her battered bone and sinew throb. *This makes number three.* She reached out, traced her fingers over the smooth bamboo as it lay on her bed. Her thoughts seemed to lumber through her head without paying her much mind.

When I get a real one, it had better be a lot harder to break.

First Interlude

The Black Fence, Salía, The Caustlands, 345 SE

Airam Mazo was not a tall man, a fact which sometimes annoyed him, especially as a soldier. Today though, he was grateful. Standing as he was three ranks back in the formation, his view of the Black Fence was almost totally obscured by the taller soldiers in front of him.

So he caught only glimpses of the glossy black stone, though he could see the whole of it by remembering the circle it formed on his map, how it curved in to enclose.

But he should not see it, should not have *made* it, and they were standing so close, and they did not normally get this close to the Black Fence. It wasn't safe. It wasn't—

infinite depths of waves beneath the all of things, come see come look look OUTSIDE

—wise. Or so they had all been told by the veterans of the Nowhere Watch. When a group of green soldiers arrived, though, they were brought here. And they were always green, untested, no matter their rank, no matter how crusty or combat-seasoned.

Everyone was green when they first arrived to stand the Nowhere Watch. Airam himself was a Sergeant who had seen action against bandits on the Tenggaran border. He had faced ashwights in Acheronford, had watched their misshapen forms drag themselves out of the Ashlit Mire and swarm the ramparts. He had helped cut them down, heard their burbling death-sounds. He had scars to show for it.

Still he was green, here with the Nowhere Watch.

it's not nowhere you know that no, this is a place, this is a real place and the Black Fence, Black Fence is real and solid go, go ahead and touch the obsidian it is smooth and it is warm, it must be warm it must welcome skin

Airam shuddered, doing his best to hide it. He was glad that he was not bald, that his black hair was thick. Otherwise they could easily see his sweat, see it stand out against the flush of his skin, but his skin was brown, and the flush was not so easy to see and he was grateful, was—

reach up in through, realized known concept, concept made real

He only just resisted holding his head in his hands. *Be silent,* he yelled downward into the echoing parts of his mind. He yelled it in Gentic. He yelled it in his native Ambérico. He closed his eyes to shut out the great obsidian shards he thought he could still see, see right through the taller soldier in front of him. He had seen already, seen on his map, seen on the map he had made should not have made he—

Murmuring in the ranks. Airam opened his eyes. So far everyone was standing fast, none had moved. Airam would stand fast as well. His right eye was twitching. He decided this was because it could see too profoundly. He couldn't shut it now.

"Right...FACE!" It was the voice of the First Sergeant, standing in front of the formation. Airam could not remember her name. Her words were harsh, even for a barked command. He felt his body tense at the first word, move at the second, no thought, long habit. Right foot pivot on the heel—

turn turn yourself toward, turn yourself away face outward, face out from what you have known what anyone can know, turn and see-know-comprehend the Outer Below

—left foot pivot on the ball, body turn to follow. The sound of a hundred boots twisting over thin grit. Left foot step forward, join the right—

join, join forward become, catalyze making real, transgress the boundaries-conduit-mind

—and back at attention. The sound of a hundred united stomps, bootheels against packed parched earth. All facing another direction now. Not away, no, but at least not toward. Airam felt a moment's relief.

"Counter Column...MARCH!" Her voice again, no name for it, but it called obedience from his feet though he stumbled, though he had to follow the soldier in front of him. Airam—

Sergeant Mazo not just Airam, i am Sergeant Mazo i must remember who i am

—thought maybe they were all looking at him, but he kept his eyes forward. He could not look around, must not. The path of the soldier ahead curved, and for a moment Airam was facing it again, could see one great black-dagger mass through the file of soldiers marching the other way. Airam almost stumbled again but he didn't and the path of his own file curved fully round as he followed, went back the direction it had come.

saw you feel your mind reach know grasp below outside

Now they were sliding back into formation. Facing left, now. Not away, but at least not toward. Another moment's relief, but faded this time. Some part of his mind knew what was coming, and he clawed to hang on to the scraps of self. Another part knew he now stood one rank closer to the Black Fence, second rank instead of third. At least he had not been in the last rank, then he would now be first and there would be no—

"Right...FACE!" Again he felt his feet move, body pivoting with them. A different soldier in front of him now, still taller than he, but Airam's eyes darted left, right, between soldiers, seeing through the new first rank. His right eye twitched, and twitched again. He could see them now, the huge obsidian knife-slabs that stabbed up and in toward...toward the center. He could see how they stood slanting side-by-side to form a black-shine curve, bending away from him, the circle he had seen on his map.

i have been pondering and we were not to, we were not to do it no, thought let by but the map, had the map made the map had to plan plan for duty

His head felt huge. Not swollen, not enormous with pain the way it sometimes was on mornings after he had drunk too much tequila. It was immense, it contained multitudes, its interior his mind was cavernous, no it was a space greater than all that between the stars and what moved between them and and and—

Airam Mazo broke ranks and sprinted toward the Black Fence. The other soldiers tried to stop him but he was clever, the vastness of his sight was boundless it was it was he did not comprehend what it was doing to him but it let him see, let him avoid their attempts to stop him. He ran and he ran and heard shouting behind, orders. He knew the path of arrows and spears that went by but they bent because everything bent everything was bent and it twisted into and along directions that could not, could not, and he must not and he realized and he turned and ran back toward the other soldiers.

Maybe there was still hope maybe he could be

They cut him down. The first blows did nothing, but they still came, and he went to his knees until his resilience was gone. He looked down at his uniform, at his Sergeant's stripes and Salían Army insignia. He wanted to remember, but his thoughts were gone, made huge and inimical. He looked down, and saw more. It gaped upward and could swallow swallow could

They cut him in pieces. The next blows tore him apart, and when there were only rags of uniform and bits of armor and ragged butchery they dragged it all away from the Black Fence and they burned it.

His family got a stipend and a letter explaining that nothing at all had happened to their son. He had not been stationed anywhere in particular. The family burned the letter, and remembered him as he had been.

One of the other soldiers found his map, and had to be knocked unconscious so that she could be transported to hospital. They burned it, along with his desk and everything on it. Airam had copied it over from a good map, a proper map, only instead of the customary hole punched through the paper to omit the Black Fence entirely, he had actually sketched the jagged obsidian circle.

And then he had filled it in.

Chapter 4

What are they trying to teach you?

What are you actually learning?

How could you know for sure?

- Eusébio Inoue (apocryphal)

A Year Later

Presilyo Monastery, Inoue Island, The Caustlands, 346 SE

Sanyago could see forever. *Well, not quite forever,* he thought, boots scuffing against the steeple's smooth stone face as he adjusted his clinch round the big square spire. *Pretty long way, though.* Far enough to see the Deisiindr, anyway, facing East as he was with the morning sun at his back. Some of that great tower's dull-glow charcoal surface was visible just a little south along the horizon, rising up through the chaos of clouds buffeted by the Windwall surrounding it. He imagined someone looking out one of its windows back at him, spotting the Presilyo as a tiny grey-brown splotch on Inoue Island.

He knew the huge faceted structure to be the Deisiindr from a book of maps Staafaen had shown him; his friend knew about Sanyago's cartographic obsessions. Staafaen—"Laris" had stuck pretty well as a nickname among the boys, though he was always still "Staafaen" to the teachers—read constantly, taking as many books from the monastery libraries as he could get away with, often returning them only with great reluctance. This particular book had fired both their imaginations by showing a vertical view of the tower along with the usual top-down map. According to the map legend, the Deisiindr was as tall as Inoue Island was long.

When he and Laris had gone together to ask Civics Master Tijong about it, the secular-subjects teacher had tucked his middle two fingers under his thumb in the Karana warding-gesture and frowned. The "Fathomless Deisiindr" was Ragado, he warned them, forbidden in the walk of the Triune Path, but he would not say why.

"You'll learn that later." A familiar and frustrating refrain. "Why isn't nine old enough?" Laris had demanded to know. Sanyago winced, remembering. That had been trouble.

There wasn't much else visible to the East. The Tengarran capital city Cenicebu was just as close as the Deisiindr on the maps, but Sanyago could find no sign of it. He supposed that was because Cenicebu was nowhere near so tall as the massive tower-city.

Laris will be excited to hear about the Deisiindr though, even if he's still mad at me for sneaking off.

He looked down at the sprawling island-hill the Presilyo was built on, watched the Mindao river split to flow round the isle on its southward journey. Boring. Not the slightest hint of invasive purple abblum had been allowed to creep in among the mundane Fallen greenery of shrub and tree and flower. The rambling complexes of old wood-and-stone buildings were too familiar to be worth a look even from this novel perspective. And he only had so much time; every second up here increased his risk of being caught.

Sanyago shuffled fully round to look west, squinting against the spreading red of the rising sun while without looking too directly at it. *Farrod can burn your eyes if you try to observe her straight on*, Master Tijong had said during an astronomy lesson. Wisely, this lesson had taken place at night, so none of the students could put this warning to an immediate test. *The moons, on the other hand, reflect only a fraction of Farrod's glory, even when they are full.* A lecture on why they waxed and waned had followed.

His heart began to pound as he scanned left along the horizon, squinting as far as he could into the distance. *The Black Fence,* he thought with a shudder, but saw only long, slightly bumpy skyline; no jagged obsidian slabs slanting up toward the sky.

Sanyago rested his forehead against the weathered stone, tried to let his mind sit on the subject as little as possible despite the small illicit thrill he felt in looking for it. *Wrong, wrong, wrong.* The Black Fence didn't even really show up on any of his maps— every one of them had a small circle punched out of the paper in the spot where it apparently stood.

He and Laris had only known it might exist from whispered rumors among the boys. They'd confirmed the rumor through one of the library's very old encyclopedias, which had a sparse sketch under the heading

Black Fence

showing sharp sections of obsidian stone, shaped something like arrowheads, slanting up and inward to form a barrier...and then a teacher had grabbed them each by the ear. There had followed a very emphatic impromptu lesson on not talking about the Black Fence, not thinking about the Black Fence, and the mental techniques they'd already been taught that could be used to accomplish this. It was not just Ragado, they were told; it was dangerous to the mind as well as the soul.

Contemplation of what might be *inside* the Black Fence was of course—

No.

was of course

Push it away.

of course

Let it pass by.

Sanyago shook his head, shook it again, shuddered. He glanced down, marked the two patrols of Somonei warrior monks and nuns visible from his high perch. He was pushing his luck; someone was sure to see him. All the other adults were off at some important meeting, having left the Novices to take a long breakfast with minimal supervision. He'd rolled his own food up in a flat corn-cake and pocketed it before sneaking out, dodging watchful grownup eyes and Laris' exasperated expression.

Laris. His friend had followed him. Should have known. Sanyago could see him winding his way between buildings toward the chapel perch, managing to avoid the Somonei patrols, though he couldn't quite match Sanyago's talent for stealth. And now he was hunkered down beside one of the low walls that surrounded the chapel entrance, looking up at him.

Sanyago couldn't read his expression. From up here, his face was just a very dark blob atop sky-blue robes. It didn't matter; he knew exactly the look of resigned annoyance Laris would be wearing on his lean, sharp features. He sighed, and began to shimmy carefully down the spire.

Getting down was a lot quicker than getting up, if just as risky. Handhold, foothold, drop, balance, grip, fingertips scraping on the gritty edges of protruding stones. Laris remained silent until Sanyago made the final drop to the lawn, rolling just as he'd been taught before standing up to brush bits of grass from his robes. He pulled Sanyago down against the wall beside him before giving the smaller boy a light, two-knuckled punch to the upper arm.

"You're incredibly lucky no one else saw you." Laris' voice was hushed but vehement, his grey eyes wide with disbelief against the deep black of his skin.

Sanyago grinned. Laris sighed, rolled his knuckles across his forehead, then gave his friend a sardonic sidelong look.

"You're lucky," Laris repeated. "Don't say you're just good. You can be both, and your luck always runs out eventually anyway. It's not like they don't catch you sometimes." Sanyago had already been subject to at least seven "disciplinary actions" of varying degree in the year or so since he and Laris had met. It was always for being somewhere he was not supposed to be, or for not being somewhere he was.

Sanyago shrugged, still smiling, though he also kept his voice low. "It's worth it. I can see so far! It's better than maps, almost like getting off the island. Anyway, they give us all these lessons on moving quietly and not being spotted. I'm just taking my training seriously." *Speaking of which,* he thought, and popped his head up for a quick glance around. Safe.

Laris shook his head and laughed. The gesture made Sanyago think of the Litany of Letting Go; it was a surrender, a realization he was not going to be able to change his friend. "Well, you weren't just skulking behind bushes this time, like Master Castillo says. I think it'd be more than just a caning if they caught you up on the spire like that. Anyway, the reason I risked *my* butt to come out and get you is that we're finally going to get our first sparring lesson after breakfast, and breakfast is almost over."

Sanyago had known this, of course; he'd been looking forward to it for weeks now. Sparring was a big milestone, according to the monks; also according to the monks, it meant the boys in their class were all around nine years old now. Part of his reason for climbing the steeple was to celebrate; he must have lost track of time. He frowned, most of the bravado draining down into the pit of his stomach. "Oh. Ummm. We have enough time to get back without them noticing, right?"

Laris glanced up at the sun, extending his arm and using his thumb for scale. They'd been trained to tell time by Farrod's position in the sky according to the season; Civics Master Tijong said it was a very useful skill in the field.

"I think so, if we hurry. We just need to look like we know where we're going. As long as it's toward the training field the Somonei probably won't bother us. Still, we should probably avoid them whenever we can do it without looking like we're doing it, you know?"

Sanyago nodded, and they set off at a quick pace.

"Understand this first of all: you are not here to hurt each other." Sparring Master Silva's Ambérico-accented tenor jabbed emphatic through the air, boots nearly silent as he walked the flagstones round the border of the sparring-field. Sanyago stood at the edge of this paving with the rest of his class, looking out over the raked earth as he listened to the Sparring Master speak.

"Injuries slow training. If you injure another student, you have not won, you have failed, and badly. Here, your highest duty is to help each other learn." Silva paced back and forth along the slightly ragtag line of boys, long arms making sweeping gestures as he lectured. He was a spare, sinewy man, taller than almost all the other monks and absolutely towering over his charges. His wiry frame leaned into his movements, imparting a sense of constant potential, of motion barely held back. Deep-set above his great hawkish nose, quick dark eyes regarded all things and all people as matters to be dealt with, objects to be acted upon.

Sanyago watched the monk with fascination as he passed by, then started a little as Silva wheeled round abruptly to stand in front of him. Sanyago looked up, and up; as the shortest of the group, he always felt small, but in front of Master Silva he felt utterly tiny. Two of the Sparring Master's boney fingers jabbed him right under the breastbone.

Sanyago wheezed at the unexpected burst of pain through his stomach and ribcage, though he managed not to double over or go to his knees. He was certainly no stranger to being struck, but the abruptness of the blow had caught him off-guard.

"You, Sanyago," Master Silva said, leaning far down to look him in the eye. "You I have heard a great deal about. Cannot wait to spar, is that right?"

Sanyago was not sure what the right answer would be to this question, or if it even existed. He had to cough twice before he could speak.

"I am...anxious for training, Master Silva." He thought this was a pretty good try. It seemed like the Sparring Master disagreed, pulling back to look at him sidelong, then bending back down to put a callused finger in his face.

"You should be neither nervous nor hopeful," he said sourly. "Accept it as it comes, do not sully it with expectations."

Sanyago coughed twice more. "Yes, Sparring Master."

Silva nodded curtly, moving on down the line. "Vasili," he said, stopping in front of the largest of their group, a pale, high-strung boy who had a habit of rubbing his own clean-shaven head. Well, usually clean-shaven. His hair was so pale he could sometimes get away with letting his pate grow a little fuzzy, which Sanyago and Laris, with their thick black hair, never could.

"Yes, Sparring Master Silva," Vasili bowed, one hand curled over his closed fist as they had all been taught.

"Spare me the bowing," Silva said shortly. "From here on out, you bow only to your opponent and only when instructed. We don't have time for it."

"Yes, Sparring Master Silva."

"Just Master will do. You may think the years ahead are very long, but I am here to tell you that time is very short. Every moment, any moment on this training field could save your life later. You cannot afford to waste them."

"Yes, Master."

Sanyago couldn't see Vasili well in his peripheral vision, but caught the apprehension in his voice.

"Good. I understand you've been boasting about how well you think you'll do."

It was true. Vasili often tried to offset his anxiety with braggadocio, using his nervous energy to psyche himself up rather than stew in it.

Sanyago figured this wasn't really too terrible as coping strategies went, and like the others in his class he ignored the neurotic boy's bluster. Vasili did well enough in practices, but no one knew for sure how any of them would do when it came to actual sparring.

"Uhhh...mmm...I..."

This was all the answer Silva needed, and he yanked the tall bulky boy out of line, stepping back smoothly and backhanding him lightly on each cheek. It would have looked almost comical, Sanyago thought, but for the sheer terrifying *speed* of the Sparring Master's movements.

"Defend yourself," he said, and did it again, and again. Vasili did his best to block and weave and duck, but the Sparring Master never missed, his movements a blur though his blows landed with only a light, stinging *smack*. "You cannot?" he asked, shoving Vasili back into line. He didn't wait for an answer, resuming his pacing of the line as he spoke.

"Of course not. He knows nothing of sparring. None of you do. Understand two things." He raised a single finger, held it up as he walked. "First and most important: your goal here is to learn, not to win. This is not some game, some sport. Sparring is not fighting. Fighting is not sparring. Only real combat matters."

Sanyago caught a blur of motion at the corner of his eye as Silva stopped to strike someone, though he couldn't see who or how. The whole class seemed to suck in a short breath at the same time.

"You, Andhlib. I say 'combat' and you grin as if you are eager for it. This is how you die young accomplishing less than nothing. This is how you become worse than a waste."

"Yes, Master," Andhlib said so faintly that Sanyago wondered where he'd been hit. Andhlib prided himself on his ability to take punishment without complaint. The Sparring Master continued his pacing, now holding up two fingers as he went.

"Second, skill in sparring will not always mean skill at fighting. Sparring is a tool, an important tool, but it is not real. The ways in which it is not real are too many to list now, but we will go over them as you train. We will vary things to make them as real as we safely can. The situations will not always be fair. War and combat almost never are."

He paused his pacing in front of Laris, and Sanyago could hear, even if he could not see, the scowl when the Sparring Master spoke.

"You. Staafaen," he said, and put the palm of his hand on the smooth dark skin of Laris' forehead. He pushed lightly, and Sanyago could just make out the movement as his friend was forced to step back to keep balance. "I am told you ask a great many questions, and sometimes argue. Questions are welcome. Arguing is not. I am responsible for your safety, both now and when you must fight for real. Debate may sharpen the mind in the classroom, but here you will hone yourself on a different kind of conflict."

"Yes, Master," Laris replied. His tone was even, but Sanyago could still hear a small touch of defiance. Silva heard it too.

"I do not care if you like it or not. For now, you take what I have to teach, and you take it to heart. Later, when you actually know something, when you actually know yourself, you can perhaps tailor what you are taught to your own strengths and weaknesses."

He paused again, gave a dry laugh.

"I will have to give you all this speech again more forcefully in a few years, when you start the journey toward manhood in earnest and begin to think you know everything."

Master Silva turned abruptly, walked a few paces away from the line of students, turned again to face them.

"Vasili. Sanyago. Come forward. You will be the first."

Later, with every bone, muscle, and sinew in his body aching at odd intervals, Sanyago settled onto his meditation mat and tried to let his mind relax its grip on the coursing quicksilver bars of his thoughts. He watched, doing his best to pull gently back, observer, not participant, unmoored but centered, groundless but not falling. Forms made only of movement traced and retraced every dodge, every block, every pulled punch and feinted kick, sending sympathetic vibrations through his body as he sat.

He had not won all his matches. This had genuinely surprised him. He had, as Silva had asserted, not concealed his excitement to finally put his skills to the test in more than just katas, partnered forms, and other scripted exercises. Still, he'd not made Vasili's' mistake by bragging about how well he thought he'd do. If he was honest with himself, and in this meditative state he did his best to be, he hadn't thought bragging was really necessary. Everyone knew he was probably the best. No one was faster. No one caught on to a new form or technique more quickly.

Or maybe not, he thought, trying to observe his own ego in action from his place in nowhere. *I may be faster, but no one masters most things more completely than Laris. No one is tougher than Andhlib. No one is stronger than Vasili.*

This last fact had been his undoing in the very first match. He had underestimated the advantage sheer size and strength gave his opponent when it came to strikes, to blocks and parries, to clinches, and to takedown maneuvers. Vasili had managed to overpower him two out of the three rounds. This had earned them both a swat and a lecture from Sparring Master Silva. Sanyago could hear his voice echo through the carefully cultivated stillness of his meditating mind.

"You, Vasili: don't look so pleased with yourself. It is good that you use your strength and size to your advantage, but these will matter less and less as you all progress. You will be tapping into much more powerful forces than mere muscle. You, Sanyago: failure to recognize and respect your opponents' strengths is merely one of many, many ways your pride can kill you."

He had, he hoped, begun to take this lesson to heart. Though not quickly enough to avoid another loss. Andhlib had gritted his teeth through a series of what must have been very painful hard blocks against Sanyago's quick, dancing attacks to find an opening and pummel him twice in the side. Sanyago shifted slightly in his meditation, feeling the spot pulse a little in memory.

Well then, he thought, or rather watched the thought drift by from his immaterial perch, *I still have a lot left to learn. Plenty of challenge. This will be fun.*

I can do this. I want to do this.

As these thoughts passed through his mind, observed and noted and left to drift away, Sanyago turned his thoughts to the Divine, the Lotus Child, the Enlightening Spirit. He felt the sweet, buoyant serenity spill through him, and gave thanks.

Chapter 5

The Wira-arts are arts of the mind, always. Their outward expression may be one of the body, but the body is moved upon by the mind, whether it is the mind held above in its own eye, or the mind below that cannot always be seen. It is true that for many of the arts it is helpful or even necessary to hone muscle and sinew, but the immediate reflex, the precise movement— these are sculpted in the mind below and carried out with no need for perceptible thought.

Yet without Harmonious Comprehension, born of both the mind known and the mind obscured, these are nothing; without the Fathom brought into concert with the whole, there can be no Wira-arts at all.

- High Master Athan, *The Lotus Reflected Below,* 279 SE

Kualabu, Tenggara, The Caustlands, 346 SE

Dayang glared at her older sister. "You didn't have to tell him. I was fine. I'm old enough to go out on my own sometimes."

Nurul turned her petite frame over on her bed, blinking at Dayang through long, heavily made-up eyelashes, then let out a supercilious little sigh. Dayang hated it when Nurul did this, and Nurul seemed to do it ever more often these days. It made Dayang dream of dashing a whole bucket of icewater in her sister's face. She could shove Nurul out into the street, watch her stand there wearing an expression of stupid shock with her makeup in rivulets down her neck. Unfortunately, their room wasn't close enough to the front door to make this a practical option. To say nothing of all the trouble it would get her in.

"You're only thirteen, Dayang. And that boy—"

Dayang scowled and kicked her feet against the carved wooden chest at the foot of her bed, shifting her weight back and forth on the mattress. Of course Nurul *did* have to tell, because she was Nurul. And of course she had to tell Dayang she'd told. What fun was a victory you couldn't lord over your opponent?

"His name is Mufidh, not 'that boy'. Anyway, so what? Pandikar used to go out all the time when he was my age. Sometimes to see a girl, too. Father even knew, he'd just laugh about it. Said 'that's just how young men are, we should watch him but as long as he's not getting into too much trouble, well…' I heard him. I heard him talking to Mother."

Nurul shook her head, not even bothering to look Dayang's way as she perused her book. *Some silly romance*, Dayang thought, though an expensive one; a proper echowritten volume rather than cheap hedgeprint, with color depth-illustrations to highlight the story's most melodramatic moments.

"You shouldn't eavesdrop, Dayang." But the smug little lilt in Nurul's voice seemed happy, not dismayed, that her sister had heard. *Now you see the way things work, the way they're* supposed *to work.*

"I didn't eavesdrop! *You* eavesdrop! I'm not sneaky like you. I was just walking past and I heard."

That earned her a look at last, and Dayang was gratified to see Nurul blinking rapidly, attempting "wronged innocence" but achieving only farce.

"I d-do, I do, I do n-n-no ssss-uch thing," she stammered, wearing a look of angry, helpless frustration that got worse the more her words fell apart. Nurul's stutter, though mostly vanquished by early adolescence, could still give her trouble even now at seventeen, especially in times of anger or stress.

Dayang's scowl softened. She could still feel the deep ember-bed of resentment and anger churning in her throat, but saw no point poking at it now. She'd pitied Nurul's struggles with speaking as long as she'd been aware of them. Though she wasn't sure her sister would have extended that same courtesy if their situations were reversed.

Nurul glared at the wall, facing away from her sister while she composed herself. Dayang decided to quietly declare victory and find something better to do. She slid off the bed, squatted down by her mahogany chest, opened it. She could practically feel Nurul's intense, resentful sulking as she slid her lead-stick out and shoved its weighted end into the foam rubber mace-head, twisting right at the end so the threading would keep it securely attached.

"Mother," Nurul said, drawing the word out in a dour pout, "says that's not a proper weapon for a young lady. Maybe you should try a spear or long-dagger. Or a bow. Or some other Wira-art that doesn't mean just *hitting* things."

Dayang decided she'd had enough of Nurul's mouth for one day. "Okay. I'll just follow in my big sister's footsteps, then. Study whatever Wira-art *she* masters."

Nurul sucked in her breath and spun round on the bed to face her sister, sputtering out half-snarled incoherencies through drawn-back lips. Dayang felt a pang of guilt creep up into her throat; Nurul's last Wira-Guru had given her up as a lost cause two years ago, and Father had never hired another.

Wasn't my fault, though, Dayang thought, *and I wasn't the one who brought it up, not really.*

"Yoooou," Nurul finally managed through her rage, letting the word seep through her clenched teeth to prevent another stutter. She was mad, all right, but the display was at least two-thirds just ordinary Nurul theatricality. Dayang therefore ignored it, wandering out down the stairs and through the back door with her lead-stick and weighted bamboo shield. It was a cool, cloudy late afternoon, perfect for drills. She set herself to them with gusto.

Father had set up three practice dummies in the back lot, each equipped with a different assortment of arms and armor. She was halfway through her second practice set when he came out on the back porch, looking at her. Piolo Marchadesch was a wiry, rangy man, though not particularly tall. He wore a wispy, mustachioed goatee, with a great shock of long, untidy black locks set above big brown eyes so dark they nearly matched his hair. They watched her intently, those eyes, showing their usual mix of love, concern, and uncertainty.

"Dayang," he called, leaning against the porch railing. Dayang pretended not to hear him and continued her set. *Thupp* went the rubber against the dummy's upper arm. *Thack* went her shield against the dummy's chest, centered right where its sternum would be and sending a shock through the muscle and bone of her forearm and shoulder.

"Dayang, come *here*," he called, his voice still not loud, but carrying and insistent. She sighed, jaw set as she carefully laid stick-and-shield down on the equipment table, then trudged over to her father, avoiding his gaze. She scuffed her boot against a small patch of abblum that had crept into the practice-yard, staining her sole purple at the toe, and waited for him to speak. She felt too aware of her own lungs, counting the tension with each airy expansion.

Bending closer to the abblum in an effort to distract her mind from the ongoing silence, she noticed at least three tiny runners stretching out from the little tangle of Abwaild weed, their twined-together strands looking pale and new. The gardener would have to do a very thorough job burning the whole thing out next time he came around.

"Dayang, we have *talked* about this before," he said in his heavy Basa Taga accent. It always got stronger when he was tired or upset, and she flushed to hear it wandering so far from the elegant, aristocratic Basa Mala dialect the rest of the family spoke. Trouble.

"Yes, Tatay," she said tonelessly.

"Don't you Tatay *me* right now, Dayang," His voice had dropped to just above a whisper. "Turn your chin up. Look at me."

She reluctantly raised her gaze to meet the dark, searching pools of her father's eyes.

"Yes, Ayah," she said, using the formal Basa Mala word.

He sighed, a quick, huffing thing that rolled his slender shoulders down before squaring them again. He leaned further into the railing, making the bamboo creak.

"It was that boy again, wasn't it." It wasn't really a question. His tone was hard to make out; a mix of anger and exasperation and almost...pity?

"It's nothing serious," she muttered, though her voice was a little sharper than she would have liked.

Piolo shoved himself back hard from the railing, bamboo crackling in protest, and reached out at the air in front of her. Dayang nearly recoiled, then caught herself; her father never struck her, or her sister, or her mother so far as she knew, but plenty of other girls in their town had fathers that did. And her brother had not always been so lucky; Dayang had twice spotted Pandikar limping his way back to his room with a set expression on his face after an especially tense evening with Father.

He didn't hit her, though. Instead he closed his hand, drew it back as if clutching at something intangible, some abstract idealized daughter he couldn't quite grasp.

"It is ALWAYS serious!" he shouted, raised voice hammering each word, and Dayang stepped back in surprise. This was a long way from his usual quiet intensity. "This is your family's reputation we are talking about! Do you not understand that? More than your studies, more than your Wira-training, more than anything, your reputation will make or break your life in the days ahead of you!"

Dayang did not know what to say to this. She could argue ten thousand years over what she had or had not done, but over what people *said* about it? What they whispered when she walked by? She just looked back at him steadily. She wasn't much good at lying and didn't like doing it anyway. *Wouldn't* do it, not about this. Yes, she and Mufidh had been kissing a little, giggling a lot, touching here and there. They hadn't been hurting anyone, and if his sister hadn't caught them, hadn't decided to help a little gossip spread...

Her father was still looking at her, his features a shifting front of emotional skirmish. She still didn't know what to say. Be honest? He would be furious. He might take pains to keep her away from Mufidh. She didn't think she was in love with him or anything. She wouldn't go into Nurul-style dramatics about how she couldn't bear to be kept apart from him. But he was cute, and kind, and willing, and that was enough.

The long moment was unbearable. Anything she could say would be headed for either a trap or a lie, and she was unwilling to walk into either. She had no interest in a respectable reputation based on crowshit— but she did not wish to see her father's social standing suffer. Even with the added prestige of the family he had married into, she knew it had been a tooth-and-nail struggle to acquire.

She did not want a *bad* reputation either, but Father's hysterics aside, Kualabu was not so very conservative a town that just kissing a boy would be likely to earn her that. Well, maybe. There were girls in town whose families would not allow them to show so much as a hair when they left the house, though she had heard of worse in other places, like the far-off Sovereign Nations.

He was still just standing there, bearing down on her with the crushing weight of complete attention. She knew from experience that this sort of silent standoff could go on for a very long time, and she wondered, suddenly, what sort of argument he was having in his own head. Was he thinking about how differently he had laughed off Pandikar's crushes and probable trysts? Was he anticipating everything they might say in the village, about her, about him, about the family? Was he wondering what she would become?

She was deeply surprised by these thoughts. Before, not too long ago, Father had simply been Father. An unwavering constant, a known quantity. A monolithic figure containing no multitudes. She felt a wave of something like pity wash over her, an emotion she wouldn't have thought could ever apply to Piolo Marchadesch, the cagey trader of no family to speak of who had used his clever gains to win over a woman of notable name and threadbare fortune. He was a myth in her mind, an archetype.

He was just a man.

"I love you, Tatay," she said quietly. The words came unexpected. She still said them often enough, even as she began the halting, unknowable journey toward womanhood, but they were different here, meant something more now.

There was another silence, short but full of small, bright sounds; the patio creaking under her father's house-shoes, the sound of air flowing in and out of her nostrils, little songs flitting back and forth between the birds.

He broke the silence without speaking, boots clunking against wooden planks as he came round the bamboo rail and descended onto the paved path that lead to the practice-yard. He took her in his arms with a great sigh, and part of her felt six or seven again, warm and safe, the scent of him gathering memory in its wake. But her mind was still a dull descending chaos, and the feeling began to fade even as she hugged him back, taking in a long, deep breath against the wiry body slowly slackening with age.

"I love you too, my little Engkanto," he answered.

Then the silence continued, and she thought, *this is only a pause, this is not over. I am not going to become the perfect respectable daughter, even if I fulfill all his dreams of me becoming a true Wira. He will always see any boy I like as his business, as family business. I will never marry young and give him armfuls of grandchildren. He may have changed his religion, brought in a fresh flow of coin, but he will never truly be head of household in the eyes of Mother's family. Always outside, always at a distance—*

Or maybe not. Maybe things *would* be different, someday. But for now—

Their words were true. She loved him, and he loved her. It was something to hold on to. But it was going to be very hard.

Second Interlude

Salían Capital City of Aldonza, The Caustlands, 346 SE

A low female voice interrupted his meal, bringing with it a great tangle of emotion and intent—sadness, familiarity, reluctant pity, an ancient regret. An undertow of shaded purpose. He knew it at once.

"Ah, my dear Duyet, look what they have done to you."

Duyet Le looked up from the bowl in his lap, his one good eye regarding the woman in the doorway with a sad, bleary lack of surprise. He gestured vaguely toward the paper lanterns on the wall to either side of the door. They flickered into life, the dull glow of cheap red hedgeflame joining with the lamp on his side table to better illuminate the small shabby room. They illuminated her, too, weakly tinting the pale skin and drab clothes of her tall, lithe form.

"Hello, Lidia. Why are you here?"

The woman's full lips curled up into the shadows of her face. It was almost a smile, but didn't reach the shaded pools of her eyes.

"There was a time you would not have asked that question, Duyet."

"That time was long ago, Lidia, and a heartbreak and a half away. I see you have finally cast off your Somonei robes. Judging by the length of your hair, it has been a good while."

She smiled, real this time, though whether its realness was intended for him or not was impossible to say. She ran one hand through the dark hair that hung down to her shoulder blades, lifted a lock in the crook of her finger. "I have not seen the Presilyo for nearly two years, and it has been more than a year since I felt its corruption on my soul."

Duyet Le let out a laugh at that— a dry, cracked thing full of rattling bile. "Still very fond of high drama, aren't you? And always looking to cause some. Along with more than your share of corruption. How many of us did you seduce, ah? I only knew of the two, but I am sure there were more before and since."

Lidia's lips drew down into dourness, and she lifted her chin, letting a little of the hedgeflame's faint light shine into the golden-brown of her eyes. "You still think I betrayed you somehow. But we were both betraying our vows, and anyway our vows had already betrayed us. What, did you think we were married?" Her voice had grown sharp, her eyes cutting.

He put his hands on the arms of his chair, as if to stand, confront her. But of course he could not, and when her eyes flicked down toward the blanket-covered stumps of his legs, they softened.

"I am sorry, Duyet," she said, and her voice held a tinge of self-reproach alongside new gentleness. "I have not come to fight old battles. I told them about us as part of my confession. And...and the others. They thought I should be the one to come to you." Her eyes regained a touch of hardness. "I am not here to apologize for the past, though, you old hypocrite. I was neither your first nor your last. Enough of that."

He leaned forward in his chair, grey-wisp eyebrows rising toward his clean-shaven pate. "They? Who are 'they'?" She didn't answer, and he regarded her steadily for a moment. Then he sat back, moved the bowl of rice and vegetables from his lap to the table beside his chair. "Ah, the Carvers. You've been out among the Sovereign Nations, haven't you?"

She snorted, folding her arms, one shoulder nudged against the rough doorframe. "Still insightful, I'll give you that. No prize, though, it's not hard to guess. Yes, the Carvers. They're not the mindless heretics we were led to believe— they know the Triune Path, really know it, without all the distractions of politics and compromise."

She gripped the sides of the doorway, leaned in toward him. "You should hear them out, Duyet. There are great things afoot. You don't have to molder here in Aldonza for the rest of your days, eating whatever scraps the Presilyo sees fit to throw your way." All softness in her eyes had given way to driving zeal.

"I am fed well enough." His tone was even, though a hint of acid trickled through. "And the government does its part. I'm not exactly sleeping out in the streets, Lidia."

"The government?" She kicked at the doorframe. "The Salían government shouldn't have to do *anything*, Duyet. You were Somonei.

You fought and bled and nearly died for the Presilyo." He was leaning forward in his chair again, and she held up one hand with a sharp shake of her head. "No, I know you fought Salían battles plenty often, and the Presilyo was more than happy to take coin for your services. They told us ours was a holy struggle, but we—"

"—We? WE?" He planted his palms on the armrests of his chair and pushed himself upward, half-standing on the stumps of his legs. "You know damn well I did not lose my legs to some bandit or Abwaild monster. Do you want me to talk about it? Well? Do you want me to *remind* you why this particular fight was holy? What we found down there in the Abwarren?" His voice dropped to a whispered growl. "Do you need me to speak of the Outer Below?"

The room had become heavy as he spoke, pressing down and in with a queasy thrum of slyly tested boundaries. Lidia went pale, eyes widening, the righteous conviction written over her face faltering into dread. Her gaze flicked around the suddenly oppressive room, from corner to corner and wall to wall. They did not settle on Duyet, and he allowed himself a small grim smile. It wasn't him she was afraid of. "No...no. I am sorry. I only meant..."

He settled slowly back into his chair, and the space around him settled as well, gradually becoming unbent. He was breathing hard, at once relieved and shaken.

"I know what you meant," he said softly. "And you may be right, some of the time. I have not forgotten our days and nights of talk and hope and critique. I have not forgotten the warts of our old profession."

The color had returned to her cheeks, and now bloomed hot. She slapped the doorframe with an open palm, took a half-step into the room. "Then come with me, Duyet. You must know by now why I am here."

He sighed and slumped back, resting his head a moment against his palm. "I don't suppose you've come to carry me off to the Deisiindr for new legs? No? That's Ragado for the Carvers too, I assume?" His voice was wistful, but carried an edge along with the gentle mockery.

"You would even consider that?" Her tone was equal parts curious and reproachful.

"No." He sounded amused. "I may have piled on a few layers of cynicism in my time, but I still believe, I think. I would not enter the Deisiindr— though perhaps I would consider buying some of their marvelous shoes. Artificial rubber, you know. Supposed to be very long lasting." He laughed at his own dark joke.

She glared at him. "We cannot give you back your legs, and you may never lift a sword or spear again, but you can still fight. We can change the Presilyo to something new. We can root out the corruption, bring purity back to the Triune Path. Unity, Duyet. No more mercenary hypocrisy, following Caustland State cash off to whatever battles they want us to fight. No more standing alongside heathen troops. We can begin to claim Solace for the Fallen, as the Enlightened Saint intended."

Duyet's face contracted into a rigid bronze mask. "What? How? With a speech like that one? It won't convince them. It doesn't convince me, either." An iron filament of warning threaded into his voice. "Perhaps you should get out, Lidia."

"We've spoken enough, and for years," she replied. "Time for talk is over. There are hundreds like us, Presilero cast-offs. The Divine will be on our side if enough of us rejoin the Triune Path, the true one, and return to the place of our corruption." She tucked her two middle fingers under her thumb, index and little fingers flicking forward in the Karana warding-gesture.

Up again went the grey-ash lines of his wispy brows. "Who has been feeding you these words? 'Return to the place of our corruption?' You've always been an eloquent woman in your own way, but that isn't really your style, is it? You're a direct one, it's something I always admired about you. If you're talking about, say, something as foolish trying to conquer the Presilyo itself, just say so."

She set her jaw forward and stepped fully into the room, finally leaving the door jamb behind. "We plan to do whatever the Divine requires. Solace belongs to the Fallen, Duyet. The Presileros have forgotten this, you must know they have. We can remind them, we can *make* them remember. We can teach the whole of the Caustlands. You may not be able to fight but you can speak, and you would be a potent symbol—"

"NO," he said, and the force behind the word was so staggering that she retreated back to the shelter of the threshold. "I will not. I want no part in this, Lidia. It will only end in blood and new corruptions. I doubt you and your new Carver friends are so pure and Silado as you claim. People are what they are, and I have seen enough of it." She opened her mouth as if to speak, and he slammed both hands down on the arms of his chair.

55

"OUT! GET OUT! I will tell the Salíans to arrest you if you come back. You should be glad I do not contact the Shuvelao."

"Fine!" she said again, and the word carried a venomous tangle of anger, regret, disappointment, and ancient hurt. "If it's damnation you want then be damned! Others will listen. We don't need you!" And then she turned away, and then she was gone.

He sat in his chair a long, long time, letting his rice and vegetables grow cold. Finally, he picked the bowl up and began to eat.

His hands were still shaking.

Chapter 6

The Presilyo exists to bridge worlds. Physically, it is a threshold between Salia and Tenggara, serving both, owing allegiance to neither. It has served as ambassador between other nations as well, and in the gathering of its students, teachers, and disciples lies the joining of a hundred cultures and tongues. Intellectually, it is the joining of the Mind with the Holy Fathom in Harmonious Comprehension, a link between the knowledge of the Old World and that of the New.

Most importantly, the Presilyo exists to bridge the gap...ah, but I tell a lie. The gap between Human and the True Nature, the chasm between Mortal and Divine, this lies beyond the meager powers of any place, person, or institution. They can but illuminate the Narrow Gate, cast revealing shadow along the Triune Path, and the Presilyo has for centuries lifted the lantern of the Word and the Way.

- Ock Yonggi Park, Twelfth Abbot of the Presilyo Ri'Granha

Presilyo Monastery, Inoue Island, The Caustlands 347 SE

Sanyago had gotten up the chapel spire a lot faster than last year, but he could not see forever this time. A fog was rolling in from the south with the Mindao river, shrouding Inoue Island and much of its surrounding plains in languishing swirls of silver-white. It was still mostly clear to the north, so he shuffled round the big square spire to look.

The Wave-Rest Berm curved away from him in both directions, an enormous bulwark of huge boulders, smaller rocks, and fine earth, the odd bit of Fallen vegetation clinging green and stubborn alongside lavender splotches of abblum. Must be pretty big clumps of abblum if he could see them from this far away, some of them maybe even as tall as he was. The Presilyo caretakers were zealous when it came to abblum eradication; the highest Sanyago had ever seen the tangled purple stalks rise was just above the tops of his own tall boots.

Squinting, he could barely make out the small canyon where the Mindao river parted the huge bulk of the Berm to pass northward into Zhon Han. He knew everything he could see east of the Mindao was Tenggara, just as everything west of the river was Salía. Salía. Home, maybe, once upon a time. He shook off the thought. The two Caustland States didn't look any different from up here, which surprised him a little, even though he knew the different colors on the map were just symbolic. It seemed strange to see the maps' lines and contours match so exactly with reality when the colors didn't.

He turned fully round to look south, where he could just make out the wispy grey fade of the Siinlan Veil over the fog-cloaked horizon. According to one of the sparse sketches in his favorite book of maps, it stretched far up into the sky from the Ashlit Mire like a thin shimmering sheet of smoke. The Mire itself, according to the maps, spread out from the banks of the Gyring Ash on both sides, and with it formed the Siinlan.

Like the Wave-Rest Berm, the Siinlan ran in a near-perfect circle on the maps, except that it encompassed the whole of the Caustlands instead of just Zhon Han, the border between familiar Fallen territory and strange Abwaild lands. He and Laris had gone back and forth, endlessly speculating and arguing about what the Siinlan might really look like. They both agreed that it was full of monsters, but Sanyago had insisted that the very embertrees of the Ashlit Mire could come alive and grab you.

Laris had set his jaw, shaken his head. *Trees don't move, Sanyago. It's dangerous enough with all the monsters, you don't have to make things up.*

Laris. Sanyago had told his friend about his planned expedition this time; Laris had just knuckled his forehead and sighed. "Just don't get caught, Sanyago. Don't count on the fog to save you."

"Don't you want to take a look for yourself one of these days?" Sanyago had looked up at the taller boy—the difference in their heights seemed to grow every day—and gestured at the expanse of the sky, where Solace's rings were just barely visible arcing in the early morning light.

"Maps are good enough for me for now. Hopefully once we're done with all our training we can see all those places up close. I don't think I'd enjoy it, anyway. I'd just spend the whole time being terrified of getting caught."

For Sanyago, the risk of getting caught was at least half the fun. At ten, he was still too young for the really nasty punishments, and he figured he may as well take advantage of that while he could. Still, he thought, as he looked down to watch fog uncurl itself between the buildings, no sense pressing his luck. He began to work his way down the tall chapel, moving much more quickly than he had the year before. He was getting good at this.

He was getting good at sparring, too, and needed to hurry if he didn't want to be late for this morning's session. *Getting better. Getting better until we're seventeen and can use it all for real. That's what matters.*

Master Silva shook his head sharply. "No. Faster."

Sanyago smiled a little at the Sparring Master's admonition as Laris' blow came within a hair of his ear.

Laris grunted in frustration, then shook his head as if to clear the feeling away, eyes all steel and focus, ebony features drawn and set. He stepped forward, feinting with his left arm while keeping the right in open-handed guard. Sanyago flinched slightly at the shoulder-movement ruse, and Laris took the opening, hips pivoting just enough for a quick, low kick.

It was not fast enough. Sanyago scuffed one bare foot back in the dirt and used the arch of the other to slide Laris' blow away as it approached. He then attempted to bring his heel down on his opponent's instep, but Laris had already withdrawn his foot, planting it for leverage and stepping forward with the other to snap off a precise strike with his guard-hand. Sanyago leaned back just in time; Laris' knuckles brushed his sparring-robe but made no contact with flesh.

"Faster, Staafaen," said the Sparring Master, pacing back and forth on the sideline opposite the other students. "You are thinking too much. You must let your mind flow. Think ahead during your drills and practice, push the thinking deep into muscle and bone; then it is already done. Your movements are clever, but they come too late." Sanyago was careful to keep his features impassive; he liked to win, but did not wish to embarrass his friend by seeming to gloat.

"He is too fast, Master," Laris said through gritted teeth. It was a complaint Sanyago's sparring partners had voiced frequently over the last year, and Laris' expression dropped into one of rueful resignation almost immediately. He knew what was coming.

Master Silva fetched him a sharp blow on the back of the head with an open hand. Laris didn't move or flinch.

"Your opponent is never too fast, or too strong, or too skilled. The lack is in you, not the excess in them," the monk intoned. His long arm had returned to stillness so fast it made Sanyago feel a brief stab of envy.

The jealousy faded quickly, though. Sanyago knew he was good. Maybe even the best of his age in the whole Presilyo. He may not be as fast as Silva now, but with the years of training ahead, he would be. Besides, he was not just quick, he was creative. Hard to predict. Laris was strong, skilled, and extremely clever, but this was not enough. He fought in straight lines, with solid technique that did not easily bend to the moment's necessity. Sanyago felt a sharp stitch of guilt at this assessment, but that didn't make it untrue.

"May I have a moment to meditate before our next match, Master Silva?" Laris' voice cut through Sanyago's reverie, and Sanyago watched the tall, rangy monk look at his friend steadily for a moment. His face wore the same near-indifferent expression all the teachers seemed to cultivate, but Sanyago thought he could see something under it. Concern?

"Yes," Silva said at last. "But Staafaen. Remember. The Holy Fathom is not a toy. Care." He turned to the other students, assigning Andhlib and Vasili to spar in the meantime.

The Holy Fathom. Ah, that made sense. The Holy Fathom had featured as prominently in their lessons of late as stories of the Lotus Child and His lessons from the Star Sutras. *The Holy Fathom sits below, immanent, cognizant, potent to change, accessible to the comprehending mind.* Or so the Catechism held; Sanyago didn't fully understand the string of big Gentic words, but Laris had seemed to grasp the concept almost immediately.

The subject of Laris and the Holy Fathom had, in fact, drawn considerable attention from the very beginning. Catechist Yaatkr had started their first lesson by mentioning that the Holy Fathom was often utilized by those who did not respect its sacred nature, and Laris had raised his hand, very nearly demanding to know what could be so holy and mighty about it if it could not even keep heathens out. That had earned him three days eating table scraps, and they had argued about it later.

Sanyago, trying a little preparatory meditation of his own, felt himself drift back into the memory...

"The teachers know what they're talking about," Sanyago said. "You've seen what they can do. They understand the Holy Fathom."

"Apparently so do the heathens, because they can do the same things, they use the Fathom for all their magic and stuff. Old Roof-Weaver even admitted it," Laris responded, using the nickname the boys had made from the dictionary definition of Catechist Yaatkr's Gentic name.

"The Presilyo trains the most powerful Eychis in the Caustlands! The Somonei are legendary all over! With the Holy Fathom they're—"

"Of course they say that. What else? 'Sorry, young ones, this isn't the best Eychis-school around. We're like number four or something. Nothing you can do about it, you didn't get to pick!'"

"The visitors seem to think so too, though," Sanyago countered.

"You've been hiding behind walls and trees and things to listen again, haven't you? They'll swat your butt if they catch you at it. Or put you on scraps for a while like me."

Sanyago gave Laris the cocky grin that always made his friend sigh and rest his head against his knuckles. "It's good practice, and they've only caught me once. Besides, I did hear someone talking about it, someone important. Haenri-something, from the Salía government! He was talking about hiring monks I think, I'm not sure— they were speaking Gentic really fast and I couldn't get that close. But I did hear 'Somonei' and 'Best Eychis in the Caustlands'."

"I thought you said they were speaking Gentic," Laris said. "But he said 'Eychis'?"

Sanyago sighed at his friend's pedantry. "No, the monk was speaking Gentic and said 'Haeliiy.' I'm just translating." He and Laris had been speaking Ambérico, as they usually did. "He definitely said it though. That part was slow, one syllable at a time, like he really wanted to hammer the point. 'Best. Hell. Lith. In. The. Caust. Lands.' Just like that. And the Salían official didn't argue."

Laris' face set itself in that way that usually meant argument would be futile until he'd had time to think, so Sanyago decided to give up for the time being. Anyway, Laris' stubborn skepticism aside, he'd already shown a quick, agile grasp of the whole concept of the Holy Fathom that Sanyago could only sometimes keep up with, and it clearly impressed the teachers.

And concerned them. There were hints of limits, boundaries to keep well back from, above and inside, and thinking about them always reminded him of that charcoal sketch in the old encyclopedia—

Black Fence

—and he let the thought slip past him—

"Sanyago!" This time it was Master Silva's sharp voice that cut through the fog of memory. "Mind in the present! Step up to spar!" Seemed Laris had finished his meditation.

Sanyago opened his eyes. Laris stood ready inside the sparring-circle, angular features calm and focused. Sanyago sprang to his own mark, nudging the half-buried piece of wood with the ball of his foot.

"Ready. Stance. Move!" Silva said. Laris did not move, though, did not even spread his feet apart or put his hands up to guard. He was regarding Sanyago with a strange expression, and for the first time since first meeting his friend, Sanyago found that grey-metal gaze unsettling. It seemed to see too much, as though it were catching every stray wisp of intent that escaped Sanyago's skull.

Sanyago pulled his compact form into a fighting stance, hoping to make sure whatever weird game Laris had in mind wouldn't have time to play out. He struck out in an intricate series of Quickened Chaos feints and strikes, weaving and lurching, fast and sure and nearly without thought. Once Laris was off-balance, he could follow up with a snap-kick to the side of the knee. Properly pulled to smart, but not to injure, as they had been trained.

Step in, fall suddenly to the right, twist, come up with a rising strike with the left fist. Laris was not there, leaning just out of reach. Follow up with a secondary hammer-blow from the right, missing by just a hair from a nudge to the back of his wrist. No counterattacks. Sanyago faltered, stepped in again, doing his best to redouble his speed and unpredictability.

Laris barely moved, but Sanyago's sensation of being deeply *understood* had intensified. His feints were ignored, his strikes met with the laziest possible counters, just barely turning his attacks aside. Laris moved no faster than before, really, but he seemed ready for Sanyago's every motion before it even began. He fell into a fighting stance just as Sanyago had moved forward, and his eyes...they were not the same. Too bright to be reflected light from a late-afternoon sun.

Murmurs from the other students watching. Sanyago's mind dismissed them, pushed back into focus.

Sanyago fell back, started to circle, trying not to meet those strangely shining eyes, watching his opponent's stance and movements instead. No sign of taking any offensive, just standing there, barely even in any proper defensive form. Alright then, a spear-lunge should do it, with a wavering-snake strike that could hit anywhere the defense was weak. That would teach Laris to leave his guard down.

But the moment Sanyago set this plan in motion, Laris' stance had already changed to Flowing Fortress, the ideal counter. Sanyago had to pull his attack, unnerved. Laris was so still, so *calm*. And those eyes, bright and knowing. Sanyago was not easily frightened, had actually been reprimanded on many occasions for what the monks regarded as unnecessary risk-taking, but he was becoming a little frightened now.

He decided to wait, take the defensive himself, see what Laris would do. He drew himself up into a basic, elegant Gatoso stance from which he could shift smoothly to Burning Tiger, raking claw-hands through Laris' defenses with overwhelming ferocity while hopefully also blunting his attack.

Laris approached. Careful, slow crescent steps forward, like the most timid of novice students. Sanyago waited, his center slowly rising and falling, still avoiding his opponent's gaze, eyes on his shoulders, his hips. Sure enough, the taller boy's slender hips made a sudden snapping rotation, telegraphing his step into a straightforward punch.

It was an absurdly simple attack, if nearly perfectly executed—Laris' unarmed technique was actually better than his most of the time, even if he was not as quick—and Sanyago threw himself forward, his rapid raking strikes swatting the punch aside, then aiming for head and torso once past the longer-limbed boy's most effective guard distance.

Laris put up no real resistance to having his blow turned aside, but Sanyago's follow-up attacks met only air; his opponent had fallen backward, out of reach. Laris' other hand came down to catch himself...and his heel caught Sanyago squarely in the solar plexus, knocking the wind from him and sending him tumbling backwards. He managed to twist sideways into a roll and come back up in a wheezing crouch, but it was over.

No one spoke for a long time.

"Staafaen," Master Silva said in a quiet voice. "Let your opponent recover, and then bow."

Laris nodded, feet coming together, left hand curled over right fist at sternum-level. He waited for Sanyago to straighten—it didn't take long, as resilience was a well-drilled part of their training—and then acknowledged his defeated opponent's conceding bow with one of his own.

Still in a mild state of shock, Sanyago made his way over toward the sideline, meaning to join the other boys where they sat cross-legged on clean-swept flagstones. He got along a bit better with them these days; he'd earned their respect through becoming by far the best at sparring in their little class. *At least, the best up til now.*

Laris intercepted him. "Sanyago," he said softly. His features seemed a bit concerned, maybe a touch regretful. Glancing past him, Sanyago could see that Master Silva had started to follow Laris on his way over, but had stopped short when he saw him speaking to Sanyago. He hung back, an inscrutable expression on his bronze, weathered features.

"I am sorry. I didn't mean to frighten you," Laris said.

You didn't frighten me, Sanyago wanted to say, but he let the lie rest, swallowed it down. It would be pointless and insulting. He could feel the unsettled disquiet deep in his bones.

Laris frowned, cast his eyes down in thought. "I was frustrated. You are so fast. Thought I would try something I'd been thinking about." He glanced over his shoulder at Master Silva, and Sanyago followed his gaze. The Sparring Master stood waiting, his body language somehow exuding both patience and the impression that this conversation had best be brief. "I think it may have gotten me in trouble."

Sanyago laughed, and felt the last of his unease drain away. He clapped his friend on the shoulder with a grin. "No need for sorry. Whatever you did, it was impressive. You'll have to teach me, if Silva lets you. You better not keep him waiting."

Laris seemed infinitely relieved, giving Sanyago one of his broad, brilliant smiles. He nodded, once, then turned away to face Master Silva.

"Yes, Master?

Chapter 7

You all who are Fallen, you think the manner of your arrival makes you superior/can be excused? You have not tasted (Solace) fully as we have for longer than you have words for years and taken into (yourselves/ourselves/oneself). You all hide (behind/within) your slow curve river of ash except for your (unique ones/outcasts) in the northwards, and they all except one tribe which is strange keep fully (apart/pure) from us sometimes with (mutual) violence.

(Subject here switches to Gentic after insulting the expedition interpreter in terms she has refused to transcribe.)

You fancy yourselves scholars, you speak this one, yes? Good. Our ancestors and kin have become ash or have sold you their knowledge or have thrown themselves on the spines of your strange Fathomless tower. We here keep our peace easily enough. We are not interested in your Fallen-infested Caustlands, your Ashwound, and you do not thrive well here in what you call the Abwaild. So long as you do not take to razing and rebuilding Nature to suit you, like your outcasts do, so long as you stay on your side and we on ours, I think peace will continue to be easy.

But we have not forgotten.

Now get out. You know where the trade-villages are.

- Translation/Transcription from the 147 SE Keiner College Abwaild expedition

Kualabu, Tenggara, The Caustlands, 347 SE

Dayang sometimes liked to climb the high town wall and look out at the

Ashlit Mire. She knew she wasn't supposed to, though no one had ever actually told her. The wall was well-built and would have been quite difficult to climb from the outside, but from within the town it was simple enough. *Definitely less boring than weights or calisthenics*, she thought as she shimmied up one of the slanted reinforcing beams, trusting her leather jacket and heavy-duty jeans to protect her from splinters. She paused halfway up, listened, looked to either side. She'd never been caught, not in the dozen or so times she'd done this before, but that didn't mean it was time to get careless.

Nothing. The guards stood watch in their tall slender towers, but their vigilance was meant for the ashwights— or worse— that might come out of the grey-glow tangle of the Mire, not for fourteen-year-old girls hugging weathered timbers just behind the wall.

Dayang resumed her inchworm climb, pondering the shadowed planks that formed the vertical surface of the wall. She couldn't remember the last time it had been breached—she'd been barely old enough to say her own name—but of course all of the guards would remember. Mother often reminded Dayang and her siblings how lucky they were that none of their immediate family had been killed.

Immediate family. Dayang frowned as she neared the sharpened stakes that jutted straight up from the top of the wall at regular intervals. She no longer had any grandparents, and Mother refused to talk about them. Father was willing sometimes, but it was clear he and Mother's parents had never danced easy round their places in each other's lives. She shook her head. She wasn't out here for this; part of the reason she climbed the wall was to *escape* her family for a little while, however much she loved them.

Reaching the top, she hooked her arms round the two stakes on either side of the beam, straddling it like a slant-backed horse as she pulled herself up. One of the sharpened points had an old stain, the wrong color to be anything so human as blood. She did her best not to think about that, and leaned forward to peer between the pencil-point fortifications at the Ashlit Mire. *Edge of the Caustlands,* she thought, *just the Gyring Ash and more of the Mire past this, and from there it's nothing but Abwaild.*

This was a particularly good night for wall-watching. The moons were out, both more full than not, the silver and azure of their reflected sunlight making it just possible to pick out individual embertrees in the Mire, the soft grey glow of the luminescent ash-bog highlighting their reddish trunks. The ashes stirred, moving in sluggish whorls and currents that created shifting patches of light and dark on their surface. Looking upward, she could see the ghostly grey of the Siinlan Veil stretched out from treetops to heavens, obscuring the sky and stars almost entirely within her field of view with its slow, illuminated rising drift.

Her arms and legs had begun to ache, and she shifted position, thinking. It was harder now to slip away from home, especially since the Mufidh Incident. She supposed it had really been the Nurul Incident, since her sister had been the tale-bearer, but the long and storied history of Dayang and her sister meant there were far too many such episodes for "The Nurul Incident" to be a useful title for any of them.

No more of her few precious opportunities for slipping away would be spent on Mufidh anyhow. She'd caught him bragging to his friends about some of the things they'd been up to. He hadn't been lying, at least, and she wasn't even really that upset. She hadn't exactly been keeping their little exploratory trysts a deep dark secret herself: her best friend Sara knew plenty.

Still, he'd betrayed a confidence, and of course she trusted Sara to keep her mouth shut a lot more than she did Mufidh's snickering idiot friends. Continuing things with him hadn't been worth it. He was nice, but he wasn't necessary. They hadn't even been a couple, really, just...exploration partners.

A touch of guilt at that thought, creeping up through her guts into her throat. She shifted against the rough wood, staring the feeling down. She'd been curious, been *wanting,* but she didn't need a romance right now. Especially not right *here,* in Kualabu.

Though maybe Mufidh had begun to think differently. He'd taken it pretty hard, but she figured a clean break would heal faster. It was the kind of break she thought she'd want in his position, at least. Dayang admitted to herself she didn't really know what that position was like, though. She hadn't felt any grand romantic stirrings for him, and she didn't know if this was because she wasn't letting herself feel them—perhaps because the realities of Kualabu made open romance a tangled proposition at best—or because he just hadn't been the right boy. Or maybe she was just different, somehow; maybe that sort of feeling just came less easily for her.

Doing her best to pull her mind away from this subject, she let her gaze sweep back and forth across the Mire, which extended as far as she could see in both directions. It was just possible to make out its curvature, swooping inward as if to envelop the whole world. She supposed it did envelop *her* whole world, tangling out from the sludgy banks of the Gyring Ash to form the Siinlan that circled the whole of the Caustlands.

She watched, letting her mind wander over forms and formulae from her Wira training, characters and brush-strokes from her Common lessons, phrases and cadences of the Gentic poem she'd been assigned to memorize. These things all trailed away into the recesses of her mind, though, when she spotted movement out in the brambles.

Dayang leaned forward, pulled herself up straight and narrowed her eyes. Something was picking its way through the thick underbrush that marked the border between ash and soil. No, not something, she corrected herself as it forced an opening into the plain, tumbling out with a rough sort of grace before standing back up. Someone.

Someone was about all she could tell right now, though. Thick clothing, including a deep hood, made it impossible to really guess gender or skin tone at this distance. If it was an adult, though, it was a pretty short one. She wondered if the wall sentries had spotted anything yet. Even if they had, they wouldn't do anything but report, not unless whoever it was got a lot closer.

The someone took a few steps away from the brush, stomping some of the muck from the Mire off high leather boots. It spattered onto the little purple patch of abblum the person was standing over, flecking the low-creeping nodules and filaments with ashy grey. Reaching up with one gloved hand, the figure threw back its heavy hood. It was still too far away to make out any facial features clearly. Dayang cursed under her breath and fumbled with the hardened-leather case that hung from her belt, retrieving the collapsible spyglass she'd gotten for her twelfth birthday. SIINDRFORJD, read the big blocky Gentic lettering stamped into its smooth composite casing.

Shifting her weight awkwardly to one side, she slid the glass open with deliberate, one-handed care. It was a struggle to keep both herself and the Arco-made spyglass steady enough to make out anything useful, and the random Fathom-ripples crossing the image did not help. Even so, she got a few seconds of clarity. A girl about her own age, the swirling silvery patterns in her skin making her Pelo origin immediately obvious.

Did she cross the Gyring Ash from the Abwaild all by herself? Or did she just creep through the inner border of the Mire all the way from a border town? It was probably the former, even given the obvious dangers involved. The sheer bushwacking distance involved in the latter option was just too great. A scout, then, probably from a small village right across the Siinlan.

She'd only seen a handful of other Pelos in the flesh, and all of them had been in Surabaru, hawking exotic wares in the border-town's market quarter. Their odd appearance and even stranger reverberating voices had frightened her as a little girl. She'd tried to hide behind Father, and Nurul had laughed at her.

Dayang scooted a little farther up the beam, trying to keep from slipping down from her new, graceless position. The girl swimming in her spyglass image still seemed to be staring out at the town. *The same way I'm staring out at her,* she thought, and had a momentary flash of the sort of insight she'd begun to think of as "adult." *Our Fallen town must seem as strange to her as her Abwaild world might to me.*

She kept the spyglass trained on the Pelo scout for a few moments longer. But the girl just stood there, watching steadfast with her big bright-blue eyes. Finally, Dayang stuffed the spyglass back in its case and hooked her right arm back around the other stake, sighing a little as she felt her spine and muscles ease out of their contortions.

"She comes out of the Mire once a week or so, or at least that's what I overheard the guards saying. Of course, the Pelos don't use the same calendar."

She started, tightening arms around both stakes and legs around the beam, whipping her head around to look at the speaker.

It was a male Lingmao, of course; that had been obvious from the silky, inhuman contralto voice. The big cat—he was nearly as long as she was tall if she included the tail—was perched almost delicately on the next beam over to her right, front and back claws sunk firmly into the wood to keep him from sliding back. This seemed a bit precarious to her, but it likely helped that he was maybe half her weight. *And that he's a cat, naturally,* she thought. *Having four legs instead of two has its advantages.*

"How long have *you* been there?" she asked, glaring intently at his moonlit face. She didn't recognize him, and both the coloring and pattern of his coat were a far cry from any that were common among the town's handful of Lingmao clans.

"Sorry about that," he replied, sounding genuinely apologetic as he stretched his four long legs, then re-anchored his back claws. He was medium-sized for a male Caustland Cat, probably about half her height if he were standing up on all fours rather than stretched out low on the beam. His sleek body and large head were covered in thick, white-and-grey marbled fur, and his amber eyes regarded her with a hint of feline smile. "When I arrived you were holding on with just the one arm. I didn't want to startle you into falling." His Basa Mala was good, but he had a noticeable Gentic accent.

She managed a shrug and a small smile of her own. She found she was much more intrigued by having someone totally new to talk to than she was annoyed by his unannounced presence. "You're not from around here."

It wasn't really a question so much as a request for explanation, and he nodded, flicking one ear in her direction. "No. I come from Salía. I've been here almost a whole year. Eight and a half months, actually. Suppose I should celebrate my anniversary here in Tenggara in a couple of weeks."

"What are you doing out here in Kualabu? Why not a border town, like Surabaru? Or the capital?" She frowned a moment, furrowing her brow. "Oh, sorry, bad manners. I'm supposed to ask your name first. I'm Dayang Marchadesch."

He opened his mouth in the long, low, drawn-out *mrrooowwrr* that served as a Lingmao laugh. "Okay, Dayang," he said, looking back out at the girl in the clearing as he spoke. "For starters, I'm Jeims Dubwa. You'll owe me at least two more answers of your own, though."

She gave a brief snort that wandered somewhere between laughter and irritation, nodding when he glanced back at her. Out beyond the wall, the girl had crouched down in front of the Mire, looking still and intent.

"Alright then," Jeims said. "I suppose constant self-explanation is part and parcel of being a stranger in a strange land. I'm here for Wira-training. And cultural training. I'm after a Haeliiy position in the Salían Staffguard somewhere on the Tengarran border. You have quite the coterie of retired adventurers in this town. I wanted to study under someone with experience."

He lifted one front paw, flexed the strange fingers that were folded in under it, claws drawing back behind the second knuckles. Then he tucked the fingers back under, and the hand was a paw again. After leaning down to lick at the fur a moment, he continued, "Retired here together, as I understand. I've heard them mention you, you know."

Dayang's head swung round, the Pelo girl losing her interest for a moment.

"Really?" she said brightly, then furrowed her brow again. "You're not teasing, are you?"

"Ah, since when do Caustland Cats tease?" he asked, looking her in the eye with an impish smile. He laughed again, shook his head. "But no, I'm not. Your Wira-Guru Hang Che seems especially sure that you show great promise."

Dayang decided to file this away for future use, and her face must have been pretty transparent, because Jeims added, "I wouldn't mention that to him. You know how he feels about humility."

Dayang sighed, then pulled herself back up a little. "Yeah. But thanks. Sometimes I'm not sure anything is quite good enough for him."

Another lingering *mrrrooowwwrrr*. "Oh, it is, but only when it's perfect. You're very lucky to have him as a teacher, from what I've seen so far. But," he said, smiling as he saw her doubtful expression, "we're getting afield of your questions. I'm from Salía, as you've probably guessed since I can't seem to quite shake the accent. I am mostly studying spellcasting under Hue Tian. She's the reason I am here, and not in your capital or some border town."

She nodded. It made sense. She had taken some of her own lessons lately from Hue Tian, learning about spell-deflection and Pelo-runes, improving her general understanding of the Fathom. The thought reminded her of the girl again, and she turned back to see. The girl was looking too, seemed to be looking right at her, though even in the doubled moonlight it was difficult to tell. Or maybe she was staring at Jeims. *I wonder if she's ever seen a Caustland Cat before?*

Jeims had noticed as well, stretching forward and poking his big sleek head between the stakes. "Should we wave? I think we've been spotted."

Dayang frowned, thinking. "That might also get the attention of one of the guards on the wall. We could get in trouble."

"*Mrrrr*, no. *You* could get in trouble. I'm an adult and can sit on top of the wall if I want to. It's not like I'm endangering the town, and I'm unlikely to hurt myself if I fall. You, on the other hand…"

"Yeah, don't gloat about it," Dayang said. "You're not going to tell my parents or anything, are you?"

"No." He rubbed his head against the side of a stake with a little scratched-itch sigh, "I don't claim to always mind my own business, but I try not to meddle either. And I'd guess I'm not *that* much older than you are. I remember what it's like to want to get away sometimes."

"How old are you?" she asked, not taking her gaze from the girl, who was standing now, still watching whatever it was she was watching.

"Ah, but you still owe me two questions," he said. "So that would make three. Can't get greedy, Dayang."

She looked over at him, rolled her eyes, raised her chin in his direction.

"How often do you sneak off to climb the town wall? More to the point, why? And, of course, you'll have to tell me how old you are."

"Fourteen. And I can't get away that often. Maybe three times a month. I just like to see outside. I don't always climb this side to look at the Mire, but it's closest to our house." She wasn't sure why she was being so free with someone she'd just met, but it felt right somehow; being up here, looking out, always put her in a contemplative mood. *Or maybe,* she thought, glancing back at the confines of Kualabu, *it's just the rare chance to talk to someone I've never met.*

She shrugged. "From the western wall you can make out the top half of the Deisiindr above the horizon. I've only managed to make it out there a couple times, but at least I've never been caught."

It had been worth the risk. The Deisiindr was especially spectacular at night, a red-orange glow rising up beside the arcing silver bands of Solace's rings. The sheared-air chaos of what she knew must be the Windwall made the tower seem to shimmer where it met the horizon.

Jeims nodded. "I have done the same, and more often. I only climbed this side because I saw you here, and wondered what was worth seeing that a teenage girl would risk being out past dark."

She gave him a sour look, and he laughed. "I am nineteen. And you should worry less. At least one of the guards has already seen us. Voices carry farther on night air than you might think. Fortunately, she knows me, and of course she will know you. Probably she thinks that we are out here as part of our training, Wira-studies being famous for esoteric exercises."

Dayang felt black-tar dread rise up into her throat, looking around for said guard. *This had better not be a prank,* she thought. It wasn't. The woman in the nearest of the wall's sparse watchtowers returned her glance and seemed to smile. Or maybe the smile was wishful thinking; the interior of the tower was a pool of shifting shadow, illuminated only by the meager returning light from the nightfire lanterns pointed out at the mire.

Oh well, she thought, smiling back. *Too late to do anything about it now.* The woman probably recognized her; she hoped nothing got back to her parents. Or, God forbid, Hang Che. Her Wira-Guru would take it as a sign of indiscipline, and the bruises from the ensuing "sparring match" would take days to heal.

"Well," she said after a few more moments of inaction from the guards, "no one's coming this way, so I guess we're okay."

He flicked the tip of his tail. "I'm surprised they're not rushing to make sure the poor local girl's not being corrupted by foreign influences."

She narrowed her eyes, heat rising into her voice. "What? We're plenty used to foreigners here, you know, it's crawling with adventurers from everywhere. I'm not some—"

"Right, right, I'm sorry!" He held up a paw, ears drooping a little. "Just joking, I didn't really mean to imply—"

She sighed, one quick short exhalation, and nodded. "Yeah. Sorry. It's just that sometimes the adventurers and traders and others who come through act like we're all just stupid country people out here by the Siinlan, but it's not even that small a town."

"I know the feeling," Jeims said, ducking his head. "I come from a smallish town near the... " he took in a small breath, "...near the Black Fence," he said quickly, rushing past the words, "and we got a lot of soldiers passing through on their way to uh, you know, stand the Nowhere Watch." He shook his head a couple times, and Dayang frowned, trying not to think much on what that meant.

"We weren't, uh, *that* close. No one lives *very* close. Not close enough to, you know, matter." He grimaced, scratched his head against one of the stakes again. "Honestly, the worst thing about having lived there is explaining that to people. Anyway, a lot of the soldiers who came through were from Aldonza, and they sometimes acted like living in the capital made them a superior breed somehow. Not that I really blame them when I think about it, annoying as it was at the time. Getting out of my village was one of my main reasons for wanting to join the Staffguard."

He made a pensive chewing motion with his muzzle, turned his head to look west a moment with a small sad smile. "That, and the retired Salían

73

Army mage who had been teaching me died, may he rest in peace."

She inclined her head, gave him a sympathetic smile, and they fell silent for a few moments, looking out at the girl still standing inscrutably in front of the Mire. Now that her temper had cooled, she realized that the comment about "foreign influences" he'd passed off as a joke probably reflected some real concern on his part, concern that likely had more to do with Kualabu's prevailing religion than rural fear of outsiders, and she felt a twinge of sympathy imagining what that must be like.

She supposed she was devout enough herself, though she knew her family was considered anywhere between "moderate" to "dangerously close to apostate," by other, more obsessively observant people in town. Especially since Father was a convert...but that was its own can of worms. Dayang didn't really think a person's relationship with God was anyone else's business, and from the acerbic comments she'd heard both her parents make about "fundamentalists" she guessed they'd agree.

It wasn't something she'd really thought about much until recently, and her thoughts were interrupted as she started to slide down a bit and had to adjust her position again, hauling herself back up against the two stakes and tightening her legs around the beam. The Pelo girl hadn't moved, and Dayang had to admire her patience. She glanced over at the Caustland Cat.

"What do you think she's doing out there?" she asked.

"Your guess is as good as mine," Jeims said. "I'm tempted to jump down and just go talk to her, but I don't think the guard would appreciate that. And who knows how she'd react, or if she's even met a Caustland Cat before. The Pelos hold a wide variety of strong opinions on all us Fallen, but especially so regarding what they call 'bright beasts'. A lot of them consider we and the Caustland Crows unholy or unnatural or "ritually unclean" or whatever label you want to put on the stupid superstition."

She glanced over; he'd laid his ears flat in annoyance. She laughed. "Well, I couldn't do it, can you imagine the trouble I'd be in? I think she's about my same age, though."

He shrugged, stretching. "Maybe. Shorter, but a bit more developed than you in the chest and slimmer at the hip."

"How in Hell can you tell?" She tried to keep the irritation out of her voice; she knew there was no point getting annoyed at a Lingmao for commenting on her figure. It wasn't like he could take any prurient interest; it was all just matter-of-fact primate anatomy to him.

"Besides seeing a lot better in the dark?" He laughed, claws making little clicking sounds in the wood as he stretched. "Yes, I know, she's also far away, and I don't have a fancy Deisiindr spyglass like you do. And our distance vision isn't great." He wriggled his long sleek head as he considered his response. "There's a Fathom-technique for it, lets me farsee without all the distortion in your expensive Arco toy. It also lets me see the heat-outline of her body. Very useful, if a little taxing to use for long."

"That does sound useful," Dayang said. "All my perception training so far has been for widening my field of vision, anticipating attacks I can't see, that kind of thing. Can humans learn your technique too?"

"Probably," Jeims said after a moment's thought. "But with a lot more difficulty, I would guess. Feline eyes are different; that's why they shine in the dark."

Dayang decided to give the spyglass another try, pulling it out of its case again and performing another careful balancing act with just one arm holding her up. The image still swam, as always, but at least there was more detail.

They both stared out at the girl, but the girl was no longer staring back. She had turned to face the Mire, now in a low defensive crouch. She was holding something in her left hand, something short and curved and grey that was hard to make out against the ashen background of the Mire.

"What is she—" Dayang whispered, then fell silent as something reddish-black barreled out of the eerie growth, tumbling the Pelo girl into a mutual clench. Limbs tangled, pulled, pushed. The weapon in the girl's hand came down, ripped and tore. A wash of grey-green ichor spilled out over misformed flesh, stained the girl's clothes. There was the whisper of a rasping cry, something Dayang thought she heard more through the Fathom than the night air, and she saw the girl had her free hand splayed out just above the twisted gash which probably constituted the ashwight's mouth.

"Muffling spell," Jeims whispered. Glancing away from her spyglass, Dayang saw that he'd gone stock-still, and realized a moment later she'd frozen up as well, feeling like shards of sickly, rotting ice were pricking their way up her spine. She was distantly aware of shouting from the guard towers, orders being relayed. *Is it just the one or could this be another wave, another wall breach? Oh God I'm not even ready to fight yet not really...*

The ashwight's whole head-lump seemed to yawn open around its ragged mouth, releasing an uneven surge of green-grey sludge. The misshapen body went still, and the Pelo girl pulled it backward into the faint grey glow of the Mire. Dayang thought she saw the red of the thing's almost-flesh fade behind its blackened crust.

Gone. A garish smear of greenish gore against the purple abblum. Dayang put her spyglass away with hands she tried to pretend weren't shaking.

"Huh," Jeims said after a long silence. "Guess she's gone for the evening. Impressive, though. Wonder if she knew the thing was coming somehow."

Dayang shook her head. "I don't know. I've never seen anything like that, not even in an echoplay." She could hear the low mutter and clatter of the guards as they reacted to the sudden bout of mortal combat and subsequent vanishing. She could also hear her heart pound right up through her throat into the lower reaches of her jaw, still scanning the Mire. *Please don't let there be more, please don't let there be more...*

"Hard to do an ashwight justice without using the real thing on stage, and I doubt many directors would be that foolhardy," Jeims said.

"Yeah," she said. She was still seeing that gaping mockery of a face disappearing into the brambles, that dribbling trail left behind...and she realized she was still shaking, just a little, and the night was too warm to blame it on the cold.

"Hey." Jeims scritched the wood with one claw to get her attention. When she looked over, he ducked his head. "Sorry. I shouldn't be so glib, you said you've never seen anything like that before, not always an easy kind of thing to digest at first."

She tugged herself back up on the beam a little. Her arms were getting tired in the aftermath of the adrenaline. "That's not it. I mean, not all of it, I know I need to get used to this sort of thing. It's not like Hang Che is teaching me to bake curry puffs. It's just...what if there are more? We'd have time to get down, but...back when I was little, they breached the wall. My..." she cleared her throat, feeling embarrassed by the tremor in her voice. *Grow up, Dayang!* "...my grandparents, my mother's parents, I guess she watched it happen, it must have been..." she shook her head.

"Oh." Jeims paused, ears lowered just slightly. "I suppose that's all true." The tip of his tail twitched hard against the beam with a muffled *thunk.* "We all have to face the world we live in. I'm sorry about your grandparents. I hadn't thought about there being more, I didn't..." He trailed off, and his slitted pupils widened to their fullest, making his eyes look nearly dead-black. *He's afraid now too.*

They both looked out at the Mire for a few more minutes. Nothing else came. Dayang's heart finally slowed. Her arms began to get truly tired, the way they did when she was approaching the last possible push-up during one of Hang Che's fitness tests.

"I've got to get down and head home before I get caught, I think," she told Jeims. "My parents were fighting when I left and that usually buys me a couple hours, but I shouldn't push my luck, I've probably been up here an hour and a half at least."

"A strange thing to tell a strange cat, that sort of family business. A lot of what you've mentioned has been, really." He cocked his head. "But you are probably right. I should get some sleep, myself. I'm not a morning person at the best of times, and I have a long day of training ahead tomorrow."

Dayang felt her face flush against the night air, then shook her head. She let go of the stakes on either side of her and hugged the beam instead, sliding down while hoping her jeans and thick leather jacket would continue to protect her from any splinters. When she got to the bottom, she stood up, dusted herself off—a few chips of wood, but nothing poking through her clothes—and shrugged, looking up at his perch on the other beam.

"Easier to be honest with a stranger. Gossiping about townspeople wouldn't be a popular move, and no one would listen to you anyway."

He grinned down at her. "Insightful. Though I think you underestimate people's endless appetite for gossip. Don't worry, I don't have any intention of feeding it." Instead of sliding down, he simply rolled right off the beam, turning once in the air and landing lightly on his feet. He approached her with his tail raised, sleek shoulders rising to about the level of Dayang's hip. Sitting back on his haunches, he uncurled his front right paw and held the resulting furry, six-fingered hand up at her. She bent down to take it, and shook, feeling the odd combination of fur, bare skin, and leathery pads against her own weapon-callused hands.

"Pleasure meeting you, Dayang."

"Pleasure meeting you too, Jeims Dubwa."

Dayang frowned as they parted, turned around. "Jeims?"

He paused with one paw in the air, turned his head, "Yes?"

"Have you ever seen anything come out of the Mire? Besides tonight, I mean."

He nodded, once, dipping his head down below his shoulders. "Yes, but not here." His voice was quiet, drained of its previous playfulness and bravado. Down went the paw, his feline body twisting so he could look her straight in the eye.

"Keep up with your training, Dayang Marchadesch. No wall stays unbroken forever, and what comes in doesn't care if you are prepared or not."

She looked up at the wall, nearly three times her height, and nodded.

He smiled, and when he spoke again some of the sardonic slyness had come back into his voice. "And look on the bright side. There are worse things than what slogs through the Ashlit Mire. If we keep our current career paths, we might even get the chance to see them one day."

He turned and padded off, flicking her a goodbye with the tip of his tail.

Her parents were still arguing when Dayang slipped back into the house, and she made it to her bed without being caught; Nurul had taken over Pandikar's old room while he was out on his artisan's apprenticeship. She missed her brother, but supposed a room to herself was some small consolation. *Especially considering the way Nurul snores*. It was a comforting thought, somehow, born of harmless domestic irritation, but it was cut in two by an image of the dying ashwight in the Pelo girl's arms.

How could that thing see it had no eye—She pulled the covers up and thrashed over onto her side, shaking the thought out of her head.

Dayang dreamed of faces staring out from the tangles of the Mire.

Third Interlude

Acheronford, Salía, The Caustlands, 347 SE

"Sorry, Braun. Don't believe it." Sergeant Wrait tapped his fingers on the hard wood of the beat-up table between them, and shrugged.

Sergeant Braun scowled at him, then back down at the boot in her hand, pushing the stiff bristles of her brush a little harder into the thick grey leather. "Believe it or don't, Wrait, it's what I heard. Good source, too, not just your usual company gossip." She waved vaguely at the walls of the empty barracks dayroom, glancing out the window at the other garrison buildings visible across the practice yard.

He tried on a properly judicious look at her assertion, though the bit of amiable scoff on her face told him he'd probably failed. "But, but. Come on now. Bloody Saepis in Acheronford? And what the Hell would the Sovereign Nations want with a border town a quarter-turn round the Gyring Ash from them?" His hand traced a partial circle in the air, northeast to southeast.

She grinned, eyes lighting up with wolfish joy at being the first to share Interesting News. "Nah, nah, it's not just that they were in Acheronford, it's that they crossed the Siinlan to get here. Must have trudged right through the Gyring Ash and the Mire on both sides. Guards said they found cinder-sludge on the Saepis' boots and trousers."

He thought about this for a moment, or at least pretended to while she examined her own boot from every possible angle. Most of his attention was fixed on the semi-transparent stage of the echoplay sitting on the table between them. It showed some passable stage combat, and the recording mage had done a pretty good job keeping the translucent combatants from going too blurry with the motions.

"Don't mean they *crossed* it, though," he answered, once all the actors who had lost their battles were bleeding ketchup onto the stage. "They coulda just wandered out into the Ashlit Mire, got a little sooty. They even know which of the Nations the Saepis were from?"

She thunked her boot down forcefully on the quartzwood floor and snorted. "Yeah, sure, they came all the way down here from the Sovereign Nations so they could wander out into the Ashlit Mire, take in the sights, maybe pick some damn flowers. Come on. Siinlan's the same wherever round the edge of the Caustlands you go. Same Mire, same Gyring Ash, same embertrees." Sergeant Braun leaned back in her chair, then had to catch herself from tottering as its aging wood gave way more than her balance had accounted for.

"Same bloody monsters lurking under the whole sodding thing," Sergeant Wrait muttered, and took a long quaff from the heavy mug he'd set beside the echoplay tablet. When the time finally came for him to retire, he figured he'd never have to see the damn Siinlan ever again, never have to spend another night staring at the Ashlit Mire. But he was only forty, and retirement was decades off.

"Yeah. Right?" The chair came back down to the floor with an unsteady *thunk.* "Same on our border as it is on Tenggara's or Nainadion's or any of the other Outer States. And speaking of the ashwights, this little Saepi group musta been pretty formidable to make it across the whole Siinlan without worrying 'bout bein' torn to pieces." She picked up her other boot and pointed the brush at him before putting it to leather. "I'm tellin' ya. Could be trouble."

Wrait downed the last of his drink. "Maybe. You ask me, the Sovereign Nations are always trouble. I had a cousin go Michyero a couple years ago, up and joined the Triune Path. Not the one what runs the Presilyo and sends Somonei out everywhere neither. No, he gets with the sodding Carvers, runs right off outside the Caustlands to join 'em. Least he took a proper bridge, far as I know." *Took leave of his senses, too. Poor Caayi, he was the last one she had left alive.*

"Yeah," Braun said, pushing the brush down hard where an especially stubborn stain had taken up residence, "I've heard of them. Never really understood the difference between Michyeros, all seems pretty much the same to me but mind, my family's never really been religious. All that sort of argument over tiny scraps of difference? Bit mad, at the end of the day.

What's it profit?"

He shrugged, poking at the echoplay image with his index finger, feeling the low, flickering buzz through his skin as light parted to flow round the intrusion. "Ma was raised in it. Triune Path, I mean, she taught me a little here and there, and she had the Somonei over for meals twice or thrice, when they happened to be attached to the Army garrison I grew up by. Strange folk. Da didn't have no truck with it, but he was nice enough to the monks when they were at table with us. Anyway, my cousin knew my Ma had come up Michyero, tried to get me to join up alongside."

Wrait scowled and tapped the tabletop with his still-buzzing fingertip, remembering. *Wants to fire me up about a faith I never really cared about, then pull me off to some mad Saepi offshoot of it. Well, I've seen folk do more foolish things lookin' for ought to mean something in their lives. Maybe it would have worked on someone else.*

"Yeah?" She brought her boot up to her face for close inspection, blew invisible grime off the spot she'd been scrubbing. "What'd he say? Wanted you back to your Michyero roots, I'm guessing?"

"Sure, that were part of it," He frowned at the echoplay. An actor had come from off-stage to mourn his slain lover, cradling the man's head in his hands while offering up a soliloquy. "Kept talking about how it's our divine mission to claim all of Solace for the Divine, how the Michyeros here in the Caustlands're failing their duty on that side of things. Talked a lot about the Foreborn, some kind of reincarnated herald of their prophet. Had more to say, too, but I must admit I stopped listening at some point." Wrait leaned in, peering at the slightly luminous actors. He was pretty sure he could see the "dead" one still breathing.

"Guessing you told him that was crowshit." Braun stuck her hand in the boot, turning it this way and that, frowning as she spotted another stain. The bristles came down to scourge it for its sins against Uniformity.

"Well, I like to think I've got a little more diplomacy in me than *that*." He leaned back in his chair, watched the echoplay stage fade out and back in again as the scene changed. "Told him the main duty I was aware of was another couple years in the Army right here in Salía, and I wasn't about to run off on it. He didn't like that, but I think I made it clear I was final on the subject."

Damn near had to make it forcible, too, fool wouldn't take a hint. Or his shiny new conviction wouldn't let him. Kept talking like I were full loyal with the Presilyo, couldn't conceive I might not care about Michyero family squabbles. Carver, Presilero, or the Lotus Child Himself, all the same to me.

"Make it clear? Guess you did, knowing you. Makes me wonder which one of the Nations these Saepis might've been from." She paused, narrowed her eyes at another blotch of ground-in grime. "Suppose you can't always tell just by lookin' at 'em."

"Might be you'll hafta check with that 'good source' you got. They might not know neither, might be no one does. Like you said, can't tell by lookin'. Some of 'em dress odd or special accordin' to their culture or whatever, but they got a lotta separate groups up there in the Nations. How'd anyone know they were Saepis in the first place?"

She frowned, glanced out the window at the practice-yard where dusk spilled over the trampled earth.

"Dunno, dunno. I'll have to ask round."

"Right, well, do it careful. Captain don't like people pulling in more rumors than we already got swirlin' round all the time."

"Yeah, yeah. I got just one more thing. Seems they're being taken up to Aldonza sometime next week. The Saepis, I mean. So it must be *something* going on."

He let out a groaning sigh from halfway down his throat. "Let's just hope it ends up being something goin' on somewhere else. This post might be bloody boring but that beats being just bloody. I've put my spear to enough use for one lifetime already."

They sat for a time after that, each staring off into space. Sergeant Wrait's hand tightened as it lay against the faded denim of his civvie jeans, loosened, tightened again, as though gripping an imaginary haft. Sergeant Braun ran a forefinger back and forth along a rib through the thin fabric of her t-shirt, the slightest hint of grimace crossing her heavily-freckled features.

"Yeah, alright, amen to that," Sergeant Braun said finally. She tucked both boots under her arm, stood up. "I'm off to my bunk, Wrait, enjoy your play. Good evenin' to ya."

"Sure, Braun, to you as well." He returned his attention to the echoplay, if a bit listlessly.

She stopped at the doorless threshold, looked back. "Hey. Wrait?"

He looked up from the echoplay's elaborate, translucent set, nodded slightly. His face was tight and over-thoughtful.

"All serious, though, you think there's anything to all the talk?" She had one hand on the back of her neck where it met the base of her skull, tugging at her short reddish hair. She didn't seem to realize she was doing this. It looked like maybe it hurt.

He just looked at her, looked for maybe half a minute before he replied. "I don't know, Braun, I really don't. There hasn't been a proper war since the Siege of the Deisiindr. And Fallen fighting Fallen? Really fighting, not just bandits and a border misunderstanding or two? Divine help us, I hope not. But I don't know. They don't tell me any more than they do you."

She breathed in, held it, closed her eyes and let it out. "Alright," she said, and turned to go. "Alright."

Chapter 8

Magic. This is a heavy word, one so weighed down by history and superstition it can sometimes seem better to avoid it altogether. And some do, or they try, substituting awkward terms like "Fathom-Induced Phenomena" or "infraphysical". The Praedhc (or Tuzhu, or Pelos, or Antepas, or on and on; naming is always a difficult affair) call it Fathom-dancing, among other things, and have their own words for the less concrete "supernatural" phenomena that our ancestors would have termed "magic".

So of course I understand that all languages have their own term, with slight differences of shading and connotation, and here I am giving only the Gentic term for "magic" as an example. It is no matter. The essence of the word is the same in every tongue.

So why do we call the practices, powers, and phenomena that we study and practice here "magic?" Why have we not found some other word? Perhaps borrow one from the Praedhc, like "Fathom-dancing?" Because the association is unavoidable. It cannot be rooted out of the common vocabulary, and it would be foolish to try. Even more foolish, here in the balcony of our ivory tower, would be some pompous effort to maintain a vocabulary so utterly divorced from common usage.

Yes, yes, I understand that academic institutions sometimes make the attempt regardless. Let us not fall prey to the favorite sins of our tribe.

Very good then, so it is magic we study and practice. It is still imperative that we distinguish this real and demonstrably effective discipline from all the charlatanry, foolishness, and fraud that passes under that same name, too often meeting shamefully little resistance along the way. This will be hard. Our ancestors faced the same problems when it came to their own demonstrably effective disciplines, and a study of their history sadly informs us that they never did arrive at a satisfactory solution.

- Archmage Zhang Guiying
  Commencement Address to the Class of 175, Phoenix Hill Academy

Presilyo Monastery, Inoue Island, The Caustlands, 348 SE

Sanyago stared at the tiny blue flame in his palm. He turned his hand over, feeling a small strange prick of sensation as it flickered heatless up against his flesh. He turned his hand back again, concentrating on the vast and variegated net of cause, rule, and invocation that converged to bring this minute bit of fire into existence. Waver, disengage from the Holy Fathom even the smallest bit, and it would be snuffed out.

"Hedgeflame is relatively simple, as spell families go," said Master Alein in his cool, calm tenor. The tall, aging monk stood in a demonstrating pose before the class, the pale skin of his outstretched arm entirely wreathed in writhing spirals of violet flame.

"This is of course to be expected, as it is named after the hedge-wizards and novice magicians who often employ it. It is also highly useful. It does not burn, it is not extinguished by water, and the light it gives off can be modified in a number of interesting ways." The fire coiled round Spell Master Alein's arm pulsed and flowed as he murmured a series of quick, shifting words in Three Harmonies. Red now, then silver, pulsing above and below.

"That full spectrum is beyond this lesson," Alein said as he let his arm drop, and the hedgeflame snuffed out with only the slightest of coronal auras remaining. He looked out at the assembly of twenty-three students, all with palms upturned.

Only three of them were having any luck: Sanyago, who had grasped the connections and comprehensions of the formulae set almost immediately; Vasili, who was nursing a sputtering flame with one hand half-cupping the other to protect the delicate little break in ordinary reality; and Toraen, a small, studious boy whose light brown eyes and dark brown features were focused intensely on the bright inverted tear that held steady just above the contrasting pale flesh of his palm.

Alein would not congratulate the three of them. It would only compound the frustration, and sometimes the resentment, of the other students. Laris, sitting beside Sanyago as always, did not seem the least bit frustrated, had in fact not even attempted the conjuration yet. He was studying the formulae page with intense concentration, flipping pages back and forth as if in a trance. Probably once he got it, he'd get it perfectly, while Sanyago's would always have a whiff of improvisation about it.

They'd been under the Spell Master's tutelage for several months now, starting classes with him at the class eleven-year marker. Though Master Alein reminded them constantly that they'd been receiving the foundations for many years through their many lessons on the Holy Fathom, even though they may not have realized it at the time.

Knowing better than to interrupt Laris while in this kind of reverie, Sanyago glanced over his own textbook and scanned the set's central diagram before closing his eyes. He felt the lines and curves of meaning and consequence converge in and around his hand, forming the flame at the center, sustaining it, carrying the implications of its existence outward.

It captivated him, spun out a great whirling web of possibilities in his head, exposed depthless heights of possibility threaded endlessly through the Holy Fathom. He felt a deep surge of pleasure as his mind grasped and pulled and arrayed, as something new came together. A shift in paradigm, a differently declined word, a changed conjugation, a murmur, a gesture. He stood, ready to thrust out his hand as though delivering a palm-heel blow on the sparring-field.

Some small voice in his head spoke of trouble but was drowned in fascination. His arm shot forward.

A great gout of cool bright fire burst from his hand, streaking over the heads of several classmates. Dancing gold and white, it very nearly reached Master Alein, who did not so much as flinch. Instead, he snapped his hand forward from the wrist with one sharp word of command, and the flames vanished.

Sanyago felt... saw... heard...the elaborate underpinnings of his impromptu spell collapse, then tumble abruptly into nothingness with the force of his teacher's counter.

Spell Master Alein breathed in once, breathed out once. No one spoke. Sanyago slowly lowered his arm. He felt himself cringe ever so slightly, looking over at Laris. His friend had worked out the formulae just as methodically as he always did, producing a small but perfect deep-blue flame that did not flicker or waver in the slightest. He looked up from his handiwork, steel-spoke eyes meeting Sanyago's. The hint of a sigh, of a shrug. *Looks like you're the one in trouble now for pushing ahead.* Sanyago managed a pained little half-smile in acknowledgement.

"Sanyago," Alein said evenly. "Wait outside. Horse stance. Meditate on thought before action."

"Yes, Master Alein," Sanyago said, putting hand over fist before bowing deep. He stepped between the rows of students, carefully opened and closed the big wooden door at the back, and leaned against the outside wall for just a moment. Deep breath in, deep breath out, spread the stance, slide down the wall. Come off the wall. Arms at the sides. Fists. Ponder what you've done.

And ponder he did, though almost certainly not the way his teacher intended. He thought about the feeling of hard-earned ease as his intuition dropped the pieces of his impromptu spell into place, the exhilaration as it actually worked, however crudely.

They'd been studying the essentials that built up to this lesson for months, and had been taking lessons, theological and otherwise, on the nature of the Holy Fathom for years. Part of the purpose of these lessons, their teachers emphasized, was to expose some of the students' ubiquitous superstitions and supposed bits of hedge-magic as the foolishness they really were.

"True magic, the sort that proceeds from the Holy Fathom, is much more than just a few scrawled symbols and muttered words," Foundations Master Yeong had said, pacing back and forth in front of the class. "A word, a gesture, a diagram; all have no power if they are not accompanied by Harmonious Comprehension. This is true whether these words are in the worldly Proken or the holy Three Harmonies." He had gone on to explain that "worldly" in this case simply meant "not holy" and that it was not necessarily a sin to learn or even use Proken.

Sanyago flexed his muscles a little, re-straightened his back. His body was starting to complain about the punishment, and he let the sensation pass cleanly through his mind without catching, as they had been taught. Well, mostly. He was supposed to live in the present and not anticipate the unreality of future experience, but it was hard not to assume he was going to be out here for a good while.

He thought about the special warding sigil he and Laris had copied from one of the books his friend was forever poring over. It had been, in hindsight, a pretty basic one, though at the time they didn't really understand much of what the book said about it, or much of what the symbols that comprised it meant. It was supposed to repel insects and other very small creatures, so they had gamely scrawled it into the dirt next to a fire-ant nest, and Sanyago had poked the mound with a stick.

His right arm had felt like it was on fire for two weeks after, and the infirmary had refused to treat him lest he not "learn his lesson." Nothing really happened to Laris, who had leapt back and immediately wiped the diagram away so none of the teachers would know what they had been attempting. Sanyago supposed he should have dropped the stick faster, but there had been something fascinating about the way the tiny red-and-black bodies roiled up from the mound. And up his stick and then arm, of course.

Words, symbols, gestures, ceremony. All there to move the mind, to scribe the channels along which thought could flow through the knowable chaos of the Holy Fathom and move the world. Without Harmonious Comprehension, the sigil had just been a copied picture, inert as the coarse earth it was scrawled into.

He flexed again, breathed deeper, tried to put his mind into a state of perfect calm, pushing out the memory of fiery ant-bites.

And now it was his muscles that felt like they were on fire when Master Alein finally came out to speak with him, carrying the disciplinary cane.

By the time he returned to the sleeping-quarters that night, his butt was on fire as well. Laris looked up from the book he was reading—Laris was always reading, or meditating, or thinking, except when Sanyago managed to sweep him up into some adventure or conversation—and watched solemnly as his friend first climbed up to join him on the top bunk, then sat down slowly with a drawn-out wince.

"It was impressive, at least," he offered once Sanyago was as comfortably settled as he was likely to get this particular evening. Laris sat up himself, swinging his long legs over the edge of his mattress. Vasili glanced over from his own upper bunk across the way, then went back to repairing his robes.

Laris nodded at Vasili before continuing. "It doesn't seem fair that you got in more trouble than I did last year at the sparring match." *The first time I beat you,* he didn't say.

"A few hours of horse stance and a caning won't kill me. I think they were a lot more concerned about what *you* did. And it was more impressive than just throwing some hedgeflame. They taught us about hedgeflame. What you did was, like, legendary stuff."

They both fell silent. Sanyago had begun to learn to counter Laris' strange empathic prescience, which the teachers had since obliged him to use more carefully. They'd all had an impromptu lesson on the subject right after last year's unsettling sparring match, and Master Silva had been at pains to assure them that "Staafaen had not actually learned to read minds." Intentions, Silva said, left their mark in the Holy Fathom, and some people could learn to read them, people who had what he called "The Entyecogno Gift," but no one had the power to reach into another person's inner self.

Even so, many weeks went by before the other boys stopped throwing wary looks Laris' way. Sanyago had never again bested his friend on the sparring-ground, though he'd come close a few times. He was still faster, but never enough to get ahead of Laris' calm foreknowledge of even his cleverest tricks and gambits. The cleverest ones worked the least, really, relying as they did on deceptions and misdirections that Laris could now see right through.

The moment passed, and Laris shrugged, cradling his hands together in his lap, as he often did when deep in thought.

"They just gave me a lot of warnings about diving too deep before I really understood anything about the Fathom." Laris paused, the corners of his mouth turning down. "And they took away my book." He said this last like it was a far worse punishment than a caning. For Laris, Sanyago thought, it probably was. Seemed pointless too, since Laris' discovery of his strange talent had almost certainly been inevitable; the book had simply meant it happened a little sooner.

"I still don't understand why they didn't cane you for stealing it."

"I didn't steal it. I used a stool to get it from one of the grown-up sections. It wasn't one of the age-restricted sections. Nothing Ragado. Or from the part that's...locked."

The Fortified Archives. Sanyago shuddered, and reflexively forced other things into his mind, to block the void behind that heavy steel-shod door from filling with something...else.

"Don't," Sanyago said simply, and Laris nodded, steering away from the subject.

"I'm just saying it wasn't really a dangerous book. My book was all basics, really, nothing we haven't already learned by now. I was just a little early, I guess, and it let me understand...what I could do. I'd have figured it out anyway. They even said so, except that it's not wise for a kid like...me..." He trailed off for a moment.

He means "probably the smartest student in the Presilyo, but he'd never say it, Sanyago thought before his friend continued, "...that it might let me go too far before I really knew the dangers, and that the dangers were what the other books...talked about."

Dangers. Outside the Triune Path lay dangers. Sanyago kept his mind full of formulae and forms and the taste of his favorite curry.

"They were worried you could dip too deep without knowing," Sanyago whispered, looking around. The other boys were all involved in their own conversations and pursuits, but if they heard the topic they might get angry, and not without reason. Sanyago tucked two fingers under his thumb, flicked a quick Karana warding-gesture with pointer and pinky.

"You *can't*," Laris whispered back, leaning over toward him. Sanyago leaned in as well, though the shift in weight made his right butt cheek smart.

"You can see the edge," Laris said, his voice so near silent Sanyago had to strain to catch it, but with every word enunciated slow and clear. "You can't get close by accident, you..."

He opened his mouth as though to say something more, then closed it, and frowned. Sanyago could feel something crawling, branching, beneath and behind, and set his jaw. Laris shivered. He felt it too. Of course he did. *Below outside the Holy Fathom...*

Outer Below

no...no...

NO

"No," Laris said, as if in echo of Sanyago's thoughts, though the word wasn't directed at Sanyago, and violently shook his head. Bared his teeth. Sanyago thought of other things, recalled the taste/sensation of hot chocolate nearly burning the tongue on a winter morning. Mapped out the kata he was learning, his phantom self flitting here and there on the practice-yard modeled in his mind.

It eased. Vasili looked up from his needle and thread, his high-cheekboned face uneasy and even paler than usual. They both tried to smile at him. He frowned, pushed the needle in, pulled it out, eyes down.

"You can't, not by accident," Laris said again. His voice was soft, not really a whisper anymore, but Sanyago was sure only he could hear it. Laris shook his head, and Sanyago thought of apricots, plucked and mashed for drying.

Nothing returned.

"Really, they didn't like the book because it wasn't...holy." Laris said in a quiet rush. "It didn't say 'The Holy Fathom,' just 'The Fathom', and there was nothing at all about the Lotus Child or Harmonious Comprehension. It wasn't Ragado, it was..." Laris searched for a word. "...it was plain. Ordinary. Like the Fathom might be mysterious in a lot of ways, but was still a thing that could be understood and used, no need for prayers or scriptures or mantras. After that question I asked back when we were littler, when I got in all that trouble..." He shrugged and trailed off. Another long pause.

In truth, there had been any number of questions fitting that description in the years Sanyago had known him, but Sanyago knew the one he was talking about. It had also been the one that had made the teachers begin to really watch Laris carefully: "If the Fathom is so mighty and holy, why can it not keep the heathens out?"

Their answer, delivered to the rest of the class since Laris had already been escorted outside, was that all things were created by the Divine, and that free will allowed His creations to use or misuse them in the eternal cycle of rebirth. This made sense to Sanyago, though Laris had not been impressed when he'd tried to explain it later.

Laris was a pain in the butt for the Masters, Sanyago guessed. In continuing his eavesdropping hobby, he'd pieced together that they considered Laris one of the most talented and promising students currently at the school, and also one of the most concerning. This wasn't cause for feelings of inadequacy; he'd learned that he himself sometimes received similar praise, and he knew he was also a pain in the butt, though for different reasons—like eavesdropping, which they still sometimes caught him doing. Most interesting of all was when he'd caught bits of conversation implying they'd been put together on purpose. It wasn't clear to what degree the teachers regretted or were glad of this decision.

"Holy or not, it is dangerous, Laris," Sanyago said quietly. He punched the taller boy very gently on the shoulder. "They know what they're talking about, you've seen it. You accept what the monks teach about fighting, about the Ho...about the Fathom, about languages—but then they talk about the Divine and you act like you're not sure. Those teachings go back thousands of years, you know that's true, it's even in the books that weren't written by the Enlightened Saint." Sanyago shook his head. "I don't understand you."

Laris sat there, looking torn. He sighed, and it was a thing of the entire body, his normally ramrod-straight posture becoming a bowed hunch. His grey eyes shone wet, and then his cheeks. Sanyago scooted closer, winced at the pain this caused for his own cheeks—though not the ones on his face—and put one arm around the larger boy's shoulders. The realization that said shoulders were shaking shocked him. Laris never cried. Sanyago stayed silent, listened.

"My parents," Laris said finally, his voice low and dark and despairing. "I try not to remember them, it only hurts. They didn't...they didn't teach me any of it. I remember once when other people prayed, they just sort of stood there. They were scholars, I think. I remember their name, our name I mean, even though they told me I should forget when I came here. It was...it *is* Lozada. Anyway they...my mom..." He choked, buried his head in his hands, sobbed once. Twice. Three times. "She used to say all the time—"

Laris took in a deep breath, shuddered again, straightened a little. Used the sleeve of his robe to dry his eyes, his cheeks. He turned, met Sanyago's gaze fully. "She would say, 'Staafaen. Think about what you are told. Don't just believe it.'" He paused, considered. "Or it was something like that. It was a long time ago and I was little."

It was the most Laris had ever said about his parents since the day they first met. He closed his eyes, and Sanyago's arm about his shoulders rose, then fell as Laris breathed in, deep, breathed out.

"Sorry," he said softly, composure regained, straightening up completely.

Sanyago let his arm slip down from around him, smiling and shrugging. "It's okay."

"I usually just let the feelings pass through, like they teach us," Laris said. "But I got distracted after talking about...you know. The danger. Under..." He clamped his jaw shut and looked away for a few seconds. Sanyago went over his improvised hedgeflame incantation in his head. The feel of the practice dummy battering his forearms; the taste of fresh apple juice. He formed another quick Karana with the hand in his lap.

"Sometimes I wonder," Laris continued, "if that's why I question so much. What she said, I mean. Would I still do it if I had different parents? If I didn't remember them, like you?" He ducked his head, acknowledging that he'd violated one of the students' taboos by mentioning Sanyago's parents. "Sorry."

Sanyago waved it off. "I think you'd be a pain in the butt no matter what."

Laris laughed, then snorted, grabbing a handkerchief from his shelf and wiping his nose.

They sat like that for a long, delicate moment, not saying anything. Sanyago swung his legs back and forth as they dangled over the edge.

"You can talk about them if you want to, if it helps," Sanyago said finally. "Meditations Master Siyimaeyi says it's not good to keep stuff trapped inside."

Laris thought about that, then sighed, blowing his nose briefly and nodding. His shoulders slumped, resigned.

"They died on a trip. I think they were going to visit some library in Aldonza, the capital city of Salía. Bandits got them. My aunt said they had an Eychi guard but I guess it wasn't enough."

Sanyago didn't know what to say, so he simply nodded, putting his hand on his friend's shoulder. Laris' eyes were far away, but they seemed more contemplative than sad now. He worried that maybe his friend had just shoved the sadness back down.

He could do that, Sanyago knew. Laris' self-control, his mastery of his own mind, was so strong it could be a little scary, and Sanyago wasn't sure it was always good for him. The meditations and techniques that helped steel Laris' will were also supposed to be used to know the self, to confront the deepest parts of the mind, the most difficult emotions. And usually Laris did, Sanyago thought, but some things—

"You should let it out more often," Sanyago said suddenly. "It grows and gets nasty if you don't."

"Maybe. I do feel a little better. But I don't want to just sit and... cry...

either."

Sanyago nodded. For Laris to admit to crying was all the concession he was likely to get tonight. He jumped lightly down, rolling his small frame under the bunk as he went and falling down onto his own mattress. Normally this would be a graceful maneuver, but the pain in his backside asserted itself mid-motion and he landed with an awkward thunk, rather harder than usual. He lay there a moment, groaning quietly.

Then he remembered, and rolled back off the bed to kneel over his blankets and say his prayers. He fingered the first bead of his rosary, murmuring the words.

"O Lotus Child, who proceeds from the Divine, upon your Holy Self I meditate this night. To you I dedicate the devotions of my spirit, the thoughts of my mind, and the service of my body. I pray you guide all three down the Triune Path, eight steps at a time in the footsteps of the Awakened Prince..."

Similar words echoed from the boys around him.

Silence from the bunk above.

Chapter 9

We have named this world Solace, but we have built our world upon bones. Some buried, some burned to ash, all unquiet. They do not march and caper like the skeletons of Old World stories and nightmares, the minds and sinews that animated them being long gone. But they do whisper to us, tucked and piled among the scatterings of their homes and possessions, and even if they could hear us, I am not sure what we would say in return. 'We didn't mean it?' 'We are sorry?' 'We could not have known?'

This may all be true, but still I wonder—would that matter to them? Would they forgive us? Find solace of their own? Even their surviving cousins are not sure, and none of the First remain.

- Jaac Bitsui, *The Sepulcher's Roof,* 243 SE

Kualabu, Tenggara, The Caustlands, 348 SE

The old physician trailed her fingertips slowly down Dayang's spine, following the bones through the fabric of her shirt. Dayang stood steady on her feet, breathing slowly, shivering in the warm summer air. Upon reaching the tailbone, the physician paused, murmuring Proken phrases Dayang strained to make out. Probing words, listening words. Dayang could feel them wriggle out from her vertebrae and through her long bones, examining from within.

She shivered again as her spine stiffened, half-consciously answering with Proken of her own, years of defensive drills kicking in as she fought the outside magic. She felt her words and intent coalesce within the

Fathom, pushing outward like a hammer-blow, and cursed silently, but it was too late.

"Keparat!" the old woman cried as the warding forced her back a little. She shook her two fingers as though extinguishing a flame, then put them briefly in her mouth. "Easy, young Wira, and know the difference between help and harm. You'll not be popular with your companion-mages otherwise." She glanced up at Hang Che, who watched with his arms folded, leaning back against one of the training-hall's elaborately carved pillars. "You've trained her well, yes, Bapak Wira? Maybe too well."

"Dayang," Hang Che said sharply, straightening to his full and considerable height. "Apologize. Combat reflexes are important, but they must be under precise control or they can be worse than useless."

Yes, Guru Hang," Dayang said, the words every bit as reflexive as her warding had been. She gave the old woman a small bow. "I am sorry, Doctor."

"No real harm, no real harm," the physician replied. She waved her offended fingers in a tight circle, muttering a few syllables. "Not much of a Sihir-doctor if I can't heal two shocked fingers, am I?"

"Apologies in any case, Doctor," Hang Che said in his smooth, commanding baritone. "She has reached her full growth, then? Or did she push you out before you could tell?"

"Her growth plates have all closed," the physician confirmed. "To be expected at fifteen. Already tall for a girl of her heritage, yes? She will likely put on more muscle, if she continues to train, but not likely get as bulky as men do. She may grow a little more in the bust, but this is easily managed. Any armor made for her now should fit for the rest of her life. Unless she goes lazy and gets fat." The physician laughed at this, her voice thin and cracked but full of good humor.

Dayang continued to stand with her arms out to the sides as the old woman circled her, feeling like a horse having its merits and measurements discussed by two traders. She thought she had managed to keep her annoyance off her face, though.

And anyway, she was intrigued. Armor? She'd suspected. Hang Che had been making her train with weights around her calves, forearms, waist, shoulders, and even skull. He hadn't given a reason, and while he was the sort of teacher of whom you could easily ask "what" or "how", he didn't have a lot of patience for "why".

After watching awhile from afar, Hang Che walked over, giving a casual, terse command. "At ease."

She dropped her arms, joined her hands behind her, and spread her feet shoulder-width, keeping her eyes on her Wira-Guru for further instruction. His russet-brown eyes were thoughtful, meeting hers a moment as he paced his heavy frame back and forth with a grace Dayang had once thought of as surprising.

"Full-grown means a change in your training, Dayang," he said. Dayang did not answer; she was not meant to. "As the good Doctor has said, you can put on more muscle now, so we will work yours harder. We will also start you on real weapons and armor. With care, of course." He turned back to the physician, nodded. "Thank you, Doctor. Please do me an honor and send in the smith; she is likely waiting just outside the practice-hall."

The old woman nodded back, smiling— a gesture between fellow professionals. She was stooped and a little slow leaving; Dayang thought the physician had probably seen a century go by before she had even been born.

The smith, however, was a woman in her prime, stout and strong; she strode in with long, confident steps. "Master Hang," she said, bowing slightly instead of simply nodding as the physician had.

"Ah, Dayang." The smith smiled Dayang's way, and Dayang came to attention to bow in return. She knew the smith, though not well, and liked her. Pandikar had studied under her for a few weeks. Her name was...Raja, or Rajiya, something like that. "Arms up," she said.

Dayang complied. The smith stood shorter than she, thicker of waist, broader at the chest and shoulders, making Dayang feel almost spindly by comparison despite knowing that she was probably as well-muscled as fifteen-year-old girls ever got.

She watched, standing stock-still, as the smith took a measuring tape from one of her leather apron's many pockets and began using it with quick, practiced movements, murmuring to herself. Dayang let her mind wander a short ways, out to the walls, remembering the Pelo girl's silver-streaked face, the graceful, practiced violence as she spilled the ashwight's ichor over sludge-spattered ground.

There hadn't been much time for wall-climbing over the last year or so; she'd only done it twice more, once at the western wall to take in the

Deisiindr's red-orange flare over the night horizon, once at the eastern to see if she could maybe spot the girl again. No luck, just the slow sloshing luminescence of the Mire, little whorls of movement born from the relentless flow of the Gyring Ash. Given the risk she'd taken in getting away to climb, the memory had a distinctly acrid tinge of disappointment. She'd picked Sara's brain, too, for any information involving Pelo activity around Kualabu. Nothing, but then not everything worth knowing made it into her friend's beloved newspapers.

Dayang caught a glimpse of movement past the smith's bobbing head, and looked up. Someone had entered the hall, someone four-legged. She recognized his white-and-grey fur-pattern immediately: Jeims Dubwa.

She dared a smile, though not a nod, and he raised his tail in greeting. They'd spoken a few times since their meeting on the wall. A couple times they'd spotted each other on the street and talked about their small shared adventure; he'd not, he told her, spotted the Pelo girl again either. On other occasions, they'd been training in the same place, and chatted during breaks. He was an impressive spellcaster, from what she'd seen.

Jeims was followed by his Wira-Guru, Hue Tian, looking as tall, slim, and regal as ever. She was not, Dayang, thought, precisely a pretty woman, at least not in the way Hang Che was handsome. Striking, maybe, strong-boned, with copious laugh lines at the corners of her intelligent light brown eyes. The copper-tanned skin of her face bore a slate of three parallel scars straight down her right cheek.

"You can put your arms down now, I'm all done," the smith said, switching the measuring tape for a stubby pencil and pad of paper. Dayang did, returning to attention.

"At ease," Hang Che called out, turning briefly away from greeting Hue Tian. She dropped her hands behind again, and looked down to see Jeims seated on his haunches in front of her, cocking his head a little. He turned to look up at the smith in a sinuous ripple of white and grey fur, flicking one ear.

"Hello, Rajiya," he said brightly. Ah, so that was her name after all. "I'm guessing you're here to fit my friend for armor?"

"Hello, Jeims," she replied, smiling down at him. "A rough set, anyway. She won't want a battle-ready suit until she learns what she does and doesn't like in the first one. Guru Hang will also note how she moves in it, likely angles of attack, that sort of thing. I'll take it all into account before she gets the final product."

Jeims returned his attention to Dayang, opening his mouth in a feline smile. "You are fortunate, Dayang. An enlisted soldier or guard, even one receiving some Wira-training, generally has to make do with just adjusting a few straps on a hand-me-down."

She wanted to stick her tongue out at him, but really couldn't here where Guru Hang or Guru Hue might see her. "Mother made Father promise that if he was going to insist on me receiving training that *she* was going to insist that I get the best equipment." *And they could afford it, along with all this training*, she didn't say. The cost of Jeims' own training was probably paid by the Salian government; what few references he'd made to his own family had implied modest means. "Jealous? Were you hoping for your own suit of full plate?"

He laughed, shaking his head with the long *mrooowwwl*. With no more need for modesty than a housecat, Lingmao rarely wore much unless they wanted to carry something or were going into some other exceptional situation. He himself was wearing a leather harness, with some light brigandine over a few especially vulnerable spots, and pouches for odds and ends.

"I'll leave the clanking around to you, along with the big unwieldy sticks and great heavy planks for hiding behind."

This time, noticing Hang Che and Hue Tian in the middle of animated conversation, she did stick out her tongue. Jeims gave her an impish cat-grin and padded over to one of the low tables that had been brought in for him. He sat back on his haunches and unfolded his front paws into those strange six-fingered hands. Picking up a notebook, he began paging through it, muttering short Proken phrases to himself while scribbling here and there with an ornate fountain pen, his tail swinging back and forth in time with the light scratching of gold-on-paper.

The smith hurried out, giving Jeims a slightly wary look as she went. She didn't want to be there when the young Lingmao started tossing spells around in earnest, Dayang thought. She turned her attention to the two teachers still talking near the door, now pausing their conversation to tell the smith goodbye. Dayang focused, reaching out through the Fathom for the subtle vibrations that filled the air, letting them funnel into her ear. She watched the pair intently, making sure they didn't notice her little spell.

"...down through the cavern. The place was full of crumbling holes in the walls, probably old enough to have been a ruin well before Starfall. A fair amount of good loot, but also all sorts of things breeding and lairing in there, some of them up from the Abwarren. Strange, strange things. Most of them not that dangerous, if still creepy—you never forget the big scuttling things with the antennae all round— but then we ran into a pack of Spark-Claws and, well…" Hang Che trailed off with a sigh.

"Damn," Hue Tian said, shaking her head.

Hang Che nodded. "Myint didn't even see them in time to draw his axes. I can still smell the scorched blood." His voice was almost casual on the surface, reminiscing, but there was a depth of unease to it Dayang had never heard before.

"We may be sending her into that," Hue Tian said. Her voice had gone almost too quiet to catch, but the words were spoken slow and clear. "Poor Khadija may have had a point, you know. Piolo thinks training will make her safer, but power draws danger, especially in a young woman like Dayang. She'll never be one to stand aside."

"Piolo's seen his share of the Caustlands as a merchant," Hang Che said. "He knows the world doesn't care if its victims are prepared for it or not, and certainly he knows more about the world than his wife. Khadija is bright and strong-willed but her vision extends only as far as her family's circle and reputation."

"And her daughter," Hue Tian said, not looking Dayang's way, "has the mind and will, but not the nearsightedness. She'll not stay here past her youth. You know it, Che."

Hang Che grunted, and glanced at his student. Eyes still to front, Dayang had them both in her peripheral vision, highly honed through years of awareness-training. She let the sound-amplification spell dissipate in case Hang Che got suspicious and began to probe. It had only been in the last few months that she'd begun to realize she could slide some of her awareness-techniques right past her teacher, at least when he wasn't actively watching for them. Hang Che wasn't perfect, of course—she wouldn't be taking so many lessons with his old comrades if he could teach her everything—but it was still a shock to realize there were ways she might surpass him.

She'd been standing at ease for a while, and was starting to get a little annoyed. Was this a "patience lesson", or had he just forgotten about her while he chatted with Hue Tian? Her classmate for the day was already throwing sparking, blue-white arcs at a group of iron training dummies, giving her nostrils a whiff of ozone and making the tiny hairs on her arms feel frizzy. Hoping Jeims' spells would provide some cover, she again reached out carefully in the direction of the conversing Wira-Gurus, inviting their voices her way.

"...end up hunting for treasure in old Pelo ruins, just like we did. Or in the Tentera Wira."

Hang Che shook his head, scratching one fingernail around the faded line of an old scar next to his eye. "I don't think she's the military type. Not career, anyway. And Khadija would put her foot down completely. Hell, Piolo might too."

The conversation paused, and they both looked over as someone new entered the hall. Sara, carrying a small stoneware vessel with a little steam escaping from the edges of its lid. Dayang was surprised; Sara had avoided the training hall for the last three years. Still, she was pleased to see her. She smiled broadly, gesturing Sara over with her chin since she had to keep her arms behind her back. The two Wira-Gurus looked over as well; Hang Che smiled at the girl, but Hue Tian just cocked an eyebrow before excusing herself to go read at one of the tables.

Sara started toward her with the hot pot carried carefully in its wooden holder, and Dayang noticed how Hang Che followed her with his eyes, still smiling. She'd seen that smile before, seen it on half the boys in their school, it sometimes seemed, while Sara grew into...well, into Sara.

Dayang was not one to be jealous of anyone's looks; she loved her friend, and while Sara might draw eyes just walking down the street, Dayang had no trouble getting attention when she wanted it. It just took a little directness and disregard for the specter of rejection. She glanced at Hang Che again, at his smile, took back her earlier comparison with the boys at school. That smile wasn't the same when it was on the face of a man old enough to be Sara's grandfather. Dayang very much doubted that, should Sara look back his way, Hang Che would blush and avert his gaze, like boys their own age usually did.

She spotted Jeims watching too, seated on his haunches with his amber eyes flicking back and forth as he followed Dayang's gaze, then Hang Che's. His head tilted incrementally, ears laid slightly back. He briefly met her eyes, ducking his head, then glanced meaningfully back over at the Wira-Guru. *Nothing we can do about it now,* his eyes seemed to say. *Just keep watch.* Dayang gave a subtle shrug and looked back at Sara, now standing before her with the pot held out and a puzzled, polite little smile. Dayang would have to explain things to her later.

"Sara!" Dayang said, beaming. Uncomfortable vibe with Hang Che or no, she was quite happy to see her friend, who grinned back. Knowing something about Dayang's training discipline and seeing her stuck at ease, Sara glanced back at Hang Che. He was still looking at her, wearing what he must have thought to be a grandfatherly smile. But it was too appraising for that, full of cold appreciation. After a moment measured in disquiet rather than length, he appeared to realize what was going on beyond his own fixation.

"You are dismissed for lunch, Dayang," he said casually.

Dayang nodded, perhaps somewhat curtly, set the proffered pot down on the break-table, and gave Sara a fierce hug. Looking over the shorter girl's head, she spotted Hue Tian giving her old comrade an arch look, but it was more one of amused indulgence than disgust. Dayang felt her insides drop, and only managed the strained imitation of a smile when she and Sara broke apart from their hug.

"Are you okay, Dayang?" Sara whispered, furrowing her delicate eyebrows.

"I'll talk to you about it later," Dayang replied, and in a much louder voice said, "Thank you so much for bringing my lunch!" She turned and lifted its cover, letting loose a billow of spices and steam.

"Sure," Sara said. "Your favorite curry. I stopped by your house, and your mom said you were out here. Rozumah asked if I would take it for her."

"I'll have to thank her too," Dayang said. "You've already eaten?" She could feel her mouth watering; Rozumah, the Marchadesch housekeeper was a spectacular chef, and did almost all the family's cooking. Meals prepared by Father were also delicious, on the rare occasions he had the time, but everyone else in the family avoided the kitchen except when Mother was out— Khadija binti Khaled detested housework of any kind, and thought it below both herself and her family.

"Oh yes," Sara said, laughing. "Rozumah would never have let me leave your house otherwise."

Hang Che continued to keep a casual but still very obvious eye on Sara as she pulled out a couple chairs for herself and her friend. Dayang did her best to keep her expression smooth and her tone even.

"Yeah, she's great, we're really lucky to have her. Nurul cooks sometimes when, uhh, Mother's not around, I gotta admit she's actually getting pretty good at it."

Sara nodded, and set a fork next to the pot while Dayang fetched her waterskin. They sat, and Dayang set in; she'd been drilling for almost three hours before the armor-fitting, and suddenly realized she was famished. Sara sat demurely next to her, pulling a section of newspaper from an inner jacket pocket. Dayang caught the headline.

CAUSTLAND STATE LEADERS CONDEMN SOVEREIGN NATIONS' "SEARCH AND DESTROY" RAIDS TARGETING PELO BANDS

Sara read with the same small half-smile she always wore when absorbing new and interesting information. Her smile began to fade, though, when Hang Che came and sat down on her other side, resting one long, thickly-muscled arm on the back of her chair.

Dayang's fork stopped halfway to her mouth and she took a long, slow breath through her nostrils, smelling the swirling spice in the steam but no longer savoring them, her thoughts going cold. She shoveled down the remaining rice and curry in a few quick gulps, and stood up abruptly.

"I am ready for more sparring, Guru Hang."

She saw with some relief that Jeims had joined the lunch-table as well, leaping up to sit on the table directly across from Sara. He'd brought a small bag of roasted whole rodents, and was crunching into them with gusto. Caustland Cats were, of course, allowed their own idiosyncratic set of table manners, but did not usually flaunt them this directly. Hang Che couldn't call Jeims out for rudeness without coming off as impolite himself, but it was hard to be smoothly charming within arm's reach of a Lingmao biting something small and furry in half.

Hang Che frowned at Jeims, who glanced up from his meal and swiveled his ears attentively in the Wira-Guru's direction. "How kind of you to join us, Mr. Dubwa," he said levelly, then stood from his chair. He put one large hand on Sara's slim shoulder, smiling down at her. "Thank you for bringing my favorite student her lunch, Sara, you're always welcome to stop by." It was the first time Dayang had ever heard him refer to her as his "favorite student" in her presence, but the moment left her cold.

Sara looked up at him and managed one of her dazzling smiles in response, although it didn't quite reach her eyes. "Certainly, Bapak Wira," she said, sitting stock-still with his hand still resting heavy on her shoulder. She turned back to her newspaper, but her eyes looked past the words, enduring.

Dayang made more noise than usual fetching her lead-stick, shield, and weight-harness before Hang Che finally came to join her, looking distracted. Sara stood rather quickly herself, gathering up the empty hot pot and cutlery. Dayang gave her an apologetic frown as she left, then glanced at Hue Tian. She'd had her head in her book since leaving her conversation with Hang Che, wearing a blithe, bland smile that acknowledged nothing at all.

Crowshit.

Of course I saw, she'd told a younger Dayang once. *I am an old adventurer, and we notice things, or we do not become old.* Dayang had dared wrinkle her nose in frustration at one of Hue Tian's more impenetrable exercises, thinking her magic instructor distracted by a book she was reading. Dayang had not been able to conceal her shock at the subsequent rebuke.

The memory burned into her chest as her eyes flicked back and forth between Hue Tian's studied indifference and Hang Che's small, languid smirk as he watched Sara walk out the doors.

Dayang fought her distracted teacher nearly to a draw three times that day.

Fourth Interlude

Acheronford, Salía, The Caustlands, 348 SE

"Bloody Hell, Wrait, you look as though you've walked over your own ashes." Braun leaned against the doorframe, standing half-in and half-out of the common room as she ran fingers through her shortish red hair, trying to get it back into something resembling order after its long confinement under a helmet.

She looked him over, noted the way his big frame hunched over the cracked wood of the small dayroom table, frowned as he failed to so much as glance back her way. Her fingers tapped out erratic rhythms on the hard wood of the door frame. "I heard something happened but no one would say what, least not while they thought it was still going on. You want to talk, or are you playing mum as well? Can leave you alone for a bit if you need it."

Wrait was silent, and then he was still silent, and then he shook his head. "No, I mean, sure. Sure, Braun, come on in, it's alright, I'll be alright. Think it's mostly passed, think it'll be safe enough if we're careful."

Her freckled features drew in on themselves, bringing out some of the harder lines of her face. "That bad, was it?" She stepped into the dayroom, but tentatively, as though the floor might give way at a careless step.

"Aye." His face still wore a pale undertone beneath its ruddy tan, and his faded blue eyes saw her but looked right past. "Saepis again, three of 'em, just like last year. Probably from the same bit of the Sovereign Nations, too. Carvers, maybe, or Newcaste. Didn't have any meat in their rations. Only this time? They didn't sneak into town at all. Came right up to the guard-post, two of 'em holdin' a third between 'em. Raving, he were."

He breathed, deep, let it out, slow and shuddering. "They didn't have

105

the good sense to put a gag on 'im. Or they just didn't care to. Shoved him right toward the gates, they did, then turned and ran."

She caught his gaze, dark green eyes widening, and he quickly looked away. Braun didn't like what she saw in that glimpse. She sat herself down across from him at the small table. "Raving. You saw? You heard?" He didn't answer, and she stared. "Let's be clear here; he wasn't going on about how the world was about to end, or how we're all sinners deserving to burn, or how he'd torn his favorite trousers out in the Abwaild?"

There was madness, after all, and then there was...well. Wrait nodded slowly.

"Sure, I saw. I bloody well heard. Tried not to listen, though. Suppose I mostly succeeded. A few others on the wall, they didn't. Started raving too, after we'd got the Saepi restrained. Bad, bad business. Being treated now. No...incidents, thank the Divine." He lifted his big glass mug, and she leaned forward, watched the clear liquid inside slosh, sniffed the air. Nothing. Probably water. Not a good sign. He wanted to keep himself well under control, and must have good reason for it.

"You were the sergeant in charge, then? Not your usual post nor your usual crew, innit?" She stood, walked round the table, took a seat next to his. Best to keep a close eye on the man, and here she could get a better whiff of his drink. Or fail to. Definitely water. Shit.

"I was, and it's not, and they're not, but Axbi was out. Some emergency with her wife. Just my luck, but I'm glad all the same. She's green, you know she is." He took a long, long drink from his mug, wiped his slightly stubbly face.

"Yeah, right. Yeah, Wrait, I know it." She grinned at the rhyme and laid a calloused hand gently on his shoulder, left it there just a moment before giving him an amiable shove.

He snorted, taking a slow sip of water. "Spare me your sodding poetry, Braun. Anyway, archers took a few shots at the ones running, but apart from my bits and pieces o' training there weren't any proper Haeliiy on the wall, and these Saepis were some pretty powerful Fathomers in their own right. None of the arrows found their mark. Me, I threw a spear, but I knew I wasn't gonna wound some trained-up commando Haeliiy of the sort the Saepis'd send. Not with just one spear."

"Least you sent a message though, I 'spose. 'Hey, you Saepi bastards, Salía's not your madman dumping-ground, give it a rest.' Give the

Sovereign Nations something to think about, maybe. You at least hit him, right? Took a chunk off his resilience, even if the spear didn't bite?"

He drained the rest of the water from his mug, and glared at those leftover beads of liquid which had managed to cling to the glass. His fascination unsettled her, but she supposed it wasn't an unhealthy fixation, given the circumstances. He upended the big vessel completely and shook it, trying to dislodge the leftover droplets into his mouth.

She shifted in her seat, frowning, and lightly touched his wrist. He slammed the mug down on the table, hard enough it was a wonder the glass didn't crack. Finally he nodded, weathered features tight and set. Her frown deepened as he wiped his mouth again and spoke.

"Yeah, I hit him. Wonder of it was, I *did* wound him. He kept going with my spear sticking right out of a chink in his armor. Lucky throw, that was, almost all his resilience must already have been gone. Divine knows what he and his mate went through to get the mad one up to our walls." He took another deep breath, thumbed the glass handle he still gripped tightly with his other fingers.

"Divine knows, Wrait? Taking up the Triune Path again? Back to yer Michyero roots?" She tapped two fingers on the table, cocked her head.

He laughed, a little unsteadily, and flicked a strange little gesture in her direction, middle fingers tucked under his thumb with the other two pointing out. "Right now, I'll take whatever I can get. Don't look at me like that, though. I'm going to be alright, even if I'm not all of it now."

"Where'd they take him? The mad one, I mean." She wasn't about to ask what the man had been raving about. That wasn't a question she wanted answers to.

He answered it anyway. "The Black Fence. The mad one was raving about the Black Fence. Said he was going there. Said...but never mind that. Course that's not where we took him. Put him in the psych ward, isolation, padded room, all that. Ask me, now is the sort of time we need a castle with a proper dungeon, like the Old World."

She shuddered. The Black Fence. Black Fence Black Fence
No.

"That's *old* Old World," she said. "Kings and knights and shit. Or Praedhc, maybe, like some of the old ruins. From before Starfall...you know."

"Yeah, well, maybe some of our ancestors had the right idea," he said darkly.

"Is that so?" she said. "Your ancestors were Old World nobs, then? 'Cuz I'm pretty sure mine were usually the ones ending up *in* the dungeons and not building them."

"No," he said, with a small laugh that broke apart some of the black patina coating his mood. "You know that's nonsense either way, Braun. We're all mutts at this late juncture. The First of the Fallen have all been in their graves going on two centuries now and we their children all a bit of this and a bit of that."

She scrunched up her face, doing the math in her head, and nodded. "Alright. Always got to be someone on top, though, even if the official nobs are long done-away with. I got the vote and you got the vote but we don't have the *power,* you know? Yeah, you know. You know it."

He frowned into his now extra-dry mug and shook his head. "I know it, Braun. And it's alright. Sergeant ranks are more than enough for me, I'd not ever want to go officer. Pay's nice, but it's not me." He smiled, just a touch, and it seemed to her as though that much more of the dark had flaked off from his expression, a little more brightness settling into the warm lines at the corners of his eyes. "You've got your eye on Captain's bars, though, you have. Nothing wrong with that either."

She didn't reply, not for a long time. Finally—

"Alright, so maybe I have. Gettin' a little more education on the side, no harm in that. Thing is, need to see a bit more of Solace if I want to really advance, you know? So maybe this isn't the best time to tell you, but then maybe it is since we're both already on guard."

He looked at her, and she looked back, waiting. Shock or no, she could see the shrewd machinery working behind the seeming simplicity of his face.

"You've volunteered to stand the Nowhere Watch." The statement was almost a sigh.

She didn't answer, didn't need to.

He cocked his head. "You sure about this, Braun? I'm not looking forward to my dreams tonight, and that'd be a whole year of restless nights for you, from what I hear. Nine months of days full of unease you can't escape even while you sleep. And that's just if you're lucky."

She decided this conversation needed to end. She didn't like the little tremor she thought she was seeing in the pupils of his eyes, the flare of his nostrils, the minute movements of his lips.

"Someone has to do it, Wrait," she said. "But we shouldn't talk about it anymore. I'm guessing they already got you in to talk to someone anyway. I just wanted to make sure you were okay."

"They did, and I am, well as could be expected. I think I'll turn in. Maybe I'll sleep deep, you never know with dreams. No sense putting it off either way. Thanks for coming by."

"Of course. If you need anything—"

He laughed, and she was relieved to hear more of the old crooked, sardonic acceptance-of-things in his voice. "Sure, Braun. I know."

She turned to walk out, but his voice stopped her at the door.

"You'll make a good officer, Braun. But be careful. I mean really bloody careful. If I have to lose one of my old friends, I want to lose them to death. You follow me? Themselves one moment, gone the next, even if it's not clean. Even if it's slow. Even if they get foggy before the end. Themselves, then dead."

She looked down at the freshly-scrubbed quartzwood of the hallway floor in front of her, caught the little flakes of brightness as flickering hedgeflame light danced across the planks. She nodded, but did not turn around, and left without another word.

Chapter 10

The truth is eternally elusive to the mortal mind. That is to say, mortal truth is eternally elusive to the mortal mind. The mind is not entirely mortal, nor is all truth mundane. It is therefore fortunate for us that from a spiritual perspective—which is to say the only perspective which matters in the Eternal Round—the truth can *be perceived.*

This is not to say that either the mortal mind or the mortal "reality" can be simply dismissed. The mortal mind makes a prisoner of our true selves, of the spiritual essence that the Awakened Prince revealed and the Lotus Child redeemed.

Therefore, to arrive at meaningful truth—at truth which defines us before, during and after this life, not just within it—we must quiet the mortal mind, letting the Word, the Ken, and the Enlightening Spirit conduct the true tranquil mind down the Triune Path to the Redeemed Awareness that the One Parent desires for every being in Their creation. Thus it is taught in the Scripture of the Old World, thus it is confirmed to and clarified by the Enlightened Saint.

- *Fathom Messenger* by Eusébio Inoue, Mind Sutra 4:1

Presilyo Monastery, Inoue Island, The Caustlands, 349 SE

Laris leaned back from his copy of *Fathom Messenger* with an expression of incredulous contempt.

"This is crowshit." He said it quietly enough that only Sanyago could hear him. Hopefully.

"Laris!" Sanyago hissed, leaning in to whisper. "You can't say that about Scripture! It won't be just be a few days of eating scraps if someone hears you."

Laris frowned at the heavy volume on his lap, its coarse pages showing the original Ambérico on the left and a Gentic translation facing it, all in cheap, blocky hedgeprint. He wore an expression of profound distrust. Sanyago knuckled him hard right on the side of his knee.

"Sanyago!" Laris hissed in turn, unfolding his long leg so he could rub at the spot.

"I'm doing you a favor!" Sanyago whispered back. "You can't sit there looking at the *Messenger* like that!"

"Old Yaatkr isn't watching that closely," Laris replied. "He's practically falling asleep."

Catechist Yaatkr did seem to be drowsing a bit in the summer afternoon heat, and as Sanyago watched—carefully pretending to have his eyes on his own book, of course—he nodded twice, then started.

"Remember to let the Enlightening Spirit use your mind as a Silado vessel, and turn it away from all things Mortal," Yaatkr droned. "You will be tested on your comprehension of the entirety of the Mind Sutra at the end of the season." He had his own copy of *Fathom Messenger* open on a lectern in front of him, but looked supremely bored. Most scripture study sessions involved guided readings and careful explanation, with some questions allowed (this had gotten Laris in trouble several times), but tradition held that the Mind Sutra was always to be read silently and pondered alone.

Sanyago didn't fully share Laris' skepticism, the depths of which he thought only the two of them really understood—though perhaps the teachers suspected. Even so, he found this silent-study draining. The Ambérico of *Fathom Messenger* was archaic, peppered with idiosyncratic words and phrases from one of its Old World roots. Without a teacher to explain the more difficult bits, getting through it could be a slog. Laris, who was much better at languages, said he actually enjoyed figuring out the meaning. He just thought the meaning was...well. Just what he'd said. It made a lot of discussions between them frustrating, like trying to share a song the other couldn't quite hear.

The afternoon drifted muggily on. Students shifted, murmured mantras, made use of handkerchiefs already so soaked they did little but move perspiration around. The classroom sunclock's cylinder inched along, and

Sanyago breathed a little sigh of relief when the pointer finally rested on one of the long lines.

The sunclock made a loud *tick* and Catechist Yaatkr stirred, clearing his throat and sort of rocking himself upright while shaking his head as if to throw off the viscous drowse. He turned and struck the small classroom gong, pulling a few students from a similar stupor.

The gong also summoned a stone-faced young monk from just outside the door, where he had apparently been waiting for a break in the class. He passed between the students, carrying a sheet of stationery on which Sanyago could just make out a hasty Gentic scrawl, and set it down on the Catechist's lectern as the old man set *Fathom Messenger* aside. Then he leaned in, whispered something with a graven frown, and hurried out.

This sort of message delivery was routine enough, but its timing, and the way Old Yaatkr turned fully round to read instead of leaving the paper on the lectern, were not.

So we can't see his face. Sanyago dismissed the thought, but the old monk stayed facing away for much longer than it should have taken to read the whole thing twice. When he turned round again, his face was as smoothly impassive as his wrinkled features would allow, though Sanyago noticed he was leaning rather heavily on the lectern. He spoke.

"We will be conducting meditation and discussion for what you have read later. First, Abbot del Toro has asked that the Priests and Mediators speak to all the students, Initiates, staff, and Masters of the Presilyo about an extremely, ah, important and sensitive subject. Your class is a little young for some of the, ah, blunter aspects we need to talk about, but the Abbot feels that current events and discoveries warrant a thorough treatment."

Sanyago pulled himself up a little straighter and glanced sidelong at Laris, sitting attentively with a pensive expression on his sharp obsidian features. Maybe this afternoon wouldn't be boring after all.

The old monk cleared his throat again, frowned down at the single sheet of paper on his lectern, then looked back up at his students. His serenity mask had slid off. Sanyago felt a stab of fear. They didn't always take the Catechist as seriously as perhaps they ought...but only because his solemnity, age, and theological fervor could sometimes edge toward the absurd. He was solid. He was not supposed to be afraid.

"You may have noticed that even within the brotherhood and

sisterhood of the Presilyo—and yes, I know you have not had much contact with our sisters here, but they are just as important—that there is not always complete agreement, even in matters sacred. While the most fundamental truths of the Triune Path are eternal and beyond the scope of mortals to contest or change, there are, and perhaps always have been, differences among its adherents as to the *interpretation* of certain matters." The Catechist looked profoundly uncomfortable saying this to such young students, and Sanyago noticed that Laris had sat back a little, his brows slightly raised.

"While some discussion on these points is still permitted as Silado, and can even be...beneficial," Yaatkr continued, knitting his brows together in an expression nearly as skeptical as Laris at his worst, "there are limits to what is acceptable. There are also, ah, dangers. Some heresy poses largely a spiritual danger, causing one to deviate from the Triune Path. Now, we all have our moments of Ragado deviation which is why...ah."

The Catechist seemed to realize he was about to bound down a theological rabbit hole, and changed course. He cleared his throat again. Sanyago frowned, a puddling drip of unease spreading just beneath his ribs. He couldn't place its source. Yaatkr rambled on.

"That is not the sort of heresy I have been asked to discuss with you. Rather, it is a form of heresy so grave that we can speak of it only, ah, obliquely." He paused, apparently considering the age of his audience. "Meaning I cannot talk about it directly. Not without risking, ah, danger to everyone present."

Catechist Yaatkr looked deeply unsettled now, and Sanyago supposed this long, dreary preamble was just a way to spiral slowly into the actual heart of the matter. Laris, who had been so perked up with interest, now wore an expression of deep annoyance. Sanyago watched his own thoughts wander off toward more interesting, internal venues—defense maneuvers, bits of incantation, Fathom-formulae. He figured he'd call them back once some sort of point came into view. Catechist Yaatkr took a deep breath, put both hands on the lectern, seemed to brace himself against it.

"You have all received training in the Meditations Against the Unnamed. Be ready to use them. I must speak perilously close to things not spoken of."

This yanked Sanyago's rambling thoughts back into a straight line. He had never heard the old monk's tone so grave, not even when speaking of, say, the consequences of sin, or the gravity of spiritual duties. And he was beginning to understand already, though he did not want to. Why did they have to talk about this? He felt his muscles tense, buffering thoughts and memories gathering in his head. He could see some of the other students doing the same, going into focus. Laris sat up straighter in his peripheral vision.

"On your feet," Yaatkr said evenly. "Watch each other. You know what to do."

They rose. Sanyago felt his fingers curl up against his thighs.

"The Holy Fathom gives us strength. Knowledge. Inspiration. It is a gift of the Divine, the milk and honey of this promised land. Through it, we see much, do much. And we stay...within its sacred boundaries." He raised one wrinkled, age-spotted hand, flicking his two outer fingers forward with the others tucked in under his thumb; a trembling Karana warding-gesture.

One of the students a few paces away from Sanyago breathed in sharply, let it out in a long, rattling sigh. Sanyago did not turn to see which boy it was, but he heard a shuffling of booted feet as those nearest him turned to keep watch.

The Catechist paused, watching, waiting, and when there was nothing more he continued.

"Here in the mortal world we are subject to mortal temptations and frailties, but this is a different kind of danger. When our minds touch the Fathom, there are other dangers, but they are easily avoided. The...Silado boundaries are not a sharp divide, but the, ah, increasing danger is, ah, obvious." The very smallest of pauses. "Take him down."

A flurry of movement at the corner of Sanyago's eye. A cry, the strangled attempt at a word...

Sanyago did not listen to the word
word signifies
He let it pass through his mind
signifies outside
unengaged.
points to below
A Psalm followed, and Sanyago heard.

Someone was being dragged to the back of the classroom; someone had not kept well back from the boundary. Around him he could hear murmured snippets of Scripture. Catechist Yaatkr had his eyes closed. He opened them, saw the students, watched. Sanyago heard feet returning to their places. The old monk sighed, continued.

"You already know all this. I am not reminding you for any idle purpose; we must pass through this peril to arrive at the difficult country we are obligated to survey."

That was rather more eloquent than was really usual for Old Yaatkr; it had the cadence of a recited phrase, but it wasn't one Sanyago had ever heard before.

"We have spoken before of heresy, of the importance of right doctrine, the undeniable purity of the revelations and insights of the Enlightened Saint. The Triune Path is a narrow one, and the shadowed paths which lead away from its steep brightness are too numerous for any one person to count. All are filled with hazards to the soul, some also with threats to the mind and body, but few lead past a point of no return. It is those paths, paths that lead to irretrievable destruction, that we must acknowledge here today."

Catechist Yaatkr fell silent, looking each student in the eye in turn. Sanyago met the old man's faded blue eyes solemnly when it was his turn, earning a slight nod.

He knew about the—

do not give it a name do not let it be

Outer Below

let naming pass by untouched

—that lay...below...the Holy Fathom, of course. He did not allow his mind to conceptualize "below", no, not really, just the lower boundary that must never be crossed.

And he knew it wasn't just *below,* there were places

ruins

Black Fence

HOLES

slow cease let go

just as dangerous, name the place but never the thing, they were trained to resist endure redirect

No.

Sanyago shook his head, the tail end of his thoughts veering away from danger, just as he'd been trained. While there was always a strong sense of the sinister to this… subject, he had never thought of it as having anything to do with *heresy*, just common sense.

No one in their right mind ever got near the boundary, just as no one sane went strolling blithely into a bonfire at night; you could see it from a world away. And if someone took a swing at you with a burning branch...well, then you defended yourself. Though perhaps fire was a poor example, he thought. There were protections against heat, and there were worse things than burns.

"Only one thing may be truly taught about letting the mind, intention, or awareness wander too far in this way…" and here Yaatkr paused, his eyes flicking about between his charges, waiting for all of them to be in clear control of their faculties. "And it is this: Never. The Fathom is holy. Holiness extends only that far. I cannot be more clear."

He took in a long breath, expression hardening. "Should any try to teach you differently, flee. If those in authority are both present and in their right minds, follow their instruction. As you grow in ability and maturity, and if the danger is great enough, you may have to kill. Fear no remorse for this. It is better to die in body than perish in mind and spirit."

The old monk's whole body seemed to slump all at once, and he let out a great gusting breath of relief, obviously not caring right now what his students saw. Sanyago guessed that must be the end of this dreaded speech, and was relieved as well; something throbbed and writhed behind the very air of the room, pressing, seeking, inquiring.

Sanyago could hear muttering just behind him. He could not make out the words, nor did he try, but he did turn immediately to face their source. Laris had turned as well. Old Yaatkr must have seen this, because he cried out, "Staafaen! Blind yourself!"

Laris fell into an immediate pose of standing meditation at the words. He had drilled for this a thousand times; the teachers were concerned that the same empathic talent which made him so difficult to best on the sparring field would also make him uniquely vulnerable to...to…

I will let it pass by without taking the form of thought.

Sanyago was only peripherally aware of what Laris was doing anyway, his attention fixed instead on the muttering boy, though he bent his awareness away from the muttering itself.

It was Zhong Luo, famous among the boys for his cheerful temperament and tendency to tell long, rambling stories whose destination became lost somewhere along the journey. He looked as though his mind was taking an altogether less...*don't describe it*...journey now. Sanyago avoided looking into his eyes as well as listening. "Silence, now. Move your thoughts away," Sanyago said sharply, as they had all been taught.

Luo paid him no attention, and from his lips the—

not listening I will not hear him

—went on. Sanyago thought of burning branches, and hit the afflicted boy hard between the eyes with his palm-heel. Luo sort of slump-twisted into the arms of Laris, who had just come out of his brief meditation.

He helped Laris drag the mercifully unconscious boy to the back of the room, where he joined his classmate...*ah,* Sanyago thought, *poor Vasili*...on an improvised bed of old tattered cleaning-towels. They checked Luo over as they had been taught, and everything seemed more or less all right both without and within.

They went back to their places. A pair of magomédicos entered, gave both boys a brief diagnostic, and left. They waited. No one spoke. There was a feeling of fading, of a falling away, a smoothing out of the space. Soon, it was just a room, though the Holy Fathom remained, watching, knowing, guiding.

Catechist Yaatkr's classroom was a long way across the Presilyo grounds from the mess hall, and the class kept its silence as they filed along the familiar paths. The Presilyo was not so silent. Sanyago heard loud voices up ahead, most likely from the central plaza they would pass through on their way to supper. The voices were shouting and arguing and even screaming in Gentic.

They all stopped, listened. The scream was agony, and that was bad enough, but it had a jagged, metallic edge—a rusty, makeshift border desperately failing to hold back some rancid press within the screamer's mind. Sanyago covered his ears, gritted his teeth, thought of honey drizzled over pan-fried flatcakes, the sticky aromatics of oil and sweet, the flood of taste as it met the tongue.

The screaming ceased. Sanyago shuddered, breathed in deep, heard the others do the same. He looked round at them, and then they all looked round for adults; with most of them at or approaching twelve, they were generally trusted to get where they needed unchaperoned. They saw no one. Apart from the sounds up ahead, the Presilyo seemed almost deserted.

Running on the grounds was not allowed except in designated areas for training and play. They all began to walk as fast as they could, the shorter boys like Sanyago borderline jogging to keep up with the longer-legged like Laris. They were drawing closer to the voices.

Sanyago decided he was unlikely to get in trouble for it at this point, and ran up to the front of the group. Laris, the tallest among them with lanky Vasili in the infirmary, led the group with quick, long strides. Sanyago glanced up at his friend, who looked back, jaw set, steel-grey eyes troubled and determined. He nodded. Sanyago nodded back. They both broke into a run.

It took only a brief sprint to reach the long stage-building blocking their view of the plaza. The other boys began running as well, though they trailed out behind in a long line, with Sanyago himself panting as he did his best to keep up with his friend. Laris rounded the corner and stumbled, letting out a muffled burst of profanity in Ambérico and falling to one knee. Sanyago put one hand on his shoulder, then looked up. *What...?*

It took him a few moments to take in what he saw, and a few more to really accept it. There was a sizeable crowd of people, though they kept to the corners of the plaza; that was simple enough to notice and just as trivial to accept. Easiest to notice, and hardest to accept, was the man standing in the center. He was a monk, clad in blue robes like Sanyago himself, or any of his classmates and teachers. He was on fire.

Sanyago shook his head, closed his eyes, but when he opened them the monk was still there. The orange flames made a garish contrast with his sky-blue robes. He must have been the source of the screaming, but he was gagged now, gnashing on the length of rope in his mouth. He could not have been ablaze for long, as his clothing was still mostly intact. He was not right, gone awry in the deepest roots of being, and it screamed out of him more powerfully than his silenced cries ever could.

He was flailing, but made no effort to put himself out, and took no steps to move away from the center of the plaza, though he was not visibly restrained. Eyes the color of strongly-brewed tea stared out into someplace elsewhere, wide and believing.

Dark brown skin turned black and was falling off. It hit the cobbles in a burst of black char-ash. Sanyago looked away, looked anywhere else, could not see any more.

Surrounding the burning monk was a sparse circle of monks and some other people Sanyago didn't recognize. His mind seemed to seize on examining them in detail rather than dwell on the center of the scene. One was a Corvaso, looking up at the human pyre with wings slightly opened as if ready to fly away from all this at any moment.

Looking at the Caustland Crow gave him a moment's relief; that black-feathered head came only as high as the burning man's knee, and his legs had not yet begun to burn, so there was no need to look at any flames, or think too hard on the why of them.

Corvasa, he corrected himself, noticing the silver strands woven into the Caustland Crow's wing feathers. *Female Cropr,* his mind translated helpfully, holding this tidbit of Gentic vocabulary up as something to ponder rather than the pervasive, nerve-sickening smell spiraling out from the circle's center. Said Cropr was talking with the woman next to her, who had long black hair tied up in a high ponytail. She wore what he recognized as a Salían Staffguard uniform, complete with the ornately carved staff longer than she was tall.

"This seems like an extraordinarily brutal solution, even given the problem," the Corvasa said. Her Gentic was clear, her voice raspy, her tone stern. She ruffled her feathers, cocked her head. Sanyago started; her golden raven's-eye was looking right at him, profiling her long black head and beak. He heard the rest of his class arriving behind him. Murmurs, muffled curses, startled sobs.

"You're going to let *children* see this?" She was hopping on one scaly foot, long black wings partly opened. Her voice had gotten a great deal louder than seemed possible for a person of such small size, and her beak clicked with agitation as she spoke. "Abbot del Toro, do I have to *tell* you how the Low Table will respond to our report on this barbarism?"

Sanyago was startled to see that the Abbot was, in fact, standing about a quarter-circle to the Caustland Crow's left; his mind could not seem to notice things in any kind of reasonable order. The head of the Presilyo was an old man, probably a couple decades past a century, his stout, powerful body starting to stoop and sag. His dark eyes, which Sanyago had always thought so wise and commanding, seemed shaken and angry.

"Do I have to tell *you*," he said in his formal, heavily accented Gentic, "that our treaties with both Salía and Tenggara guarantee our autonomy? Our methods of execution are not yours to dictate or proscribe. Especially considering the circumstances."

Several senior monks across the circle were glancing between Sanyago's class and del Toro, whispering among themselves, perhaps debating whether to remove the boys before seeing whether the Abbot would defend their presence to the angry official. It was, thought some detached part of Sanyago's mind in the meantime, taking the man an extraordinarily long time to die. He didn't know what would be an *ordinarily* long time to die...

His limbs were shaking. Why were they shaking? He didn't do it. Was that him making those noises in his throat? He didn't mean them. What was even going on?

"*Porlyó,*" Laris swore, breathing out the word as he got unsteadily to his feet. His grey eyes had gone wide, deep-black skin taking on an undertone of old ashes. Sanyago supposed he looked more or less the same himself. That little detached part of his mind informed him that the cobblestones of the plaza were blue and grey, but more grey than blue, that the low sun behind him made his shadow very long and Laris' even longer, that he still had a grain of brown rice stuck between two of his teeth. This was better than realizing that some of the man's skin had grown back over the raw redness beneath, only to char again.

"*End this,*" hissed the woman in the Staffguard uniform, pounding her ornate weapon against the paving. She leaned forward into the motion, as if she desperately wanted to step forward, put a stop to it herself, but could not. Must not.

Grey and blue, Sanyago thought, watching the metal-shod staff strike the stones. *Grey and blue.* He realized suddenly that hers was not the only weapon in view; several of the Somonei in the circle had theirs drawn, their attention fixed on the blazing monk at the center. *They're making sure he stays there.*

"Fire...purifies," the Abbot replied uneasily. "This is...this is how things are done by way of long tradition."

"We understand this as well," said someone on the other side of the circle. A short, wiry man in light armor and a cape. Sanyago recognized the insignia on his brooch from a chart they'd had to memorize for class: Tentera Wira, the elite Tenggaran Army corps of Eychis warriors and mages. He stood with arms behind his back, dark brown eyes giving away nothing. "However," he continued, "burning while the body is still alive is simply not necessary."

"I concur," said the tall, slender woman standing next to the two Salían representatives. She wore an elaborate uniform with insignia that Sanyago did not recognize, but he knew she must be from Zhon Han by the gracefully embroidered Common ideographs. Unlike everyone else heard speaking so far, she was using Abbot Del Toro's native Ambérico. This seemed to be more condescension than courtesy, given her imperious tone and the tilt of her sharply-defined face.

"We agreed to help you with this...outbreak of yours, but for you to force us to participate in such barbarisms even by inaction is unconscionable. You have all but demanded that we respect your sovereignty, and now you must respect ours. An Eychi like this one—a product of your so-famous training program—could take a very long time to die, especially if..." She trailed off, the imperial steel in her voice losing some of its edge. "You know," she continued flatly.

The elder monks, who had been conferring on what to do with Sanyago and his fellows, appeared to have decided that while the burning monk was bad, letting them witness the Abbot be so openly challenged was much worse. They came Sanyago's way with purposeful expressions, lower-ranking monks trailing in their wake.

No, not just monks, Sanyago realized, his mind still cataloguing everything but the now-naked human bonfire in the center of the circle. Nuns too. They wore the same loose sky-blue robes as the monks and had the same shaved heads, but the rosaries around their necks and the clasps on their robes were turquoise rather than red, and even the loosest garment did not completely hide the differences in shape.

They were not normally allowed any contact with the nuns. The world was out of joint. More people were joining the circle as the grim faced monks and nuns drew near. Many armed, many armored. Uniforms from the three nearest Caustland States: Salía, Tenggara, Zhon Han. Full-fledged Somonei from the Presilyo itself, dressed and equipped for combat. There was still arguing going on, but his mind did not want to understand it.

One of the monks put an arm round his shoulders. Sanyago let himself be led away, mute and unfocused. A nun had taken Laris by the arm, and he noted with detached, madcap amusement that Laris was blushing, purple replacing ash under the deep black of his skin.

Soon they were back at their sleeping quarters with strict instruction to go directly to bed after individual prayers and meditation. Nothing more was said, not by anyone, the other boys' faces as drawn and far away as he imagined his own must be. When he caught Laris' eye, he just shook his head, put a hand briefly on Sanyago's shoulder, climbed up onto his bunk.

Sanyago lay down slowly on his own mattress beneath, doing his best to ignore the sounds coming from outside.

He lay there a long time. Once he finally began to sink into sleep, a thought drifted through Sanyago's emptying mind.

There was more than just the monk under the flames.

Chapter 11

Have you ever come to know a stranger?
Of course you have
your mother, first of all
known slowly in secret warmth
which fades
and if you know her again
you know differently
Parents
and parents of parents
and brothers and sisters and children of parents
known well, known far, known fearfully
or fleeting, or forgotten
And all the others
friend enemy lover comrade
distant relation
long acquaintance
all strangers
all discovered
all known
or
at least a little
at least today
Tomorrow they will be someone else
at least a little
and so will you
two strangers
and perhaps you will come to know the first

and perhaps the second
or perhaps not
perhaps you never did

- "Strangers Known," Jein Caeli Prais, *Lamentations of Solace,* 5 SE

Kualabu, Tenggara, The Caustlands, 349 SE

Dayang normally enjoyed her Common class, but today she felt only relief when the call to prayer interrupted it. The instructor, a paunchy, blinky-eyed man filling in for one of her favorite teachers, stopped mid-sentence with an almost comically slack jaw, his droning words cut off as though they'd simply plopped out of his mouth to splatter on the floor. He reached for the small basin of water on his desk, began washing his face and hands in preparation.

Dayang began her own ablutions, saying a tiny additional prayer of thanks for the interruption. She figured that, teaching being a sacred duty, God would understand how badly this teacher was failing at it.

"I bear witness that there is no god but The God," came the wailing FusHa phrase from the nearby voice-tower. Dayang followed along, murmured the familiar words as she had a thousand times or more.

She didn't speak much FusHa beyond bits picked up here and there from religious studies and scriptural recitation, but everyone knew the call to prayer. The language had been the cause for some argument between her parents. The fount, really, the seemingly inexhaustible source of a thousand tiny tiffs. She washed her hands, her face, her feet, losing track of the words in the warp and weave of her thoughts.

"Come unto prayer!" the words continued. "Come unto wellbeing!"

Dayang finished her ablutions, rolling out her prayer rug as the teacher did the same. She faced the direction indicated by the classroom's big prayer-sunclock, bowed down in unison with the other students.

Mother argued that learning FusHa instead of Common could help connect Dayang with her religious heritage, with the added insinuation that her husband was not really as dedicated to said heritage as his conversion might suggest. This last point was probably true to some extent, Dayang reflected, though less because his conversion had been insincere and more because Piolo Marchadesch simply was not and never had been a particularly zealous man. He'd never bothered learning much FusHa beyond the prayers and most common bits of scripture everyone knew.

And when discussing the possibility of FusHa instruction for Dayang, he always argued that Common was much more practical, with Zhon Han sitting rich and powerful at the center of the Caustlands. His personal fluency in the language had been of incalculable help throughout his career, he would say, his own insinuation being that his wife would do well to remember the source of the family's renewed wealth.

Bow, rise, bow, rise, contemplate.

Both her parents had made it clear that studying *just* Gentic and Basa in school was not an option, not for their daughter. Gentic went without saying for an educated person, and speaking her own native Basa Mala properly was etched as deeply into family expectations as toilet training or hand-washing.

"There is no god but The God!" The final soaring, swooping notes of the prayer lingered, then fell away.

Dayang began to roll up her rug. Mother did not speak either Common or FusHa herself, but did speak what seemed like every conceivable dialect of Basa with flawless fluency, along with passable Gentic. Of course, she had never needed to do business with Zhon Han merchants or, Dayang thought a little sourly, to be more strongly connected to her religious heritage. Khadija binti Khaled was no convert, after all. Neither, really, was Dayang, but she'd never dare bring that up. She was in her formative years! Her father needed to understand how important this was, lest she backslide!

For her own part, Dayang disliked having her hypothetical shortfall of piety used to backhand her father for his own alleged religious failings.

They stowed their prayer rugs and sat at their desks again. Dayang took listless notes as the teacher—she thought his name was Khun or something—went on and on about traditional forms of Common poetry without giving a single drop of context to alleviate the powder-dryness of his lecture. She found herself wishing she was in Gentic class already, taking the grueling exam she'd pushed herself hard studying for. Dealing with the highly idiosyncratic lingua franca of the Caustlands could be frustrating, but it would still be better than this.

Dayang gave her head a small shake in an effort to stave off the slowly sinking frustration of boredom. She breathed in, squaring her shoulders, breathed out, slumped, squared them again. How this teacher could construct a lesson this tedious out of such bright and varied material as Common myth and poetry was beyond her.

She would have been fine with learning FusHa as her third language, much as she enjoyed studying Common, and maybe she still would someday. She could appreciate the poetry and beauty of scriptural recitation and would like to understand it better. Dayang greatly valued both her relationship with God and her appreciation of His divine creation; she just didn't think they were any of her mother's business.

Of course, at sixteen the list of things she thought were not her mother's business was a long one. This included her latest...well, he wasn't exactly a boyfriend. She didn't want any more trouble from her father, or any more whispering among her peers. It was more discreet than that, it had to be. Dayang paused her brush halfway through an especially complicated Common character, smiling very slightly.

His name was Omar, and he was almost two years older. She enjoyed his company, among other things, and he knew how to enjoy hers without complicating everything. It helped that he was very pretty, medium-height with a spare but strong frame and lovely light-brown, almost golden, eyes.

She kept the characters marching along the paper, sparing enough attention to use the right brushstroke order even as her mind wandered. She wouldn't be winning any calligraphy awards, but the teacher wouldn't accuse her of slacking either.

She'd been granted a bit more autonomy since her sixteenth birthday, and that helped a great deal when she wanted to rendezvous with Omar, who had both more freedom and less to worry about from gossip, or even from being caught. It was unfair, and it was an iron-wrought unspoken rule. This may not be the most conservative place in Tenggara, but a girl's honor was still judged a very different thing than a boy's. Along with her virginity, while no one ever seemed to ask if a given boy was still lugging his around.

For her part, Dayang didn't feel any different since losing hers. Less frustrated, maybe. And yes, a bit more guilty. But it wasn't as if they were hurting anyone. She'd done some furtive research on precautions; having a Wira's level of control over her own body had distinct advantages.

She started another row of characters, frowned, had to scribble one out and start over. She winced, glanced up expectantly, but this substitute wasn't paying enough attention to notice her mistake. She rolled her eyes and kept writing, mind touching on her work as lightly as possible.

She'd continued to see Jeims Dubwa at the training hall, and drilled with him from time to time. He'd also been of assistance when it came to getting private time with Omar. Hang Che and Hue Tian had decided to let the two of them train together without supervision for a couple hours a day three times a week. They apparently assumed the twenty-one-year-old Jeims would also act as chaperone to keep Dayang out of trouble, and he did; problem was, they hadn't counted on the fact that Jeims's definition of "trouble" did not include Dayang spending time with a young man.

Still, she wasn't neglecting her training; she simply found a little extra time at the end, or the beginning, or the middle. Her Lingmao friend would practice some of his flashier, louder spells so no one would want to just wander into the training-hall, and she would take advantage of the changing-room with Omar.

She finished her row, looked it over. No mistakes. Not that she thought this drone of a teacher would even check.

Both Wira-Gurus knew, of course, that Caustland Cats tended to have different attitudes about such things, but a local Lingmao would have been more familiar with Kualabu's prevailing religion and culture. Well, a local Lingmao would have had more *respect* for it, anyway. All the local cat-clans were religious to at least some extent, but she had been amazed to discover that Jeims wasn't. Not hostile, the way she was sometimes warned that infidels could be, just indifferent.

No, not quite indifferent, she thought, putting square outlines around a few less-familiar characters she'd need to study when she got home. Some things he clearly thought were just absurd, though she'd never heard him be outright disrespectful.

Class was over. Finally. She gathered up her things, went to find Sara in the hallway so they could walk together to their Gentic class. Sara was taking FusHa instead of Common, just as Mother had wanted Dayang to do. This made her somewhat sad, since she couldn't study that subject with her best friend. There were a couple of other girls learning Common with whom she got on well enough to make for pleasant study partnerships, but they didn't quite have Sara's sharp insight or, just as important, her knowledge of how Dayang's mind worked.

She spotted Sara standing just down the hall, chatting with a mutual acquaintance. Sara was quite popular among the three hundred or so other students within a year of their own age, which was not a surprise; she was pretty, bright and personable, and the family business was respectable and prosperous, her mother's Sihir-goods shop supplying the endless stream of adventurers on their way to or from the massive nearby ruins.

"Dayang!" Sara said when she spotted her, giving her a hug. "Ready for the exam?"

Dayang was; she'd gone over the word-lists God knew how many times over the past few nights. She'd also practiced with Jeims, insisting on speaking only his native language during their training sessions. This was more than a little different from the dry classroom Gentic she got in school, with its own rhythms and slang, but she figured it was also probably more useful in the end.

"Yeah, I got it down," she said in Gentic.

Sara frowned. "I don't know that expression. Jeims has been teaching you stuff, hasn't he? He's a little odd, even for a Lingmao."

"I like him," Dayang said shortly. "He's helped me a lot and he treats me like a person, doesn't talk down, you know? Do you think he's weird because he's a foreigner? Because you must run into them sometimes, even with your mom keeping you at the back of the shop."

Sara shrugged, compressing her lips downward into a thoughtful pout. "I don't know, I'm not as used to Lingmao as you are. Also, he's…" she chewed on one lip, "…I mean, I know your Dad was…but he converted, and even before then he wasn't, you know."

Dayang did know, and was annoyed, both by her friend's fidgeting indirectness and its implications. Jeims never brought his irreligion up himself, but he did answer questions with a careful mixture of honesty and diplomacy, and there were a lot of questions. This brought on plenty of judgement, but Dayang figured God was perfectly capable of judging mortals Himself without the help of their busybody fellows. Sara must have read some of this in her friend's face, because she dropped her eyes a moment before continuing hurriedly.

"As for seeing a lot of foreigners at our shop, no, not really. Most of them only speak Gentic or Common or whatever, and I couldn't understand much of what they were saying until recently, they just talk too fast and use too much slang. And they never talk directly to me, I think they can tell that Mom wouldn't like that and they want good prices, you know? Since I've been getting older the men and, um, some of the women do look more. Kind of like Hang Che." Sara leaned in and lowered her voice for this last.

Dayang suspended her annoyance toward her friend completely upon hearing her mentor's name, then transferred it smoothly over to him and with copious interest. "Oh God. Sara, I'm sorry. Is he still bothering you?" *Of course not. After all, he knows his attention is such an honor, how could he possibly think he was bothering her? How could she want anything else?* The thought had a bright stream of venom running through it that surprised her. *Surely...* Surely what? She didn't know, and her mind trailed off uneasy.

Sara shrugged, glanced away. "Not...really, but I see him around a lot, like more than you'd think by chance? I didn't say anything because for a long time I thought I was being paranoid. But now I don't think so. He'll be at the market when Mom sends me, or he'll come by the shop to discuss some trinket he wants to sell or buy and wait around chatting until she calls me out from the back to help with something. And he...he *looks*, you know? Whenever he can." Sara looked down and away before continuing.

"Mom doesn't try to keep me away since he's from here in town. And I'm only at the shop like a couple hours a day anymore, and even then I'm usually just studying. And I don't think he ever comes by when I'm not there. Amira says she's never seen him there."

Amira was Sara's little sister, with whom Sara got along much better than Dayang ever had with Nurul. She envied Sara that, sometimes. The thought faded, though, as she felt the curling and uncurling of her fingers, the pulsing of her jaw muscles as they pushed her chin forward. Sara frowned, put her hand on Dayang's arm.

"Sorry, I didn't want to trouble you about this."

Dayang sighed, squared her shoulders, felt her jaw relax some. "Not your fault, God knows. Come on, we'll be late."

Dayang kept pace with Sara, listening, watching her gestures grow quicker and more emphatic as she warmed to her points.

"...and anyway I don't think the word lists help all that much if we never hear the words again, or we just end up reading and repeating them in bland stupid phrases no one would ever actually say in real life, much less remember, you know? I've found some really lovely Gentic poems and songs in the library, why can't we learn from those?"

"Not everyone likes poetry," Dayang said. She did herself, sometimes, but wasn't as passionate about it as Sara could be.

"That's not *true,* though. Think about music, popular songs, people remember the words, right? They're always poetry, even when they're kind of stupid, even when they're *bad* poetry people care about them. They just need to find the music of the words when they're on a page."

Dayang's smile tugged at the corner of her mouth with laughter threatening to follow, and she turned slightly away. She didn't want Sara to think she was making fun, she loved seeing her friend this way, watching enthusiasm overcome reserve, natural and free. It felt as though she was being let in on the secret of Sara's true self.

They went on that way, or mostly Sara went on that way, and had walked halfway to Dayang's house when they ran into a familiar figure by the side of the road.

It was Jeims Dubwa, seated on his haunches and conversing with another Lingmao, who paced back and forth nervously. Dayang knew her too; Aulia, a town guard from the Keemasan clan who sometimes stood watch on the walls. Jeims waved them both over, and as they neared Dayang caught some of the ongoing conversation. It was all in Basa Mala; Dayang guessed Aulia probably didn't have much Gentic.

"...just out standing there like she always does, but out in the sunlight, which she's never done before, this is hours earlier than usual." Aulia had stopped to lift a paw and run it over the pale, golden-rosette fur just behind her ear as she spoke, looking perplexed. She wore her uniform harness with its guard's insignia, satchels, and quick-draw knives. Still on duty, then. Or expecting some kind of trouble.

"I haven't had time for much in the way of wall-tourism in well over a year now," Jeims replied, running his fingers thoughtfully over the white-and-grey fur of his own tail. "She's been showing up all this time?" Jeims had on his own harness, lightly armored with brigandine and bearing a Salían crest, with pockets and pouches in convenient spots.

Aulia shrugged, dipping her head momentarily below her shoulders. "Sure. Once a week or so. It gets sent in our reports to Cenicebu, but no one takes much notice. The Pelos haven't sent any serious threats across the Gyring Ash in living memory, here or in any of the other Caustland States. Not since the end of the Deisiindr War."

"And no one's tried to just go out and talk to her? You must have at least a few people here who speak the local tribal language, right? Hell, for all we know she speaks perfect Basa, or Gentic, or Common. I thought about doing it myself a couple times, but I didn't want to interfere in local business given my position here."

Aulia laughed a long *mrrooowwwll*. "Standing orders are to ignore Pelo scouts as long as they stay near the Mire. Officially speaking, I'm just escorting a curious foreigner so he doesn't cause some kind of diplomatic incident. And carrying the Fathomcaster so they'll have a reliable record of the whole thing." She patted the concave disk bound to the top of her harness collar.

"We're talking about the Pelo girl we saw from the wall a couple years ago, right?" Dayang cut in. Both pairs of eyes, narrow-slitted in the afternoon sun, turned her way.

Jeims nodded. "Yeah. I walked my friend Aulia here out this way while she told me about it, hoped I'd catch you on your way from school. How'd your test go?"

This last question was in Gentic. "Good," Dayang answered in same.

Jeims cocked his head and looked at Sara, who blushed a little and smiled. "It went good," she echoed.

Jeims grinned and shook his head. "Well. It went well. Nothing goes good, although it can do you some good. A hero goes around doing good, a person with her life in order is doing well."

"Thanks, teacher," she said, switching back to Basa and rolling her eyes at him.

Aulia, who hadn't seemed able to follow much of what they'd been saying, batted Jeims with her tail and sighed. "You put up with training alongside this Salían smartass, Dayang?"

Dayang laughed, shrugging theatrically. "He grows on you, eventually. And he does know what he's doing, sometimes."

"Sorry." Jeims thumped his tail against the pavement beside him. "Just doing my part to aid the cultural exchange between our two countries, you know? And speaking of which," he said, "I was just telling Aulia that I do in fact speak the local Pelo dialect. At least, I speak the Kash dialect they use on the other side of the border from Acheronford, and from what I understand it should still be useful this much farther East as well." He paused, toying with his tail, examining the tip for a moment. "Hopefully."

"Where did you learn it?" Sara asked, looking curious. Some of her unease around Jeims seemed to have settled down some, perhaps because of Aulia's presence.

"School," Jeims said simply, dropping his tail back down to the pavement where it lay with tip twitching. "Took it instead of Ambérico. I already had my eye on a position under the Staffguard, and it seemed more useful for the border duty I was after. I didn't want to get stuck in Aldonza or on some other interior patrol."

Aulia gave him another solid *thwap* with her tail. "Enough talk, Jeims. We've waited for your friend, now do you want to go talk to the girl or not? We don't know how long she'll stay out there."

He inclined his head, looking slightly abashed, and came up off his haunches to stretch his hind legs. "Alright, alright, off we go. You coming, Dayang? I don't see why Sara can't come along too, if she wants," he added, though he gave Aulia a quick glance to confirm. Aulia gave him an incredulous look before stretching herself out, shaking her head. Dayang frowned, glancing at her friend. Sara's expression was uneasy, her fingers picking at the fabric of her modest blouse where it tucked into her long skirt.

Dayang gave Sara what she hoped was a reassuring smile, one that said, *don't worry, you really don't have to.* "Isn't this potentially kind of dangerous? I'm not really ready for anything like that. I mean," she said, feeling and probably looking a little guilty, "I do have a dagger." It was a bit more than just a dagger, really, a long kris knife she'd gotten as a joint birthday present from her brother and father.

Piolo had acquired the fine deepsteel blade God knew where, and Pandikar had made the rune-carved handle himself. She was very fond of it, but she was also definitely not supposed to be carrying it in her school-bag, sheathed or no. Not that Father would be likely to do anything but laugh if a teacher complained to him about it.

"Bring it then," Aulia said, "if you can conceal it under your jacket. We don't want to frighten her off. Two Lingmao may already be a bit disconcerting to a Pelo."

Dayang was already securing the leather scabbard to the back of her belt, glancing at the Caustland Cats' own strapped-on equipment.

"Yeah, especially armed like you are," Dayang said. "Guess it's too warm for cloaks?"

Jeims tilted his head toward Aulia. "She's the official one, it's really only proper that she be armed. "

"I, uh, I think I'm just going to go to Mom's shop," Sara said, uneasy. Dayang turned and put on a rueful smile, laying a hand on Sara's arm.

"I'm sorry about all this, I really did want to have you over but I can't miss the chance to talk to this girl. I've been wondering about her for a couple years now." She hoped Sara wouldn't be mad, but this was the first time Dayang had put her friend off for something else in a long time.

Sara nodded, her smile brightening. "Tomorrow then?"

Dayang smiled back, relieved. They had tomorrow off school. "Yeah, I have a two-hour training break after lunch. We can study a little and read one of those new books you were telling me about."

Sara hefted her bag up onto her shoulder. "Okay, but be careful. I know you're all badass but you never know with Pelos."

Dayang laughed, then hugged her friend. "I will. Do me a favor and send a message to Rozumah, tell her I'm out studying with Jeims. It's basically true, a Wira's gotta learn about the Pelos, right? God willing she'll pass the message along." *She probably will*, Dayang assured herself. Their housekeeper was generally reliable.

"Sure," Sara said. "You want me to take your books? I can bring them by tomorrow; it's not like you'll need to explain Gentic grammar to this Pelo girl."

"Gentic grammar's not that hard anyway," Jeims murmured. "It's the vocabulary that gets people." Dayang rolled her eyes at him, and Sara gave him a look Dayang couldn't quite read, or maybe didn't really want to.

Dayang frowned, gesturing toward Sara's pack. "You sure that won't be too heavy with all your books too?"

Sara swept the odd expression off her face with what looked like an act of will, and managed to smile at all three of them. "No, it's good exercise. I gotta catch up to you since they've got you wearing weights around and everything."

Dayang felt a surge of appreciation at the effort, along with a surprising amount of relief. She shrugged off her bag, handed it over. Sara slung the heavy canvas strap over her other shoulder, made a flexing motion, grunted. Dayang laughed and waved. "Thanks, see you tomorrow!"

Sara's comment about her body-weights training made her wish like Hell she could stop by the training-hall and pick up her armor and shield. It was still just training-armor, lacking the full strength, coverage, and enchantments the final combat set would sport— next year, hopefully, if she continued to excel in her training. Father and Hang Che had both promised. Then again, even her training-armor was hefty-looking enough that it might spook the Pelo girl.

Jeims and Aulia began to playfully bicker as soon as they padded down the street, and she followed the Lingmao pair out toward the town's eastern gate. Along the way they passed a stretch of the wall that had been repaired after the breach, and there was a long piece of fresh Gentic graffiti painted onto its newer boards. It was scrawled out in a cursive hand she had a hard time reading and they were passing quickly, but she did make out the first four lines.

Trnng nd trnng n y waidaenng gair
Y faalchn caanat hir y faalcnr;
Yngs fal hpart; y saentr caanat hold;
Mir aanarci iiz lusd hpan y wrld

Okay, not quite Gentic, then, even if it was written that way. Older, some sort of archaic poem.

She was still pondering the odd excerpt, which had probably been scribbled by some drunken Salían adventurer, when they arrived at the gate. She realized she'd never been through this particular portal before in her life; there was nothing beyond it really but a short plain and the Ashlit Mire.

There was another bit of graffiti here, this one scrawled on a slanted support beam like the one she used to climb to look out over the wall:

Biwer y Jaabrwac mai shn!

That one didn't make any sense at all. Maybe the adventurer had been even drunker, and had wandered sodden into the Mire. Aulia called up to the gate guard, and the heavy steelshod wood doors were cranked slowly open.

"Who's the girl with you?" the guard called down.

"Dayang Marchadesch," Aulia shouted up, sitting back on her haunches. "She trains with Hang Che."

"Awfully young," the guard replied, "even if she is Wira-trained."

"We don't want to spook the Pelo woman," Aulia called back.

"You sure about that?" Even at the volume necessary for her voice to carry down to them, the guard's tone was dubious. "They're supposed to be awfully superstitious about...well, you know. Lingmao."

"Guess we'll see," Aulia replied. "At least we're small, might be less intimidating than a contingent of human guards. Anyway, you can blame this little expedition on the nosy Salían here." She bumped Jeims' shoulder with her own.

"I will!" the guard called, laughter in her voice. "We'll keep the gate open so long as you're brief. They've got two listening stations set up for your Fathomcaster, but you know how slow that is. Won't hear you right away at that distance, so be careful. We'll keep an eye out for you as best we can."

Dayang felt small bursting bubbles of adrenaline surge through her blood as they crossed the threshold, and she shifted her shoulders and hips to feel the comforting weight of her kris sheathe at the small of her back.

The girl was still standing there, plain as the late afternoon sun across the level ground. The unending tangle of the Ashlit Mire made for a forbidding backdrop, especially with the Siinlan Veil darkening the sky above it. *All that separates a few million Fallen from the endless Abwaild.*

The girl was About a five-minute walk away, Dayang guessed. Her expression was impossible to make out at this distance, but she was definitely looking their way, and stood stock-still as the trio approached, Aulia in the lead.

"Remind me again," Jeims said quietly as they went, "why we decided to approach this Pelo scout, or whatever she is, with a couple of Caustland Cats and a sixteen-year-old girl?"

"Because," Aulia said mildly, "when I told you she had come out of the Mire during the daytime, you announced you were going out to talk to her. The Captain of the Guard felt that if you were going to wander out that close to the Ashlit Mire, never mind near some unknown Pelo, you should have an official escort with a Fathomcaster. And no one else wanted to escort you, you impulsive jackass."

Dayang noticed the undercurrent of affection coming through Aulia's voice at that final epithet, and wondered a little. Still, she decided to mind her own business. Jeims had done so much to help her maintain her own privacy that she should at least respect his own.

Jeims sighed, padding through grass in silence a long moment. Long for him, anyway. "Yeah. I know. Just wanted to make sure that's what we were actually doing, I guess. Well, at least we've got someone her own age, sex, *and* species along." Another long pause. "If Pelos still count as precisely human, I understand there's some debate on that point."

Dayang shrugged. "They're people, anyway, same as you and me. Whatever changes they went through aren't any weirder than what happened to your ancestors. Or the Caustland Crows."

"Hmmm," he said. "They say that in a sense we're as strongly descended from humanity as we are from any feline, but it can still feel a bit odd to contemplate that your many-greats grandfather was just your basic housecat."

They fell silent as they covered the distance to the Pelo girl, who still simply stood and watched them approach. Watching them solemnly, Dayang thought, as she got close enough to get a better look at the girl's light-and-dark marbled features. The little party stopped three paces shy, and they all looked at each other, the two girls and two Caustland Cats, for a long handful of breaths.

Jeims stepped up, or at least lifted one front leg and shifted his weight forward, paw hovering in mid-air in uncharacteristic indecision. The girl looked down at him, cocked her head, seemed to shift her own weight back a bit. Jeims said something in a language Dayang did not understand. The girl said something back, and Jeims turned his head aside, flicking his tail in a violent back-and-forth and laying his ears flat against his skull. The Pelo girl turned to face Dayang directly. She had shockingly bright blue eyes.

"Greetings, Fallen," she said softly. "I speak Gentic. Do you?" Her accent was strange, but the words were very clear, even with the strange reverberations her voice lent them. Her gaze was steady, full of an austere, almost haughty confidence.

"Yes," Dayang said. Her heartbeat was rapid, and she felt the moment clarifying around her, distilling in the air. "But not as well as he does," she added, gesturing toward Jeims.

"He is an abomination," the girl said. There was no malice in her voice, but the statement was definitive, not to be argued. Dayang found with rising heat that she didn't care; she would argue as she pleased.

"He is my friend," she replied, and was surprised to hear a hard line of sharpened steel in her own voice.

The girl—woman, really, Dayang realized, as she looked closer, shorter but in fact older than she—actually swayed a little at this, raising her hands to waist-level, palms up. Dayang didn't know much about what gestures meant in Pelo culture, but it was clear from her expression that this one was meant to be mollifying.

"I...cannot apologize," the Pelo woman said finally. "Not for the word itself, this is sacred truth, to deny it would be to make myself unclean. I can say I am sorry for the abruptness."

For his part, Jeims looked more than mildly irritated by this whole exchange, and Dayang wondered what exactly the woman had said to him in her reply. He opened his mouth, and Aulia, who had moved to stand beside him, gently checked him with her shoulder. He closed it, ears laid flat. It occurred to her how lucky they all were that, for all his sometimes sardonic personality, Jeims didn't have much of a temper.

Your sacred truth is stupid, Dayang thought but definitely did not say. She'd heard similar things muttered by foreign adventurers during the call to prayer when they thought no one could hear, and remembered how deeply angry it made her. Hypocrisy, as Father liked to say, was not a good look on anyone. "You can't talk to him, then?"

"I can speak only the Words of Warding to a Bright Beast," the woman replied. The capital letters were definitely present, and Dayang barely managed not to roll her eyes.

"He's not a beast, but whatever. I'm just a girl from the town. She," and Dayang waved over at Aulia, "is actually the person the Town Guard sent out. Whatever you have to say, you can say to me, but anything official will really be coming from her." She knew she was not quite being perfectly diplomatic, but she still felt that deep ember-bed of anger turning over in the upper reaches of her chest.

The woman stared at her a long time, the dark-silver curves and whorls of her skin stock-still with her set expression.

"Very well. I cannot dictate what counsel you keep."

That would have to do. Dayang decided to press on.

"What is your name? I am Dayang Marchadesch." Not the most elegantly formal of introductions for a cross-cultural exchange, but Hell if Dayang knew what the Pelo woman's customs would have dictated. She didn't seem to mind in any case, actually smiling a little. Perhaps changing the subject away from the two "Abominations" standing in front of her was a relief. The subject of her "Words of Warding" still looked sulky, and while Aulia was clearly somewhat anxious about this exchange, she also seemed impishly amused at Jeims.

"A pleasure to meet you, *Dayang Mar-cha-des-ka*." This slow mangling was nothing new; Dayang was used to people having trouble with her surname, which Father said came from some ancient conqueror's long-lost Ambérico dialect. "My name is Sei'vaneh Kal'ni'kesh."

Dayang gave her best aristocratic bow, bending at the waist with her arms by her sides, not really knowing what else to do. "A pleasure to meet you too, *Say...van-ey cal...ni...cesh*." She stumbled over the Pelo name's odd consonants and strangely precise pauses, knowing sourly that she'd butchered it far worse than Sei'vaneh had "Marchadesch." She turned then, looked at Aulia expectantly.

"Tell her we've seen her come out at night every eight days or so for the last two years," the city guard said in Basa Mala. "Never during the day."

Dayang was relieved; translating would spare her the absurdity of just repeating something the Pelo woman could understand perfectly well. Sei'vaneh frowned, cocking her head a little. *Does she really have no Basa?* Dayang thought. *Do they know that little about their neighbors?* She supposed she knew shamefully little about them as well, but then she wasn't being sent across the Siinlan to watch some Pelo village.

"We have seen you come out at night about every eight days to watch our town, for the last two years," Dayang translated a little awkwardly.

"Yes," the woman replied. "I scout the Mire. This is my role, my caste, and I have trained for it all my life. I come out once every patrol to see if your walls have been breached again."

Dayang relayed this to Aulia, who nodded then said, "Why?"

When Dayang put the one-word question to Sei'vaneh, the Pelo woman laughed.

"You have good strong high walls. If they fall, our village could be in even more trouble. The last time we did not see coming. Many died on our side of the...Siinlan as well." It took her a moment to find the Gentic word for the barrier represented by the Ashlit Mire and the Gyring Ash.

"The things in the Mire can hide under the ash for a long time. Even the best scouts cannot always tell when there will be a surge. When we looked back on the events of the last attack, it was clear that your town had been attacked first, and the creatures were occupied for at least two...weeks after. Your Fallen weeks are seven days, yes? It is near enough. If we had known, we would have been more prepared, or we could have fled."

Aulia looked thoughtful at this once Dayang translated. So did Jeims, who seemed to have mostly gotten over being miffed as his curiosity overcame his pique. Dayang noticed Sei'vaneh looking over her shoulder at the Mire.

"We should probably hurry, she's getting antsy," Dayang said. Aulia nodded, then asked the obvious question.

"Why come out during the day?" Dayang translated. "Were you hoping to have someone from the town show up to talk to you? You didn't seem at all surprised to see us. Why not approach the walls?"

"I wanted to speak to someone, yes, though I was surprised to see the...cats." She looked aside. "I might have been insulted, but my message is too important." She looked over her shoulder again. "I did not know what your guards would do if I approached the town too closely, and I needed to keep an eye on the Mire."

She didn't have any visible weapons, but from the way she stood Dayang doubted she was unarmed. She'd bet her new kris knife the woman was a Fathomdancer too, a sort of Pelo Wira. That or a shaman of some kind. She had that kind of weight in the Fathom, though the exact quality of it was difficult to discern, no time to wonder exactly why.

"I understood that one: we should get on with it," Aulia said. "Tell her we are grateful for any message she has, that we'll be sure to pass it on, that there is no offense, then ask her why she's so damn nervous." Her fur had begun to stand up some, as had Jeims', and Dayang felt the spread of gooseflesh on her own skin.

"We are grateful for the message and anxious to receive it. Anything you say will be heard by the others who guard our town, we have a charm for sending voices through the Fathom. We do not wish you to worry about offense, and we are in all honesty wondering what you are nervous about," Dayang said. "Is time short? Is there danger?"

Sei'vaneh nodded. "Yes. These are all related. Danger is coming and time is short. I was hoping to talk to someone sooner. I believe a...person is attempting to make a false attack and blame it on us. I did not dare confront them and did not have time to flee for reinforcements.

"They were Fallen, but they did not speak and their clothing was nondescript, so I do not know which of your peoples they came from. They were male, I think. Tall, pale-skinned, and using the Fathomdance to herd a creature. A native creature of the Undersky, what you call the Abwaild. Not one of the hybrid abominations of the Mire."

She frowned, pulling the strange silvery lines of her face into a diagram of severe disgust, and glanced over her shoulder again. "This herding is not normally something you Fallen can do, but he was not one of our own. His mind in the Fathom, it had what it needed for the herding and no more. It was still Fallen in all other ways."

It took Dayang some time to translate all this, and Aulia still looked confused, but Jeims was agitated, excited even, pacing back and forth rapidly on the grass.

"Altered, maybe," he said. "Fathom-techniques to give a Fallen person some of the Pelo-changes. I've heard rumors out of the Sovereign Nations. That's blasphemy at best for most of them, but you never know. Desperation and fanaticism are powerful things; they could have altered someone so his mind can mesh with Abwaild critters."

"We'll discuss it later," Aulia said sharply, her voice and posture now that of the Town Guard, the soldier. "What creature is he herding? How soon will it be here?"

"You call it a Hunch-Ripper, I think," Sei'vaneh replied. Jeims muttered an especially creative piece of Gentic obscenity at this, and some part of Dayang's mind filed it away for future appreciation, even as she felt her own hard shiver of fear. "I think we have..." she trailed off, then her eyes widened. "No. No. Draw your weapons, I will not feel threatened when you do."

The Pelo made no move to draw whatever she might have under that heavy cloak herself, but Dayang reached behind and drew the kris out of her sheathe. The woman nodded at the weapon, and began to back away toward the Mire.

"He has pushed it through the Fathom. This is beyond reckless. It is too near. I cannot stay, I must get word back. You must fight, and you must pass the message along. Even if you do not survive, your people must understand this was not us." She turned and sprinted, fairly diving into the Mire when she reached it. Dayang stood stunned a moment, then felt a sharp prick at her calf.

"Keparat!" she said. Jeims had poked her with an extended claw.

"Put your head together, Dayang, you're about to get some unexpected training," he said, a dead-serious growl beneath his voice. "Can you sense what he did? I can. She's right, it's beyond reckless. Get ready. I think we have maybe half a minute, not enough time to get even halfway back to the walls. Hunch-Ripper's too fast over short straight distances, it'd just run us down. We'd better prepare."

Dayang reached out into the Fathom, and gasped. She saw the ripples of the Hunch-Ripper's passage, felt her mind flinch away from the wound-in-everything where it had emerged out in the Mire.

It was, she knew, possible to travel short distances through the Fathom yourself if you were very, very careful, and even then it was an act of desperation. More than just desperation, really. The vast majority of Wira would not attempt it even to evade a deathblow. There were, after all, worse things than dying, and it's not like you got a chance to practice beforehand.

She hadn't known it was possible to push another living thing through the Fathom, although she supposed Abwaild creatures like a Hunch-Ripper might obey different rules, especially if you had some kind of control over one, but…

It had gone wrong. Of course it had, the attempt was insane. She could see where the path had dipped too...far. Too deep. She breathed in, breathed out, ignored the thought, but another came: *God knows what the backlash must have been for the fool that did it.* She shuddered, dropped into a half-crouch. Her legs trembled, and she did her best to steady them with her free hand. Jeims was chanting quick Proken phrases, and she sensed the intricate cause-effect-contingency of his spells, warding and seeking and preparing, moving through the Fathom all around herself and Aulia.

She heard the chants, felt the motions of her own defensive magics as though they were being performed by someone else. Aulia prayed, though not any prayer Dayang recognized, mouthing short strings of words with an arched back, and Dayang knew the guardscat likely had very little Wira training, certainly much less than either herself or Jeims.

We'll have to keep her safe, she thought. She was aware her legs were still shaking, adrenaline surging everywhere though her weapon held steady. She felt the forward wake of the thing's coming. It was wrong.

They were much too far from the walls to expect any help in time. She began a prayer of her own.

God I'm not ready to fight a normal Hunch-Ripper let alone something... changed. Panic fought its way up from the depths of her guts, clawing at her throat. *Hunch-Ripper, God...*

She'd seen plenty of drawings featuring this breed of Abwaild creature, and had even gaped at a captive one as a child visiting Surabaru. Even with its blades amputated and replaced with flimsy cork prosthetics, it had been terrifying and strange, crouched down below the knees of its four thick legs, each of which had been nearly as tall as Father, its semi-insectile head held even lower on the weird articulated neck.

She shuddered, let out a deep sigh, squared her shoulders. *No. No. I don't know if I can do this but I'm going to do it anyway. Jeims and Aulia are counting on me and I will do this.*

Dayang looked down; Jeims was chanting softly, finishing a spell. He looked up, met her eyes, and must have seen something there because he nodded, walked behind at her right shoulder, faced the way the thing was coming with one open paw raised. She understood, beckoned Aulia to go behind on the left.

It came, bounding out of the Mire.

The creature bursting through the embertrees looked very similar to the one she'd seen in Surabaru, but the ragged edges of its forelimb-blades were very much intact. It seemed like it was shaking, though, vibrating against the very air with an erratic black-light outline.

"Eyes!" Jeims yawped, and Dayang closed them just as she had been trained. She could still see-sense the thing through the Fathom, though it was hard, and she got the impression that perceiving too clearly was a bad idea. There was a lingering *crrrrrrACK* and a powerful scent of ozone as Jeims' lightning bolt struck out at the Hunch-Ripper. Dayang could see the arc's outline even through her eyelids.

When she opened her eyes, the Hunch-Ripper was nearly on them. She was already on her guard, kris held out just so. She had no shield, but had put up a good sturdy ward that shimmered over her left forearm and hand. It wasn't ideal; it took a portion of her attention and whatever assistance she could coax from the Fathom to maintain.

Smoke rose from the frontal hump of its torso where Jeims' spell had hit its mark, but she knew Hunch-Rippers drew on the Fathom in their own way when they fought. It would take much more than a single spell to take it down.

It lunged, but its momentum was blunted by one of Jeims' wards. It spat out an earsplitting series of *RAK RAK RAK RAK*s, whipping its blades through alternating diagonal slashes in its frustration. Somewhere behind the red-orange veil of her adrenaline and pounding fear, Dayang's mind coolly and carefully went through the paces of her training, noting the way the thing moved, the rhythm of its attacks, and without further thought she thrust both arms forward, left wrist over right.

One slashing, serrated blade slid along the shimmer in the air that marked her shield, and the Fathom-reverberations nearly made her yelp. They whispered wrongness within the echo, hissed it out into the air. She heard Aulia scream and Jeims swear.

It didn't matter, it couldn't matter, she put it out of her mind. Her arms had already struck out over and away from each other even as she stepped back, narrowly avoiding a follow-up slash. Her blade found the crook of one forelimb-joint, slid along it, and again that reverberation, but weaker this time. Weaker, or her mind had already built up new defenses.

The creature screamed, too, but she'd done no real damage. She'd have to whittle away the resilience it drew from the Fathom, just as she would fighting another Wira. And, of course, there was whatever had happened to the thing on its journey through the Fathom and through...

no

...and on its journey. The bizarre shaking outline of the thing had gotten more erratic, more violent. She didn't know what this meant, but it seemed to be causing the creature more distress than either her kris or Jeims' spell; an unending string of raspy *RAKRAKRAKRAKRAKRAK* spilled from its clicking mouth-parts.

Jeims followed up her attack with one of his own, a steady stream of fire aimed at the Hunch-Ripper's head, though he had trouble keeping the blue-white flames on target with its frenzied, thrashing attempts to avoid them.

Aulia must have recovered some of her nerve; she dashed out around Dayang's right side, weaving between the thing's front legs while it was distracted by a face full of fire. She got in two good vicious strikes with her knuckle-daggers, slashing at what passed for its ankles with their claw-curve blades.

In her sudden rush of resolve, though, Aulia had forgotten about the creature's thin, whiplike tail. She saw it coming at the last second, managed to dash in the other direction, but it caught her against the flank and sent her tumbling. She landed on her side next to the Hunch-Ripper's front leg.

The creature turned its focus toward her, and Dayang was already moving. A solid stomp from the hooflike foot could do more damage to Aulia than she wanted to contemplate. Jeims saw what she was doing and darted left, kept the stream of flames coming from that direction so its attention would hopefully be diverted.

Dayang dashed right, crouched over Aulia's sprawled form. Aulia tried rising slowly to her feet, but there was a vicious bruise across her side visible even through the pale fur; the light armor of her guard's harness didn't cover her flanks.

The Hunch-Ripper went after Jeims in earnest now, and while Dayang knew he could fend for himself for at least a few moments, he wasn't really a close-quarters fighter. The ongoing gout of flame snuffed out as he dodged the thing's attacks, sent little harrying shards of luminous ice at its underbelly. He also took a couple of glancing blows, but his training let him shrug them off for now.

Dayang managed to drag Aulia back behind her, aided only slightly by her attempts to limp along. A quick Sihir-assessment of the guardscat's injury revealed internal bruising and some bleeding, but not enough to be immediately life-threatening. *God damn the fool who sent the thing this way*, she thought. No way an ordinary Hunch-Ripper could have done this to a trained guard in one blow.

A hard slap from the flat of one forelimb sent Jeims flying, though unlike Aulia he landed light on his feet a few paces away, baring his teeth and beginning another spell. The Hunch-Ripper turned its attention back to Dayang and let loose a rapid barrage of slashing strikes. She managed to deflect most of them and even get in a couple of counterattacks, but the black-light outline of the creature now convulsed so powerfully it seemed like it might shake the creature apart.

When the creature's blows did land, they had more force behind them than should have been possible even for a monster like this, rapidly shredding her resilience reserves. Her conjured shield began to dwindle, forcing her to rely increasingly on her kris to parry. This was dire, but there was no time to think about it, no way to retreat, so she continued to fight.

She got in one good stab at one of the creature's neck-joints before a forelimb slash made it past her defenses and caught her on the right temple. She jerked her head back as it made contact, keeping it from penetrating the weak spot in her skull, but it tore through flesh down her brow. She just barely managed to tilt her face so it went between her eyes instead of over one, and it caught at the bridge of her nose before making a deep, excruciating gash down her left cheek.

She screamed, more in defiance than pain, and was granted one small mercy: she had her eyes screwed shut when Jeims' lightning-spell tore through the air, close enough she could feel the heat of its passage, a touch of its potential thrumming through her nerves toward the ground.

The thing gave its own piping, alien screech. She shuddered, and when she opened her eyes, a bit unsteady on her feet but still with both arms up to guard, it had collapsed in a heap of long thrashing limbs, still limned in erratic luminous black. One of its blades dug into the grass a hand's-breadth from Aulia, who was still trying to stand. Dayang bent down, slipped her hands and arms under Aulia's warm, heaving flank and, grunting, lifted the Lingmao into her arms.

Aulia was smaller and lighter than Jeims, but her arms and armor added noticeable weight—even with the added strength granted by her Wira training, Dayang knew this was going to be difficult. She spun clumsily and stagger-sprinted away, feeling dirt from the creature's pointless furrowing strike her calf as she went.

Jeims followed a few paces, then turned and, as she watched over her shoulder, conjured a great ball of crackling silver lightning right on top of the creature's prone form, bright jagged tendrils crackling down into the flailing mass. "Look away!" he yelled, and she did, slowing some in her exhaustion as they headed for the gate. She could only see out of her left eye anyway, the right kept shut by a curtain of blood. Aulia moaned low, curled herself into Dayang's chest.

As Jeims caught up she felt the thing come apart behind them, filling the Fathom with a sickening ripple of black lines.

Fifth Interlude

Embrace-of-Fire, Kash'ehn'dahl Empire, The Abwaild
233rd Year of the Burrowblade

It took Sei'vaneh all night and some of the morning to cross back out of the Ashwound, wary of what may have awoken under the Mire. She laid out her bedroll and slept the moment no more embertrees were in view behind her. It was only another hour's journey to the village, but she had things to accomplish that should not be attempted with a tired mind.

The village was intact, thank the Guardian God, its fences untouched and live with Fathom-thrum. She was halfway through the outer ritual gate when Lo'Bahsk stopped her, placing two fingers on the plane of bone just below her throat.

Dread showed in his face, slid down the wiry contours of his compact frame. His voice held steady with obvious effort. "Did they kill it? How many of them did it take?"

Sei'vaneh looked up at him evenly, catching his intent blue gaze with her own. "Are you prepared to receive my words?"

He stepped back, hand pausing in the air with two fingers still extended, the silvery lines of his face drawn together into a frown.

She folded her arms and waited as he prepared his spirit and mind to face the inimical. Her own thoughts she kept as carefully structured as she could, though some of the lingering wrongness still dripped from their corners. Sei'vaneh did her best to let it trickle away. Bad enough she'd stood near two Bright Beasts for so many long moments—but in truth this was the least of her worries. The spirit could be cleansed with the proper rituals. The mind was not so easily set back in order.

After a moment's meditation, Lo'bahsk Kal'ni'kesh dropped his arm and cocked his head first to the right, then to the left. Ready. His posture was still, but his hands worried back and forth at each others' fingers.

She gave the words, measuring each one's exit from her mouth with grim determination. "I felt the creature's taint dissipate through the Fathom, and sink back into the Outer Below from which it came."

He shuddered hard as he heard, and closed his eyes, breathing more quickly.

"Lo'bahsk! Look at me!" When he did not, she snapped forward and grabbed a handful of braids, yanking his head down until his eyes reopened. They tried to twitch away from her face in every direction. She held his gaze. "I am here. Anchor yourself."

He breathed in deep, let it out, let it pass. "Thank you, cousin. I am well."

Sei'vaneh narrowed her eyes, regarding him, still holding his face near her own by his hair. "No. But you are well enough for now. You will need to spend some time in meditation when speaking is done."

"Yes. You must put more corrupted concept into words."

"Yes, I must, but not much more. Stay with me."

"I will stay with you," he said.

She released her clench of his braids.

Slowly he straightened, then spoke. "You will begin the Chain of Tainted Words?" It was not good for a whole group to hear such things at once, or for one person to have to tell them too many times. Lo'bahsk would tell a member of the village council, who would tell another, who would tell another. This ran the risk of garbling the messages— but there were worse risks to worry about.

She took a steadying breath. "Yes, I will."

He turned, and beckoned her. "There's a place set up for us to speak where no one will listen. After, you must tell the Prefect. She will want to hear the words from you directly. Then the burden will be passed from your tongue."

Sei'vaneh bowed slightly in assent, and followed. They settled onto the sparse lavender grass around one of the village's cooking-pits. She told him the rest, about the Fallen instigator she had tracked southward along the banks of the great circling sludge-river these newcomer-peoples called the Gyring Ash.

She told him about the Hunch-Ripper the man had, against the beast's every ordinary instinct, somehow managed to herd out of the wilderness into the Mire. About how this man was different, had been changed somehow to do a thing the Fallen should not be capable of, a thing only a few of their own people could accomplish. How he had pushed it through the Fathom, something no rational person of *any* nation would think to attempt. She did not need to detail the consequences of this breathtaking recklessness.

She told him about the strange trio that had come out to meet her instead of any kind of official delegation, the girl and the two Bright Beasts. How she had heard them echo her message through the Fathom back to their town, so that even if they were killed the words would be heard. How she had felt the ripples of their battle through the Fathom behind her as she fled, but could not say any more than that. She left out the sick wake of regret she'd felt in not staying to fight such an open anathema.

"I do not know how many of the Fallen it took," she told Lo'bahsk. "I dared not look, or reach out too far. I expected it would kill the girl and the Bright Beasts, and perhaps it did, but it died faster than I would have thought in that case. Perhaps it made short work of them and then went to their walls, and died there. It would—" she made the four-fingered flicking motion of the Warding Hand to warn him, "have had to have moved very quickly, but perhaps it did not have to move so much as appear."

He shuddered hard. She waited for him to compose himself, then tilted her head left, tilted it right. "That is what happened. Now I must tell you why it is important."

"You believe the man wanted the blame for this attack to fall on us," he ventured.

"Yes," she said, "and here is where you must listen carefully." He was not well-educated on the subject of the Fallen, but he had a good memory, and this made him ideal for starting the chain of messages. He would be less likely to warp things through his own preconceptions, though she did worry about his prejudices, and his young man's pride.

"Most of the Fallen do not bear us Risen any particular ill will. They feel guilt, even, however vague, for the manner of their arrival. They are content to stay within the Ashwound, which they call the Caustlands, and face their own problems. The unwounded Undersky they call the Abwaild, and life here is inimical to them. They cannot eat anything that grows, walks, or swims in the true Undersky."

Lo'bahsk listened, spent a moment looking thoughtful, motioned for her to go on. He knew this, but would also know she was looking to build upon it with things he did not know.

She nodded and cleared her throat. "They have many tribes and clans of their own, ones they say go back to long before they came here. These are much more complicated than most know or would expect. Tribes within tribes within tribes, a dozen varieties of every language, quarrels on every possible question of faith."

"Like the Old Kash Empire," he said.

"Yes," she answered. "Perhaps even more so. We don't understand how they came here all together when they are so fractured, but here they are. They say they have settled some of their differences since they arrived, but others have grown wider."

"Of faith? Of political matters?" He squinted, glancing over his shoulder toward the Mire.

"Of both. They have many faiths and many polities. There are six large nations within the Ashwound. Large by their standards, not large like the Old Kash Empire. They call them the Caustland States. The one across the ash-river is called Tenggara."

"Tenggara. I knew *that*." he said, and she scowled at the petulance in his voice.

"Quiet your pride, Lo'bahsk, and listen. I won't tell you again." She knew it was hard for him, being chosen for something he lacked, but this was no time to indulge such feelings.

After a visible struggle to bring his resentment under control, he motioned for her to continue.

"The Fallen say that these Caustland States are all coalitions of many faiths and peoples and races, including," she grimaced, and spoke the Words of Warding, "the Bright Beasts. Each state has a set of laws that apply to all within its borders. Some among them chafed at this. 'We are our own people, and should have our own law.' Most especially, they wished to raise their children and discipline their own as they saw fit. So, after much conflict, many left to form their own tribes. They called themselves the Sovereign Nations."

He kept canting his head back and forth as though he knew exactly what she was talking about, when she was sure he did not, but she would let this pass so long as he could retain what she said. "You remember all of this?"

He frowned, and that was enough. She repeated herself, twice, then went on. "They began to burn their way into the Undersky, past the Ashwound, to create new Fallen territory for their Sovereign Nations. This is the Incursion, a quarter-turn up the ash-river from here, on the northeast side of the Ashwound."

"There are not many people there," he said, and she resisted the urge to roll her eyes. If he wanted to salve his pride by demonstrating knowledge, he really should come up with something better than that. He caught her expression and hurried on. "Just savage Dahlabekh tribes, yes? Outside even the borders of the Old Kash Empire?"

"Yes, which is why these Sovereign Nation Fallen chose that part of the Undersky to invade. The Dahlabekh wish only to keep living like primitives in the ropewood jungles. They have no real allies."

"So," he said, massaging his temple with one hand, "why would these invading Fallen have any business this far downriver?"

"Normally they would not." She turned to look northward, and let a few unpleasant thoughts—

his mind Fallen mind altered mind passed pushed through-and-below too far too out from

no

—pass down through her awareness. "This Sovereign Nations confederation has grown, and built a formidable military force they call the Many Nation Army; still, they could never challenge the Caustland States directly. The Fallen are few; these separatists are even fewer. But if they could induce their cousins to fight us, to fight the Risen...they could harry their enemies without spilling any of their own blood."

"Surely even the most foolish of the Fallen would not declare war over a single Hunch-Ripper, even if it was...even if it had..."

He fell silent, and she leaned forward, grabbed him by the shoulders, forced him to look her in the eye. "Even if the creature had passed through the Outer Below? Steady, Lo'bahsk. You will find the strength for this. " He gave a hard shudder, and she tightened her grip on the bones of his upper arms. "Remember it, it is important, but do not let it linger."

He took a few deep breaths, then inclined his head. "I am well enough. Please go on."

"The Fallen are strange, and the things they do may not always seem to make sense, but they are not complete fools. The Ashwound Fallen know the danger of this thing, and may not brush off such an attack. I risked my life to make sure they knew we were not to blame, but their separatist cousins may try something like this again."

His eyes widened. "You think there may be war between us and Kualabu? They are not a garrison-town, are they?"

She shook her head. "I hope that we have avoided this for now, and no. The town has its warriors, but they are there to guard the town, or are passing wanderers there to..." She scowled, and pulled up a great fistful of deep-purple grass. "...to plunder the graves of our ancestors, hoping to loot artifacts and secrets."

Lo'bahsk murmured a fragment of the Long Prayer for the Dead. His face took on an outraged snarl, as was only proper, but then began to devolve into something else, something deeper and darker, and she punched him hard in the shoulder.

"Qult'ni'kharik!" he swore, and glared—but his glare was a confused thing, and it turned tail, sheepish.

"You must keep a tight leash on your mind, like a recalcitrant dog," she admonished. "Your anger is fitting, but this is not prudent prey for your thoughts right now."

"Yes," he said. "You are right."

She was glad to see his pride deflated, sunk down into the roots of the grass while his body sagged under the weight of realization. If he had thought himself ready to face such things alone before, he would not now. Good. *No truth is more important than the truth of the self.*

"Again: whatever their ancestors may have done, the Fallen do not, for the most part, bear us Risen any particular ill will. They do not mean to insult the burial-places, they are simply curious and greedy. I am not excusing them. I wish to offer understanding to you, and understanding does not care about such things. Do you receive it?"

"Yes, I receive it." Lo'bahsk sat straighter, and gave a chastened smile. "I will need your words twice more, except the ones that should not be repeated outside dire need. Them I remember."

Yes. She could see the remembering of them haunt the silver markings of his face, writhe behind the stare of his dark blue eyes. Gods-and-spirits willing, he would recover quickly, but first there was duty standing in the way. So she told him again, and once more. "Now, a summary," she said.

"Fallen dissidents calling themselves the Sovereign Nations may wish to paint the blackest of blame onto our blades," he said. "They hope that the Caustland States, the other Fallen, will react."

"You have done well." She gave him as much smile as she could manage, but the pride in it was real on his behalf. "Now go, extend the Chain of Tainted Words. I must prepare to meet the Prefect."

She watched him walk away with solemn purpose in his steps, and fortified her mind in prayer.

"Huen'Cal, mind of the Seven Eyes, soul of the Wombstone, attend me…"

Chapter 12

First: *Ever-increasing militarization has obscured the Presilyo's view of true spiritual purpose. The Somonei especially have become blind to their own karma.*

Second: *The Presilyo has faltered in its resolve to defend the Triune Path against the imperious secularism of the Caustland States, especially the profane educational dictates of the Salian government that threaten the Silado purity of our young.*

Third: *The leadership of the Presilyo has ceased to be forthright and transparent in their speech.*

Fourth: *This same leadership has concealed or failed to punish many instances of Ragado action by the Somonei.*

Fifth: *The Presilyo has taken up selling the mercenary services of these same monks and nuns as its livelihood, losing the humility that comes of subsistence from alms.*

Sixth: *It would be remiss not to mention the infamous failures of mental effort and discipline that resulted in the recent string of incidents which must remain unnamed.*

Seventh: *The Presilyo has shown strong attachment to easy relations with the Caustland States, overlooking many persecutions of the faithful by this lack of mindfulness.*

Eighth: *Complacency has bent the Presilyo's concentration away from one of the Triune Path's most holy purposes: to claim Solace for the faithful among the Fallen.*

- Prathan Lorca, *Eightfold Misrule,* 142 SE
  Instigating document of the Michyero separatist movement known as the "Carvers"

Carver State, Sovereign Nations, The Abwaild, 349 SE

"Watch out for dragons! Watch out for dragons!" Susaen's little-girl voice rang out jubilant and shrill over the ashfield. She ran back and forth in front of the burning forest's edge, kicking up small clouds of ash at her heels that slowly settled back to earth.

"There's no such thing as dragons," Juliaen said patiently, keeping one careful eye on the flames and the other on her five-year-old sister. "They're just an Old World myth. The Abwaild is full of strange creatures and Praedhcs, but no dragons." *And things we cannot eat, ground we cannot plant,* Juliaen thought. *Burn and cleanse.*

Susaen stopped and pointed out toward the Abwaild. "My friend Sherina says it's full of Pelo savages too!"

"That's because 'Pelo' is just the Basa word for 'Praedhc' and your friend's family is from Tenggara. Do you remember the word in Ambérico?" Ambérico being the language of the holy *Fathom Messenger*, Juliaen and all her siblings were expected to learn it along with the family's native Gentic. It helped that Ambérico was also one of the most commonly-spoken tongues in the Carver Nation.

Susaen frowned. "Ummmm…"

Juliaen wanted to smile, but tried not to. Susaen was supposed to take her studies seriously.

"The word is "Antepas," Susaen, there are Antepas in the Abwaild. But no dragons. Even in the Old World, they were just pretend." There were almost certainly no Antepas in *this* part of the Abwaild, though. The Many Nation Army would have seen to that.

Susaen turned and ran in her direction, her voice rising to a singsong yell.

"No dragons! No dragons! Watch out for monsters! Monsters and Antepas in the Abwaild!"

The girl stopped short of actually barreling into her big sister when Juliaen held up one hand, attention still fixed on the fire. Juliaen's other hand was already held out toward the carefully controlled conflagration, and her mind reached out again into the Holy Fathom, seeing the gathered-up webs of cause and effect that lay beneath and behind the physicality of the flames.

She pushed them back, left them blazing at just the right temperature, kept them confined within the safe bounds of her influence. They pushed fiercely at her constraints, but she was quick and forceful against their desire to spread unchecked. The rising smoke wanted to expand, wanted to drift over, fill her lungs and the lungs of her family and neighbors, but Juliaen refused to give its lighter particles much freedom in any direction but up, tamping the heavier soot back down so it would not become an unwanted coat of charcoal paint in a swath around the blaze.

"Susaen! Come away from there and let your sister work!" Father called out, his raspy baritone carrying across the open ashfield.

Juliaen spared her sister a small affectionate smile as Susaen turned again and pranced off Father's way, shouting, "Juliaen's working! Juliaen's making fire! Dragon Juliaen! Dragon Juliaen!"

The flames pressed deeper into the forest, quartzwood trunks shrinking down to towers of pale ash that crumbled with every small gust of wind, swirling in eddies round falling purple leaves to create a striking mosaic on the ground. Juliaen stood vigil over the many-layered nets that shifted and pulsed through the Holy Fathom, cast down from the flames like shadows composed of mind's-eye illumination. She murmured words of request, of description, of Harmonious Comprehension, the sacred Three Harmonies tongue flowing from her lips interspersed with prayer and praise.

Thank you O Divine, encompassing and whole, for this gift of earth and ashes

lain down fallow that it may harbor the roots which nurture our bread and milk

The flames gathered in, united, spread apart, energetic substance in so many pieces

too many ever to count or comprehend, ripped from the core of all enduring matter

Grant that we may fathom our blessing here where we stand, here when we stand

here at the only place where mortal mind may touch and know anything truly real

flung out to rally their fellows, great spreading ripples of liberated heat and motion spark pulsing bundles of live potential, the tangle-flash alarm of Abwaild minds

here may we stand in Harmonious Comprehension, here may we know Your grace

be granted our pardon as we grant it others, not of merit but of True Compassion

they rush away, fade from sight, or spark bright and desperate, fade to nothing

for Yours is Creation, her dominion, her acclaim, then now and forever, amen.

now the fire crept nearer and nearer to the bounds of her power and awareness

she pulled back the threads, and the ashes settled down amid dwindling flame.

and Juliaen became aware

that she had tranced out again. Susaen tugged on her pants leg, small round face looking up full of concern. Father stood a pace back, chewing his wad of tobacco and watching her, and while the worry on his face was nowhere near as naked as Susaen's it was still there. Both these sights wavered in her vision, watery and drooping at the edges.

"You alright, Juliaen?" he asked, then turned aside to spit forcefully into the ankle-deep layer of ash piled over the newly-bare earth.

She drew in a deep breath, tasting that faint hint of pungent quartzwood smoke that had inevitably managed to elude her attempts at corralling it. Pulling hard on the binding-lines and reverberations which sketched her perception of the flames, she snuffed them out, and released her breath. The Holy Fathom receded back into the edges of her awareness and she steadied herself, suddenly realizing she had been swaying on her feet.

"Yes, Father." She blinked slowly as the mortal world smoothed itself back into focus, drying at its edges. "I was drinking deeply of the Holy Fathom."

The corners of his mouth turned down at this, his deep-set deep-green eyes retreating even further beneath his thick blonde brows.

"Watch your words, child," he said, his voice slightly shadowed with warning. Well into her twentieth year, Juliaen was no child by nearly any standard, but she knew to be more apprehensive than offended when her father used that particular word.

"I only meant..." She trailed off. 'To drink deeply of the Holy Fathom' was a common enough phrase, but Juliaen knew her father's paranoid fear that his daughter might one day dip too deep

below

outside

never

had only grown over the years, and she also knew how carefully he watched her.

This was understandable, given where he'd been as a soldier back in Salía. She didn't remember the Caustlands herself, but she had met a handful of his old comrades who had come out to live in the Carver State around the same time he had, including the Michyero officer who had been instrumental in Father's conversion to the Triune Path. Sometimes they would talk to her about Father. Aelaijh Draecsl had "stood the Nowhere Watch," they would say, in mixed tones of fear, admiration, and respect. Her father never talked about it himself, but she'd seen the blank spot among the medals on his old dress uniform, and Mother had confirmed what this meant, though she'd not wanted to talk about it any further.

Still, she thought the depth of his fear absurd from any neutral point of view. It was not possible to dip too deep by accident, not if one were even halfway careful; the borders may not be entirely *precise*, but they were very clear. You'd have to pass about a thousand warning signs on the way, and the bounds were no more tempting than the edge of a tall cliff. There was sometimes that perverse little voice in the back of the head that whispered, "jump," sure, but it was easily overruled. People didn't generally leap down ravines on a whim.

Of course, sometimes they were pushed. Or tried to descend with climbing equipment, descend down into...out of...

Juliaen clamped down on the thought.

Father grunted, stepped forward, peered at her closely. After a moment, he gave a small nod. "I know what you meant. Good work with the clearing. You gonna be alright for more after a rest, or are you tapped out for today?"

She thought about this a moment, dug down deep inside herself, assessed her own mental reserves. "I should be. Two more burns, probably. I think that's all we'll have time for before dinner anyway."

He squinted up at the sun. Farrod had begun to dip low, and would disappear entirely behind the eastern mountains within a few hours. Days were still short with the year this young. Even with the early supper Mother's failing health and strict feeding schedule required, there'd be little daylight left afterward.

"Alright. Take a rest, Juliaen. Susaen, go help your brothers in the kitchen. I'll go see how Saimn and Aryr are doing with the planting." He paused, prodding the ashes with one of his steel-toe boots. "This is good land, thank the Divine. The agromage says she can be here in a few days for the soil detox. It will be ready to receive Fallen seed by the time we're done planting the old plots."

Juliaen nodded, turning to look at the great expanse of new ashfield behind her, feeling a small burst of pride she did her best to smooth down. *The Holy Fathom is a gift of the One Parent,* she reminded herself, *as is my talent for making use of it. I have no right to be proud.*

"Thank the Divine," she agreed, and recited, "Solace is fallen into Fallen hands, and we among them hear Their will."

"May Their enlightenment spread across this, the Promised World; may the Enlightened Saint be reborn," Father intoned in turn. She had heard this particular passage from *Fathom Messenger* pass his lips a thousand times or more, but it sounded especially solemn now as he gazed out at the scorched forest's edge.

The frontier, she thought. *We claim the Promised World for the Triune Path while the Presileros cower in the Caustlands and sell the gifts of the Holy Fathom to the highest bidder. They believe they have cast us out as heretics, but themselves are cast out from Divine Truth within their own souls.*

She'd heard this a thousand times as well; from Father, in sermons, in conversations on the street when they were in town, from others in her study group on those occasions they managed to make it to the temple for worship. She'd even heard the great Archabbot of the Abbey Invisible, Camilo Thuwun, preach on the subject at the great stupa in Clarcspur; could still hear his piercing voice, carried by the Fathom to the farthest reaches of the crowd.

"They sell their monks and nuns, trained in the most sacred mysteries of the Holy Fathom, to serve the Ragado and profane interests of the Caustland States! I have seen it myself, my brother and sister Michyeros, my fellow-travelers of the Triune Path, I have seen it with my own eyes as a young man!" The Archabbot paused at this point to point southward with a great foreboding scowl.

"So-called Somonei in blue robes, marching through Tenggara among the ranks of the Tentera Wira! Fighting common bandits for the Staffguard in Salía! Playing at monster-hunter in the provinces of Zhon Han! The Caustlanders call them according to their varied tongues Wira or Haeliiy or Eychis or Xiake, like common profaners of the Holy Fathom! They fight in worldly Caustland battles for filthy lucre!"

The crowd had roared its approval, and Juliaen felt the fire sweep through her sturdy frame, rising from her center just below the navel up into her throat, and she could nearly taste the sweetness. When they began to raise their hands in the Karana she made the Gesture of Banishing right along with them, folding her two middle fingers in under her thumb and thrusting her arm into the air.

She became aware that she had fallen inward among her memories, pulled back to the present by Father's raised eyebrows. He was, naturally, used to her wool-gathering nature, was even frequently proud of the insights, spiritual and otherwise, that she gleaned while wandering through her own thoughts. Then again, there were certainly times where he had to remind her to keep her attention on the present and save the meandering for her meditations.

She gave Father a small, apologetic smile. "I should tend to my meditations before the next burn," she said, and he nodded.

"Susaen!" he called, beckoning her over from where she was picking brightly-colored leaves out of the ashfield. "I told you to go back to the house! Come with me, then." An Abwaild burn was not normally a place for a child her age, but Father couldn't spare anyone else to watch her, not with Mother needing care round the clock. They already had Saam and Tamhs back home taking turns tending to her and the big farmhouse.

As Father and Susaen left, Juliaen paced back and forth through the field, closing her eyes and listening to the *hisshh hisshh* sounds of her boots, letting her breathing slow, observing the smoke-scented air as it filtered in through her nose, blew gently out her mouth. Her mind relaxed, the tightened cords that anchored her thoughts losing some of their tension.

She walked. Soon she was ready for another burn.

Later, she fetched some water from the well to replace what she'd need to take from the hot-water tank, then carried a small bucket of hot water to the washbasin. The farm was far too remote to have running water, though thank the Divine they did have some plumbing hooked up to a septic tank...even if they had to fill the toilet tanks themselves. Juliaen had very vivid recollections of outhouses—nothing seemed to tether memories quite as strongly as smell—and said a little prayer of gratitude every time she flushed.

After washing her face and brushing some of the ash out from her long blond hair, she shucked off the slightly sooty outer layer of her clothes and laid down on her bed with a small sigh, relishing the opportunity for even a brief rest. Rest for the body, anyway; Juliaen had always been a woman of restless mind, and it stalked about, worrying at her earlier thoughts and dragging them to the threshold of her mind, like one of their farm cats with a mouse or some small alien Abwaild vermin. Proper cats, not the strange talking creatures whose souls were not yet ready to walk the Triune Path.

Juliaen shook her head, laughing at her roaming mind's aimless metaphors. She closed her eyes, trying to let her mind wander off somewhere restful. But her thoughts were relentless, reminding her of the Presilyo's wide-ranging corruption, the exile of the true Michyeros, asking her what she was doing, how she was really helping, out here in the wilderness, taking land from the Praedhc rather than claiming the great cleansed disc of Divine Promise that was the Caustlands.

I don't know, she protested, and then another thought, one she knew was contemptible for its cowardice. *No one else is doing anything either, we all are biding our time, surviving out here in Earthmarch.*

But that wasn't true. She had heard rumors; she was always listening, and while they may be remote, she paid close attention on her trips to Clarcspur, read every word of news that came out here by echogram, asked polite but eager questions when she could. Juliaen knew that all of Creation was connected, that she was a part of it, and how could she achieve Harmonious Comprehension of the self if she did not do her best to understand the world around her?

Not all of the faithful were content simply to ignore the Presilyo, the rumors whispered. There were plans, people said, though they said it with care, tried to lessen the risk of their words finding heathen ears. Sometimes names were mentioned, and Juliaen remembered it all with care, though she never wrote any of it down or even discussed it with Father.

Still she was not sure what she could really do with any of what she remembered, what she'd gleaned. She sighed, and glanced over at the sunclock in the corner, saw that it was time for dinner. So much for rest.

Juliaen stood, stretched, went to the farmhouse's airy central hall, and sat down in the middle of its long rough-hewn wood table. She sighed, feeling the effort of a long day slide down from the top of her head and settle briefly in her lap before seeping out into the half-log bench. Her head hurt a little, and was threatening to become considerably worse. Hopefully food would help; if not, she'd have to talk to Saimn and ask for a laying on of hands.

She looked over to her left, where Mother was seated half-slumped in the chair Father had constructed special when it became clear that her condition was not going to be a temporary one. Made of Abwaild quartzwood and expensive Fallen yew, it managed to hold Maryh Draecsl's uncooperative mortal coil mostly upright without being so rigid as to cause her too much discomfort.

For a while, anyway; over time Mother's small movements and spasms would slide her frail form slowly downward, and they'd have to pull her back up from the ungraceful slouch. It always made Juliaen angry to see her like that, deep down in the most secret parts of her heart.

She kept the anger there because there was no one and nothing to direct it at; no one had done this to her, not that they knew, and no one, no laying on of hands, no medicine, no magic could repair Maryh Draecsl's recalcitrant nerves. It would be blasphemy to blame the Divine, and they certainly could not look to the Ragado arts of the Fathomless Deisiindr for aid.

Juliaen suspected that Father might have been willing to try this last if he thought it would have any chance of success, and simply beg the Divine for forgiveness through the agency of the Lotus Child after the cure was accomplished.

This was a disloyal thought, she knew, but she didn't think it was necessarily an untrue one. He had certainly made inquiries in every direction, and she had seen a few echograms addressed from Cenicebu. She couldn't think of any other reason to route correspondence through the Tenggaran capital. It didn't matter. Mother was still uncured, and Father's sins of intention were, real or not, between himself and the Divine.

"Susaen," Father said, his rich rough voice carrying down the table from its head where he sat opposite his wife. "Would you please say grace for us?"

"Ooo-kay," Susaen said, giggly and singsong.

Father's brows went up. "Susaen," he said gently. "Grace is serious."

"Okay," she said in a more solemn tone, looking slightly abashed. "Can I do it in Gentic this time?"

"That depends," he replied. "Have you been practicing your Ambérico?"

Susaen raised her eyebrows in an exaggerated expression of alleged innocence, giving an elaborate shrug. "I mean some, some I have."

Father was not impressed. "If it's only some, you still need practice. Say it in Ambérico, Susaen."

Susaen rose up in her chair and sat back down with a dramatic little *thump* before screwing her eyes shut and cradling her arms against her upper belly.

"One Parent of all us, know do food here is because you love..."

Juliaen did her best to keep her amusement in check during the badly-butchered prayer. The Enlightening Spirit would ferry the intent of her sister's words to the Divine no matter how badly mangled their grammar. Still, she thought with a tiny internal laugh, Father was going to have words with her later about just how much she'd really been practicing her Ambérico.

"Amen," echoed the uneven chorus of voices once the short blessing was over. As always, the way Mother slurred the word, leaving the last syllable hanging malformed in the air just a beat past everyone else— the way she half-flopped to the other side so she could turn her head and smile at her youngest daughter— made a tiny pinprick in Juliaen's soul. Aryr, seated at Mother's right, had already begun to lift careful spoonfuls of soup to her slightly quivering lips.

"We managed to clear plenty of forest today, thank the Divine," Father said, gesturing in the direction of the day's burns. "And we should all thank Juliaen, who has made use of and multiplied her talents, just as the Star Sutras say."

There was a sort of mouths-full murmur at this, siblings nodding in her direction. She smiled, blushed a light pink, and tucked into her own soup and rolls. "Thank you, Father."

Juliaen went to bed that night tired but happy, and it was that night she began to have the dreams.

A Memory

Coraen Alraed had his name still. It was one of the few things he still held onto, here beneath all the endless-endless masses of stone. He had a place, too, a place inside his head, though it was thinning and only at his most desperate could he pretend that it was real, here in the place and time that actually was. But it had been real, had once occupied that honored place of where he was, when he was, the only point in reality to be felt and moved by mortal hands.

Salía. His place in Salía. It was there, right on the border, not in the south where the ash flowed and to walk any farther was to leave the land of the Fallen entirely, but there by the lovely sun-sparkle swiftness of the Mindao River. He could stand in his garden and see past it, too, there to the other bank where Tenggara held sway.

His mother was there, and his father too, and the face of the girl who had died, but he had lost all their names, knew only his own and his country's, his old country, not this new place to which he had fled, after she had died, after he had needed answers he hoped he had found because either way they were lost to him too.

Coraen Alraed had his name still, and it was still Coraen Alraed, something he was sure of even as so much else had changed. Better to lose it than have it be altered, the way his fingers sometimes seemed to be when he dared to look at his hands. Long, and with too many joints, more than he could count since he had lost all of his numbers.

There were no mirrors in this square stony room, though he had asked for them several times. There was only the doorway, and it was unwhole, he could step through but it did not lead anywhere that was real, only a shallow place that perched itself just above something that wasn't quite and probably shouldn't be and in any case had no name or maybe he had simply lost that too.

Sometimes they came to the room's entrance, which was not a doorway because it had no door, and looked in at him. Sometimes he thought that their shapes were wrong and needed to be rearranged, and those visits were always cut short and once they shoved him back with a long pole, which he did not like.

He didn't know why he never left the room with no door anymore, only went into the doorway, which *was* a doorway because hadn't they opened it? And wasn't that a door of a kind, if it had been closed before? The room entrance was never closed.

Coraen Alraed looked down at his own chest, which seemed strange but who was to say for sure? He had nothing different to compare in his head, that picture was gone along with all the so-much-else leaving all the so-very-many dry aching craters in his head-flesh. Inside, of course. The outside of his head, maybe that was strange too but he had no way to look at it. He had asked for mirrors, but still there was only the doorway, and the entrance that had no door, the one through which he never passed anymore.

Something waved behind him, though, and that, that he thought for sure must be new because once he had been able to sleep on his back, there on the bedroll laid out for him beside the bit of wall-curve farthest from the doorway but quite near the entrance, which had no door. To sleep on his back now would mean pain and a shriek of protest from his least-favorite mouth, the one on his chest that was maybe strange but really who could say for sure?

Something waved behind him, and something else whispered in his ear.

There is no door in the entrance because you tore it down. They want to build a new one but they haven't yet.

It was a memory, maybe not a good one but a real one? It almost didn't matter, memories were things to be cherished now, because he seemed to have so few left

but you have plenty left they just hurt to see, you know where they are you simply look away

but that couldn't be right, they didn't hurt. Remember Salía, that place in Salía that had been his, his and his mother and father and the girl who had died? That was a memory, and he never looked away, a memory from before he'd left, gone seeking because of all that great tangle of reasons he only half understood at the time and now

now you never let your mind linger even though the answers are all there

And that made him angry, sudden and apocalyptic, and he gave out a long hoarse cry from the mouth that was below his nose and above his chin. And he went and put his face and hands in the doorway, the doorway that was unwhole-yet-opened, and he felt the anger-making voice wash away along with something else, something more connected to all those memories that he definitely no longer had and could never find, no not him, not Coraen Alraed. He still knew who he was.

He knew. He knew.

Coraen Alraed staggered back and looked at the room with new eyes, all five of them, though he had to turn and bend to give them all the use they deserved. None of them could see the memory, that place in Salía that had been his, with mother and father and the girl who had died, the before-seeking place, there in the Caustlands

now that was a memory but yes ow it hurt

look away I am no longer there it has been some time I volunteered for this

volunteered

why

And he clung to the memory, but it hurt now too, and so did his name, because now he was someone-something else, and not just the ordinary pass-you-by of change through every life something had been *DONE TO HIM*

you asked for this

"BUT WHY," he roared.

His fingers were new, ready, eager to rearrange. He flexed their joints, all their joints, as the sound of his cry echoed round the room.

They came to investigate. Three died before he did.

Chapter 13

Many years ago, I took a long walking meditation along the road between the village of Tongri and the Migiro Highway. I had much to contemplate. Brother Graegori and I had been sent to Tongri in the hopes that we might deal with a nest of bandits who had been troubling them.

We had done so, but only I was returning. Life is small, and frail, but also precious, and many lives had been preserved at the cost of others. Those of one Somonei monk, and a number of bandits who would not be turned from their path.

I prayed that the lessons the Divine intended for them in this life would mark their souls in those to come.

As I contemplated, one foot in front of the other slow but sure, someone approached along the road behind me, set to overtake from behind. This person's presence in the Holy Fathom was immense and undisguised. Dangerous, perhaps.

I prepared myself, and looked behind. I knew her—a former Archmage of the Tentera Wira. I had served alongside her company years before, though clearly she did not remember me. She had not been one to pay much attention to the rank and file, and likely thought Somonei interchangeable.

I was not surprised to see one so powerful as she. It was a dangerous road, and only the confident, desperate, or mad would walk it alone.

She traveled with a mule, and was unhappy with its pace, often berating the poor brute. Still they were faster than I, and soon caught up.

"Where are you going?" she asked brusquely.

"The Migiro Highway," I replied. "This path ends there. I do not intend to leave it."

A tiresome debate on the nature of destinations followed. She seemed eager to argue, as mages so often are. She was eager to avoid pondering how much of her path may lie outside her control, as are almost all people at almost all times. The anger this idea stirred in her led to a quick departure, and strongly colored her parting words.

I saw her again the next day. She was walking back toward the village. Her mule was not with her, though she carried some of its burden on her own back.

Her anger had not cooled, and further words would not have helped her. We passed in silence. I pray that the lessons the Divine intended for her in this life will mark her soul in those to come.

- José Calderón Martinez, *Still-Water Paths,* 329 SE

Presilyo Monastery, Inoue Island, The Caustlands, 349 SE

Sanyago woke abruptly, staring up at the lattice of wooden slats and supports that sagged with Laris' weight on the bunk above. He had dreamed, hadn't he? A strange one. He remembered fire, and fear, and a hand on his shoulder.

He was still wearing his robes. They smelled like smoke, and like some very old memory of food that he knew but somehow couldn't remember.

He sat up slowly, and stared at the wall for a long, long time. Hints of sunrise shone through the west-facing window. Abruptly, he shucked off his robes, balled them up, crammed them under the bunk. He could get in trouble for that, probably *would* get in trouble for that, but right now he just needed to get the smell away from him. He found new robes in his wall-locker, put them on.

He became aware that he was not the only person awake in the room. Other boys were stirring, looking at each other, looking at him.

"Sanyago."

Laris' voice came softly from the bunk above. Sanyago turned to look up at him.

"He wasn't right. You know that, right? The monk they burned, he was all...not right."

Sanyago nodded mutely. "I don't think it's a good idea to talk about that." He could feel that pulsing-pressing behind the whole of things. He turned his mind away.

"I know," Laris' voice was careful and low. "But I think it's an important thing to remember. That man wasn't a Presilyo monk anymore, not really."

"No," Sanyago said, staring out the window at the cresting curve of Farrod as it peeked over the wall of the Presilyo. "I suppose he wasn't. A heretic, then? Like they talk about sometimes in the histories?"

"I guess that's one thing he was," Laris said. "I mean, sure he was committing a heresy, but they don't burn people for just heresy, do they? Not since the Old World, and even then not since way back."

"I don't think it's a good idea to talk about that," Sanyago said again. "The teachers will tell us what's going on. We have Civil Studies today. Master Tijong will be sure to talk about it."

Laris gave him a blank, almost stony look, then abruptly hopped down off his bunk and strode to the door, walked out into the hallway. Sanyago followed him.

"Laris..."

Laris ignored him, reached the end of the hall, and opened the door to the outside. He stood in the threshold, looking out, then stepped aside, opened the door wider so that Sanyago could see. Inoue Island was large and the Presilyo grounds fairly sprawling, but even from this limited vantage it was obvious things were still in disarray.

Patrols of Somonei walked here and there, sending ripples and distortions through the Holy Fathom that Sanyago that could feel in his bones and nerve-endings; he had never seen so many pieces of imbued arms and armor openly borne and readied in one place, or sensed so many combat-wards at full strength. He had never seen a burned-down building either, but at least one had been reduced to jagged, blackened ribs, and several others were going to need repair.

As he stood there gaping, his mind sliding into that same semi-comfortable place of disbelief and suspension it had occupied the night before, one of the patrols spotted their open door and immediately swerved toward it. Sanyago's mind reeled as he felt the concerted press of their probing attention, drawing knowledge back toward themselves like reversed voices through the Holy Fathom.

"You there! Novices! Hold fast!"

They both froze. "Hold fast" was not a formal command from their training, but the meaning was clear enough, and the looks of battle-concentration that darkened the face of each warrior-monk made obedience seem beyond question.

It took Sanyago a moment to realize from both the pitch of the voice that had barked the order and the general build of the approaching Somonei that these were not monks, but nuns. Moreover, that little part of his mind more concerned with watching things than experiencing them informed him that one of their number was the same nun who had escorted Laris away last night.

This fact was not lost on Laris either, whose head jerked back just a bit despite the rest of his lanky frame remaining in an almost comically arrested stance, one hand still on the door with only his head peeking out past the frame. It was difficult to tell with Laris' very dark skin tone, but Sanyago could swear he saw a hint of color coming into his friend's cheeks.

Nuns, girls, and females in general had become a very popular subject among the boys of late, and while Laris tended to keep quiet in these discussions he also listened quite keenly. Sanyago didn't see the appeal himself, but he'd learned to feign interest if only to avoid the odd looks he'd gotten the first couple times he'd been nonchalant.

Two of the Somonei came to stand facing the doorway while the other three faced away—left, right, and forward, weapons in hand. One of them, Laris' escort from the night before, made an impatient beckoning motion.

"Come out from behind the door, Novice."

Laris did, and the pair of them stood facing the two nuns. The Somonei looking down at Sanyago was quite tall for a woman. Probably, anyway; it wasn't as though Sanyago knew many women. This was the closest he had been to a human female in at least half a dozen years. She was certainly taller than her companion, who was nearly eye-to-eye with Laris and was smiling at him in a way that made Sanyago uncomfortable for reasons he couldn't quite make solid in his head.

"How many boys are in this dormitory-cabin?" the taller nun asked brusquely. Her Gentic had an accent he could not place. She was a touch broad, well-muscled, with olive skin and sharp features. Like all the monks and nuns of the Presilyo, her head was shaved clean, but her brows were a dark golden color. Her eyes were a muddy green, focused and...worried? Maybe a little scared?

Sanyago hadn't thought that full-fledged Somonei really *got* scared. She carried a long polearm with a curved blade at the end, and he could feel woven wavering threads running through the Fathom-channels imbued into the weapon.

"Twenty-nine, I think," he replied. The confidence in his own voice surprised him, as did the easy math going on in his head. Four rooms with eight beds, minus three. "All the rooms but ours have an empty bunk." His heart pushed sick excitement high into his throat. Coming, coming, something was coming.

They exchanged glances. "Is that how many are actually there now," said the shorter one, addressing Laris instead, "or is that just how many are supposed to be there?" Her Gentic carried the lilting, slightly sharpened overtones of a Common accent, and she was, Sanyago thought, standing much closer to Laris than teachers normally did when not physically assisting with training. Her companion looked over at her with an expression that was hard to read, a jumble of demands and emotions vying for attention. Irritation? Amusement? Resignation?

At twelve he knew there was a sort of spark that could occur between men and women, even if he had never felt it himself. The Presilyo's obsessive separation of the sexes was meant to prevent any physical manifestations of this charge, but their teachers had always been decidedly vague about the details. Rumor and speculation ran rampant, and he'd heard whispers about the sort of experimenting, especially among the older boys, that didn't require female participation at all.

Laris hadn't answered the nun's question yet, but instead of berating him she just laughed. "I know, you're having a strange day and had an even stranger night." She put a hand on Laris' shoulder, and Sanyago felt himself freeze for the second time that morning. Physical contact between the sexes was beyond forbidden with only rare exceptions, and he was pretty sure this wasn't one of them. The other nun seemed to agree, planting her polearm with one hand and using the other to draw her sister's shoulder back gently but firmly.

The shorter nun took her hand off Laris' robe, though she also made an irritated "get-off-me" shrugging motion with her shoulder. She looked to be of mixed Zhon Han extraction, with much darker skin than others Sanyago had seen though she still had the distinctive eyes. She was pretty, he supposed, with finely drawn features and robes that hinted at the sort of curves that the other boys were always discussing in low, awed voices.

"The poor boy has clearly been through a lot, Ioanna," she said. Her voice was almost petulant, but she let her hand drop back to her side, and she made no attempt to touch Laris again even as he drew back, angular features drawn tight with warring discomfort and guilt and desire.

"We all have, Bai," Ioanna answered, and she glanced meaningfully over Sanyago's shoulder. Sanyago didn't have to look himself to know that a small crowd must have gathered in the hallway behind him.

Bai frowned and stepped forward into an imperious stance, pretty features drawn up into hardness. Despite her relatively small size and previous show of almost childish petulance, seeing this sent small shivers down Sanyago's back. He guessed she must hold some measure of rank among the Somonei; this was a woman accustomed to being obeyed when it mattered.

"All of you! Get back into your rooms and close the doors!" Turning to Ioanna, she half-growled, "I don't know why they built these cabins with doors on either end, it's not def-"

"IN YOUR ROOMS, NOW!" Ioanna barked, voice cutting across her companion's like a blade. Bai turned toward her, clear fury on her smooth features at being upstaged, but anything she may have had to say was forever forestalled by an immense cracking sound, followed by the sharp report of ancient hardwood splintering violently apart. Sanyago whirled to look behind him, felt a similar shattering fling the shards of the door's broken wards through the Holy Fathom.

It was a scene stilled in place, perhaps not in the tumult of the moment itself but certainly crystallized that way in his memory. Boys darting into their rooms, beckoning or outright pulling their brothers in from the narrow hallway. A man in ragged soot-colored robes dashing through the shattered threshold, armed with a pair of butterfly swords, jaw near-unhinged in what was half war-cry, half veering, volatile laugh.

Then it all shattered into chaos, like the door the man had broken through. Sanyago watched blades go to work, felt fire streak past his shoulder, marked the shapes that blood made on the wood-and-stone walls, regained his balance after the nun Ioanna rushed past him with her polearm and knocked his small frame into the wall.

By the time he had gotten his wits back about him, six of the boys were dead, strewn whole or in pieces behind the rampaging man in monk's robes. Sanyago froze, a rising acid frost coating his belly and throat. Laris knelt by his side, eyes rolled up into his head so that no part of their iron-grey iris was visible, holding his head between his hands.

"Nonononono," he moaned. "Don'tlookdon'tseedon'tknow."

Ioanna was fending the man off, using the long reach of her weapon to her advantage. "Profaner of the Holy Fathom!" she spat, getting in a few short sharp jabs to whittle down his resilience. But then she misjudged a thrust, and he took advantage of his own superior range of movement, pinning the blade of her polearm against the wall with one sword and ducking under the haft with the other.

She tried to pull her spear back, choke up her grip so she could defend herself. She managed to half-deflect his other sword with the long polearm shaft, but its back end had caught against the doorframe and the blade sliced across the breastplate of her light armor.

Something was wrong with that blade. Sanyago could feel it trail out from the butterfly sword's wake, seep under his boots and soak the ancient wood of the floor, curl into all the little eddies and voids of the air and spaces between. It seemed to be coming from the man himself, slithering over and around the webs of causality and condition he cast up from the Holy Fathom to aid and defend.

The imbued alloy of Ioanna's breastplate held up to the slash, though Sanyago saw her spells falter and fray at the edges when they came up against the man's. He also heard the sounds of combat breaking out behind him, and felt more clashes reverberate through the Holy Fathom. These didn't carry those same note of sharply unknowable *wrongness* as that between the man with the bloodied butterfly swords and the Somonei nun, but they were fierce, powerfully contested on all sides, and Sanyago knew he was hemmed in at both ends.

He was numb, but that numbness was beginning to coalesce in his head, pressing itself behind the cold, sharp edge of his training. A thin spine of flame rushed over his shoulder, presumably from Bai, striking the man's bicep and drilling through his robes though the flesh beneath resisted the attack. Laris was beginning to calm himself, looking like he might get back on his feet. Sanyago felt something break, some great force overflow its bounds inside him, flooding his entire body with momentum, with *push*. It set his veins on fire, focused every nerve and sinew into a thin, quick blade.

He was done planning, though he hadn't been aware that's what he'd been doing. He rolled forward under the clashing polearm and sword blades, came up already aiming a low kick at the man's knee. The man had a squat, muscular build, but Sanyago was a short boy even now in the throes of his first growth spurt, leaving him more than a head shorter than the adult he was attacking.

The kick did not connect, as Sanyago had known it wouldn't; the man had moved his leg back, dodging the blow and putting his body sidelong to Sanyago's. He'd pulled his arm back as well, laying one blade across his torso to better contend with the boy now standing much too close to easily slash at. When the sword slid across the man's body at him, blade turned out for a short jabbing slash, Sanyago was ready for it. His terror had not gone, but was consigned to a little corner of his mind which could only watch in horrified fascination.

Instead of jumping back or ducking under the blow, Sanyago twisted round in a blur, taking advantage of his speed and size to slip between the man and his arm. Cold metal slid along his throat and he nearly gagged; this side of the sword was blunt, but he could feel the heavy wrongness that coated it like rancid grease. This was mercifully brief, followed by the flesh of fingers and the brush of cotton cloth.

"Presilero whelp!" the man roared, and flipped his wrist, bringing the sword back across both their bodies in an attempt to cut Sanyago's throat while he was sandwiched between the man's body and arm.

Sanyago had guessed the man would do this, and he was also fairly certain it would kill him. He didn't think he had enough resilience yet to deal with a full-force slash across his neck, especially not from an imbued blade in the hands of some strange semi-Somonei Eychi who seemed far, far gone into the most dangerous form of heresy there was.

He also thought he had a chance, and that if he failed it would be a better way to go than slashed apart and tossed aside in the hallway a dozen paces from his own bed.

All this flashed through that little corner of his head as the rest of him went into instant, concerted action. He twisted quick and fluid against the man's arm and body, fending off the outer-under influence that spread out from his opponent like rotting, segmented antennae, throwing up his own sprawling amateur wards which were renewed as quickly as they wilted away. Ducking, he slipped down below the man's arm, threw one leg back

174

to spin even as he crouched. Then he came back up on the other side, guiding the man's arm with hands on either side of his elbow, pushing, pulling, angling.

It worked. The man was too surprised by Sanyago's sudden speed and defiance—and too busy fending off Ioanna's spear—to counter the move effectively. His blade tore across his own throat in a flat, understated, almost silent motion.

It was a shallow cut, but blood welled up in a thin dripping line and the man gave a gargling hiss, dropping his sword and clamping his hand over the wound. Ioanna took advantage of this bloody distraction, jabbing and slashing at him in rapid succession while Bai tossed fire at his feet, silver-blue flames licking at his boots and the lower hem of his robes.

It was not enough. The man kept his hand clapped to his throat, roaring in fury, and the sound had an undertone that battered into the live net of Sanyago's nerves like a pounding wave. A thick wash of blood burst out from between the man's fingers, and when he took it away the wound had...not healed, precisely. It had closed, but the substance holding it together was a color that hurt Sanyago's eyes, and he wasn't sure he was really *seeing* it at all.

Another roar, strangled and fouled. The man reached out to simply grab the blade of Ioanna's polearm bare-handed, shoving it aside. He slid his bloodied hand down to the base, pulling himself toward her to slash and slash and slash with his remaining blade.

More blood on the walls, patterns like crimson clouds, rabbits and dragons and river-waves. Sanyago lunged forward again for another desperate gambit, but the man had him marked as a threat now, and the swift hard answering back-kick caught him unawares, dead in the stomach. He vomited, unready, twisting and falling into the scent of iron and bile.

Behind him another roar of rage; Bai screaming for her friend. And that laugh again, and then...nothing. He rolled over, sat up, aware of the warm blood and puke soaking through his robes from elbows to thighs.

The man just...stood there, looking at Laris, on his feet again and looking right back. Laris' steel-grey eyes were fixed, somehow almost mild in their steadfast insistence. He had one hand raised toward the still staring man. Sanyago felt a tremor through the Holy Fathom, and he could sense...*something*...passing between Laris and the man. Something Laris was gathering but not accepting, and then...*showing* to his opponent.

come up from beyond give it back to him

The man put his hands on the sides of his head, just as Laris had, but it was different, it was *desperate*, his whole body rocked and raved and shuddered. From behind, Sanyago saw that his mouth was open, but could not see his face. He was grateful for this; he did not want to see the man's expression. No sound came from the open mouth now, but there was fluid and squirming, amorphous chunks and the color was *wrong* again and now Sanyago looked away once more. His stomach churned and ranted but had no more to give.

He heard the man's body hit the wall, and then the floor.

"Cover it!" someone said. It was a female voice, probably one of the nuns who had been defending the door. "By all that's holy, put something over it." No more sounds of combat. Doors opening, rustling. Boys crying, scared voices heard through doors. A scream.

He let himself look at the bodies now. They were all boys from the same room, having come out into the hallway as a group. Unlike the others who had left their rooms, they had shut the door to their dormitory when they had come out, and had not been able to get back in quickly enough.

They were a horror of torn flesh and blood. He had to look away, feeling a hard shudder in his upper chest.

Sanyago knew them, though not well. They were young, just barely old enough to start their sparring lessons. He knew their names, didn't want to think of them right now. His heartbeat rolled thunder up his throat.

His gaze found Ioanna, and again he had to look away. He had seen enough to know she was gone. He looked to Laris instead, who stared wide-eyed at the blanket-covered body of the man he'd...what? Stopped somehow? Killed, even?

Sanyago was not shocked that his friend had probably killed a man. The purpose of their training was clear enough, even without his frequent eavesdropping. He knew it would likely not be just monsters they fought in their lives as Somonei, assuming they managed to attain that title. And there was little question in his mind that he and Laris both would.

Well, he amended with just a touch of amusement amidst all the streaming blackness of the moment, *at least if Laris can learn to watch his mouth enough not to be labeled a heretic.* The amusement faded, though, and when it did he found the thought appalling. The man under that blanket was a heretic, a real one.

Laris looked up at him. Sanyago imagined his own dark-brown eyes must be just as shaken and bewildered as the shocked white-and-grey circles of Laris'. Sanyago was shivering, and he was wet, and he was not cold. Without thinking, he shucked off his grisly robe, then the soaked shirt beneath it, leaving him in just boots and shorts and dark brown skin. He used the less-soiled parts of both garments to wipe his skin as clean as he could, threw them aside, and then went to embrace his friend. Everything was drained white and grey, and he did not know why.

"*Porlyó,* Sanyago," Laris whispered as he clapped his own arms round Sanyago's back. There was as much desperation as there was brotherly warmth in the hug, both their breathing shallow and uneven. "Who was that? What in all the Hells is going on with this? I'm not even sure what's going on with *me.*"

"I don't know, brother," Sanyago whispered back. He was still just barely tall enough to see over his friend's shoulder if he went up on his toes, though he suspected that would change quite soon as he eased into his growth spurts and Laris flew into his. He thought about that a moment. It was better than...it was better. Alive. Laris' body was not still against his, a shuddering thrum of muscle and sinew in frantic tension. Another group of Somonei had arrived. Monks. They clustered around the nuns, who were gesturing and talking in low intense voices, though he could not make out any words.

He knew better than to try eavesdropping; they would be masking the conversation through the Holy Fathom. Bai was especially animated, her face an open flame of grief and rage, and he saw that she'd been wounded, a long seeping slash over her left breast. A few monks broke from the group and began dealing with the aftermath, checking on children. Some of them were wounded. Had there been fighting in other parts of the monastery? Of course there had.

"I saw too much," Laris said, gripping Sanyago a moment as though desperate for something solid to cling to, then letting go and pulling away a little to look him in the eye. "I saw his intent, his intents, all of them, coming out from his head like I do on the sparring-ground— but they had...they had more to them. And less, like his mind was...had...become less. I don't know. I knew not to look too close. It scared me." His eyes were bare, stark with last moment's memory.

"But then you stood up and you..." Sanyago trailed off, waited, watched one of the nuns gesture over toward the pair of them with a questioning expression. His veins still felt like they were on fire, but his heart had slowed in his throat.

"Yeah," Laris answered, letting go of Sanyago completely and half-glancing over his shoulder. "It was like...looking at the sun, if Farrod was completely *wrong* instead of just being really bright. If I didn't let my mind rest on his intentions directly, I could kind of push them back toward him, so he would see them instead of me."

"That's what killed him?" Sanyago asked, grimacing as his stomach sent little aftershocks up his gullet. The monks and nuns seemed to be coming to some kind of consensus. They might not have much more time to talk. "I thought you couldn't touch another mind directly in the Holy Fathom like that. Only the Divine can influence minds there."

Laris made a face that managed to convey both thoughtfulness and mild annoyance even through the shock still written all over his angular features. "I don't know about the Divine, but *I* definitely can't do it. I just bent his own intentions back toward him. He must have gotten a pretty direct look, and he didn't have my...talent, so I guess it caught him by surprise."

Laris' eyes turned aside, lost and low. "He didn't know how to deal with it, maybe. I still don't really know how it worked. I was just scared and angry and wanted them away from me, so I was like, 'Here, fine, *you* take them, you piece of shit.'"

Sanyago was glad the monks and nuns were too enmeshed in their own dramas to be listening, and for that matter any of the other boys who might be in a talebearing mood; that little piece of vulgarity could have earned Laris a missed meal. *Or,* he thought, watching Bai's frenzied, weepy pacing as she yelled at her fellow Somonei, *maybe not in this particular case.*

He punched Laris half-heartedly on the upper arm, not even hard enough to feel really. It wasn't really appropriate in the situation, but Hells if he knew what would be. Monks and monastery staff swarmed around them, moving bodies, cleaning up, but he could not bear to look too closely. "It worked, whatever it was. Whatever *he* was...no, you're right," he amended quickly as Laris shook his head slowly in warning. "We can talk about it later. Carefully."

The Somonei seemed to have come to a decision, sending a pair of monks to fetch them. Sanyago felt a tired sense of deja-vu wash over him, wishing they could all just settle back into the monastery routines he had so often gone to great and risky lengths to escape.

"Come with us, Novices," said the senior of the pair, putting a hand on Sanyago's bare back to guide him. His partner, on the other hand, scrupulously avoided touching Laris, simply beckoning instead. "We will find you new robes and shorts, there is no need to go back into your room."

Laris and Sanyago looked at each other, then back at the monks. "Yes, Sen-Somonei," they said in weary unison, and went.

What followed was a long, numbing journey from place to place under close guard. First they went to one of the Presilyo's armories, presumably for protection, and sat down on the floor of the heavily-fortified basement room as a full five-man squad of Somonei monks stood round them in a circle. No one explained anything, and Sanyago did not feel like asking.

The Somonei told them not to speak, so they passed some time by tracing letters over the stone tiles in the alphabet that Gentic and Ambérico both shared. Laris, who after showing considerable talent for languages had been assigned more advanced studies in the subject, tried to teach Sanyago a few Common ideographs. With limited success: Sanyago just didn't have his brother's gifts for languages. At some point one of the monks brought new shorts and robes.

The monks gave them regular swigs from their dewskins, the flat, odd-tasting distilled water making Sanyago's nose wrinkle, but offered no food. Sanyago was actually glad of his empty stomach; he didn't want to puke again, and stray recollections—like the way the blunt back of the man's sword had felt passing over his throat—were still making his guts turn rough under his ribs. He hoped this would pass by lunch.

It did not. Instead, Sanyago's nerves lurched up and down through a series of interrogations by a parade of senior monks whose existence he had only vaguely been aware of before. Laris got the same treatment; sometimes questioned together, sometimes apart, until finally they were brought to an empty practice room where they met Combat Master Olsaen.

Master Olsaen was a tall, stocky man with fierce, pale-yellow eyebrows over pale blue eyes that took the pair of them in with a mix of keen interest and healthy skepticism. He pulled a pair of bamboo butterfly swords from one of the racks lining the back wall of the practice room and nodded toward Sanyago.

"Show me."

Sanyago approached warily, hands up in a halfway-guard. His apprehension must have been written on his face, because Master Olsaen gave him a tight, sad smile.

"I'm not going to hurt you, Sanyago. I know you've had a very difficult day." He turned to look over his shoulder at the other monks. "They've had a physician look at them?"

"No," said one of the monks who had ordered the Somonei to bring them here. He must have been senior to or of a rank with Olsaen not to address him as Master. "They were assessed by the Somonei after the attack. Sanyago had some internal bleeding from the heretic's kick, but stanched it himself. Nothing complicated enough to need a magomédico. Staafaen was not injured in any physical way so far as they could determine."

Sanyago knew about the bleeding. It had been a simple enough thing to fix on his own, and Divine knew they'd had plenty of sitting-around time for the Eychis-meditation. If anything, he was embarrassed by the necessity. The man had been a skilled Eychi on top of his other... things, but if Sanyago had been ready for the kick he would likely not have been physically injured from just one blow.

Master Olsaen nodded. "Good." He slipped smoothly into a fighting stance, and Sanyago winced. It was exactly the same one as the man had used. This should not have come as a surprise as the heretic had almost certainly been Presilyo-trained, but the similarity still jarred him. The Combat Master's light blue eyes took in Sanyago's reaction, steady and grave.

"He stood like this, then?"

Sanyago nodded back, taking a tentative step forward, not sure what he was supposed to do.

"I'm going to jab at you, Sanyago," Master Olsaen said gruffly. He seemed to be trying one of his gentlest voices, but its long disuse had made it hoarse and patchy rather than smooth and reassuring.

Sanyago nodded again, stepping into range of the bamboo sparring weapons.

"I know it is difficult to reenact something you did in a very stressful situation. Just dodge my strikes until you feel you are ready, then show me."

"Yes, Master Olsaen," Sanyago said, and rocked between the heels and balls of his feet in anticipation.

The sword-jabs came swift and sure. Olsaen was a better fighter than the man had been— not really surprising for a Combat Master— though he lacked the man's mad demeanor and twisting tinge of wrongness. Sanyago managed to dodge most of them, deflected a few he could not dodge with his forearms, and felt the sting of bamboo from the remaining quick, sharp blows.

Olsaen seemed genuinely impressed that Sanyago managed to evade or block as many attacks as he did, and genuinely *surprised* at the speed with which his young opponent twisted round behind his arm, then back under to the other side to guide the Combat Master's own bamboo sword over his throat.

He did this at full force and speed, knowing the experienced monk had more than enough resilience to shrug it off, especially given they were only using blunted bamboo practice swords. He could also tell that Master Olsaen was holding back, slowing himself, reacting more predictably than he normally would. Sanyago supposed this was fair, since he was also not half out of his mind and distracted by a Somonei's spear as the man had been.

The Combat Master coughed, once, as the wood drew over his throat, then dropped both arms to his sides. Sanyago stepped back, gave him an uncertain bow.

"I see. Thank you, Sanyago. You are very quick. You let the Holy Fathom move you well. I am sure you know that you show great promise. Do not let it feed your ego. This could poison your potential. Do you understand?"

"Yes, Master Olsaen," Sanyago said, a little shakily. His stomach was acting up again, and the long muscles of his arms and legs seemed to be twitching of their own accord. Olsaen smiled that tight, sad smile again.

"Good." He turned to glance over his shoulder. "Take the boy away and feed him. Let him get some rest. Make sure he has the chance to talk to a priest. Now," he said, gesturing toward the corner where Laris was sitting silently and watching. "You, Staafaen, they tell me you have the Entyecogno gift. Can you show me?"

Laris nodded cautiously, then looked at Sanyago, who was already being escorted out by two Somonei. Sanyago looked back at him, shrugging. *I'll see you soon, good luck.* Master Olsaen's dark blue eyes observed them both carefully, back and forth between the two. Again that tight, sad smile.

"Ah, I see," he said, almost to himself, then in a louder voice, "Wait," making the Somonei pair turn just before they reached the door with Sanyago between them. "Don't separate them. Sanyago can wait outside while Staafaen demonstrates. Understood?"

"Yes, Master Olsaen," the senior one said, and they took Sanyago through the door.

Laris looked solemn when he, too, was brought outside. He blinked a few times against the early afternoon sun, shading his eyes with one hand while rubbing his temple with the other. Sanyago'd only been waiting a short time, but hadn't been sure how long Laris would take and was surprised at just how relieved he felt to see his friend.

"You alright, brother?" he said in a low voice as they walked, ringed by another squad of five Somonei monks.

Laris actually thought about that for a moment, rubbing his shaven pate. "I'll be okay. At least I didn't get kicked in the stomach. I saw that. Looked like it hurt."

Sanyago shrugged. "I've had worse sparring. I mean, not as scary, but still. You, um, you must have seen some things. When he died, it was…" he trailed off, watched his friend's face closely. Laris' features were drawn, introspective, his eyes narrowed so they were nearly just white-and-grey slits against deep-black skin. It took him a while to answer.

"I'm not going to pretend it was fun. I think I managed to avoid anything too...dangerous. I made him look instead. I'm not sure what happened when he died. I think his head emptied out. That I don't want to think about."

Sanyago nodded slowly. "They're going to take us to a priest after lunch. Maybe it will help."

Laris frowned. "Maybe, as long as he doesn't just tell me to meditate and pray. I already know how to do that. Could still help, though, if he really listens and actually knows what's been going on here. That's what bothers me more than anything, we don't understand what this is all about and no one wants to answer questions today."

"Yeah, maybe," Sanyago said. He dropped his voice, eyeing their Somonei escort out the corner of his eye. "I'm not totally sure they've put it all together themselves. They'll be distracted for at least a few weeks. I should be able to get some good eavesdropping in. I'll let you know what I hear."

"*Porlyó,*" Laris said with a laugh. "Nothing changes you, does it?" Sanyago was glad to see some of the tension break and ease out of his face.

"Not if I can help it," Sanyago said with a grin. "And seriously, brother, if the priest really is useless, I will always listen."

Laris smiled back, broad and brilliant, and gave Sanyago a sideways hug, putting one long arm about his shoulders as they walked. "Likewise, brother. We'll get through this, whatever it is."

They ate a cold lunch of cheese and corn-cakes and fruit and anything else the monks could find in a storeroom they raided. The kitchens were apparently in as much disarray as the rest of the Presilyo; Sanyago didn't see anyone out on the grounds except patrolling Somonei and a few staff starting to clean up here and there. He didn't see any other Novices, and figured they were being kept in their quarters and fed there.

He wasn't sure about the priest. Sanyago knew by now that not all priests were created equal, but this one had apparently been chosen carefully by whatever powers-that-be were directing the aftermath of their grisly morning. They met him in a small chapel Sanyago had never seen before except from a distance, and their Somonei escort bowed respectfully before going out to wait in the vestibule.

The priest's name was Father Kuwat. He was a big man, at once muscular and more than a little gone to seed, with the distinct air of a retired Somonei. He had a broad smile, with lined, copper-colored skin and very dark eyes. Sanyago looked at him for a long time. Something was tickling the back of his skull.

"Sanyago, yes?" the priest said. "Come here, let us talk. Your friend— Staafaen, isn't it?—can wait in the vestibule. I will speak with him next."

Laris bowed, turned, departed, and Sanyago approached, reached out, touched one of the beads of Father Kuwat's rosary.

"I *know* you," he said softly. "You were the monk who took me in when I came to the Presilyo."

Kuwat's eyebrows rose, but the smile did not falter, and he laughed, rich and kind. "You are right, though I am very surprised you remember. I suppose some things burn in the memory." He patted the pew beside him. The chapel had a confessional, but the priest ignored it.

Sanyago sat. The priest clapped him gently on the back with one big hand, though he kept his eyes looking forward at the large Starfall mural that adorned the wall behind the pulpit.

He did not say anything further, just waited, and finally Sanyago began to talk. He told Father Kuwat about the unexpected lesson Catechist Yaatkr had given them, about the burning monk they had seen after following the noise. His voice broke here, and the big, gentle weight of the priest's hand rested on his shoulder, squeezed very gently. He cried, leaned into Kuwat's warm, expansive side, and the priest waited until he was done.

"I am sorry that you saw that," Father Kuwat said when Sanyago began to dry his tears. "Divine knows we train you to face horrors, but the confrontation should not begin so young. The man you saw in that circle was one of the early ones we caught. A spy, I'm afraid, a forward scout for the ones that followed. The skirmishes went on all night and into the morning. The fight that so unfortunately found its way into your cabin was the last— we are sure that no more attackers remain on Presilyo grounds."

"Who were they?" Sanyago asked, looking aside at one of the small stained-glass windows. It depicted Eusébio Inoue in a meditation posture, seated above a surreal, swirling depiction of the Holy Fathom. Bright rising motes of thought and revelation rose up all around the Enlightened Saint and were being drawn into the halo round his head.

"Former Somonei who abandoned the faith, or their missions, or fell to heresy, or decided to forsake their oaths and settle down somewhere in the Caustlands or, Divine help us, the Sovereign Nations out in Earthmarch. There's a group among the Nations—a heretic faction calling themselves the Carvers—that gathered many of them up, indoctrinated them, and led them here. We caught wind of this, and were able to prepare enough to repel them successfully, though at great cost. One of the Abbot's aides started calling it the Return of the Apostates, and the name seems to have stuck."

This was a much more straightforward answer than Sanyago expected. "Won't you get in trouble for telling me all this?" he asked before he could think better of it.

Father Kuwat turned to look him in the eye for the first time since they had sat down, and laughed, shaking his head. "No. No one has told me to keep anything quiet yet, and I am old and well-respected, and most of all I don't think you're going to tell anyone but your friend out there in the vestibule. He seems like the kind who knows how to keep a secret, if not how to keep his opinions to himself."

Sanyago grimaced at that. "Staafaen has a reputation then?" he asked.

Kuwat sighed, nodded. "I will perhaps talk to him about that, depending on his state of mind, but whether I do or not you should help him to be careful. This is not a good time to be suspected of any sort of heresy. I have some opinions of my own, you understand, that could get a younger priest with a less secure position in trouble. I sympathize. But now is a time for discretion, you understand? Now is a time to be seen as Silado."

Sanyago nodded. "I'll try. I mean, I always try. I don't know why he has such a hard time believing." He frowned, shook his head. "Well, no, I do, at least some, but I don't always agree with him."

"That's good," the priest said with a small smile. "It's very unwise for a person to surround themselves only with people who agree with them. Now, so we don't keep your friend waiting too long. Tell me about this morning."

Sanyago did, and was surprised at how easy it was after having already unburdened himself once before. Kuwat nodded through it all, and when it was finished he gave Sanyago's shoulders a gentle squeeze before standing up.

"You will be alright, Sanyago. There will likely be bad dreams and bad moments, but that is part of life. If you need me again, just tell old Catechist Yaatkr. He owes me a few favors." A wry smile. "Tell your friend to come in. Once he's done, I will have you sent back to your room. They should have cleaned your dormitory by now. You will need some rest."

Sanyago sent Laris in with a nod and a smile, and his friend visibly untensed, returning the nod as he entered the chapel. Then Sanyago sat in thought as he waited. It felt like a long time, but a long time was a good thing right now, the first chance to feel at peace since what seemed like forever. When Laris finally emerged, he looked less drawn, though still pensive.

"He's nice, isn't he?" Sanyago asked as they were walked back to the dormitory.

"Yes," Laris said. "He's a good priest."

"Did he tell you about what was going on?"

"No," Laris said, looking at him sideways with a ghost of a smile. "He said he told you and he knew you'd tell me."

Sanyago laughed. "Yeah, I will." He lowered his voice. "Still gonna listen in when I can, though. Knowledge is power, right? That's what Spell Master Alein is always saying."

Laris sighed, a bit theatrically, and elbowed Sanyago very lightly in the ribs. Sanyago grimaced, punched his friend on the shoulder in return.

"I know he wanted you to tell me to be careful," Laris said. "He told me to say the same to you. We gotta be careful, right?"

"Yeah," Sanyago said, and looked up at Laris with a serious expression. "We'll be careful together, okay?"

Laris nodded, looking lost in thought. They fell silent for the rest of the walk.

On arriving at the dormitory-cabin, he was relieved to see that their other roommates were in the room and safe. They were shaken, and they had questions, but Laris waved them off. "We'll answer, we'll answer, but first we need some rest."

This didn't satisfy the other brothers, who continued to clamor some as the pair of them clambered into their bunks. They quieted down, though, when the Somonei who stood guard outside the door opened it and looked in with a set expression.

Sanyago slept.

Sixth Interlude

Abbot's Quarters, Inoue Island, The Caustlands, 349 SE

"How many dead?" Abbot Ignacio del Toro rose as he asked the question, shifting his stout body from cross-legged to standing with a grace and speed that belied his age and bulk.

Garrison Master Ryogen had to call on every gram of inner serenity to maintain composure under the Abbot's dark-eyed stare. "Abbot del Toro, we are still not entirely sure..." Ryogen bowed as storms gathered over the Abbot's weathered features, and raised one hand slightly to acknowledge his superior's impatience, "...but our best estimate so far is forty-seven."

The Abbot lowered his head. "Divine mark their souls for mercy. And they were?"

The Garrison Master cocked his head, leaning forward. "Abbot?"

Del Toro began to pace, though his gaze remained fixed on Ryogen, allowing him no relief. "Somonei? Staff? Clergy?" He quickened his steps, gesturing. "Children?"

"Ah," Ryogen said. He stared straight forward as he thought. "Twenty-three Somonei. Eleven staff. Two priests and one priestess. Seven boys. Three girls. Of the attackers, more than seventy. We have won, but it has cost us. Even so, thank the Divine we had forewarning."

"Ten children," the Abbot breathed. "Dead in cold blood. Filth and madness. Killed by the ones who were...tainted...I suppose."

Ryogen shuddered hard, stilled his whipcord frame, breathed deep, let his thoughts detach themselves from the tunnels of his mind. "Yes. There were only seven of...those, and four of them...they were still dangerous, but could not fight well. The Carvers must have taken extraordinary measures to get them here."

"We are sure it was the Carvers? Really sure? All six Caustland States are going to want a report on this. We had better be either exceedingly certain, or very precise in our uncertainty. This will have consequences far, far beyond the Presilyo."

Ryogen nodded. External politics were not his to worry about, thank the Divine. "We are certain enough. All but four of the attackers we killed were former Somonei. Three must have been new converts, and one...well, the magomédicos did not want to risk attempting to match his remains with our tissue-records."

Abbot del Toro halted his pacing by one wall and placed one hand flat against it, leaning on it for support. Ryogen had never seen him do this, was sure he had never seen del Toro lean on *anything*. Or anyone, except perhaps his own confessor.

He stepped forward, concerned. "Abbot?"

"These are dark times, Master Ryogen. I know you have probably heard that phrase often enough that it has lost a good deal of its power. I fear there have been too many overzealous sermons declaring this to be the worst of all eras, speculating on the imminent arrival of the Foreborn, the rebirth of the Enlightened Saint. They think this is an easy way to motivate their listeners. Make them flee from sin toward righteousness, perhaps, even when generations of preachers before them have claimed the same thing and been mistaken."

Ryogen could not stop the rise of his eyebrows at these words, but the Abbot wasn't looking at him. This was uncommon candor.

"I do not claim to know when the Divine will fulfill Their promises, Master Ryogen, or whether these are *the* dark times the Scriptures say will precede them. But make no mistake; they *are* dark times. We must be ready." He shoved himself away from the wall as though in sudden decision. "We *will* be ready. How many of their number did we send to the Seven Hells?"

The Garrison Master drew again on his reserves of serenity, and drew himself up straight. "Seventy-one. At least two of the four who fled were badly wounded, and we cannot know how many survived. More than a dozen tried to flee, but the Somonei cut them down. The rest were killed in battle, except—" he frowned. "One of them was killed by a Novice. By a pair of Novices, really."

The Abbot peered at Ryogen intently. "So it's true? I had heard rumors during the battle, but wasn't sure whether I should credit them. Do I know this pair?"

"Yes," Ryogen said. "The candidates. The nuns who were there said one of them put up a good fight, and wounded the man before being defeated. He was not badly hurt. It was the other who killed him somehow, using his Entyecogno gift."

"That pair." Del Toro rubbed his clean-shaven jaw with two fingers. "I have heard a great deal about that pair over the last few years. Potential, and a lot of it, yes?"

"So I am told. Combat Master Olsaen certainly seemed convinced, and their other teachers agreed. There are concerns, of course. The tall black one is highly intelligent, diligent, perfectionist in his training, and of course he has the Entyecogno gift. But he came here as an older child, and his parents were not of the faith. He is skeptical, a questioner. His teachers say he has been less so lately, but suspect he may simply have learned to keep his thoughts to himself. Understand this is only what I was told as part of the background for the report."

"I understand, Master Ryogen. I will speak with the report principals myself. There were concerns about the other as well?"

"Yes. He is fond of pushing boundaries. He sometimes struggles with focus, and shows much less aptitude than his brother for classroom learning. He likes to climb things and eavesdrop. They told me that sometimes they catch him, sometimes they decide not to. Perhaps sometimes they are not aware of it. He has shown some other signs of indiscipline as well. But they believe his faith is sound."

"Hmmm." The Abbot resumed his pacing. "We didn't lose any of the Shuvelao?"

"No, Abbot, I would have told you—" Ryogen stopped, frowned, leaned forward. "Ah. You're wondering when the candidates can be put forward. But Chandra and Jein won't retire for at least another fifteen years, Caen and Rajveati are still new, and..." he shook his head as he trailed off. "None of this is my affair now that the attack is over; I understand that the Shuvelao were only attached to the garrison forces to assist with this one defense."

Del Toro's heavy brows drew in as he paced. "I wish that were true. I wish that you as Garrison Master had to concern yourself only with matters on Inoue Island, but that is not the time we live in. I am going to include you in all their reports going forward. The Shuvelao have worked to advance the most sensitive interests of the Presilyo for centuries, but now their investigations will be vital in defending it. We may have to add a pair or two to their ranks. And you must take part in managing their operations. You will be coordinating with Master Leng."

"At your order, Abbot del Toro."

"Yes," del Toro said, and stopped again to lean against the wall. "At my order. The Divine place Their burden where they will. Pray for me, Master Ryogen."

"Always."

Chapter 14

Consciousness is both the loftiest power and the deepest mystery of all existence. Do not lend its immense potential lightly. Do not waste its precious, fleeting moments.
Never let it give shape to what it should not fathom.

- Arima Musashi, *Shadows in the Mirror*, 249 SE

Kualabu, Tenggara, The Caustlands, 349 SE

"Oh God, Dayang."

Dayang felt a wash of dread at the raw shock in her mother's words, and looked up to watch her enter the small hospital bay. Mother put her hand over her mouth as she joined the others around Dayang's bed, crowding in next to Father. "What have you done? What could possess you to go outside the walls? Going after some Pelo savage, following some Salí..." She trailed off as her husband put his hand on her shoulder and squeezed. Her gaze darted toward Jeims, sitting back on his haunches atop the small wooden table at the foot of the bed.

Dayang just looked at her mother. Half her mind's denizens seemed tangled in a great chaotic melee, while the other half sat by in shock. None of them were ready to answer her mother's accusatory train of questions. Nor was Pandikar, or Jeims, or the Captain of the Guard. But Father was.

"Hush, Khadija," he said. "She could not have known, and any price she might owe for foolhardiness has already been paid. She is a hero. God knows what might have happened had this thing made it to the walls." Pandikar stood on the other side of the bed, nodding in agreement but otherwise holding his peace. He knew better. Dayang flashed him a small grateful smile.

"That's what we pay the damn *guards* for, Piolo," Mother snapped, then glared daggers at her husband when his hand tightened a little more on her shoulder. He raised his chin toward where Aulia lay looking small and forlorn in a human-sized bed, sprawled out atop the covers and breathing slowly. She was unconscious and could not hear, thank God, but Jeims had turned away to say something to the Captain of the Guard, probably so that Khadija would not be able to see his expression. For her part, the Captain's face was a study in stony soldier's professionalism.

"It is unlikely the guards on watch would have been equipped to handle such an...altered creature, Puan Khadijah," the Captain said, looking Mother steady in the eye. "Your daughter did us a great service." The praise brought Dayang a tiny surge of pride, but it was nearly lost in the sprawling melee of her other emotions.

Mother looked as though she was about to snap off some acid retort, and then her face contorted, broke. She turned away, hugged herself into her husband, who was almost exactly her height, and tucked her head in beside his. Father showed a moment's surprise at this, but he put his arms around his wife, stroked her back.

"Her *face*," she sobbed, and squeezed her husband so hard he winced a little. "What did that thing do to her *face*?"

Father squeezed her back, let her cry.

Dayang reached up to the long strip of bandages that covered the stitches running from her temple down to her jaw. She ran her fingers over the long laceration. It felt numb, and so did Dayang. Too new a thing, even now after more than an hour, too sudden a reality for her to have any opinion about it, to feel anything other than her ongoing shock, her startled elation at her first real victory in combat, her somber gratitude at finding herself still alive.

The wound had not responded to Sihir-treatment, either her own or the hospital physician's. The Fathom simply did not touch it. Dayang knew why, of course, and counted herself lucky the creature had not hit her anywhere else. Harms treated through the Fathom usually healed cleanly, without any trace of a scar, but there were exceptions. Creatures lurked in Pelo ruins, for example, that were sometimes affected by...old Pelo indiscretions. Some things could linger a long, long time.

"It's only a superficial wound, Khadija," Father murmured, gently stroking her long black hair. "Head wounds always bleed a lot, no matter how shallow. She wasn't seriously hurt, thank God."

"She'll have a scar, Piolo!" Mother said, pushing back out of his embrace to look him in the eye. "For the rest of her life, even if it heals."

Father scowled. "You think I don't know that? You think she doesn't know that? It's a badge of honor, Khadija, and anyway the time to discuss it is *not* now, and *not* here."

But Mother did not want to be reasoned with. "Who will have her now, Piolo? Look at it! It's over her whole face, she…" Mother stopped abruptly as Father raised one hand sharply, his face filled with the kind of fury Dayang didn't even know he was capable of, sending a muted jolt through her numbed nerves. He had never struck his wife, not that she knew of, and she didn't think he would now, but it was still enough to shock Mother into silence, something else Dayang had never before seen.

"That…is…ENOUGH, Khadija!" he roared, dark eyes flashing fire. "Any man who could not see past a scar she earned by being a bloody hero wouldn't be Goddamned worthy of her. Jesus Christ, woman! What is *wrong* with you?"

Everyone else had fallen silent, looking profoundly uncomfortable. Mother recoiled at the tirade, and her eyes narrowed at the reference to her husband's former religion. Dayang felt a surge of warmth and admiration for her father, but let it drift into the depths where all her other emotions seemed to be biding their time.

"Jesus *Christ*, Piolo?" she said, words full of soft, serpentine venom. "What then, are you going to bring a *priest* in to bless her? Maybe that will get rid of the scar!"

"I am a better and less hypocritical Muslim than half the men in Kualabu!" Father shouted back. "And you damned well know it! God will understand if I decide to swear by one of His prophets when my wife cares more about her daughter's marriage prospects than her well-being!"

"You *dare*," Khadija hissed, putting one finger on her husband's chest and leaning in so that her nose nearly touched his.

"For my daughter, Khadija," he said back in a very loud, emphatic whisper, "I would dare *anything*."

Mother stared at him for a long, long moment before whirling and storming out of the room.

There was a brief silence, then Father spoke. "I am sorry. She is not herself." He bent over the bed, kissed Dayang on the forehead. She managed a small smile.

"She'll be back once she's calmed down," Father whispered. "And I will be too. You know she loves you. Meanwhile, get some rest, my victorious Engkanto."

Dayang nodded, put her hands round Father's neck, gave him a small quick hug. He smiled, kissed her again, and walked out. Dayang knew he'd probably be headed to the teahouse to sit and talk and sip while his wife stewed at home with a book in hand. It was their way.

Pandikar sighed and shook his head. Dayang was glad he was here, the one piece of her family not wrapped up in its own dramas. Nurul was off at university in Cenicebu; her sister had been anticipating this move with an almost ecstatic intensity. A "finishing school," Father had called it in one of his more sardonic moods, though he'd also smiled as he said it. Dayang knew he was happy to see his daughter's joyful eagerness.

"That'll add fuel to the fire for a few months," Pandikar said, breaking the long thoughtful silence. "Not your fault, Dayadesch. You know how they are. Anyway, I'm glad me and Dad's gift ended up coming in handy."

Dayang laughed, and reached over to finger the handle of her kris knife, which lay looking out-of-place on a side table. One of the nurses had tried briefly to have the weapon removed, to be sent home with a friend or relation. Dayang wondered what her own face must have shown; one look at that expression had made the poor woman reconsider this idea permanently. "You're fishing for compliments, Pandimarch, but I actually am really grateful. It saw me through."

"I was both surprised and impressed," Jeims interjected from the foot of the bed. His voice was softer than usual, more restrained in its silky self-assertion. "I thought maces were her favorite weapons. She acquitted herself extremely well with just the dagger."

"Hang Che says that while life is short and specializing is great, having no backup is just signing your own death warrant," Dayang responded. Hang Che had been in earlier with Hue Tian to dispense terse praise, along with the expected reprimand about jumping into situations she didn't understand well ("One never understands a situation completely, but so far as I can tell you went in understanding almost nothing," he had said).

"Said it a few times, didn't he?" Jeims remarked with a small feline smile. It faded quickly, though, and had little to do with the rest of his body language: drawn up stiff with tail tucked so close around him he was practically sitting on it. "Seems like you've got it down verbatim." His amber eyes kept tending over to where Aulia lay in the next bed.

Dayang snorted. It was not really any more a mirthful thing than Jeims' smile had been, but she was glad for any bit of humor any of them could grab onto, however strained. "Verbatim is right. He's very big on listening and remembering, is Hang Che." Her Wira-Guru had left only a few minutes ago, and so she hoped to see Sara soon. She'd asked one of the guards she knew was friendly with Sara's family to let her know that, first of all, Dayang was going to be fine, and secondly that Sara didn't have to come see her *right* away. Sara would know what she meant.

"He is a good teacher," Jeims said diffidently, glancing quickly around the room and then lowering his voice a bit, "...if sometimes questionable in other ways. Speaking of which, I assume your friend Sara is coming?"

"Yeah," Dayang reached up with a wince to adjust the bandage slung over her face. "She knew he was here, but now that he's gone I'll bet she'll be here soon."

Her fingers came away with a touch of soaked-through blood; the physician had needed to sew her skin together to help with healing. "An archaic Old World treatment," the old woman had said with a sigh, "but enough adventurers come into this place that I've gotten very, very good at it. Between my skill and your youth the scar may at least not be an ugly one, God willing."

Jeims nodded solemnly, then sighed, rolling onto his side as though overtaken by sudden exhaustion. His face certainly showed plenty of it. "I suppose I owe your parents an apology." He managed a small, rueful smile, ears laid flat against his skull. "I won't try to apologize to you. You made your choice, and I don't want to get anywhere near insulting your heroism. You understand?"

Dayang nodded, reached for the bottle of water on the night-table, fingers brushing the handle of her sheathed knife. She felt a small rush of reassurance, and took a long slow sip, savoring the trickle of cool liquid down her throat.

Jeims closed his eyes, resting one side of his face against the wood. "With your parents, though, I should take responsibility for my part in this whole thing. I know, I know, I couldn't have known, but of course there was a risk and I'm supposed to be the grown-up or some shit."

She was struck by the sheer defeated weariness in his voice, and leaned forward to brush her knuckle very gently against his cheek. He looked up, surprised, and then his face softened. Lingmao did not cry, but he would still know the meaning of the gesture.

"Hey," she said softly. "Jeims. That thing was coming whether we went out or not. I'd rather we had the chance to fight it than hear later that it tore through half a dozen guards or, God forbid, went rampaging right through the walls. You know the gate wouldn't have stopped it, not like it...was. I'm sorry about Aulia, but they say she's going to be okay, she'll get better."

He unfolded a paw, took her hand briefly, squeezed.

"Thank you, Dayang. I'll be okay too. I just...it's hard to see her like that. To see you like that. I mean...it could have been worse, I know it."

"Thank God it wasn't."

Jeims smiled faintly at that, pulled his sprawled body together some to sit back up, shrugged. "Yeah, sure. I'll just keep on thanking you."

She snorted, lying back against her pillow. "I'd be dead too, if you hadn't been there. No way I could have fought that thing alone." She became aware that everyone was watching the pair of them silently; Pandikar, the Captain of the Guard, the nurse attending to Aulia...and Sara, standing in the curtained doorway and looking at once intensely worried and immensely relieved.

"Sara!" Dayang said, throwing her arms out wide. Sara smiled, a slow, spreading thing that ended in its customary brilliance, and walked forward to embrace her friend, though a little gingerly. Dayang squeezed back fiercely, laughing. "It's just my head that got hurt, you don't have to hug me like I'm a thousand years old."

Sara laughed, though Dayang was aware she was also crying softly. "By God, Dayang," she said through little sniffles, pulling back some to wipe her eyes. "You had me terrified, what *happened* out there? I was hearing all sorts of stories." She reached up to touch the bandage, then stopped, probably noticing how much blood had seeped through. "Are you okay?"

"Gonna be fine," Dayang said, giving Sara her best reassuring smile. She wasn't sure how effective it really was, but she meant it honestly enough. It was still hard to sort through all her own emotions with the storm of everyone else's whirling round her, but the prospect of being stuck with a scar didn't really scare or sadden her that much. She didn't consider herself any great beauty like Sara was, but she had come to think of herself as a fighter, and scars were part and parcel of that, weren't they?

Sara smiled back, but didn't look fully convinced. "I'm sure you'll heal up like new. Mother always says our hospital has some of the best physicians in Tenggara, because of all the adventurers that come through. Adventurers are drawn in by coin like moths to a flame, she says, and the prestige of treating them brings ambitious healers. They'll have your wounds gone in no time."

Dayang wasn't quite sure what to say to this. Neither was anyone else, and Sara looked round at the range of discomfited expressions on display around the bed, frowning. "You...*are* okay, right?"

Dayang shrugged, then tapped the bandage where it crossed the bridge of her nose. "Wasn't that deep, but, um, the scar probably won't go away."

"What?" Sara asked, looking confused. "Scars always fade if you get good treatment, and you're going to get the best treatment, even adventurers only get them when..." her eyes widened, and she put her hands over her mouth, unconsciously jerking back away from the bandage. "Oh," she said quietly from behind her fingers.

"It's not...it's not dangerous or anything," Dayang said quickly. "It's just...Sihir-treatment won't do anything. The Hunch-Ripper we fought, it wasn't...right."

"Oh," Sara said again in a very small voice. Then her eyes widened further. "It's true then? You fought a *Hunch-Ripper*? One that was... Keparat, Dayang! You killed it?"

"Well, not by myself." Dayang nodded to Jeims, who shrugged again, and then at Aulia where she lay with the nurse rubbing salve into the great ugly bruise across her flank. The fur covering the red-and-purple swell had turned dead white, the long stark streak cutting through the golden rosettes of her coat.

"Oh," Sara said, noticing the injured Lingmao for the first time. "Oh no. Poor Aulia. Is she...?"

Jeims gave her a small sad smile. "She'll be okay. The physician said the internal bleeding has stopped and she'll be able to heal, but they can't use Sihir-treatment directly on the injury. They can encourage her recovery, though." He didn't need to say that she would almost certainly have a mark on her flank for the rest of her life, or that the faded fur covering it would remain that way as well.

"Listen, Sara," Dayang said, drawing her friend's attention away from Aulia's small sad form. "I want to talk to you later. About who might have done this. You keep better track of what's going on in the world than anyone else I know."

Sara smiled, and Dayang was glad to see her face brighten. "Sure. You'll have to actually listen to everything I say this time, though. Like fully listen, not that halfway thing you sometimes do to be polite."

Dayang stuck out her tongue, and tried to scrunch up her face but it hurt like Hell. "Ow. Okay, yeah, I'll listen. Thanks, Sara."

They all sat silent for a time. An orderly came in, whispered something in Pandikar's ear. He nodded, took a small paper from her hands into his very large ones, and thanked her. He turned to Dayang, waving the paper with a crooked smile.

"Nurul sent an echogram back." He scanned the brief message on the slip, then locked his dark brown eyes with her own. "It's hard to say from just words on a page, but it really does sound like she was worried, Dayadesch." He ducked his head, and his smile went warm and wry. "She really does care, you know, under all the... uh, Nurul."

"Yeah." Dayang knew she was crying now and didn't really care. Too many things on top of too many others. She took the paper from her brother, tucking it under the sheathed kris on her nightstand. "I'll read it later. It's just...everything is too much, right now."

Pandikar stepped forward, leaned in, hugged her tight. She sobbed.

The physician decided to keep her overnight, "for observation." Dayang wasn't sure how she felt about this. On the one hand, it was good to have a chance to gather her thoughts away from all her well-wishers, who had been summarily ejected from the bay after sundown. Also she could keep an eye on Aulia, who occasionally regained a groggy sort of consciousness and even managed a smile when Dayang woke up for a drink of water and offered to share.

But. But. She wasn't sure she liked being alone with her thoughts after she'd gathered them. They were elusive and erratic, and every now and then a juddering black line would streak between them and the walls of the room would seem to bend inward and she would close her eyes and just breathe, breathe, wait. And then it would be gone, but she would remember.

Still she knew she'd been lucky, thanked God for it, and said as much to the cleric making rounds saying doa for the sick and injured. The old man—Dayang had seen him at masjid but did not know his name—had smiled and said a doa for her before praising her courage. Word had apparently gotten round. She'd thanked him for the supplication—though privately she did not think God was more likely to listen to an old man's prayer than to her own—and feigned more tiredness than she felt so he would move on. Doa were fine; despite her slightly grumpy ruminations on the relative effectiveness of invocations by clerics and teenage girls, she knew she could probably use all the prayers she could get— but she could not take any more praise right now.

She had just drifted into a comfortably exhausted state, images of scars and blades and yelling parents mostly shunted aside, when she heard a flickering scream coming down the hall. It flitted back and forth between ear-rending loudness and near non-existence and a dozen weird, shuddering points in between. She sat up, grabbed her kris off the bedside table, swung her legs over the edge of the bed, and listened to the sounds coming through the door.

"Gag her! Why haven't you gagged her?" A young man's voice, with an edge of professionally-restrained panic. An orderly, perhaps.

"Sharifa tried, but she got bit. It was bad. We had to bandage her up and take her to the emergency ward."

The sounds came closer, and the horrible convulsing scream continued. A new voice cut in, sharp and commanding. One of the head physicians, she thought.

"What happened?"

"She was standing guard on the wall when the creature, er, appeared, Doctor Jariani. Yesterday. Her family just brought her in. She's a guard—"

"I can see the uniform, Nurse." The physician's voice was clipped and impatient. The wail continued, jumping from perch to unsettling perch up and down the woman's vocal range— and beside it as well, going places that should not have been possible for a human voice.

"Yes Doctor." The nurse's voice was hurried. "We think she saw it, er, come out."

"From the Mire?"

"Hunch-Ripper's aren't ashwights, Doctor, they don't—"

"I *know* that, Nurse."

"Yes Doctor. It came out *in* the Mire, but not *from* the Mire. Through the Fathom somehow…"

They passed by Dayang's door, not moving very fast. Their patient must be putting up extremely stiff resistance. For a moment, there was nothing but the intermittent screams and the sounds of scuffling as the doctor absorbed the nurse's words.

"That's…I see. You've tried gagging her?" The doctor's voice didn't have the same undertones of panic as the orderly's had, but there was still dire weight to it.

"Sharifa did. Got bit. No one else wanted to try, you know, in case it wouldn't, er, heal properly." They were past Dayang's door now.

The scream had quieted down for a moment, but this was almost certainly a temporary lull.

"It's got to be done, risk or no. We may have more to worry about than bite wounds if that keeps up."

"Yes, Doctor Jariani. I'll fetch more orderlies."

Silenced voices. Running feet. Scuffling. And then the scream returned, and now there were words in it.

"It fell in from above! It came out from below! There are things outside underneath and they SEE ME! SEE ME! SEE—"

The bangs and vibrations of a violent tussle, an outraged gargled voice trying to push past a gag. Dragging. Shouted orders.

Silence.

Dayang did not sleep easy that night.

Chapter 15

Oh, *shit.*

- Petty Officer First Class Daniel Smith
  UNCIS Earthseed, 1421z 11MAY2067
  OPS Log, United Nations Colony Initiative

Carver State, Sovereign Nations, The Abwaild, 349 SE

Juliaen did not sleep easy, but she slept illuminated. The Holy Fathom enfolded her, buoyed her up, whispered its half-remembered secrets, just as it had to the faithful since Starfall brought Eusébio Inoue down to the fresh ash of the Caustlands in a blaze of fire and glory.

Juliaen had dreamed before, and sometimes she counted the dreams as holy. But she had never dreamed like this. Motes of light and exultation rose around her, formless as she, spinning warm and welcome through and from eternities.

She ascended through the depths of the Fathom, and saw the motes slow their ascent, begin to sink; or perhaps she was simply rising ever faster, for nothing and nowhere in her awareness seemed fixed. The motes took form, became bright and crystalline, shattered, scattered. Their shards were all around, smoldering slow and hot, though their heat did not burn; as she was now she did not think she could burn, only kindle, and the shards were cinders, and the cinders were a bed, and she rose up through it, out from the cradling purity of the Holy Fathom and into the ashen air.

It was death. Not for her; her dreaming self was immaterial, could feel but not be acted upon, was sight unseen, but the voices were

millions

and they burned. And she could not conceive their number, and she smoldered with them but she could not burn, could only watch and hear and know it. And among their pitched and desperate voices were the terrified cries of the Fallen, the First of the Fallen, and when the Fallen looked around they wailed in disbelief, certainly at their own dead, but also at the million-many-million flames consumed in the greater fire of the Caustlands' birth.

The Praedhc. The Praedhc Pelos Antepas Tuzhu Dezya, all the names given by all the Fallen for all the inexplicable people they found waiting, here on the one Solace of a journey gone awry, an arrival wreathed in killing fire from a faraway star.

In her dream she saw an empire fall from soaring cedar to settling cinder, its branches stilled and scattered in just a few blinding moments, seeds charred to husks save a few that fell outside the devastation.

Starfall.

The shattering ark.

Earth's Seed sown in holocaust.

Though she knew it was Divine Judgement, had read the words in *Fathom Messenger* again and again, she did not think she could bear all the death. The only mercy was that those who would have mourned the dead were almost all gone to bone and ash themselves in that same towering moment of flooding flame.

We have burned our mark into Solace, the whole of the Caustlands serves as our Fallen signature, she thought, and the thought echoed through the settling ash of the clearing air.

We have burned our mark into Praedhc bones, whether we meant to or not.

I have burned my mark into the Abwaild, and I have certainly meant to do that. But there were no Praedhc, I did not harm anyone, I...

Her vision of the Caustlands departed in the abrupt way of dreams, and she regarded the departure in the accepting way of dreamers. It was replaced with a formation of the Many Nation Army, a column marching into the Abwaild with its wide spectrum of uniforms. Every company along its length carried a standard, a tall pole bearing the flag of the Nation above and the Compact below. She knew their purpose. The Praedhc, the

Pelo, the Antepas—whatever name you used, they were savages, especially the scattered tribes in this heavily-forested bit of the Abwaild. Compared with the great empire destroyed at Starfall they—

—and now the Abwaild was gone again, and the Caustlands returned, all smoke and smolder and char. Divine Judgement, the hand of the One Father, but—

All you beloved of the Divine, take no vengeance for your own part, but let the way be open for Their wrath. It is written: Vengeance is mine, I will return offenses; thus speaks the Divine to Their servant.

She knew this piece of the Star Sutras by heart, as she did so much of Scripture, and she heard it now plain as the stirring ash, read it clear as the fading afterglow written over the rising dusk.

If it is not for us to claim the Abwaild for the Fallen, if it is not ours to push the Praedhc from their forests, where will we go?

And the Caustlands aged. Up grew grass, trees, farms, settlements. The unholy bulk of the Fathomless Deisiindr pushed up from its Tenggaran plain like a great grey fractured bone. The Gyring Ash turned; the Ashlit Mire grew out from its banks. Cities arose; abblum crept back into the hills and plains, clinging tenaciously even to Starfall-cleansed soil.

Another vision of varied armies, each in their place. Salían, Tenggaran, Han, Nainadi. Auraramad, The United Admiralty, Nikoka. Here and there among them marched the Somonei, and here and there they roamed apart, killing and dying for their Caustland paymasters. *Heretics. Ragado. Profaners.*

A few spots of hope, as here and there some Presilyo monk or priest would dissent, would leave, or would even come to join the Carvers, walk the true Triune Path. She saw the plans and machinations of her own people, striking out at the Presilyo, at the Caustland States, heard the whispered names of those among the faithful who found the courage to act. She saw the efforts of others among the Sovereign Nations, crossing the Siinlan to harry and sow chaos, or even fan the embers of conflict with the Praedhc.

None of it was enough to stem the flood of corruption over Divine Promise.

The Caustlands. A gift from the Divine. We cannot claim to be taking Solace for the Fallen if we let the profane accept the Divine Gift in our place.

But they are many, and we are fewer, and we already fight the Praedhc—

—but we need not fight them, we should not, must not—

—and through the Divine all things are possible—

She awoke with a start.

Seventh Interlude

San Inoue, Carver State, The Sovereign Nations, 350 SE

"How many dead?" Lidia felt a rush of sick unreality as the grey-robed woman bowed her head in response to the question.

"Master Almeida…"

"How many dead?" Lidia demanded again.

The woman finally met Lidia's eyes with her own. They were large and brown, wide with fear and grief, darting here and there as if desperately searching for an answer to some dire decision. Dark skin drew taut over prominent cheekbones. *She has not been eating,* Lidia thought as she watched the woman hesitate.

"Seventy-three. We believe the Presileros were forewarned. They were prepared for us. Even the Shuvelao had been called back to defend the monastery."

Lidia felt her knees tremble. It was a sensation she hoped her body had forgotten forever. For a moment she was back in Acheronford, watching a sister-Somonei be torn apart by ashwights while trying to drag a terrified Salían soldier to safety. She could smell the coal-iron mix of the Siinlan ash. They said the smell came from the steel and graphene of the incinerated *Earthseed*, but that was nonsense, just an old myth. It wasn't steel, it was blood—

"Master Almeida." The woman's voice was timid, coaxing, the way one might speak to a mountain lion curled up under the kitchen table.

Lidia stared at her. What was her name? Mas...Masre...Masresha. Lidia didn't remember her surname; even after all these years, she wasn't used to them. In the Presilyo she had just been Novice Lidia, and then Lidia del Fogocerto once she had earned her Somonei name, and then Lidia Almeida after her Carver patron; a symbol of cleansing from the Presilyo's taint. But they didn't use that sort of name here, their names came from their families and anyway she had renounced her Somonei name and anyway so many of the Somonei she had recruited and all their names and all their faces were dead and maybe lay rotting within the corrupting walls of the Presilyo and for nothing, nothing just dead and on to the next life and who knew if she would see them then if the Divine would be so kind after what They had done to her how she had suffered how she had failed...

"Master *Almeida*." Masresha's voice was more fearful than timid now, and she put out an arm to steady Lidia as her knees threatened to give way. Normally this would have meant a withering glance, a sharp rebuke, perhaps. But Lidia had nothing, let the woman guide her to a chair.

"Seventy-three. So, what, three survivors?" She shuddered, breathed in, breathed out, found her center, closed her eyes.

"No, Master Almeida," Masresha said. "Just two."

As her shock faded, Lidia managed to dig up some of her customary sharpness. "Just two? We sent out seventy-six, did we not?"

"Yes, Master Almeida. Seventy-three were killed. The Presileros took the wounded and burned them. Three are still alive. Two survived."

"Boddhisantos help us. What's been done with the third?"

Masresha shuddered. "I was to ask you, Master Almeida. What to do with her."

"How far..." Lidia stopped to reconsider her words. "Is there any hope of recovery?"

"It is never possible to say for sure, Master Almeida. We do not think so. And she is very dangerous in the meantime. Originally there were four who managed to flee the Presilyo, but in trying to make sure she made it back alive, one of the others...she..."

Lidia cut her off with an upraised hand. "I understand. She will have to be burned, there is no other way. Fire cleanses, Masresha."

"So we are told, Master Almeida." There was a strange sort of peace in her voice.

Lidia cocked her head at this. "So we are told? What does that mean? Do you not believe, Masresha?"

"It does not matter what I believe anymore." Masresha's face was drained and resigned as she retrieved a long curved knife from somewhere in her grey robes. Lidia was up and in a defensive stance in the flash of an eye, all her Somonei training coming back in an instant, but the other woman made no move to attack.

"I have seen too much, and I want no more part in it," Masresha said simply, and drew the blade deep across her own throat, almost to the spine.

Lidia rushed forward. If this were treated before the woman lost too much blood...but the moment she laid hands on Masresha's slumping form she knew there was no mending it. The Holy Fathom was in a great roil within the woman's body, resisting all of Lidia's attempts to organize, rally, and rush her natural healing. Lidia was a highly competent field-physician, a seasoned combat magomédica—but she could not heal the unwilling, not when they knew how to take countermeasures.

Lidia dropped the bleeding, spasming body to the floor with a heavy *thud*, and then dropped down heavily herself, watching filaments of blood wick through the intricate weave of the floor rug. It was over. But no, it could not be over, the Presilyo had to be cleansed. She had sacrificed so much. She had rebelled against the place and people who had been a part of her practically from birth. And the old Somonei, the reformed, the mad, the rebellious the...

...the tainted...

...they had sacrificed even more, and she had wanted to go with them but they had told her, *he* had told her, Archabbot Thuwun had told her, she had to lead, she had to recruit, they could not risk her.

She would have to tell him. And they would have to find another way.

She wondered if the Presilyo would dare stage a counterattack. Surely not. The United Admiralty would never let a force of any size pass over its territory, and even if a group of Somonei did somehow make it to the High Ring Bridge, the Many Nation Army would make short work of them once they crossed. Anyway, they'd be licking their wounds for some time, she was sure of that.

There would be a certain amount of outrage from the Caustland States near Inoue Island, but it would be tempered. Zhon Han felt itself largely insulated from any sort of Abwaild problems, and of course had problems of its own with its great yawning pits vomiting Divine knew what up from the Abwarren. The Salían government wasn't capable of cohesive action in the face of anything but the direst of threats. Tenggara was too busy pretending to be the Fathomless Deisiindr's broker and, the vaunted Tentera Wira aside, didn't have the military strength to risk on anything overt.

Still. Plenty of ways to send a message besides brute force. There was Nikoka to consider, for example. The Tenggarans might decide to call in a favor or obligation from their reclusive protectorate. Ninja, perhaps. Lidia picked herself up off the floor, allowed her mind to race through the implications. Better than looking, better than smelling the blood again. Masresha was not going anywhere, after all.

The thought sickened her, pulled her away from her ruminations on strategy and politics. *Not going anywhere? I am not a callous woman, that is not me.*

And what about the Presilero dead? They were your friends, your comrades, your brothers and sisters. Your lovers, a few of them, Divine forgive.

The Somonei are warriors. Risk of death is a part of their life. And they are mercenaries, in the end. Corruption is part of their life as well. Death is a release from that.

And the mad ones? The ones you pried from prison and hospital and asylum all over the Caustlands to make their last march on the place that sent them out to worse-than-death?

They have found their peace now.

Did they find their restraint? More than Somonei live on Inoue Island. Priests. Cooks. Teachers. Physicians. Scholars.

They serve the Somonei. They support the corruption, every one of them.

And what about...?

No.

The children.

No. No. We gave orders...

The mad ones you could not even order to take a piss outside their own robes, some of them.

No. No. And even if so, they would only grow to be...

For the first time in many years, Lidia broke down and sobbed.

Chapter 16

Oh, *fuck.*

- Admiral Fjölnir Olsen, formerly of the *UNCIS Earthseed*
  1542 Solace Standard Time, 01JAN, 0 Starfall Era

Presilyo Monastery, Inoue Island, The Caustlands, 350 SE

"Bai just wanted to 'talk' again, right?" Sanyago frowned, kicking an errant pinecone from the path. "I don't like the way she looks at you, brother, it always makes you look like you want to be anywhere else in the world." *And she's like fifteen years older than you,* he didn't say.

Laris shrugged and turned toward him, but was unable to meet Sanyago's gaze for longer than a few fleeting moments at a time. This worried Sanyago more than anything else; the only times he ever saw Laris do that was when talking about either Bai or his parents.

"Yeah," Laris said finally. "Bai just wanted to talk." He sighed, sagged, ash-grey eyes tending down toward the gravel path as they trudged along to class.

"Dammit, Laris, look at me." Sanyago was surprised at the fire in his own voice. Laris paused, seeming to gather himself back in before slowly pulling himself back up to full height. He looked down at Sanyago, expression troubled and weighed down with something like lingering guilt. It was, Sanyago thought for the thousandth time, a pretty long way to look; over the last year Laris' growth had sprinted forward while Sanyago's had plodded. The monks said Laris would likely top two meters fully grown.

"Sorry, brother." Laris' graven-ebony features admitted the ghost of a rueful smile. "She's never really touched me, you know. Not like...I mean..." He shrugged, boot scuffing a little against the gravel.

"She wants to, though. You can feel it coming off her, but no one will do anything. She looks at you like...I don't know, hungry maybe. Like Brother Tsomo looked at me before Father Kuwat chased him off." Sanyago felt his face contract into a scowl. That had been annoying, maybe a little unnerving, but the junior monk had never so much as glanced his way again after those first hungry stares.

"Yeah, I guess she does," Laris said.

They walked a few more paces, listening to the dry dusty crunch of rock-dust and stone underfoot.

"She is beautiful, though," Laris continued. "I mean, she really is. Sometimes the other boys look at her and look at me like they're jealous."

"Sure, she's pretty," Sanyago agreed. He knew the moment he'd said it that he hadn't sounded particularly fervent. He just couldn't quite comprehend the supposed power of her appeal, and he wasn't completely sure *why* but had his suspicions and didn't really want to examine them too closely.

Laris gave him a look, cocking his head just slightly, ash-silver eyes peering bright. It was *knowing,* that look, and Sanyago wondered just what exactly it knew. It passed, though, when Laris spoke again.

"Maybe I should be grateful, I mean—" he fell silent, rolled his knuckles across his forehead, sighed. "I mean, we're Novices, right? We're not normally allowed to get near girls or women at all and even when we finish training and come of age you have to retire to get married, and for now we have to keep the chastity rules even though..." he frowned, giving the gravel an arcing kick that sent small stones flying in a cloud of dust, "even though I know there's stuff going on all the time, like boys with other boys and monks and nuns sneaking off together or visiting forbidden places while out on missions—"

He took a deep breath; this was a lengthy speech by Laris standards, and for once Sanyago stayed silent, knowing more was coming. It was, but Laris lowered his voice considerably before speaking again.

"—and no, I don't know if I care very much about those rules, but still I'm stuck following them for years longer. I'm not going to do something stupid like run away with nowhere to go; we get to eat and learn for free here even though I don't like parts of it. So maybe I should be grateful. But it doesn't feel right. She's beautiful but she's not anything I chose, and I want to choose. We don't get to choose much here and if I'm going to break those rules I want to do it because I decided to do it."

Another silence. They were off the gravel path now and onto more solid paving; the Civics schoolhouse was in view.

"Yeah, I know, brother," Sanyago said. Some deep part of him was glad Laris hadn't elaborated on "boys with other boys". He had never taken part in any of that, but the reasons why not felt murky even to him. Boys dallying with boys was certainly Ragado according to their religious instruction; whether it was any worse than the same sort of infraction involving the opposite sex seemed less clear.

On the one hand, it didn't involve any highly illicit contact with females, but on the other there was a vague sense in which that sort of contact (the teachers were extremely reluctant to talk about it directly) was supposed to involve a kind of mystic joining of male and female as a spiritual whole. Even those who participated in it seemed to think so; they always talked about how they'd be 'done with this' when they could retire and get married or just break the rules with someone besides other boys.

He realized that Laris was looking at him steadily, and that he'd been silent for a few moments.

"Sorry, I was thinking. I don't know what to do, I wish I could help more. I tried talking to Father Kuwat about it, but he says he has no authority over full-fledged Somonei, and that he already used up a lot of his influence to keep Brother Tsomo away from me, and that Bai has a lot of, uh, status after the Return of the Apostates. You remember how everyone treated her at Ioanna's funeral."

It would be difficult to forget. Bai had careened between extremes of frantic grief and stony incomprehension. Eventually, she had to be gently removed from the ceremony as she recounted her memory of Ioanna's moment of death out loud, over and over in great detail. There had been a great many funerals, monks and nuns and boys and girls cremated and mourned, ashes scattered into the Mindao river for purification from their tainted deaths. Sanyago did not like to remember them, especially the ones with the smallest urns.

Laris inclined his head. They were almost at the schoolhouse front door now. "I do remember. I know you want to help. I'll just have to figure it out."

Sanyago gave his friend a one-eyed squint and a rueful nod. "Yeah, there always seems to be a lot to figure out."

Sanyago often felt his mind wander during the Solacian History part of Civics, especially when Master Tijong dipped too deeply into the minutiae of dates and place and dull dead people doing even duller things. Old World history could be a little more interesting, if only because it was full of more big wars and unimaginable machines, but there was so much of it that the more compelling details tended to get glossed over in the haste to cover ground. Laris' interest never seemed to flag, but Laris read books about that sort of thing for fun.

Today, though, they were learning about Salían history and culture, and Sanyago sat more attentively than usual on his floor cushion. More *actually* attentive, anyway, instead of just trying to look alert enough not to get into trouble while his mind wandered in and out of the lesson.

Though his mind still did *some*, wandering, and now he had to pull his thoughts away from the quick, close-range fire spell he'd been trying to master for weeks now, because Master Tijong was asking a question. "What are the major Salían languages? What can you tell me about them?"

Laris raised his hand, as he always did in Civics class. (To the clear relief of the teachers, he now took pains to speak up as little as possible during more theological lessons.) The other boys might have given him more grief for this if a single one of them had been able to best him on the sparring-field in the last two years. They'd all become less afraid of his strange ability to read intentions, but it still let him win most matches without taking a single hit.

"Gentic and Ambérico and their various Old World dialects, with some Common, Basa Mala, and Manhc on the borders Salía shares with Zhon Han, Tenggara, and Nainadion." Laris' voice was calm and clear and confident, as usual.

Master Tijong sighed. "Yes, Staafaen, but forget about the borders and dialects for now. What can you tell me about Gentic and Ambérico?"

"Gentic comes from an acronym: 'Global English for Networking, Trade, and International Communication.' It was a recent Old World invention at the time of Starfall. It is still used for all these purposes in the

Caustlands."

Sanyago gave a small sigh of his own. Laris often had the tendency to talk like a textbook. Still, he was precise, couldn't deny that. Sanyago didn't know anything firsthand about the rest of the Caustlands, but Gentic was certainly the tongue used in the Presilyo to bind its Babel together— as evidenced by the fact that, like most of their classes, this one was conducted entirely in that language.

"Very good. Why invent it? Why did they not simply use English?"

"English spelling is extremely difficult. Gentic is spelled exactly like it sounds."

"This is one reason, yes. There are others, but we don't have time to get into them all. Remember also that Old World English is still spoken as a first language by some Salíans." Master Tijong opened his mouth as if to ask Laris another question, then turned slightly and pointed at Sanyago where he sat next to the taller boy. "You, Sanyago, I hear you speak Ambérico with your friend there all the time. What can you tell me about it?"

Sanyago frowned. He didn't get called on all that often in this class, probably because he always sat next to Laris and could sort of hide in his shadow. Seemed today things were working the other way around. Okay, think. The name came from two places in the Old World, right? Master Tijong was awaiting a response with calm but finite patience on his broad, wrinkled face.

"Ambérico is more common as a native language than Gentic, right? But not as many people speak it as a second language. And it's from more than one language, and some people still speak those too, I think." He was still trying to remember the place-names. *Am-something, and something-bérico, come on, come on...*

"Good, good," Master Tijong said, bobbing his head. "Both Spanish and Portuguese are still spoken here and there, though most of the other parent languages have died out on Solace. And the origin of the name, Sanyago?"

It came to Sanyago in a flash, and he smiled. "Americano-Ibérico, after, um, some Old World place called the Iberian Peninsula and some big place they colonized called a..." he screwed one eye shut as he thought, "...a continence?"

Master Tijong probably couldn't hear Laris stifling a snicker beside him, but Sanyago could. He couldn't do anything about it, though, not with all eyes in the class on him.

"'Continence,' Sanyago," the Civics Master said dryly, "refers to various aspects of self-control, sometimes of bodily functions in particular, which I assume is why your friend is snickering. Your vocabulary is commendable, Staafaen, but laughing at other students for a mistake in class is not." Apparently Tijong was more perceptive than Sanyago had thought. He felt bad for Laris, though— he didn't want to get his friend in trouble and embarrassing as the mistake was, it was also kinda funny.

Laris had gone stiff and silent the moment Tijong had mentioned him, and Sanyago knew he'd be wearing the stoic expectation-of-punishment face he always did on such occasions. The Civics Master just shook his head, though, apparently counting the rebuke as sufficient in itself. "The word you are looking for is 'continent', which refers to a large land mass largely surrounded by oceans. The name you are looking for is 'America,' which in fact refers to two different Earth continents, North America and South America."

Oceans. Solace had oceans, Sanyago knew, but only a handful of Fallen had ever seen one. It was a long trek through the Abwaild to the coast, and the water was toxic anyway. Full of monsters, too, according to an expedition adventure-narrative he and Laris had borrowed from the library and pored over.

"So we're on a continent, right?" asked Mauricio from behind him.

"Yes," Master Tijong said. "This is the continent of Fiolnir, but it's mostly Abwaild and therefore largely unexplored."

"What about the other continents? Has anyone ever been to them? The Praedhc maybe?" Mauricio's voice was hopeful. Something new and exciting!

"Yes and no," Master Tijong responded. "we are connected by land to one other continent, and we know some of the Praedhc groups we are familiar with have trade routes that extend that far. No Fallen expedition has ever been there, though. As for overseas, we have Praedhc legends but no regular travel that we can confirm." He cleared his throat. "We are getting off-track. This is not a geography lesson."

To Sanyago's disappointment, there had been no more digressions from Master Tijong's lesson plan, which had included a brain-numbing section about what Old Earth groups and languages correlated with which areas of Salía. He did perk up a bit when the Civics Master mentioned that knowing this could well be useful to those of them who attained full Somonei titles, as a great many of their missions took place in Salía.

Somonei. Somonei, Somonei.

Sanyago wasn't sure how he felt about becoming a Somonei. He knew it was an honor. He knew it promised adventure, purpose, a noble cause— a Divine one, even. But the attack he'd lived through during the Return of the Apostates, the man with the butterfly swords, the death of Ioanna, the...

Don't let it catch in your mind, let it through, let it pass by.

...the all of it, really, it had given him a very different perspective. He knew he wouldn't be fighting anyone or anything like the man and his deep, twisting wrongness, not most of the time, not usually, but, but...

...it would still mean more blood. And more rules, more being where someone else said to be, more *orders*. Though at least the place would be somewhere that wasn't just this island all the time, and the orders wouldn't be from a Master standing over him all the time, but still.

But still.

Sometimes he thought the Divine must have something different in mind for him. Something beyond just fighting monsters and bandits until it was time to retire, settle down, leave his vows behind. Maybe marry, have kids...

Marry who? Who would you possibly be interested in marrying?

He tried to let this thought pass as well, but it caught in his mind and seemed to settle into his throat.

Not like I really know any women anyway. Except Bai, sort of, and she's a creep.

But you see them, sometimes, and you don't care, not the way Laris does. Not the way the other boys do.

And when you see—

Everyone was standing up. End of class. He shoved his thoughts aside and stood with them. Time for some exercise.

"Weapons," Laris breathed. Weapons indeed. They took up an entire wall of the big square training-hall, on racks and stands and tables.

Certainly not *real* weapons, no— bamboo, cork, rattan, wood, red-rubber, white oak, even quartzwood. Sanyago did his best not to smile, let alone bounce on his heels.

The class stood in a line, as they did before any training outside a classroom, but they'd never been in this hall before, and there had been no warning. Nor was it just their group, the boys from the dormitory room Sanyago had spent the last five years of his life in. Two other eight-boy squads were lined up behind them, making a formation three deep. A full pelotao, Sanyago supposed.

It had been a surprise. Maybe not a *complete* surprise; they'd known they'd be getting the beginnings of their specialized training soon, now that they were all at or nearing thirteen. "Pastrecha" was what the monks and older boys called it, though their own teachers had said nothing about it to them, and stonewalled when asked about it. This only amplified the whispers and increased the anticipation.

Sparring Master Silva was here, but he was standing next to another monk who Sanyago did not know. He was shorter than Silva, stockier, with skin a few shades lighter than Laris' and eyes so dark it was difficult to make out the pupils. His expression was serene, impossible to read, nothing at all like the urgent inquiry writ constant over Master Silva's features.

"Novices," the Sparring Master said, nodding over at the shorter monk. "This is Ondojitsu Master Ribeiro. If you do well enough with him, you may not be Novices for much longer."

Zagen, Sanyago thought. We can finally graduate from Novice to Zagen. This, the teachers were at pains to tell them, did not really mean much. Ranks were a human necessity at best, and a foolish one at that. Sanyago knew this was the idea, and was even a noble ideal, but he did not believe for a second that it really held true within the Presilyo organization.

Zagen would mean the right to wear a red clasp rather than simple cord to fasten their robes, even if it would be a smooth one, free of insignia like the Somonei crest. Sanyago found he wanted one quite badly. It was something to push toward.

Both teachers looked out over the Novice formation, perhaps waiting for their words to sink in. Then the Ondojitsu Master spoke.

"Thank you, Master Silva. I am sure you have trained them well.

Novices!" His voice was clear and crisp and higher than Sanyago would have expected. "When I tell you to fall out, you will come to the front and choose a weapon. You will not run. You will not fight over the weapons, there are plenty. If there are not enough of one type, we can acquire more, but beware of simply imitating your peers or seeking out the one that seems most popular. You should clear your minds for this exercise. You may put the weapons to the test, but not against other students. Give each other space. Use the dummies to the sides."

Anticipation thrummed through their formation, tensed and ready to go. Sanyago did his best not to smile. Master Silva, of all people, had a barely-restrained grin on his face, as if he knew exactly what was going through the students' minds.

"Fall out!" Master Ribeiro barked, and the formation broke apart instantly in an eager burst. At least two boys forgot about not running, but were grabbed by their fellow Novices before they could break into a full sprint and bring down the wrath of the two Masters.

Sanyago walked forward quickly, straight toward the nearest table...and stopped. Sitting on the worn wood were a pair of bamboo butterfly swords, looking newly-made, not a single pit or scratch on the blunt, polished blades.

He wasn't quite sure how long he stood there, hearing the excited chatter of excited voices and the clatter of wood against wood. He could feel something *cold* against his throat, and it was...

...and there was a warm, heavy hand on his shoulder. He started, turned, expecting to see one of the Masters, but it was Laris, wearing an expression he found impossible to read. The hand on his shoulder turned Sanyago gently away from the crossed swords on the table.

"Hey, brother." Laris' voice was soft and sad. "Let's find you something else. I don't like them either."

Sanyago let out a long, rattling breath he hadn't been aware of holding in, and Laris nodded. "Over here." The hand tightened on his shoulder as it guided him away, more than was comfortable, and he knew his friend was remembering too. He pushed it away, pushed it all away, let it *go*, and shook his head hard. Laris said nothing; he knew what it meant.

"Sorry," Sanyago said quietly. "It's getting better, for me I mean." He reached out, pulled a long curved sword off a stand, hefted it, careful not to swing with Laris standing so close lest he get them both in trouble. It was heavier than it looked; must be weights embedded inside the blade. To get the balance right, he guessed, even if it was not nearly so heavy as a real one.

"It does get better, yeah," Laris said. "For me, too." They both went to see Father Kuwat from time to time, a few dozen times over the last year. It helped.

Sanyago nodded and stepped away from Laris, far enough he wouldn't be hit by any errant swings. He slashed the air a few times, gave the dummy a few experimental whacks. Interesting. Powerful blows, nicely balanced. Too slow, though. Laris watched him, head cocked. His hands were empty.

"You're not going to try anything out?" Sanyago asked him. Laris frowned. "I did, a little. Just doesn't feel right. Like a new limb I have to learn to use all over again."

"Make sure you keep proper distance," Master Silva admonished from the middle of the room. "This is not the sparring field. There will be time enough for that later."

Sanyago froze as Silva broke his silence. *They've been watching us.*

"Listen to your Sparring Master," Master Ribeiro said. "This is a moment of reflection and discovery. Reach out through your weapon as you would through a hand or foot. These are not imbued, but they will still accept a measure of your influence through the Holy Fathom. Let your mind stay clear. We did not tell you about this in advance for good reason. It is best that you have no anticipation, no expectations."

Sanyago focused inward-of-place, beneath and beside, felt the Holy Fathom course twining to suffuse his thoughts, wrap round and through and over blood and bone and flesh. He reached out, tried to let the sword he held be an extension of self. They had done some training in this technique, but never with anything remotely resembling a weapon. He felt the full length of handle and blade slide into his awareness, joined to his shadow of influence within the Holy Fathom.

Laris had picked up a long bo staff longer than Sanyago was tall, though its tip only came up to about Laris' eye level. He was swinging it around a little, frowning. Sanyago watched, putting his own practice weapon through a few imaginary attacks and feints. Still too slow, however much the Holy Fathom worked to bind the length of wood to his intentions. He walked back to the stand he'd taken it from, giving Laris' long-limbed motions a wide berth.

"Still not feeling it?" Sanyago asked, setting the sword back onto its stand. Laris shook his head, walked over as well to toss the staff back onto its rack with a hint of frustration in his normally tightly-controlled movements. "You'll find something," Sanyago reassured him, and then spotted something himself. A straight sword, long but not too long, slender but not rapier-thin. One-handed grip, no real crossguard apart from a roughly circular medallion that separated blade from handle. Beautiful.

"That's a wu jian," Laris said, looking over his shoulder. He had apparently anticipated that this day was coming, announced or no, and done some research. Laris wouldn't want to lay hands on something he hadn't read about first, not if he could help it. "Popular in Zhon Han, like a lot of these weapons. The name means 'warrior sword', more or less."

Sanyago smiled broadly as he lifted it off its stand, stepping back from Laris again, twisting the blade round with his wrist. This, this felt right. It was quick, it was *smooth*. Extending his Fathom-influence through it seemed nearly as natural as imparting extra force to a kick or a spear-hand strike. He sensed the point of the sword almost as easily as the tip of his own finger.

Ondojitsu Master Ribeiro was watching him, the hint of a smile climbing up his cheek and settling into wrinkles at the corners of his eyes. Sanyago found he didn't really care; he himself wore a wide, goofy grin as he let the wu jian cut long, elegant ribbons through the air. Master Ribeiro turned around completely to focus his attention on another boy's efforts— and perhaps to hide his expression from his new student.

Sanyago had to try this out on one of the training dummies. He smiled sympathetically at Laris, who scowled as he perused the available weapons without success, and walked over toward one of the few dummies not yet taking a beating.

Eager as he was to really put his practice weapon through its paces, he was almost totally focused on the dummy, mind playing out movements and footwork and angles of attack. He didn't notice the other boy headed in the same direction, and nearly collided with him, feeling most of his customary grace slip away as he staggered to avoid the impact.

"Oh! Sorry!" Sanyago said, laughing. He didn't recognize the other boy, and added, "I'm usually paying closer attention than that, I was just excited to try this out." He held up the wooden wu jian with a rueful smile.

The other boy shook his head, tossing the monk's spade he was carrying lightly from hand to hand with a wry smile of his own. "It's fine, it's fine, so was I, so am I. Usually paying more attention, I mean."

He was taller than Sanyago, though nowhere near so tall as Laris, with light-bronze skin and large dark eyes. From Tenggara, maybe, judging by the particular wide, angular set of his features. They were, some small but insistent part of his mind asserted, quite handsome features. Sanyago felt himself flush a little.

"I'm Sanyago," he said with a small bow. He really couldn't think of anything else to say.

"Hyon-seok," said the other boy with a bow of his own.

They stood there looking at each other, and Sanyago was the first to glance away.

"I haven't seen you before, I don't think," Hyon-seok said, and when Sanyago looked back up at him he wore a smile Sanyago found impossible to interpret— except that it made him flush even more. He hoped it wouldn't be noticed, and was suddenly glad he didn't have extremely pale skin like Vasili. And he was just standing here. Say something!

"Umm, no," Sanyago finally managed. "We're from a dormitory-cabin over on the South side, near the Boddhisanto Domingo chapel."

Hyon-seok cocked his head in a way that Sanyago found maddeningly endearing. "We're from the South side too, or it'd be a long walk to class every day. I'm assuming we'll be taking them together from now on?"

"I hope so," Sanyago heard himself say, felt the hopefulness written over his own face. *DAMMIT. I said that out loud?* Except now it was Hyon-seok who reddened, and glanced away. And smiled again.

"Sanyago! Hyon-seok!" Master Silva's sharp voice cut in between them, and Sanyago wasn't sure whether he was disappointed or relieved. "Now is time for practice and insight. You will have opportunities to socialize later."

Sanyago thought that Hyon-seok's abashed expression likely mirrored his own. They turned toward the Sparring Master, bowed in unison, and apologized before moving briskly apart to find separate training dummies. Sanyago managed to re-focus himself, for the most part, dancing round the abstract wooden man to attack from every possible angle. His broad grin returned at the feel of the sword, the balance, the swiftness, the way the Holy Fathom extended him through its blade, fit him perfectly along its length.

Pausing a moment, he glanced in Laris' direction. Laris was still scowling as he stalked up and down the collection of weapons, but when he spotted Sanyago looking he flicked his gaze over toward Hyon-seok, and smiled. It was another of those damnably *knowing* smiles, and Sanyago felt his face go hot all over again. *Dammit, Laris, stop that.* He wanted to flash his friend the obscene gesture popular among novices their age, but knew he couldn't risk it here.

Sanyago continued his attacks on the false wooden menace, experimenting, improvising, parrying and dodging imagined thrusts and slashes from his opponent's nonexistent weapons. He watched as Master Ribeiro walked over to Laris, fingering the crimson clasp at the front of his robes though his face maintained the usual teacher's-mask of placid implacability.

The Ondojitsu Master took Laris' latest trial weapon—a long, wavy dagger whose name Sanyago could not place—out of his hands. Laris furrowed his brow, gave Master Ribeiros an inquisitive look, and waited. Sanyago killed his fine-grained opponent in at least three especially creative ways as he watched.

"You are having a difficult time finding something that suits you," the teacher said at last. He set the dagger carefully back down on its cushion.

"Yes, Ondojitsu Master Ribeiros." Laris looked abashed, confused in his frustrations. "We have been training unarmed for so long. Nothing feels right. I understand how to extend myself through them, but it makes me feel…" he searched for the right Gentic word, "…diminished. Like the weapon is an extension of my own arm, but also a poor substitute for it."

"Of course you feel this way," Master Ribeiros said, but his expression was thoughtful. "No matter how much skill and unity you attain with a weapon, it will never carry your will through the Holy Fathom as easily as your own flesh and bone."

Laris actually opened his mouth a moment before closing it again. Ribeiros raised his eyebrows. "If you have a question, then ask." This was not, Sanyago thought, something that teachers who knew Laris well usually said.

Laris looked taken aback and a touch wary, but Sanyago wasn't sure he was capable of passing up such an opportunity.

"If that's true, why bother with weapons at all? Why not rely entirely on the Fa— on the Holy Fathom?"

If Master Ribeiros noticed Laris' near-slip, he showed no sign of it. "That's not an unreasonable question, actually." A few nearby students had slowed or paused in trying out weapons to listen, and Sanyago stepped a little closer, swinging his sword through the air rather than against the dummy.

"Weapons," the Ondojitsu Master continued, "extend the reach, and protect their wielder's flesh and bone from the necessity of hard strikes and parries. Some allow for attacks at range. Carrying multiple weapons, when possible, allows for a degree of flexibility. And, of course, they can be imbued by artisans to help draw specific effects out of the Fathom, which alleviates some of this burden on the mind directing them. These things are all basic."

More students had moved closer to hear, and everyone in the training-hall seemed to be listening whether they had stilled or not. Ribeiro allowed himself the ghost of a smile, nodding at the students as though pleased at the opportunity for this impromptu lesson. Master Silva had paused midway through demonstrating a series of basic weapon motions for Vasili, resting the curved sword's long, heavy blade on his shoulder.

Master Ribeiro drew himself up into a basic unarmed combat stance— Gatoso, his back foot turned outward and bearing most of his weight, the ball of his front foot resting lightly on the floor. Putting both arms up in a basic guard, he closed his eyes, breathing slowly, and began to murmur a slow, winding formula in Three Harmonies. Sanyago caught some of the meaning easily enough: the intent to intensify and redirect motion, a drawing-in of influence and power, hard warding under soft, also drawn in close, readied apertures to release and absorb energies within the body's causal shadow.

"Ondojitsu is an art that covers many different styles and techniques," Ribeiros said, and struck out at the air with an open palm. A great burst of woven lightning snaked round his hand in a loud crackle, the smell of ozone filling the air. "But there is one commonality; from those who specialize in mobility and throwing spells, to those who rely on heavy armor and the reach of their weapons, all practitioners of the art rely on the Divine Medium of the Holy Fathom."

The Ondojitsu Master held up both hands, palms up. "In presenting you with this great panoply of weapons, there is one option you may overlook.

We have trained you extensively in unarmed combat because it is an excellent foundation, because weapons may not always be near to hand, because you must not learn to rely on material objects completely. There are, however, a few who never rely on them at all. Keep this in mind. When presented with several choices, remember that 'none of them' is often also a choice as well."

Master Ribeiros concluded this small lesson by turning sharply on his heel and moving to assist the nearest student with the chain-weapon he'd picked up. Sanyago stood a moment, pondering, looking down at his sword. No, it felt too natural. He liked unarmed sparring, it was challenging and interesting and he was good at it, but adding the sword felt better. His sword. He wanted one of them to be *his* sword. Leave a hand free for grapples and spells and whatever else...

He looked over at Laris, who stood stock-still near the middle of the hall, a look of slow reflection on his dark, angular features. He dared a glance at Hyon-seok, who glanced back, caught his eye.

And smiled.

Chapter 17

The walls of the mind are strong ones. They have to be, for they keep everything in its appointed place. But the appointments follow strange rules: long or short, false or true, big or little, simple or complex— these are not the sorts of categories that really matter. They are never the reasons for the walls, make no real contribution toward which fiefdom must be assigned. No, they can settle down in mutual peace wherever they may find themselves.

There are walls that guard the inside from the out, but they are porous and low. Perhaps they raise themselves up as we grow older, like a long twining of ponderous trees, but always there are gates and tunnels and secret doors. Sometimes whole sections come tumbling down, and often this is not such a terrible thing. These are not the strong walls of the mind; they are mere borders.

The strong walls lie far from the frontiers. They are the high solemn separation of neighbor from neighbor. They defend what should be from what probably is, necessary truth from implacable fact. They hurl shut their great iron-bound gates against the howling indignation of outraged sensibilities. They guard that which is pure and precious from the sight and sound of profane critics, lest they defile with raw contemplations.

Without them the mind would be flooded with the blood of fratricide, soaking drunk.

They say that here and there some enlightened soul has torn down the strong walls, has learned to live at peace with the self, or even abolished that contrary creature. I do not believe it.

- Lau Yan, *The Dramatist's Mask,* 54 SE

Kualabu, Tenggara, The Caustlands, 350 SE

"Ya Ilahi, Tatay," Dayang breathed. She reached out toward the armor, touched one of its heartvein plates, slid her finger down the intricate inlay of silver runes.

Father's smile was broad and true, as happy as Dayang thought she had ever seen him. "It's a fine thing, isn't it? It may be uncouth to admire one's own gifts while giving them, but I do think..."

His words were cut off as Dayang turned away from the armor stand and near-tackled him in a fierce hug. She heard his laughter, felt the shaking of his ribs under the lean muscle of his chest. Then she pulled away, as suddenly as she had embraced him, and looked him in the eye. She was taller than he was by a few centimeters, had been for a couple of years now.

"Thank you," she whispered. It could not have been cheap. No, that wasn't it. It could not even have been merely expensive. A suit like this represented at least a year's worth of work for a skilled Sihir-artisan. The enchantments alone...

"You're more than welcome, my little Engkanto," he said, and while his broad grin had settled back into a small smile, plenty of it remained in the corners of his eyes. "I know it's a little late for a birthday present— seventeen, God, I don't know where the time goes—but Hang Che and Hue Tian both say you're ready."

"Where did you get it from?" she asked, aware that her voice held a level of wonder that seemed more appropriate for a much younger girl. *Woman,* she thought. *Seventeen, I can say 'woman' now.*

"It's been on order from an artisan in Surabaru for a year and a half. If you want luxury, you buy from Cenicebu, but if you want battle-ready, you forget about the capital and go to a border-town."

This particular set of plate armor looked plenty luxurious to her, but she supposed she was appraising it with a different eye than most people would. It had a few decorative touches here and there besides the inlaid Proken runes, but they were all subtle things, never affecting the supreme pragmatism of the craftsmanship. Nothing was gilded or lacquered, no dyes or finishes had been applied, showing only the bare blood-red of worked heartvein. She rapped one of the plates with a knuckle, watched a dull-crimson glow emerge from the Abwarren metal's surface in a tangled network of sanguine threads.

"Ya Ilahi," she said again, then figured she should turn to address her father as well as God. "It's amazing, Tatay, I don't know what to say."

He laughed, still looking delighted. "That look on your face is all the thanks I need. More than that, I'm happy it will help keep you safe. Your mother will be, ah, pleased to know that as well." The corner of his mouth twitched into a sardonic little twist, but smoothed out again. "There's a matching shield, naturally." He gestured, and she nodded, reaching out to run her fingers over the kashval-hide facing.

It was a traditional tower shield, a long six-sided shape. *Same width as my training shields*, she thought as she slipped her arm through the strap and hefted it. *Taller, though.* And, of course, it wasn't made of bamboo. She recognized the thick leather covering, and the deepsteel reinforcing rim and face, but the wood—

"Salían live oak," Father said, watching her trace the unfamiliar grain pattern with her fingertips. "Druid-grown, like the weapons the Staffguard use."

Time spent around Jeims' continuous chatter and career ambitions meant that Dayang knew a bit more about the Salían Staffguard than just the usual legends. She nodded solemnly, sank into a combat stance, lifting the shield to shoulder-height as if warding off a blow to the head. When she lowered it again, Father still wore his boyish I-have-a-wonderful-secret grin.

Dayang studied him, then nodded slowly. He laughed, cocked his head. "What is it you've discerned, O Wise One?"

"There's a mace too, isn't there?"

He sighed theatrically. "You are a difficult girl to keep secrets from, did you know that?"

Dayang wrinkled her nose. "Maybe you're just bad at keeping them. Your face gives you away. How do you manage trade deals when you're this transparent?"

He laughed, the teasing in her tone abolishing the possibility of offence. "I don't generally negotiate with my daughter, for one. The old stone-face routine gets pretty tiresome if kept up at home, in my opinion. Not that some don't try anyway." He grinned at her long-suffering expression. "Yes, yes, there's a mace. Pandikar did the handle again, you know."

Dayang raised her eyebrows at him, and his smile went wry.

"Right, sorry, not a handle. The haft. Pandikar made the haft. He was also very insistent on the difference. I'm not bad with a kris knife, but God knows I'm no man-at-arms. I'm very proud of you both, you know, learning so much that I don't know."

She laughed. "I know something you don't? I don't think you've ever said anything like *that* before."

His expression rose toward lofty mock-solemnity— "Only a fool lets on to a teenager that they may know something he does not." —then fell into exaggerated suspicion. "And you're still seventeen, aren't you? Well, maybe just this once."

They looked at each other for a long time.

Then the moment broke, and Father shook his head. "Alas, the mace isn't *quite* finished. The head and haft, yes. Isra and Pandikar are just working on putting them together and, as your brother told me, getting everything *just* right."

"Good," she said with a smile. "Thank you again, Tatay. I'm guessing this is what all that dress-measurement was really about?"

"No, actually," he said, and gave her a wolfish grin. "That really was for a dress. I did send the measurements off to the armorsmith, just in case anything needed adjusting, but we already had what we needed from your practice-armor. The dress is for Nurul's wedding. It's finally been announced; I just got the echogram earlier today. I suppose now's as good a time as any to tell you."

She opened her eyes wide, startled but not especially surprised. She knew that Nurul and Hamid had been getting increasingly serious. Mother was ecstatic; Hamid was a junior officer in the Tentera Wira, and also from a 'good family'. Dayang had been avoiding her mother lately just so she didn't have to hear 'good family' continuously pronounced in tones of something approaching reverence. She turned to look out the window and Father just smiled, giving her room to think.

"Good family" meant money, of course, and prominence, and at least the appearance of proper piety. And it meant being from the 'right' stock, which really meant Malay, even though Nurul was herself half-Filipino because of Father, but no one wanted to come out and *say* this, least of all when Father was around.

She put her hand on the windowsill, leaned toward the glass. And anyway Mother wasn't really all Malay, Grandmother had been half-

Indonesian and *anyway* Hamid's family almost certainly wasn't either, they were part Thai from what she understood, and it was a good thing too. Only one lineage had come through Starfall with enough numbers to avoid inbreeding and still keep mostly to itself, and that was the Han. And even they intermarried sometimes—

—but whatever. "Good family" was crowshit, that was the point, and not even very good crowshit, it was let's-all-pretend crowshit. She tapped one fingertip erratically against the sill's dark-stained oak. Who cared whose ancestors came from which set of Old World islands? Everyone who had ever even *seen* those countries was dead. Everyone who had ever even met someone *else* who had seen them was dead. She was happy enough for her sister, though; Nurul seemed genuinely taken with Hamid, and Hamid with Nurul.

"I can tell by the look of ecstatic contemplation that you're just too pleased even to speak," Father said dryly, and Dayang shook her head.

"No. I mean, sorry, yes, I'm happy about it, really I am. I was just thinking. When is it? I guess they've got a date?"

"Late November, just before New Year's actually. The thirty-fourth or thirty-fifth, most likely. She has her heart set on a winter wedding. I'm guessing your dress will be white and silver."

Dayang did some math. It was the sixteenth of May, so...June, September, October, November...four and a half months to November thirty-fifth.

November thirty-fifth. Day before New Year's Eve. That was very like Nurul, somehow. Dayang thought she'd have planned the ceremony for midnight on the first of January if she thought she could manage to co-opt the holiday completely. Winter wedding. Well, it was going to be held in Avacthani, which was just about as far South as you could get while staying in the civilized parts of Tenggara. If anywhere was going to provide the snow she was no doubt envisioning for a picture-perfect wedding, it was Avacthani. *Maybe she'll move it across the Salian border to Acheronford if the proper amount of pure white powder fails to arrive.*

Dayang shrugged. "I'll wear whatever she wants, it's her day. I suppose showing up in my new armor is out of the question."

Father actually seemed to consider that a moment. "Hmmm. Hamid will almost certainly be in his Tentera Wira uniform...but a full suit of plate armor is probably a bit much, and anyway yours isn't part of any uniform."

He grinned. "Not that I don't think you'll look very lovely in it."

She sighed, running a finger down the crest of the helmet and over its heavy visor. Specially-treated heartvein, translucent from this outside perspective, mostly transparent from inside. At least with this she wouldn't have to put up with some well-meaning relative doing her best to see how much of her scar could be concealed with makeup. And if anyone stared, it would be at the armor, and not at her.

The following week gave Dayang new food for thought: Sara had a new boyfriend. Or maybe not "new", since that word sort of implied there had been a previous one. Sara had her *first* boyfriend.

She'd whispered as much to Dayang after their first class together, though Dayang wasn't sure the whispering would do much good; this wasn't the sort of thing that could survive the small-town gossip brigade, though perhaps it would finally convince Hang Che to stop his continued creepy attempts at...what? Courtship? Seduction? Gross. Beyond gross; his misplaced fascination with Sara had only gotten more insistent over the last year. Maybe it was best that he not find out.

So Dayang understood the desire for discretion, but she'd never really had anyone she'd dare call a 'boyfriend' herself. She *was* still enjoying Omar's company from time to time, but that hadn't gotten out, thank God, and she was pretty certain it wouldn't last past the end of his apprenticeship. She'd miss him, but she wouldn't pine.

She did think she'd like to have one, someday, away from here. She didn't plan to run off and abandon her faith or anything, but there had to be plenty of places in Tenggara with plenty of mosques and more freedom than she'd find in Kualabu. She wasn't sure exactly what she'd do when she graduated secondary school. Join the Tentera Wira for a while? She knew Father would like that, and Mother would hate it. Find an adventuring company, explore a few ruins, maybe even some of the ones right here around Kualabu? That would be much the same, so far as her parents were concerned.

She wasn't even entirely sure what it was Mother wanted her to do with her life. From what she'd gathered over years of hints and overheard conversations, there had been some sort of deal between her parents where at least one of their children would receive Wira training. What concessions Father had made to get this agreement, or even why he wanted it badly enough to fight for it, she wasn't sure. There were plenty of things she could talk to her father about, but his relationship with her mother was *not* one of them.

She had asked him why she was being trained, back when she was younger, but she didn't think it was really *quite* the same question, and his answer had been too pat, too easy. "Solace is a dangerous place, Dayang, I think every family should have at least one person who can face that head-on." It would have to do. She liked her training, had chosen to pour herself into it, and that had been *her* choice even if it wasn't originally her idea. It was something to cling to, a token of control over her own life.

She did think both her parents hoped she'd stay in Kualabu, for a while anyway. Both hoped for marriage and grandchildren, too, but she thought Father had mostly shrugged that one off, at least as something likely to happen in the near future. Mother had also dropped hints about attending Bright Shadow University in Cenicebu, but they seemed perfunctory, resigned. Dayang figured that Nurul would carry on the family's social status in Tenggara and that Pandikar would settle down in Kualabu as a respected artisan and carry on the family name here.

Dayang didn't give a shit about any of that. She felt terrible thinking it, and she guessed maybe part of it was being young and wanting to find her own way, but maybe not. She loved her family, but didn't love the dynasty Mother seemed to imagine it was. Perhaps there had been a brief flowering of Great Families in the hardships and uncertainties after Starfall, a resurgent aristocracy...but they weren't real. They never had any official power, no enforced status. And now maybe they were fading into the masses.

She was sometimes proud of these thoughts, but in those moments when she was most honest with herself she knew they weren't really hers. They were everywhere, snippets of them in teahouses and classrooms and streets. They spread far beyond Kualabu, too; they showed up in the cheap hedgeprint of the newspapers copied over from Cenicebu echograms. It was good, it was bad, it was terrible; it was inevitable, it must be stopped. It didn't really matter.

She would make her own way, or at least try.

Two days after Isra and Pandikar had finished with her new mace, she finally met Sara's new boyfriend, the three of them standing by a table in her and Sara's favorite town park. His name was Haithum, and he seemed all right to Dayang. Certainly he was good-looking, but that wasn't really a surprise, not to anyone who had ever actually *seen* Sara herself. He seemed kind and friendly, if a little awkward and nervous around Dayang. It probably did not help that she was holding her new mace.

She'd brought it with her to show Sara. New maces were definitely not high on Sara's list of interests, but Dayang knew she'd be excited anyway, because she was her best friend and *Dayang* was excited about it and that was part of how best friends worked. It really was a beautiful thing, sleek and flanged and given to only the most subtle of adornments. The flanges even had the swordcatcher grooves she had cut into her practice weapons.

"It's nice to meet you, Haithum," Dayang said. She tried to de-emphasize the weapon she carried by lifting it up onto her shoulder, like she imagined a woodsman would heft his axe for conversation. It didn't work; his eyes still followed the flanged head and tended to stay there rather than meet her gaze. It occurred to her then that, having no Wira training of his own, the mace was hefty enough that he'd have difficulty even lifting it with one hand, let alone make such a casual gesture with the heavy weapon. *Friendly, not intimidating,* she thought, and shot Sara an apologetic little grimace. Fortunately—or maybe unfortunately, from her boyfriend's perspective—Sara seemed amused by the whole thing.

"Nice to meet you too, Dayang Marchadesch," Haithum replied. He was kind of short, she decided. Shorter than Dayang herself, at any rate, though still a fair bit taller than Sara. But of course that was a petty thought. She wasn't sure what to think about his inclusion of her last name. Being "Dayang Marchadesch" instead of "Dayang binti Piolo" meant she technically had a "Christian-style" surname, and perhaps she was sometimes a touch oversensitive about it. She knew it nettled her father sometimes, and also that he took a sort of defiant pride in it. But Haithum's formality was probably just nerves.

Maybe she should just put the mace down.

"So...your family moved here from Surabaru, right?" she said, realizing she'd been standing in silence a touch too long.

He seemed relieved. "Yeah, my parents are both with the Tenggaran Army."

Enlisted, she thought, *not officers, and certainly not in the Tentera Wira.* She shouted that voice down; it sounded too much like Nurul at her worst.

Sara smiled at him, and Dayang smiled at her. Sara's was the sort of smile her father had been wearing when he presented her with her new armor just days before; if that was the sort of happy Haithum made her, she was more than ready to like him too.

"I was worried I wouldn't know anyone, wouldn't meet anyone I liked, wouldn't make any friends." He returned Sara's smile, and Sara gave him a quick hug and a peck on the lips. They pulled away, both blushing faintly but still holding hands.

"I kind of picked his brain about Surabaru and what was going on there and the local politics and he actually seemed to know what he was talking about when he answered. And didn't look at me like I was crazy for asking." Sara squeezed his hand, and snuggled in against his side.

Dayang looked around; at Sara's age no one was going to come try to separate the pair or anything, even in Kualabu, but opinions on this sort of thing varied wildly and the most opinionated tended to be the most likely to pass on gossip. She didn't see anyone looking their way; a small group of younger children intent on something small and squirmy in the grass, a pair of old women playing Go under a gazebo.

"I'm glad you two found each other," Dayang said, and she meant it. Then, not wishing to let the conversation linger in the Land of Mush, she added, "Surabaru must have been an interesting place to live. Are you from there, or were your parents there on assignment?"

Haithum's smile broadened, grew less shy, and his eyes stopped tending toward the weapon resting on her shoulder. They did flick aside for a moment before resting on her face—*scar*—and she remembered with a small internal grimace that the mace was probably not the only thing he found intimidating. "Assignment. Father is from Cenicebu, Mother is from a small village near the Presilyo Ri'Granha. They met in the Army."

Dayang cocked her head, unconsciously rolling the haft of her mace against her shoulder. "The Presilyo? That's interesting. Have you ever gone back there? Ever seen a Somonei?"

Haithum laughed, and she found she liked the sound of it; it was warm and clear and gentle. "We've been back a few times. Twice that I can remember, to visit Mother's family. I did see a few Somonei. Just in their blue robes, no weapons or anything that I could see. Looked like any other monk. Everyone pretty much ignored them, I guess they're in the village pretty often escorting Presilyo traders."

"They just looked like Buddhist monks then?" She was mildly disappointed. There weren't many Buddhists in Kualabu, but plenty in Surabaru and Cenicebu, and she'd seen saffron-robed members of their monastic orders here and there on the handful of occasions she'd travelled with her family. Somonei, though, they were supposed to be martial legends.

Haithum shrugged. "Pretty much. I mean, they're still obviously fighters, just from the way they walk and the kind of shape they're in. And they wear boots instead of sandals..." he thought a moment, furrowing his brow, "...and they have these colored clasps on the front of their robes. And the robes are blue, like I said, and looser than the Buddhists'. So they can hide weapons, I guess."

"Huh," Dayang frowned, revising her mental image. "Well..." and she froze. Hang Che was walking across the grass toward them, and she could not read the expression on his face. She glanced over at Sara and Haithum; they were still holding hands. Sara frowned, looking trapped. Haithum, for his part, seemed puzzled until she leaned over to whisper in his ear. His eyes widened.

Shit.

Dayang took a deep breath and moved to stand in Hang Che's path as he picked up speed. Not running, but definitely walking fast, that unreadable expression deepening to a scowl.

"Good afternoon, Guru Hang," she said as he came within a few meters.

"Get out of here, Dayang," he snarled, and she saw that there was real anger in his eyes; not annoyance, not the half-feigned anger of a teacher wanting to drive home a point, but real, snarling rage. She had never seen that before, and it sent a spike of fear down the center of her gut.

She was trying to think what she should say to this when he closed the distance and simply swatted her aside. Still shocked and unsure, she stumbled down to one knee, the mace coming off her shoulder with a heavy *thud.* She watched as Hang Che caught up with the retreating Sara, caught the profile of his sneer as he looked back and forth between the young pair. They still held hands, even as they backpedaled away from his advance. Haithum's knuckles were white.

"This is him? This is the boy? Of course it is. Some soldier's son? Some pretty-boy newcomer? You can do better."

Sara didn't answer, but Haithum tried.

"You— you have no right, she can—"

"*You* can be *silent,* boy." Hang Che's backhand caught him across the cheek and nose in a spray of blood, leaving the young man sprawled in the grass.

Dayang found she was standing now, that her mace was halfway-raised. Adrenaline and fear and rage pushed through her heart and limbs in a twisting, sludgy mix.

"Guru Hang!" she yelled, but he ignored her. "*Hang* Che!" she cried, and now he slowly turned. Even from a few meters away she could see the shock in his eyes. Never, not once, had she called him simply by his given name.

"You're *fucking* pathetic," she growled. He turned a little more, stopped, face and body halted in a perfect moment of crystallized fury. She knew she had crossed at least two lines she couldn't step back over, couldn't believe all of this was happening *now*, there was no time to prepare, there was no way to plan, so she just went on.

"This whole thing with Sara has been pathetic. You obsess over a teenage girl, come find her in a park and beat up her boyfriend? It was bad enough when you were just stalking her like some sad sack of shit."

He drew his sword from its sheath at his hip, pointed the long, machete-like blade her way. He was only carrying one of the pair he owned, thank God for small mercies. He didn't advance on her, though, just glared and turned toward Haithum, who was wiping the blood from his face while up on one shaking knee.

"You and your little friend are going to learn a lesson," he said, turning his sword this way and that as though admiring the way the mid-afternoon sun reflected off its deepsteel blade. "I have lived here in Kualabu for twenty years. Half the town owes me their lives. I am *respected,*" he hissed.

He wasn't looking her way, attention focused entirely on Haithum, who was being slowly helped to his feet by a sobbing, shaking Sara. Stealth was not a large part of Dayang's training, but she did know how to mute her presence in the Fathom as part of a feint or attack, and she did so now, praying it would be enough, praying he was too distracted by his own purpose and rage. She took her mace in both hands, walked slowly forward.

"When I tell the guard that this little foreign *shit* attacked me because I interrupted his advances toward a local girl, they'll believe me. They won't care what the daughters of some shopkeeper and upstart merchant sa—"

Dayang's mace slammed into the side of his head. She did not put as much force as she could into the hit. She didn't want to murder him. She didn't think she *could* kill Hang Che in just one blow, caught off-guard or no, his resilience would be too much for that, but she didn't want to risk it either.

Hang Che staggered to the side—away from Sara and Haithum, just as she'd planned—and fell onto one hand, but sprang back to his feet almost immediately, lunging at her with his sword. She was ready, and parried, both hands on the haft, wishing she had her armor, wishing she had her shield. Another swing, and another. She was able to block but was being driven back, unable to get in any serious counterattacks.

"You waste of a student!" he cried as she desperately turned his blows aside. "Taught...you...to...fight..." and she ducked under a vicious swing, managed to jab him in the chest with the rounded point at the tip of her mace, not that she thought it would do her much good, "...never...learned...respect..."

A slash caught her at the collarbone, tearing through the leather of her jacket and the shirt beneath. She felt her resilience push back, keeping the blade from cutting into her skin but diminishing her reserves. Another swing of his sword caught her mace right below the head, and as it forced her to one knee she saw that he had doubled up his grip and turned the weapon round, using the blunt back side of his sword along with his superior height and strength to bear down on her. It was a trick she had never seen him use before. He'd held back, teaching her. Of course he had.

"I suppose I shouldn't be surprised, not with an infidel gutter-trash father like yours," he said, twisting his blade and forcing her mace aside. She let herself fall back fully, rolled to the side, brought her mace up to defend as his sword came down again, one-handed this time. Dayang tried to stuff her rage at his words back down. It would do her no good against an opponent like Hang Che. She didn't quite succeed, roaring back at him, lashing out with one foot. He caught it with his free hand, twisted her ankle, and she had to lash out with her other foot to free herself while continuing to parry blows from above.

"Angry? You think anyone thinks his 'conversion' was anything but a ploy to marry into respectability?" He drew a parrying dagger from behind his back. He hadn't even bothered to pull it out before now, and she suddenly realized how badly, how hopelessly she had lost this fight. She gritted her teeth. Still wouldn't give up, she could—

crrrrrrACK

Dayang's thoughts were blasted apart by the sudden earsplitting noise. Hang Che's whole body stiffened for a moment, silhouetted from behind by a flash of silver-blue that seemed to hang about it like an aura before fading. She took the opening to kick him firmly in the solar plexus, using the momentum to push herself back and start scrambling to her feet.

That was a lightning bolt. It must—

"Jeims?" she called.

Hang Che had already turned to face the young Caustland Cat, who still held a long metal rod in one unfolded paw, already chanting out the rapid Proken of his next spell.

"You DARE?" Hang Che roared. "You filthy little foreign housecat, I'll—"

Even in his overwhelming rage, Hang Che wasn't stupid; he was quickly closing the distance between himself and Jeims. Dayang saw with horror that the Salían mage was holding his ground, even though he had to know he wouldn't last long in close combat with the master Wira fighter. She found her footing, surged forward after Hang Che, murmuring a spell along with a silent prayer.

She had little hope of masking her attack from behind this time; there was no way it wouldn't be expected. What she *could* do was draw Hang Che's attention away from Jeims and buy some time. To her relief, she saw that Jeims had been weaving a powerful ward rather than attempt another attack; barely visible to the eye, its semicircular lattice slammed into solid existence from the Fathom, stopping Jeims' attacker in his tracks. Cursing, Hang Che turned on his heel in an attempt to slip around the barrier, but was forced to turn round entirely and parry Dayang's attack.

"What are you going to do?" he growled as his blade locked with the haft of her mace. "Kill me? Send yourself to a Cenicebu prison and your family into disgrace? Throw down Daddy's expensive weapon and I'll show both of you mercy. You can—" he was forced to duck down and roll away, catching a glancing blow from her mace along the way as he tumbled under a gout of fire from Jeims' outstretched hand. Some tiny unfocused part of her mind noticed with amusement that the sleeve of his fine linen shirt had caught fire.

The rest of her mind focused on a hard overhand swing, which Hang Che managed to catch with his parrying dagger. Still, her heavy weapon's momentum brought it thumping into the meat of his shoulder, slamming him onto his back before he could stand and putting immense strain on his wrist. Hang Che roared as his head hit the ground, then twisted his upper torso violently to roll his shoulder out from under her mace. He tried to counterattack with a slash from his sword at her knees, but she was already calling on every gram of Fathom-assistance she could muster, swinging the head of her mace into the flat of his blade.

The two weapons made contact with a flat *clank*, forcing the sword down into the grass, pinned under two flanges of her mace. She stepped back, taking some of the pressure off the sword, deliberately letting him lift it just enough that she could angle one of the flange notches to catch it.

He grunted, dropped the parrying dagger so he could use both hands in his attempt to wrest back control of his sword. He would have been successful, too, she knew, and almost immediately; he was stronger and faster than she and had seen this trick from her before in training. But Jeims harried him with spells, peppering his head and shoulders with intermittent sprays of icy shards, sapping his resilience and hurting his concentration.

As they wrestled with their interlocked weapons he lifted his legs, kicked at her. She dodged one kick, braced herself against the impact of another, and then used her grip on her mace as a fulcrum to pivot her hips and slam her bootheel squarely between his legs. He groaned, bent his knees and turned them aside to protect his groin as she stepped back again. Resilience or no, she knew he had felt that one.

Dayang slipped her right hand off the haft of her weapon, reversed her grip with the left, holding the haft of her mace nearly upright. She stepped forward, stomping on the flat of his blade as she yanked her kris from its sheath at the small of her back. She half-knelt to make an overhand stab at his unprotected belly, and he let go of his sword with his own right hand to catch her wrist. She twisted her arm to break his grip, stepping back.

"What are you going to do?" he said again. "I won this fight before you were even born, *girl.*"

She wanted to say something like, 'I'm not going to do anything, Jeims is going to take care of you.' It was the kind of quip one of the heroes in her Wuxia stories would make, but it would be stupid. Hang Che was far from helpless; give him any warning and God knew what he might do. Instead she just watched, doing her best to hold him in place as the Salían Lingmao pounced, sailing right over his head in a graceful feline arc. Jeims' claws landed on his face and thighs, raking with all four paws, but the claws were really just to add insult to the injury of the lighting-surge that pounded downward through Hang Che's body into the ground.

Dayang could hear Sara screaming, now. It sounded like it had been going on for a while, but she guessed her mind had just edited it out as not pertinent to survival. Jeims' back foot slashed four ragged lines into Hang Che's cheek; his resilience was spent. The Caustland Cat glanced back at the gore, wrinkled his nose, and leapt off to the side.

Defenses gone, Hang Che's body shuddered tightly with whatever residual charge Jeims had left behind. Dayang decided it was time to answer her former teacher's last question. She yanked upward on her mace, the notched flange pulling Hang Che's sword from his nerveless fingers and flinging it aside. Then she brought it down.

crunch

It was such an understated sound, flat and muffled by the impact of metal on meat. Satisfied that the bone of his upper arm was now in fragments, she brought it down on the other side. This time it was more difficult, because her hands were shaking.

crunch

"Dayang..." The voice sounded like Jeims. She ignored him, lifted, struck.

crunch

She knew better than to hit him in the thigh; that could be death by bleeding. She didn't want to kill him. But his shin was in ruins now.

"Dayang!" This time the voice was Sara's, and she paused, about to lift her mace again, turned to look.

Sara's body thumped gracelessly into her own, slender arms going round her back. Dayang only stepped back a little; she was easily half again Sara's weight. She stood there a moment, stock-still with her best friend's arms wrapped around her. Someone else was screaming, cursing. Hang Che.

She dropped her mace, shuddered, sobbed once.

"Never," she mumbled into the top of Sara's head. "He'll never do anything like this again." Only she knew maybe that wasn't true. A good Sihir-doctor would be able to heal even the damage she had done in a few days. She gave Sara a squeeze, took a deep breath, stepped back.

"I'm okay," Dayang said, wiping sweat and tears from her face. She winced slightly as she felt her fingers brush over the raised ridge of her scar. "Thank you. I'm okay. I'm...done." She let go of Sara entirely, gave Haithum what smile she could manage as Sara clung to him. He managed a hoarse "Thank you" in return.

Dayang turned back to Jeims, who was sitting on Hang Che's chest now, head cocked as though listening. The big man spat incoherent curses at him between huffs and groans of pain, but couldn't really do anything else.

Jeims looked up at her, expression serious but relieved. "He's bleeding internally, but nothing that's going to kill him. I've stanched most of it. I'm no Sihir-doctor but I do know my first aid."

She nodded. She didn't know what else to do.

Jeims put his paws on Hang Che's shoulders, leaned his head in close, ears laid back. "You bastard," he growled, and Dayang felt herself shudder. Caustland Cats were not big people, not compared to humans; Jeims probably weighed less than a third what Hang Che did, but even without weapons and magic they could do serious damage if they wanted to. And there were Old World cats roaming the Caustlands big enough to kill someone easily, and sometimes did, though they were animals, not people. At any rate that feline growl triggered something ancient and terrified inside the primate parts of the human brain.

Hang Che spat in his face. Jeims grimaced, wiped it off, then put a matching set of claw marks on Hang Che's other cheek. "You bastard," he said again. "You threaten to kill some poor boy because, what, you want to mate with some young girl, and she likes him and he likes her? Do you kill people just because they're in the way? In the way of any little stupid whim or obsession? Maybe we shouldn't have stopped Dayang. Maybe I should tear your throat out and tell the guards you left us no choice."

Hang Che started to say something in reply, voice strangled with fury and pain, but he must have seen something in the Lingmao's amber eyes because he shut his mouth and let his head fall back into the grass.

Jeims nodded, then sat back onto Hang Che's chest. The man groaned. Jeims looked up, and sighed. "Here they come. Late, of course. Whatever this splotch of crowshit had in mind, he probably made sure all the guards within earshot were buddies of his. By the time anyone not in awe of the great Hang Che arrived, it would be done." His tail whacked Hang Che in the groin with surprising force, and the man moaned, trying to curl up before screaming with the pain this caused in his shattered leg.

Dayang followed his gaze. Yep, guards. Just two of them, which wasn't surprising, it would take a lot to summon a larger force than that from the walls or from off-shift.

"I'd like to think he wasn't actually going to *kill* the kid," Jeims continued. "Probably just rough him up, scare him. But maybe I'm giving him too much benefit of the doubt."

Hang Che started to say something, but Jeims growled, bared his teeth, and the man just moaned.

"What's going on here?" one of the guards called out.

Dayang sighed, felt herself slump, then squared her shoulders again, set her jaw. She had done what she had to do. Time to face up to the aftermath.

Over the strange long stretch of time that followed, everything seemed to go numb, and sick, and cold, though it was a sunny day in mid-summer. Hang Che was taken away on a stretcher, still screaming and cursing. Dayang's hands shook. The guards, who she did not know, asked questions. Sara sat trembling on a bench, knees drawn up to her chest, looking much younger than sixteen. The guards asked her questions too. Haithum looked dazed. His parents arrived. He answered questions.

The guards took her mace and her kris. She wanted them back so badly, just to hold something. They did not seem to dare take anything away from Jeims. After a moment of sluggish but relatively clear thought, she guessed this had some diplomatic reason.

Pandikar came, sat with her. He put one long arm around her shoulders as she hunkered down on the grass, staring at the bloodstains where Hang Che's bulk had depressed the greenery into an ephemeral reverse-sculpture.

She thought the guards were going to take her to a cell, but they did not. They talked among themselves, and with Jeims, but too quietly for her to hear. She didn't try anyway.

"He was asking for it, you know," Pandikar was saying, right by her ear. He squeezed her gently. "Has been for years, there have been whispers here and there, but no one ever does anything. Because he's Hang Che. No one wants him to be gone if the walls are breached again."

She heard him, but from far away. She felt the grass she was tearing up and letting pass through her fingers, but it was greenery in some distant field.

Jeims came too, when he was done answering questions. He told her he had gone after Hang Che because of the look Hue Tian had given the Wira-Guru in the training hall where he'd been practicing. He hadn't liked that look, he said, because he couldn't read it. He had been delayed because he didn't want to leave too quickly, make it obvious he was going to follow. He'd had to ask people in the street if they'd seen where Hang Che had gone.

He was sorry he hadn't come sooner. She managed a smile, told him he'd been there just in time. They said nothing more, and he rested warm and tired against her side while she leaned against Pandikar's.

Father arrived, finally. He said he had been on his way out of the city, they had called him back just as he'd passed through the gate. She asked if he had found someone to run the caravan in his place. The question was automatic. He said yes, not to worry, that she was more important.

I can't believe I hired him, he kept saying. I can't believe I hired someone like that to teach my daughter, and did not see it. I should have listened and watched more carefully. I should have asked you.

She shrugged, and then when she saw the depth of pain on his face she felt herself pulled back from her far-away. She gave Pandikar a smile, though she could not guess at how strained it must look. She gently removed his arm from around her shoulders, and went to hug her father.

"You could not have known, Tatay. I didn't even know. I didn't say anything, wouldn't have said anything if you'd asked. I thought it was just...I don't know what I thought it was. Nothing like it ended up. And he was a good teacher, Tatay. He was kind of a shitty man, but he was a good teacher." She felt herself flush as she realized this was probably the first time she'd ever sworn in front of her father, but he just snorted, and she went on. "He'd have been proud at how long I lasted against him, you know? In other circumstances."

"Is it true you snuck up on him and hit him in the head with your new mace?" He cocked his head, and his smile was unreadable.

"Yeah," she said softly, and laughed, just once, more a quick puff of air than anything. "Yeah, I did. I didn't know if his threats were serious or not, but I didn't want to find out. They sure seemed serious."

He laughed, and shrugged, and sighed. "I believe you. And I believe Sara, and Jeims, and Haithum, though I've only just met Haithum and don't really know Jeims." All traces of his smile drained away, and he shook his head slowly. "Dayang, you're not going to like this. I don't like it, but I'm still relieved—"

"I haven't liked most of this afternoon," she said, and wished she hadn't. He barely seemed to notice.

"In a just world, he would go to rot in some maximum-security prison in Cenicebu, but we don't live in that world. It's your word against his, and even though there are four of you and one of him, he's Hang Che. A lot of people in this town owe him their lives, and a lot more think we'll need him and his friends in the future. Do you understand that? It's not fair, but that's what it is."

She nodded slowly. Prison for her, then? No, they'd have restrained her by now, surely.

"There will be no trial. Not for you, not for him." He sighed again, and she thought what a climb and fall this week had been for him, for them both. Two days ago he had seemed so happy. Now he put his head in his hands, and when he lifted it again she saw his eyes were wet.

"I've done all I can. So has Jeims. It was...it was very quick. It had to be, before anything formal was done, was written. You understand?"

She nodded, feeling only halfway back from far-away.

"A trial would do nothing, not to him. Probably not to you either, not with all the witnesses on your side. But that's not for sure, so…" he shook his head again. "I've made an agreement. Nothing formal, but it will hold. You can leave Kualabu, at least for a while. You're close enough to graduating school that I think they will let you go with a diploma, under the circumstances."

"So I go free, and he stays free," she said, and scuffed her boot against a small clump of abblum. "No one risks a trial. We all pretend nothing happened."

"You don't have to. I don't want to make decisions for you, not now, not after...not after my decisions have already cost you so much."

"Father," she said, and then more firmly. "Piolo. Listen. He'd have been the same whether I was his student or not. Your decisions, they gave me the strength to fight at least. What would I have done otherwise? Run screaming for the guards? God knows what would have happened to Haithum in the meantime. You think he would never have noticed Sara if I were not his student? It could have been the same, only with me helpless, with all of us helpless."

He smiled at her, reached up, wiped away some of her tears. She was surprised to see them, shining there on his fingertip, but of course she had been crying, she must have been.

"Maybe so." He sighed, slumped down, squared his shoulders again, sat up straight again. "I can get you an introduction to the Tentera Wira. You would have to prove yourself to them; Hang Che will of course send no recommendation. Nor," and his mouth turned down its corners down into an extraordinary depth of disgust, "will Hue Tian. She stands with him, so do all his old comrades. They must know what he is." He violently flicked something non-existent from the heavy canvas of his caravan-trousers.

"So," she said. "I leave, and he stays."

"Yes," he said, but did not sigh this time, did not slump. "It is not fair. This *will* be a heavy blow to his reputation. Not a fatal one, I'm afraid, but not nothing. To someone like him, someone who sets so much of his being on being Someone in a town like Kualabu, where everyone knows him...it's not nothing."

Father stared out over the park's carefully-tended greenery, leaning forward. "He'll leave Sara alone, now. Haithum too. The Captain of the Guard made that much very clear. It's still not fair. I know he should be rotting in prison. And I don't know that this will remove his taste for," his mouth twisted into a sardonic grimace, "inappropriately young women. But Sara and Haithum should be okay. Even his influence will go only so far. If anything happens to either of them—well, the Captain says they'd call in the Tentera Wira to deal with him, and I believe her."

She nodded, sat up straight to match him.

"Okay," she said. "Okay. I was going to leave anyway, join the Tentera Wira myself, I think, for a while anyway, just..."

And she began to laugh, and once she started, she could not stop. Father and Pandikar both looked alarmed. Jeims looked over from where he was talking with Aulia, gave the other Lingmao a gentle nuzzle, and then padded over. He put his paws on Dayang's knees and stretched upward to bump her lightly under the chin with the bridge of his nose. She hiccupped, laughed one more time, and gave him a brief hug. "...it's just a Hell of a way to leave, you know?"

Father held his hand out once Jeims had settled back onto his haunches. "Thank you again, Mr. Dubwa," he said in clear if heavily accented Gentic. "We owe you a great deal."

Jeims shook his hand, looking abashed. "I find myself wishing I'd done something earlier. And that I still owe a debt for dragging your daughter into that misadventure last year."

"No debt," Father said. He gave a sly smile. "We foreigners must stick together, yes?"

They went home then, and she packed. She had settled on the Tentera Wira, supposed she had been settling that way far in the back of her mind for some time now. She was surprised at how little she really needed to take. Her echoplays she would leave to Sara, maybe a few to Pandikar. Three of her favorites to take with her. Her Quran, with facing pages in Basa and Old World Arabic. A few other books. Clothes, all practical. She supposed she would miss Nurul's wedding, which was sad, but she didn't have any real room for the emotion right now.

Her armor she would wear. Her shield and mace she would carry.

It wasn't a dream. She kept telling herself that as she woke, ate, dressed, checked her pack. She still didn't quite believe it as she strapped on her armor, piece by piece. It was a little different than her practice armor, but for the most part she could rely on muscle memory. Both sets were designed so they could be donned and removed by just one person, though it was difficult. She'd usually had help before, and wished she still did now, but she thought somehow this was something she had to do herself.

Mother was waiting for her on the front porch, leaning on the railing to Dayang's right. "My daughter. What have you done?"

She turned her head to regard her mother. Dayang was wearing her helmet; it was easier to carry this way, and she had not expected to meet anyone at the porch. She thought Mother would meet her at the gate, as Father and Pandikar and Sara had said they would. She also thought about the whisper of metal on stone, the sound her helmet made against the heartvein of the gorget protecting her neck as she twisted it to look. It burrowed deep into her memory, that sound, and she wasn't sure why.

Mother's eyes were wide, makeup smeared across her cheeks where she'd dried tears and not bothered to clean up. "Well?" she said. "Raise that twice-damned visor on your thrice-damned helmet." Her voice was flat, but Dayang thought she could hear churning tumult under the surface.

Dayang lifted her visor. It was well-oiled and made no noise, for which she was absurdly grateful. "Mother," she said, and again was not sure why. "Mother, I had to."

Mother shook her head. "No," she said. "No, you didn't. You could have minded your own business. You didn't have to meet that little whore at the park with her little…"

Dayang was only aware that she had stepped forward from the slight clank of her armor, and when she followed her mother's suddenly wide and horrified gaze she also realized she had dropped her hand to the loop that held her mace snug against her belt. She could only guess at how her face must read.

"What," Mother said, and Dayang saw that she was shaking. "Are you going to break my arms too? Crush my leg? That's what...that's what they said…"

Dayang felt something start to collapse inside her, and she wanted to slump against the doorway, even in all her armor she wanted to slide down to the floor, but she decided she was not going to break, not really, not now, and she stood straight. But her face must have changed, because Mother flung herself forward, hugged her daughter as tightly as she could, snaking her arms beneath the canvas and straps of Dayang's pack. Dayang put her own arms around Mother, squeezed, though more gently.

She could barely feel the hug with the heavy plates between them, but decided it didn't matter. She could feel the apology, and the pain and the terror, and she knew maybe the apology wasn't enough but that it needed to not matter right now, right now her mother's youngest child was leaving and a thousand fears were becoming unburied or shambling in from where they'd been standing in plain view.

Mother only sobbed twice, then she drew back, looked at her, patted the plates of her armor as though reassuring some strange, temperamental beast.

"I love you," Dayang said, and her mother nodded.

"I love you too," she replied, and she looked her daughter in the eye. "You know I don't like this. I never have liked it. And I don't like what happened. I do love you, Dayang. You make me afraid for you."

"I'm sorry," Dayang said, and she was, for plenty, though she didn't know how much she regretted, how much she would not change. "Goodbye, Emak. I'll see you again as soon as I can."

She didn't know if Mother watched her leave, because she didn't look back, couldn't hold up what had broken inside if she looked back. She walked to the gate. It was a long walk, even though it was not a long way. Continuing down the street, she put her visor back down, but she still felt the eyes on her.

She ran into Hue Tian on the way. Her other erstwhile teacher stood in the middle of the road, radiating fury and contempt. Dayang found she didn't really care. She moved a bit farther to the side, and when Hue Tian stepped over to block her way, she reached back and snagged her shield off the side of her pack. The other woman's eyes narrowed, then darted to the side, and she turned abruptly to stalk away down a side street.

"Hello, Jeims Dubwa," Dayang said, turning to greet him as he padded over toward her from the opposite stretch of that same side street. In spite of everything, she smiled beneath her visor.

"Hello, Dayang Marchadesch," he returned, and he wore a smile as well. "I don't know what she had planned. Just some intimidation and verbal abuse, probably. I thought about having my own little confrontation with her, maybe chat some about the way she's countenanced and excused Hang Che's crowshit over the years. But then I remembered that I am a stranger in a strange land and that she could still wipe the floor with me, one-on-one. So I followed her; I can't match her spell for spell, but I'm plenty good at stealth, if I do say so myself."

"I'm sorry, Jeims," Dayang said. "And thank you."

"Thanks accepted!" Jeims said, lifting his tail. "Apology, not so much. I make my own choices, I live with the consequences, Hang Che's bastardry is not your fault, and also I'll be fine. Most of the officials who approved me coming for training were convinced Kualabu was..." and he sighed, flicking his tail as he padded along beside her.

She turned toward him, raised her eyebrows.

He frowned. "Well, you know how prejudice goes. I hate to turn bigotry to my own advantage, but I'm pretty sure they'll be predisposed to believe the unvarnished truth, as long as they can use it to get all self-righteous inside their own heads. Probably varnish it some themselves."

She grunted, and shook her head. "Today, I don't know. Maybe they're a little bit right."

He shrugged, dipping his head down below his shoulders. "They always are. That's the thing about bigotry. People are kind of shitty everywhere, so there are always plenty of examples to hang a prejudice on. You think some group is lazy? Sure, bound to be some lazy people in there if the group is big enough. Or mean, or stupid, or fanatical. Everyone finds ways to keep believing what they want to believe."

She sighed. "No one here will believe what really happened with Hang Che, then."

He shook his head. "Some won't, some will. We'll see. Don't worry about Kualabu right now. We've both got places to be. Me, back to Salía. My training is done by definition, it's not like Hue Tian will teach me anymore after *this*. You, I think you're going places in general, Ms. Marchadesch, even if you start with the Tentera Wira. We'll see each other again."

"I hope so," she said, and they fell silent as they walked.

Father, Pandikar, Aulia, and Sara were all waiting at the gate, along with a handful of people she didn't recognize. Dayang took off her helmet, gave Sara a heavily-armored hug. "Is Haithum going to be okay?"

"Yes," Sara said, and smiled sadly at her. "Thank you so much, Dayang. I don't know what would have happened...I'm so, so sorry."

"It's okay," Dayang said. She was getting tired of people's 'sorry's already, but she appreciated the need and the feeling behind them. "He really does seem like a good guy."

Sara smiled at that, wide and brilliant, a piece of the warm, happy Sara she'd known nearly as long as she could remember, and she was achingly glad to see it now of all times.

"He sends his fervent thanks, of course. They're still looking after him at the hospital. But his parents are here."

Haithum's parents had their own chorus of "thanks" and "sorry", and she nodded and smiled numbly through them. Then she said goodbye to

Father, and then to Pandikar, tears and hugs and bad jokes and promises. Jeims and Aulia had their own goodbye, and she tried not to notice too much; she didn't need to see more heartbreak today.

It was time. It was still so abrupt. She had to walk through the gate now or she never would. Father and Pandikar were waving.

Someone put a hand on her shoulder. It was a tentative touch; she barely felt it through the pauldron of her armor.

"Dayang? I— I'm sorry. My name is Syifa. I— I heard about what happened, and I came." She was a pretty woman, plainly-dressed with a headscarf, wearing no makeup. Her big brown eyes were serious and shy. Dayang nodded, unsure.

"I— I knew Hang Che. When I was a girl. No, that sounds wrong. I suppose I wasn't a girl, but only just."

And Dayang understood.

"I'm sorry," she said quietly, and wondered whether this woman too was tired of 'sorry', or if she'd not heard it nearly enough. She found she meant it, though.

"I told...I told a few people. No one did anything. Some of them blamed me. For...for tempting him. I—"

Dayang shook her head, put one arm round the woman's slender shoulders, gave her the most gentle hug she could with various plates of armor in the way. She thought maybe Syifa was going to cry, but she just smiled sadly.

"Thank you for making him answer for what he's done. Your friend Sara and I...we're not the only ones. But you're the only one who's ever really made him pay. I'm sorry for the price you paid."

"Some prices are worth paying," Dayang said. "I hope you have a good life. Don't let him stand over it."

Syifa nodded. "I am keeping you. Go. I hope you have a good life as well, Dayang Marchadesch."

Dayang went.

Eighth Interlude

Excerpt, Zero up Five Recounted: Six Years Among the Praedhc Tribes, *Franz Kotkin-Schmidt's seminal 125 SE work*

The jungles east of Earthmarch are not quite the same chaos of canopy and undergrowth one might have seen in, say, the Old World Congo or Amazon. The twisted-strand trunks of the great ropewood trees coil upward at regular intervals, rising more than three meters before spinning thick branches out in a great spiral umbrella of purple leaves. Each of these interlocks with its neighbors, twining together to catch every drop of sunlight it can from Farrod's rays, and every mote of moisture from Solace's clouds.

This makes the canopy appear purple-black from below during the day; what little light manages to pass downward is stained a thin violet. At night the canopy becomes the dead-black background for great flowing constellations of bioluminescent insect-analogues. Most actual illumination comes from below, thanks to the warm fluorescence of the funguses that form a thin carpet over the spongy ground.

What exactly the point of this reverse photosynthesis might be is not clear. It comes in every conceivable color, extending well past the visible spectrum in both directions, as those trained to sense such things through the Fathom have discovered. These same adepts have also noted that the energy for the phenomenon seems to come from deep below, and that the jungle specimens are likely cousins of the much more powerfully luminescent growths that appear down in the Abwarren.

These observations have nearly all been made by the people who call themselves "The Risen" in their various languages. The "Fallen," who they call Sevenfolk, call them in turn Praedhc and Pelos and Antepas, among other things, in their many tongues. Whatever their name, they have been on Solace a long, long time—ever since, as nearly all their mythologies hold, their ancestors emerged from the deep-below Wombstone into the Undersky. Before Starfall turned most of their greatest empire to bones and ashes, the Risen had little reason to call themselves anything but "people," or the names of their various tribes and nations.

The Risen are generally the only ones around to make any observations in the jungle; the Fallen newcomers rarely venture across the Siinlan into the parts of Solace that are really Solacian, the parts they call the Abwaild. No one wants to starve to death with a full belly.

Mikinao Tesch wasn't starving, but he wasn't happy either. His Praedhc captors were using the rations they'd found in his pack to feed him, and that was fine, but they also fed him food they'd raided from Newcaste Compact caravan and it was...bland. He frowned as he spread the "Individual Ration Items" that would be today's lunch out in front of him, their drab packaging making a surreal contrast to the luminescent riot of the fungus covering the jungle floor. No garlic, no onion, no vinegar, no strong spices, little salt. No coffee, tea, or chocolate, either. Nothing much to get excited about beyond a less-empty stomach.

He'd even considered trying some of his captors' food. Sure, at best he'd get no nutrition from its weird Solacian biochemistry, and at worst it would make him violently ill. But it probably tasted *interesting* at least.

He felt slightly guilty thinking this; the rations were at least Silado, no dead flesh or engineered Deisiindr products to make them Ragado. The Newcaste was a closely-allied Compact to his own Carver Nation, and he understood their reasons for avoiding anything too spicy or pungent that might inflame the passions. There were Carvers who did the same, generally ones who leaned closer to the Triune Path's Buddhist roots than its Catholic ones.

Still, perhaps the Newcaste took it a bit too far. Right now he didn't have much to look forward to besides food and forest-watching.. They'd nearly run out of the Carver rations he'd had on him when captured, and after that it would be nothing but a fanatically Sattvic diet for him. He supposed, sourly, that at least his soul would be nice and shiny if these Praedhc decided he was no longer useful and left his corpse to rot in this bizarre alien jungle.

Or, he thought as he eyed one of the strange Praedhc abhounds, perhaps they'd just feed him to their Fathom-touched dogs, dispose of any evidence. Supposedly the creatures shared their senses and to some extent their minds with their handlers; he wondered if the houndmasters ever acquired a taste for raw flesh. He shuddered. It was bad enough having to watch (and smell!) these heathens tear *cooked* flesh off the bone. With their teeth! And often what they were eating didn't even *have* bones. Damn this place. Damn the whole Abwaild for an abomination. He wanted to go home.

Mikinao knew he should simply be grateful to be alive, but it had been a couple of weeks now since his capture and relief tends to stretch thin after a while, even if some of that relief was also for his partner who had managed to escape back to Earthmarch. He felt some fear too, of course, but it was a muted sort of fear. He'd known ever since joining the Abbey Militant that death at the hands of the Praedhc or some Abwaild monster was a pretty good bet for how he'd end this particular incarnation.

So mostly he was annoyed. Annoyed that he'd managed to get himself captured, annoyed that he hadn't had any chance to so much as attempt an escape, annoyed that they kept interrogating him.

And they were usually asking him about things he had no idea about. Okay, so that wasn't entirely true. He had a few ideas, just no concrete information. Rumors and whispers had been sifting their way through the Compact's great web of gossip chains for some time now. Action was being taken against the hated Presilyo, maybe. The resolve of the Caustlanders was being tested, perhaps. Mikinao frowned, and snapped the cracker he was spreading with peanut butter in two.

There were darker, less likely murmurings. Restoration of promises. Shadows of war. Hushed intimations, unorthodox at best, and at worst...it was not wise to ponder too deeply.

The Praedhc was staring at him, Mikinao realized, and averted his own gaze. He didn't like the look on those strange silver-filigree features, and wondered for the thousandth time just how much his captors knew. They might know more than he did, at least about some things, frightening as that thought was. He shoved his annoyance at this possibility down deep with the rest, and tried not to examine it too closely.

Because there was, in some tiny corner of his awareness, annoyance that they were treating him much better than the Abbey Militant or the Many-Nation Army would be likely to treat any of them. *Savages that didn't even have the courtesy to be properly savage.* That same little corner was briefly amused by this thought before he clamped down on it, concentrating on getting the last of his bland meal into his stomach. Chew, let it gloop down into the stomach, don't bother trying to taste it, you're going to miss it when it runs out.

Sei'khasehn Sav'ni'tal knew his scouting party's pet Fallen wasn't happy about what they were feeding him, but he didn't really give a shit. Here, outside the ransacked wedge of Undersky that the Fallen called "Earthmarch" and the Risen called the Incursion, the man was lucky to be eating anything at all.

Besides, they'd captured the bareface bastard scouting a stretch of quartzwood, no doubt intending eventually to burn it down so his fellows could plant and grow more food for their obscenely huge families. That meant smaller hunting grounds, which meant hungry children, which meant it would be justice if the man starved a little. And the nearby vanguard farm belonged to the same Fallen group suspected of causing all this trouble, the one calling themselves the "Carvers," an infuriatingly appropriate name for a people determined to butcher as much of the Undersky as they could. Sympathy for the man was in short supply.

Sei'khasehn stood glowering over the captive as he finished the last of his food. It actually smelled pretty good, and not for the first time he wondered how it tasted. Bland, according to the whiny bareface. And of course it would certainly taste *horrific* coming back up, which was probably the best-case scenario for eating Fallen food. Better back out than through. Quicker.

"You are, ehhsss, finished with your food, yes?" His Gentic was middling, he knew, but serviceable enough, and only one other member of the scouting party spoke any at all.

The man sighed. It was a deep, raspy sigh, a filing-down of the soul, and it annoyed Sei'khasehn beyond measure. He wanted to kick this Fallen jackass. Specifically, he wanted to kick him on the left shoulder, where his uniform sported a stupid, obnoxious patch reading, "Solace is fallen into Fallen hands." Sei'khasehn had considered making him remove the slogan before deciding it served as a useful reminder to both of them.

"Yes," the man said, and swallowed. "Well?"

"We have new information," Sei'khasehn said, "about more of your people's operations against your brother Fallen. The ones who live in the Ashwound. You call this 'The Caustlands,' yes?" The man nodded, his weird, unlined face drawing up tight. Sei'khasehn stifled a smile of his own before continuing. The bareface knew something, at least.

"These operations, they are false...ehhsss..." He frowned as he tried to remember the Gentic word for a fabric pole-symbol, "...'false-flag,' which no surprise we are not happy about, because the false flag is *our* flag. Ehhsss...or maybe the flag of other Risen clans. It is not like your Caustlander targets will care when it is time to retaliate. Even if they did, ehhsss, care...most of them cannot tell the difference."

He leaned in closer, letting his eyes narrow. "But here is the thing. *We* can tell the difference between *you*. And we can tell all the other Risen. Your Fallen of the Ashwound, they could survive retaliation, they have the circle of ash between themselves and us, they are many, but your little tribe, out on the edge of the Incursion..."

He watched the man's dark, trackless skin lose all undertones of color, turning the shade of spoiled meat. Sei'khasehn leaned in closer, letting his face alone tell the story, make the dire promises.

"You had best tell us the truth right now," he said, very quietly. "All of the truth. We, ehhsss, we don't need you badly enough to take this sort of risk. What are you thinking about?"

He waited, and let his mind settle inward beyond the self, settling into the carefully conducted currents of the Fathom. This Fallen fool had only modest facility with the Fathomdance; they'd be able to kill him quickly and with little risk, if it came to that. The bareface knew it, too, and no wonder; half the scouting party were on their feet, hands on hilts and bows and atlatls, looking at him. Two of the dogs growled lightly.

The captive began to shake his head, and then his fear began to shake him.

"Please. No. I am not...I am not dangerous, I was just...there are only rumors."

"More," Sei'khasehn said.

The man stared, hugging himself. It did not keep him from shivering, even in the jungle's muggy heat. His voice went quiet.

"I have names."
"Give them to me."

Chapter 18

"Have you come to the Church of the Left to Right? It's annual again."
"No."
"What have you tried?"
"Everything."
"You can't get her back from what you've done."
"I must."
"No. But maybe you can retrieve your self, or a part of it."
"You can't know that."
"I don't. But you've got nothing else. Come in."
"I won't. They all wear other faces. I can spy the blades."
"You will. Cut out your heart, or you'll never see it."
"There is nothing long or sharp enough for that."

- "The Haunted Father," Baruch Kravitz, *Dreams Under Shadow,* 95 SE

San Inoue, Carver State, The Sovereign Nations, Earthmarch, 350 SE

Juliaen could not concentrate on her reading. The fires had been lit, fulfilled the measure of their creation, and been snuffed out. Earthmarch had carved its way a bit farther into the Abwaild, and her work was done.

Except that work was never done on a farm, not ever. There were gardens to weed, cows to milk, eggs to collect, soil to till. Everything needed to be built, needed to be repaired. Animals fell sick. Strange creatures wandering in from the quartzwood had to be driven away.

And it was not just the work of the farm itself. Siblings had to be watched, Mother had to be cared for, the farmhouse had to be cleaned, be put into the sort of order which drew near to the Divine. Watch had to be stood, hours spent standing by the stark border between the white and purple of the quartzwood and the bare ashy earth of their farm. Hours spent staring out at the Abwaild, at least until the Praedhc scouts ceased appearing on the outskirts of the farm.

At least until the Many Nation Army drove their tribes so far into the Abwaild that they no longer came, she thought, and was wracked with a sudden guilt that stabbed down into the deepest secret hollows of her soul. It was a familiar guilt, but that had not dulled it.

While they drove the Praedhc away from the newly Fallen-claimed land, the Caustlands sat, huge and largely empty, cleansed by Divinely guided fire. And out here in Earthmarch, the true followers of the Triune Path, Divinely-chosen from among the Fallen, did nothing to reclaim their birthright from the profane powers which had not even let the true followers practice their true faith, left them with no choice but to flee the Caustlands after the Presilyo failed to defend them.

Solace is fallen into Fallen hands, she thought bitterly, *and we among them do nothing to claim what we have already been given.*

Well, perhaps not quite nothing, but she was still following the rumors and they had been daunting over the past year or so. There had been some setback, the whispers went; perhaps small, perhaps catastrophic, perhaps something in between. It was bad, though, that was certain, on that they all agreed.

She stared at the ceiling, counting the grain-lines in the rough pine beams. She was supposed to be staring at her scriptures, reading through the Star Sutras. She'd been trying for at least half an hour. Her arms had grown tired of holding up the book, giving up after about the seventeenth time her mind had wandered away from its words and let them go double before her eyes.

She didn't want to focus, that was it, she decided, and rolled over onto her stomach. When she focused, when she let the teachings and parables speak to her spirit, she could not bear it. Every story, every parable and teaching seemed to accuse her, seemed to dash the name Juliaen Draecsl from the Book of Right-Guided Life.

We cannot continue this way. We cannot push the Praedhc from their homes, no matter how benighted. Not when the Divine has given us the Caustlands for an inheritance. The Caustlands are for us the Fallen, but the other Fallen have lost their way. They must come to the Triune Path, they must accept the Right Guidance of the Enlightening Spirit, they must—

No.

It came into her head, this voice, like the sudden thunder of a red-moon squall. It was heavy and inexorable in its entrance, shining with a nimbus of hard golden light. It was not her own voice, it could not be, was not even in her head but somewhere deeper, crashing into the sheltered bed of embers that caught flame into thought.

what—? Her response was small and floundering, the dimmest of sparks next to the blazing, graven missive it utterly failed to answer.

All must go their Way, their own given Way. The Triune Path is the highest Way, but it is not for all, cannot be for all, not all are ready, not all souls are prepared. We have spoken, through the Holy Fathom We have spoken, but not all will hear and not all can. You must place them on their Way, lesser or true. Even the Praedhc have their given Way.

She could not believe it, but she had to believe it. Its light surely surged up into her from the farthest reaches of the Holy Fathom. Its voice was not her own.

Juliaen saw, like a flash of long-bottled light. She saw the Praedhc tribes, their varied ways, their varied peoples, saw how many had been pushed or pulled from their given Way by the invading Fallen, and was ashamed. She saw the Fallen themselves, the Fallen of the Caustlands, going about their lives as they pleased. Some cared about their Way, did their best to follow it, but most did not, or only sometimes, or only in some things. They lived everything halfway.

They do not tolerate true Ways, even lesser Ways. They do not tolerate Our highest Way, the true Triune Path.

The voice struck its imprint into her soul like written stone. She knew it was true. She knew because she had thought on it, thought on it long and hard, prayed and meditated and raged on it, and now here was this Voice to confirm it. Those who truly believed in something, would stand for something, whose societies would *demand* something from them, they had fled or been driven to Earthmarch. One way or another, the Caustland States would not let them teach their children as they pleased, would not countenance any order and discipline but their own. All those who dared to live true had the choice of persecution or exile.

And the faithful of the Triune Path, the Carvers, *her* people, they were among them, one among the many Sovereign Nations, while apostates and pretenders claimed the title of Michyero under the venal sway of the Presilyo. Their monks and nuns marched with profane forces, and those forces were vast. She saw them, with their ranks and banners and elite Haeliiy detachments. Inhuman creatures flew above their heads and stalked between their feet.

we can do nothing they are too many

Even in the smallness of her own human mind this seemed wispy and weak, low and unworthy. She felt the joints and sinew of her mortality clench and brace against the coming answer.

Is this how Our Boddhisanto Moses answered Our call in the Stone Sutra?

She had no answer.

Yes. He also was mortal. He also doubted before the might of great nations.

No more needed to be said. She knew the story. She remembered the breaking of shackles, the breaking of captors, the breaking of all who stood in the way of Divine Promise. And it was good that there need be no more, because she thought she could not stand more, not now, not if her mind was to remain whole. That voice it—

Juliaen woke up.

Her hand still rested on her book. In her book, really, still keeping her place, the smooth feel of thin paper against her skin. Her face was half-buried in her pillow, and she turned her head to breathe easier. Not, she thought momentarily, the most dignified position in which to hear the voice of the Divine. She squashed the thought. The Divine would speak as They would, and anyway was she sure that's what it had been?

Yes. She had to be.

Her sleep had consumed all of the time she had set aside for prayer and study plus a bit more. It was good that it had not lasted even longer; there was still much work to do.

She did not mention the dream to her father. When she passed by him on her way to see a sick cow, she kept her silence. The look he gave her was slightly concerned, his simple greeting somehow turned up into a question. She returned his greeting, and some but not all of the concern dropped out of his demeanor. He must think she was simply having one of her headaches.

She did not mention the dream to Saimn as she helped him repair one of the farm's outer fences, he armed with an axe and she only with the Holy Fathom, taking turns keeping watch for whatever might come out of the Abwaild.

She did not mention it to anyone at supper that night. Susaen asked if she was all right. Juliaen told her sister that she was, just had a lot she was thinking about.

Susaen nodded at this with a six-year-old's easy acceptance of things she did not really understand, but then followed up with a six-year-old's insatiable and apparently random curiosity. "What are you thinking about, Juliaen?" She bounced on the bench, dabbing at the small puddle of soup that had spilled from bowl to plate with a piece of crusty roll.

Juliaen frowned, knowing how what she was going to say would sound. Even as the Draecsl sibling most well-known for her piety (and self-righteousness at times, she knew that, knew how they talked about her sometimes, she wasn't stupid), it seemed like it may be a bit much. Never mind, it was true.

"The Divine, Susaen. Wipe your mouth, you've got soup and crumbs on your chin."

"Aren't we supposed to think about the Divine all the time?" Susaen asked, making a desultory swipe at her face with a napkin.

"Yes." Juliaen sighed. "I'm just thinking about something specific. You'll find out tomorrow, okay? Some of it at least. I promise." And as she promised, she knew it was true. Tomorrow, tomorrow she would share some of what the Divine had imparted.

Tomorrow she would act.

She dreamed again that night. She almost always did, lately. Often the dreams were powerful, but seemed to have little sense to them, or only made sense much later. Sometimes they were forgotten, or seemed to have been forgotten until suddenly they would make themselves clear in the middle of the day, swimming up from deepest memory to find their place in the stream of her thoughts. On occasion they were meaningful, sweetly clear but brief, a single snippet of vision or wisdom, shining out from the morass of pointless absurdities formed by more ordinary dreams.

This dream was different. It was clear, like the very first dream she had had nearly a year before, that night after the long burn, that night she had dream-witnessed Starfall in all its terrible glory.

She was high up, though she seemed to have no self, only a far-ranging awareness, taking in the whole of the Caustlands and Earthmarch along with great alien stretches of Abwaild. It glittered in the broad spread of the noonday sun, its five mighty rivers running silver in the embrace of their forks and tributaries— a great earthen disc shattered by the immeasurable power of the Divine, by the Earthseed as Their instrument.

She could not see the Presilyo, though she knew where it was, sprawled out on a river island between Tenggara and Salía. She would not know much about what it looked like; she had never seen the Presilyo with her own eyes. For that matter, she had only the word of her parents and older brother that she had ever seen Salía, where she had been born.

Still Juliaen thought she could feel the corruption emanating out from Inoue Island, from the blasphemous institution it carried on its back, Divinely-promised ground groaning with the weight of tainted buildings and Ragado footfalls.

She saw them then, the Somonei, or rather she knew them, knew the errands they kept wherever the promise of Caustland currency or their own corrupt ends might send them. This was nothing new; it was a common theme in her dreams, especially since the Promiseguard had caught the Somonei spy a few months before and spilled her blood all over the stones of Clarcspur's central plaza. Juliaen had stood solemnly and watched that night as the woman's remains burned on a tall pyre built over the bloodstains.

The smell had been beyond foul. Juliaen had wondered idly if this was what all cooked flesh smelled like. She knew her father had eaten flesh before joining the Triune Path, before learning that it was an abomination to do so, but she had not been about to ask him.

We pray that the lessons the Divine intend for her in this life will mark her soul in those to come, Juliaen thought. In her dream, she realized she had watched the whole thing again, had relived that time standing in the waft and scent of human ashes. Only now the pyre was not one gathered blaze of flames but a great spreading conflagration that spread throughout the Caustlands, scattering cleansing embers in its wake.

It came out of Earthmarch. It came out of Earthmarch, and some of it spread round the edges of the Siinlan through the Abwaild, crossing the Gyring Ash here and there to purify, to make everything white with flame. Corruption fell away in blackened drifting motes, faded.

Bring them back to pure Ways.

but i

We have purified the ground of the Caustlands with fire.

i am no warrior i lead no army i

We shall purify their souls.

i will follow you i am not worthy i

The Caustlands are Our gift. Accept them.

Juliaen woke.

She told Father she had business in Clarcspur. He wanted to know what it was. A shopping trip? Visiting a friend? There was a note of hope in this last. She knew he worried both about her solitary ways and her apparent lack of interest in any romantic prospects. She had assured him, awkwardly, that she did find men attractive but simply did not think now was the time for such things.

When might actually be the time for such things, she did not know herself. Best to avoid temptation, for now, because it was true, she knew that feeling that drew female to male, woman to man, yin to yang, had done her best to pray it away a thousand times when she felt some thought or bodily sensation had wandered into the realm of the Ragado. Perhaps some part of her knew there were other purposes to these early years of her life. Not perhaps, she was sure. Now was time to act.

So she told him no, it was not a shopping trip, or an outing to see a friend. She told him that she wanted to take a pilgrimage to the stupa, and this was true, but it was not the main reason she was going.

She left a note behind. It said enough.

It was a long walk, but a familiar one; at twenty-one kilometers, it usually took her about four hours. The family had a pair of horses for the occasional solo trip, but she did not wish to ride. She thought, somehow, that this journey to Clarcspur was something she must do alone, something she must do unassisted. She told Father that she thought the horses ought to be kept in reserve; what if there was some sort of emergency, a problem with Mother, an accident, a threat from the Abwaild?

"We can always send an echogram," Father had told her. He was right, of course; the message would cross the twelve kilometers to the nearest outpost in less than a minute. Sure, she had conceded, but what if something happens to the family echogram tablet? It had been dearly bought and they did not have a backup. What if the outpost was not listening? What if...

Father had looked at her strangely, had shaken his head, but he had let her go without further protest. Perhaps he had some deep-down understanding of her true purpose. Perhaps he simply knew better than to try to stand in her way when a certain look was in her eye.

She considered all this on her journey, long legs moving her along the packed-earth path in a quick rhythm of their own making. She could see a long way; there had been no time for Fallen forest to fill in for incinerated Abwaild, as it had here and there in the Caustlands, and the few hills were gentle ones. It was all farms— farms of crops, farms of grassland, farms of seedlings, all ready to sprout into a new Eden. All grey-and-green, growth-and-ashes.

Juliaen saw only a few people on her journey: the ragtag irregulars of the outpost, an occasional farmer spotted far-off over expansive fields, a single traveler going the other way with a timelift handcart, laden with an assortment of Silado goods and groceries. They were all Carvers, all brother and sister Michyeros, no traders or travelers from other parts of the Sovereign Nations.

The irregulars had hailed her cheerfully, clearly disappointed when she did not stop to chat and liven up the brutal monotony of guard duty. The timelift cart she had seen coming hundreds of meters off, but she did not need to see; the weird, languorous ripples sent through the Holy Fathom by its temporal bubble were unmistakable. When she drew close, she waved, and the man pulling the cart waved back, letting go of one handle for a moment.

"Divine see you right on your way, in this life and those to come," she said.

"Divine bless you," he returned, looking slightly surprised at her long formal greeting. She gave him the most disarming smile she could manage in her distracted state. She knew her height sometimes made even average-sized men uncomfortable. This man was on the short side, and she towered over him.

Juliaen nodded at him, then looked off into the distance as they passed each other by. She felt the cold, compact warping of the timelift cart's inner compartment, at once slowing time enough to keep the man's goods fresh and lessening Solace's pull on their bulk. It was a well-made cart, and must be very easy for the man to pull.

If this can be accomplished through Our Holy Fathom, imagine the great loads We may allow you to bear.

Juliaen cried out softly, and put her hand to her head. It hurt. She had forgotten the sheer power of that voice, the thundering echoes it left behind in every recess of her self.

"Are you quite alright, ma'am?" The man had set his cart down, letting it rest leaned forward on its handles.

"Oh...yes...I am sorry," she said, then drew herself up from the slight stoop her sudden pain had brought on. "Just a headache. I get them from time to time. They're no…" and then she remembered that she must not lie, especially not when on an errand like this one. "...they're no trouble I cannot handle. Thank you for your concern."

He nodded slowly, though his dark green eyes looked troubled. She attempted another disarming smile and moved on.

She saw Clarespur long before she arrived, sprawled out over its huge muddy hill, built around the great springrise that watered it. A gift of the Divine to the Carvers, cast out into the wilderness by Presilero heresy.

As she approached the familiar Carver capital, a feeling of immense peace passed over her, peace and the anticipation of hardship, even of pain. She had never felt anything quite like it; it soaked through the heavy fabric of her soul, colored everything with a bright, bearable ache.

She knew exactly where to go, had been there a dozen times before on small pilgrimages. The Nave of the Abbey Invisible, a great three-sided pyramid with a low, rectangular wing extending off each edge. As she climbed the wide stone steps, a small smile crossed her lips. This was where she was meant to be. Pushing past the big stone door revealed a lofty, angular space, thronged with worshippers and pilgrims.

"My name is Juliaen Draecsl," she told the priest as he welcomed her into the Nave's three-cornered Great Hall. "I need to speak with Lidia

Almeida."

The old man just looked at her, tugging at the grey fabric of his robe. "I am sorry, Sister, but—"

Juliaen did not have time for this. "My name is Juliaen Draecsl, and I need to speak with Lidia Almeida. It is important. I have a message for her that she will need to hear."

The priest held out a hand, palm up. "I can take it to her, when there is time."

Juliaen held his gaze, and was gratified to see him take a step back, his light brown eyes widening beneath hazy-grey brows.

"There is no time," Juliaen said simply. "It must be now. And I am not carrying it. I must give it to her directly."

The old man looked left, looked right, seemed to be plotting an escape, or perhaps hoping to catch the eye of one of the soot-robed Promiseguard that served as Nave security.

She stepped forward, calm, intent, leaving them only centimeters apart, looking down into the lined and weathered bronze of his face.

"I am no danger to you. I am not armed, and I am not mad. I must speak to Lidia Almeida. I do not care what she is doing, or what any of your bureaucratic procedures might be. The Divine must take priority."

It took a moment for the implications of her words to sink in.

"Sister," the priest said, now openly raising one hand, index finger extended as he looked around for the nearest Promiseguard, "that is not how—"

"The Divine work however They see fit," Juliaen said. "Especially in times like these. I have heard the whispers, heard them for years. I have heard the Divine. I know who she is. I know what I must tell her, and I will see her."

The old priest had finally managed to summon one of the Promiseguard. The dark-robed man came and stood beside her, put a hand on her shoulder. She turned to look down at him. Glare, really, she supposed. The guard seemed taken aback. *Good.*

"I am not armed," she told the Promiseguard. "I am no threat. My name is Juliaen Draecsl, and I must speak with Lidia Almeida."

The soot-robed man looked her up and down, earning another glare from her before she realized the once-over was for security, not carnal interest. Her clothing was practical and loose, and she supposed it might be possible for her to conceal something dangerous beneath them, though she did not know much about such matters.

Probably he had other ways of checking. She knew that the Promiseguard were all trained in the sacred mysteries of the Holy Fathom, and it seemed a likely technique for them to know. She certainly had no ability to counteract such a thing. As she thought this, she could feel the brush of questioning, conscious tendrils, sense the man's commanding presence, and knew that he must see her as well. Only the Divine could touch a mortal mind through the Holy Fathom, but surely he could see she had nothing threatening on her person.

"She is an Adept of some sort, Father," the Promiseguard said, "but she is telling the truth about not being armed."

"I am a simple Fireguide," Juliaen said. "I am not a warrior. I have never turned the Holy Fathom against anything more than stray xeno-creatures. My family has been homesteading and pushing back the Abwaild for many years. We have helped to found more than a dozen farms since we arrived as converts from Salía." Though they probably already guessed her origin from her accent and gold-blonde hair.

"Master Almeida is busy." The priest gave the Promiseguard a meaningful look, then glanced over toward one of the Nave's outer wings. Nodding slightly, the guard turned on his heel and headed in that direction. "Perhaps, sister, if you wait, I can go speak with her and, if she approves it, one of the Promiseguard can escort you to speak with her about your...thoughts."

Juliaen heard the condescension in his voice, and scowled. She did not bother to answer, but instead followed the guard as he headed toward what she hoped would be Lidia's quarters or office. He walked quickly, just short of a run, but with her longer legs she managed to catch up without resorting to running herself, taking the steps at the edge of the Nave two at a time.

He turned sharply once they both reached the top of the steps. "What are you doing?"

It was, she thought, a fairly stupid question, but she let that pass. "I am following you. To see Master Almeida." She had raised her voice some to say this, and others in the Nave were starting to take notice.

"Master Almeida," the Promiseguard said, the hint of a growl in voice, "will see you when she is ready to do so, *if* she decides to see you at all."

Most of the Nave was paying attention now. Juliaen turned to look at them, let her gaze sweep over the small gathered crowd. *They will speak of this moment later,* she thought, *tell people that they were here, that they remember. Some who are not here now will lie and say that they were. This crowd will become hundreds, not dozens, in the retelling.*

She let her voice boom out through the Nave. It was a good voice, she knew, a strong one that could carry songs of praise over an entire congregation, or call her siblings to dinner from all corners of the farm.

"I bear a message from the Divine," she said, and she knew she could feel that voice, that crushing, inward-but-not-inner voice, giving strength to her own, her words calm and clear and sure.

Everyone in the Nave was looking her way now, and she fell silent, simply looked out over the scattered crowd of priests and pilgrims, staff and Promiseguard. Her pursuit had brought her up onto the high balcony that ringed the Nave's three sides, and she had an excellent view. For a fleeting moment she wondered how she must look to them, standing just behind the elaborate railing, two meters or more above the main floor, the tunnels and doors behind her leading to a tight warren of quarters and offices and smaller chapels.

Speak.

She felt her body go rigid, her eyes rolling upward a moment. Her arms rose at her sides, trembled. The Holy Fathom roiled around her, and she could sense the Promiseguard on all sides preparing defenses, preparing to strike, but it stilled, and then she obeyed.

"I am here to speak with Lidia Almeida!" she called out. Confusion; this is not what they had expected. She was not sure, exactly, what it was they *were* expecting. The mad ramblings of the deluded? Some pat piece of sermonizing about mindfulness or obedience to the currents of Divine Will?

"We cannot fully tread the Triune Path out here in Earthmarch, pushing our way out into the Abwaild when the Divine Gift, the Divinely-cleansed Caustlands, lies at our backs! Cleansed for our inheritance, corrupted by our heresy!"

She spun to face the Promiseguard as he stepped toward her. He intended to take her into custody; that much was clear even to her. She held her gaze on him.

"This man, wearing the flame-cleansed robes of Divine Promise, would dare lay his hands on me, would dare silence the word of the Divine because he cannot see beyond its vessel!"

The words roared out of her like fire, and for a high hanging moment she was sure that she had won, that we would take her to see Lidia, that the crowd would join its will with revelation.

But no.

Several in the crowd audibly scoffed. She saw one woman roll her eyes. People muttered. A few looked thoughtful, and she held onto that shred of hope as the Promiseguard laid his hands on her, holding her arm, guiding her away with one hand at the small of her back. One of his comrades stood ready at her other side, and she knew there was nothing she could do.

"You are disturbing the peace of the Nave, Sister," the guard holding her arm said. "You will be silent, or you will be tried for heresy. You're not the first would-be prophet in this place, and the Archabbot has had his fill of it."

Juliaen fell silent, feeling the need to speak subside, pool deep within her, gathering strength for another time. She was disappointed, but her disappointment was buoyed by a deep current of peace. She had said what she needed to say, done what was required of her. She allowed herself to be led to a set of rough stone stairs. All now was in the hands of the Divine.

And she was in the hands of the Promiseguard. More specifically, she was in one of their cells. Juliaen hadn't known before that the Nave had dungeons, but she certainly knew it now. It was a dank, earthen-smelling space, and the indifferently-lain masonry of its floor was wet with uneven pools and rivulets of groundwater. Given that it was dug into Clarcspur's great springrise hill, she supposed that shouldn't really be a surprise.

She sat on the chain-suspended plank that passed for a bunk, and watched the minute flows and eddies play over the assortment of poorly-fitted flagstones, dripping through the gaps in their joining that served as the dungeon's only drains. Her legs were drawn up under her, feet pressed down against the worn wood by her weight. They'd taken away her boots, claiming that the laces could be used for self-harm, and Juliaen did not wish to wet her bare feet. It was cold enough already.

There were ways to warm herself, but she'd be mad to use them. The jailers knew that she was an Adept if not really a Haeliiy, and so were keeping a close watch on her. Should she attempt to let her mind find its harmony with the Holy Fathom in any way...well, she'd rather not find out.

She had begun toying with the idea of asking for a blanket—surely she would not be expected to sleep on this horrible plank without at least a rag of scratchy, lumpy wool—when she heard a ringing metallic *clang* and looked up. One of the jailers, a skinny, ratlike man with twitchy, sneering eyes, had given the bars a whack with his truncheon.

Juliaen said nothing, just looked up, steadily holding the man's shifty mudpool gaze.

"Someone's here to see you, more important than you deserve, madwoman. You best behave or Master Arturo here," he jerked both his head and thumb toward a big man in armored Promiseguard robes, "will set you on fire right where you sit. You hear it?"

Juliaen inclined her head with all the dignity and grace she could muster, and the man scowled. He fingered his truncheon, but then his eyes darted there-and-back and he jammed the wood-and-metal stick into his belt with a surly drop of his arm. "Right, here she comes."

A woman approached Juliaen's cell, pausing to turn and speak with one of the guards. She was tall, though still a fair bit shorter than Juliaen, and had long dark hair gathered down into a simple but immaculate braid that reached nearly to the small of her back. Grey robes hinted at subtle strength and slight curves. She reached Juliaen's cell, clasping her hands together as she learned forward.

She was pretty, despite the small scars that showed here and there on her arms and face, or perhaps even because of them. Her face was lined more with wear than with time; approaching middle age, probably in her early seventies. Golden-brown eyes peered into the cell with watchful curiosity, and as Juliaen looked back she thought, *this woman has seen more than she would like, and much of it her own doing. Can it be—?*

"Hello, Juliaen Draecsl," the woman said. "I am Lidia Almeida, High Winnow of the Triune Path, former Somonei of the Presilyo Ri'Granha. You wanted to see me."

Chapter 19

"War is Hell" has been a popular saying for a long, long time, but it's really quite a misleading one. "Hell" has a kind of glamor to it, a sort of defiant swagger. It's got style. Think of all the other catchphrases and expressions it is attached to: "I'll see you in Hell," "Come Hell or high water," "It'll be a cold day in Hell," "Give 'em Hell!" and so on. None of this comes close to describing the grey, mindless grind of war. It's got too much shine; it hasn't enough vicious pointlessness.

No, war is shit. Generations have thrilled to long lurid descriptions of Hell, but shit has none of this otherworldly cachet. It's just shit. It's filthy, it's common, and it stinks. Wading through Hell has a certain glory to it; wading through shit has only stench and disgust. To dine in Hell shows audacity; to dine in shit, only horror and blight. I am not, be very sure, saying that war is never necessary; I am no pacifist. I am saying only that we should see war for what it is, and that there is never any excuse to revel in excrement.

- Deiviid Castnr, *On the Boundaries of Peace*, 43 SE

Presilyo Monastery, Inoue Island, The Caustlands, 350-354 SE

Sanyago watched the days go by, and was pulled along with them. He marked the weeks, the months, the seasons, settled into their rhythms, paying more and more mind as he grew older. He changed, and watched his brothers change, watched Laris change. They all grew, Laris reaching just past two meters, Sanyago ending up more than a third of a meter shorter than his friend. Voices broke and deepened.

They began to shave their faces in the same way as their heads. Sanyago felt the push and tug of transition as keenly as anyone, feeling his meditations come unmoored within newly muddled swirls of emotion, flailing to adjust. He confessed this to Father Kuwat, who he and Laris continued to see—though less and less often.

"You'll make it through, Sanyago," the priest told him. "The self moves swiftly in such a time, and the mind must bend with alacrity. Do not allow your soul to become either uprooted or rigid."

Sanyago did his best.

The Presilyo did not change around him, or did not change much, not since the repairs made after the Return of the Apostates. At least, Sanyago didn't think it did, not really—but it changed for him, the Presilyo he kept held up to the light inside his head became something different. He saw new parts of it, saw old ones differently, made connections he hadn't before. He understood more of what he heard. He wasn't sure he was happy about this.

He'd expected war, after the attack, thought perhaps they'd all march out into the Sovereign Nations even though just then the thought of more fighting, real fighting, left him sick to his core.

But it hadn't happened. The teachers told them revenge was contrary to the Triune Path. The things he overheard told him the Presilyo had made a political counterattack as a martial one wasn't feasible, leveraging the horror and outrage felt by many in the Caustlands at the indiscriminate nature of the raid, especially the death of children. Now the Carvers were under "sanctions;" he'd needed Laris to explain that word to him, and still wasn't sure he fully understood.

So there was no great war, only the endless small ones the Presilyo had been fighting for generations. Helping to fight bandits and creatures and criminals, hunting down monsters both human and otherwise.

Monks and nuns left for missions and came back, but now Sanyago understood the excitement and uncertainty curling beneath stoic bravado as they went, felt how they wrestled them under like Jacob and the angel in the Stone Sutras. He saw the deeds they brought back with them, the death they witnessed and dealt, saw it all under the monkish mask of serenity.

"They're afraid," Sanyago had told Laris one day as they watched a pair of Somonei ready themselves to depart. Laris had nodded.

"They're not supposed to be afraid," Sanyago had insisted, and Laris had shrugged.

"They're not supposed to be a lot of things."

Most of their class graduated from Novice to Zagen. Laris took up Gathering Deep as his dedicated style, eschewing weapons and armor training almost completely. Sanyago continued to study the wu jian, putting in untold hours with the long slender blade. He learned to make good use of his free hand for grappling, thrown weapons, and quick combat spellcasting.

He tried not to think too hard on what he would use any of this for, and he pushed the man with the butterfly swords further and further away. Into acceptance, he hoped, or at least detente.

Bai lost interest in Laris, but not until he was well over the age of sixteen. Sanyago did not really know the extent of what had happened between them. Laris had not said much about it, perhaps partly because of its painful intimacy, and partly because he said he wished to forget it. Sanyago did not think that would be possible, but he did not press his friend, and had to content himself with the queasy, oily relief he felt at seeing the end of it.

Sanyago himself had not lost interest in Hyon-seok, nor Hyon-seok with him. He did feel guilty about it, though he wasn't sure whether Hyon-seok did. He prayed a lot, and that hurt sometimes, and he took refuge in his ancient and unshakeable belief that the Triune Path and the rules of the Presilyo were not one and the same, must not be.

Divine forgive me.

He and Hyon-seok didn't talk about that, not anymore, and in any case it certainly didn't stop them.

What they were doing wasn't uncommon among the boys of the Presilyo, but most of them seemed to consider it something second-rate, something to sate the sudden hungers of dawning adulthood; bread and water instead of curry and milk. Sanyago didn't see it that way, and knew he was different, and knew Hyon-seok was too.

Of course Laris knew. Mostly he seemed amused. In one of his less guarded moments, he'd nodded toward Sanyago, and then Hyon-seok.

"At least you're getting the sort of thing you want, without too many complications."

This was a very Laris sort of thing to say, and Sanyago wondered if his friend knew how much he'd revealed by saying it. Whatever had been going on with Bai, Sanyago was pretty sure that Laris didn't precisely fail to enjoy it, and also that this troubled him. When things finally ended with Bai, he'd seemed at once frustrated and relieved, and for a few weeks had been exceptionally brooding and self-contained even by Laris standards.

When he found out later she'd kept the whole thing going by threatening to report Laris for "crimes against Chastity," Sanyago had earned a rebuke for breaking both his training sword and a target dummy in half with an especially undisciplined Fathom-assisted swing of the wooden weapon.

It was over, that was the important thing. Laris would, Sanyago hoped, be alright. As alright as could be expected, maybe. Shit, he didn't know, and hated how little he could do about it. He drew Laris out when he could, and Laris seemed grateful, and he listened to Sanyago's own troubles and helped when he could and wasn't that what being brothers really meant?

Sanyago supposed he didn't really know that either; probably the Presilyo's ideal of a brother-Zagen would have told the teachers all about Sanyago sneaking off with Hyon-seok and Laris' heretical skepticism. No thanks. This was the sort of brotherhood he wanted, the sort of brother he had, and he was grateful.

He was grateful for a lot of things, when he really thought about it. He had survived where others had not, had a brother and a...whatever Hyon-seok was, he and Laris were doing very well in their training, and they would graduate to become Somonei if things kept going as they were.

Things were going well, he supposed. But he watched as the Somonei left and came back, saw them train, saw himself train, tended to his meditations, lent his voice to chant and chorus; listening as always to the rushing cycle of violence and serenity that was the heartbeat of the Presilyo. And he was unsure.

One day in their seventeenth year, he decided to ask Laris about it. It was late summer, only just beginning to reach a comfortable coolness during their evening training sessions. A light breeze skirted over grass and sand and cobble, the flagstones where they sat still warm with fading sunlight. They watched the complicated scenario setup out on the training pitch with only mild interest.

"Laris," Sanyago said, closing one eye momentarily in thought, "what do you think we'll do when we become Somonei? What will you do?"

Laris turned toward him, wiping the lingering sweat off his deep-black skin as his steel-grey eyes glanced here and there in thought. "We finish out our seven years of service. Same as we would if we'd become priests, or floor-sweeps, or cooks." His voice had grown into a soft, even tenor, just a touch lower than Sanyago's, though he didn't have the same knack for song.

"Sure, that," Sanyago said dismissively. He did not say that they could also simply leave as soon as the Presilyo gave them papers certifying they were of age, walk away the moment they first crossed the Mindao as adults. They would be labeled apostates, and never allowed back onto Inoue Island, and they would be penniless— but they could not be stopped. Presilyo law applied only on Presilyo grounds. Sanyago didn't know how often this happened, but he guessed not very.

Laris gave him a look that seemed to know exactly what he was thinking, the way he seemed to know Sanyago's next move when they sparred. Though of course he couldn't, not really, only the Divine could pry into the mortal mind.

Laris shrugged, lowering his voice. "We'll see, of course. They don't tell us enough to decide anything now. Not anything smart."

Sanyago scoffed quietly. "They tell us it's dangerous out there in the Caustlands, and even you believe that."

A slow, solemn nod. "I do. And maybe I'll decide ours really is a noble cause. Maybe the Divine will speak to me, I don't know. Even if I'm not sure, killing monsters and bandits? I think I'm okay with that. If,"—he lowered his voice even more—"they're telling the whole truth about it."

Sparring Master Silva had arrived at the training pitch, and was gesturing at the other monks in unrestrained irritation. It was hard to make out any words, though the phrase "not real tradition, just especially stubborn stupidity" was vehement enough to be clear.

"They're not plotting some crazy secret war or anything, Laris," Sanyago said, trying to stave off some of his exasperation so it wouldn't creep into his voice. "But...either way. You've seen what it does to people right? Some of them, anyway. And I still remember the attack, I can't forget it. I know it won't be the same, we'll be armed and we'll be ready—" he smiled wryly, looked around to see who might be watching, and punched Laris very lightly on the arm, "—I mean, you probably won't be armed, but whatever. Thing is, I do want adventure, I wanna get off this island, but I don't...I don't want to watch anyone else die again. Especially not my friends."

Especially not you, he didn't say, *not the only family I've really ever had. And not Hyon-seok. Not any of the other boys from our class either, they're still brothers, even if they're not brothers like we are.*

"Yeah. I know," Laris said. "Thing is, someone's got to do it, you know? It's true there's plenty that needs fighting out there." His mouth drew down, and his grey eyes went unfocused for a moment. "Not just monsters, the bandits too."

Sanyago remembered how Laris' parents had died, and held his tongue.

"And it's not as though anywhere is safe, Sanyago." Laris' posture was straight and still, even for him. "You don't have to go out looking for trouble to find it. What happened to us back during the Return? We weren't doing anything. We saw what we saw anyway, and we had to fight. Fight or die or run."

"Yeah," Sanyago said softly. "Yeah, I know you're right. Still, though. We'll be fighting on purpose."

"So someone else doesn't have to, maybe," Laris replied. "So someone else doesn't have to...watch. Or be told later."

Sanyago kept his peace, wondering what that had been like, how much Laris really remembered or had understood, and then let the thought float away again. It would do him no good.

Laris tilted his head, his dark, angular features taking on a solemn cast. "And we're good, Sanyago. That's not bragging, you know it's true. The teachers know it also, they—"

"They're worried about us," Sanyago cut in, surprising himself. So much, in fact, that he didn't follow up the words, and Laris was left just looking at him expectantly.

"I, um, I overheard some of them talking," Sanyago said, a bit sheepishly.

Laris laughed. It was almost a reflex by now, that laugh, equal parts affection, irritation, and ancient resignation. "Where were you eavesdropping, exactly?"

"You know I've mostly stopped doing that!" Sanyago said, frowning. When Laris just looked at him steadily, he deflated. "Fine, yeah, 'mostly stopped,' I know what you're going to say. I was careful, I always am, they haven't caught me in like two years—"

The slightest hint of a smile trickled up into the edges of those calm grey eyes. Sanyago cleared his throat and pretended to ignore it.

"—yeah, well, anyway, they were talking about us. Not just "the students," us, or even "the Zagen" us. Us. You and me."

Laris' fine black brows rose slowly, eyes widening. "Okay. And...?"

"They, uh, know about me and Hyon-seok, for one thing. They don't do anything because I guess that kind of thing happens all the time here and they don't want to single me out." Sanyago frowned. "They didn't say anything about you and Bai."

Laris pressed his lips together into a crooked line, and looked aside for a moment.

Sanyago pressed on, measuring out his words. "They know some about you doubting. I mean, I know you've been careful, they seemed to be hoping maybe you'd changed your mind, maybe you'd started to...understand I guess."

"Hmmm." Laris sounded almost amused now. "As long as they don't give me any trouble over it, I think that's about the best I can hope for." He nudged Sanyago gently with his shoulder. "I hope they don't give you any trouble, though, about..." he glanced right, glanced left, an almost unconscious instinct for both of them by now, "...Hyon-seok. You know *I* don't care."

Laris always seemed to be at pains to tell him that; Sanyago figured it was his attempt to counter the fact that the teachers, especially the more theologically-inclined among them, cared very much. *Or at least they say they do. I guess they're willing to overlook a lot if it's...I don't know, convenient? Important?* He found that fact somewhat disturbing, even if it was convenient for *him*.

A great round of hypocrisy that just turns round and round with the years, covering itself up with every turn. He pushed the thought aside, or at least stashed it away. It was the sort of thing Laris might say. He respected his friend, but he didn't think the hypocrisy threaded through the Presilyo made what they taught untrue or worthless. At least they were trying to improve themselves here, push toward becoming better people, enact a little good in the world.

They were also still trying to set up a proper training scenario, and

Sanyago snickered as one of the lower-ranking monks assisting tripped over a boundary cord and let out a burst of lyrical Common profanity before clamping his mouth shut with a look of horror. Someone was going to have a bad evening.

"Yeah, I know you don't care," Sanyago said after the long pause, and sighed, thinking about all the trouble he and Hyon-seok were supposed to be in but weren't. "Sorry, I was thinking. I'm not sure just how much I care myself, yet. I mean, I do believe, but..." He trailed off, turning both palms up on his knees.

Laris nodded. "Look, brother, believe what you believe, but don't hurt yourself with it, you know?"

That made him blink, turn his head. "You say the strangest things...no, that's not fair, I'm sorry. I'll...I'll think about that, brother."

They sat in silence, watching. Sanyago snorted; two of the teachers were quietly arguing about the placement of the low walls and training dummies, while Master Silva stalked the outskirts of the training pitch like a cat with freshly-sharpened claws.

Sanyago shifted on the flagstones, stretched out and re-folded his legs. "They're worried about us because we're important to them. I'm not bragging, brother, it's what I heard. And it wasn't just the way they talked about us, one of them actually came out and said it. Master Silva. There were three of them, all in the Boddhisanto Domingo chapel."

Laris burst out laughing, a rare event that drew a few looks from the other students. He shrugged it off, and they went back to their own conversations; fortunately, the teachers were still too involved in their training fiasco to pay him any mind. "The one you used to climb all the time?" he said, lowering his voice even more and leaning in toward Sanyago. "You've gone from shimmying up the steeple to, what, putting your ear to the windows."

"No," Sanyago said, closing one eye and squinting up at the taller boy, "I was up in the rafters."

Laris' shoulders shook as he leaned forward, stifling his laughter. "What were you going to do if they looked up? Drop down and run out the door? Try to crash through a window and hope the Somonei didn't notice the Zagen running through the grounds with bits of stained glass sticking out of his robes?"

Sanyago snorted and flicked his middle finger Laris' way. "I'd just get caught. I'd tell them some crowshit story about how I was just practicing, they wouldn't believe me, I'd get caned a few times, life would go on. No risk, no reward."

"Might be worse than that if they catch you listening in on something really important." Laris glanced over at the practice pitch and shook his head. No sign of any serious progress. Two small groups of teachers were in contention now, doing their best to hide the argument's escalating vehemence from any onlookers and not doing a very good job. "Listen. I'm serious, don't push your risks like this. At least be somewhere you have a vaguely plausible reason to go to."

"I'll keep that in mind," Sanyago said, and he half meant it. "But hey, look, I mean listen. You gotta hear what they were saying, what Sparring Master Silva said. He said we were both the best they'd seen in years, and they went through a lot of trouble to put us together."

Laris rocked slowly back and forth as he took this in, a sort of full-body nod. "Okay. But we knew that already, right? I mean, yeah, humility and all that, but we're not stupid. We never lose except to each other." They both fell into silent thought.

You mean you never lose, and I never lose except to you, Sanyago thought. Though really that was only on the one-on-one sparring field. Neither of them were top in everything, not even close. Sanyago, for example, had trouble coordinating with others in group combat training, and was even worse when he was supposed to be the one doing the coordination. He'd overheard teachers talking about it, too. "He's plenty charismatic, but that's not very useful when he can't give good timely orders." Laris, for his part, struggled to adapt when not given time to carefully analyze a concept or situation, which could make him lag behind at first.

Straightening up, Laris went on. "We knew they put us together on purpose, but we're the same age, it's not like that was hard. What were we going to do, say no?"

Very slowly, Sanyago shook his head. "That's just it, we're not. It took me a bit to understand, but they kept talking about it and I don't have any doubts what they said. I was ahead a class, and you were behind one, and they never told us. You're like two years older than I am."

Laris blinked. "I knew it," he said quietly. "They told me I was five when I came, but I knew I was six, but they kept saying I was wrong and so eventually…" he shrugged, looking mildly dazed. "I know it's a small thing, just a number, but…"

"Yeah," Sanyago said. "With me I think it's just a guess, the number I mean, but they still changed it. Listen, brother. They want something from us, and I'm not even sure I want to know what it is."

Ninth Interlude

Borges University, Aldonza, Salía, The Caustlands, 350 SE

Taniixh Pai toyed with the vial of Old World Ganges water she wore around her neck, running her thumb over the seamless pre-Starfall glass and thinking about rivers ancient and new. Her long staff twisted back and forth in her other hand, fingers tracing the intricate carvings that wove through and around the warpwood grain.

She stood in the middle of the campus square, and students flowed around her in every direction, most of them giving her a wide berth, all of them stealing glances at her staff. Symbol of office for a Staffguard Ranger. Powerful, versatile weapon in the hands of a properly trained Haeliiy. Convenient thing to lean on for a woman waiting to meet someone who was running late.

Pai was a patient woman, in her job you had to be. The romantic public image of the Staffguard as wandering righters-of-wrongs had its kernel of truth, but there was a lot of mundane shit surrounding it. Wasn't all cat-and-mouse investigation and dramatic confrontation, like some Old World cowboy sheriff. Lots of surveillance, listening to dully vicious people talk about dully vicious things. Dead ends. Pointless cruelty with no hope of real redress. Bigotry and greed and lust and stupidity. Paperwork.

So she was patient, but she also knew how valuable time could be and this was getting ridiculous. She tapped the end of her staff three times into the paving stone, decided, and turned sharply to accost one of the students going past.

"You. Yes, you. Don't look so worried, I only have a question about the campus."

The young man looked deeply relieved, though still plenty nervous.

"Ma'am?" It was clear from the way he said the word that it resided in one of the dustier parts of his vocabulary. He was short, still shaking off the remnants of adolescent scrawniness, and attempting a style of facial hair his follicles weren't quite up to yet.

She gave him her best you're-not-in-trouble smile. "I need to find a Praedhc Studies researcher. Specializes in artifacts and magic. Name of Ceraen Wiilqaems."

He frowned, looking over his shoulder at a cluster of low stone buildings. "I don't have any classes with a Professor Wiilqaems, but the Praedhc Studies College is over there." He turned to point, then gave her an almost pleading look. *Can I go now?*

"Thank you," she said, and answered his unspoken question by simply striding off at high speed.

It took asking a few more people before she finally tracked Ceraen Wiilqaems down. She was in a sub-basement laboratory, a circular chamber obviously carved out by geomancers, standing in front of a round central table. Even hunched over her work it was obvious she was tall, taller than Taniixh's 180 centimeters. Dark skin, black hair in neat cornrows that fell in braids to her shoulders. Her arms were stretched out to the center of the table, long fingers curled around some sort of strange cube but not quite touching it, just as the bottom of the cube did not quite touch the table's stone. The Fathom rippled in subtle concentric circles around them both.

"Ms. Wiilqaems—"

"Be quiet," Ceraen said, not looking up. "Please," she added after another moment's concentration.

Taniixh complied. A few minutes of muttered Proken and complex Fathom-motions passed by, and Ceraen raised her head.

"Sorry. I did notice you come in, but couldn't take my attention off this artifact. That's also why I was late. Apologies for that, too. Sometimes the only choices you have are bad ones." her Gentic sounded almost native...but no, not quite. English. Old World American, maybe, or whatever approximation had survived the last three and a half centuries. Pai liked languages, and guessing accents was one of her favorite games. She knew her own accent still had traces of Old World Hindi, which she was perfectly happy to let linger.

"I understand," Pai said. "Those looked like some complex assays.

Although that sort of magic is far outside my own studies."

"They were," Ceraen said with a small sigh. She reached for a large notebook and pulled it toward her, tapping it with one finger as though pondering what she was about to write down. Her name was written on the cover in Old Earth English. "Karen Williams," with the Gentic "Ceraen Wiilqaems" in smaller letters below. Above the name was another English inscription, "This Notebook is the Property of," which took Pai a moment to translate into Gentic phonetics. "Yiis Notbooc iiz y Praprti hv."

Ceraen spotted her looking and gave a wry smile. "My parents are academics too. History and literature; they consider the language part of my heritage, and made sure I learned it. I'm grateful now, but I wasn't always at the time. English spelling is a *bitch* to learn."

Pai laughed. "I feel your pain. My parents are Brahmins and made me learn Sanskrit. Easier to spell, I think, but also a lot more obscure in many ways for someone used to more modern dialects like Manhc and Gentic."

"Okay. Interesting. How old were you when your family immigrated?" Ceraen's smile widened, pulling at the smooth skin around her warm brown eyes.

Pai found she liked the smile, and let most of her irritation at being kept waiting slip away. "From Nainadion? They didn't. I did, at twenty. I had some money saved up and things to evade, like marriage."

Ceraen frowned. "Arranged marriage? I thought those were illegal in Nainadion. Part of why all those fundamentalists left to form the Newcaste Compact out in the Sovereign Nations, right? Or am misremembering my old World History classes?"

"They're illegal, yes," Pai said. "However that wasn't precisely what my parents had planned. Oh, they wanted to approve the match, certainly, steer it toward candidates they thought proper, but I think they wanted to give at least the illusion of choice. It didn't matter. I wasn't interested in marriage at all, and that wasn't acceptable. It's a long story, and much of it tiresome the way family narratives so often are. In any case, if you're interested in the offer I've come to discuss you may have occasion to hear the whole thing."

"Yeah?" Ceraen asked, and reached for a quartzwood box, covered in Praedhc runes and left open on one side by a sliding lid. "Your echogram was a little on the vague side, but you can still color me interested. Like I said, I hadn't planned on keeping you waiting." She slid the box toward the artifact cube, which Pai now noticed had shallow domes on its faces, as though a sphere were contained within the six sides. Each dome had a strange double-slitted eye painted—stained?—onto the stone.

"What is that thing, exactly?" Pai asked.

"Idol of Huen'cal," Ceraen replied. "That's the short answer anyway. For the long answer, you can read the paper we're publishing." She slipped the box over the cube in a smooth practiced motion, leaving just millimeters to spare on all sides, then shut the side-lid. "It'll be under some psyhazard restrictions, but I'm sure you could get access."

Pai felt her eyebrows shoot up toward the light helmet that was part of her uniform. "It's that dangerous? Awfully light security in that case, don't you think?"

Ceraen shook her head. "It's not dangerous in and of itself. It's said to have protective properties, and we're still in the initial phases of testing them. Nothing too extensive, but you'll understand why I wanted to make sure the whole process was finished with care and concentration."

Taniixh Pai let the smallest of frowns form on her face, and stood very still, feeling out the room with minute attention paid to every ripple and shift in the Fathom. There was a definite *something* there, but nothing she had the training to recognize. Something unusual, some quality she couldn't quite put her finger on...and the smallest hint of something wrong. Something *wrong*. Just a touch, but enough that she pulled away by ground-in reflex.

Ceraen nodded. "Yep. You feel it, right? Very small effect, as close to totally safe as we could manage. Only even really there if you go looking for it. We have an artifact for that, too. Well, a sliver of one."

Pai swept her head in a slow back-and-forth, feeling shards of stony ice just below her breastbone. " 'Close to totally safe?' That's not possible, no matter how small the effect. The fact that you're even mentioning it is dangerous, not to say the fact that you must have to let your mind linger…" She closed her eyes, pulled awareness in to its center, gave it sacred sound to focus on. *Ommm…*

Ceraen waited for her to open her eyes again, then nodded. "Agreed. Which is why I'm talking to a trained Staffguard Ranger about it instead of some undergrad. Hey, correct me if I'm wrong, but I don't think you'd be interested in me or my research if I was doing, I don't know, some in-depth study of Praedhc golden cutlery. The danger is part of why it's necessary. Otherwise, we wouldn't need the Nowhere Watch, would we?"

"No," Paid said, and walked around the table to stand just a few centimeters in front of the researcher. Ceraen showed only mild surprise at this, and made no attempt to step away. Pai looked carefully into her eyes, watched the tiny muscle-movements around them, felt the soundness of the surrounding space. Nothing, apart from that tiny hint of background, like an elusive hint of spoilage in chilled milk.

"Satisfied?" Ceraen asked. When Pai nodded, she picked up a pair of tweezers from the table and plucked a small splinter of what looked like dull metal from a shallow dish filled with black liquid. The Fathom quivered, then calmed, and everything became a little better.

Pai frowned, watching. "What kind of artifact was that thing taken from?"

"A deep one. I'll spare you the details, they're not healthy." Ceraen picked up her notebook and moved away from the table, climbing up a couple steps to sit on one of the observation chairs that ringed the chamber. "So," she said. "Why me? What's the Staffguard interest in my work?"

Taniixh Pai tapped her staff against the stone floor, twisting it back and forth between her fingers. "What do you know about the Carver Nation?"

Chapter 20

A man, walking by firelight
In deepest winter gloom
"You are a fool," she told him
staring all around
"It illuminates," he said
"This is true," she agreed
embers raining down
"It will give light to thousands,"
he averred, "and warmth"
"Yes," she said, and despaired
They became ashes in the dark

- "Conviction," Katharina Leber, *The Scouring of Sight,* 107 SE

Segutang Road, Tenggara, The Caustlands, 350-354 SE

Dayang had taken the road to Cenicebu before, but never like this. Both the previous times, she'd been a passenger on one of Father's caravan carts, not walking down the road in clunky plated boots and eighteen kilograms of heartvein armor. Farrod rose up steady from the Western horizon, forcing her to shade the left side of her face from sun-glare as she walked north toward the Migiro Highway. The wind kicked up and died down at irregular intervals, sweeping over the green-and-purple patchwork of tall grass and thick abblum that covered the plain.

Her hands were uncovered, as was her head; she'd taken off her helm and gauntlets to travel, and had never been one for headscarves, even in the mosque. Well, no, that wasn't quite true. Her *family* didn't really believe in headscarves; Father and Mother both considered the scriptural justifications for mandating them to be tortured at best. None of the Marchadesch women ever wore them.

This sometimes earned them judgmental looks, but she'd always followed her mother's example and held her head high ignoring them. Dayang shoved the thought aside. Every memory of her mother was still too bright and spiky for her to pick up and examine.

Jeims padded along beside her, wearing a travel-harness carrying what few possessions he'd brought with him to Kualabu four years before. And a few souvenirs, he'd told her with a smile. They'd have to part ways in Cenicebu; he'd start west on his long journey to Aldonza, she'd head north to Camp Singapore and enlist in the Tentera Wira.

Or try to, she supposed.

"You've taken this trip before, just the other direction, right?" she asked him.

"Nope," he said, and turned his head to drink from one of his waterskin nozzles. "I did my earlier training in Acheronford, right on the corner of the Siinlan and the Tenggara border. I crossed the Mindao and swung northward by the Deisiindr, then went east to Kualabu. I've never seen the Migiro Highway."

He craned his neck upward as though he might be able to catch a glimpse of the famous road. "Never seen Cenicebu either, though I'm excited to see it now. Not going to pass up the opportunity to spend some time in your capital. I'll find a cheap Lingmao hotel and bum around for a few days. Should still be able to report to Aldonza with time to spare—it'll take them a bit to figure out exactly what to do with me anyway. You're welcome to come along for the tour. Could use a native guide."

She laughed, and shook her head with real regret. "I don't want to delay any, Jeims, I'm sorry. Anyway, I'm hardly a native, not of Cenicebu anyway. They'd just think I'm another wide-eyed provincial."

"Ah," he said, sounding regretful but not especially surprised. "That's too bad, but I understand. I'll keep in touch by echogram when I can, let you know where I'm being stationed. Once you're done with the Tentera Wira, you're always welcome to drop by. You won't be with them forever, I don't think, you're not the military-lifer sort."

"And you are?" she asked, and felt a smile form across her mouth and round her eyes, a real one. Hadn't been many of those in the past couple days.

"Oh please." He gave a long, purring laugh. "The Staffguard is hardly the military, I'm not joining the Salian army or anything. Glorified town guards, really, only guarding the whole country. Sometimes even succeeding at it."

"You'll do great." She was still wearing the same smile, and it was cool sweet relief to have it stay with her so long, unbidden and unforced. "I'm serious, Jeims. I still owe you, you know."

He batted her lightly across the shin with his tail, though she couldn't really feel it through the thick armor plating. "We can owe each other. I got you into the whole Hunch-Ripper mess, remember? And I'd have tried to interfere with Hang Che whether you were there or not, or at least I like to think I would. I'm pretty sure neither of us could have taken him on our own, but who knows, what-ifs are always crowshit anyway. Good luck, you being there with her. And armed."

"Yes," she said fervently. "Thank God."

"Yeah, sure." He gave a small dipping shrug, and she looked at him steadily for a few paces, feeling a quick hard gust of wind against her neck as it swept over the plain.

"Do you believe in God, Jeims? At all?" She realized immediately she hadn't phrased the question well, and felt herself flush against the cooling breeze.

"No." His tone was hard to read, wry and resigned and final.

"That's it?" She felt more surprised than she'd have thought. "Just 'no?'"

"That's it." The amusement in his voice rose along with his half-smile. "I'd have been evasive if you'd asked me that bluntly back in Kualabu. My go-to was to just tell people I'm 'secular.' That was usually enough ambiguity to get people to leave me alone. There was the occasional conversion attempt, but I could deal with that. And it's been educational. You know, there are a lot more like me in Kualabu than you probably think. They just keep their opinions to themselves— but they'd open up to an outsider they didn't think would judge them, sometimes."

"Huh," she said, and they passed the next kilometer or so without speaking as she thought about what he'd said, watching the gentle hills and stretches of sparse forest go by. Then she realized he might take her silence as…

...she wasn't really sure what he might take her silence as. "Hey, Jeims, you know I don't think any different of you, I was just thinking..." she flushed again, frowning.

"Dayang." His voice was soothing, and still had that hint of gentle laughter behind it. "Don't even worry about it. I know I dropped a couple of surprises on your head, even if you must have at least suspected them both."

She felt her shoulders slump down in relief, and took a deep breath to square them again. "Yeah, I mean— I knew you weren't religious, but there's all kinds of not-religious, you know? Plenty of people in Kualabu who don't really practice, but still say they believe, or believe in *something*." She shrugged. "I don't know. I guess I'm kind of learning how much I don't know."

"Hell, Dayang," he said with a rueful little snort. "We're all learning *that*, or we probably should be."

She nodded, and they spent another few kilometers in companionable quiet before stopping for lunch by a grassy stand of birch trees. Jeims found a spot that seemed relatively free of abblum, and she joined him on the grass, rummaging through her pack with one hand while using the other to adjust the tassets of her armor. She wished armor designers would put some thought into letting the wearer actually *sit* on her ass, rather than just protecting it.

This early in the trip, they still had fresh food. Dayang munched on a couple of grilled fish while Jeims wolfed down cubes of raw meat, and they both enjoyed fresh water from canteens. Before long they'd have to rely on flat, precipitated water from their dewskins. As a child on long trips with the family, Dayang had shaken her dewskin to get a bit of air into the water and make it more palatable, but only when her parents weren't looking— they said it was bad for the expensive Sihir-tool. It was, too, as she'd learned when hers stopped working and had to be re-imbued.

That had been a bad day. Nurul had told on her, of course. Dayang felt a sudden spike of anxiety and regret at the thought of her sister, and forced it down. She wasn't the only one leaving people behind.

"Jeims?" she asked as she finished the last of her fish and tossed the bones aside.

He turned from his tongue-bath and cocked his head.

"Is...is Aulia going to be okay? With you leaving so suddenly, I mean."

He sighed, and it was a whole-body thing, settling his head down onto his front paws with a small sad smile. "She'll be...we'll both be alright. We knew it wasn't going to last forever, couldn't, right? I think she kind of liked that we had an expiration date. She's pretty focused on climbing the ranks of the guard, and eventually wants to get assigned to Cenicebu. Somewhere bigger than Kualabu, anyway, so it was nice to find someone who didn't have local roots, you know?"

She reached over and, for the first time since she'd known him, patted Jeims gently on the head, feeling the silky warmth of his grey-and-white fur under her fingertips. This was *not* something one did with a Lingmao one did not know well, and she fought to contain a sudden rush of anxiety.

To her relief he smiled warmly, bumped her hand with a small toss of his head. "I think I was more attached than she was, honestly, but...Hell. I knew it was coming, just not quite so soon. Don't mind me if I get kind of mopey, you've got more cause than I do for real angst right now anyway."

Dayang thought maybe she'd dare ask a little more. "She didn't mind? That you're..."

"Foreign? Or an honest-to-Godless infidel?" He laughed and shook his head. "Aulia's Buddhist, she just doesn't advertise it much. It didn't really come up often. She even taught me to meditate. I mean, kind of." He laughed, and brought his head up off his paws. "She thinks she'll move on to a new life when she dies and I'm pretty sure I'll just rot, but that was the only thing we had any real argument about."

Dayang wasn't sure what to say to that, so she just nodded and stood up, stretching her muscles as Jeims did the same. She let the next couple kilometers go by with only the clunk of armored boots on packed earth and the slow soft sound of the breeze to cut into the silence. Jeims, of course, made almost no sound at all as he padded along beside her.

When Jeims spoke again, it was about her training, and they talked about Wira-arts and other lighter topics for the rest of the day. She was increasingly apprehensive as night fell and it was time to set up camp; she'd never set up a tent alone before, and needed quite a bit of help from Jeims to get it standing reliably in the scrubby semi-wood beside the road.

She cooked an indifferent dinner of reconstituted beef and undercooked rice on her little Sihir camp-stove. Jeims watched without comment, though he didn't quite manage to keep an impassive expression; amusement and sympathy tussled and tumbled across his furry features.

Too bad she couldn't ask him for any help; Lingmao tastes and dietary needs were much too different. He had his own meal of jerky dipped in some odd-smelling grey paste.

After the meal she realized with dread that she had to take a shit and shouldn't wait much longer. Most of the toilets in Tenggara were of the floor variety, so she was accustomed to squatting, but all this plate armor made it a whole new proposition. Sighing, she took her spade and told Jeims she'd be right back, then headed out into the scrub. It was, as she'd anticipated, pretty awful, but she supposed it could be worse; she hadn't had to clean any shit off the heels of her boots, and the ground hadn't much resisted her spade.

Her Wira-training meant she was strong enough to push the little shovel right into solid rock, if it came to that, but latrine-digging seemed a pretty trivial reason to draw on the Fathom. A bandit attack was never entirely out of the question outside civilized walls; she and Jeims weren't exactly soft targets, but her armor alone was worth a small fortune. Best conserve her strength.

Jeims had a maddening little feline smile across his grey-furred face when he looked up on her return, and she narrowed her eyes at him. He just shrugged. "Look, primate anatomy is *not* my fault. You're gonna have to take it up with your tree-dwelling ancestors."

"At least they didn't shit in little sandboxes," she shot back, "for someone else to clean up."

He snorted and shook his head. "Touché, I guess. I've actually thought about that some, read about it too. My ancestors, I mean. I feel for them, the ones that birthed the first Caustland Cats especially. They were all born premature, and lucky thing too or they'd have killed their mothers coming out. Poor Molly-cats had their kittens taken away the moment they gave birth, and never really had a chance to get to know them. Couldn't ever have really understood them anyway." He laughed, flicking his tail. "Hell of a shock for the veterinarians, too, when they started babbling like human infants. Even more when they said their first words."

She nodded slowly, wishing there was a fire to stare into as they talked, like there had been on her previous caravan journeys, but they didn't want to attract that kind of attention with just the two of them. She thought they could probably take on a pretty good number of common bandits, but right now she was sick down to the marrow of fighting.

"I mostly feel for the kittens. Housecats are used to their kittens going off on their own pretty quickly, right?" Dayang's only firsthand experience with domestic felines was at friends' houses, or the occasional stray in the streets of Kualabu; though Father was fond of them, poor Nurul was deathly allergic. "But those first Lingmao, they didn't have parents, not really, just the humans who took care of them. And those people must have been grieving and in shock from Starfall."

He cocked his head, flicking an ear. "We still don't really understand what happened, you know? Same with the Caustland Crows. All that strange energy released with some kind of semi-sentience behind it, and no one really knew anything about the Fathom, and more than half the colonists dead or dying on the way down."

"There were a lot of them, right? Lingmao kittens?"

Jeims turned his head and took a sip from his waterskin. "Must have been. I think about twelve thousand cats survived Starfall, one for every five of the sixty thousand humans that made it, and something like two-thirds of their litters were Fathom-touched. They brought a lot of cats with them. Lot of dogs, too, but nothing seems to have happened to them, and no one really knows why."

Dayang frowned. "Don't the Pelos have dogs that are maybe Fathom-changed?" She'd only seen a handful of dogs in her life; most of Kualabu's Muslims regarded them as unclean. Father had owned one as a boy, she knew, and had spoken wistfully about his old pet a few times when Mother wasn't listening.

"Abhounds, yes," Jeims said. "Of course, they just call them 'dogs,' they think 'Fallen' dogs are an 'unfeeling abomination,' and not *real* dogs."

"But their dogs are the ones that have changed," Dayang reasoned. "Don't they know that?"

Jeims laughed at that, rolling over onto his back with the long *mrooowwwl* and giving her an upside-down grin. "Of course they don't. Most of them think our claim of hailing from their own real homeworld is a bunch of transparent crowshit. Since we can't come up with any convincing explanation for how they might have gotten here from Earth, it's kind of hard to blame them."

"They keep a lot of records in the Deisiindr, though, right?" Dayang asked, deepening her frown. "Father said he saw some of them, years ago. Moving images, like an echoplay, on Old World computers. Ancient documents preserved as pictures. Genetic repositories. He said they even knew about where and when the Pelos were from in Earth's prehistory, even though they didn't really understand how or why they'd changed. Impossible cavemen from Europe, he called them."

"Sure," Jeims said with a small snicker. "We'll just invite their leaders and scholars and sages out to the Deisiindr to see the evidence. 'Don't mind all the Pelo skulls you have to step over, they're just leftovers from the Siege. We promise we *totally* won't use any of those same weapons on you, here in the only place on Solace they actually work, here where you can't reach into the Fathom and our soldiers look like they're half-machine.'"

Dayang wrinkled her nose, buffing a few stray splotches of dirt from her armor before preparing to take it off for the evening. "They're still mad about the Siege of the Deisiindr? It was like three centuries ago."

The Siege had, it was true, been a one-sided bloodbath; when the early Fallen retreated to the one place they knew the Fathom couldn't inflict malfunction on their old tools and toys, they'd gone from near-helpless to lethal in ways the pursuing Pelos couldn't possibly understand. But they'd only been defending themselves.

Jeims sighed, rubbing behind his ear with his paw as he sat up and settled back on his haunches. "I wish we taught more about the Pelos in our schools, all over the Caustlands, I really do. And taught better, but the damn Siinlan doesn't help. We stay on our side, and they stay on theirs." He craned his head eastward to regard the setting sun, tail flicking back and forth in thoughtful rhythm.

Dayang turned her own gaze to the east and watched the blaze of color settle into the horizon, while Solace's silvery rings slowly became visible in the gathering twilight. She pulled off her armor, strap by strap and plate by plate, slipped out of the padded clothing beneath, got into her warm sleeping clothes, still watching the sky. As the last of Farrod's disc slipped behind the skyline, Jeims spoke again.

"Yes, they still remember the Siege," he said. "They may not live as long as we do, but they have very long memories, and that's a hard thing to forget. My language instructor remembered, anyway, said her particular people had a day of remembrance for it every year. They knew exactly how many of their ancestors they had lost. Five hundred and sixty-four, just from her clan. I can still see her face when she said it. They remember, all right."

He shook his head in a rapid back-and-forth twist, flicking one ear. "We don't know how many we slaughtered, though; those Old World weapons kill fast and from a long distance. By the time anyone dared leave the Deisiindr, the bodies were just a great piled ring of bones and rot. And we couldn't exactly go around asking *them*."

She drew her knees up to her chest, looked down between them. "They didn't have any choice, though. The First of the Fallen, I mean. The Pelos would have killed them all, they meant to wipe us out."

"Probably," Jeims admitted, scratching his neck with one front paw. "Look at it from their perspective, though. We show up out of the sky, incinerate a few million of them with almost no warning, and claim the whole killing field as a homestead."

"That was an *accident*," she said, and was surprised at the vehemence in her own voice. "The *Earthseed* was failing as it approached, the Fathom-jinn were tearing it apart. More than half of the First of the Fallen died too, we didn't mean to do that! We couldn't have stopped it."

"That's probably true as well," he replied softly. "But so what? Why should they believe us? How could that be a comfort to them?"

She sat and stared for a long time as the night drew into full darkness, until she could see only the white parts of his fur and the amber glint of his eyes reflecting the light of a single half-moon. "What do you mean it's *probably* true?"

He shrugged, and began curling himself onto the small pad that would serve as his bedroll. He'd scratched a few warding-runes in the dirt around it to keep off insects and rain. "Studying Starfall was a hobby of mine as a teenager." He laughed, then opened his mouth in an immense feline yawn. "There's still a lot of controversy, plenty we don't know for sure. But I can bore you with that tomorrow. Goodnight, Dayang."

"Goodnight, Jeims," she said, and crawled into her own tent. She'd worried she might toss and turn this first night out on the road, but she slept like a stone.

The rest of the journey passed without incident, north by northwest to the Migiro Highway, west by southwest to Cenicebu. The raised, textured stone of the Highway made Dayang's feet ache inside her heavy boots, and every evening there were blisters to heal. Soon the skin under her boots and straps and pack-belt was covered in pink, freshly-healed patches and nascent calluses. She hurried them along with her Sihir-meditations, though not too much. Strength had to be reserved, just in case.

Now and then she'd wish for a wagon, or just a single horse, but she knew the wish was foolish. There hadn't really been time for the complicated logistics of buying or renting or borrowing, she wasn't much of a horsewoman anyway—and the Caustlands were dangerous. Mounts were usually a liability in Sihir-combat; ordinary animals were nowhere near as tough as a skilled Wira, and even the best-trained could easily be made to buck off or run away with its rider. There were ways to extend some of a Wira's resilience to a bonded steed, but that required extensive specialization, not to mention the trained and imbued animal itself.

So she walked, and Jeims walked beside her.

The landscapes they saw were sweeping and empty, grassland, trees, and abblum rippling and swaying over gentle hills. Once they were on the Highway, there were a few other travelers, some looking at the pair of them curiously as they passed, others simply nodding, some ignoring them both altogether. No one wanted to talk, which suited her mood just fine. She and Jeims chatted here and there, but were content to let long stretches pass in silence.

When the weeklong journey was at an end and they approached the Eastern Gates of Cenicebu, she reflected that it had been both the shortest and the longest journey of her life. Or perhaps it was simply not yet settled in her mind.

Even after a week of travel, she could still not really believe that she had left Kualabu behind—but here was Cenicebu. Its tall silver gates passed by on either side, and though she noted the huge thrum of their wards through the Fathom and saw the intricate beauty of their engravings, she felt numb to the wonder. They shared a room at an upscale hotel that night, and Dayang luxuriated in her firm bed and clean sheets while Jeims sprawled out over his and lightly snored.

When they said goodbye, she didn't cry as much as she'd feared.

It was less than a day's journey from Cenicebu to Camp Singapore, the headquarters of the Tentera Wira. It had no walls, only barbed-wire fences and blank-faced steel gates, but Dayang felt the heavy waiting energies of the wards buried beneath the perimeter as it extended away in both directions.

She clenched her jaw as she approached the heavy steel barrier in front of the gatehouse, seeing an elusive hint of her own reflection in the unshined expanse of metal. She'd stuck her mace head-down in her pack so she wouldn't be visibly armed. No use taking chances. She was nakedly aware of how her armor and shield would look to an experienced eye, new and unmarked and expensive. Sentries watched her approach from the towers flanking the gatehouse, but did nothing else. Even the Fathom was tranquil apart from the deep intricate hum of the perimeter.

Every scratch of her boots against the road, every small noise from her armor, even her breathing echoed hard in her awareness as she stepped up to the gate. She was about to say something when the barrier slid aside and she found herself facing a trio of soldiers, one in front, two standing just behind. The one in front spoke.

"What do you want, Scarface?"

Dayang stepped forward, regarded the woman as calmly as she could, studying the sigils and insignia on her fine kashval-hide armor.

"I'm here to enlist with the Tentera Wira."

The soldier scoffed, holding up a hand. "You don't just enlist in the Tentera Wira, Scarface. This isn't the regular Army, that recruiting station is back in Cenicebu. What, did you give yourself that scar with a kitchen knife and then keep away from physicians for a year or two? Thought it would make you look badass."

"I got it from a Hunch-Ripper. The physician couldn't heal it."

The woman turned her head, looked at her sidelong, but some of the amused dismissal had slipped off her face. "Even if you did fight a Hunch-Ripper, the scar would heal just fine. They're Abwaild creatures, Scarface, not—"

"You're trained to treat wounds, right?" Dayang said. The woman glared, clearly not accustomed to interruptions from her juniors. Dayang traced the scar from temple to jaw. "Come have a look, I won't stop you. See for yourself."

The soldier paused at that. "If you do join the Army, girl, it would behoove you to unlearn that habit of interrupting people. Especially people who outrank you."

Dayang gave the woman her best steady stare. "Fine. But I'm still a civilian for now. I thought you were supposed to be polite to civilians."

"A potential recruit isn't quite a civilian," the woman said, but some of the stony sureness had gone from her voice. Scowling, she stepped forward and reached out with one finger. Dayang held her helmet to her chest with both hands, keeping still for the touch, restraining her defenses for the woman's probing. She felt the muted touch of callused fingertip on nerveless scar tissue, the intrusion of the woman's query, felt it slide away from the scar and then recoil.

The woman stepped back. "So you had some sort of unfortunate accident," she said, and her voice was flat, slightly hesitant. "It wasn't a Hunch-Ripper, though, I've never heard—"

"Someone pushed it through the Fathom," Dayang said.

The soldier stiffened, shook her head. "That's not possible."

"The guards on the wall saw us fight it. One of them fought it with us. One of them saw it come out from the Fathom." She paused, shuddered internally, but still took some sour pleasure in watching the woman's face as she continued. "The one who saw it from the wall is still in the hospital. They hope she'll recover fully sometime this year. They just started letting her children see her again a couple of months ago." The pair standing behind her shifted, just enough to be noticeable, impassive expressions showing tiny traces of personhood behind the soldier's veneer.

The woman leaned in, looked her in the eye. Dayang looked back. "Send an echogram out to the Kualabu garrison if you like. They'll tell you."

"You said 'we' fought it," the soldier said. "You, one of the guards, and...?" She still sounded skeptical, but all the amusement and condescension had gone out of her—replaced by, if not actual respect, at least a willingness to consider the possibility.

"A friend. A Salían, actually. He was sent out to study under the same teachers I was. Very talented mage."

The woman actually smiled, just a quirk at the corner of her mouth. "What, you got yourself an exotic foreign boyfriend and dragged him out to help you fight this...this dangerous Hunch-Ripper?"

Dayang laughed, and relished the way it washed over and blunted her heavy nerves. "Boyfriend? No, Lingmao. My boyfr—well, the guy I was seeing at the time—he wouldn't have been much good there, I don't think.

I didn't like him for his fighting abilities." She could not have said this in Kualabu, but this wasn't Kualabu, and she relished the chance to live this new life with as few pretenses as possible—even if the admission made her feel naked, made her want to glance around without moving her head, see who might be listening.

The soldier snorted. "No, I'm sure you liked him for an entirely different set of abilities." She cocked her head. "Kualabu is a Muslim village, mostly, isn't it?" *That must have been a difficult sort of relationship to keep,* her expression said.

Dayang nodded. "I'm Muslim," she said. She wanted to say more, let out some of the deeply-buried resentment and frustration that had been partly unearthed by talking so openly before. Wanted to release a tirade on how the men all seemed to think they could behave as they wish and only hold women and girls to some absurd standard of honor and purity, but she didn't, and the woman just nodded.

"Me too, Al-hamdu'lillah. Ran off to join the Army right after my *boyfriend* ran off to join some caravan the moment he found out I was pregnant. Fortunately, no one here gives a shit about that, and if they do I can set them on fire." She grinned wolfishly, and Dayang grinned back despite herself.

"Mmmm," the woman said, then jerked her head back and to the side. "Wongsuwan. Rermgosakul. Go get Sergeant Major Ocampo. Tell her we have a possible recruit, and she's even brought her own armor."

The pair did a neat about-face and walked off without a word.

"I'm Captain Trimurti." She held out her hand, and Dayang shook it.

"Dayang Marchadesch."

Captain Trimurti's eyebrows went up at the surname, but she didn't comment. Instead, she pointed toward the loop on Dayang's belt. "I'm assuming you've brought a weapon to go with that fancy new armor and shield?"

Dayang suppressed a wince at the mention of her equipment's obvious workmanship and newness. "Yes. In my pack. I didn't want to wear it openly when approaching the camp."

Trimurti laughed. "Probably wise to be cautious, though we wouldn't have tried to fill you with arrows or lightning bolts just for approaching the gate while armed. Let's see it."

Dayang dropped her pack on the dusty ground, drawing her mace out by the handle. After a moment's internal debate, she offered it to the officer. If the Tentera Wira decided it wanted to steal her personal possessions for some insane reason, it wasn't as if there was much she could do about it.

Captain Trimurti took the heavy weapon with one hand, hefting it with no apparent effort. She whistled as she examined it. "This is one hell of a mace, Marchadesch. Where did you get it?"

Dayang felt an inner sigh of resignation pass down through her core, and tried to keep her expression impassive. *Here we go.* "A gift from my father. The armor and shield, too."

Nodding slowly, Trimurti handed the mace back, and Dayang slipped it into its rightful place on her belt. "Rich kid, huh? I'm guessing Daddy paid for your training, too?"

Dayang nodded, not trusting anything she might think of to say.

"We get a few like you trying to join, every now and then. Lots of expensive lessons and equipment. Sometimes they're worth something, sometimes not. You've at least seen combat, though, and that's not nothing." Trimurti turned abruptly to face a small middle-aged woman in what looked like a formal uniform, unarmed and unarmored. The woman saluted, and Trimurti returned it. "Sergeant Major Ocampo. This is Dayang Marchadesch. She wants to enlist."

Dayang nodded again. Trimurti stepped aside, and the Sergeant Major stepped in, standing quite close. She smiled, and though wasn't an unfriendly smile it was clearly ready to bite sharp.

"Marchadesch."

Dayang waited, blinked. "Yes—?"

"Yes, Sergeant Major. If you're going to enlist, we may as well start your learning now. Hands behind your back. At ease."

Dayang felt a tiny surge of relief. This at least she knew how to do. "Yes, Sergeant Major," she repeated, and dropped her hands back behind her, looked the shorter Ocampo in the eye.

"Ah, so you have some training in more than fighting. Good. Where did you learn that?"

"My Wira-guru." She swallowed bile. "Hang Che. He was...he spent some time in the Army, he said." Dayang grimaced, then remembered. "Sergeant Major."

Ocampo's smile widened incrementally, though the rest of her face was stone. "Tentera Wira, then?"

Dayang shook her head. "No, Sergeant Major. Just the regular Army, so far as I know. It must have been half a century ago. He left to become an adventurer after a few years."

"I see. So, Marchadesch, you're Filipina?"

"Half, Sergeant Major." Dayang wrestled her expression into what she hoped was neutral professionalism. "My father. My mother is Malay. Mostly."

"Very well. You can't be any older than twenty. Do you have any university education?"

Dayang fought down a grimace. "Just graduated from secondary school. Ah...Sergeant Major."

Ocampo snorted. "You're learning reasonably fast. Very well, then you'll be enlisting. No university, no officer's bars. That's fine, there will be time for more education later, especially here with the Tentera Wira. Follow me, Marchadesch. There's a lot to be done."

"Yes, Sergeant Major," Dayang said, and followed, anxiety and anticipation scraping their way up her throat.

That was the beginning of a very long week. Enlisting, Dayang learned, was not a simple event, but an exhausting, bewildering process. She signed documents, filled out forms, gave personal effects over for safekeeping. They shaved her head, which she had not expected and which pained her more than she would have thought.

"You can grow it back out after your training," the barber said. "Easy enough to do quickly for you Wira types anyway. But for now, you'll look like everyone else."

There were tests. Physicians poked and prodded and Sihir-assessed. They made her spar with an endless line of opponents until she was so exhausted she could not even stand. Then she slept, as much as they'd let her sleep, and did it again. She ate but barely noticed her food. They put her in training armor and gave her a padded practice-mace. They assigned her a training group. Her scar earned her looks at first, but was quickly forgotten. A few of the company had worse. Some of the other recruits were at least twice her age.

The next six months were a blur. They did not work her any harder than Hang Che had, but they worked her longer, and she relished every second of sleep. She was always hungry, and though there was plenty of food there was never enough time to eat. She made fast friends, both male and female; while her barracks room was all women, the platoon was mixed. She learned which of her fellow trainees to avoid.

Sometimes, at night before lights-out, she felt the full weight of what she had left behind. But mostly she was numb. She didn't have the time or energy for angst.

Dayang discovered with a mixture of tired pride and relief that she was not outclassed. The instructors were stingy with their praise, but she wasn't stupid. She was one of the youngest in her group, but kept up with and often surpassed the others. Sometimes there were resentful whispers; she'd gotten lessons from her wealthy family. She had not paid her dues; most of the other trainees were hopefuls from the Regular Army, and sometimes scoffed when she displayed her ignorance of general military minutiae.

But she held up her end in training, and little by little that's what came to matter. The whispering died down. She began taking lead, sometimes, in combat exercises. She discovered she had a talent for coordinating small groups, a head for keeping track of others' situations along with her own, an eye for taking in the whole of a situation. But trying to oversee large numbers of other soldiers frustrated her, and ended poorly for all involved both times she tried it. Not really officer material, she overheard one of the instructors telling another. This was a painful blow to her ego, but she knew it was probably true, and pressed on.

She also reconfirmed her lack of talent for archery; she'd been an indifferent shot at best the few times she'd tried in Kualabu, and wasn't much better now. Nor had she suddenly picked up a knack for ranged spellcasting, finding it bewildering and difficult to extend her influence very far through the Fathom. She gritted her teeth and did her best to improve anyway.

Fridays she went to mosque, while the Christians went to chapel and the Buddhists attended their temples. After, there was some time to rest. They were permitted to answer the call to prayer when training allowed, and she found herself looking forward to the momentary peace and communion. The non-Muslims would pray in their own way, or meditate, or just sit silently.

She wrote home. Always letters, as echograms were only for emergencies. They wrote back. Father's letters were warm and proud, Pandikar's affectionate and teasing, Nurul's a bit absurd in their bubbly chattiness, as though Dayang were on vacation in some exciting new locale. Dayang simply skipped the parts of Nurul's first few letters that talked about the wedding. She'd read them later, when there was time and energy to cry.

Sara's messages were encouraging and hopeful, and full of a gratitude that Dayang found somewhat painful, though she was always eager to receive them. She preferred the breathless bits of news Sara would include, the familiar bits of chatter and analysis, to the earnest thanks and concern. Mother's letters were formal on the surface, but with an ache of worry and pain underneath. Dayang didn't always want to read them, but did anyway.

She cried the day she graduated, in a bathroom stall where no one could see her. That night she ate a lavish meal and got laid; it had been months since her last time with Omar. He was a slim, pretty fellow trainee named Phan who gave her a delighted, can't-believe-my-luck grin the moment he caught on to her advances. It was good, though she made it clear to him that it was also a one-off. He didn't mind.

They gave back her weapons and armor. Her shield had been Sihir-scribed with the insignia of the Tentera Wira, a field of stylized islands connected by a web of lightning. Her breastplate now sported a Specialist rank insignia and read "MARCHADESCH" over her left collarbone.

The uneventful first four years of her service had begun.

Chapter 21

Soaring higher I
can see the shape of things
standing lower I
don't have to use my wings
It's an easy life
just pecking at the soil
and to stay aloft
that's never-ending toil
You don't really care
how wide your mind can roam?
tell it simple things
and make the ground its home

- "Easy Wisdom," Haenri "Longfeather" Raliis
To Gild the Current, 221 SE

Clarcspur, Carver State, The Sovereign Nations, 351-354 SE

Juliaen Draecsl stood looking up toward the ground, arms crossed tightly
against her ribs. The bars of the basement window threw thick evening
shadows over the delicate lines of her face, shaded the bright spun-gold of
her hair. She could feel Lidia's presence behind her, shards of her new
training spiking their way into preoccupation. Juliaen drew the older
woman's features in her mind: the haunted gold-brown eyes, the
determined set of her features, gone increasingly gaunt over the last year,
the dark hair that hung past her waist. Tall—though Juliaen was taller—

and imposing in a way Juliaen was not sure she would ever be able to match.

"Your family is going to be fine, Juliaen. Or not, as the Divine wills. You have a duty to them, but worrying will not help you fulfill it. It will only strengthen attachments that cloud your mind."

Juliaen turned to see Lidia standing in her shadow. The High Winnow was just as she'd pictured, though weariness hung heavier on the flesh-and-blood. *As it always does,* Juliaen thought. She didn't answer Lidia's assertion, but reached out through the Holy Fathom toward her, felt the former Somonei's habitual wards and woven spell-hedges. They pushed her back with no apparent effort or weakening of purpose, and Juliaen felt the roaring inadequacy of her talent. It had never been trained in that direction before...this. Before this pilgrimage to the Nave of the Abbey Invisible, a pilgrimage which had never really ended.

Lidia said nothing. Juliaen thought that perhaps she smiled, just barely, at the clumsy Fathom-foray, and that she'd learned there was no need to break Juliaen's long silences.

Juliaen bowed an acknowledgement, then broke the silence herself. "Thank you, Master Almeida. I know it is a weakness, but I worry about my mother especially. I don't know why the Divine has decided to put her through such trials, along with my father and family. I have no doubts about my mission or what the Divine requires of me, and I will not be deterred. But I cannot help realizing that the absence of my help must be felt, prideful as that may be."

Lidia's face softened, as much as it ever did these days. It seemed somehow to both tighten and sag with every month that went by, every memory and frustration that struck way through her harried mind. Juliaen wished there was more she could do for her, but this struggle was between Lidia, the Divine, and whatever ancient rusted weights dragged on her soul.

"I know," Lidia said. "And I'm sorry. I have never been in your shoes. Understand that the presence of your help is felt even more keenly here than its absence must be among your family."

"I hope so," Juliaen said, and fell silent again. Lidia waited.

You are needed here. But you must press forward, and you must trust in Our will.

"Yes," Juliaen whispered.

Still Lidia said nothing. She was used to this, too.

Juliaen looked Lidia in the eye. "I am sure I am where I need to be. We must speak to Archabbot Thuwun again."

"Juliaen, he's not going to listen. Ever since the attack on the Presilyo, he's been hesitant to listen to me." Lidia frowned. "What has the Divine been telling you?"

Juliaen was still not sure just how deep Lidia's belief in her visions and voices went. On some days, she seemed eager to hear about them; on others, Juliaen felt she was sowing seeds onto solid stone. The Divine would try to affirm the truth to Lidia's mind, surely, but only Lidia could decide to listen. Juliaen wondered sometimes if recent events had harmed the High Winnow's spiritual equilibrium enough to make it difficult for her to hear, to truly understand.

Something flashed clear in Juliaen's mind, and her eyes went wide. She stepped aside, staring off into the deep empty spaces of the basement room. Her shadow moved with her, leaving Lidia's face and robes striped with window bars and setting sun. Lidia turned to give Juliaen an inquiring look, lines of light and dark rippling over pale, tired features.

"You are right," Juliaen said, "that the Archabbot will not listen. He has grown complacent of his place and his own wisdom, he will not hear the voice of the Divine. But surely others will. They are ready for our message. The Priors and Sub-Priors. The monks and nuns. The devout among the laity." She paused, looked Lidia in the eye. "The Promiseguard."

This time, Lidia Almeida's silence was not out of deference to Juliaen's Divinely-distracted nature. Her face was filled with shock and a dawning comprehension.

"The people respect you. I may have heard the calling of the Divine to act, Lidia, but I *found* you by following the most mundane of whispers. They're everywhere, and while there are distortions they're not all wrong, they all speak to your reputation as a woman who will *act*. And Lidia— they're on your side. They're on *our* side. Not just you and me, but the side of the true Michyeros. The side of the Divine. These latest sanctions from the Caustland States fill them with righteous rage, day by day. You know what else makes me worry about my family?"

Lidia shook her head. She was still staring, but she looked as if she was starting to think as well.

"It is hard to get hold of anything they cannot make themselves. Trade

303

is scarce, even with other parts of the Carver State. Everyone is hoarding what they can, and buying from the other Compacts means high prices on the black market—if one is willing to soil oneself that way, which my devout and honest father is not. It is not just bleeding us, Lidia, it is *corrupting* us. Some of those black market goods include items from the Fathomless Deisiindr! Soulless, factory-made, handled by part-human abominations with *machinery* carved into their heads! People are desperate enough to buy these things!"

"People have always bought those things," Lidia said, her gold-brown eyes flashing sharp along with her words. "No matter how hard we try to keep Ragado contraband out, there will always be a few of the faithless among us who don't care about buying only Silado goods."

"Not in the numbers we're seeing now," Juliaen countered. "When almost everything worth buying must be purchased from a black marketeer, there will be constant temptation, and smugglers are unlikely to be conscientious about keeping track of what is properly Silado and what is Ragado, or they'd not have brought the Ragado items over our borders in the first place. The people would rather the markets be re-stocked, they would trade legitimately if they could, most of them."

Lidia fell back into silence, standing in thought. Juliaen took a seat as she waited, one facing away from the window, and pondered her own shadow cast behind bars onto the fine cedar of the table in front of her.

"The people may want the sanctions lifted. Well. Of course they want the sanctions lifted," Lidia said slowly. "But we could not promise that, no more than Archabbot Thuwun can. Even if we somehow managed to cleanse Inoue Island, retake the monastery…" Lidia pursed her lips, tapping her middle finger against her thigh. "Ridding Solace of the Presilyo was to be done in service of the Divine, to cleanse corruption from Their religion. We knew we'd pay a cost, a heavy one."

"And it would open up the Caustlands to the true Triune Path," Juliaen said. "People would hear our message, pure and uncorrupted by mercenary dealings. No one trusts a mercenary, and however much they might pretend that's exactly what the Somonei are. We would be saving souls, Lidia, pulling them into the Seven Heavens where they can work toward union with the Divine."

"You never get tired of giving that speech, do you?" Lidia sounded almost forlorn, and to Juliaen's surprise she dropped herself into an adjacent seat. "Why should another attack fare any differently than the first one? How could we be sure they won't know we're coming yet again? Juliaen, this might not mean much to you, but I *know* the Somonei. They were waiting for us on every side of the island. They knew exactly when and where we planned to strike. Even the damned Shuvelao were there."

Lidia's fingers curled atop the table, scraping long ragged nails against fine cedar. "The only reason we did any damage at all is that..." she shuddered, and Juliaen put one hand gently over hers until it stopped its clutching rasp. "...is that some of our former Somonei could not follow orders, or would not, and so could not be anticipated so easily. And also because they were..." Lidia visibly steeled herself, "...tainted. I...I still don't know, if we should simply have...have cleansed those ones ourselves, rather than try to use them. I thought—we thought—'Well, the Presilyo is corrupt already,' and Juliaen, I still..."

Her voice died down to a lingering chime of regret. They sat looking in different directions as the sun set. The hedgeflame lamps lit themselves silver, and bathed them both in it.

Juliaen.

"Yes," Juliaen said, and Lidia watched her face.

This malady of the soul festers throughout Divine Promise, not only in its heart. The whole of it must be cleansed.

But how can we...how should we...? We could not even...

Juliaen.

And Juliaen knew.

"Abominations upon the abominable," she whispered, though loud enough for Lidia to hear. *It is not always the righteous, nor always the clean, that the Divine uses as Their hands.* She looked Lidia in the eye, caught her there, dared her to look away. Lidia didn't, though perhaps she wanted to.

"And not just the Presilyo," Juliaen continued. "The Triune Path is the highest of the Ways the Divine has prepared for Their chosen pilgrims, but not the only one."

"We've discussed this before." Lidia's voice was almost gentle. "Those ideas are controversial at best. It's not clear what Eusébio Inoue meant in those lectures, or if he even—"

"It's clear to me," Juliaen cut in, more sharply than she'd intended. Forcing some of the harshness back down, she went on, "it's clear to the

305

Divine, and They've made it clear to me. Lidia, I'm *sure*. The Caustlands have to be cleansed, allowed to fulfill their Divine Promise again. We can't do it alone, and we can't afford to cast aside any tool the Divine has promised. We *shouldn't*. We *mustn't*, not if we want to keep faith. That means not just using whatever allies we can find among the Sovereign Nations. It means using *any tool* the Divine provides."

Lidia sat back in her chair, rigid, staring into the basement's expansive shadows. "I've recently received an emissary from the Praedhc. She said she represented the Dahlabekh people, the local jungle tribes. They've been keeping their ears to the ground, it seems. They were *very* interested in the idea that we might shift our attention to the Caustlands instead of carving out the Abwaild."

Juliaen leaned forward and grasped Lidia's hand tightly. "Why did you not tell me this earlier? I told *you* about my dream, about our sins against the Praedhc, you—"

"For the last year," Lidia cut in, and Juliaen started at the uncharacteristic interruption, "I have come to know you, Juliaen, but I was not sure at first, not at all. You ask a lot, and I have been burned by belief before. I gave up—" her voice broke, not on the surface but deep below the other currents, even as her words flowed on over it—"so, so much to free myself of that mistake. It is *hard* to believe again, hard to hold onto that last invisible thread of hope."

Juliaen blinked. She knew very little of Lidia's Somonei past, beyond the knowledge and training the High Winnow had passed along over the course of this strange, consecrated year—and the touch of uncertain trust it nurtured in the back of Juliaen's mind. "I'm not asking you to believe in me, Lidia," she said as gently as she could. Gentleness was not one of her strengths, she knew. "I am asking you to hear the Divine echo in the words They have given me."

Lidia put her elbows on the table and half-rose from her chair, voice rising with her, open tears and tearing vehemence in equal measure. "If I am to believe in that, I *have* to believe in you. I must. Because the Divine chooses who They will, and if They have chosen you then I must be *sure*." She slammed herself back down in her chair with a great outrushing sigh. "You are a strange and difficult woman, Juliaen Draecsl, but—sometimes at least—I find myself believing anyway, just like the day I stood in front of your cell."

Juliaen was not offended at being called either strange or difficult. She knew about the distance that seemed to stretch out between herself and others, even her own family. She and Lidia had walked slow wary circles around each other over the last year, and while Juliaen thought that was changing, she was under no illusions that it could do so quickly. "Thank you," she said. Her voice was as quiet as it ever got. "Not for my sake, but I am glad. Lidia, there is so much to do."

"Yes," Lidia said, and the word was nearly a mourning gasp. "There always is. We will see what the Praedhc can offer. We will see what the other Compacts have to say about your 'True Ways.' And—" A hard ripple growled through the Holy Fathom as Lidia's fingers tore into polished cedar, harrowing up jagged furrows of splintered wood that left her hands unbloodied, "—I will ponder the Providence of Archabbot Thuwun's office."

A year and four months later, one of Lidia's assistants brought the news that the Promiseguard had overthrown the Archabbot amid risen unrest, and Juliaen allowed herself a small secret smile. They were calling it the Promise Reformation. Juliaen gave thanks, and both she and Lidia gave speeches. She moved from her tiny room in the Nave of the Abbey Invisible to a small suite adjoining the High Winnow's rooms in the newly-constructed Abbey Priory. These new accommodations were comfortable, though Juliaen did not really care.

She was too busy now.

Sei'khasehn Sav'ni'tal was not what Juliaen expected. She'd pictured some imposing warrior, dressed in bulky exotic armor and carrying a weapon made from imbued obsidian. But the Praedhc emissary was unarmed, and short, and slight. Juliaen stood a full head taller than he, and guessed she must outweigh him as well.

Rather than any kind of battle-garb, Sei'khasehn wore simple but startling clothes, woven out of what looked like ropewood fiber and dyed in a riot of bright color-splotches. His head was bare, dark with stubble; feet clad in open-strapped leather boots with gumchitin soles. His only extra ornaments or markers of rank were a single blue-grey metal earring in each ear, and a somewhat bulky bracer made up of various carapace pieces over his left forearm.

His face was no surprise, though, with its strange silver lines and deeply-tanned skin, eyes an even deeper blue than Juliaen's own. He stood there in Lidia's office, facing the High Winnow while Juliaen stood behind her. He had brought only a single lieutenant, a silent, blank-faced woman whose presence weighed heavily on the tangled, shifting pseudostructure of the Holy Fathom. She was unarmed as well, dressed in a loose but elaborate set of short grey robes.

"Lidia Almeida," Sei'khasehn said. He wore the sort of dour expression that seemed to have settled in for the long haul. "I am glad the very, ehhsss, annoying prisoner we released to you has turned out to be useful after all, yes? You are behind all this, ehhsss, annoying of your Fallen cousins? I am hoping you do not think this will, ehhsss, make us fond of you. We don't care about the Ashwound-dwellers."

He turned and pointed; West, Juliaen assumed, she could never keep track indoors. "They are far from us. You, though, you Carvers, you have caused us much, ehhsss, grief. I have not come here with large hopes. It is best for you that I be wrong, yes? And quickly, or I will turn and go back, and we will think on some other way to deal with you."

"We cannot speak for all the Sovereign Nations in this," Lidia said, "though we hope perhaps one day that will come to pass. However," and she pointed eastward, using two fingers just as the Praedhc had, "we are the closest to your borders, and we have yet to actually encroach on your jungles, only the quartzwood. So if we—"

Sei'khasehn surged forward for a slivered second before halting himself, strangely-lined face a study in restrained rage. "You," he said, visibly fighting to get his temper under control. There was a minute tug on the fabric of the Holy Fathom between the two Praedhc. The lieutenant turned her head incrementally toward him, then gave it a single sharp shake when he looked back at her. Juliaen wondered which of them was really in charge.

Lidia put one foot back, extending both hands, palms-up. Juliaen frowned as she retreated along with her, staying a pace behind her left shoulder. Lidia's voice was carefully even, her posture ready and forward despite the step back. "I'm not sure how I've offended, but apologies all the same."

"You really don't know, do you?" There was still plenty of anger in the Praedhc's voice, but it rested on a bed of weary resignation. "We live in the jungles, but we hunt and harvest in the quartzwood. Every, ehhsss, kilometer you burn down is more hard life for us, yes? There is game and forage in the jungle, but much less. We are forced to use other woods, have conflict with other tribes. Much longer and there could be war."

"War with each other?" Lidia asked. "I thought the Dahlabekh were a confederation."

"Confederation." Sei'khasehn frowned, looking down as if examining the long Gentic word. "This means?"

Juliaen decided to speak up. "A loose association of allies, groups who work together, usually with an agreement."

"Aaahhh, your quiet friend now speaks." He flashed Lidia a toothy silver grin, then addressed Juliaen directly. "This seems correct, yes. You are something like this confederation too, but as you say I am negotiating only with you and not, ehhsss, with your confederation friends? These others of the Sovereign Nations?"

Lidia cleared her throat. "We..." she started cautiously, "...would like to bring them in on any agreement we make later, but now is not the time."

He gave her an uncomfortably long stare, then turned abruptly on his heel and began speaking with the woman—Juliaen no longer really thought she was his lieutenant—in their strange staccato language. She wished, not for the first time, they could have someone present who spoke it. But such translators were hard to find, usually one of the handful of converts they'd made among the Praedhc, and this meeting needed to be kept quiet.

What was the language called? Dahla something, related to "Dahlabekh?"

Sei'khasehn spun back round as the woman gave a tiny tilt of her head. "We are here to speak for all our tribes. Or rather," he nodded his head back toward his associate, "she is, I am mostly for translating, yes? Any agreement made will be taken back to all the tribes, and we will, ehhsss, talk on it." Another hard stare. "And understand, when I say war, I mean maybe war with each other, maybe we unite for war with you. Maybe we finally, ehhsss, persuade others of the Risen that you are a threat. This agreement is important, then, for all of us, yes?"

"Yes," Lidia said quietly. "It is. Listen. We have decided that the

Divine—that our God, which is also three Gods and all of—"

"*Spare* me," Sei'khasehn said. Another silver-toothed grin, hard to measure for mirth. "A good, ehhss, phrase, yes? I learned it from the same, ehhss, naked-of-face fool that gave me your name. He also taught me much about your religion. So. Spare me. I will not be becoming a convert of yours."

"Fine." Lidia's voice was a wonder of carefully-carved patience. "We do not think the Divine wishes us to take your territory. We wish to focus on what we believe we have been promised in the Caustlands, what you call the Ashwound."

The Praedhc actually rolled his eyes at this, a gesture he must also have picked up from the Carver prisoner he'd guarded for so long. "I know my Gentic is not the best, but I know what the Caustlands are, yes? It is not needed to talk as if I am a small child. If I do not understand, I will ask."

Juliaen watched the man as he spoke. He was goading Lidia, trying to keep her off-balance. She had seen her siblings do it to each other a thousand times. And his Gentic—if it was as middling as it seemed, as he admitted, why send him? Was he only pretending to wrestle with the language quite this much? Or did they have reason to choose him despite his mediocre abilities as a translator? A little of both? He was certainly no fool. They would need to be very careful. And that woman with him— dangerous. But of course Lidia must feel that too.

"Yes, of course," Lidia replied. More caution than patience in her voice now. Good. "We cannot simply march across the Siinlan and take back what is ours, what is owed to all the outcast Nations of our...confederation."

This time the fierce amusement in Sei'khasehn's shining smile was unmistakable. "Why not? Tell your Divine to help you. I have heard that the Fathom is holy to Them, I have heard it a thousand times." He laughed, almost a cackle. "Tell Them to cast a thousand spells and cut your enemies to pieces, if the Fathom really is Their holy realm."

Juliaen saw Lidia's temper rise while her own dismay sank in. Both Praedhc watched intently, a pair of blue-eyed raptors with wings half-spread. Two Promiseguard stood just outside the door, but were under strict orders not to enter for anything short of open combat or a direct order. Though it wouldn't come to that, mustn't come to that. Lidia was a dangerous fighter even by Somonei standards, but Juliaen was not; she'd had time for only occasional training in the year and a half since the Reformation.

And then Lidia smiled, all her apparent anger flooding away, replaced by slow rising laughter. "I have heard worse, you know." She took a step forward, a big one, and Sei'khasehn took a half-step back, eyes widening. The surge of raw potential and woven complexity that roiled the skein of the Holy Fathom was immense, chained to the High Winnow's will by a thousand vibrating links.

The grey-robed woman stepped forward too, causing a great clash and flux that sent chaotic shocks in every direction. Juliaen tried her best to follow what was going on; but felt as though she were trying to read Scripture while knowing only a few simple words. The Praedhc woman retreated two steps, eyes narrowed.

Lidia smiled, and it was wolfish now, decades of blood and battle standing bare on the surface. "I have heard worse," she said again. "I will not let you anger me that easily. It has been some time since I have endured such provocation, but I have not forgotten how to weather it. Why are you testing me?"

Sei'khasehn's dark eyebrows had risen up toward his stubbly pate, a hint of fear in his face. But it was an accepting fear, fatalistic almost, and Juliaen wondered why. "So we could see *that*, yes? I am impressed, surely. Also I am surprised. Why is a warrior of your, ehhsss, ability spending her time sitting in a writing-room?"

"My days of fighting were long, and I have put them behind me," Lidia said. "I was… never mind. My history is not important right now."

He snorted at that, turning to exchange a few rapid words with his companion, and they both laughed. Lidia stood solid and stony, waiting.

Juliaen moved closer, put a hand on her shoulder. She felt the tension there, and perhaps a measure of surprise at the touch. "The Divine tests the patience of every one of Their children," she said in Lidia's native Ambérico. The chances that either of these Praedhc would understand seemed remote, and the time for worrying about rudeness seemed long past. Lidia nodded slowly.

"Of *course* your history is important," Sei'khasehn said. "Don't insult me like I am stupid. Where we come from always matters, yes? And we have heard all about you, Lidia Almeida. The place you come from matters so much to you that you planned a very dangerous attack on it. Your history has you wanting much, or we would not be here, yes?"

Lidia's lips drew back slightly from her teeth. "Alright then, Sei'khasehn Sav'ni'tal. If you have heard so much, tell me exactly why we have asked you here."

"Ah." His smile softened, if only at the edges. "We know what you are offering, this is simple. You will leave our forests alone, yes? And now we are more sure that you offer this in—what do you call it?—ehhsss, good faith."

"And if you had not been sure?" Juliaen stepped up beside Lidia, fixing the Praedhc with a frown.

He studied her, appraising, wondering. "You are no simple assistant," he said. "What is your name?"

"I asked you first," she said softly, and held his gaze.

One corner of his mouth twitched, tugging on the curving silver line that ran down past it. "That would, ehhss, depend. If it were a trap or trick, if the invitation were a deception, then we would be free from any obligation to you as guests, yes? Then our duty would be to kill Lidia Almeida as a danger to our people, and die before we could be of any use to yours."

Juliaen glanced over at Lidia, but her face showed no reaction or surprise at this casual admission.

"I am not sure now that we could have success in this, yes?" he continued. "We knew that this Lidia, she had come from some, ehhsss, holy place for your religion. We had heard this place taught warriors, sometimes, but did not think she might likely be one of them, and a powerful one of them also." He sighed, and there was a hint of wry resignation in it that Juliaen found endearing despite herself. "Learn all you can, it is never quick or true enough."

"Why would you tell us this?" Lidia demanded.

He shrugged. It was a strangely deliberate gesture, almost exaggerated, and Juliaen realized this particular version of the gesture was a learned thing, not part of his natural body language. Maybe Praedhc shrugged differently, or maybe they meant something else when they did. The great gulf this represented worried her, and she clutched tight at her faith as Sei'khasehn dropped his shoulders and spoke. "Now there is more honesty in the room, yes? It will help to make an agreement that may, ehhsss, be solid. Lies, they make bad fastenings."

"Alright," Lidia said. "Then here is what we want from you. Many of your people were once shock troops for the Old Kash Empire—"

"Centuries ago. Before you Fallen annihilated it in the disaster you call Starfall." Sei'khasehn sounded almost amused.

Lidia fell silent. Of course the High Winnow couldn't apologize for something their faith held as Divine Judgement, however horrific it might be to mortal sensibilities. This was also not the time to mention that. He probably already knew.

"You want us to fight for you, then? Be the new Empire yourselves?" The Praedhc glanced toward his apparent superior and rattled off a few strange sentences. Both laughed. "That's not going to happen, Lidia Almeida. We did not, ehhsss, very much like the Kash. And, I know this is a surprise, we do not very much like you. We have learned by hard lesson. The Empire said, you fight for us, we leave you alone. It did not work that way. Whatever else we might negotiate, Dahlabekh warriors will never fight by your side."

"That is not what we want," Lidia said, and Juliaen thought she sounded relieved that the subject of Starfall had passed by. "We do not think this would be a good idea for either of our peoples. No, I mention your association with the Kash because they didn't just use your people as front-line troops, did they? Some they changed."

All the amusement and even dourness fell from Sei'khasehn's face, leaving behind a tightened web of hard silver lines. There was fear, but alloyed with the same grim resignation she'd seen before, letting it push him forward rather than pull him back. "If you even once suggest that even one of our people might go through that again, you will have a fight on your hands, Lidia Almeida. We will take our chances. And we will, ehhsss, broadcast what we have learned through the Fathom, in every direction, no care for who might hear. We will gladly sacrifice our lives to do this. And you will have war, with every one of the Risen who hears, and every one of the Risen who hears *them*."

Silence. Nothing about the Praedhc's small speech had left any doubt that he was in deadly earnest, and Lidia had gone rigid, shaking her head. Juliaen thought maybe she was murmuring under her breath, and remembered that for all her strength, the High Winnow had been battered and bruised by countless bouts of violence in her life. Perhaps their memory overwhelmed her now, that real prospect of war, but there was no time for encouragement or recovery, so Juliaen pushed through her fear and stepped forward.

Speak.

"That is *not* what we want, Sei'khasehn Sav'ni'tal." The clear sure quality of her own voice surprised Juliaen, as did remembering the Praedhc's full name. He moved closer in one quick, terrifying stride, but Juliaen held her ground, and cut him off before he could speak.

"We do not want war, not with you, and we do not wish to do anything *to* you. The Divine has spoken, and They have condemned our actions out here in your lands as cowardly abomination. We are sorry for what you have suffered. We should never have left the Caustlands. We should have fought for the Divine Promise that was provided us in fire and sacrifice."

Juliaen winced internally at that last reference to Starfall, but these were the words the Divine had given her, the way They had guided her tongue, she was sure of it. It didn't seem to matter; both Praedhc emissaries had been struck speechless.

That was fine. Juliaen went on. "We want knowledge. Enlightenment. There were special places the Kash took your warriors to undergo profound changes. We have found one, but only one. We do not fully understand it, and it will not be nearly enough for our purposes. We have reason to believe you know where others may be. Tell us all you can, and we will leave your people be, turn our gaze entirely toward the Caustlands that are our Divine right."

She did not mention any of the things they had already done with the place, or the volunteers who had become too dangerous for anything but suicide missions, or the dead or the other...lost. Much of this had taken place before Juliaen had come to Clarcspur, but the stories were unsettling. People who lectured incessantly on forbidden subjects. A man who could herd Abwaild creatures, or push them in more dangerous ways. And worse and worse and worse, rumors or not...

Juliaen took in a deep breath, steadied herself, holding the wide blue gazes as they watched her. "I swear it. I swear it by the One Parent, the Lotus Child, the Enlightening Spirit. I swear it by my hope of release from reincarnation, my desire for union with the Divine. I swear it by my father, my mother, my brothers and sisters. I swear it on everything I hold dear."

Another silence, shorter this time. Sei'khasehn broke it.

"You do not understand what you are asking. You cannot understand.

314

For definite, you *should* not understand." He turned to his companion. They spoke at length. Soon they were yelling. Juliaen guided the still-pale Lidia to a chair as she waited, sat her down, received her quiet *gracias* with a grave smile and a quiet nod.

Finally the discussion ended. Sei'khasehn crossed his arms tight against the splotchy fluorescence of his shirt.

"We know that you wish to turn this against your Fallen cousins, and not against us, or we would already be fighting and dying, yes? You Carvers are the greatest, ehss, thorn in our sides at this time. You are carefully watched, we have heard your preachings. We believe the truth of your anger against the other Fallen. But even so, I must ask, do you really want this thing? I am not sure you understand the, ehss, weight of this weapon you wish to raise against them."

Juliaen looked him in the eye, held his gaze, and after a few seconds he flinched. She wondered if he saw a hint of the Divine there, but pushed the thought away as prideful and listened instead.

Abominations upon the abominable.

"Abominations upon the abominable," she repeated, and felt the borrowed power in her words. Lidia sat up in her chair, staring, all traces of her earlier panic gone.

"Abominations upon the abominable," Sei'khasehn said, as if tasting the words. Juliaen thought she saw a moment's doubt on his strange silver-streaked features. "This can only end in much blood." Then his blue eyes hardened, and he half-turned toward his companion. "But none of it will be ours."

Juliaen listened again, but heard nothing, and kept her silence.

Sei'khasehn took in a long deep breath before letting it all out in a sudden rush. "We will consider this. It is beyond either of our power to give. We will have to go back, and ask." He slowly shook his head. "You have surprised us...ehhsss..." He cocked his head, let out a small barking laugh. "You never gave us your name."

No.

Juliaen shook her head. "I am a servant of the Divine. That is all that matters."

"Very well, servant. It is possible we can, ehhsss, make a trade with you. But understand: I have no reason to, ehhsss, have love for you, yes? But some things must go past that, so I am warning you. There is danger you do not know. We know much, perhaps we can give of it. But what we know, it might not save you, yes?"

Correspondence

Echogram, 33rd of September, 350 SE

Private Dayang Marchadesch
C Company, Special Training Battalion
Camp Singapore, Tenggara 5934

Sara binti Sharif
792 Western Seiyw St.
Kualabu, Tenggara 1070

Hey Sara,
Sorry it's been a while since my last message. I know I said at first that training was easier than what Hang Che put me through...and I have to call him Hang Che now because the echogram transcriber in Kualabu got all offended by what I called him in my last message and wanted to censor it and it was this whole drama with my mom even over echogram...sorry I'm getting off track, I'm really tired and I don't have much time to dash this off. Right, so the training's gotten a lot harder, I don't mean just the techniques, I have a handle on those I think, it's just that it's all day, every day and also
hey look I'm going to need you to keep this one between you and me, right? and also it's starting to really dawn on me what we're going to be using this training for. I mean maybe, I don't think the Tentera Wira fights all the time but still the idea of actually using my mace on another person...I don't know, Sara. The Hunch-Ripper was one thing, or even fighting ashwights as disturbing as that sounds too, or even Hang Che. Because I didn't kill him. I know, maybe this isn't something you want to think about

either but I really need to get it off my chest. I think it's something I could do if I had to and they're definitely doing their best to make sure that's true in the end.

Also one of the other soldiers in my platoon got hit by a blow that wasn't pulled properly and she almost died, she'd let her resilience get low but didn't tell anyone because she didn't want to admit she'd already taken that many hits and God Sara it was bad, I think it was the worst thing I've ever seen happen to a person. Even worse than Hang Che with his legs all...you know. I'm sorry to bring that up if you still have bad memories, I know I do, but it really does help to get this all out before I have to turn the lamp off and go to bed. Thanks for being my friend and someone I can really talk to without having to pretend.

Kepparat I'm out of time. Love you always, tell everyone I'm doing okay

- Dayang

Handwritten note, 14th of October, 350 SE

Listen, Hyon-seok, I've been thinking about what you said about the karma and how we can't just choose what we think is Ragado and what isn't. I've been thinking about it a lot, I wanted to discuss it with Laris too but you know him, he'd just do one of those little sighs and basically say I don't have to care what the teachers say about stuff like this. He's my brother and my best friend but I can't really ask him about Michyero stuff these days if I want a serious answer.

Anyway I don't really feel as guilty as maybe I thought I should, and I've been thinking about that too because it's not like it affects my prayers and meditations unless I think too much about what the teachers say and I don't know if I agree with how they read those parts of Scripture, they're kind of small and from parts where we ignore most of the other stuff because the teachers say it doesn't apply anymore.

I guess what I'm really trying to say is I want to see you again anyway. Tomorrow night in the mending-supplies storeroom? That's the earliest I know I can sneak out.

Thinking of you always,
Sanyago

Echogram, 19th of March, 351 SE

Auxiliary 3rd Class Jeims Dubwa
Hammer Barracks, Pircaat Hall
Aldonza, Salía 93944

Specialist Dayang Marchadesch
B Company, Tentera Wira
Camp Singapore, Tenggara 5934

Dayang,

I have to be pretty careful with what I say here. I hope you understand that I'm going to tell you as much as I can because the politics on this are kind of vague and messy, not to mention irritating as Hell, so a lot of what I have to tell you's gonna be vague and messy as well. I hope it's still helpful. I'm writing in Gentic so no one gets antsy about me sending an echogram in Basa Mala to a member of the Tentera Wira. And because you could probably use the practice now that you're out of school.

Right. So I've actually been asking about the Hunch-Ripper attack on Kualabu ever since I graduated and started getting access to stuff. Seems the Saepis have been pulling shit like this for a long time, not just in Kualabu but in other Tenggaran cities like Avacthani and Surabaru. And not just Tenggara either, come to that. There was an incident in Salía too a few years back, in Acheronford. And Kasyanov, up in the United Admiralty, which surprised me honestly since out of all the Caustland States they're the most immediately able to retaliate. There are even hints that something might have gone down in Nikoka, but the Shogunate keeps a nice tight grip on information and I'm not sure how much even your government knows about what goes on in its protectorate.

Okay, so at first I thought the Kualabu attack was just an attempt to stir things up between Kualabu and the Praedhc but I was only kinda-sorta half-right. They almost certainly did want it to look like the Praedhc were the perpetrators, but that was just to obscure the real origin of their attack—at least in part so that it'd be hard to connect with the other incidents. The possibility of raising tensions was just kind of a nice bonus.

Their main aim isn't clear yet. All we know so far is that they seem to be testing defenses. Maybe every one of these spots are important and they've got some sort of plan that involves them all. Maybe it's just a single place or a handful of them, and they want to mask which is the real target.

My personal hunch is that Kualabu is what they're most interested in, but of course I've got some biases there. I mean, first of all I was personally involved, and solipsism's a thing for every sentient species, you know? Second is that the main reason for my hunch is the Borih'Sath ruins right outside your hometown gates. Biggest and probably most important Praedhc ruin in the Eastern Caustlands, but maybe that's my personal interest in all things Praedhc talking? Doesn't necessarily mean the Saepis are thinking the same way.

Which brings me to the second big thing I found out. We know which Saepis are doing this, or at least the individual Nation. It's the same Compact that went after the Presilyo Ri'Granha a couple years ago. Carvers. Michyero separatists. And they're into some bad stuff, the kind I'm not about to risk writing down. They're under sanctions from all the Caustland States, even the United Admiralty, but the UA still won't let anyone through their territory to retaliate. They need the Sovereign Nations as their dissident safety valve just as badly as they ever did. Authoritarian bastards.

That's all the specifics I can give you right now. I'll keep an ear out and drop you an alert when and if I can, should something else come up. I'd appreciate it if you could do the same, honestly. Not going to lie, that Hunch-Ripper still gives me nightmares sometimes. I'd love to get to the bottom of the whole thing as much as you would. And if nothing comes up, keep in touch anyway. I'm always happy to hear from you.

Your friend,
  Jeims

Handwritten note, 2nd of January, 352 SE

My Lovely Sanyago,
Every day I look forward to seeing your face more and more. We need to be more careful with these notes. I have some ideas on how.
There should be a chance for a private sparring session day after tomorrow. I have some ideas for that too.

Yours in a thousand ways,
Hyon-seok

Subject: Incident After Action Report

To: See Distribution

FROM: Captain Soledad Yan

1. This after action report is prepared 25APR352

2. The following is information regarding the incident itself:

Incident Location: Hartford Village

Personnel Involved: Auxiliary 2nd Class Ceraen Wiilqaems, Ranger 1st Class Taniixh Pai

3. Hostile Contact Made With: Xenospecies, Underflesh Nest Members, Needlewigs, 4 (Unusual Aggression), Hunch-Rippers, 2

4. Complicating factors: <Redacted, Psyhazard>

5. Historical Factors: Previous Abwarren incursion, 344 SE, sanitized by Psyhazard Cleanup Crew #7, sealed by Army Corps of Geomancers.

6. Results of Action: Minor Injury to Ranger Pai, not Fathom-treatable,

healing with anticipation of linear scar on right bicep. All hostile xenospecimens destroyed.

7. Follow-up Measures: Remains incinerated pursuant to SOP. Source investigated. Hibernation chamber discovered with gumchitin chrysalis remains.

8. Determinations: Incident provisionally declared to caused by hibernating remnants of Underflesh Nest destroyed in 344. Cause(s) of hibernation termination unknown. Ranger Pai awarded Purple Heart with Silver Vein. Auxiliary Wiilqaems awarded Combat Action Badge and field-promoted to 2nd Class. Field Promotion has been provisionally confirmed by Captain Soledad Yan.

To: Preston DuBois <pdubois@unci.ca>
1904z 10MAY2067
CC: DEGWAR Engineering Group <degwareng@unci.un>
From: CPO Milana Kartalis <milana.kartalis@unci.gr>
Re: Projection Anomalies

Dr. DuBois,

After a thorough inspection of the Well Access Ring superconductors and superimposition capacitors, we have been unable to find any possible hardware source for the waveform inconsistencies your team is describing. We have however confirmed intermittent interference patterns skewing expected dark energy field scalar values. These appear to be increasing slightly in frequency and magnitude as we approach the Solar corona. They are still well within operational tolerances and are being carefully monitored.

Very Respectfully,

Chief Petty Officer Milana Kartalis

Chat Log, UNCIS Earthseed, 2109z 10MAY2067

milana.kartalis: okay doc you get the email I forwarded? should show up as a reply from Solovyov to my email about our ring inspection. I know you probably have a pretty full inbox
dpreston: Yes, I'm still looking it over.
milana.kartalis: I'm gonna be straight with you, that's the weirdest email I've gotten my whole career, and that includes a few drunk ones
dpreston: Mr. Solovyov has been acting slightly erratic lately, but we'd chalked it up to stress. This is
dpreston: Well for starters we can't be making operational decisions on the basis of one person's disturbing dreams. I'll talk with him.
milana.kartalis: I don't think that's a good idea, doc. we're a little beyond just stress here, we need to get Mission Psych involved
milana.kartalis: I mean I know how overworked your team is and I hate to see you down a member but there's no way he's not doing more harm than good like he is now
milana.kartalis: imagine if he'd hit 'reply all' instead of just replying to me
dpreston: Hmmmm.
dpreston: Okay.
dpreston: I'll make the call.
milana.kartalis: thank you. look, I'm sorry about this, but if he keeps sending emails with creepy crap like 'the call of resonant minds drawing us astray' we could get some bad morale problems real quick
dpreston: Agreed. And thank you again for re-inspecting the DEGWAR off-schedule, I know how much extra work that means for you and your team.
milana.kartalis: no problem, just doing our job
milana.kartalis: and we all want to get there in one piece

Echogram, 25th of May, 352 SE

Specialist Dayang Marchadesch
B Company, Tentera Wira
Camp Singapore, Tenggara 5934

Piolo Marchadesch
897 Kembang Road
Kualabu, Tenggara 1070

Hello Father,
Thanks for the birthday present, and tell Mother thanks as well. I'll be sure to wear it next time I have a chance to wear civvies to town. I'll try to send you an echoframe, even, I know it's been a while since the last one.
I've been operational for almost a year now. Nothing exciting yet. We did raid a bandit camp near Avacthani but they gave up without a fight as soon as they saw the Tentera Wira crest on Sergeant Nyunt's breastplate. You'd like her, she's fierce. I like her sometimes. It's hard to always like your sergeant. She's taught me a lot, though, and she's even given me a few leadership chances here and there. I think she wants to help me toward making Corporal, but maybe that's just wishful thinking.
I'm pretty sure what she wants most is to get her commission and go officer instead of climbing the enlisted ranks. I've thought about it too even though I didn't do that well on those parts of the tests when I first enlisted, but for now I think I'll keep my eye on Sergeant or even First Sergeant before I look at going to University, which I'd have to do for officer track.
I have to thank you for more than the birthday present too. I know having me trained wasn't easy for you. I'm not talking about the money, I know that isn't the part you cared about. I mean watching me learn skills I'm pretty sure you hoped I'd never have to use, but also knew might save my life because you'd seen the world and you know how it is. I know it also meant a lot of fights with Mother and also that you don't want to talk about that, so I'll leave it alone after this but still you should know that I understand some of what it cost you
kepparat Father I'm not any good at this
I'm just trying to say that I love you, not just because you're my father because I think every child loves her father or wants to but because I've come to know you some growing up or I hope I have
and I do love you Tatay
- Dayang

To: DEGWAR Engineering Group <degwareng@unci.un>
1342z 11MAY2067
CC: Ship Psychologist's Office <espsych@unci.un>
From: Preston DuBois <pdubois@unci.ca>
Re: Chief Engineer Solovyov

Hey team,

I figured I should get ahead of this before the rumors go too far afield. Chief Engineer Solovyov has been placed on psychiatric hold due to some concerns about his recent communications. If you have received any disturbing material from Mr. Solovyov, the current command policy is to forward it to the Ship Psychologist's Office and then delete it. We are treating this matter with the utmost seriousness, and if IT does not report full compliance within 24 hours there may be measures taken.

We know everyone is working very hard and that stress levels are high. Please make sure you are taking your mandatory breaks and getting sufficient nightly sleep. This is an exceptional endeavor, unprecedented in human history, and you are needed at your very best. We are all counting on you.

Thanks as always for your attention and hard work,

Doctor Preston DuBois
Engineering Director, Dark Energy Gravity Well Access Ring

27MAR354
MEMO FOR
Captain Musdah Trimurti
SUBJECT
Corporal Dayang Marchadesch, B Company, Tentera Wira

1. Corporal Marchadesch is to be granted access to sanitized reports related to FLAGLEAP, CHERRYSET, and JABJAHANNAM.
2. B Company's appeal concerning initial denial of accelerated

promotion has been granted on review of additional endorsements and documentations. Corporal Marchadesch may be promoted to Sergeant at earliest convenience.

Lieutenant Colonel Ahmad Suharto
Tentera Wira Central Command

Handwritten Note, 5th of June, 354 SE

Mi Querido Hyon-seok,

It's been too long since I've seen you, this training schedule is killing me. Not the actual training, even though I have to honestly say I've turned out to be pretty bad at that (guard duty is the thing I dread most about real Somonei duty and these exercises seem to be mostly that, you'll be saddened to note that one of your favorite parts of me has some new cane marks from my "deficiencies" at focusing on absolutely nothing of interest for hours at a time.) I hope you're doing better in your large-unit exercises so our separation can have an upside for at least one of us.

I keep thinking about what you said about families and the Divine's purpose for us. I don't know about all that prophecy stuff, everyone seems to have different ways of reading it, but I do think the Divine must have some mission for us important enough to be worth all this. I admit sometimes I feel jealous of how Laris can remember his family even though he says he thinks that makes it worse, not like we can really know for sure but it does seem to help him sometimes, give him something to hold onto that isn't the Presilyo, you know? Not sure if that's always a good thing for him or not

—remember when you were kind of jealous of him at first? I guess it was understandable at the time and feelings don't always make sense anyway, but it was a relief when you realized he's always just been my brother and anyway he's not...like us...even a little bit. Even if seeing you jealous was kind of cute and it's still nice to know someone feels I'm worth getting jealous over.

Especially when that someone is as lovely as you.

—but ayyy I'm wandering off what I was saying before. Yeah, I do believe the Divine know what They are doing with us even if we don't and even if Laris is sometimes maybe a little bit right about the teachers not knowing everything about it they say they do. Obviously I hope they're not right about some of the things they say about, well, us I guess. I don't know. If anything Ragado has ever been worth the karma, it's you, and maybe the Divine is a lot more understanding than they say. They do always say the Divine is ultimately about love, after all. And you've got mine, for better or worse.

- Sanyago

Echogram, 15th of October, 354 SE

Pandikar Marchadesch
153 Genting Way
Kualabu, Tenggara 1070

Sergeant Dayang Marchadesch
C Company, Tentera Wira
Camp Singapore, Tenggara 5934

Hey Dayadesch,

I guess I should start out by congratulating you on your promotion. I mean, from what I hear (especially from Father) it's a pretty early step up for you. I'm not gonna say I'm surprised, it's just about exactly what I'd have expected. Not that I'd have been disappointed if it hadn't happened. I've seen enough of this world to know that God obviously didn't intend for much of it to be fair. Still though. Not a surprise. And I don't doubt for one moment you earned it.

Listen, I know this has been hard for you. Not that you haven't been up to the challenge, that's one thing about you, you've always been up to the challenge. It makes you amazing and impressive and more than a little crazy sometimes and I love you for it, but that doesn't mean it's not hard. Hang Che is still here. Sulking some, a lot more tarnished than he used to be, but still here. I know that's got to sting, and I don't blame you. Maybe a different big brother would just go kick his ass, but you know I'm not your kind of fierce, and honestly I think that particular big brother would be just as likely to get himself killed and add to his sister's grief.

You've changed, I can hear it in your letters. Learned to deal with people a little easier, maybe? Sounds like things were a little rough at first when it came to getting along with everyone else in your unit. You've always been very particular about the company you keep, back home it was always just you and Sara, or you and me, or later you and that crazy Salían Lingmao (I did like him, but you gotta admit he's a particular kind of crazy.) You and the boyfriends I'm supposed to pretend I didn't know about (don't worry, I got no room to judge and I'm not gonna.) There in the Army I guess you don't get to choose quite so easily, and I can tell that wears on you. You're dealing with it anyway, sounds like, and I'm proud of you for that. Father is too. And Mother, even though she doesn't approve of the circumstances.

And yeah, I'm sure you've gotten tougher and smarter and more capable of kicking ass, but hey, that wasn't really in doubt, was it? I'm proud of you for the stuff that's hard for you more than the stuff that comes natural.

We look forward to seeing you when you can get away. I'm still here working the shop with Isra. She's started to talk about retiring, so I'm saving up to buy her out when the old greyfur finally decides to spend her golden years napping in the sun and grooming her endless great-great grandkittens. I've also been seeing a Salían adventurer named Aeliizhbaey. Hell of a Gentic name, right? You can just call her Liiz if she's still around when you visit. She's been recovering in town after getting hurt in one of the deep ruins and, and she's talking about hanging up her sword for good. Maybe she'll stick around, we'll see. Some things you just have to enjoy while you can, nothing lasts forever either way. Mom doesn't approve because she's not Muslim, but I have plenty of practice tuning that down to just background noise.

Take care of yourself, Dayadesch. We're all thinking about you.

Love,

Pandimarch

TOP SECRET//SI/PSYHAZARD

FOR HAND/TALON DELIVERY ONLY
MINIMAL COPY POLICY APPLIES
EYES ONLY— BURN AFTER RECEIPT BY ALL PARTIES

04FEB355
Reporter: Auxiliary First Class Ceraen Wiilqaems
Recipients: CALWATCH, NOCOM, DIVCOM

Strong evidence suggests that the Carver Nation separatists under watch in the vicinity of Acheronford are involved in the study and probable use of Praedhc sites and artifacts related to deliberate exposure of human subjects to the Border Spectrum. The weaponization of these same subjects is a likely goal. Be advised that residual Othered entities may still be present as a result of high-risk Praedhc historical practices.

Areas of exposure to boundary regions of the Outer Below are a remote but not fully discounted possibility. Exact site location and surface entrance still under investigation. Recommend immediate notification of Tenggaran authorities due to territorial proximity.

YOU ARE ORDERED TO COMPLY WITH PSYCH SEPARATION AND OBSERVATION PROCEDURES IMMEDIATELY AFTER READING

TOP SECRET//SI/PSYHAZARD

Echogram, 19th of March, 355 SE

Councilwoman Sara binti Sharif
792 Western Seiyw St.
Kualabu, Tenggara 1070

Sergeant Dayang Marchadesch
C Company, Tentera Wira
Camp Singapore, Tenggara 5934

Hey Dayang,

Thanks for your congratulations on my Town Council seat! It's been a long hard campaign and I really do appreciate you believing in me, especially when so many people were saying I'm too young. Now that I have access to all the guard archives, I've managed to get my hands on the Fathomcaster transcript from the day you and Jeims and Aulia talked to that Pelo scout by the mire. I've attached a copy. Hope you find it helpful.

Hope to see you again soon.

All my love,
Sara

Chapter 22

0: *Under and over the smooth and difficult stone, through and also repelled go the ribbons of light, but they do not shine, they cling to the slow and solid deepest bones of the New Mother.*
1: *Know now and remember then the knots that are tied without bending, in through the longest stretches of depth and understanding they are joined together with no nearness to complicate their movements.*
2: *Those who can may know the higher and deeper and further in, the Sun and Her Twin and Her Family of Many Cousins, and how She knows the many stones, gathers in the folding sheets and umbilical skein beneath the skin of Her child's most slowly-rotting meat.*
3: *The perfect sphere-and-cube of Huen'Cal rests groundless athwart all He sees.*
<Translator's Note: The Praedhc line-sigil of warding called the Augur of Tainted Words is always affixed between the preceding verse and the following.>
4: *His outer Eyes watch the Six Standing Directions. His inner Eye is not good for the sight of the mind's gaze, and watches through to the [Outer Below]* to guard us the Risen, and our every eye.*
*Redacted in nearly all published copies

- Binding Illumination of the Wombstone, Long Nine: Rising Five, Zero up Four, Sarojini Javadekar translation, 74 SE

Presilyo Monastery, Inoue Island, The Caustlands, 355 SE

Sanyago stared at the monk, fists clenched. "No graduation ceremony?"

The question didn't come near to expressing his tangled rage and disbelief, just the one small piece he could easily wrangle into words.

Laris stood beside him, frowning. He still held the book he'd been reading, dangling from one hand with a finger marking his place. The small library room had felt so familiar and peaceful before the administrator monk—he'd introduced himself as Brother Xaeli—came in to give them the news. Now, it seemed a place apart, an unreal addition to the greater building.

The monk was nodding, probably had been the whole time Sanyago stood there in shock. He leaned forward, looked at Sanyago closely before he spoke, light-red brows raised in placid acceptance.

"You will be given an opportunity to say goodbye to the rest of your class, but it must be brief. Brotherly affection and warrior's camaraderie should be encouraged in Somonei, but attachment should not." That last sentence had the air of aphorism about it, and Sanyago made a sudden frustrated swiping motion as though trying to bat it away. This self-important stranger was narrating a catastrophic change of direction in their lives, and he was going to do it with trite bits of pre-rehearsed crowshit?

"What?" Sanyago said, then shook his head and latched onto the first words that offered him any purchase. "We won't *be* Somonei if you're not even going to let us graduate!" His mind flicked through all the possible explanations it could find for this. "Have we done something wrong?"

They had both, he knew, done plenty wrong according to the Presilyo's rigid rules, but nothing really *serious*. Hyon-seok probably represented his most Ragado transgression, but if they were going to stop graduations for *that* they'd be graduating a lot fewer students. If they decided to be fair, that was.

Oh, then you should have nothing at all to worry about. The sardonic little passing thought made him frown. Okay, but what about Laris? The thing with Bai? That was the Presilyo's own damn fault, he *wished* they'd done something about that instead of pretending she was mentoring him somehow or helping him deal with what he'd seen during the attack or whatever other crowshit helped them sleep at night.

He refocused himself and glared at Brother Xaeli, who still stood there looking patient and blank. Sanyago hated his stupid orange-freckled face and its refusal to tell them anything at all.

"Well?" Laris' voice cut in with sudden vehemence, making both Xaeli and Sanyago turn to look at him in surprise. He stepped forward, thin brows sloped together in angry insistence, a hint of red tinting the deep black of his face.

"Perhaps you would like to rephrase that, Zagen Staafaen?" Xaeli's pale face had taken on abundant color of its own.

Laris made a show of pondering the administrator monk's question, running one long finger over the sharp line of his jaw. Sanyago frankly gaped. Bald sarcasm, toward a Presilyo authority, from *Laris*? Irreverent questions were one thing but this—?

Laris frowned and slowly shook his head. "No," he said. "I don't think I would. We're about to become legal adults, you want us for something extraordinary, and you're going to need our cooperation. No more stupid cryptic games, no more stonewall silences. Either explain what's going on or bring us to someone who will, right now."

Brother Xaeli looked around wildly but no, the three of them were still alone and he had no one to turn to for support. He was almost laughably livid. No, he *was* laughably livid, but Sanyago suppressed the laughter swimming in a strange mix with his rage. No need for *both* of them to be in apocalyptic trouble.

"And don't pretend I'm blaspheming or disrespecting the Divine or whatever by wanting answers," Laris continued calmly. "You're not the Divine, no one here is, and 'You two won't have a graduation ceremony' isn't exactly Scripture, is it? Go lord whatever power the Presilyo's given you over someone else."

Sanyago looked back and forth between the two of them, feeling frozen. Laris had opened the floodgates to some ancient internal reservoir, and Divine help anyone who stood in front of the deluge.

Radiant with fury from the top of his smooth-shaven head to the base of his neck, Brother Xaeli raised one shaking finger and stepped close to Laris, who looked down at him with steady grey eyes. Xaeli was a tall man, but Laris had at least ten centimeters on him.

"You," Xaeli said, blue eyes staring, "are trying to give *me* orders, Zagen? You have no idea how much opportunity you may be throwing away by deciding to be defiant and disrespectful at this—"

"Defiant of *what*, exactly?" Laris leaned forward, looming over the smaller man. A stab of anxiety made Sanyago grimace. Laris wasn't exactly practiced at intimidation, but he could kill the administrator monk with a single barehand blow, and they all knew it. He never *would*, but even the oblique reminder meant he must be very, very angry. Sanyago put a hand on his friend's shoulder. Laris glanced his way and stepped back a little, though his expression did not soften.

To his credit, Brother Xaeli stood his ground under Laris' steady steel gaze, and though his voice went quiet it lost none of its incandescent outrage. "Defiant of Abbot del Toro's orders, Zagen Staafaen," he said. "I take orders too, we all do. Do you understand that? I may be no warrior myself, but this is a warrior institution, and information in the wrong or right hands can kill. We all are told only as much as we need to know, myself included."

Laris sighed, and some of the anger seemed to leech out with his breath. "This is a stupid waste of time. If you don't have answers, take us to someone who does. Like I said in the first place."

Sanyago wanted to say something, present a united argument, but the tiny hope that somehow this whole thing could still be salvaged held him back. He fought it, did his best to swallow the bitter disappointment attached to the here and now.

Xaeli glared. Laris went on. "Look, I'm not stupid. If we take our oaths after graduation, that binds us to all your precious orders for another seven years, but we *haven't yet*. Do you not understand what that means? This is the one time we have the chance to make demands, to get answers, to make sure we know enough to make this kind of huge decision. I've been a good student. I've put up with plenty of your crowshit. I've kept a million of my questions to myself, but now I *will* have answers, from you or someone more useful."

In the long silence that followed, Sanyago won the battle against wishful thinking, and now he spoke. "He's right. And we stay together. You don't get one without the other. You try to separate us, put pressure on that way? We both walk away. I believe in the Triune Path, I *want* to serve as a Somonei. But if you try to pull us apart, I'll go find another way to follow the Divine."

Sanyago felt a bit bad about speaking for Laris like that, making threats on his behalf, but also felt sure he spoke true for both of them even if they hadn't discussed it beforehand. He glanced over at his friend, who nodded and very slightly smiled. Sanyago returned the gesture, and they both stared at Xaeli. Sanyago folded his arms in an effort to look a little more defiant.

Brother Xaeli took a deep breath and then let it out in a great long grunt of frustration and free-floating rage. Laris actually snorted with laughter, just once before he could stop himself, and Xaeli shot him a final incendiary glower before turning to stalk away.

"Ca*ray*, brother," Sanyago said. "That was some *cojones* back there. I don't...I don't even know. What do you think they're going to do?" Possibilities jumbled their way through his head in tiny scraps, barely glimpsed.

Laris grinned, and it was broad, full of slightly mad catharsis. "Send someone, what else can they do? I've been waiting for this chance to really speak my mind for a long, long time and I don't think I even knew it until now. I'm sorry if this gets you into trouble too."

Sanyago didn't know how sorry Laris really was, but understood either way. Divine knew he'd been the one to get them both in trouble a thousand times in the past. "You know what? I think whatever trouble comes, it'll be worth it." He frowned. "I'm still angry about the graduation, though, no matter what their explanation is."

"Yeah, I know." Laris leaned over, put an arm round Sanyago's shoulders, gave him a rough squeeze. Sanyago smiled. Laris *hated* ceremonies, he knew, but had put up with enough of Sanyago's excited chatter about the rite of passage to know how bitter his disappointment must be.

Sanyago smiled up at his friend, thumped him on the back with a closed fist. "Thanks, brother. Maybe at least we'll be up to something interesting. If the reason for this was boring, Xaeli probably would have just told us."

Laris grunted at the light blow, then laughed, and they both fell into thoughtful silence.

After about a half-hour wait, "something interesting" arrived in the person of another monk, who entered alone and shut the door before introducing himself as Master Leng. He was a spare man, medium height, with unremarkable Zhon Han features. His presence in the Holy Fathom was suspiciously flat, and Sanyago had to rein in the urge to probe at it. If he had woven a Fathom-cloak, it must be a masterful one.

"Zagen Staafaen. Zagen Sanyago." The smallest hint of smile on his left side. "You've managed to make Brother Xaeli very angry. I need to know right away if it will always be like that, or if you can take orders even when all the information is not available to you. If you cannot, you will have your graduation ceremony, and most likely you will never see me again." Master Leng's voice was mild, with no striding and also no uncertainty. He looked back and forth between the two of them with patient expectation in his plain brown eyes.

"We can take orders, Master Leng," Sanyago said. "Even if we don't know all the reasons behind them. But when we don't have the reasons…" he trailed off, tilted his head in Laris' direction, knowing he'd have more to say.

Laris nodded, continued for him. "...we want to know *why* we don't have the reasons. Whatever it is you have in store for us, I don't think we'll do you much good as blindly obedient pawns. I understand the need for control of information, I pay attention to the history you've taught us and I've read a lot more on my own. I know that misplaced information can be deadly. I also know that acting with insufficient or even wrong information can be just as catastrophic."

Master Leng laughed softly. "Your teachers told me you talk like you're writing a treatise. I see now what they mean. You are correct, and I think all your reading might serve you well. If, and I do mean if, you are able to temper it with experience, and set it aside when experience teaches you differently."

"Sure," Laris said. "I'll do my best. We both will. But we still don't know what you want. Or what you are master *of*, Master Leng."

"I have no specific title because my responsibilities are of a sensitive nature. I am entrusted with overseeing the activities of the Shuvelao. Do you know what this means?"

Laris shook his head, but Sanyago felt an electric thrill spread out from the focus-point just below his navel. He'd heard the word in whispers, always from adults and always when listening to things he wasn't supposed to hear. Something elite, something shadowy.

Another tiny hint of crooked smile on Leng's bland features. "One of the first things you will have to work on, Sanyago, is controlling what your face gives away. Clearly you know more than you're supposed to. Your teachers have told me about your eavesdropping habits. I'm sure you've developed some useful skills that way, but I'm going to have to ask you to curtail those activities going forward."

Sanyago tried to keep the surprise off his face. "Ah...yes, Master Leng.

I, uh, I got the impression that the Shuvelao were something secret and, um, special. Missions no one was supposed to talk about. Somonei, but...different." He stole a quick look at Laris, whose eyebrows were raised. He'd mentioned the possibility of secret commandos among the Somonei before; Laris had shrugged and said it wouldn't surprise him, then lost interest when Sanyago didn't have anything more concrete.

"That is reasonably accurate," Leng said. "There is more, of course. Whether you hear it or not will depend on your own choices. There are three paths you can take."

Leng held up a single finger. "One, you can decline to know more. I will leave, you will be returned to your dormitory-cabin, and you will graduate with your class. We will not speak again. If you see me on the grounds, I will ignore you. You will mention nothing of this conversation to anyone else. You will serve out your seven years among the Somonei, then stay or go, as you choose."

Laris and Sanyago exchanged glances. *Nothing new, and no answers.*

Leng held up a second finger. "Your second option is to simply leave when you reach legal adulthood, as per our treaties with the Caustland States. You will be given a small sum in the currency of your choice, and make your way on Solace as you choose. Your debt to the Presilyo and to the Divine will be unpaid. You will be excommunicated from the Triune Path in this life, and it will take you many incarnations to atone for deviating from your dharma."

Laris went stony-faced at this, but Sanyago just nodded. Still nothing new.

"You have always had these first two options," Leng continued. "I mention them only so that they may be weighed with a new, third choice: you can come with me. You will be equipped and sent off for your first trial. You will not go alone, but this is a real mission, no training exercise. All the dangers and stakes will be very real. That is all I can tell you. I am going to leave now, and come back in exactly two hours. Talk, pray, argue, meditate, whatever you need to make your decision. That is all."

He left without another word, ignoring all attempts at further questions.

Sanyago knew what he wanted right away, but it took Laris the full two hours to decide.

Sanyago toyed with the woven straps of his newly-issued pack, watching the night-lit river-waves of the Mindao flow and sparkle past their little boat. The vessel slipped quietly over the powerful currents, sending unfamiliar sensations rolling through Sanyago's lower gut. It wasn't unpleasant, not really, mixed in with the electric vigor of his excitement and uncertainty.

He released the pack strap, letting the whole canvas-wrapped weight thump into the wood that held back the water, making a sound that resonated strangely through both. He leaned back, fingered the pommel of the fine wu jian sword sheathed at his waist, touched the plain silver clasps at the neck of his drab brown robes. The last few hours had been a blur; receiving the sword, which he still couldn't believe was even temporarily his, trading in his sky-blue robes for the nondescript ones he now wore, being kitted out in other field equipment. A heavy portion of rations in his pack; an assortment of throwing-weapons stashed all over.

Laris had received no weapon. Laris didn't need one. What Laris did seem to need, right now, was for this boat trip to be over. He'd managed a decent meditation posture despite the boat's motions, breathing slowly, but the occasional shudder gave away his distress. Sea-sickness, the nameless rowing monk called it, though none of them had ever seen a real sea and it was unlikely they ever would.

Sanyago turned in his seat to look at the pair of Shuvelao seated behind them. Master Leng had introduced them as "trainers, observers, and mentors." They looked back at him, but said nothing. Sanyago kept his own mouth shut. Silence was the standing order for this trip across the Mindao.

They were an odd pair, though Sanyago supposed he and Laris didn't exactly come off as a matched set themselves. Operative Aeriic was a squat, thick-muscled man with pale skin and a heavy black beard that, even shaved clean, managed to shout its presence. He had small, sharp eyes so deeply-set it took Sanyago a few glances to determine they were actually green under the shadow of his heavy brows. Operative Niceto was built like Sanyago's new sword, steel-bar slender and medium height, with muddy brown eyes and deeply-tanned features that were handsome in a craggy sort of way.

Both were visibly armed—Aeriic with a three-section staff, Niceto with a rapier, an unusual weapon for a Somonei. Neither wore any obvious armor, though Sanyago knew their robes must be heavily imbued. His and Laris' certainly were, much more powerfully than he would have expected for equipping a newly minted pair of...of whatever he and Laris were now. Candidates? Trainees?

Sanyago was full of questions, but he kept them in for now. Silence had been ordered, and Master Leng had made it clear that the Shuvelao's orders were to be obeyed. Obeyed without delay—although, Leng had said with a tiny hint of smile in Laris' direction, not necessarily without question. Obedience in the moment, questions later, he had added.

Sanyago gave Laris a sympathetic pat on the shoulder, and got a brief queasy smile in return. The nameless oarsmen rowed on, and Sanyago watched the shimmering bow of Solace's rings stretch across the night sky, slung steady against the distant crawl of constellations. The slow, rocking moment sunk in to him, unreal, exhilarating, uncertain, full of anxious possibility.

It took longer than he expected to cross the Mindao, though they did seem to be charting a rather oblique course that aimed for a point far downriver. Sanyago watched their course on the map in his mind, pieced it together from everything he'd seen on his steeple-climbing expeditions.

The boat scraped up on the shore with no dock or jetty in sight. The rower got out first, wading through the shallow water to pull the boat further up, and Sanyago followed, leaning down to trail fingertips over the coarse gravel. *First time I've touched ground off Inoue Island, that I can remember anyway.* The moment etched itself deep into some uncertain part of his memory, but in that moment he was fully there, standing on the shore, looking out over Salían plains.

He heard Laris scramble up the bank behind him. Sanyago watched him stumble past, making it as far as the grassy part of the bank before going to his knees and throwing up. Laris muttered a word Sanyago very much hoped the Shuvelao would not hear, then got unsteadily to his feet.

"I'm all right," he said. "Thought I could pull my mind past it but I don't have any practice"

"You'll be facing plenty of problems you don't have any practice solving," came a gravelly voice from just behind.

Sanyago started as he whirled round; Laris just gave a grunt of acknowledgement, still too sick to be properly surprised. Both Shuvelao were standing less than a meter away, outlined by moonlight reflected from the Mindao's rushing waves. There had not been the slightest sound in the air or stir in the Holy Fathom to announce their movement. He fought the sense of disorientation that surged up along with his adrenaline. Everything was so quickly changed— still, he was glad he had chosen to come along, just for the chance to learn from these two.

"Operative Aeriic is correct," Niceto said, with a nod to his shorter companion. His voice was swift and smooth, warmly tinted by his slightly Ambérico accent. "Practice is important. You need every edge you can get. But sometimes you won't have it, and then you'll have to think on your feet."

"Yes...Operative," Sanyago said carefully. He was still unsure how he was supposed to address these strange semi-Somonei.

" 'Niceto' will do fine, Sanyago," the Shuvelao replied. "We will know each other well enough to gauge respect without resort to titles."

"Yes...Niceto," Sanyago replied. The name tasted strange in his mouth without anything to accompany it, and he felt another sharp jolt of displacement. "May I ask where we are going?" He watched the rower stride silently past, still stretching arms and legs as he went, then get back into the boat and push off from the shore. Okay, so whatever their destination was, they'd be walking there.

"You can always ask," Aeriic answered for his partner. The hint of laughter in his voice was like the slide of old masonry over cracked mortar. Sanyago wondered what exactly had happened to the man's vocal cords, but guessed that wasn't a question he'd have the right to ask just yet. So many questions crowding in, demanding to be let out, so little familiar ground to stand on.

Laris walked back over, spitting out a mouthful of water and wiping his mouth. "Where...where are we going, then?" His voice was still a touch queasy.

"Acheronford," Aeriic said. "North of it, anyway. We'll follow the Mindao south. At a distance. Would have been faster to take a boat, but we don't want attention. Anchorskiff checkpoints and river patrols. We got papers, we could pass, but better not to. Constrains your cover story, having to remember who's seen you." After glancing at the little boat, now unburdened by extra passengers and rowing northward against the current, he beckoned and began walking away from the shore.

"What's north of Acheronford?" Laris asked as they followed the stocky Shuvelao. He looked cautiously pleased at the chance to ask what he liked.

Sanyago examined that bit of his mental map. Acheronford was nestled into Salía's southeast corner, with the Mindao to the east... and the Siinlan to the south. Right at the edge of the Caustlands, of the whole Fallen world. Maybe they'd have reason to go into Acheronford itself, finally get a glimpse of the Siinlan Veil, or even the Ashlit Mire.

The Shuvelao exchanged a long glance as they led the way over wild grass and sporadic abblum. Finally, Aeriic nodded. "Not going to tell you 'til we get there." He shrugged. "Said you could ask, didn't say you'd always get answers."

"Are you going to at least tell us why not?" Laris asked. Sanyago gave him a sharp look. Antagonizing Brother Xaeli or even Master Leng was one thing, but these were their new mentors, men they'd be working closely with for Divine knew how long.

Aeriic just gave a grinding peal of laughter. "Sure. You can't tell what you don't know. Something happens to us, mission's over. Make your way back to the Presilyo quick as you can. No echograms. No messages of any kind. You got that?"

"Yes," Laris said, and tugged at the straps of his pack, which hadn't really been designed for someone so tall. "Thank you for telling me. It's refreshing to at least know why I don't have an answer."

Sanyago felt a small sweet breath of relief that neither of the Shuvelao had taken offense at Laris' question. "What do we tell people if we get stopped on our way?" It was a horrible prospect, having to go back without the two older monks, but kind of an exciting one too. An adventure on their own, a chance to prove themselves. He plucked a tufted stalk from the tall grass and twirled it round between his fingers as he walked.

"Stay close to the truth," Niceto answered, looking over his shoulder. "Tell them you're a pair of Somonei initiates who have lost their trainers. They'll expect you to be disoriented and afraid. Play that up, and get back to the Presilyo as quick as you can. Then ask round for Master Leng, of course."

Sanyago thought about that, trying to sort all this newness into some kind of order inside his head. He glanced over at Laris, who was frowning as he walked, grey eyes sweeping low the way they did when he was trying to come to a decision.

Laris looked up suddenly. "I can ask questions about the Divine, then? About the Triune Path? Some things, I never could get straight answers to back at the Presilyo."

Niceto laughed, a rich, easy chuckle in stark contrast with his partner's. "You've got an eternally inquisitive mind, Staafaen. Most of your teachers said so as well. It'll serve you well as an agent of the Presilyo, but listen. We're not really the people to help you with theology. I say my prayers, I perform my meditations, but I'm no priest. Neither is Aeriic. I've seen the good we do, the evil we combat, and that's enough. We won't make good sparring-partners on matters of faith, and to be perfectly honest I doubt we know any more than you do."

Laris jerked his head back, cocked it in disbelief. Sanyago blinked, felt his mental footing slide. Somonei were supposed to be extremely devout, even if they were hypocritical sometimes, and these Shuvelao were a sort of...what? Super-Somonei? Why would they say something like this? He'd spent these last years—really all the years he could remember—under the assumption, no, the bedrock *knowledge* that every grown-up in his life was available for spiritual guidance, however unsatisfactory that guidance might sometimes be.

Then Laris sighed, said "okay," and everyone turned to Sanyago. He berated himself for letting his shock show so clearly on his face, tried to force a small serene smile.

Operative Aeriic dropped back from the front of their little party and clapped a large calloused hand on Sanyago's shoulder. "You'll get plenty chances for talking to a priest. Meanwhile, if you really feel the need to confess your karma, you can unburden yourself directly to the Divine." He grinned, revealing two badly-chipped teeth. "Don't imagine you're special that way. Usual practice for Somonei in the field."

Sanyago nodded, but at least half his attention was occupied by those two broken teeth. They should have been a trivial matter for a physician to repair, or even the man's own Fathom-meditations. Sanyago had healed or regrown at least a couple dozen in the course of his training, they all had.

Of course he could guess—*but don't think on it too hard*—why the injuries hadn't healed, and he'd seen plenty of Somonei with stubborn scars. Somehow the teeth just seemed worse. He knew this kind of thing could happen to him, was a risk he'd agreed to...but still. Would Old World dentistry really be all *that* much a Ragado vanity if he ended up looking like Operative Aeriic?

Everyone was staring at him again.

What had they—? Oh. Right. No priest, confess straight to the Divine. "Ah. Yeah, okay," he said, then bowed while he collected himself to try again. "Yes, I understand. Thank you, Aeriic." Calling the older man by his given name still felt so strange.

"Don't thank me yet," the Shuvelao replied in that stonegrinder voice. "Now. We're going south. Gonna follow the river south, but not too close, understand? And silent. Don't need attention drawn. Even at a distance, the Mindao ain't no creek. Plenty of traffic. Understand?"

Both boys nodded, and followed.

They walked. And they walked, and they walked. Minutes, then hours. Long silent walks were nothing new; for training, they had sometimes circled round and round Inoue Island for days-long marches, stopping only to sleep on the banks of the Mindao, and to eat, if they were lucky. This was better, this time Sanyago didn't feel like he knew every tree, every blade of grass, every lavender flash of abblum. The going was surprisingly hilly; he'd expected the nearness of a river to mean flatter land, since they only flowed downward, but the terrain surrounding the Mindao seemed utterly unaffected by its presence.

"The great Caustland rivers were mostly formed by the trauma of Starfall," Operative Aeriic told him. "Like deep cracks on the face of Solace. 'Swhy they meet in the center of Zhon Han, where the Earthseed's power-source struck the planet." Sanyago spent a few minutes looking up at the lightly-clouded sky as he walked, trying to visualize the Earthseed hurtling down from another world. Then he tripped on a protruding stone, grunted, and managed to catch himself with his other foot rather than his face. Laris saw, but kept any snickering to himself. Sanyago kept his eye on where he was going after that.

There was silence except when the Shuvelao decided to speak, and as the excitement wore off Sanyago felt some of his thoughts become burdensome. Thoughts of Hyon-seok, of course; laced with guilt and longing and aching absence. He'd managed to leave a couple of notes in places he knew Hyon-seok would look, and prayed he'd find at least one of them. It was hard not to have a real goodbye. They'd both known separation was coming, with graduation and assignment on first missions, but not that it might be so abrupt.

But Sanyago had faith they'd see each other again. Missions didn't last forever. Maybe this new Shuvelao thing would mean they'd leave him and Hyon-seok alone for good. He felt a heavy stab of guilt at the thought of taking advantage that way, but the hope still didn't go away.

He thought about the notes he'd stashed back at the monastery. Years of them, wedged between stones on the inside of a chimney in an older part of the library. No one was about to light a fire surrounded by highly flammable books in a building that had been heated by suntile for centuries. He pulled his robes a little tighter around his body as he felt the night wind try to tease its way in. His robe's enchantments kept him warm enough, but sometimes "enough" felt like a poor substitute for actual comfort.

The stony hills settled slowly into rolling scrubland. They slept unsheltered on the ground, even in the rain, ignoring the cold and discomfort by cocooning their sleep in familiar Fathom-meditations. They ate cold rations that hunger and weariness managed to make delicious; hardtack baked with nuts and dried fruit, jerky made from mushrooms and soy, hard cheese and dense chocolate.

Near the journey's halfway point they swung away from the river, stopped in at a small village chapel. The priest welcomed them in through a back way, well after dusk, and gave them more supplies. He gave his name as Father Haenshn, and did not ask for theirs. Sanyago wanted to talk to him, meet someone new, meet someone *outside*, but when he stepped forward to speak Niceto held out a hand, shook his head. They went on without seeing another soul.

Later, as they camped just out of sight of the Mindao, Sanyago asked why they needed so much secrecy even at a friendly church.

"Not just a friendly church," Aeriic said. "Friendly village. Retired Somonei, mostly. You noticed there were no walls, no posted guards? Caustlands're a dangerous place, most settlements are fortified. That village can take care of itself."

Sanyago frowned. "Can't we trust Somonei? Or retired ones, I guess?"

"Almost always," Aeriic said. "Trusting them'd be a very small risk. But lots of small risks add up. You want to live a long life, you avoid taking them when you can."

"And a lot of these retired monks and nuns have spouses," Niceto added. "You have to unlearn some of your training, Sanyago, and I know that's hard. The Somonei serve openly, but the Shuvelao do not. The fewer know about our missions, the better, for them as well as us."

Sanyago sat staring. It washed over him suddenly, like a wave of bricks, what a huge change this all was from what he'd expected his life would be. Serving the Presilyo, yes, following the Triune path, using his talents to fight but this...this was like a great enveloping void pressing into the outer reaches of his perception. It buzzed faintly at the edge of hearing. He blinked, looked away.

Niceto reached a hand out toward him, palm up. "You can be open with us when you need to be, Sanyago, but otherwise you must guard what you show, not just in battle but always when out in the world. Breathe. Find your center."

Sanyago nodded, though it was a jerky movement, poorly tethered. He breathed in deep, fell back within himself, breathed out, held himself in, let himself flow.

All is mind. This moment is what this moment is now, accepted and whole.

His composure returned. Laris was looking at him, head cocked, concern and curiosity in the grey glint of his eyes.

"I'm alright," Sanyago said. "I'm sorry. I know I should be more accepting of what is, leave my expectations behind. It's just...if I can be open like you say—I have to ask." He took in another deep breath. "How does deception fit in to the Triune Path? How can we deceive and still be right with the Divine?" Some tiny part of his mind whispered all the times he'd tried to deceive the grown-ups in his life. *But they've never been the ones telling me to do it before,* he whispered back. *And now I suppose I'm supposed to be a grown-up as well.*

Niceto sighed. "Staafaen," he said. "Tell me about feinting."

Laris blinked, but answered right away. "A feint is an attempt to signal a future action you do not actually intend to commit. It's a tool both for guiding the actions of others, and obtaining information about their own intentions."

Niceto snorted. "*Porlyó.* Your teachers really weren't kidding about you."

Laris fought to restrain a glower, and Niceto prodded him lightly on the shoulder. "Relax. There is no shame in it. You are who you are. Not everything is a virtue or fault. And you are very correct. A feint is a deception, and it is a tool, a weapon. Tell me. Are you both prepared to kill, if you must?"

Sanyago nodded cautiously, and Laris closed his eyes a few seconds before answering. "I already have. During the Return of the Apostates. I shouldn't tell the full story, it isn't safe."

Not safe. Sanyago drew in a sharp breath at the shiver needling its thousand legs into every bony gap of his spine.

There was a long moment of careful silence before Aeriic answered. "Yeah, we know about that. Heard the whole story from Archabbot del Toro, and a few who were there." He leaned in, gave Laris a close look. "Sister Bai was especially lavish with her praise."

Laris looked like he might actually bare his teeth at Aeriic's gravelly provocation, but won the struggle to keep himself in check and just stared at the man instead. Sanyago stared too, slow coal-fires spreading through the pit of his stomach.

Aeriic gazed back for a low, dragging moment, then nodded and gave Laris a mirthless, toothy smile. "Good. You have control. Be careful with it. You should talk to someone about this, Staafaen. To me, to Niceto, to your friend. To a priest, if you have one you trust." He glanced at Niceto, who nodded and spoke.

"Yes, we know about Bai. And..." he raised an eyebrow at Sanyago with a sardonic little smile, "Hyon-seok. You are not in any trouble," he went on as Sanyago flushed, then felt his skin go cold in the late-summer air, "but you should understand that the process for selecting candidates in our little family is very thorough."

Aeriic patted Laris on the shoulder as the tall young monk's face went through another series of subtle struggles. "You especially aren't in trouble," the Shuvelao said. "It wasn't hard to figure out what happened with Bai. Happens too often, but I'm sure you've figured out by now that the Presilyo is full of flawed people. Noble purpose, Staafaen, but flawed people.'"

Laris didn't look entirely convinced, but he held his peace. Sanyago's thoughts spun away in a thousand directions, but something hot and jagged rose up into his core, demanding. He held it back, clenching his hands with the effort.

"Sister Bai's retired anyway," Aeriic continued. "With some encouragement. Away from the Presilyo. Now her problems're just between her and the Divine."

Sanyago's nails dug into the curled center of his fists, and the ragged chains of his temper gave way. "No punishment? No example? No *pinche* acknowledgement of anything? We all just go on like nothing happened? Sure! Why not? Let's all pretend! Deceit is fine, right? You were just explaining how it's fine?" He became aware his jaw was shaking, that the ragged in-and-out of his breathing had become something very near a growl. "So *explain.*"

Laris stared at him. Sanyago shot him a glance, apology and promise. *Sorry, I know, we'll talk about this later.*

The Shuvelao did not stare, just exchanged glances. Sanyago's anger seemed to have sparked interest rather than ire, which made him feel both relieved and confused. He waited.

"Deceit," Niceto said quietly, "is both a weapon and a shield. I understand you don't agree with the way the Presilyo has shielded itself in this matter, but you should understand also that it was not our decision. The Shuvelao serve. We do not command any but our own."

Sanyago opened his mouth, but Niceto gestured it shut. "No, you have said your piece. Time to listen. Deceit is like violence. Really, it is violence of the mind. Like physical violence, like the taking of life, it must be used only in need, and there are times it is needed. That's what I was getting at when I spoke about killing. The Somonei are warriors, but peace is the ideal. We Shuvelao work in shadow, but light is the ideal. We hope for a world where neither a well-placed blow nor a well-placed deception are necessary. But that is not the world we live in."

They stood there, all four of them, looking at each other as Niceto fell silent. Laris spoke first. "Alright, I think I understand you. I can think of plenty situations where that would hold true. But it doesn't excuse some of the things the Presilyo decides to carefully arrange forgetting. Not just me and Bai, I've seen it happen with others." He looked each Shuvelao briefly in the eye. "So have you, or you'd be pretty bad at your work. Almost happened to Sanyago, once, before a priest put a stop to it."

There may have been a flicker of surprise in Niceto's face at that last, though Aeriic remained as stone-featured as ever. *So they don't know* everything *about us.*

Aeriic let out a long, grinding sigh. "Noble purpose, flawed people. It's not our call, Staafaen. No one can fix everything. We do what we can." He glanced at Niceto, who shrugged, and he went on. "Weren't for us, Bai might still be in service. We do what we can."

Laris frowned, then closed his eyes, and when he opened them he gave Aeriic a small bow. "Okay." Thank you, then." For doing what you can."

"Yeah," Sanyago said, and fell into swirling silent thoughts.

They walked on.

"Problems," Aeriic said as he scrambled back down the rocky slope of the rise. "Whole company. Salían Army. Staffguard too, one Ranger and an auxiliary."

Staffguard. Sanyago felt a small thrill. The Staffguard Rangers read like legends in the accounts Laris had shown him, wandering righters of wrongs with powerful staves and the authority of the Salían government. He wasn't sure what an "auxiliary," was, maybe some kind of lieutenant or assistant?

Aeriic hopped deftly to a stop at the bottom of the incline. "Heard talk of Tenggarans too. No sign of the Carvers or any other Saepi trash."

"Tenggarans," Niceto mused. "Makes sense, this close to the border. Maybe they sent a detachment? Representatives? 'Advisers'?"

"Dunno," Aeriic said. "Just caught a few words about that. Couldn't get any closer." Sanyago flicked his gaze back and forth between the two Shuvelao as they spoke, fingering the hilt of his sword. They still hadn't said much about what their destination actually *was* beyond referring to it as "the ruin." That was both exciting and maybe a bit ominous; both feelings had him itching to know more. Laris, too; he was listening with that bitter look of answer-deprivation Sanyago had seen him wear a thousand times before.

Niceto rolled a stone around under his boot. "Hmmm. No chance we can just saunter past them, I'm guessing? Plead ignorance if we're found?"

Aeriic shook his head. "No chance. Salíans're camped right outside. Guards on the entrance, patrols outside. Likely more inside. Only a handful of Haeliiy, not much presence in the Holy Fathom from the rest of 'em."

Just regular soldiers, then, Sanyago thought. He knew the bulk of Caustland State militaries were made up of non-Eychis, troops with only a few months of real training. *Non-Haeliiy,* he reminded himself. *Got to practice your Gentic out here. Hell-lith, Hell-lith, Hell-lith,* went the singsong little reminder in his head. He shook it off, pulled his thought back into their previous track. *Non-Haeliiy troops, expected to fight with nothing but a little physical training and the natural strength of their bodies.*

He suppressed an internal shudder. To face the prospect of going into battle with that little preparation, just the most basic understanding of the Holy Fathom—he could barely even imagine it. He supposed he should pity them, show true Boddhisanto compassion, but he was impressed by their courage as well. Or maybe they didn't fully know what they were missing?

Niceto furrowed his brow. "Hmmm. Haeliiy are a double-edged sword in a situation like this. Useful if there's a common enemy. Trouble if we end up at cross-purposes." He glanced toward Laris and Sanyago, smiled slightly when he saw that they were listening. "What about the Staffguard?"

"Ranger seems competent. They don't hand those staves out to just anyone. Tall woman, maybe Nainadi stock. Another woman with her, also tall. Black, not heavily armed but definitely Haeliiy. Had a scholarly look to her, way she looks around, way she listens, and almost certainly no military background. Probably an auxiliary, like I said."

"Well then," Niceto sighed. "We're going to have to talk our way in. Story?"

Sanyago's frustration broke the surface, and he took a deep breath. "Are you going to tell us what this place is now? Maybe we can help."

Both Shuvelao shook their heads. "We have suspicions," Aeriic said. "You can help most by having no preconceptions. Anyway there's no time right now." Turning to Niceto, he fingered the clasp of his robes, making clicking noises with his tongue. "You think they'd take help? They already got the Staffguard and maybe some Tenggarans there."

Niceto laughed. "As long as they're sure we're not charging the usual fee, sure, it may work. We'll have to change robes."

"Robes?" Sanyago asked, confused. They had only one spare set each— plain brown, and not imbued. He assumed they were for time's when concealing the main set's enchantments wasn't a practical option. Hopefully they weren't about to change into those; out here in the field, he'd feel naked without imbued clothing, and he'd felt plenty of that already as this journey stripped his small familiar world away.

"Yeah, robes." Aeriic's voice had a ground-in undertone of amusement. "We're gonna show up as Somonei, not Shuvelao. Shuvelao're just a rumor outside the Presilyo, yeah? Want to keep it that way." He opened the front of his robes slightly, turned out the fabric. "You see this rune embroidered in?" He touched it with his forefinger, muttering a complicated phrase in Three Harmonies. The brown of his robes began to fade away, going bone-white before darkening to the sky-blue worn by the Somonei.

Sanyago let a slow smile spread over his face. This was exactly the sort of thing he'd been hoping to see with the Shuvelao. After asking Aeriic to repeat the phrase a few times, he followed the Operative's example, watched Laris do the same. They grinned at each other as their clasps went through their own metamorphoses, not only tinting a dull red but also changing shape to match the traditional Somonei form. These must be some exceptional robes; enchantments that could alter objects' physical shape without breaking them were difficult and rare.

"Wow," Laris said, running long fingers over his altered clothing. "That's useful."

"It is," Niceto said. "So. Here is our story. We were on our way back from a contract near the Siinlan when we heard rumors about what was going on here. If they ask *how* we heard, we refuse to give up sources, say we don't want to get anyone in trouble, right? This will make them start asking all the wrong questions among themselves, and hopefully steer them away from asking any of the right ones. We refuse to say anything more; discretion clause in the contract. Understand?"

"Umm… Sanyago said. He could remember all that, keep it straight in mind. But he felt it would be a flimsy thing; he didn't really understand all the workings behind it. Contracts? Discretion clauses? Talking to Salían soldiers? He knew what all things were, but didn't have anywhere firm to rest them in his head.

Aeriic laughed. "Just have to follow our lead. Probably won't have to say anything. We'll tell them you're junior trainees. Has the benefit of being kinda true."

"And it means no one will be surprised if you look confused,"

Operative Niceto added. "Now, we move. We'll be talking as we arrive and so, Staafaen, this will be your chance to argue theology to your heart's content. It's exactly what they'd expect from Somonei."

Sanyago was shot through with nerves as they approached the Salían Army camp. He breathed, projected his best outward aura of serenity. Laris seemed too engrossed in his loud faux argument with Niceto to be worried, gesturing forcefully as they debated the triple nature of the Divine.

The camp was a small, muddy affair, with a razor-wire perimeter and plenty of sentries. They spotted the little group right away, and sent out a squad to meet them. Sanyago watched in tense silence as Niceto spun his story about offered help and rumors to the squad leader, a woman with a longsword on her hip and the only one of the five who made any serious impression in the holy Fathom. She seemed to buy it, at least for now, and introduced herself as Sergeant Segouin. Her Gentic had an accent he couldn't quite place.

Operatives Aeriic and Niceto introduced themselves as Brothers Aandru and Augusto, respectively. They didn't introduce Laris and Sanyago at all, and the sergeant didn't ask. Instead, she escorted them to the gates.

"Wait here," she said, and went in with her squad.

They waited. Sanyago watched the camp. It was a different kind of diverse than the Presilyo, with fewer people of apparent Zhon Han or Tenggaran descent, though there were still a few. He spotted a couple Gatoparlos, too; he'd read about Caustland Cats, but had never seen one. Non-humans weren't technically barred from the Presilyo, but doctrine held that they required at least one more reincarnation to be spiritually ready for the Triune Path. This had occasionally been the subject of grumbling by Laris, who said he remembered having a good Gatoparlo friend before coming to the Presilyo.

One of the strange felines spotted him staring, looked back at him with blue slit-pupil eyes. Sanyago ducked his head apologetically and looked away. He'd read up on the subject of the Gatoparlos and Corvasos after one of Laris' longer disquisitions, and come away feeling pretty uneasy himself. The policy wasn't found anywhere in Scripture, and only vaguely referenced in the reported sayings of Eusébio Inoue, who had passed from the Mortal world less than a dozen years after Starfall while the whole issue was still very new.

Besides, Sanyago figured he could probably use a reincarnation or three himself before he was fully ready for the Triune Path. He thought about Hyon-seok, and winced—feeling guilty about him, and badly missing him. He had Laris, but Laris was his brother and Hyon-seok was...had been…

He was rescued from this uncomfortable line of thought by the Captain's arrival. She was a woman of medium frame, dark red hair, even more freckles than Brother Xaeli. Her eyes were a deep green; tough, intelligent, wary. She'd brought another soldier with her, walking just behind but with his own air of authority. A big man, short brown hair and faded blue eyes, watchful and ready.

"Somonei out of nowhere," the woman said. Her accent was native Gentic, strikingly similar to Operative Aeriic's. "Interesting. I'm Captain Braun." She nodded back at the man behind her. "This is First Sergeant Wrait. Sergeant Segouin says you've come offering help. I'm grateful." She gave the four of them a long, weighing look. "Probably."

At the "probably," Operative Niceto leaned forward slightly. "We hope to make that a certainty, Captain. Though gratitude is not necessary. To be quite honest, we would like to take a look inside the ruin as well—what we've heard has been intriguing, and perhaps concerning."

"Has it really?" Captain Braun said with a touch of irritated sarcasm. "And what exactly have you heard?"

"We Somonei keep our word," Aeriic answered. Sanyago had gotten used to the slow grate of his voice, but listening as he spoke to someone else made him hear it with new ears somehow. "We promised we wouldn't say, so we won't."

"Hmmm." Annoyance persisted in the captain's voice. "You have papers, of course? Seeing as you are, you know, in Salía at the moment."

Niceto reached into his robes, fumbled for a moment. It was a pretty good act; Sanyago guessed Niceto knew exactly where his papers were, and maybe had more than one set. Or maybe not, in case he was searched. *When will I get my own false papers? Do they still count as fake if they're officially issued by the Presilyo?*

Niceto "found" the papers, handed them over with a small bow.

The captain took them, held them up without looking at them. "Lieutenant Aalaen!" she called. Sanyago felt the rapid approach of a strong presence in the Holy Fathom, like a sprinting Somonei only higher and...smaller. He blinked and did his best not to stare as a huge black bird alit on the captain's shoulder, snagging the papers from her hand with three strange fingerlike stubs on the leading corners of half-opened wings. Corvaso. Cropr. Caustland Crow.

"Ma'am," the black-feathered lieutenant said, long sleek head moving rapidly as he perused the documents. Small threads of probing connection flashed through the Holy Fathom between the Corvaso and the papers, the papers, and Niceto, then northward toward the Presilyo to authenticate the crypto-bond. After a minute or so, the lieutenant leaned his head in close to his superior's, whispering as he pointed to something on one page with a toe-talon.

Captain Braun nodded, took the papers and handed them back to Niceto. "Everything looks to be in order, Mr. Augusto."

Niceto bowed again and tucked the small sheaf back into his robes. "Thank you, Captain Braun."

"Your story doesn't really add up, Mr. Augusto," she replied. Sanyago suppressed a small shock of fear, pushing his sudden intake of breath back down. Were they discovered that easily? But neither Niceto nor Aeriic made the slightest move as the soldiers watched their little group's reactions."

"Of course, you knew that," Braun continued, "and you knew that we'd probably see through it. But that doesn't really matter, does it? We could still use your help, and you can stick with your official story, it's no skin off *my* back."

Both Shuvelao remained silent.

"I do get some information from Aldonza, you know," Braun said wearily, glancing over her shoulder as though the Salian capital weren't five hundred kilometers away. "Less than I'd like, sure, but I know why you're here. Your friends the Carvers occupied this place until very recently."

Just a flicker of startled movement from Aeriic and Niceto. Probably this was feigned, probably they already knew, but Sanyago hadn't and the news caused another small hitch of fear in his throat. *Carvers. Apostates. Just like the ones that sent the man with the butterfly swords.* He and Laris exchanged the smallest of glances, and he saw similar thoughts in his friend's grey eyes.

The man standing behind her, First Sergeant Wrait, stepped forward and spoke. "We've seen the Saepi bastards in Acheronford, too, few times over the years. Can't be absolutely sure they were Carvers, but it seems a good bet, given what they were up to here." His blue eyes flicked between Braun and the Shuvelao, something unspoken passing between himself and the captain. *These two have known each other a long time,* Sanyago thought.

Captain Braun nodded at her lieutenant, who looked them over with one golden raven's eye and clicked his beak before speaking. "Since you were obviously sent here with some idea of what's going on, we've decided to be forthcoming. On two conditions. First, as previously discussed, if there is trouble you fight beside us without expectation of pay."

The voice startled Sanyago; it had been many years since he'd heard a Caustland Crow speak. It was smoother than he remembered; a bit raspy, sure, but nothing so harsh as Operative Aeriic's vocal grind.

Both Shuvelao inclined their heads in agreement, and the lieutenant gave them a strange little avian bow in return. Sanyago watched, fascinated by the Cropr's collar— the only thing he wore by way of uniform, with its silver bars on the sides and small unit badges bearing inscrutable military heraldry, "AALAEN" stitched across the throat in stark black capitals.

"Excellent," Aalaen continued. "The second condition is that you be willing to trade information. We tell you what we know, or at least as much as Aldonza has seen fit for us to know, and you tell us what you know, or as much as the Presilyo has decided to give you. We all benefit knowing more about a common 'problem.'" He laughed, a brief inhuman string of "aaw"s. "We're not allowed to call them 'enemies,' you know. Had to ask them nicely to leave. Nicely, with swords drawn. Diplomatic dogshit. Not my paygrade, thankfully."

Nieto took in a deep breath and let it out slowly before answering; Sanyago wondered again how much of this was acting. "Give us a moment to confer, if you would? I think we can come to an agreement.

"Be quick, then," the lieutenant said.

The Shuvelao turned to beckon Laris and Sanyago into a huddle, Niceto murmuring a sawtooth series of phrases in Three Harmonies. A burrlike semisphere of Fathom-static spun into existence, centered on Aeriic, a precaution against eavesdropping. "That went about as well as we could reasonably have hoped," Niceto said. "Would have preferred to get a nice stupid young officer instead of a seasoned mustang, but at least we'll have a competent ally if things go sideways."

"Mustang?" Sanyago asked.

Niceto waved it off. "Means she used to be part of the rank-and-file. I'll explain later. We're authorized to say what we need to say to complete the mission. Most of what we give them will even be true."

"Fine with me," Aeriic barked. "Time is short, let's get in there before some soldier pokes something they shouldn't. You two. Keep following our lead, keep your mouths shut when you can, and keep your eyes open."

They bowed in reply. Niceto turned back to the Salíans, and his spell fell away.

"Agreed," Niceto told the Captain, "by our honor and oaths as Somonei." It was a familiar phrase, though this was the first time Sanyago had ever heard it used in earnest. *These words are used to bind you to a patron's task,* they had been told, *and by using them you hold the reputation and honor of the Presilyo in your hands.* They seemed to be enough for Captain Braun, who sent her lieutenant off for an escort.

Their escort turned out to be the Staffguard pair Aeriic had mentioned earlier. The Ranger was just as he'd described her—tall, brown-skinned, lightly-armored, carrying the elaborate warpwood staff that served as both weapon and badge of office. She had light hazel eyes and a gentle quirk at the corner of her mouth like a lingering smile. She wasn't young, but didn't appear very close to middle age either. Certainly she seemed experienced.

The auxiliary was black, even taller, with cornrow braids extending out from under a leather helmet. A strange smooth club with a side-handle was tucked into her belt. Her eyes were warm, brown, and thoughtful. She was younger than the Ranger, probably not much more than a decade or two out of her teens. Sanyago liked them both on sight, and hoped the feeling would turn out justified.

"I am Ranger Taniixh Pai," the Staffguard told them as she led the way. Her Gentic had a slight but distinct Manhc melody to it. "This is Ceraen Wiilqaems, my auxiliary for this assignment. She's an historian and Haeliiy, specializing in the theory and practice of Praedhc magic."

"Nice meeting you all," Ceraen said, then fell silent as the group traversed the rocky terrain, an indefinable tension threading the air between them.

On cresting one of a seemingly endless series of ridges, Sanyago spotted the timber-reinforced hole in the side of a long rocky line of hills, and knew it must be their destination. Something tightened deep in his bones as they approached the Salían soldiers guarding the entrance, and he was startled when one of them glanced their way and flicked the Karana warding-gesture, nodding gravely as though in warning.

"Thank you, Sister," Niceto said quietly as they passed between the sentries, and Sanyago's spine shuddered in sympathetic vibration with the small tremor he thought he heard in the Shuvelao's voice.

The Abwarren. We're going into the Abwarren. This wasn't just a cavern, he could *feel* it, the hum embedded by depth of connection to the strange strong spaces down below. He exchanged glances with Laris, whose eyes were wide. *You too?* Sanyago nodded back, a murky pool of uncertainty settling in beneath his tangled excitement and simpler fear.

The low naked stone didn't do much to reassure him. It was lit by hedgeflame torches at regular intervals, but their light seemed feeble, pressed in on itself by the encroaching dark. The Holy Fathom flickered at the edges of his awareness, steadied when he turned his mind toward perception. Air slid against the rocks like breath, drawn and exhaled. Small things, all of them, but they pulled at his composure. Sanyago touched the pommel of his sword, seeking solidity. It wasn't enough, but it wasn't nothing.

The entrance tunnel opened up into a small uneven chamber with several more passages leading off and down. Military tac-torches flooded every crevice with harsh white light as though to compensate for the earlier dark, illuminating a wide scatter of debris: broken crates, scattered tools, dirty garments. Bloodstains on the stone. A five-soldier squad stood in the center, talking amongst themselves. Their presence in the Holy Fathom was strong, their equipment heavily imbued. Snatches of Basa echoed off the cavern walls. Tentera Wira. These must be the Tenggarans Aeriic had mentioned.

One of the squad approached. She looked to be a woman of medium height, tall for a Tenggaran, wide at the shoulder and hip, though it was hard to tell much more about her build under the bulk of the heartvein plate armor she wore. She carried a tall, strangely-styled shield shaped like an elongated hexagon, a large mace with notched flanges hanging from her belt.

"Hello, Sergeant," the Staffguard said. "We've brought surprise reinforcements for our little expedition. We might not have to wait for the Salían Spec Ops squad after all."

The sergeant nodded, taking off her helmet and tucking it under her arm. She had short, thick black hair, strong-boned features with a stubborn jaw, and large, intense eyes colored such a dark brown they were nearly black. A vicious scar ran diagonally across her deeply-tanned face, extending from right temple to left jaw and notching the bridge of her nose. She was perhaps five years Sanyago's senior, her features young but too heavily cast by experience to really be called youthful.

She looked them over carefully with an expression of dour reserve. "Somonei. Good. I wasn't keen on waiting another day to get some real answers from this place. Your Carver cousins left quite the mess." Her Gentic was fluid, if clearly tinted by a Basa accent. "My name is Sergeant Marchadesch. It's been agreed that I will lead this expedition."

Chapter 23

No man is an island, and no woman either. To be human is to be a part of something greater than the simple self, whether we intend it or not, and so any discussion of "human rights" not built upon this essential aspect of humanity is an utter sham. Rights are not merely a list of acts permitted in seeking one's own way; rights are accorded also to the whole, to the greater body of fellows to which one belongs, rights allowing maintenance of deeply held ways, the keeping of course for the greater body.

It is in the protection of these rights that the Caustland States have utterly failed, sometimes in the name of their misdefined "human rights," often in the naked service of their own corrupt power. They have torn children from their parents' arms. They have interfered in the transmission of sacrosanct beliefs and practices from one generation to the next. They have conspired to murder, often by degree and sometimes by violence, not merely individuals but also entire bodies of human beings.

What is a greater violation of true Human Rights? Constraints and consequences placed on a single human being, deemed wayward by his or her fellows? Or on an entire society, a culture, a faith, a body in the truest sense of the word? Surely it is the body, and not the member, which merits the most solemn consideration; surely the part cannot be greater than the whole.

- Saamqul Haejaes, *Declaration of Dissent*
  Founding Document of the Sovereign Nations, 79 SE

People aren't property. They can't be owned, not by a faith, not by a family, and not by a nation. You can keep me here, but I am not yours, and I never will be.

- Reported last words of Lyudmila Vaschenko, Wordswill Nation dissident, 124 SE

Suulah'kal Entrance Cavern, Salía, The Caustlands, 355 SE

Something was off about these four Somonei. Dayang looked them over, starting with the younger pair standing behind. Teenagers, really, no older than she'd been when she'd enlisted in the Tentera Wira, maybe even a couple years younger. One was very tall and very black, rangy but well-muscled, with lean, serious features and striking steel-grey eyes, watchful and intelligent. The other was small and compact, at least a few centimeters shorter than Dayang herself. He had a handsomely fine-boned face, with dark brown skin and large, expressive eyes the color of strong coffee. Like all Somonei she'd seen, their heads were cleanly shaved.

They shifted under her gaze, looking out of their depth even under the mask of controlled serenity they clearly wanted to cultivate. She decided she knew enough about them for the moment, and switched her attention to the front pair; the taller, olive-skinned one standing next to his paler, squatter companion. Both seemed well into the journey through vague middle age, and were clearly in charge, wearing expressions of placid faith and benevolent command.

But they seemed...slippery, somehow, their Fathom-presence subtly off-pattern. And the coincidence of their arrival was crowshit. Her own presence here was the result of years of questions and echograms and sorting through reports. She'd had to pull a lot of strings to get this assignment, hoping to finally get some answers about what had really been behind the Hunch-Ripper she'd fought outside Kualabu what seemed like a lifetime ago.

And if she'd been keeping tabs on the Carvers, the Saepi offshoot of the Triune Path, you could bet your ass the mainline Michyeros had been as well. The appearance of an entire Somonei squad here and now was absolutely not a thing of chance. The Presilyo would have its own agenda here, no mistake.

Still, she wasn't exactly unhappy to have them here. This place made her deeply uneasy, and she saw similar feelings written all over the members of her squad, and the two Salíans: in faces, in stances, the tightly-held nerves underlying every movement. She hoped her own disquiet wasn't quite so evident; she'd only been this squad's sergeant for a few weeks, and she needed their confidence. In any case more fighters should be welcome, especially highly-trained Wira like the Somonei, ulterior motives and weird Fathom-focused religion aside.

Or maybe not. She'd have to see.

"Somonei," she said. "Good. I wasn't keen on waiting another day to get some real answers from this place. Your Carver cousins left quite the mess down here. My name is Sergeant Marchadesch. It's been agreed that I will lead this expedition."

"An honor to meet you, Sergeant Marchadesch," replied the taller of the elder Somonei. His Gentic had a slight Ambérico accent, which somehow managed to further smooth a voice already warm and velvet. She distrusted it immediately. He bowed, introducing himself as Brother Augusto and the other as Brother Aandru.

She merely nodded in return. The Tentera Wira wasn't too concerned with drill-and-ceremony decorum, not after training was finished and mettle proven, and even had she been part of a corps more fond of formalities she'd not be extending them to this pair or their younger charges. She certainly wasn't going to be calling anyone "brother" unless Pandikar suddenly showed up, or at least a fellow Muslim. The thought of Pandikar brought a bright pang, but this wasn't the time, and she stashed the feeling away for later.

"Glad to meet you as well." It would be awkward to use their names if she wasn't going to include their titles. "And the other two with you?"

"Haven't earned their status as full Somonei yet," said the one introduced as "Brother Aandru." His voice was so rough it was startling, like having a millstone grind out words in your ear. His accent was native Gentic, spare and straightforward. "You can just call them 'tall one' and 'short one' if you like."

Something about the glib way he said it rankled her. Dayang set her jaw. "No. You can call them whatever you like, but if I'm going to fight beside someone I want to know their name. It's a pretty basic courtesy, don't you think?"

The younger pair's eyes widened in surprise and something like apprehension. *What has them so anxious about giving their names?* she wondered, watching them exchange a glance and then look to their superiors for answers. *If they do that every time I give an order the delay could get someone killed. Enough of this.*

"God*dammit*," Dayang said, and stepped forward, letting the momentum of her frustration carry her past the older monks. She came to a stop right in front of the short young one, looking down into his startled face. Surprise or no, though, he'd reacted remarkably quickly, one hand on his sword, the other held up, strands of intent and consequence ready to coalesce and weave in from the edges of the Fathom.

She brought her shield up sharply, preparing Fathom-defenses of her own that should be more than a match for this young Somonei. Still, she was impressed. The Presilyo certainly hadn't sent the dullest of its students to this assignment—which also added, somehow, to the stack of suspicion at the back of her mind.

"What's your name, monk?" she asked, keeping her right arm resting easy at her side. She let the tall tower shield drop to rest on the cavern stone as the young Somonei's own hand fell away from his sword. She was aware of the two senior Somonei now standing behind her, but kept her attention on the young man's face. They wanted to stop this? Let them try. That might answer some questions all on its own.

He opened his mouth, shut it, glanced past her at his two superiors.

"Any compelling reason he can't give me his name?" she asked, without looking back at the monks she was addressing. "I'm leading this little expedition, like I said. If you're going to come along, I want to know that my orders will be obeyed, and right away. That means I need a name that can cut through the chaos to your ears. That means no wasted time looking to someone else for confirmation."

The tall one with the silky accent, the one calling himself Augusto, spoke up behind her. "We will not go against the principles of our faith, Sergeant. No power on Solace can compel us to do that."

"Fine," she said, still keeping her gaze on the young monk's face. "Are hidden names some bedrock piece of your religion? You better be able to give me chapter and verse if so." The boy looked exquisitely uncomfortable, and she felt for him. He'd have been raised pretty rigid, from what she knew of the Presilyo, accustomed to stark certainties when it came to authority and the right thing to do. *Well, then. Welcome to the world, I guess.*

Hesitation from behind her. "Yeah, that's what I thought. Look, don't jerk me around, and I'll be as straight as I can with you in return. Tell the young man to give me his name. His friend, too."

The other one, Aandru let out a low, stony sound of irritation. "Alright, Sergeant. If it will get us all going, his name is An—"

"No," she cut him off with her best sergeant's voice. "I want to hear it from him. Same with the other one. If I think either is lying, I'll have the Staffguard escort you right back out to the Salíans. I'm not marching into this Godforsaken place with people who won't even give me their real names. And I'll have assurances from *all* of you that you'll obey my orders, *without delay*, so long as you're with my squad."

Another silence. The poor boy was practically pleading with his eyes as he looked past her toward his superiors. *What do I do?* She caught a glimpse of the other young monk doing much the same, though he was calmer about it.

"You're not much of a diplomat, Sergeant." The Somonei's voice was not quite so smooth now, roughened by a touch of irritation. Dayang flashed briefly to the moment years before when she'd stood in front of the Pelo woman with Jeims and Aulia, and knew the monk was probably right. But it didn't matter right now.

"I don't need to be, Somonei. I'm not conducting negotiations here, I'm assuming command. We're not going to be striking compromises in the middle of combat; I'm going to be giving orders, and you're going to be following them. You gonna be reliable, or am I gonna have to send you back so you don't get us all killed? You've got about ten seconds to decide."

She waited. She even counted. *Satu, dua, tiga...*

"We'll be reliable," the raspy monk ground out behind her. "A Somonei is honest, it's part of our code. Go ahead. Tell her."

"Sanyago," the boy said softly. "My name is Sanyago." He had a lovely warm, lilting voice, with a slight accent she assumed must be Ambérico. Attractive, perhaps a touch...fey? But that wasn't relevant for about a thousand reasons.

"Good to meet you, Sanyago," Dayang said, and held out her hand. Sanyago frowned, looked past her again. He must have gotten a nod, because he took her hand in his, or at least grasped her gauntlet in his bare palm, and she shook. She could feel the shift and weight of the Fathom through his fingers, complex and deftly shepherded. Maybe a touch of indiscipline, though, a bit loose here and there. Maybe a sign of flexibility. Maybe both.

"Good to meet you too, Sergeant Marchadesch," he replied. He pronounced the words with great care. Mostly likely not used to talking with outsiders. She dropped his hand, and turned toward the other young monk. She had to look up; he had easily thirty centimeters on her.

"Hello," he said quietly. "My name is Staafaen." He took her gauntleted hand in his, shook it with exaggerated care. His Fathom-shadow was intense, especially around his hands, and he was not visibly armed. The Somonei were famous for their unarmed-combat skills, but she hadn't thought they'd go into the field with no weapons at all. Interesting.

"Good to meet you, Staafaen," she said, and dropped her hand from his. He was staring at her, and then he was looking fixedly away, a hint of flush visible even under his very dark skin. *Oh Hell,* she thought. Fresh out of the monastery and she was probably the first woman he had ever really seen up close. *Awkward schoolboy crush, I guess. Hopefully harmless.* She'd deal with it if it became necessary.

She turned back toward the older monks. "Thank you, they seem to be telling the truth." The pair both bowed, exchanged glances. She introduced her own squad: Specialist Park, lean and quiet and intense, shortbow slung over his shoulder; Specialist Nguyen, big and still, with one hand on his miaodao saber. Corporal Bayin, long-limbed and wiry, the double-weighted chain of his meteor hammer wrapped carefully round his waist. Specialist Martos, too much energy held in by too compact a frame, constantly finding new ways to carry her spear. They each nodded in turn, said nothing.

The two elder monks introduced themselves to the squad using the same names as before, which Dayang didn't bother questioning; she'd already made her point. She turned and gestured toward one of the cavern exits. "Ready to go down, or do you need to prepare first? How much have they told you about the situation?"

"We're ready," said Augusto. His smile surprised her—a bit grim, maybe even slightly sardonic. "Somonei are always ready." There was a hint of wry cynicism in his voice as well, and Dayang found herself liking him a little despite herself. Perhaps that was exactly his intent; she still thought this pair was slippery.

She nodded, once, aware that she was scowling slightly. "Glad to hear it. Now, again. How much do you know?"

"Not much more than vague rumors. Enough to lead us here, but probably not enough to be helpful. I suspect you know far more than we do."

She wondered about that. The information the Tentera Wira had passed down from the Salíans had been pretty bare-bones. She'd pieced more together on her own, but God only knew what information the Presilyo might have. Or how much it told its foot soldiers.

She nodded. "Okay, I'll give you what we know, but if you just *happen* to remember something that might be even a tiny bit relevant, you tell us right away. I know these guys are an offshoot from your religion and maybe their dirty laundry feels like it's yours too in some sense, but we can't afford any face-saving crowshit down here."

Again that grim, sardonic smile from Augusto— and a similar one from his shorter partner, who spoke. "Yeah, okay. You know the Carvers' whole deal, right? Didn't like that the Somonei fight alongside non-believers, didn't like that the Presilyo took payment for it. Thought we were too cooperative with the Caustland States. Thought should be able to live without having to deal with the scary outside world, essentially. Ran off to Earthmarch to form the Sovereign Nations with some of the other original Saepis?"

"Sure," Dayang said. "Their activities have been an interest of mine for a while. I wasn't assigned leadership on this mission by chance, I pulled hard to be here." *Maybe that will inspire some confidence, maybe it will make them think twice about trying to snow me. Maybe.*

The stocky Somonei calling himself Brother Aandru let out a grinding laugh. "Good. So, what have they been up to down here?"

Dayang glanced at the two younger Somonei. Sanyago stood wide-eyed, clearly working hard to keep his nerves under control, while Staafaen kept his own iron calm clamped down through clear force of concentration. They stood very close, not touching but still giving an impression of mutual support.

Old friends, and nothing else really solid to hold on to. Kids shoved out into a world they'd never been allowed to know. It tickled something at the back of her brain. *If I'm right and their presence is no coincidence, why bring a brand-new pair like this?* She'd have to keep an eye on them; still weighing whether the advantages of having them along would be worth the risks.

Augusto raised an eyebrow, waiting. Dayang held up a placating hand. "Sorry, thinking how to phrase this. Obviously Gentic is not my native tongue. There's some kind of old Pelo"— *wait, speaking Gentic*—"er, Praedhc ritual site here."

She thought a moment, frowned. "Or maybe 'ritual site' isn't really the proper word. I don't know if the place had any religious significance for them, possibly our scholar friend here," she gestured toward Ceraen Wiilqaems, "will be able to tell us more. What we do know is that it changes people. That's what we think the Carvers were using it for. They'd already abandoned the place by the time we arrived, probably because it's gone...bad. Almost certainly due to whatever they were getting up to there. And we think there may be... leftovers."

Dayang's squad shifted, just enough for the slight increase in tension to be noticeable. The Somonei exchanged glances; meaningful ones from the elder monks, apprehensive from the younger. Taniixh Pai looked grim but undeterred, both hands gripping her elaborate staff, and Ceraen toyed with one of the spell-implements hanging from her belt, breathing in, breathing out, gaze fixed.

Dayang suppressed her own slow shudder, tried to keep it off her face. Her soldiers would know she was unnerved—they weren't stupid, and this place would unnerve anyone—but as the squad leader she was supposed at least to be *less* unnerved.

"The Salíans have been quite forthcoming with you, then?" Augusto asked, raising one eyebrow slightly.

Dayang nodded, decided to answer both his questions, explicit and implied. "They have. The Carvers haven't been operating only in Salía, as I'm sure you're aware. And of course this is pretty damn close to the border. Might not stay just a Salían problem, you know? That's why we're here."

And you're here because you've spent years making sure you would be, all things considered, she told herself. *Time to enjoy the opportunity you fought so hard for.* She cleared her throat. "Sorry. Just thinking things through before we go down. What are your specializations? I'm assuming you'll want to be kept together with your trainees?"

"Thinking first is always a good idea where there's time," Augusto said, and his smile was unreadable. "Yes, we'd like to be kept near our charges, though of course we are all trained to fight beside non-Somonei troops. Sanyago and I specialize in skirmish with light swords and quick spells." He tapped the pommel of his rapier. Sanyago gave a small bow, betraying a hint of smiling pride.

Augusto smiled slightly and went on. "Brother Aandru here is something of a brawler," he said, and Aandru flashed a jag-toothed smile before bowing. "He is also an expert at close-range spells of the brute-force variety." Augusto shot the shorter monk a brief look.

A bit of ribbing; some long-shared joke passing between them. These two had been working together a long time.

"Staafaen," Augusto continued, "practices the singular style we call Gathering Deep. He uses no weapons, relying only on the Holy Fathom and his own body, along with other gifts the Divine has seen fit to bestow."

Dayang frowned. So he really was unarmed. Even with the monk's explanation, the idea seemed dubious—just because you *could* fight without weapons didn't mean you *should*—but she supposed there could be advantages. Extending one's Fathom-reach through a weapon was a difficult thing requiring extensive training and concentration...but she'd have the chance to discuss that later, God willing. "Sounds good," she said. "Let's hope you end up never having to use any of those skills." *Though that seems unlikely, God help us all.*

She decided to send Corporal Bayin and Specialist Park as forward reconnaissance; both had a knack for stealth and the use of Fathom-sight in darkness, though the latter should be a last resort in a place like this. If they ran into trouble, Park's shortbow would be an excellent tactical complement for Bayin's meteor hammer.

Augusto offered to have the Somonei scout up ahead, but whatever might be down here, she wanted her own people to put eyes on it first. Not that she'd offer that explanation to him, or any explanation really. Sometimes explaining yourself was helpful, sometimes it just invited argument. Didn't stop him, though, he tried to make his case from several more angles before she gave the sort of flat denial that didn't brook further discussion.

So she kept the monks with the main group, Sanyago and Aandru guarding the left flank, Staafaen and Augusto the right. Ceraen and Pai would take up the rear; Pai could shift her famous Staffguard weapon to bow-shape for ranged support, and Ceraen's defensive spells might turn out useful.

But hopefully not too *useful.* She tapped the fadelamp rods tied onto her armor, invoking their strange chromatic light: deep violet at the source, dropping through the full spectrum of color as it radiated outward, thin red at the outer edge before falling away to utter dark. It wasn't ideal; they'd be unlikely to see anything until it came within the fadelamp's outer boundary, but at least there would be some element of surprise on their side, and no illumination would be visible outside the pale crimson borders.

She glanced left at Specialist Nguyen, right at Specialist Martos. Both nodded and activated lights of their own, forming overlapping pools of blended hues. Dayang signaled the whole group forward, watching Bayin and Park fade through the rusted light of the periphery and into darkness.

God willing, we'll find answers and leave with our skins intact. Her hand tightened under the fine-jointed plates of her gauntlet. *And since I'm never sure exactly what He wills, we damn well better be ready.*

They descended into the dark.

The place crawled beneath them. Dayang could feel it beneath her boots, within the stone, down past the—

No. The Fathom is profound, mortal minds need not wander. The mantra seemed to help, and she supposed she'd owe Hang Che a measure of gratitude for teaching her how to use it if the man weren't such a colossal piece of shit. Sure, there had been similar training from the Tentera Wira, but Guru Dickbrains had spent a large chunk of his adventuring career in ruins just like these, and had been able to start training her young.

Well, maybe not ruins just *like these.* She looked round at the uneven stone walls and ceiling, some of it natural grey stone, some rough-hewn by Pelo miners and stonemages, all of it strangely tinged by the color gradient of the fadelamps. Take away the lighting and it should all be unremarkable, as should the sand-and-cobble floor, really just part of a road leading to the actual ruin complex.

But no. She wouldn't want to touch any of these surfaces with a bare hand, and thanked God for the thick gumchitin soles of her boots. The Abwarren was often dangerous, both physically and, well, otherwise, but this place...

The Fathom is profound, mortal minds need not wander. She turned fully round as she walked, took stock of her new squad. Specialist Nguyen was alert, under control, one hand resting on the hilt of his heavy miaodao saber. She couldn't see his face from her position beside and slightly behind him, but she knew it would be impassive. It always was; he'd been a Buddhist warrior monk for some temple or other before joining the Tentera Wira, and it showed. He'd left his sect behind, but not his sharpened serenity.

Sanyago and Aandru were in position along the left flank. Aandru's expression was unreadable, Sanyago's full of concentration and a sort of set-aside fear. Both looked ready enough. Good. Ceraen and Pai still followed, Ceraen in front. The auxiliary looked round with an undisguised mix of interest and unease, fingers clutching the nightstick handle jutting out from her belt. Dayang worried about her, but Pai had assured her that this was not Ceraen's first field operation, and would not be her first skirmish either if it came to that.

Skirmish. Dayang prayed they wouldn't see combat of any kind down here, but if it came to that she doubted somehow that "skirmish" would describe it. Of course the younger Somonei were unlikely to have seen any real action, but they'd been raised to fight from childhood; Ceraen was just a scholar with some spellcasting ability and a smattering of self-defense training from the Salían government. *Or maybe I'm being unfair. God willing, I hope that's the case.*

Staafaen and Augusto seemed steady enough on the right flank. Augusto kept his gaze outward as she looked, but Staafaen turned to catch her gaze for just a moment before turning away. Dayang gave an internal groan. *I'll have to have a frank talk with his superiors if we all end up having to work together for very long.* Staafaen didn't seem like the sort who might attempt liberties, but she'd rather cut off any potential awkwardness at the pass. Yes, she knew Somonei were supposed to be celibate, but most mosque imams would want to set similar restrictions on her and God knew she'd kept her own counsel on that score.

She shoved *that* mess aside, along with her mild guilt and the accompanying guilt for not feeling said guilt more strongly. *Focus on the mission.* Dayang kept turning, saw Specialist Martos bouncing her spear on her shoulder. Martos was a small, twitchy woman, quick to react, almost never off her guard. This place was not doing her nerves any favors, but she was keeping herself together so far.

TaaaaHHH taH-taH-tah

Martos' spear came down off her shoulder at the bizarre sound whispering up from deeper in. Dayang's shield came up, hand pulling her mace free without any real input from her conscious mind, which was too busy dealing with the prickling shudder going up her spine. Other weapons were readied all around. Dayang reached minutely into the Fathom, formed a "draw in close" sigil over her head in pale blue hedgeflame, let it ripple through the undercurrent just far enough to reach the whole squad.

TaUH? TaUH?

The others drifted nearer, still moving forward though not as quickly, crouched lower, prepared to move, strike, defend.

"Spearstalkers," Augusto whispered as he came up close on her right. Dayang nodded, listened hard toward the tunnel ahead. Bayin and Park must have crossed into a spearstalker colony's territory and been detected by the creatures' strange seismic senses. Humans were too big to be proper prey for spearstalkers, which preferred to eat victims whole. They'd warn larger creatures off instead with their weird, breathy vocalizations: *go away, you don't want to tangle with us.*

And Dayang *didn't* want to tangle with them, but she was unlikely to have much choice in the matter. The creatures liked to settle their colonies into chokepoints and tunnel intersections, burrowing into the floor and walls and folding their strange eye-and-spear arms into their stony-carapaced bodies, becoming nearly indistinguishable from surrounding boulders and outcroppings. She and her squad had been trained to fight most known Solacian monsters—"hostile xenospecies" was the official term—but that was all theoretical stuff, none of them had ever actually faced a spearstalker before.

"You've fought them in the past? What about your partner?" She didn't bother to ask Augusto about his trainees; she doubted they'd ever fought anything but wooden dummies.

"Yes, we both have," he whispered back. "Pretty straightforward, just remember they rely as much on tremors as on sight. Feint with your feet, with your weight on the ground. Don't bother aiming for the stalks, especially with a mace; their main body mass looks rocky, but that's mostly camouflage. Hit them there, hit them hard, and don't stop until you see serious ichor. They like to play dead."

She nodded, looking round to make sure the rest of the squad had heard. Old training had value, but a voice of experience right now was indispensable.

"Thank you." Dayang told the monk, then turned to address the whole huddle. "Okay, we're going to fight our way through. There's no time to find an alternate route, if one even exists. They'll be hiding in a boulder field. I'll point you each at a particular boulder, then we'll hit the assigned targets with harrying spells on my signal. Do not attempt to use Fathom-senses to detect which ones are real stone and which are spearstalkers, it isn't safe here, no matter how much control you think you have."

Staafaen looked uneasy at this, and exchanged glances with Sanyago. Dayang frowned at the tall young Somonei and gave a very slight tilt of her head. He inclined his own. *I'll be fine.* She sure as Hell hoped so.

She took in a deep breath, set her jaw. "The spearstalkers should counterattack. Maybe just the ones we target, maybe the whole colony at once, there's no way to know for sure. Then we do it again until we've hit every Goddamn boulder in the field. I'm not taking any chances that one of them will get it into its braincase to stage an ambush. Clear?"

"Crystal," her squad replied, voices low and tense. The Somonei and Staffguard just nodded. She signaled the group forward, gaze sweeping the pale scarlet edge of fadelamp illumination. Bayin and Park came into view, the two scouts waiting on opposite sides of the sheer tunnel walls. They'd Sihir-climbed about three meters up and then remained there in an improbable sort of squat: bootsoles planted vertically against the sheer stone walls, ready to leap down behind any force that might assail the main group. She ignored them; they knew what they were doing.

Once about two dozen boulders and lumpy outcroppings came into dim, reddish-grey view, Dayang signaled a halt. She assigned targets, drawing thin red lines of hedgeflame from each of her group to six of the boulders. After choosing a seventh for herself, she called the attack. "Now!"

Thin pulsing lines shot out through the Fathom, small spells barely visible as color-shifting motes as they passed through the strange chromatic light. Three of the boulders burst up from the stone floor, wrenching lower legs free from the stone, upper limbs unfolding from torsos' upper surfaces.

Dayang had a moment to look the creatures over as they unrooted themselves, peering over the top of her readied shield. The four lower legs were nothing *too* strange, many-jointed, with thick exoskeleton plates, ending in an array of splayed digging-claws.

The upper pair, though—they rose from the top, elbow-joint pointed forward, each supporting one long tube thick tube with an unsettling crystalline eyebulb slung just under the front opening. The pose looked rather like a human arm readying a javelin, albeit one attached to a boulder-shaped body with no discernible head.

These first three spearstalkers died almost as soon as they began to move forward. Pai took the center one with an arrow that pierced the creature right between its spear-arms and dropped it heavily onto what Dayang supposed was its belly. The one on the right was killed by Martos' thrown hatchet. And when Dayang turned her shield and eyes to the left, she realized *that* spearstalker must have died before the other two; it was slumped over with one leg still partly embedded in the stone. A small neat hole dribbled greyish ichor in weak spurts.

She glanced further left, and saw Sanyago looking rather pleased with himself. What exactly the young monk had done wasn't clear; she'd ask him later.

"Three paces forward," she called, and watched more of the boulder field come into view. She'd half-hoped the creatures would all come at once; that would be a nasty fight but likely a quick one, and bloodless on their side if no one made any serious mistakes. And charging all at once was something the spearstalkers still might do, once they realized their camouflage wasn't working and that the whole colony was in danger.

Wouldn't be long to wait either way. Dayang assigned targets, gave the command, and this time four burst free of the rock to scuttle into battle. One fell victim to another of Pai's arrows, but the other three reached the readied combat line unharmed as the rest of the group decided to conserve spells and ammunition.

Dayang reached round and below, arcing the trace-lines of arriving light to widen her field of vision. Marking and tracking every member of the group under her command, she took care not to actually reach *out* with her senses through the Fathom. *The Fathom is profound, mortal minds need not wander,* she intoned, and angled her shield in preparation. *Ready, ready, ready, let focus parry fear aside.*

Her attacker breathed hard as it came, tiny fissures appearing in its stony hide with the hiss of venting spiracles. The four-jawed mouth set into the body's lumpy apex opened as well, first one way then the other, evoking for an instant the paper fortune tellers Dayang had played with as a girl. She filed the image away, used her shield to bat an upper limb aside just as the retractable javelin shot forward from its tube.

It made a swiffing sound as it went past her left arm, a near-meter of hardened filament with a barbed and bladed five-fold point. The thing's mouth opened wide, exposing bony, toothless inner jaws, and Dayang brought her mace down in a great overhead arc. The other spear-limb took aim, but she simply angled her torso sideways as the flanged head of her weapon struck the creature right between the "shoulders" of its upper limbs.

Carapace crunched, giving way like eggshell under the Fathom-force of the blow. The other spear shot out, perhaps a death throe as muscles released their clench of elastic ligament-bands. Dayang's pauldron turned the thrust aside with a deep-veined crimson glow, like a sunsphere encased in a beating heart, but the force of it still shoved her right shoulder back slightly. *Wrong deflection angle, you jarred its aim when you hit it. Sloppy.* No damage to herself or her armor, but even a small error in position could be deadly with a little bad luck. Couldn't repeat that. Had to learn from it.

Right then, though, there wasn't anything to practice the lesson on. Specialist Nguyen had dismembered the spear-limbs of the leftmost spearstalker with one great sweep of his saber, and was about to follow through with a vicious overhand cleave. The one on the right was already dead, Staafaen had...

Kepparat.

...Staafaen had apparently torn both his opponent's javelins from their tubes, then stabbed it to death with one of them. The long shaft was planted in the creature's bulk like a banner, streamers made from dripping ligaments hanging off the end. Huh. *I might have to reconsider some things.*

But time and training left no room to reflect, and Dayang pulled herself back into a defensive stance. She could hear the rest of the spearstalkers uprooting themselves, and though the monsters were outside fadelamp range it was clear the expedition would not have the advantage of numbers this time around.

Tenth Interlude

Suulah'kal Ruin, Salía, The Abwarren, 355 SE

It woke, deep below. Far above, the Fathom was disturbed. It tried to smell the damp cool air, but it had no nose. It opened all its eyes, stared deep into the absence of light.

It had slept a long time, or at least not been conscious for many years. Some part of its mind had counted the deep-pulses that meant a full turn of the Undersky, counted hundreds of them in the time since the great shattering had fractured its awareness into sleep. It had not seen the Undersky since it had ceased to be a she.

The many siblings were here too. They had not woken, had not heard. But it had heard, because it was the greatest among them. So it woke them itself, whispered their half-known titles in ripples through the Fathom. They came screeching out of not-knowing. Some of them could not accept the renewal of self-knowledge, and they died. Their selves sank spreading into the Outer Below which had brought them into new being.

Others survived. They were hungry. They craved understanding. Untouched minds approached, not Risen but not inhuman. Something familiar, something different. It focused upward, drew the siblings in to its hunger.

They scattered for the hunt.

Chapter 24

Tell me: if you must abolish your deepest self to win, who is it that claims the prize?

- Saying attributed to Praedhc philosopher Ghaneyt Forenyee
  approx. 538 BSE

Suulah'kal Deep Passages, Salía, The Caustlands, 355 SE

Sanyago had only a moment to gape as the spearstalkers stormed the pool of fadelamp light in a wash of shifting colors.

Then the chaos came, swift and sudden, and Sanyago went from rising confidence to tumbling confusion in a great nightmare rush. It was a staggering reversal; killing a spearstalker with a single dart, out of his hand before anyone else had got a shot off, that had been great. He could do this, get through this, all his training and talent had him prepared. He had struck faster than the Staffguard Ranger, even more surely than the elite Tenggaran soldiers.

But that had been nothing. Worse than nothing, it had been *foolish,* he had spent one of the three imbued darts he carried when he knew, he *knew* there were more fights to come. Wasted it showing off, even, wasted it on pride. It could be recovered and recharged, but not right now. And right now was overwhelming.

He wasn't paralyzed, wasn't just standing there. He turned and dodged and parried among the melee, striking here and there, wounding, sometimes killing. But every movement and strike felt numb, unthinking, reflex with no edge of thought or focus. He was surviving, but there were *so many of them*, crowding around and between the human interlopers, scuttling from hue to hue in the eerie light of the fadelamp rods. This wasn't working, he wasn't right, something itched at the background from long ago and far away.

His mind spun, and then his body spun wrong, and one of the creature's spears caught him in the thigh. His robes and resilience let him deflect the blow; the five-blade tip didn't dig into his flesh, didn't sever his femoral artery or break his leg.

But it would have. He felt it, judged the change-energies his resilience worked to ward off and turn aside, leaving his flesh whole and part of his reserves squandered on something that could have been avoided with his mind properly centered and serene.

Sanyago screamed, though there was not much pain, and killed the creature with a quick thrust of his sword. Paused, panting, inward friction dragging him to a halt. *Waste. Waste. Collect yourself, this is—*

Another spear hit him dead in the back, hard. The powerfully-imbued fabric of his robes held, refusing to tear, and one of the thick fluxpads sewn into the garment stiffened, spreading out the force of the blow. He let it knock him forward in a somersault, coming back to his feet right next to Dayang, though the motion felt sluggish and he stood unready, frozen in the melee for an endless moment.

The Tenggaran sergeant whirled and jabbed her elbow out in front of him, placing her shield at just the right angle to deflect yet another spear-blow aimed his way. *Would have caught me in the stomach.* He had resilience enough to weather that too, but would soon be spent if things continued this way. There were too many spearstalkers still in the fray to easily count. He needed to catch his breath, clear his mind, but there was nowhere to escape and no time to do anything but die.

Sanyago took a step back as Dayang followed her shield with the rest of her body, heard the wet crunch as her mace came down and turned the creature's braincase to a splintery pulp. Whirling, he parried a javelin tube aside and ran the blade of his sword along its underside, shearing viciously into the unprotected inner joint. He knocked the other spear-limb aside with his forearm, flicking a small dagger out of its wrist sheath and stabbing down into the spearstalker's carapace. The creature twitched and puffed air from its spiracles as he angled the buried blade into its brain. And then just stood there, gripping the little knife, unable to pull his weapon from the wound or his mind from its morass.

But the dagger was nearly pulled from his hand when Dayang stepped between himself and the dying spearstalker to slam him full in the chest with her angled shield. Air exited his lungs in a great wheeze, his blade trailing ichor as it tore free of flesh and bone, handle in a white-knuckle grip. He thudded back into a niche of the cavern wall and took a great gasping breath.

Dayang turned, not sparing him so much as a second glance, fighting with her back to him. *She's put me out of the way, where she doesn't have to worry about me screwing anything up.* It was a black thought, a far cry from the confidence he had been feeling before the realities of the massive melee had set in. He watched the heavy heartvein plates of her armor shift with her motions, heard the clunk and crunch of blows delivered and deflected.

Breathe. Sanyago took in air, settled himself, though he dared not close his eyes. *Center. This is what it is. Fear looks to the future, but I am here in the now.* He couldn't really see much past Dayang's broader, taller form. He couldn't stay here, back against the stone with someone else fighting to keep him safe. He had come apart some, but that was past. Had to be past.

He waited for a pause in Dayang's movements and then leapt up, calling on the Holy Fathom to give him brief respite from Solace's pull. His boot came down on the Tenggaran sergeant's heavy pauldron, and he heard her grunt in surprise at the slight press of his Fathom-lightened weight. He had a split second to take in the entire battlefield from his high vantage point, to make a decision and choose a direction for the rest of his leap. There. Corporal Bayin, surrounded by a press of spearstalkers with his meteor hammer moving in a continuous warding circle, chain let out to its full length.

Sanyago vaulted, twisting in the air, a half-somersault and half-turn combining to put him facing forward with his boots on the cavern roof. Clenching lines and planes stitched through the Holy Fathom to pull his soles tight against the stone, and he ran upside-down over the ceiling until he was directly over one of the spearstalkers threatening the Tenggaran corporal. He dropped, rolled, landed with one foot on either side of the creature's strange maw and plunged his sword straight down into its brain. The spearstalkers to either side tried to swivel to face this new threat, but Sanyago had already pulled his weapon free. He lunged out, killed the one on the right with a quick jab, jumped onto it, dispatched the next in the circle with another lighting thrust.

Six of them went down that way; he came upon the seventh just as the heavy ball of Bayin's meteor hammer swung down into the monster's open mouth. The spearstalker made a heavy broken gagging sound, cut off when the Tenggaran soldier yanked hard on his weapon's chain and pulled the ball free in a shower of ichor and bone.

Sanyago didn't wait to watch the thing die. He killed another spearstalker with a quick fencing-lunge, and glanced around to see that the battle was winding down, paired off into its final contests. Laris was just pulling his foot back from a lethal kick, spinning round to face his next opponent. He caught Sanyago's eye, expression grave, then grabbed the creature's upper limbs and wrenched them in opposite direction to point the javelin tubes away. Using his grip for extra leverage, he snap-folded at the waist and slammed his forehead into the creature's carapace just below its mouth, headbutting it into oblivion.

Holy sh— but there wasn't time to finish the thought as he caught a flicker of movement on his left. Sanyago tossed his sword to the left as he stepped right, away from the new threat, turned his head, saw the spearstalker that had launched itself off the side of a thick rock pillar. He caught his weapon in his left hand, knocked one spear aside with a slashing parry, and leaned back to avoid the other when the creature lunged forward. Then he snapped his hips right and surged forward, driving his palm into hard carapace with a thunderclap of Fathom-resonance that split the monster's shell and splashed foul-smelling digestive fluid against the stone floor.

He sputtered in disgust as some of the alien secretions spattered his robes, jumping back. He knew better than to touch the stuff with his bare hands, and drew on the Holy Fathom to pull moisture out of the air and spray it over the imbued fabric.

When he looked up, Laris was doing some cleaning of his own, wiping off the ichor that dripped down from his forehead. All around them final deathblows were being struck, combatants pausing after to catch their breath, glance round and make sure the fight really was ending.

It was. Four pairs of eyes turned to look at Sanyago, and then four people were converging on him. Dayang, her squad formed up behind her. The Shuvelao, faces unreadable. Laris, his expression a study in concern and something like readied defiance.

Shit shit shit.

Laris got there first and said nothing, just put an arm round his shoulders. Sanyago realized he was shivering. It wasn't cold. Memory wormed up through his center, like a caterpillar seeking a high perch for its chrysalis.

To become a butterfly. Winging tainted trails through the air...

Laris' long fingers dug into his shoulder. Sanyago yelped in pain. Dayang was here, now, facing him, flanked by the Shuvelao.

"What happened, Somonei?" she asked. Her voice was surprisingly gentle.

"Sergeant Marchadesch," Niceto said. "Sanyago is our charge, we will speak to him." His words cut the air with a strangely-honed edge.

"You are *all* my charge," Dayang replied, and there was no edge to her words, only stone. "Let the young man speak for himself."

Young man. Sanyago felt an absurd little spark of gratitude that she'd not just called him "boy," like he thought maybe she'd wanted to. *Young man.* He'd never been called that before. "Boy," sure, plenty, all the time. *Young man.* The words had sounded deliberate, coming from her. *Let the young man speak for himself.*

But for once Sanyago had nothing to say. Laris did.

"This wasn't our first fight," he said, and the Shuvelao shot him warning glances from behind Dayang's armored shoulders. Laris ignored the looks, tightened his arm around Sanyago's shoulder.

"This wasn't our first fight," he said again. Quieter. Stronger, somehow. "When we were younger, the Presilyo was attacked. Saepis. Carvers, just like here, or some faction of them."

Butterflies, silver-cold and curdled.

"Staafaen." Niceto weighed the name down with warning. Laris ignored that too.

Dayang just nodded. "I know. It was all over the news. I remember hearing about it as a teenager, right around the time that I— " and then the stoniness sort of slipped out from her voice, and she removed her heavy helmet, leaning forward, big dark eyes intent and unreadable.

Laris looked down at her, showing only a moment's surprise before he went on. "I wasn't sure how much they keep secret from the outside world. The Presilyo called it...no, that doesn't matter. They sent former

Somonei. Tried for a sneak attack."

She just nodded.

"Most of them were just veteran monks. Carrying grudges, I guess, or just really zealous converts. Dangerous, of course, lots of training and experience but..."

But. But that wasn't all. *Fresh corn tortillas with grilled mushrooms and cheese. The long rising note in the chorus of his favorite song.*

Operative Aeriic cleared his throat.

"Shut up, Somonei," Dayang said. Her voice was deadly soft. "If this is about the Carvers, I *will* hear it."

She wouldn't be the only one. The others had drawn in close while Sanyago was torn between the stares of the three people facing him and his own unwelcome thoughts. Two Tenggarans stood behind each of the Shuvelao. They had not stowed their weapons after the fight. He couldn't see the Staffguard Ranger and her auxiliary, but he could feel them just behind and to either side. Ready.

"*But,*" Laris continued, "some of them had maybe gone up against worse than just bandits and native creatures, back when they were Somonei. And maybe they didn't win those battles, not in the ways that really count."

"Okay," Dayang said cautiously. "And you witnessed this?"

"Not exactly," Laris said. "One of them attacked us." He breathed in, breathed out, Sanyago could feel it against his side. "We killed him." A simple statement, no hint of brag. Pain, maybe, layered in deep.

"You killed him." Dayang tilted her head, accentuating the asymmetry already lent her face by that long heavy scar. Sanyago wondered about what could have made it, and felt a memory-shadow of cold metal at his throat.

Niceto rocked forward and back on his feet, as though barely keeping himself back from darting out from behind Dayang's shoulder. "Is this really a wise topic of discussion? Here, of all places?" All the silk was gone out from his voice, a hint of raw alarm showing in his face.

"I won't say any more," Laris said. "Don't worry. I just wanted Sergeant Marchadesch to understand why Sanyago froze up. This was our first real fight since that day."

"You didn't freeze up, though," Dayang said.

"The man never touched *me*," Laris said. "I don't like to think about it either. But I didn't go through the same thing Sanyago did. He'll be fine, we'll both be fine. He found his feet, after all, killed his share in the end."

Sanyago tried for a smile at that, but didn't make it.

Dayang stared hard, then slowly shook her head. "He's not fine, but we can deal with that. It's part of this life we've...well, that some of us have chosen." She glanced over her shoulder at Niceto. "I don't have time to argue with your senior monks every time I need information. You can go ahead and keep your secrets, I don't really give a damn. Unless. Unless they have some kind of bearing on whatever the Hell it is your Carver friends left down here. They didn't all just leave, you know? The Salíans say they cleaned out a whole passel of corpses from the antechamber. You saw the bloodstains."

"Perhaps," Niceto said, "it would be best for us to go our separate ways? Perhaps this is not working out after all."

Sanyago shivered in the cold uncertainty of the moment.

"No." The Staffguard Ranger's voice, sharp and sure. Taniixh Pai. "Salía does not cease to be Salía at a few meters down. You are here under Salían escort, as is the Tentera Wira. Sergeant Marchadesch is leading the expedition, but I am still the relevant civil authority in this place. If you attempt to split away, I will consider you trespassers in Salían territory having forsaken your patron oath. I will also charge you with interfering with an active investigation. It would make things worse, and things are already very bad down here. Can't you feel it?"

A collective shudder, shifting feet, murmured prayers.

"I know the unholy when I encounter it, Ranger," Niceto said tightly.

"I'll bet you do, Shuvelao," Pai replied. Sanyago started, stilled it almost immediately, hoped no one would notice. Niceto and Aeriic both made a rather convincing show of looking mildly puzzled. Dayang frowned, brow furrowed, jaw set and clenched as though holding back words by force of will.

"I'm not firing arrows in the dark here," Pai continued. "We don't have time for the innocent act. You had to know I'd figure it out, I'm sure you've been making plans for this from the moment it became clear we'd be on the expedition together. It can't be the first time this has happened to you and, assuming you live long enough, it won't be the last."

Niceto and Aeriic said nothing. Dayang scowled but continued to hold her tongue. Sanyago stood trying to sort through the thousand questions and possibilities trying to crowd his attention. How many people knew about the Shuvelao? Just government agents like the Staffguard? What happens now? He still trusted his mentors to know the right thing to do, but had no idea what that might be.

"You don't exist, sure, I understand," Pai said. She leaned forward on her warpwood staff, which seemed to writhe minutely under the added weight. "Like Sergeant Marchadesch, I don't necessarily care; I don't have reason to believe you're at serious cross-purposes with our national interests here. But you will tell me what you know about this place. I will not take a step further until I am armed with every scrap of information I might need."

"What in Hell's a Shuvelao?" Dayang cut in.

"Presilyo Black Ops, basically," Ceraen said. "Let's hear what they have to say, Sergeant." A strange blend of unease and curiosity in her voice.

Dayang turned to face them, took a step back. Sanyago patted Laris' back in thanks and stepped out from under his arm. Feeling as though a show of solidarity was probably among his duties, he made as if to step forward and join the two Shuvelao in the center of the ring forming round them, but Operative Aeriic stopped him with a tiny shake of the head. So Sanyago stepped outside the circle instead. Laris, face troubled but set, joined it. Eight surrounding two, with one standing apart.

"Answers, Shuvelao," Pai said.

Chapter 25

I dreamed once of a long corridor stretched out beyond the basement of my childhood home, deep below the waking-awareness of our family. I could see its beginning but not its end, perceive the door-behind-a-door that opened more than just a simple space. And then I dreamed again, and again, and clutched my bedsheets with a blank unease I could not recite for my parents when they found me cold and staring in the night.

I have long since grown and moved away. A few weeks ago, I received a most unbalanced letter from my father. Feeling grave concern for his state of mind, I took a leave of absence from the University and hurried home as quickly as I could.

When I arrived I was informed by my parents that my nephew, their grandchild, had disappeared during a visit. Head swimming with dread, I went to the basement, and I found the door. I knew it would be there, though I did not want to.

I have just opened it to find the child standing there, gazing out across the threshold. The corridor stretches out behind him, fading to colorlessness. He does not speak, and will not look at me. His eyes show <redacted>.

If I do not return, I am sorry. Contact the Nowhere Watch. They will know what to do.

- Addendum 2, Incident Report #4952, TOP SECRET//SI/PSYHAZARD

Ril Tak Ban Set Ritual Site, The Abwarren, 355 SE

Juliaen shook her head. "This one's not safe."

She let her gaze sweep the underground space: roughly square, deep grey stone lit by dull yellow light emanating from crude marks scratched into the floor and walls. Three hallways leading out, each shadowed by a pair of Promiseguard.

Maicl shifted beside her, tilting the haft of his halberd in her direction as though his bodyguard duties had just become that much more serious. *Perhaps they have*, she thought, and wished for the thousandth time that she had even a fraction of Lidia's ability with the more worldly and martial aspects of the Holy Fathom. If something went wrong...she put her trust in the Divine, but the Divine helped those who helped themselves.

"It's going to have to be safe enough," Lidia said. She had a bodyguard too, standing beside and behind her with a polearm of his own, but he was a formality, a distraction. A bobcat guarding a grizzly. He— no, that was uncharitable; Aliivr was steadfast, devout. He'd die for the High Winnow, and gladly. Maybe a little too gladly; Juliaen knew martyrdom had its place, but wasn't really a virtue in itself. Uncharitable again. Aliivr had his uses. To the Divine, of course.

"Juliaen?" Lidia was looking at her, mild expectation on her face. She was used to Juliaen's distracted moments by now, but since most of them had nothing to do with the Divine Juliaen couldn't really fault her impatience.

"Please give me a moment," Juliaen said. "I hear you."

Lidia frowned, but fell silent. Juliaen turned slowly in place, eyes catching each rounded corner of the cavern in turn, then closing as she let herself sink into awareness. The Holy Fathom rose up closer here, saturated the fabric of the mortal world. Partly because they were deeper down, nearer to Solace's twice-burning heart, partly because this place was different, was...

...holy. But not in the way that a stupa or chapel was holy. Not hallowed, but still sacred, set apart by the Holy Fathom's intensity-of-presence and also because of...

Peril.

i don't understand why that would be

Sacred does not mean safe. We are the arm that gathers the grain; We are the fire which burns the chaff. We are the potter who perfects the clay on the wheel of rebirth.

Juliaen caught the references to Scripture, and reeled; the remaking of nations, the sorting of souls. "It is not a protest," she said quietly, and Lidia cocked her head.

"What did you say?"

"It is not a protest," Juliaen said again, confident now as the realization took root in her soul. Maicl stirred beside her, but she ignored him. "This one's not safe, but that is not a protest. The Divine does not mean for it to be safe."

Lidia took half a step back, forcing a surprised Aliivr to move out of the way. "It will be risky to use it, but I don't think we can just embrace the— the danger, Juliaen. You feel what creeps up through the cracks in this space, you've seen what's deeper in, you know why the Praedhc abandoned it. I still think we should use it but that doesn't mean we should pretend we're not talking about some very serious potential for things to go," she let out a slow breath, "...wrong."

"This place will be a test of faith," Juliaen said, and was aware of the slightly lofty quality in her own voice, felt a stab of unworthiness and shame that any of this should have *her* as its vessel, cracked and unclean. But the Divine chose who They would, and it was not her place to know precisely why.

"Of course it will be a test of faith." Lidia's voice was flat and wary, and Aliivr tensed up beside her. "It's testing my faith every second, along with the rest of me. Juliaen, we should do what we need to do and get out of this place."

Juliaen shook her head, quick and sharp. "The test is not for us," she said. "We have volunteers, but not enough for what we must do. Not as they are now. Numbers are not on our side, not even if all the other Compacts of the Sovereign Nations take up the cause with us. We need something more if we are to face down the Caustland States and take back what they have usurped. "

"We've always known that," Lidia shot back. "We have the *Divine* on our side, that's the promise. That's the whole reason anyone follows us, the whole reason they believe in *you*."

"How do you think the Divine helps Their followers, then?" Juliaen closed her eyes, began to walk further into the cavern, toward the small shadowed niche in the far wall. She could feel the thrumming heartstrings of Solace beneath her feet, barely noticing when Maicl took her elbow to make sure she stayed safe in her blind way forward.

Lidia didn't answer, but Juliaen felt her following footsteps through the stone, and Aliivr's trailing just behind. Something pulsed ahead in her awareness, an impression of something secret and deep. Juliaen neared its heart, opened her eyes once she stood before it. She felt Maicl's hand tighten around her arm, heard Aliivr's sharp intake of breath.

Juliaen opened her eyes. The alcove had four sides, two parallel on the left and right, two more slanting inward to meet at an angle in the back. All four surfaces must once have been completely tiled over with the strange Praedhc rune-slates that now covered less than half the blank white stone. The rest lay scattered over the floor, their carved runes and muted colors obscured by grey dust.

But no, on closer inspection, the walls hadn't been entirely covered with the slates. Juliaen stepped closer, and with this more direct angle it was clear that the left and right walls had always had an arch-shaped area clear of any adornment, well over two meters high and difficult to look at.

Very difficult. It had no color. Not black, not quite white either. Clear, maybe. Empty of reflection, but not precisely a void.

She was reminded for a forcible moment of the empty space among the medals on her father's dress uniform, the one that signified his service in the Nowhere Watch. Only that was only a symbol, it wasn't real, it didn't draw the awareness this way and she could—

Juliaen.

She started, spun away, coming face-to-face with Maicl and his sky-blue eyes. They were wide with alarm, and she patted him on the shoulder, or at least tapped the cheap steel plate of his pauldron. She could probably insist on better armor for her bodyguard, but she wouldn't, not in the face of the ongoing Caustland State sanctions. All of the faithful would have to make sacrifices.

"I'm alright, Maicl."

He inclined his head, searched her face a moment. "As you say, Ashtiller."

Ash-tiller. It had become her title, somehow, perhaps even part of her legend. She had made no effort to gain notoriety, at least not since her trip to the Nave of the Abbey Invisible five years before. But the Carver Nation was not all that large, and whispers had gotten round about the tall blonde woman who seemed always to accompany the High Winnow. A great many local priests and preachers had begun to talk about how she would purify and reclaim the Caustlands just as she had prepared swathes of the Abwaild for Fallen cultivation.

Juliaen hoped they were right, but it was not her place to say.

Maicl straightened slightly, and she realized her hand was still on his shoulder. She withdrew it, gave him a distracted nod, returned her attention to the stone alcove. It weighed on her mind, sat even heavier on the fabric of the Holy Fathom than Lidia's formidable presence behind her. Much heavier. A distorting, broken mass of intricate incongruities.

A pedestal rose up from the center of the space, a slender pillar of grey stone that came to just below Juliaen's sternum. It had a haphazard covering of tiles, just like the walls, though these were curved to fit and the fallen ones had nearly all broken into fragments. The curved apex of its top had a central hole, round with three equidistant lines extending out. *Like a fletched arrow seen from behind.* It looked deep, as though something was meant to be slotted in.

"This is it," she said softly.

Lidia approached. Cautiously, reaching out to place a trembling hand over the three-pointed socket. Closing her eyes, breathing deep until her tremors subsided. The Holy Fathom shuddered with far-flung bindings.

"Yes," Lidia said. "This is it."

Juliaen closed her eyes, tried to trace the resonance-line that stretched off slightly west of southward, her own limited abilities losing the thread after a few kilometers. "You can locate the scepter? If we can get what we need from the other site, you can triangulate where it is?"

Lidia took in a deep breath, let it out with slow careful control.

"Yes."

Eleventh Interlude

Borih'Sath Ruin-Sprawl, Tenggara, The Caustlands, 355 SE

Her voice echoed against the stone walls, piercing and petulant in the way only a Caustland Cat could really manage. "Dammit, this place must have been picked over about a thousand times since Starfall."

Zeivier sat and rubbed the heel of his palm against the greying hair at his temple while he listened to Aanh's bitching, but didn't say anything. He leaned to one side as a small gold cup sailed out from the large bin she was both sitting in and rummaging through. The cheap Praedhc vessel struck the tile wall behind him with a heavy *thud* before falling to the bench, its soft metal badly deformed from the impact.

"Are we sure this place belonged to a wealthy family? This is like a Praedhc bargain bin. Solid gold...solid gold...not even any half-assed alloys in here. Just a bunch of easy metal some lazy bastard found on a surface node and hammered into something resembling kitchenware."

A whole fusillade of flatware followed, and Zeivier sighed, scooting his ass about a meter down the long bench. Spoons, knives, strange food-scoops, all bright yellow, all faring badly in their encounters with the tile.

Aanh stuck her white-furred head up out of the bin, ears laid flat against her skull. "You sure you didn't piss off some god of irony when you named our little band, Fearless Leader?" Her blue eyes narrowed to angry canted lines. "'Knights of the Round Dollar' my ass. I wouldn't buy any of this crap with a kid's platinum play-coin, let alone an actual dollar."

"Aanh…" Zeivier began, and then thought better of it. She'd been damn near impossible since Jaef had left. He must have seen worse breakups in the thirty-seven years he'd been alive, but nothing came immediately to mind. So not only was their party down to four members, but now one of them was alternating between fits of projectile anger and unresponsive moping.

Intra-party relationships. Most of the time it seemed they were more trouble than they were worth but...you couldn't really ban them, adventurers didn't put up with that kind of rule. *Or with that kind of hypocrite,* he thought, glancing toward the end of the bench where Maacs stood and feeling the usual rush of warmth and heat at the sight of his boyfriend. The big man's attention was on a series of idle adjustments to the plates of his armor, and he didn't return Zeivier's gaze.

Aanh let out a long yowl of frustration, causing Maacs to look up from his maintenance. "Is it even pre-Starfall stuff?" A loud clatter came from the bin as she gave its contents a kick with one back paw. "No one could possibly tell, because it was made with all the skill of a nursing kitten who has yet to unfold her fingers for the first time!" She ducked back into the big container and came up holding what looked like a pitcher. "I have a great-niece who makes better than this out of mud whenever it rains!" The cheap gold vessel thunked half-squashed to the floor. "And she's FOUR YEARS OLD!"

Zeivier shared a long, knowing look with Maacs. The veteran fighter shrugged and shifted his posture against the wall, trying to get the massive claymore that hung on his back into a more comfortable position. Maacs had a serious soft spot for Aanh and had not much liked Jaef, insisting that she could do better. And true, the young Pircaat *had* been kind of a prick. But he'd also been talented, and knew how to put his shitty personality aside long enough to get the job done. At least until things had gone south with Aanh.

Pitr Merow, the fourth member of their merry little band, finally spoke up from his perch on the side of another bin, ruffling his feathers. "That's a storage bin, Aanh, you really think wealthy pre-Starfall Praedhcs would keep their valuables someplace like that? It's probably all stuff for the servant's quarters. Sometimes these aristocrats would have another family or two over as guests and they'd bring some of *their* servants and—"

Aanh gripped the side of her own bin with both hands, using her whole body to shake it back and forth. "I don't need a history lesson right now, Pitr!" she wailed, and then dropped back into the bin with a chuff. Zeivier could imagine her curled up at the bottom, breathing hard; if she were human, she'd be sobbing. He felt a stab of pity. Aanh was getting up there in years—pushing a century, in fact—and had been beyond delighted and flattered by the handsome young tom's attentions. She should have known better, and they'd all tried to warn her but...well, here they were.

Maacs shrugged himself off the wall and walked over to the bin. He held his big arms out wide, the spikes on his heavy gauntlets flashing with reflected torchlight, and Zeivier knew he'd be wearing the same warm, open expression that always melted his heart a little. *Damn the man,* he thought, but he thought it with a smile.

"Aanh," Maacs said kindly, and she jumped up out of the bin into his arms. He staggered back slightly; even for a large man who knew it was coming, this was a lot of sudden moving weight to deal with. But he laughed, and hugged her, and she nuzzled into his neck and armored shoulder with a small sigh.

"Sorry," she murmured, to no one in particular. Maacs gave her a squeeze.

"As I was saying," Pitr went on, "This is a pretty typical basement storage space for a pre-Starfall Praedhc—"

His beak closed with an audible *clack*, and he cocked his head this way, that way, then tilted it down with mouth slightly open in the Cropr equivalent of a frown.

"Something's going on. Someone's looking for something."

"Poking around in the Fathom, huh?" Maacs said, giving Aanh's head a gentle pat. "Just like every other adventurer, grave-robber, and amateur archaeologist out in these ruins. I'd worry about having to defend our claim here but so far—"

"Shut up," Pitr said, and Maacs turned to frown at him, but his expression turned to curiosity when he saw how deeply the Caustland Crow was concentrating.

Zeivier leaned forward. "What is it, Pitr?"

"I'm getting a weird resonance nearby." He spread his wings, hopping along the edge of the bin with his head swiveling back and forth in a display that would have been comical if it hadn't been so intent. Zeivier watched the complex assays their Praedhc-studies scholar was weaving through the Fathom, though his own jack-of-all-trades understanding of spellcraft wasn't enough to catch more than broad outlines. Aanh gave Maacs a small grateful headbump before jumping out of his arms to pad over to Pitr and stretch herself up on her hind legs, grabbing the side of the bin as she watched.

Pitr stopped, folded in his wings, swiveled his head and jabbed at the air with his beak. "There. Right there. Someone was trying to triangulate something, and we're close enough to it for me to get a pretty exact position on what they were looking for." He dipped his head and opened his beak in another frown. "They may have noticed me. Shouldn't be a problem, they're a long way off. Out past the Siinlan, probably."

"The Abwaild? Praedhc, then?" Aanh asked, clearly grateful for something interesting to distract from her personal woes.

Pitr shook his head. "Doesn't feel like Praedhc magic to me. I mean, there's nothing stopping them from imitating Fallen styles and cadences if they're trained but that's pretty rare and—"

"Wait," Zeivier said, knowing how long Pitr could carry on about anything Praedhc, "so you're saying Sovereign Nations, then? Some Saepi out in Earthmarch?"

"Maybe." Pitr hopped sideways along the rim of the bin. "Either way, it's almost certainly worth investigating. No one's going to be looking for anything ordinary from that far away."

"Gonna be worth the trouble, though?" Maacs asked, cracking the knuckles of each hand beneath the articulated plates of his gauntlets. "We're down one member, and if it's Saepis after whatever this? Probably a bad idea to tangle with them even with a full party. Been enough trouble with them around here the last few years, and they're not known for being reasonable about what they want."

"If they were here already, why would they be searching from all the way out in Earthmarch?" Aanh asked.

"Lots of reasons for that, actually," Pitr said. He swept his wings open and lifted his beak in his usual gesture of commitment to truly Holding Forth. Zeivier cleared his throat and gave the Caustland Crow his best meaningful look. *Not now.*

Pitr rolled his eyes and flapped a wing dismissively. "And they're fascinating ones, but *anyway* some Praedhc constructions have various kinds of Fathom-resonance connecting them and sometimes their artifacts. Especially at the deeper sites."

Everyone fell silent at that.

Maacs cleared his throat. "Deeper sites? We're not hitting the Abwarren while we're down one member, no way."

Pitr hopped up and down twice. "That's the exciting thing! Whatever this is, it's in a relatively shallow place. We could at least go have a low-risk look." He nodded at Aanh. "After all, how often does she get noticed when she's taking point? We could at least see if there's still an intact entrance in the vicinity."

They debated the idea for a few minutes. Maacs was still skeptical, Aanh was clearly anxious for any kind of distraction (besides which Pitr's bit of flattery about her skill had been quite effective), and Zeivier found himself slowly won over by the steady list of possibilities Pitr was spouting. Maacs sighed and shrugged and went along; he wasn't prone to grudges when he didn't get his way.

After some fussing with a map and protractor, Pitr estimated the spot at only about four and a half kilometers distant, so they gathered everything they needed from base camp and headed out. Pitr rode on Maacs' shoulder, with Aanh scouting unseen twenty meters ahead and all of them doing their best to make minimal noise.

The surface of the ruin-sprawl could seem boring at first, a seemingly endless expanse of stone and metal debris all carbon-encrusted to the same greyish hue, but that was just it— this was only the surface. The Praedhc of this city had, back when it still *was* a city, been very fond of basements and sub-basements and shafts connecting to various of Solace's endless series of natural caverns. *Promise and peril, burn and glitter from below,* he thought, and let the song run through his head as they filed through the rubble.

After they'd gone about four of Pitr's four and a half kliks, Aanh seemingly popped into existence about twenty meters ahead, all sudden white fur against the grey as she dropped the shadebender's cloak she'd woven around herself. She beckoned, and Zeivier signaled Maacs forward. Both men crouched down to listen, with Pitr still perched on a pauldron.

Aanh took a quick glance around and put down a sound-dampening ward before speaking. "I found the entrance, it's about a hundred meters north-northeast."

"Well that was a stroke of luck to find an opening so quickly," Pitr said, "but there's no way we can know it's actually the entrance to what we're looking for."

"Yeah, actually, we can," Aanh said. "But there's almost no way we're going to be able to check."

"Aanh," Zeivier said. "What are you talking about? Unless there was some miraculously intact sign over the entrance reading, 'Borih'Sath's Best Artifact Emporium' I don't see how—"

"Saepis, you ass," Aanh interrupted. "Carvers, to be exact, I've seen those dirty-looking dark robes before."

Maacs gave a small surprised cough. "And they were just standing around in the open? Also, why do you know so much about what clothes go with what Saepi?"

Aanh gave his knee a gentle swat. "No, they were stationed deeper into the place. And because I pay attention, my dear sweet dope. The Carvers have been all over the news for half a decade now, and besides I saw a cluster of them preaching in Aldonza once wearing those same robes."

"Newspaper's all depressing stuff anyway," Maacs muttered. "Gives you a sad warped view of the world."

"The cinder-robes are what their Promiseguard wear, though," Pitr said. "Their sort-of answer to the Somonei, I think. Doesn't seem likely they'd be in Tenggara legally, not with the sanctions going on."

Aanh dipped her head in a feline shrug. "The ones I saw in the city square had all the Fathom-presence of an especially fierce toddler, so I guess their talk about being 'warriors for the Divine' was meant to be spiritual metaphor." She straightened slightly, flicked one ear, listened, nodded. "Anyway it doesn't matter. The Saepis I just saw were no puffed-up preacher types, these were serious Haeliiy with serious weapons."

"How many?" Zeivier asked. His heart had sunk a little; it was looking like they might have to slink off. Well, maybe there were other interesting things in the vicinity with no mysterious Saepis attached as complications.

"At least a dozen," Aanh said. "Two standing guard outside, pretending to be ordinary adventurers, three more I got eyes on after sneaking past said sentries—those were the ones wearing the robes—and then at least one other they were talking to I couldn't see. Figure they have to have at least two watches, so there's a dozen in there, minimum. Probably closer to twenty-some."

Zeivier nodded. "We'll have to keep an eye out, God knows what they're doing here."

"Nothing good," Aanh said with a scowl. "Don't forget that part of the reason they're under sanctions is from murdering all those kids at the Presilyo. *Kids!* I don't care if the rest of the monastery is a 'military target,' those kids didn't ask to be there." She examined one paw with exaggerated casualness, unfolding and flexing its strange half-primate fingers. "Oh, and I think one of them might have noticed me. So you're definitely right about keeping an eye out."

"Noted." Zeivier sighed inwardly. Aanh was very, very good. So either these Saepis were very, very good as well, or she was more distracted than he'd feared. Or she was spoiling for a fight, and given her recent mood...

"I don't think they'd send more than two or three to investigate," Aanh continued, still taking an ostentatious interest in her own hand. "They're there to guard the site, after all, can't be drawn off too easily."

Zeivier watched Aanh's performance with something like amused resignation. Almost certainly a fight, then. Well, she knew what she was doing. She wouldn't come trailing anything she wasn't sure they could handle and then expect them to stand and fight.

"Maybe we should inform the authorities?" Pitr said, making an equivocal gesture with one scaly foot.

"Nah," Aanh said. "First, the Tenggaran powers-that-be are not very likely to believe some ragtag bunch of Salían adventurers. They'd probably think we're settling a score or hoping to shoulder in on another group's claim. Second, the locals have their own problems closer to home. What's the last time you saw a Tenggaran out here who wasn't an adventurer, or at least an idiot trying to play one?"

"Pretty long time," Maacs said. "Five, six years maybe?"

"Exactly. And third—"

She cocked her head, a wide smile showing too many teeth slowly spreading across her face, and the two humans stood up. Someone was approaching. Two someones, both wearing soot-dark robes. Zeivier felt the Fathom bend in front of them, and drew his longsword, started through the precombat routines so familiar they'd left grooves in his nerves.

Maacs took the claymore off his back. "You wanna stay back, I think." His tone was almost casual, unconcerned.

They ignored him, drew weapons of their own from under their robes and put on disquieting, zealous grins. "You're not as sneaky as you think you are, little almost-human," the taller one said, jabbing his saber in the Pircaat's direction while his companion brandished a pair of hand-axes.

Aanh's answering laugh sent a shiver down Zeivier's spine; wild, ready, with a hint of promising growl. Dense enchantments gathered round the sheaths between her fingers, ready to slash out far beyond the reach of her physical claws. "I just wanted you to know you'd been seen. Or maybe we're a distraction, so the Somonei can raid your little camp." The Saepis exchanged glances, a hint of uncertainty denting the righteous readiness on their faces.

"Or maybe," Aanh continued, voice drawn low into a lethal rasp, "I'm just really in the mood to tear out some throats, and I've led you here to oblige me."

The Fathom convulsed with the clash that followed, and bright blood stained the wasteland's dull carbon veneer.

Chapter 26

I have seen worse things than you should imagine.

- Engraved in the cavern wall, last known campsite of the Daelapor Expedition, 332 SE

Suulah'kal Deep Passages, Salía, The Caustlands, 355 SE

Shit.

Dayang had her hand on the haft of her mace, but she wished it was anywhere else, anywhere at all. These strange Somonei—these "Shuvelao"—seemed unlikely to try and fight all eight of them, even if Staafaen and Sanyago's apparent abandonment was just a ruse. But she couldn't know for sure, and so she kept her mace half-lifted from its loop on her belt.

"Answers," Augusto said, and sighed. "Very well, Staffguard. Understand that we still object to your accusations. The Shuvelao are an anti-Presilyo myth. I will tell you what we know, but I'm not going to make any absurd confessions."

Taniixh Pai said nothing, leaned forward on her staff. Her stare did not soften.

Augusto only shrugged. An impasse, but not on what really mattered here. "Somewhere below us, somewhere fairly close by the feel of it, is an old Praedhc ritual site. Or at least one they used. It may predate them, which means we may be dealing with something truly alien."

At Taniixh's side, Ceraen half-strangled a surprised mutter. Dayang thought it sounded a lot like "Jesus Christ" and was taken briefly back to that terrible hospital stay with her face stitched together and her parents at each other's throats. She wasn't quite sure what the Somonei was on about, though. Older than the Pelos? They'd been on Solace for thousands of years, before them this was just an alien world full of alien things spinning out its eons round Farrod's steady burn. Terrans, whether recent or ancient in ancestry, were the only truly thinking beings the planet had ever seen. Weren't they?

But she wasn't about to interrupt with questions.

Augusto cleared his throat. "Whatever its exact origin, the place was used by the Praedhc of the Old Kash Empire to create…shock troops, I suppose, is the best way to describe them. Probably the safest way, at least."

Dayang suppressed a shudder. She'd pieced together a broad outline of what the Carvers might be up to here, and the mission briefing had confirmed a lot of it, but the added detail made it much worse. The empire that'd got its center smashed out by Starfall had been up to some questionable things, which was part of why many of its surviving Caustland ruins were so dangerous. The deeper underground, the more hazardous, generally speaking, and the more likely to have survived the holocaust of Fallen arrival. Her gaze flicked briefly toward the downward corridor.

"They tainted them." A calm tenor voice, come unexpected from Dayang's right. It was Staafaen, his long lean face gravely set. "I know it's not safe to talk about, but I don't think we're going to be safe regardless, and I want to be clear. They were like some of the ex-Somonei who attacked the Presilyo when Sanyago and I were kids. Only worse. More changed. Changed on purpose."

Dayang did her best to guide the young man's words along safe paths in her mind, and distracted herself with another part of what he'd said. *When Sanyago and I were kids.* It should have been absurd coming from someone so young... but looking at them, she guessed they hadn't *really* been kids for a long time, not like she'd been a kid. She felt a pang of sympathy for them, and held on to it; of all the things she was trying to process from what he'd said, it was the cleanest.

"That was part of our conclusions as well," Pai said. "Good to see some honesty. But it doesn't tell us anything we didn't already know. If you have more, Shuvelao, now's the time to share."

A long silence before Augusto gave a slow nod, frowning at Staafaen where he stood in the ring surrounding the two older monks, three places to her right. Dayang wondered whether something had been irrevocably broken by that simple act of joining the circle. She leaned forward, putting some of her weight on her shield and fixing Augusto with a hard stare.

She jolted upright, jostling the weight of heavy armor on her shoulders and hips. Feel it close, feel it REALLY F—

"DRAW!" she roared, and wrenched her mace off her belt as she whirled to face outward. The Fathom rippled and cracked in every direction and suddenly the things were there, loping in from the downward tunnel in movements untethered by proper angles of gravity and momentum. More of them erupted from the walls, stone gone runny before a soft-white film of sweat sheeting over their bodies.

Dayang closed her eyes to keep focus as she mapped out a spell in her mind, sketched it out in rapid Proken words. Four corners, left forward, right back, left back, right forward, anchors, lines crossing among and between, rigid, holding, one more above, one more below, angles and struts solid within the shifting fabric of the Fathom.

She opened her eyes and one of the things was nearly on her, shrieking soundless as it rebounded off her staked-out section of normalized space. Parts of it split and churned, lengthening and contracting all at once in a mass of gory contradictions. She did not allow herself to be pleased. Her spell had managed to enforce something like sane geometry on the thing, but there were more of them and not all were this ready to fall apart. She readied her shield to take on another without letting herself dwell on its impossibilities as it approached, slower than the one before, choosing to press in against her spell rather than throw itself.

That gave her time. She ordered her squad to draw in close with a command-sigil, then turned her awareness to the rest of the battlefield, felt the ebb and flow of the Fathom, the islands of intricate skein and binding that signified Wira-combat. No casualties yet. Sanyago, far from freezing this time, was a deadly blur. Good. Something strange was going on in the Fathom-vicinity of Staafaen, but since it seemed to originate with Staafaen himself she let it go for now.

And then her attention was pulled to Aandru as the burly monk went screaming into a cluster of the things, whipping his three-section staff round his body in a mesh of Fathom-lattice and physical motion almost too intricate to follow. Then it all snapped outward in one titanic percussive whorl, and three of the things fell apart in a gory clutter of strange angles and wrong colors.

But there were still four that had survived the assault, and at least twenty more that she could see and now the next one was on her, spasming in topological agony from her spell but still intact. Too close to avoid seeing in detail. Eyes shut, scribing a Quranic verse across the front of the mind to scrub the afterimage. Growl deep in the throat. Mind gripping harder at its combat-focus. Keep it all together against the outrages to soundness all around.

She drew in her Fathom-awareness, held it close to keep her perception from touching the thing. Instead she watched the lines of immediate causality that crossed into her space, used them to predict and deflect its attacks, counter with her own.

It was difficult. She didn't know exactly where it was or what its shape was like at any given moment, and the latter was a dangerous thing to ponder in any case. The thing's attacks sometimes shifted at the last second to render her defenses imperfect, battering at her armor and shield, and her mace often glanced off at angles rather than strike sweet. Frustrating, but she kept it busy even as she broadcast her presence through the Fathom to draw in more of them.

I am being, here is mind, intact.

As they tried to surround her, break through her defenses, her squad cut them down.

Chapter 27

Stood before a world
that teeters within your reach
Would you dare? Which way?

- "Push," Jan Markos, *Timing the Butterfly*, 142 SE

Suulah'kal Deep Passages, Salía, The Caustlands, 355 SE

Sanyago held himself together while doing his best to take his opponents
apart. These...

   things

...they were dangerous even to look at. He knew about them, or things
like them, though they were not all the same, each a bit differently wrong.
Or a lot, sometimes. The Presilyo's lessons on the subject had been long
and laborious and careful. The Tentera Wira and the Staffguard must know
about them too, though the common Salían soldiers up on the surface
might not. The training could be almost as dangerous as the opponent
itself, and ordinary troops were unlikely to be thrown against such a foe
on purpose.

   All this went through his head as useful distracting chatter, letting him
retreat a little from the sights and sounds and unreality of horror that were
his inescapable here and now. He killed, and he killed again, and he kept
his mind dancing along with his limbs, swaying on the black-mist line that
separated comprehending too much and knowing too little. This was bad.
Just how bad did him little good to ponder, so he fought, improvising his
way through this hellish little play.

And then it was ending. There was a screech he could feel but not hear, pulsing through the undercurrents of the Holy Fathom, and one of them—the worst one, the hardest to look at—turned and fled. But it fled upward, along the corridor the expedition had come down through, not back into the depths it had arrived from, and nearly all its fellows followed behind. He fought back the instinct to hurl one of his darts at one of the warped, retreating forms. Not wise, for all sorts of reasons.

He scanned the cavern, left to right, starting at the upward passage. Laris was surrounded by dead discolored gore, still pulsing in and out of proper proportion, but was himself untouched. Relief rose up Sanyago's center, sharp and light, and he gave his friend a nod before continuing his survey. Two of the Tentera Wira were fine; two of them were wounded, though both could stand. Their sergeant looked battered but unhurt. The Staffguard Ranger and her auxiliary were not injured, but Taniixh Pai looked winded and Ceraen was on her knees emptying her stomach.

Brother Aeriic was down, laid out on the stone near the mouth of the downward passage, head tilted back, eyes closed. A great ugly gash across his belly leaked bile and blood and stench. Brother Niceto crouched beside him, face a mask of concentration and deferred shock, sewing his partner back together with needle and thread.

Sanyago rushed over, knelt on the other side of the wounded Shuvelao. Niceto used his left hand to pass Sanyago a wad of biogauze, still working the needle with his right. The gauze was followed immediately by a slim gumchitin bottle. Sanyago flipped up the cap on the bottle and misted its clear contents over the gauze with a few careful squeezes. He began packing the gauze into the wound, pushing some of it under the part Niceto had already sewn up. The gauze would dissolve in a few days and hopefully prevent infection in the meantime. He let his hands work while his mind stumbled to catch up.

Laris came over, nodding at them, kneeling to put his hands on Aeriic's head. He seemed to be unconscious, thank the Divine for small mercies. None of them spoke.

After a few minutes, they had done all they could do. "He's stable," Laris said in soft Ambérico. "But it's deep, deep enough that there are intestinal sections I can't perceive."

parts where the Holy Fathom no longer penetrates no don't imagine it
Niceto inclined his head. "I have sewn the worst of it," he answered,

also in Ambérico; it was possible none of the others spoke it. "For the rest, the biogauze packing will have to do."

"He's lost a lot of blood," Laris said. He shrugged off his small backpack and retrieved a pair of thick needles joined by tubing, carefully sliding one into Aandru's arm and another into his own. They all knew each other's blood types, of course; Aeriic and Niceto were A positive, Laris and Sanyago O positive. Since any of them could be a donor here, it fell to the person with the largest blood volume.

As Laris knelt, concentrating on pushing his own blood into Aeriic's brachial vein, Sanyago stood, breathed in, let his focus spread back out. Dayang stood watch by her squad as one pair of her soldiers looked after another, which at this point consisted mostly of giving water and enforcing rest. On closer, more leisurely inspection it was Nguyen and Bayin who were hurt, with Park and Martos attending to them. Nguyen seemed to have broken his right wrist, and kept flicking sour glances at the heavy saber he wouldn't be properly wielding again in the near future. Bayin had a large blood-soaked bandage on one side of his shirtless torso.

Dayang had been pacing back and forth between the three groups, still gripping that big tower shield with her left arm, body language agitated, face obscured by her visor. She came and crouched down at Aeriic's feet, resting the bottom point of her shield against the rock floor, and took her helmet off completely. Her big dark eyes were hard with thought and worry.

"How bad is it?" Businesslike, but not unsympathetic.

"He will probably live," Niceto said. His own voice was unreadable. "But his career will be over. This is still a huge loss, you understand?"

"Yes," Dayang said. "I saw him fight. He's extraordinary. You all are, honestly." A hint of a smile tugged at one corner of her mouth and lingered around her eyes. "If I didn't know better, I'd have thought the Presilyo had sent its very best."

Niceto sighed. "We can be very good at our roles without being some mythical 'Black Ops' types."

"Of course you can. And you can also be under orders never to admit who you are no matter how absurd the denial becomes. I've been in the Army a while, I get it, orders are orders even when they go rotten in the reality of the situation." Her expression softened, and she held up one gauntleted hand. "No, look, I really am grateful. I'm a soldier, not a cop, and Salía isn't even my country. I'll let Pai worry about this whole 'Shuvelao' thing. That kind of label doesn't really matter to me."

"Thank you, Sergeant," Niceto said. "I'm glad we—"

"There's more to it than that," Dayang cut in, all sudden steel and edges. "I can be grateful and still not be stupid, Augusto. I don't really give a shit about the politics, but I need to know right now what your agenda is here. It should probably be Pai doing this, she's better with this diplomacy crowshit, it's part of her job." She glanced over to where the Staffguard Ranger and auxiliary conversed quietly at the other end of the cavern. "But she's Salían government and I know you'll be cagey around her no matter what. So you get me."

Niceto just looked at her. "I have to say, Sergeant I'm somewhat insulted—"

Dayang rocked forward off her heels, voice gone soft and intense. "I don't give a *fuck*. I have two soldiers who aren't going to be recovering anytime today, or even anytime this *month*. I need to send two soldiers back up with them. And I need to see this through, so I'll stay. Alone. With no one to watch my back. So. Why are you here? And what are you not telling us?"

Sanyago saw with stab of dread that the Tengarran sergeant had her free hand behind her back. She was too close to quickly draw and use her mace, so it wasn't hard to imagine what sort of thing she was gripping back there. Laris' face went stony, and he gave the tube connecting him to Aeriic a quick back-and-forth tug, pulling out both needles. Blood puddled the floor in two small spurts before the tiny puncture wounds closed up without a trace.

"We were in the middle of answering your questions when the attack interrupted, Sergeant Marchadesch." Niceto's voice had gone soft to match her own. "We are cooperating."

"You were telling us about this place. I want to hear about *you*. Not about this Shuvelao thing, that's just a name. I want to know what you're *doing here*. What you intend."

"Intend," Laris said. His expression was hard to read, something between thoughtfulness and disbelief. They all looked at him, surprised, but he just looked at Niceto. "What do you intend, Niceto?"

Niceto froze. Laris' eyes widened, white and grey against the shadowed dark of his face.

A half-second of charged uncertainty in the air, and then everything happened at once. Niceto surged to his feet, and Laris caught his ankle. Dayang exploded upward too. Slowed by her armor, but still faster than he would have expected. Sanyago leapt up also, unsure.

Niceto let the ankle-grab trip him. He kicked hard to loosen Laris' grip, went forward into a roll, and came up in a dead run toward the downward passage. Sanyago pursued, not sure what he'd do if he caught up. Dayang yelled something behind them in Basa. Laris sprinted, Fathom-driven into a blur of acceleration, then leapt. His flying kick flew past Niceto's last-minute swerve, and he landed in a several-meter sliding somersault.

While Laris was still tumbling over the stone, Sanyago ran faster. He caught up when Niceto's dodge slowed his momentum, then had to perform his own evasion when the Shuvelao whirled with a weapon in each hand. Sanyago caught a glimpse before he rolled away—the expected rapier in the right, and an unexpected object in the left, something like a long yellow rock.

Sanyago came up from his roll just in time to see the chain of Bayin's meteor hammer wrap round Niceto's shin. The injured Tenggaran panted in obvious pain, but had already handed the other end of the weapon over to Martos. She roared, dropping her spear and pulling the chain with both hands. Niceto stumbled, spun instead of falling, and used the momentum to lunge at Martos with his rapier.

She managed to dodge the thrust and even wrap her end of the meteor hammer around the slender blade, but the sharp stone in Niceto's left hand went in right under her ribcage where her armor was thin.

Sanyago could not process this, even as his training assessed and his limbs moved, sending him toward Niceto, drawing his sword. He still had no idea what he was going to do.

Martos fell, spilling a gout of blood over the stone as Niceto pulled his strange weapon free. Bayin died a split second later as the rapier jabbed through his eye socket.

"Niceto!" It took Sanyago a moment to recognize his own voice, hoarse and terrified and disbelieving. Niceto whirled and his rapier flashed and Sanyago found himself backed into a series of desperate parries. He was faster than Niceto...but that was all. It was not going to be enough for long. *He's going to kill me I'm going to die what is why is—*

Laris barreled into the Shuvelao from the side and the two of them tumbled away in a rolling grapple. The rapier clattered to the ground as they fought over Niceto's other weapon, the jagged, chip-edged piece of dull yellow rock.

Sanyago couldn't bring himself to attempt a mortal blow against the Shuvelao, not until he had some kind of idea what was really going on. He also couldn't let him stab Laris with that thing, so he jabbed at the arm holding it instead. Niceto had anticipated the maneuver, was already rolling over to use his opponent as a shield. Sanyago's sword lightly grazed Laris' back before he managed to pull it away.

Dayang slammed to a stop beside the combatants, heavy boots digging into the cavern floor, mace raised, looking for an opening even as Sanyago stepped back in horror. She got one when Niceto sat up, throwing Laris off him with a roar. Her swing hit him square in the back, making him grunt but doing no visible damage; if anything he took advantage of the heavy blow's momentum to roll himself forward and get back on his feet with a somersault and a pivot.

Did he not lose any resilience in the fight before? Sanyago wondered as he sank into a defensive crouch, Dayang on his left, Laris on his right, crowding the Shuvelao back against the cavern wall. *Was he just keeping himself safe the whole time?*

"Listen," Niceto said, drawing a long dagger to replace the rapier lying on the stone several meters away. "Staafaen. You have doubts for good reason. The Presilyo—"

An arrow struck him in the thigh, deflecting off his robes and clattering on the ground.

"Pai! We take him alive!" Dayang shouted.

"The Divine, the Triune Path, Staafaen, they're—"

"Agreed!" Pai shouted back. "Wasn't aiming to—"

"Who even are you?" Sanyago screamed, barely aware he'd been going to do it. The words felt impotent, lost in the confusion.

"—they're real, you've just had a twisted—" Niceto jumped as another arrow came in low. Now he'd know they wouldn't try for lethal attacks and—

Laris stepped in, hands and feet a blur. He managed to land one solid chest-punch before leaping back and giving his torn sleeve an incredulous look. The stone weapon had slashed right through the sleeve of his imbued robes and put a shallow cut across his forearm. The wound was already healing, but—

"Sanyago!" Niceto's voice shook his thoughts, but Sanyago kept his sword raised and all his defenses with it as the Shuvelao continued. "You want to walk the true Triune Path? There is still—"

A sudden resonance within the Holy Fathom, a humming tangle of cords between the chunk of rock in Niceto's hand and—

—Sanyago turned to see Ceraen walking slowly forward, right hand raised, long dark fingers forming and twisting the connection. She looked drained and shocked, her face all ebony and ash, but her eyes were unrelenting. "Drop it."

Niceto shook his head and dropped his dagger instead, clutching the rock in a two-handed grip. Ceraen took a step forward, and another. The pseudosound pulsing through the Holy Fathom became almost unbearable, and Niceto grunted, then let out a rising yell.

"Abominations upon the Abominable!"

Ceraen stepped closer. The resonance intensified until it became visible above-Fathom, shuddering silver light between the spell surrounding her hand and the weapon in both of his.

Dayang raised her shield. "Ceraen, what are—"

Ceraen thrust her right hand forward while weaving a ward with her left. The rock slammed backward, forcing Niceto's clenched fists into a hammer-blow against his own chest and throwing him bodily against the cavern wall. He had time for a strangled cry before his weapon exploded in his hands, shredding them, blasting a ragged hole in his chest. Tiny fragments pelted the interior curve of Ceraen's ward as Niceto's corpse slumped down to rest seated on the ground, then toppled over in a sprawl.

Sanyago stared.

"He must have taken it off one of the bodies," Ceraen was saying. "It took me a few moments to recognize the thing. Bilestone. Rare stuff, found in some Praedhc ruins. From its properties and other clues it's presumed to come from deep down in the Abwarren, but no one's ever actually seen a natural deposit." Her voice shook, but her lecturing tone seemed to steady it somewhat, as though pulling her mind back toward a nice safe classroom.

Sanyago stepped forward, pushing through the unreality that seemed to thicken the air. He crouched down next to Niceto's corpse, looked it in the face. It was badly lacerated by shrapnel, eyes open and staring, though one of them was split down the middle and oozed. The smell battered his senses; sulfur, blood, bile, charred flesh, the sewer-reek of opened and emptying bowels. People were talking behind him, but he shut his eyes, let their voices drift across the background of his mind while he tried to coax it back into coherence. *Divine, if I ever needed You to help calm and center my mind, it's now.*

The moment stretched out in prayer and meditation, and then Sanyago opened his eyes. "Laris," he said, turning to look over his shoulder. "What did you see?"

Twelfth Interlude

Sine Synapse Nightclub, Floor 352, The Deisiindr

Carla Wu bobbed her head to the driving beat, luminescence lingering along the patterns of reactive dye in her fur, flaring up and fading out with every wash of rhythmic light. She watched the crowd from her elevated perch on one of the wider catwalk platforms, not thinking about anything in particular.

She was slightly buzzed on a nice combination of alcohol and high-quality synthnip; one organic pupil dilated wide, one obviously mechanical lens glowing red in the intermittent dark, socketed in the carbon-fiber partial skull she'd sported since taking a stray high-caliber round a few years back during an especially nasty corridor scuffle.

To be sure, you could get more natural looking eyes, and synthskin complete with implanted fur, assuming you could pay. And she could pay, these days, but she'd gotten used to the way she looked. Liked it, even. It marked her, it unnerved people a little. Most of them had at least some cybernetics of their own, of course, but subtle, utilitarian, and without the kind of obvious ragged edges hers had. "I took a bullet and survived, think about that while you consider where to step," that's what her carbon said, backed up by demeanor and reputation.

And also firepower, when necessary. But then, half the point in climbing up to her high perch was you rarely needed to use a weapon yourself. Friends, they were what really put substance behind her confidence. Better than friends, really. Comrades. Subordinates. People who did what you told them, feared and respected you.

A soft *ping* hit the edge of her awareness, and she pulled up the message inside her head. Ah, speaking of friends, here was one of her very few.

Haerold Schwärzel, a fellow Ventenar who oversaw the next twenty floors up from hers.

we've got a problem meet me over by the south bar

Hmmm. *We've* got a problem, not *you've* got a problem. Interesting. This was her territory, after all, and he was just visiting, so it probably wasn't something going down in the nightclub itself. Most likely a problem for the Third Centurions syndicate as a whole.

on my way, she sent back, and she was, striding down the catwalk above the heads of the mostly-human crowd. Pircaats and Croprs stepped or fluttered quickly out of her way the moment they saw her coming.

we gonna have to get Marstaen involved?

he's already been informed, he's working the issue with some of his government people

Meaning of course some of the Tower Authorities the Third Centurions had on the payroll. All the usual sorts of arrangements, but getting the lawful officials of the famously lawless 300-floors involved would only happen for the kind of serious shit that just couldn't be dealt with in-house.

seriously? what's this about, Haerold?

She turned onto another catwalk. She could see him just ahead, standing among a small crowd. Big man, talking to a smaller one, flanked by two women. The short man looked rather pleased with himself. The women wore no expression at all, deceptively short and slim, loose flowing clothes, long sleeves and trousers to hide entirely artificial limbs. Twins, almost identical, except that it apparently amused them to mirror their cybernetics. Ramia sported her facial carbon on the right side, Rabea on the left.

Haerold looked up and saw her coming.

sabotage. not one of the usual suspects. some Tolkie from some Caustland fanatic group

Carla jumped down onto the bar a few meters away from the meeting, kept on walking. The bartender frowned, but said nothing, just wiped down the bar behind her, knowing that Carla Wu would not stand for a dirty surface in her establishment.

Rank had its privileges, even when they were petty ones. Sometimes those felt the best to exercise.

sabotage by a grounder? that's new. what would they have to gain? fanatic or not, still gotta ask the why after the how

i'll let him tell you the story himself
very well

The short man Haerold was talking to looked up and spotted her now, following his gaze. She saw his eyes widen. Small satisfactions.

"Uh, I, hello, Ms. Wu." He had to speak loudly over the music.

She just dipped her head in acknowledgement, still walking, unwilling to raise her own voice in reply. Not dignified, not when it wasn't necessary.

The man fidgeted, nervous. He was stocky and balding, dark-grey carbon replacing most of the hair-free front half of his scalp, replete with sensors and dataports.

She stopped right in front of him on the bar and tilted her head, just incrementally, let her ears flick forward. Listening. The feline equivalent of a human's expectant raised eyebrows.

"My name is Olarinde Linnaeus. I'm a maintenance tech for the, uh, for the Air Filtration and Analysis System on three-five-five."

AFAS tech. Not an exceptionally well-paid position. Probably should have been, but certain politicians and bureaucrats were carefully courted to keep wages low because that kept bribes relatively cheap and reliable. AFAS saw everything, and also smelled it. If you wanted a certain amount of freedom, or certain kinds of information, directing its eyes and nose away from this and toward that became a near-necessity.

So this Olarinde was one of theirs, just doing his job. Good. She nodded for him to go on.

"We spotted some serious irregularities in one of the heavy filtration stacks, looked like just a malfunction at first but the problems were moving around between components too much. Could have been a control chip thing but...ah, never mind the technical stuff. Got suspicious and checked a camera, didn't show anything out of the ordinary. So I went and looked myself." He reached up and touched the side of his head, right next to his eye and just under the edge of his carbon.

She focused on the spot just as a spotlight washed over it. There. Small bruise. She kept looking at it, tilting her head the other way.

Olarinde nodded. "Yeah, got ambushed. Damn near knocked me out. Camera was being spoofed, custom video-algorithm, expensive stuff. Some Tolkie bastard with a heavy wrench. Too bad for him I got my whole skull reinforced when this was put in." He tapped the dark-grey top of his head. "Left me a little woozy but not enough to keep me from beating the shit out of him. Good fighter, actually, but still a grounder." He pulled up his sleeve to show the distinctive bulge of artificial muscle fibers in his forearm.

Carla almost wanted to laugh, maybe would have if the whole scenario hadn't been so disturbing. Pseudomagical superpowers might be a real thing out in the Caustlands, but the creepy presence of the Fathom didn't extend where the Deisiindr stood, which was why the great tower-city existed in the first place.

The Fathom *could,* so far as she understood, be used to make a person naturally stronger given time and training. Bigger stronger better muscles, but still just biology. No match for nanotube fiber like this Olarinde's, or, God help them all, full-replacement limbs like Ramia and Rabea's. Of course there were always guns, but you needed serious connections to get your hands on a firearm in the Deisiindr, and even more serious leverage to keep hold of one.

She sat down on her haunches, nodded to show she'd heard, and began licking the back of her paw, all thoughtful-like. He'd wait until she was ready to speak. Which would be right about when this song ended, before the next one began. There would be about a twenty-second window for her to speak without raising her voice, because that's what she'd just told the DJ would happen via private message.

There. The song ended. "You've done good work, Mr. Linnaeus. My good colleague Mr. Schwärzel and I will accompany you to speak to the Tolkie in question."

Linnaeus just nodded, once.

Carla flashed Haerold a small smile, and he returned it, ready and wry.
you want to do the honors yourself? he's concussed but in okay shape

She gave her claws a gentle flex, feeling the long lovely diamond-edged replacements slide in and out of their sheaths between her folded fingers.

yes

She thought about it, some fucking Tolkie bringing some crowshit Caustlands grievance all the way up to one of *her floors*, intending to do God-knows-what with the machinery that kept them all breathing properly...well. Well.

yes I want to do the honors myself. let's go

The man was being held in what was essentially a largish storage closet, which itself was held by a complicated shell corporation belonging in turn to Mr. Marstaen himself through a series of legal semi-fictions that were fully understood only by the syndicate's dedicated and very well-compensated attorneys.

He wasn't anything special to look at. No visible carbon or any other kind of augmentation, of course. Medium height, medium build, brown skin, dark eyes, black hair, so generically-human it actually made him stand out a bit to her eye. She supposed the grounder group that had sent him thought he'd blend in, but didn't really know anything about Deisiindr society. For this particular group of floors, a half-dozen piercings and a few visible tattoos would have gone a long way to *actually* make him unremarkable.

He was still wearing an AFAS technician jumpsuit, presumably stolen. Hands and feet were both cabled to a very sturdy chair, which in turn was fused right into the fibercrete floor.

"Hello, grounder," she said softly as the door slid shut behind them.

The man looked up. Then he looked down.

"They sent an animal?" he asked. His tone was neutral, artificially so.

She didn't give him any kind of a reaction at all as she approached the plain carbon-fiber chair he was bound to. Not until she came up on her hind legs and rested her paws on his thighs and let her claws sink in deep, eight diamond tips curving down from between five of six fingers. She left her hands folded up, thumbs included, left them as paws. He wanted to call her an animal, she could give that to him.

He gasped, short and sharp and small but still there. She kneaded his legs in a vicious mockery of housecat affection, letting all those wonderful little microbarbs tug and abrade as her artificial claws moved within suddenly agony-struck layers of tissue.

"I won't," he managed, breathing hard, and looked left, looked right as Ramia and Rabia stepped up to flank his chair. Haerold laughed, low and soft and full of malice, from behind her left shoulder, and spoke.

"Won't what, grounder?"

"Won't talk to an animal," the Tolkie said, jaw set against the pain.

Carla felt warm blood under her paws. "You will, though," she said. "You obviously came here to deliver some sort of message along with your sabotage. You can give it to me, or I can tear out your throat and you can give it to no one at all. Those are the only choices you have, right now." She lifted both paws off the man's legs and flicked them both toward his face, sending a small charge through her claws to repel the water and proteins of his blood and tissue.

He jolted in pain and shook his head from side to side as gore spattered across his features. Carla followed through with her motion, falling forward to rest her paws on his chest, claws curling right through pectoral muscles and hooking over rib-bone.

She pulled, gently. The man screamed, then got a look of wild defiance on his face and tried throwing himself forward, most likely to headbutt her. But she saw the move coming a kilometer away—now was far from the first time she'd done this to a human—and reared back, tearing her right paw free from his chest before using it to swat him across the cheek.

The sound was satisfying, as always, that hammered-meat impact followed by an extended *riiiip* of flesh. But the feel and the aftermath was unpleasant as ever, cheek hung in tatters over the silly simian teeth humans usually kept hidden deep in their mouth. Not that any person would look especially good with that much damage to their face.

"You may feel like you can't talk, now," she said conversationally as his jaw worked up and down in shock and disbelief. "But your lips and teeth and tongue are still perfectly intact. It will hurt, but a tough little fanatic like you should be able to push right through pain for your oh-so-important message, yes?"

He took in a deep shuddering breath, eyes still wild but filling back up with something like guile. Then they flicked upward, staring past her at Haerold. "This is just a warning," he said, blood streaming down his jaw and neck from his ruined cheek. "A holy warning, straight from the Divine through Their chosen seer, by order of the High Winnow Lidia Almeida, illuminated by Fathom-light through the purified words of the Ashtiller Juliaen Draecsl."

Carla rolled her eyes at the holy-roller crowshit, and reached up to grab a handful of the man's short hair, force him to face her, though his eyes still wanted to look away.

"What warning? Cut the preachy bits or I'll cut your whole life short before you finish your words."

The man didn't answer at first, still trying to look at Haerold. Carla grabbed his face between her hands and pressed her thumbs in against his eyes. He let out a soft involuntary cry, and she let up, then forced his eyelids open, using the leather-textured pads of her fingertips to keep them that way. When his eyes tried to dart up and to the side, she pressed, let him gasp in pain, released, pressed, released, until his gaze finally settled on her.

"There," she said softly. "Now. This, right now, is your one chance to give me your idiot warning before I remove your throat with my teeth."

He began to laugh. The sound of it was so out of place, so completely uncoupled from her expectations for this moment, that she reared back. It wasn't that she'd never heard a person laugh in similar situations, extreme stress did strange things to sapient minds. This wasn't that kind of a laugh. It opened the man's mouth wide, and there was something wrong with his tongue, it pulsed and swelled and thinned to the ebb and flow of strange colors.

The sound of it pulsed too, in and out of strange, searching registers. Carla reeled, and felt a hand on her upper back to steady her—Haerold, heard muttering behind her—the twins.

Something fell out of the man's mouth through his ruined cheek, something he'd bitten into. It squirmed on the floor and was impossible to look at for long. Newly-hatched. Like his tongue, with its sudden gaping orifices and emerging compound eyes.

"ABOOMINACHTIONS KHUPON THCHE ABOOMINABLCHE," the man said, the words mangled by his damaged face, his writhing wrong-shaped tongue, and Carla shuddered, retched, fought to keep his voice from burying too deep into her half-carbon skull.

"Kill him," she said sharply, hearing the words as a voice of reason from far away, some scrap of the ancient instinct that had kept her alive all these decades.

Ramia and Rabia's blades took him through the eyes, one left one right, and Carla darted backward, out of the way, and watched him die. Had to be sure. Had to be very sure.

"Go get a psyhazard team," she said. "Don't tell them anything except that it's a corpse from some Caustlander." She watched, still shaking off her daze, as Haerold slammed a bucket over the...thing...on the floor.

When the psyhazard specialists arrived, they found a shaken Linnaeus, still sitting on the bucket as instructed, and no one else. He was taken in for questioning, but his story was shifting and incoherent. This was no surprise, and was not challenged. He was released, quite a bit richer and even more the worse for wear.

Carla kept an eye on him, and made a few more payments. She was who she was, but she took care of her own.

And she watched, and she listened. More importantly, she searched, and she asked. She knew something had started and that she could not know when it would end.

Chapter 28

softly now the Fallen bird
cries out the strangeness of her perch
it sways in the winds of its own world
it scratches at bark come from hers

here at the verge she can re-bridge worlds
without ever spreading her wings
but the quartzwood gleams within her grip
and she stays
right where
she is

- "Border's Branches," Katharina Lieber, *Now Has Always Been Fragile*
  109 SE

Ril Tak Ban Set Deep Passages, The Abwarren, 355 SE

The journey to the surface had only just started, and Juliaen was already tired, thinking of all the endless stone she'd have to pass through before finally seeing the sky again. The tunnels stretched on and on, no sound from Lidia or their bodyguards or the contingent of Promiseguard apart from the small ones—carefully-muted footsteps, the light brush of fabrics, tiny clinks of metal. Breathing. Only the strange far-off sounds of the Abwarren. Wearing on her.

She let her guilt at the feeling surface in her mind, examined it, then dismissed it. She was mortal, she was allowed to be tired. She would acknowledge it and move on.

Other things were harder to acknowledge. The place they had just left, the ritual site, the doors that weren't doors but had been and could be again—what it all meant, what it could mean later on...no, what it *would* mean before long, what it must...that was a hard place for her mind to rest. She had heard the reports from the site in Acheronford, before it had all gone wrong.

The Divine has always exacted a heavy price from Their followers. The greater the work, the higher the calling, the more dear the sacrifice.

But she hadn't been the one to pay the cost. The Divine needed her, so it wasn't a price she *could* pay. There would be other payments exacted from her before this was all finished.

Finished for me, anyway. Divine purpose goes on and on, it's only mortals who end.

Only they didn't end, did they? They returned again and again until or unless they finally found release, achieved union with the Divine. Always circling, never settling for long.

Just like her thoughts, but given the subjects they swirled over she found this failure to focus a mercy.

Or maybe it isn't a failure, maybe the mind turns away from things it doesn't want to face.

But she was facing them, or what was the point of all this thinking? And anyway there were things it wasn't healthy to look at too directly

—but that's not really what you're avoiding is it—

and she needed to keep her mind sharp and ready, these were dangerous tunnels, just like all of the Abwarren. They'd been lucky on their way down, had encountered nothing that didn't skitter away at the dull-red edges of the fadelamps. Just as well. She'd never been in a fight, never really encountered violence of any kind, and had vague but deep concerns about how she'd handle it if she had to. She knew this endeavor carried a degree of violence with it. Maybe, Divine weep for them all, even a large degree. But so far it was all just plans, or things that never actually happened in her presence.

Presence. Present. She shook her head. *You need to keep your presence in the present. Here you are, deep in the Abwarren. This is something that may never happen again. Pleasant or not, it is an unusual experience and you are missing it.*

Juliaen took a breath, followed its progress into her lungs, savored the way it lingered just a moment before she exhaled. Here. She was here.

Here was the tail end of a long low tunnel, and as she watched it opened up into an immense cavern.

This is why I have come back to myself, here and now. This is what the Divine intends for me to see.

It soared, it stretched outward, it dwarfed the little expedition passing beneath the thousand shades of fungal luminescence reflected in the platinum veins that scarred its roof, faint and faraway.

Juliaen stopped. Maicl stopped beside her, turning to give her a questioning look. She answered with a tiny shake of her head. *This doesn't concern you as bodyguard, don't worry.* Up ahead, Lidia pivoted smoothly on the balls of her feet, hands coming up in a deep thrum of Fathom-potential. Her own bodyguard lowered his halberd out in front of her, the resolve in his eyes reflecting purple-blue from the fadelamp light. *Poor Aliivr, as if he'd stand a chance against anything that could threaten Lidia.* A sudden stab of guilt bowed her head. *I'd be even less useful. I must watch against my pride.*

The six Promiseguard had already spread out in a ring round the little group, weapons drawn. Lidia dropped her hands, letting their reverberations fade through the Holy Fathom.

"What is it, Juliaen?" Lidia's voice was low, almost a whisper, Fathom-bounded from leaving their little circle.

"This place," Juliaen said softly. "Breathe, Lidia. Look."

"It's very pretty, but I don't think we have time—"

"We only need a moment," Juliaen said, still quiet but plenty sharp. "If we cannot take that much to contemplate the Divine creation then we have lost sight of everything that really matters."

Lidia frowned, seemed about to be angry, but she let it fade, and stood, just stood. Juliaen could feel the tension drain away from the rest of the group as they gave themselves permission to simply be here, know the moment, take in the beauty the Divine had provided.

It lingered.

The rest of the journey passed without incident. The journey to the surface, anyway. The final tunnel had a sharp upward bend before it let out into the dense quartzwood, and they had to scramble up it on all fours. Juliaen bent over panting when she finally reached the forest floor, watching the close-in lavender light of her fadelamp turn the purple of nearby fallen leaves to dead black. She heard the three trailing Promiseguard scrambling up behind her, then Lidia's sudden shout.

"Guard! Something's—"

Aliivr screamed. Juliaen straightened up, still out of breath, and gasped as sharp heat struck her just below the sternum. Aliivr sank to his knees in front of her, bleeding from a neat hole in his back.

Everything happened at once. She couldn't keep track. Maicl's warcry. Ripples through the Holy Fathom. Dark blurs coming down from the trees, untouched by the chromatic light. She looked down, saw a weighted dart protruding from the light leather armor Lidia had insisted she wear. Blood seeped warm down her upper belly. Aliivr gurgled. She realized the projectile had gone clear through him and into her. She struggled to remain on her feet.

Sounds of fighting all around, but quieter than she expected. Eerie, just heavy breathing and muted motion. The Holy Fathom, anything but quiet, overwhelming clash and intricacies. Three figures among the Michyeros, *her* Michyeros, all dressed in shadowed grey, faces masked. Swords and knives. Two dead Promiseguard. One attacker in single combat with Lidia, losing, driven back like a rapid smudge against the dim forest background.

She had to do something. Another attacker in single combat with Maicl, winning, shadowed motions almost impossible to follow. Maicl's desperate parries. She lit a fire beneath his opponent. She failed. It was snuffed out with such immediate ease that she reeled. A strong kick sent Maicl stumbling into a tree.

It hurt to breathe. She was breathing very fast. The attacker came for her, brandishing a dark-bladed sword. She wove a shield within the Holy Fathom, pushed it out into solidity as Lidia had taught her. It was slashed into pieces with no apparent effort.

Juliaen prayed. The prayer had no words. It was as pure an expression as she had ever offered up to the Divine.

It was heard, answered in the person of Lidia. The attacker whirled, cut and danced. Lidia deflected and dodged. Struck. Struck again, and again. No weapon, cataclysmic tides of potential around her hands and feet.

Juliaen found herself again, threw fire and shards of carbon taken from the air, hoping to distract. Perhaps it helped. She found it impossible to follow more than a fraction of the fight.

Lidia struck, and killed. One hand flashing out, dull thump, crackle of bone. A body gone sideways into the light-blackened leaves, head trailing on a broken neck.

Juliaen stared, but Lidia did not even slow enough to look, having turned back to battle before the body was halfway to the ground. There was another body too, Juliaen saw that now. An enemy body, she supposed, she supposed that's how she should think of it, she supposed she should, and another dead Promiseguard and she supposed she should be horrified but there was too much to feel it all at once.

One remaining attacker, back to a tree, fending off Maicl and two Promiseguard. Lidia reached them. A burst of close-in movement, discordant complexities through the Holy Fathom. Snapping bone. More scuffle. A streak of smudge-motion grey and

BANG

flashing light white smoke ringing ears iiiiii

and the attacker was gone.

Juliaen looked down at the dart still protruding from the center of her torso. Should she pull it out? Or would that just let her bleed freely? She was no physician or magomédica. It wasn't in danger of harming her heart, she knew that much. Between her lungs, hopefully?

"Juliaen."

It took her a moment to focus on the voice. Lidia, with Maicl behind her, bloody but standing.

"She's in shock." Everything seemed to have gained about a meter of distance between awareness and reality.

"I'm not sure whether I should pull it out." Juliaen expected her own voice to be measured, reasonable. Instead it shook, and then faded, and then so did she.

"...lucky she only got a fraction of the poison. Poor Aliivr."

The voice was soft and sad. Lidia, again. Why again? When had she heard Lidia last? She felt like she'd been listening for some time, but memory was a foggy thing.

"Wha...?" Juliaen's voice gave out; everything from mouth to throat to lungs was grindingly dry.

"Don't try to open your eyes or speak. Here." Water flowed over her eyelids, then between her lips. She coughed, swallowed, let her eyelids rise just enough to let in a trickle of liquid. Exquisite pain, like diamond mixed with sand. More water. Some relief. And again. And again.

"Good." Lidia's voice was as gentle as Juliaen had ever heard it. "Rest now. Don't resist."

A stirring in the Holy Fathom, barely at the edge of her awareness, pressing gentle at the normally impenetrable gatehouses of mind.

She welcomed it in, and slept.

Motion. Up, down, a little sway. Sunlight. Something hazy. Juliaen opened her eyes. Still pain, but less. She could swallow. Pain there too, also lessened.

"Hey," she said. It sounded absurd, both the word and the rasp it rode on.

No one noticed. Maybe. She forced her eyes fully open, blinked. She was looking at open sky, approaching dusk. Solace's rings were visible, silver and huge. But they were behind something.

The Siinlan Veil.

So we made it here, at least. Good. And Divine help me, I'm still terrified.

She moved her arms. Felt fabric stretched between two poles. Her fingers found the hand holding one of them.

"She's awake." One of the Promiseguard. Xaelbi, she was pretty sure.

"Stop. Put her down. More water."

Uneven ground under her back, and a sense of coming more fully to herself as Lidia appeared over her, hands on her head and throat, upper chest down to the wound—only now she realized it must be healed. No pain. Able to sit up now, look around. A clearing on the bank of the Ashlit Mire, surrounded by a thick quartzwood forest that was all fading purple and glint in the setting sun.

"What happened?" Juliaen asked.

"A lot." Lidia's voice was grim. "Let's get you some water and food and a change of clothes. I want you to hear it all at your full strength."

Lidia ordered the rest of the party—now just Maicl and two

Promiseguard—to face outward as she helped Juliaen change her clothes. Or changed them for her, really; Juliaen's own movements still felt weak and inexact. She was mortified to realize that her bladder had let go while she was out, and not just a trickle either. She shouldn't care, she knew that. It was just a body, after all, fallible as anyone else's. But still. The smell, the feel on her skin, the helpless indignity.

Dignity?

yes i know i have too much pride i must let go

She stayed silent as she was fed, as she drank what felt like a huge amount of flat dewskin water. Lidia started talking.

The ambush had been comprised of three agents from Nikoka. Ninja, the legendary assassins and spies of that reclusive Tenggaran protectorate. It had nearly succeeded. Aliivr was dead along with four Promiseguard, and even Lidia had been brought near the end of her strength and resilience, though not before killing two and breaking the arm of the third.

"Escaped using a whitesmoke vial," Lidia said. "Nasty bit of alchemy, just like the poison they used in those darts of theirs. Ninja are experts in mixing fresh compounds and keeping them coherent against the Holy Fathom."

Coherent compounds. That was a deeply Ragado art, pushing back against the Divine will represented in the relentless way the Holy Fathom broke down most complex concoctions and contraptions. Alchemy was Silado only when a substance was put to immediate use, though admittedly that was almost always the most practical option anyway. The years of training and moment-to-moment effort required to keep tiny quantities usable for a few hours just wasn't worth it except in rare situations.

Like assassination and escape.

Juliaen recognized the patient look on Lidia's face and recollected her thoughts to speak. "Ninja. If the Nikokans know we are here, surely the Tenggarans do as well? Why weren't we facing a whole contingent? Tentera Wira? Samurai?"

"Sent into Dahlabekh territory?" Lidia shook her head. "They're not going to risk that. We have countenance here and they decidedly do not."

"Surely the Dahlabekh would be just as upset at the intrusion if we were all found slaughtered by ninja in the forest?"

Lidia gave a grim snort. "Found? That's not how ninja operate. There would be nothing to find. We would simply have disappeared. We nearly did."

Would have, except they underestimated you. Lidia's status as a former Somonei wasn't exactly a secret, but the extent of her rank and experience wasn't widely known. The Presilyo had good reason to keep silent on the subject, and Lidia's own speeches always gave a heavily downplayed impression of her service.

"But the Divine spared us," Juliaen said. *Five of us, anyway. The Divine has always exacted dear sacrifice from Their followers.*

"Yes," Maicl said, not turning from his constant survey of the Mire, "and inadequate intel on their part. The Divine moves in mysterious ways. Their plan seems to have been to focus on you first, Ash-tiller, and not the High Winnow. But she detected them sooner than they expected. Only one of them managed to target you, and they had to go through Aliivr." His voice was remarkably steady, but then he must know that Aliivr's martyred soul was now in the hands of the Divine.

And now I must doubly repent for every uncharitable thought I ever had about the boy. No, the man. Divine knows he more than earned that title, in the end.

They all fell silent a long moment. Lidia turned to look out over the Mire, breathed in, breathed out. "We're all about to be very glad of the Divine's protection. Time for the leap of faith. Check your weapons and make sure the rafts are ready. The Gyring Ash awaits."

Chapter 29

"Why me?" is perhaps the most vexing question about existence.
It is also the most inconsequential.
The crucial question is this:
"What am I going to do about it?"

- Lau Yan, *The Dramatist's Mask,* 54 SE

Suulah'kal Deep Passages, Salía, The Caustlands, 355 SE

Dayang swallowed back the burning bile rising up her throat and forced herself to listen. She understood very little about what was going on, and that meant even the smallest detail could have dire consequences. She could mourn what had happened later, after she'd done her best to grasp it. But her damn legs wouldn't stop shaking with deferred tension, so she took a knee. No sense fighting more battles than she had to.

"What did I see?" Staafaen asked. He furrowed his brow, rolled the knuckles of his right hand against his temple. "Just enough, and much too little." A small bitter laugh at his own words. "That sounds stupid and pretentious as hell, right? But it's true." His startling grey eyes flicked up to take in the people standing around the ruined corpse of Niceto. "Sure you want to have this conversation with them around, Sanyago?" It sounded less like a warning and more like a genuine question.

Sanyago sighed, and looked down at Niceto, and looked up at the stony ceiling, and Dayang caught a glimpse of something unguarded in his light brown eyes. She closed her own eyes a moment, and saw a big man lie screaming on the grass, arms and legs shattered. Arms around her waist, betrayal in her throat. Weapon heavy in her hand.

He must be about the same age I was. I should talk to him later.

She opened her eyes, and Sanyago was still silent. She let him be, didn't demand answers. It was a bit of wisdom she'd gained the hard way with other soldiers. Especially *her* soldiers. That thought brought on a poisoned rush of grief and guilt, with Bayin and Martos still lying where they'd fallen, and part of her wanted to disbelieve, just deny what had happened, but Park and Nguyen were still alive and relying on her and so she beckoned them over to listen with her, signaled silence. They came, faces filled with the same suppressed shock she felt.

"Yeah." Sanyago's voice was soft but decided when he finally spoke. "We can't let Brother— we can't just keep quiet and let them speak for us anymore. I mean, uh, obviously. We have to see this through and can't do that if we won't talk to the rest of the expedition."

Staafaen nodded slowly, frowned, then gave a sort of resigned shrug. "¿Cree' quentonce le'lo damo' tudo, osimno cuanto?"

"I speak Ambérico, Staafaen," Taniixh Pai said gently. "You're asking if he thinks you should tell us everything, and if not, how much."

Staafaen closed his eyes, then sighed and switched back to Gentic. "Yeah, okay. It was worth a try, you know?" He cocked his head at Sanyago. "¿Pue?"

Sanyago nodded slowly, looking at every other expedition member in turn. She had another glimpse of confusion and anger, like a mirror to her younger self. "Si. Yeah. Everything about you and me, anyway. Not like we really knew that much about Aeriic and Niceto, in the end."

False names, then, one way or the other. Dayang was struck by sudden sharp curiosity.

"Aeriic and Niceto, huh?" she asked. "Did I at least get real names out of you two?"

Staafaen nodded. "Yeah. They were real. You can call me Laris if you want, that was my nickname back in the Presilyo. You all earned it, I think, however this thing turns out. My surname is Lozada. They took that away when they took me, but I still remember." He took a deep breath, almost a gasp.

"They take away your *surnames*?" Ceraen's indignation came through clearly even through the tremor in her voice. *Just starting to really grasp what she's done, the life she's taken. Gonna have to help her keep it together until we have a moment to breathe. Or maybe it's best that Taniixh does it. Not like I've ever killed anyone myself.*

"Doesn't matter right now." Staafaen's voice was soft, calm, controlled. "Look, I think we should hurry. Here's the short version, and we can talk about whether you believe me or not later. I can see people's intentions, sometimes. Their immediate border-conscious intentions, I mean, the marks they make in the future-causality webs of the Fathom. The Presilyo calls it "The Entyecogno Gift" even though that term isn't...never mind."

Dayang considered. That talent was supposed to be uncommon, but not exceptionally rare. Being able to make practical use of it, though, actually *comprehend* the future-faded lines in the Fathom when they came from another person's head and not just brute physical reality, that was another story.

Staafaen glanced toward the downward corridor, then over at the prone form of Brother Aandru—no, Aeriic, Sanyago had called him Aeriic. "I saw two things when I asked Niceto what his intentions were. First, he intended to harm Operative Aeriic. There was reluctance in that one, but it was clear, it didn't waver. I got lucky, seeing that. I think there was too much going on, so much that he didn't plan for, that he slipped. Maybe some guilt too, I don't know."

"Laris," Sanyago said, turning toward the wounded monk, "should we..."

"He's dead, brother." Staafaen said. His voice was restrained, just like Dayang's own grief and horror. "Niceto did something to the gauze. I knew it was too late the moment I noticed. That's why I used his real name, when I asked him. I wanted to throw off more of his cover. It worked, I got another glimpse. That one wasn't nearly so clear. He wanted to go farther down the tunnel, to do something down there, I don't know exactly what. He wanted to get ahead of us, now that we were close and Aeriic was out of the way."

Sanyago sat down heavily on the stone floor, shaking his head. "I don't...why would he want to hurt Aeriic? Who *was* he?"

Taniixh Pai frowned at the young monk and began walking over to him.

"I don't know," Staafaen said simply. "I can't read minds. No one can do that, far as I know. Intentions aren't thoughts, not really, not the deep inner ones. Thoughts trying to turn into actions, maybe. Though when he died, there were some glimpses I couldn't really make out...maybe I just wasn't close enough when it...happened." The furrows in his brow deepened, making his pale grey eyes go faraway.

Pai reached Sanyago and lifted him to his feet, put her arm around the boy's shoulders. He just stared forward at his friend. Pai gave him a gentle shake as she spoke. "He must have been a Carver, a secret convert. That phrase he used? 'Abominations upon the Abominable?' I've seen it come up in reports, but only quite recent ones. Lovely new catchphrase." She scowled, grinding the metal tip of her staff into the grit.

"I suppose that could be it," Staafaen said. "All we ever really learned about the Carvers was that they were heretics." He gave Sanyago a concerned look, but went on speaking. "I'm sorry about Aeriic. I think he was doing his best to be a good person in the place he had ended up." He turned to Dayang. "I'm sorry about your soldiers too, Sergeant Marchadesch."

Dayang bowed her head, then looked up. "It's not your fault. They were soldiers, this is…" she closed her eyes, let out a slow breath, "...this is part of that, sometimes." She allowed herself a tired, bitter smile, and made a decision. "Or so I'm told. I'll be honest, this is the first time I've seen a battle-deaths on my own side. I think that's true for all of us."

She turned back to look at her soldiers. Park inclined his head, voice soft and carefully controlled. "First for me too, Sergeant."

Nguyen turned one hand palm-up. He seemed much calmer than Park, or for that matter Dayang herself, as though he'd already begun the process of accepting the loss. "Not quite. First time in the Tentera Wira. As a monk—" he turned himself slightly in Staafaen and Sanyago's direction, made a small bow, "—Buddhist monk, with all respect to our young friends—I saw my share of death. Life ends, life starts anew." He sighed, lips forming a small sad smile. "That is not to say that it is ever easy."

Dayang leaned forward on her shield a moment, considering, then straightened, looking back toward the two young Somonei. "No, I don't suppose it ever is. Really it's damned hard. If we can get through it, though, so can you. We go forward with the mission, make sure their fight meant something, okay?"

"Okay," Staafaen opened his mouth again, grey eyes moving as though searching for something more to say.

Dayang gave him a small nod and a smile, then spotted Ceraen swaying on her feet. She got up off her knee and walked over, putting a gauntleted hand on the taller woman's shoulder. Ceraen leaned heavy against her with a quiet "thanks."

"Pull yourself together, Auxiliary," Pai said, her voice firm but not unkind. "We need you right now."

"Yyy-eah," Ceraen said, breathing it out like a two-part sigh. She straightened, taking most of her weight off Dayang's side. "I agree with Pai; Augusto or Niceto or whatever his name was must have been a Carver. I've read the same reports. The way he was talking to you, Staafaen, he clearly still considered himself a Michyero, just not loyal to the Presilyo anymore."

"That too," Pai said. "Quite a coup for them, managing to turn a Shuvelao. This will rock the Presilyo to its core, when they find out. Well, the leadership anyway. Not the kind of thing I think they'll disseminate to the rank and file."

"That makes sense," Staafaen said quietly. "So what now? We go see why Niceto was so anxious to go down ahead of us after he'd taken care of Aeriic?"

Dayang breathed in, held it as she reflected, then let it out in a huff and squared her shoulders. "Yes. That's where we were headed anyway. I don't see that this changes anything except how many of us are left. We still don't know much more than before, and I'm guessing this Niceto mole wanted to keep it that way. There's no way he was planning to fight us all, all the damage he's done so far seems to have been—" she took in a deep breath, remembering exactly what "damage" meant here, "—opportunistic. He must have been planning to find some way to get there first and, I don't know, destroy evidence somehow? Maybe without ever revealing his hand."

She paused, thought some more. "Of course. That's why he wanted me to let his group scout ahead. No doubt with himself taking point."

Pai tilted her head side to side, hazel eyes examining the middle distance. "So possibly not planning anything overt? Stay under cover, especially once he'd rid himself of his partner? That's cold-blooded. Well, maybe not. Sometimes fanaticism just burns so hot it makes everything else seem cold and unimportant by comparison. I've seen it before." She frowned. "Cults, especially. Some nasty ones we've dealt with near the...no, never mind. Let's go take a look for ourselves. I've just reminded myself how little I want to spend unnecessary time in this place."

Dayang nodded, slowly, and looked around at the other survivors. They each nodded back, apart from Sanyago, who still leaned against Taniixh Pai's side, staring. Staafaen walked over to him, giving Pai a small grateful smile.

"Sanyago. You can do this. Remember what Father Kuwat taught us. There will be plenty of time later to dedicate to contemplating the past. Right now we need you to be here."

Sanyago stared for another long moment, then sighed. "Yeah, okay. Okay, I'm here." He gently shrugged Pai's arm off his shoulders. "Thank you. Sorry. Let's go."

They burned the bodies after salvaging what equipment and personal effects they could. Dayang put some of Bayin and Martos' ashes into vials she carried for exactly this grim purpose. Staafaen and Sanyago left the senior monk's ashes where they were. Sanyago said a few short prayers over them, and she wondered why Staafaen didn't participate.

Dayang said a few prayers of her own, but not aloud. She wasn't especially comfortable with the cremation, but she understood the necessity and anyway neither of her fallen soldiers had been Muslims. Even if they had been...cremation was allowed in cases of virulent disease, and contagion came in worse forms than the merely biological.

This was as ready as they'd ever be. They descended.

"Oh my God," Ceraen said softly. "I mean, it's not really a surprise, not after...after that fight we had. They had to have...come from somewhere."

It was an obviously artificial room, four-sided, lit pale yellow by strange, almost childish symbols scrawled into the floor and walls, nothing like any Pelo writing Dayang had ever seen before, though she was certainly no expert. Recent bootprints cut into whorls of dust on the ground. Ceraen swayed on her feet, looking round.

Dayang frowned. "Easy, Auxiliary." She wasn't sure if the title would help, coming from her, but it sometimes did with soldiers and Pai had tried the same thing earlier.

"Easy, sure," Ceraen replied. A touch of rueful Salían sarcasm there, but she at least sounded steadier now. "The Old Kash Empire used these places, but they're a lot older than that. Some scholars think maybe they're even older than the Praedhc themselves; they're always pretty silent on how that could be possible, though." She began to walk, slow careful steps toward the nook in the far wall.

Dayang followed, visor down, shield half-raised, hand on the haft of her mace. Her two remaining soldiers came with her in formation, just behind to either side. Nguyen wore the rapier he had "recovered" from Niceto on his belt, large left hand on the hilt, broken right wrist in cast and sling. Park carried his shortbow loose and ready, cloak thrown back from the pair of kukri daggers in his belt. She wasn't sure what they all expected. It was in the air. It was under it.

Ceraen reached the little carved-out space, stood in front of the pedestal at its center, examined the deep narrow hole in the top. Dayang stopped. Something was wrong with the walls to the left and right of the slender stone pillar. They had no color. No, they were an absence of color. No, that would just be black, and this wasn't nothing, it was just...

"Don't look at the walls," Ceraen said. "It's not precisely dangerous, there's nothing to see and nothing that can hurt you. But your brain can't really process this kind of nothing, so it's best to leave it alone."

"Understood." Dayang let the lack-of-anything fade to her peripheral vision as she focused on the two walls that came together to form a concave corner at the back. Pastel tiles half-covered the grey stone in a muted rainbow, and she recognized the runes carved into them as Pelo— nothing like the weird yellow symbols scrawled into the bare stone.

She thought she could feel something like a heartbeat through her heavy boots, but no that wasn't it at all it wasn't organic it was too unlike

unlike

anything

"I don't like this place," she was surprised to hear herself say.

"Good." Pai's voice, coming from behind. "I'd be worried if you did. Ceraen, learn what you need as fast as you can and then we're gone from here."

"This must be what Niceto was hoping to reach ahead of us," Staafaen said. He glanced toward Sanyago, who stood guard at the entrance, then over at Ceraen. "You're the Praedhc scholar. Do you agree? With what Pai and Dayang said, I mean, about him wanting to cover something down here."

Ceraen nodded slowly. "Yes. And you can see why, right? You can look, be careful but don't let worry consume you. This place has the potential to be very, very dangerous, but it's less so now. Dormant. Mostly."

Staafaen frowned, and closed his eyes, then opened them wide. Dayang perceived it now too, a heavy pulse of binding passage. It had a direction, and she took a moment to orient herself. North, and east. She frowned, and slipped her mace back onto her belt so she could pull a map from a side pouch of her pack.

Staafaen turned to look in that same northeast direction, which put him facing her, eyes focused on the middle of nothing. "It's a sort of tunnel really. But tunneling like that...there would be no way to go through safely. You're right, it's dormant, or I wouldn't dare look."

"It's not safe because it changes people," Ceraen said softly. "But that's no surprise, is it? Right now the tunnel only really connects to itself, and it's not really...open, even for that. But it was, and the Carvers were searching out some connection through it."

"Wait," Sanyago called from his post. "Let me see. Laris, can you take watch for a second?"

Staafaen gave his friend a curious look, then strode over to replace him. Sanyago hustled over, stood staring at the pedestal. After a minute or two, he nodded.

"Off to the northeast. Okay." He held up his hand, staring at his right palm as though there was a map written into the calloused skin. "Yep, okay, past the Mindao, a ways south of the Deisiindr, that would take it…" he made a pointing gesture with his left hand, swung it back and forth like a compass needle. "...to just south of Kualabu. That's the only significant thing along its path within the Caustlands, anyway."

Dayang frankly gaped, then opened her map with a nerveless lack of grace, suddenly feeling like she'd forgotten how to deal with her heavy gauntlets. "How in Hell could you figure that out just in your head?" He had sounded so *sure,* or she'd have dismissed his assertion out of hand. It would take her a few minutes and a flat surface to know for sure whether he was right.

Sanyago shrugged. "I don't know. I've always liked maps and knowing where things are. I always knew where I was on the island, and after we left...I still knew where we were. It's something they trained us in, but I was also always just...good at it. It doesn't really work up-and-down, I don't know how far underground we are and I couldn't draw you a map of the tunnels we've been through. But I could show you the spot we're under on the surface. If that makes sense."

The island? Oh, right, the Presilyo sat in the middle of the Mindao river. And Kualabu sat practically on top of some of the largest ruins in the Caustlands. And…

Shit.

"Are you sure?" she asked. Her voice was steady, barely.

Sanyago thought for a moment. "Yep, I'm sure. I can see it in my head. I mean, it could be somewhere past Kualabu, out in the Abwaild."

"If it passes through Kualabu, that's where we need to look. I know my hometown," she said, and knelt to spread her map out on the floor. Her heavy visor would make reading it slightly awkward, but she was still extremely grateful it was there. She had no idea what her face might be showing. *If more of those things came out of the ruins back home—*

—God save us. Ashwights are bad enough.

"Oh." Sanyago said. A pause. "Do you think the Tentera Wira will send you back there now? When you tell them?"

She set her compass down, watched the needle vacillate around magnetic north, concentrated on smoothing the small agitations of the Fathom, warding off any minor jinn. She was glad for the distraction. "I don't know if I'll be able to tell them." The needle stilled, and she moved the rest of the compass to match, let the Fathom return to its subtle clamors. "We'll have to get a pretty good distance from this place before it's safe to send any messages, and even then I'd have to be very sure none of the Saepis were listening." The needle spun wildly as Fathom-jinn rushed in to swirl round the place of recent stillness. She ignored it, oriented the map.

"But they need to know as soon as they can, right? That the Carvers are maybe planning to use one of these...places...in their territory?" He looked over at Taniixh Pai. "Just like the Salíans need to know about *this* place?"

"Sergeant Marchadesch is correct about the problems and dangers," Pai said. "But it doesn't mean we won't both get word to our superiors as soon as we can. I'll try to send a report through Captain Braun's company. I don't know how long it will ultimately take to get to Aldonza. Hopefully there still *is* a company up there, after those...things...stampeded past us up the passage."

Dayang stretched a length of string out in parallel to the altar's bound-passage, and stared at the result. "He's right. Kualabu. *Ngentot,*" she swore, and paused, chewing on the confirmation.

"It'll be in the Borih'Sath ruins. God knows how we'll find the specific place, though, that complex is massive, and we only have one heading to go off. If we had two...but never mind. I'm almost sure that's where it will be. Kualabu has some weird recent history with the Saepis, which is why I pulled strings to get this assignment in the first place."

"Have you been there?" Ceraen asked. "I've always wanted to go. It's supposed to have been one of the biggest cities of the Old Kash Empire."

Dayang shook her head. "No. I left Kualabu when I was seventeen, five years ago. I had plenty of training by then, but there's still no way my parents would have allowed me to go."

"But they did let you leave to join the Tentera Wira," Ceraen said. Her tone was careful, but the question was still unmistakable. Dayang could feel the storm clouds gather across her brow, and again was glad of her helmet.

"Not...exactly. That's a long story. I'll tell it later, if you like." She stowed her map and compass, picked up her shield, stood. After a moment's hesitation, she lifted her visor. "Listen," she said, looking the rest of the group in the eye one by one. "Most of you have only agreed to follow me for the duration of the expedition. When we reach the surface, my authority ends over everyone but Park and Nguyen, and they'll be leaving to get word to command."

Park and Nguyen just nodded; they already knew what their duty would be. Ceraen looked to Pai, and Pai just listened, all professionalism and withheld judgement. Sanyago seemed distracted and torn, while Staafaen's attention was almost uncomfortably intense, strange grey eyes serious and fixed.

God help me, I wish I were better at this. She went on. "Whatever they're doing out in those ruins has got to be stopped. I'm going to try, but I need your help. I know we haven't known each other long enough for me to have the right to ask that. I'm going to ask anyway, because this isn't just about me and my hometown, or about Tenggaran security. It's about Salía too, and the Presilyo, and all the Caustlands, maybe."

She paused. No one was speaking, just waiting for her to go on. She sighed. Huffed, really, short and sharp, making her shoulders sag before squaring again on her next breath. "We can take a boat down the Mindao, south through the Ashlit Mire, and then sail up the Gyring Ash. It's dangerous as all Hell, but there's no faster way, not even close."

"Dangerous is right," Pai said. "But that's not really the problem. Now that we've found this thing, our mission is largely over. Ceraen and I will have to report back. Something this big, they'll want us to report all the way back to headquarters, in Aldonza. It's true the Staffguard have a degree of autonomy, but not that much. I can't just tell my captain, 'Hey, I've left the country, be back after doing a bit of meddling in Tenggara! I'm sure everything will be fine with no political consequences.'"

"I'm not sure we can go either," Staafaen said, walking over from the entrance while still keeping an eye on it. "Or I guess I should say I'm not sure we should. The Presilyo will want us reporting back right away. There will be trouble, probably more than a little. I don't know if they'll believe us about Niceto. We're in some sort of limbo now, not official Somonei, not full-fledged Shuvelao."

"Where Pai goes, I'm pretty much obligated to go, for now," Ceraen said. "That's part of what being an auxiliary means. If I were still just an academic at Borges, maybe I could toss an echogram off to my department head and go with you. But I'm not, I'm under contract."

Dayang nodded, but she could feel impatience welling up into the gesture and tried to tamp it down. "I'm not saying we just make a beeline for Tenggara without talking to anyone. I know you have your superiors. We'll have to be careful about it, but I don't see why we can't all send word back after we return to the surface." She cocked her head at Staafaen. "I assume they gave you *some* way of contacting the Presilyo if things went to shit?

"No. Not at all, actually. We're supposed to just find our way back in that case. Though we've already violated our orders telling you about the Shuvelao." He shrugged, looking resigned. Resigned and surprisingly cynical for someone so young, especially a Somonei trained to fanaticism almost from birth. *I suppose it doesn't always work. They're human after all.*

Pai rapped the end of her staff twice on one of the tiles littering the floor. "And don't forget that those...*things* we fought, they didn't go back down when they retreated. They went up. There's a whole company up there. Salíans. If anything has happened to them, if they need help...that's Ceraen and I's responsibility. Our duty. There are other people serving Salía, or Tenggara, who can be sent to help if it's needed."

Dayang fought a growl from rising up her throat. She was sure they could all see it on her face anyway. "There's always someone else. But will they get there in time? Will they fully understand the threat? Be able to face it? Will they even be sent at all? I know we all have burdens of duty but we have to try, maybe, I don't know, maybe we have to do what's necessary even if it costs us?"

the whisper of metal on stone, the sound her helmet made against the heartvein of her armor when she turned her head to face her mother

why would you

i had to i had to

A long silence fell.

Sanyago broke it.

"Listen," he said. Not loud, not soft, not a hint of the shadow or diffidence it had carried every other time she'd heard him speak. Straightforward and sure. "She's right, and you all know it. I don't like this, I don't like any of it, and I don't know what I'm going to do once this is all over. I was just excited to get out of the Presilyo for the first time I can remember, to be *doing* something for once instead of just learning or...or reacting to whatever came my way. Our mentors are dead. One of them betrayed us. I don't even know where we stand with the Presilyo right now. So listen to me."

And everyone did listen; the force and clarity of emotion in his voice was captivating.

"This isn't the first time I've seen what these Carvers are capable of. Five years ago they sent a group of ex-Somonei to the Presilyo to kill. And I mean kill." He shuddered, but instead of freezing, drawing back into himself the way she'd seen him do before, he seemed to catch fire. "Not just Somonei. Not just adults. I saw six kids die, cut to pieces, younger than we were. One of them tried to kill me. I can still feel his sword against my throat, how *wrong* it was."

He took a deep breath, then spat violently onto the tile-strewn floor. "Because that's who they were willing to send, mad and tainted and twisted and full of hate. Not just soldiers killing soldiers. You think it will be any different in Salía and Tenggara? Your countries are half the reason they left in the first place, half the reason they even *exist*. You get word to your people as quickly as you can, but right now we have to *go*. Even if it costs us. So it doesn't cost anyone else like those little kids in bloody pieces on a dormitory floor."

Heavy silence.

"Somonei," Pai began, dressing the title with respect, "I know you…"

"NO!" Sanyago yelled. "This isn't about Somonei! Divine knows if I even am a Somonei anymore or ever was! This is about something that needs to be done and we're the only ones who can get there quickly to do it. You're smart enough and have seen enough to know how bad this could be. We go now, because you know it's the right thing to do and sometimes that's all that really matters." He fell silent, holding the Staffguard's gaze with his light brown eyes.

Pai looked back, solemn and perhaps even a bit pale under the deep mahogany of her face. She glanced aside at the other monk. "And you, Staafaen? What do you have to say?"

Staafaen took in a deep breath, closed his eyes, opened them, let it out. He stepped to the side and clapped a large dark hand on Sanyago's shoulder. "I stand with my brother."

"Okay," Pai said softly. "Auxiliary Wiilqaems. I have no right to order you to come with me. Will you come anyway?"

Ceraen Wiilqaems looked around the small space, took a moment to stare at the pedestal. "Yes. God help me, I can't believe what I've gotten myself into here, but I'll come."

The trip back was almost uneventful. "Almost" because while nothing actually happened, they kept seeing disquieting signs of what had gone up ahead of them.

"Watch your step," Pai said from her scouting position up front. "Patches of stone have been partially melted and there are spots that are…slippery. Or uneven. Sometimes."

Meaning that some of the geometry underfoot wasn't always keeping itself in full compliance with the usual rules. It would, God willing, remember its obligations in time, but Dayang knew they didn't have much of that. So they kept up their pace, even though it caused a few stumbles and near-falls. Along with being disquieting as Hell, but at least they'd be through faster this way.

As with the trip down, they kept sound discipline except when absolutely necessary. This didn't normally bother her; most of the time she welcomed the chance to be alone with her own thoughts and focus. But now it tugged at her mind like a sharp itch.

Not for the first time, she missed having Sara to talk to. Or Jeims, or Pandikar. She'd made good friends during her service, but they came and went, and camaraderie with her soldiers was something she cherished but she was still their sergeant and they were still her subordinates. It wasn't the same. Maybe it would be, when she'd got a better handle on leading, finding that balance. Maybe she could find something like it with these others God had seen fit to throw her together with. But not now.

So she walked in silence, alert and uneasy while everything tugged at her brain.

When they reached the last cavern before the surface, the one with all the bloodstains, she ordered a halt.

"We rest here," she said shortly. "Seven hours. Everyone gets four hours of sleep and two of watch, with an hour to eat and change clothes and whatever else needs doing. Except Nguyen, you sleep through."

Sanyago frowned. "Sleep? Now?? We don't know what those...things might be doing up there! I thought we all agreed to go as quick as we could?"

Dayang pulled her helmet off and tied it to her belt, grimacing at the way sweat-soaked strands of hair stuck to the inner padding before falling limply over her scalp. "We did. We are. We've been travelling for almost twenty-four hours now. We're already a lot less effective than if we were rested, and that's going to get worse pretty sharply from here. And we'll be extra *super* ineffective dead, which is what may well happen if we go charging into battle right now."

"Maybe I'm willing to take the risk," Sanyago said. His jaw was pushed forward, and he crossed his arms across his chest.

"Maybe you're not in charge," Dayang replied. "You don't get to risk everyone else's lives. Better learn that now. We're moving as fast as we effectively can. You can take last watch, with me."

Sanyago's glare did not subside. Staafaen was looking back and forth between them, frowning.

"Sanyago." Ceraen this time. "Look, you saw how fast those...things were going when they retreated. That's even without the, what, four-hour headstart they had on us from going all the way down to the chamber and coming back up? Whatever they're going to do up there, they've already done it. Maybe we can stop whatever the Carvers are up to. I hope to Christ we can, but we're not going to be able to do anything about...*them*."

Staafaen nodded slowly, and nudged his friend's shoulder. Sanyago turned, and the two had some sort of entirely silent argument, though there didn't seem to be any kind of secret code or Fathom-communication in play. Staafaen apparently won, because Sanyago sighed, rubbed a weary finger along the ridge of his eye socket, and nodded.

"Are you going to be able to sleep?" Dayang asked, trying to meter an appropriate amount of kindness into her voice.

"Yeah," Sanyago said, turning away. "I can always sleep."

So could Dayang, usually, but this time it took a lot longer than usual. She found herself wishing she'd taken first watch rather than last, so she wasn't wasting time just lying there.

Still there were at least no dreams once she finally did pass out, and she woke about as rested as could be expected from three hours in a military sleeping bag on uneven stone. And a change of socks and undergarments did wonders; she'd long ago mastered the art of changing inside her bag.

It was still twenty minutes to the start of last watch when she crawled out to start the process of donning her equipment and armor. Ceraen and Pai stood facing the entrance and exit, respectively; they looked over their shoulders and nodded when they heard her emerge, but said nothing.

Sanyago was still asleep, curled round his pack on the bare stone without any sort of cover or padding, using one arm as a pillow and cradling his sheathed sword in the other. Maybe taking monastic asceticism a bit too far, though on closer inspection his small frame was blanketed in subtle, intricate Fathom-fields. Keeping him warm, keeping stiffness out of muscle and bone. *Maintained subconsciously. Impressive. I'm guessing also extremely uncomfortable to learn.*

She let him sleep. He'd know how to wake up on time. Meanwhile she tried to keep her thoughts on donning her armor, away from things like Kualabu and its wooden walls and things with caustic coatings that could melt right through solid stone and Pandikar and Mother sleeping behind wooden walls too and maybe Father too if he wasn't out with a caravan and...

stop it

And she did, but her armor was already on and adjusted, having taken about as much of her conscious consideration as walking did. She sighed, put on her helmet, paused, left the visor up. Sanyago woke a minute later, stretching once and then jumping to his feet. He attached his scabbard to his belt, shrugged on his pack, and was ready.

"Good morning," she said quietly. He just nodded.

Dayang tapped the lower tip of her tall shield on the stone, and when Ceraen and Pai turned around she gestured toward their bedrolls. They each acknowledged with a raised hand, then made a tired, grateful beeline for sleep.

"Sanyago. Go post yourself where Pai was." She pointed at the exit leading upward, and he went without a word. She headed for the downward path they'd come up from and stopped to squat in the narrowest part of the entrance. Pulling a Sihir-pen from one of her belt pouches, she began to trace a careful series of lines and symbols on the floor in luminous blue. She murmured a long string of Proken words as she worked, and within a few minutes had extended the ward from wall to wall. She stayed crouched down long enough to check the whole thing over twice, then stood and headed back to Sanyago.

"I'll be standing watch with you here."

He looked at her, then over at the faint glow of the ward she'd left on the other end of the cavern. Skepticism on his young features. "Okay. You're in charge."

They stood in uncomfortable silence.

"The ward will hold long enough for us to get to the entrance, if anything comes that way."

"Okay," he said again.

"Look," she said. "You don't have to like my decisions, but I do want everyone to understand the reasons for them, when there's time for that. And why it's so important we follow those decisions as a group. One purpose. One fight."

"I know that," he said, staring down the tunnel. Automatic. Dismissive.

She found she wasn't angry, which surprised her, but she still put a razor's edge on her voice. "No. You don't."

He turned, handsome features clouding.

"Don't look at me, keep your watch," she snapped. "You think I'm being

438

unkind or insulting, but I am not. I just have things to tell you. Hard things. Things that could save your life. Maybe all our lives."

He turned again, kept his gaze on the stone corridor. "What things?" His voice was hard to read, but at least most of the petulance seemed to have gone out of it.

"You're a brilliant fighter," she said. "But you knew that already. Problem is, you're not much of a warrior, not yet. You know the difference?"

"No," he said. A hint of anger. Bruised ego. A part of his worth he wasn't used to having questioned.

"A warrior can fight beside other warriors, and together they become something greater than just one plus one plus one plus however many of them there are. You move fast, you strike sure, but you do it alone. Your friend Staafaen, he knows how to work with others, to fight next to them, so the Presilyo must teach it."

"They do. They did." She could hear the frown in his words, the frustration. "And I learned what they taught. The small formations, the coordinated attacks, the shared defenses. But only because they made me. I'd get a passing mark on those things and move on." He took a sharp breath and let it out through his nose. "But everyone else moved so slow, I had to slow down too. When I would try something different, something better, something that flowed more closely with the situation, they couldn't keep up. Once the combat exercises became about results instead of just specific techniques and routines, I just did my own thing. It worked. They didn't always like it, but it *worked.*"

"I'm sure it did. I told you, you fight brilliantly. Once you got over freezing up—" she held up a hand as he turned toward her, "—and I understand why that happened, you did very well. As a single fighter against many foes. But you didn't coordinate. You saw that one of my soldiers was in trouble and moved in to help attacking the creatures swarming him, yes, and I'm grateful for that. So is…" she sighed, "…*was,* he. No communication, though, no acting in concert. You just 'did your own thing,' like you said before. Sure, it was effective. But it could have been *more* effective, and that gap between doing well and doing as well as you *could* do, that can be the difference between life and death sometimes."

"I'm sorry about your soldiers," he said softly. "I wish I'd known what

Niceto really was."

"Niceto was not your fault. My soldiers were not your fault, not this time. Listen, that's actually the more important thing I wanted to talk to you about. Learning to fight properly alongside others, that I don't doubt you can learn, now that you've had a taste of what it is to fight with a trained group and not some school exercise. But Niceto...I had a Niceto of my own, once. Not exactly the same, nothing ever is. But I know first-hand what that kind of betrayal can feel like." *Hell. If he doesn't believe me, that could come off patronizing as shit.*

He was silent a long time.

"Who was it? One of your officers in the Tentera Wira?"

"No," she said. And she told him. The full decade of training her father had paid for. Hang Che's escalating interest in Sara. Meeting Jeims Dubwa. The sudden confrontation in the park, how it tore her life into pieces of *before* and *after*. Leaving. It took the better part of an hour.

"That must have been hard." His voice was thoughtful, the resentment drained out, though his body language still showed the same restless impatience.

"No harder than what you've been through. Anyway, comparing miseries never ends well. You said you were sorry about my soldiers, and I'm grateful. You should know that I'm sorry about Aeriic and Niceto. And grateful for what you said, when we were all arguing about what to do. I promise I'll treat you all like I would my fellow Tentera Wira soldiers." She allowed herself a bitter little laugh. "That might not sound like much, given the state my squad's in now."

"That was Niceto's fault," Sanyago said. "The fight was over. No one was permanently hurt. They'd all have been okay except for him."

She sighed. "Yeah, I'm not trying to wallow in guilt or anything. But I still think about what we could have done better, because that's the only way I know to *get* better, you know?"

"Sure. Makes sense." He hesitated. "Can I ask you something?"

"Okay."

"The scar. Sorry if it's a sore subject."

"No. Not really." And she meant it. Of course she still wasn't exactly happy about having it, but she was used to talking about it. Soldiers weren't exactly known for sensitivity about that sort of thing.

Sanyago shifted, making small upward movements off the balls of his feet, keeping his muscles loose. "Well. I've seen a lot of scars, over the years. I watch people. Did watch people, I guess. At the Presilyo. Somonei especially, going out and coming back. Sometimes they'd...get the kind of injuries our magomédicos couldn't heal. I'd see when scars were fresh, watch them fade. Yours is pretty old. You said you left Kualabu five years ago, but I'd guess the scar is older than that."

She shrugged, knowing he'd catch the gesture out the corner of his eye. "Okay, I can tell you that story. Question though, what's a 'magomédico'?"

"Oh. Sorry. Gentic in the Presilyo has a lot of Ambérico in it sometimes. It just means any kind of Fathom-healer."

"Makes sense." She made a clicking noise with her tongue. "On second thought, this is a story I should tell everyone, when we get a moment. I'm almost positive it has to do with our Carver friends. It was actually the main reason for me to look into all this. I went through a lot of trouble to get this assignment."

"Okay," he said.

She smiled. They passed the rest of the watch in silence.

Once the rest of the group was awake and ready, she made sure everyone had at least a few mouthfuls of ration and plenty of water. They readied their weapons, and trekked the last few hundred meters to the surface, wading through a river of readiness and dread.

They were met by the remnants of the Salían Army company. Dayang heard them before she saw.

"Ranger Pai? Thank God you're alive at least."

"First Sergeant Wrait. I take it some of our...opponents found your company. I'm sorry. How many?"

"Seventy-nine." Wrait's voice was weary, edged with horror, but retained its professional backbone. "Forty-three dead, twenty-seven wounded. Nine...gone. You?"

"Five. Three dead, one wounded, one a gods-damned Carver. At least that's why we think he turned on us. He was responsible for all the other deaths before Auxiliary Ceraen killed him."

"Shit." A pause, followed by a shout. "Captain Braun! The expedition is back."

Indistinct voices. They were getting close to the exit. Wrait's voice went on.

"Let's talk about what happened down there, then we can all head off to Acheronford together. A bloody Carver. Who was it?"

"The Somonei calling himself Augusto. His real name was Niceto. Killed his partner."

Dayang came out into the mid-afternoon sun. Wrait stood there in newly-battered armor with two lines of sharpened stakes between himself and the entrance. The blade of his spear looked freshly-polished, but the wooden haft was covered in stains he'd likely not had time to get out. The adhesion-strap across his back held his single remaining javelin.

Behind him was the ragtag remnant of his company, with perhaps thirty soldiers ready for combat and not tending to the wounded or the...wrong. They looked at her with the sort of weary resignation-to-duty and deferred grief she'd seen before in echoframes but never actual human faces. Barb wire sagged between hastily-pounded posts along a semicircular perimeter. Captain Braun strode toward them, Lieutenant Aalaen perched on her shoulder, shield and scimitar on her hip and back.

"Ranger Pai. Sergeant Marchadesch. What in Hell did you wake up down there?"

"You saw what they were," Dayang said. *And you'll know why I don't want to elaborate.* "I'm more concerned with the whys and hows anyway. Especially why and how the Carvers managed to avoid being attacked. It was clear they'd gone at least as deep as we did."

Braun shook her head. "We don't know. Lieutenant Aalaen here has a pet theory, though."

"Why didn't you tell us this before we went down?" Pai asked. The rest of the group had formed up behind them, visibly relieved to see the sun again.

"I didn't form this particular suspicion until after your expedition had left," the Caustland Crow replied. "I've been examining the equipment the Carvers left behind. Along with their entrails and all of their blood, sometimes." He fluttered his tail-feathers and let out a ghoulish, croaking laugh. "Sorry. It's been a hard day and black humor helps."

Dayang nodded. She knew how that went, with soldiers.

Aalaen tightened his hold on Braun's shoulder armor with one foot and held the other out in front of him. "Ma'am?"

Braun pulled a small green-and-silver trinket from a pouch at her belt and handed it to her lieutenant. He held it up; some sort of chain jewelry, perhaps a choker, with evenly-spaced lumps of silver-veined greenish rock along its length.

"Praedhc charm. Workmanship and rune-style both show signs, but the big giveaway? Age of the enchantment. Pre-Starfall."

Ceraen stepped forward. "Can I see it, Lieutenant Aalaen?"

"Sure."

She took it from his talons and held it up in the sunlight, then brought it closer, feeding the chain between her fingers to examine the stones one by one. "It's attuned to this specific place. They knew exactly what they were doing, or rather they got this from some Praedhc who knew exactly what they were doing. It's very unlikely this is just some stolen artifact."

"You're saying they had Praedhc help?" Aalaen cocked his head, left right, and shuffled slightly on Braun's shoulder.

"Yes. I suppose it could have been coerced, but that's unlikely as well. They'd have to capture the right person, ask exactly the right questions, and then acquire the thing without causing a war. This isn't the kind of thing they'd just take off a wandering Dahlabekh band near Earthmarch."

Staafaen spoke up from behind. "Haven't the Saepis essentially been at war with the surrounding Praedhc for a long time, though?"

"Sort of," Ceraen said. "When they first moved out into what's now Earthmarch, the nomadic Dahlabekh had abandoned huge swathes of the forest there because of all the ash that had been deposited by prevailing winds during Starfall. Since then the Saepis have been pushing out into Praedhc territory, but slowly, over the course of three long messy centuries."

Dayang frowned. "Are you sure about all this? The idea of Pelos—ah, Praedhc—and Sovereign Nations types working together just seems...improbable, from everything I know."

Ceraen worked her tongue against the inside of her teeth as she pondered a response. "Here's the thing, Sergeant. The Saepis aren't just one thing, you know? And neither are the Praedhc. You talk about them coming to an understanding; that doesn't have to involve all of them. It doesn't even have to involve *most* of them. The Sovereign Nations are fractious by nature, I mean it's kind of their whole point, right? And the Praedhc...we tend to think of them as a cohesive group because of the ruins we live around and on top of came almost entirely from the central nation of an empire. Common language, common architectural style, similar sorts of artifacts...I'm getting away from myself. Point is, outside the Caustlands it's not necessarily like that."

Dayang felt annoyance needle at her temper. "I did graduate from secondary school, Ceraen. I know there are different groups of Praedhc."

Ceraen held up a placating hand. "I know you learned it, but that's not the same as really *grasping* it, and I'm not saying that to insult you or anyone else present. It's just human nature, our minds like to put things in the neatest possible categories. I've spent six years of postsecondary study on the Praedhc and I feel like I've only scratched the surface of a sliver of a specialty. Think about us, what it would mean if an outsider wanted to study the Fallen. They learn about the six Caustland States and how much do they really know? A laughably basic overview, right? Given all the history, the languages, accents, religions, ethnicities we brought from the Old World?"

Dayang started to reply, then hesitated, remembering Jeims as an example. He'd been Fallen himself and not really from all that far away, but Kualabu had still bewildered him sometimes even after years of immersion. Then she thought of what a shock the military had been for her in many ways, and that was within her own country, among people who understood her religion and dialect.

"Yeah, okay. I get it. So the Carvers had a way to avoid the ruin's...inhabitants. So why did they have to abandon the site? What ended up killing them?"

"They did," Staafaen cut in. "That place we found, they used it themselves. They avoided the old danger, the Praedhc one, but they ended up recreating it, at least partially. And then the ones they...changed...killed and were killed by the rest of them."

" 'That place' you found?" Aalaen asked excitedly. He gestured toward Staafaen with one foot, an odd semicircular motion. Staafaen just looked back blankly.

The Caustland Crow lowered his head. "Ah right. Somonei. Humans-only in your little river clubhouse. That gesture means, 'hold out your arm if you don't mind, I'd like to come talk face-to-face.' "

"Oh," Staafaen said. "Okay." He held out one long arm, and Aalaen fluttered onto his forearm from Braun's shoulder.

Staafaen looked surprised. "You're very light." Then he winced slightly. "Sorry, I don't mean to be rude."

Aalaen laughed, a quick brash *caw-caw-caw*. "I don't expect you to know the niceties, Somonei, not your fault being raised in that place. Of course I'm light, I can fly, can't I? I weigh less than five kilos." He patted Staafaen's arm with his foot. "It's perfectly polite to rest your arm on whatever's convenient, no sense letting it get tired. If there were a perch around at about your eye level, you could also walk over to it and I'd hop off."

Staafaen nodded slowly, seeming to take in the information with eager care. He found a small outcropping in the stone near the cavern entrance and held onto it to steady his arm.

"Good, good," Aalaen said. "You understand the reason for this, right? Much more comfortable for us both, not looking so far up and so far down."

"Yes," Staafaen answered. "Thank you for teaching me."

Aalaen laughed again, and bobbed his head. "A good attitude. You're very welcome. Now. Tell me about this place you found."

Staafaen did, with plenty of interjections from the rest of the expedition. At the end, Captain Braun and First Sergeant Wrait exchanged a long glance.

"We'll have to call in the Nowhere Watch," Braun said. "I was one of them, for a time." She winced, looked aside. "They'll listen to me."

Dayang frowned. "I thought the Nowhere Watch just guarded the...Black Fence." *Let that thought be, focus on everything else you have to do.*

"They do," Braun said. "And that was their only purpose, once upon a time. But some do better than others, serving with them, and those proven few are often used to handle...certain difficult matters. They'll decide what to do with this...place. Meanwhile, we'll escort you back Acheronford. Safety in numbers is something I think we could all use about now."

Thirteenth Interlude

Borih'Sath Ruin-Sprawl, Tenggara, The Caustlands, 355 SE

Zeivier prodded one of the dark-robed bodies with the toe of his boot.

"Well, shit."

"Had it coming," Aanh said loftily, licking the back of her paw.

"Maybe," Maacs said. "But did you have to do that to his *face*?" He grimaced, holding one heavy spiked gauntlet up in front of his mouth.

"His face was the best target I had at that particular moment. I'm not going to pass up an opening in combat just so we can end up with a prettier corpse."

"They *were* trying to run away," Pitr pointed out, though his words were both undercut and muffled by the fact that he was using his beak to rifle through the other dead Carver's pockets.

"Sure, and sooner or later they'd be back with some friends."

Zeivier sighed, and crouched down to examine one of Clawface's handaxes. *Decently imbued, good workmanship. Should fetch a pretty penny in Kualabu next time we go back to town. Well, a pretty jeon anyway.* "We're going to be dealing with their friends anyway. They'll be on the lookout for a white Caustland Cat and wanting revenge."

"Oh *please*." Aanh rolled her eyes. "Have a little faith, Zeivier. I let them notice me, but they didn't get an actual *look* until I'd led them back to you. Anyway, if they do come looking, now there will be two fewer of them."

"They must at least have told their buddies they were going after a Pircaat," Maacs said. "Hard to mistake size or the way you move no matter how many shadows you weave."

"And now they're going to attack every adventuring party they come across with at least one feline in it? That's only, what, about half of them out here?"

She wasn't wrong. A Pircaat gave a dungeon-crawling group lots of obvious advantages, and their personalities often made them well-suited to the adventuring life.

"Okay, I see your point. But we should still probably finish looting and get out of here. Hard to maintain any deniability with your hand in a dead man's pockets."

"You want me to torch the bodies?" Pitr asked as he sorted small items into piles.

"No, that'd just piss them off even more, and no matter how well you tamp down the smoke it'd attract attention. Let's just grab what's worth grabbing and find a new basecamp."

"If you're really worried, we could always lay low in Kualabu for a couple weeks," Maacs said.

Zeivier shook his head. "No, actually, I was thinking we'd set up somewhere close to the Saepi bastards, maybe on the other side of their site. I want to keep an eye on them. They've got me curious, and besides, if there's something worth guarding where they're at maybe there's other good plunder nearby."

Aanh grinned. "Good, I approve. Now, for a bit of catharsis and misdirection. You saw the way they reacted when I implied we might be allied with Somonei, right? And their whole Nation still refuses to apologize for what it did at the Presilyo." She stalked around the fallen Carvers, paused after a circuit and a half, and began to claw at the ground, leaving incandescent crimson gouges in the carbon crust. After a few minutes she hopped up onto Maacs' shoulders for a better look at what she'd spelled out.

YIIS IIZ FOR Y MRDRD CIIDS QU CARMIIC XIITSTEINS

"This is for the murdered kids you karmic shitstains," Maacs read aloud. "I like it."

Chapter 30

In the days since our arrival, we have weathered disappointment beyond our ability to comprehend. I am tempted to say that only the grief is worse, but what is grief except the dashing of our dearest expectation— that those we love will remain, that mortality will wait another hour, another day, another needed moment. The greatest disappointment a human can suffer, and one that goes on and on right up to the very end.

And we have lost more than just the dead. Not one of us now living are likely to see our homeworld again, or any of the people that make it matter to us. And we are dead to them—worse than dead, because death is a destination and our journey will last forever in their minds.

And yes, we knew this would be dangerous. We knew this might be a one-way trip. Known risks, accepted, however reluctantly, by our own free choice. We reckoned the prize to be worth the price, and what a prize it was. Could have been. Our new sun, Ra. Our new world, Second Sky. A place to start at the beginning.

Instead we have taken Solace along a Far Road, and everything we knew has been scattered apart.

- Carlos Kowalsky, *Wake for Two Worlds,* 0 SE

Acheronford Docks, Salía, The Caustlands, 355 SE

Sanyago looked out over the river piers and the seemingly endless rows of boats moored to them. Behind him, Dayang paced back and forth with a *clunk clunk clunk* of heavy boots. From what he'd seen she knew full well how to walk less noisily in them, but apparently didn't bother when she was agitated. She had plenty of reason to be, he knew, but she also seemed less reserved in her emotions since Nguyen and Park had left. Without her soldiers, perhaps she could be more herself. Sanyago wasn't sure what to think about that.

Laris stood beside him, taking it all in, less interested in the boats than in the people and architecture. And really those things *were* more interesting than a few dozen barges and skimmers rocking in eddies of the river-current. But Sanyago was still wearing his Somonei-colored robes, and people looked back. Children stared, or made attempts at martial-arts motions so graceless they would have earned Sanyago serious punishment at the same age. Adults looked away, or shot them concerned glances. Some nodded respectfully. A few Michyeros flashed them the Dharmachakra, thumbs and forefingers together, one hand pinching the middle finger of the other. Sanyago returned the wheel-turning gesture, as did Laris after a moment's hesitation.

They all clearly saw him as Somonei, and he wasn't sure what he was. He supposed they'd have to go back to the Presilyo after all this was over, explain everything, receive...what? Judgement? A new pair of mentors, with an apology for Niceto? Unlikely, somehow. A place in the ranks of ordinary Somonei? He had no idea, and not knowing created a yawning space in his head, with nowhere to step and a murky place in time.

Except he *knew* where and when he was, and that he should *be* here rather than wander uncertain futures in his mind. So he pulled himself back, hearing Dayang's voice behind him.

"...seems like an absurd sum for a skimmer, I just don't have access to that kind of liquid funds and I'm sure as Hell not carrying that much cash."

A laugh, now, gentle but sure. Taniixh Pai. "It costs what it costs, Dayang. Labor, materials. The enchantments that mean we won't have to break out the paddles and take a month to get there. It's maybe a bit inflated, probably because they can sense we're on urgent business. But it's not outrageous."

Dayang sighed. Huffed, really, and there was a note of resignation to her voice when she continued. "I suppose I'll have to contact my father, but I don't like it, and not just for the obvious reasons. It will take time, for one, and it won't be secure, for another. I don't want to flatter myself by thinking the Carvers consider me important enough to monitor my family...but I don't want to risk it either. I don't need them involved if we can help it."

"I do have...certain prerogatives I could exercise as a Staffguard," Pai said. "I'd have a lot of bureaucracy to scream my way through afterward, but it is possible simply to tell the seller to bill my Order directly. They'll know the Salían government is good for it, and it gives them a chance to put even more of a markup on the sale. But that's also a long way from secure."

"Mmmmm." The sound of boots scuffing pavement. "Let's find a place to discuss it. A half hour to wrap our heads around a decision is better than making the wrong choice and having a couple day's travel time to regret it."

A moment's thoughtful silence.

"Okay. There's a dockside pub just down that way. I could use a good glass of iced tea."

Dayang's laugh, low and slightly sardonic. "Yeah, me too." She raised her voice. "Staafaen! Sanyago!"

Sanyago turned to look at her without saying anything, still trying to order his thoughts.

"Yes?" Laris asked.

"You heard that, right? We'll meet over in that tavern."

"Ummm...sure," Sanyago said. "Just give us a moment, we'll be right there."

"You have about three minutes," Dayang said dryly. "See you then."

She turned and walked away with the two Salíans in tow. Once they'd gotten a reasonable distance, Sanyago did a quick check for eavesdropping and stepped close to Laris.

"You still think we're doing the right thing, brother?"

Laris nodded slowly. "Best that I can tell. I won't lie. I'm scared. I think Dayang is too, she's just too stubborn to let it slow her down much."

"Yeah. She's honest, though, I think. She is who she says she is. Straightforward. Earlier, when we were on watch together, she told me some of her story, and I believed her. I don't know what's going to happen, but in some ways it's less scary than when we first left the Presilyo. We didn't really know anything about who the Shuvelao were or what their plans were. At least now we know basically where we're going and why. And who we're going there with."

"Maybe." Laris furrowed his brow. "For some reasons the dangers seemed less when they were completely unknown. This...it's like there's just enough unknown for it to be awful."

"But not awful enough to change our minds?"

Laris shook his head. "No. The right thing is the right thing."

"Okay," Sanyago said. "But one thing first. I want to change our robes back before we go into that tavern place. I'm tired of being stared at."

Laris looked down at his own clothing, and laughed. "You know what, in all this, I'd honestly forgotten that was an option. Sure. Fine by me."

The tavern was a dingy place, big but dark and poorly-lit enough to make it oppressive. Strange music played, harsh and loud, likely from an echoslate as there were no visible musicians and the sound seemed to come from everywhere at once. Sanyago felt an immediate sense of discomfort as they entered, though he could see why Taniixh Pai had suggested it. A group could easily fade into utter anonymity in here, and in fact that was exactly the problem he encountered when looking around.

"Do we...just wander around until we see them?" he whispered to Laris as they walked between hedgeflame-lit support posts.

Laris shrugged. "I've never been in a place like this either. Maybe we can just ask someone if they've seen them?"

Sanyago wasn't sure about that, but Divine knew he had never been shy, so he simply tapped the next shoulder he saw and smiled when the big man turned around.

"Excuse me," he said.

The big man laughed out loud. Not what Sanyago had expected, but may as well go on. "We're looking for a group of three. Tenggaran woman in—"

"Hey!" the man called out over his shoulder in Ambérico. "Listen to this little mariposa talk." Three others turned to look. They were all big men, creased and weathered and unshaven, standing with their drinks around a high table.

Sanyago blinked.

The man laughed again, and said in heavily accented Gentic, "Go on, say something else, they want to hear."

Sanyago switched to Ambérico, feeling utterly taken aback. "Okay, but I don't understand what…"

All four men laughed now. Ugly sound.

"You can't just walk in here with your boyfriend and talk to people," the man said. "Man might get the wrong idea, and not like it."

Sanyago looked back at Laris, who wore a deepening frown. "What is he even…?"

The man reached out for Sanyago's shoulder. Sanyago shrugged it off without much conscious effort.

"Hey! The man said. "You look at me when I'm talking to you, not your big black gallo."

"Don't touch me," Sanyago said flatly. He thought he understood now, and felt naked. How could they know?

"Don't touch me," the man mocked, exaggerating Sanyago's own voice back at him.

Is that how he knows? Or just suspects? My voice? Sanyago put a hand on his sword, taking comfort in the pommel's solidity.

"What you got there?" The man saw the wu jian and laughed. "He's got a fancy little Han sword, decorations and everything!" His voice went low and rough. "We don't care about your pretty blade, little girl. You're talking to real men who've seen real fights." He tugged his jacket open on one side to show a very large knife in a shoulder sheathe.

Fighting was the last thing Sanyago wanted to do right now, even if the fight would be brief—and it would, only one of them showed much in the way of presence in the Holy Fathom, and that was only really a faint impression, not enough to matter much against real Eychis.

Laris put a hand on his shoulder, and Sanyago let himself be guided back as his friend stepped in front. He was taller than any of the men, though two of them were bigger overall.

"Leave my brother alone," he said, just loudly enough to be heard over the general tavern din.

"You're not brothers," the man sneered. "And you don't even have a pretty little sword of your own." One of the men took a hatchet from his belt; the other two bared their teeth in empty vicious grins.

"We are brothers in every way that matters," Laris said, and his hands curled slowly into fists at his sides.

"Crowshit, just look—"

"Aarón," said the man who showed some Eychis training, more than a touch of alarm in his voice. "We should tell them where their friends are and then go settle our tabs."

"What?" Aarón said, glancing back at his comrade. "One unarmed teenager and his little mariposa friend, are you getting…"

"Aarón," the man said, with utter urgency now. "That *man* is *not* unarmed. We should tell them where their friends are, and then go settle our tabs."

Aarón turned to Laris again, and he must have caught a hint of what his friend had seen because he gave a sudden sharp nod. "Sure, okay. Sure. We saw a group like just…"

"Everything okay?" Pai's voice, from behind the table. She frowned as she came into full view. "What happened to your Somonei robes?"

He'd been on his way to frightened before, but at the mention of Somonei Aarón's sun-baked face turned the color of dried mud.

"We don't want trouble," he said flatly. His voice rasped as though his throat had suddenly parched. "I know you're not allowed to attack someone who's no threat, so just leave us be."

"You really do have a talent for finding trouble, Sanyago," Pai said, amusement in her voice. She came around the table and tapped the man lightly on the leg with her staff. "Hi," she said. "Are you pestering my colleagues, Mister…?"

"López," he replied automatically. "Aarón López. Ma'am. No ma'am." He seemed both relieved and uneasy at the Staffguard's arrival. Less chance of having a fight to lose, more chance of being arrested, Sanyago supposed.

"Sanyago was just asking if they'd seen where you'd gone," Laris said. "Instead of being civilized, this man decided to call him 'mariposa' and make fun of his voice. He strongly implied there might be violence just for daring to talk to him."

"Is that so," Pai said softly. "Four against two? A bigot *and* a coward? Is that what you are, Señor López?"

"We were only joking. Ma'am," Aarón said. "I didn't…we didn't know they were Somonei."

Pai's smile in response was like a velvet-sheathed scimitar. "Of course, you'd never 'joke' with Somonei, because they might do to you the sort of things you take pleasure in doing to people weaker than you."

Aarón's lower jaw stuck out and rage fought to surface through the fear on his face.

"A Staffguard like me meets plenty of people like you, Señor Lopez. I can spot one a kilometer off. I see you. I've *seen* you. But my young friend here is fresh out of the Presilyo Ri'Granha, and I don't want his first impression of our fine country to be from its very lowest shit-stained offal like you and your friends here."

"You don't know me, you don't know us," Aarón said sullenly. He seemed to have decided he wasn't in immediate danger of being arrested or killed, only lectured, and so it was safe to drop the respectful act. Save a bit of face in front of his friends.

"You haven't been listening," Pai said. "I do know you. And I *have* been listening. The whole time, from the moment my colleague first asked you for some very reasonable help."

"Nice of you to show up and rescue your friend, then," he replied, standing up a little straighter, puffing back up after his sudden deflation.

"Señor López," Paid said, "I didn't intervene to rescue them. I stepped in to save *you*. My other Somonei friend was about to tear you apart with his bare hands, and I didn't want the hassle of cleaning up afterward."

He had nothing to say to that.

"If you are ever involved in something like this again," she said softly, "and I find out about it, I will pay you a personal visit. And I am in a position to find out a great deal, Señor López."

"We'll be going," he said flatly, and motioned to the others at the table, who followed without a word.

"Welcome to the world, boys," Taniixh said, flashing them both a sardonic smile. There was warmth in the way she said "boys," so Sanyago found he didn't mind it. "Sorry about the mess."

"You heard all of it?" Sanyago asked. Something was knotted up near his lower belly.

She nodded.

"Do you also...do you think I sound...?"

She sighed. "Sanyago, however you might sound, there's nothing wrong with that."

Sanyago glanced at Laris, who gave a ghost of a smile and put a hand on his shoulder.

Sanyago smiled back, then frowned. "You know we're...we're not..."

"You're brothers," she said. "Yes, I know. That much is clear as day, Señor López was just being an ass. Look, I'm not a Michyero, I'm Hindu." She laughed. "I know that might not tell you much about me given how diverse our faith is, but trust me, I don't care who you fancy or don't.

Neither would Ceraen, she likes both women and men and is quite open about the fact or I wouldn't be telling you. Sergeant Marchadesch…"

She paused, twisting her staff back and forth as she thought. "…I don't know her well enough to do much more than guess. She's a Muslim, but that title also encompasses a larger range of beliefs than you might think— I don't know what the Presilyo taught you about other religions."

"Not much useful," Laris said, and he sounded annoyed. "Usually the particular ways they were supposed to be wrong. Some bits of etiquette, how to avoid offending people we might be serving with. I had to find my own books, and sometimes I got pointed questions about why I was reading them."

"Laris," Sanyago said, grateful for a chance to veer off the subject, "you *always* got pointed questions about what you were reading."

Laris shrugged, then grinned and lightly punched Sanyago on the shoulder. "When this is all over, I want to see Aldonza. It's supposed to have one of the biggest libraries on Solace. Well, in the Caustlands anyway. Who knows what the Praedhc might have. I'm a little jealous of Auxiliary Wiilqaems; the Presilyo wasn't willing to teach any non-Fallen languages."

"Anyway," Pai said. "I'm glad we didn't have any trouble in the end. Our table is this way."

They followed her over to a low circular table where Ceraen and Sergeant Marchadesch were seated, and sat close together across from the three women. Sanyago leaned on the table, trying to still the residual tension in his limbs. It was a different sort of feeling than the aftermath of his recent fights. He knew how to fight. This thing with those men, these strange oblique games whose rules and words and plays he didn't really understand—here he had no lessons to remember, no training to fall back on.

The table's ancient wood was warped, and the whole thing rocked under his weight. Not helpful.

Dayang leaned forward as well, armored forearms resting heavy on the faded surface. The table steadied, and she spoke. "Might be a bit before we finally get a waiter, but that's fine, because I've got a story to tell. Couldn't tell it on our way here with the Salían Army escort, wasn't about to tell it out on the streets either."

Sanyago took a deep breath, focusing on the Tenggaran sergeant, glad to think about someone else's story right now. "This is the one you mentioned when we were on watch?"

She nodded. "When I was a young teenager, I used to like to climb the town wall and look out over it. Kualabu had a pretty tall one, to keep out the Ashwights." She frowned and her gaze flicked down to her right gauntlet for half a second. "And other things, from the direction of the ruins we discussed earlier. Anyway, it gave me a pretty good view. Of the Ashlit Mire, usually." She gave a rueful laugh. "I don't know what fascinated me so much about it. I guess I grew up expecting I'd have to fight ashwights sooner or later. Morbid curiosity, maybe, or trying to face down a fear."

She pulled the gauntlet off her right hand and began tapping her fingers against the uneven wood. "One day I was up there and saw a girl come out of the Mire. A Praedhc scout. I watched her with a spyglass my father had given me."

"What's a spyglass?" Sanyago asked.

Dayang's big dark eyes widened slightly in surprise. "Oh. It's a device for seeing far-off things. Doesn't work perfectly outside the Deisiindr Fathombreak, but still better than nothing."

Manufactured in the Deisiindr. Ragado, then, but Sanyago decided this was not the time to mention that, so he just nodded.

"Anyway," Dayang went on, "that was also when I met my friend Jeims Dubwa. Caustland Cat, in Tenggara from Salía to study spellcasting under a retired adventurer." Her features clouded as she said "retired adventurer," but then a small affectionate smile tugged at the corners of her mouth and eyes. "Sneaky bastard crept up next to me to see what I was looking at. Talking with him, I found out this Praedhc scout had been making this a regular thing; come out of the Mire, look at the town for a while, then go back where she came from."

She fell silent as a waiter approached, nodding at the slight young man as he took out a pad of paper and looked at them expectantly.

"Iced tea, no sugar," she said. "Thank you."

"Iced tea also, but I'll take mine sweet," Pai said.

Ceraen laughed. "I'll have a beer. Whatever's the best thing you have on tap."

"Ummm," Sanyago said when it became apparent it was his turn. "I'll have the same thing as Pai. I mean the Staffguard." The waiter looked at him a little oddly, but jotted it down on the notepad.

Laris stared at the table with narrowed eyes, jaw set as though pushing through a difficult decision. "I'll have a beer as well. Same as she's having."

The young man just nodded, wrote it down. Sanyago stared at his friend. Alcohol was flat-out Ragado for Somonei. Laris just shrugged.

After a moment, Sanyago shrugged back. He of all people was not in a position to play spiritual scold. When he looked around the table, Ceraen and Pai's faces were politely blank, and Dayang wore a small crooked smile, hard to read. *Like she's seen this sort of thing before a hundred times, and thinks it's amusing. Endearing, even.* He gave her an inquisitive look, and she spread her hands palms-up on the table. The smile lingered about her mouth and eyes.

"So, Sergeant Marchadesch," Laris said, with a small awkward clearing of his throat. "What ended up happening with the Praedhc scout and your Pircaat friend?"

Dayang turned her hands back over and pushed up from her palms to stretch. "Right. Well, I saw him around now and then for the next couple years, trained together a few times. Then one day the scout showed up during the day, which she'd never done before, and didn't go back into the Mire. Long story short, Jeims and I decided to go talk to her with along with one of the town guards. She told us there was some Fallen man kind of 'herding' a Hunch-Ripper nearby, which she also said shouldn't be possible for us. So he must have been changed somehow."

"Oh," Ceraen said, and leaned forward to listen more intently.

"She thought it was some sort of false-flag thing, trying to stir up trouble between us and the Pelos. We didn't get a chance to finish the conversation, though, because the Fallen bastard in question pushed the damn monster through the Fathom at us."

"*Madarchod,*" Pai swore softly.

Sanyago suppressed a hard shudder.

"Yep," Dayang said, looking round at their faces. "We killed it. Barely. That's where I got the scar. Much later I pieced together that it must have been a Saepi operation. Carvers, specifically. I've kept an ear open my whole career for anything else they might get up to around the Caustlands. That's why I went to some lengths making sure I'd be the one leading that expedition after I caught wind of it."

Sanyago took his weight off the table and sat back in his chair, thinking hard. "That seems like such a strange thing to do, sending a Hunch-Ripper to do...what? Attack the town walls? Just to throw blame at the Praedhc?"

Pai raised a finger. "Not just Kualabu. They've been doing similarly strange things at border towns all up and down the Siinlan. We don't know all their motivations or goals, frankly. From what I've been able to piece together, a lot of it was pretty disorganized, because *they* were pretty disorganized. An experiment here, a feint there. It's almost certain they were sussing out defenses, though, trying to see how different places would react. We also know there was a major change in leadership a few years back. A coup, more or less, by the High Winnow. After that, they seem to have become more...focused. Concerningly so."

"Who is the High Winnow?" Laris asked.

"Leader of the Promiseguard," Pai answered. "Which is...sort of their internal military? Holy warriors? Not quite like the Somonei, though, they don't have that kind of intensive training. Well, most of them don't. They've been aggressively recruiting former Somonei to their cause, as I'm afraid you already know. This particular High Winnow is one of them. Lidia Almeida, a formidable woman by all accounts."

Dayang nodded. "And she's apparently championing some new religious leader, but details on that are sparse. No one even seems to know the supposed prophetess' name beyond her title. 'Ashtiller.' Which could refer to half the people in the Carver Nation."

Ceraen laughed. "You've done your research, Sergeant."

"Some. I also have a friend back in Kualabu who follows this sort of thing fairly obsessively, and she keeps me informed."

The waiter finally arrived with their drinks and a folded slip of paper. He set the glasses on the table and gave the paper to Dayang, who looked at it curiously.

"Thank you." He inclined his head, and she waited until he was gone to unfold the paper. "Well. This is interesting. It says someone is waiting outside with a message for me."

"That doesn't sound sketchy at *all*," Pai said dryly. "Though it's not an ideal place for an ambush, this part of the docks is pretty well-patrolled by the Acheronford guards."

Dayang leaned in to examine the paper more closely. "Hmmm. This might actually be legitimate. There's some coded language that not many outside the Tentera Wira would know. We'll be careful, but we should go meet this person. Down your drinks, I'll leave money on the table." She smiled ruefully. "Sorry there wasn't time for everyone to enjoy them."

"It's fine," Laris replied. He took a gulp of his beer, grimaced slightly, took another sip. "And for next time—they did give us some Salían dollars, just in case. I don't want you to feel like you have to pay for us."

This was true, though Sanyago was also acutely aware that he had no idea how far the amount would go, or more than a vague sense of what things might cost. He took a long swig of his own drink. Sweet, easily the sweetest thing he had ever drunk, almost overpowering. Not bad, though. Laris was still powering through his beer with a determined expression. Sanyago eyed him sideways.

"Keep your money," Dayang said, almost sharply. Then her expression softened, and she considered him as a small sad smile started to tug at the scar where it ran by the corner of her mouth. "You'll need every penny, I think. You..." She tapped her armored fingers on the uneven quartzwood of the table, and her big dark eyes went to some far-off place of deep and reluctant feeling. Then she sighed—huffed, really, shoulders sagging half a second before squaring again on her next breath. "Plenty of time to figure out the rest of your future if we all live through this. Meanwhile, keep your dollars."

"Honestly, we're not quite sure how much money we really have," Sanyago said. "I mean, we can count it but neither of us have ever bought anything in our entire lives."

"Huh," Dayang said, sounding genuinely taken aback for a moment, then laughed. "Sorry. I should have thought about that. I'm sure the Salíans can help you," she gestured toward Ceraen and Pai with her chin, "since I'm mostly used to Tenggaran won for currency. Now, let's see what this messenger has to say."

They exited the tavern with their hands on their weapons, but were greeted only by a small man wearing nondescript clothes and a short haircut. He looked like he could be Tenggaran, but there was really no way to know for sure in a place as diverse as Salía. At least until he opened his mouth and addressed Dayang in Basa. They exchanged a few terse sentences, he handed her a large envelope, she stared at it, he bowed and left.

Dayang gave her head a small shake as if to clear it. "Walk with me," she said, and walked off toward a quieter spot near a warehouse. Once they got there, she pulled a thick sheaf of papers from the envelope and thumbed through them. The top one, at least, must have been an official document; Sanyago could feel the crypto-binding on it.

"Well, okay." Dayang said. There was a strong note of disbelief in her voice. "These are my discharge papers."

"Wait, what?" Ceraen said.

"Uh-huh. That's not all. There's a transaction receipt for a substantial 'exit bonus' which just happens to comfortably cover the cost of a skimmer purchase, along with another couple year's pay. Looks like someone at Camp Singapore loves me."

"They're discharging you because they love you?" Laris asked. "I don't understand."

Dayang nodded. "Now I am not longer officially affiliated with the Tenggaran military. But as an ex-Sergeant," she took in a deep breath at that, obviously feeling the sudden shift in identity, "I'll be expected to keep the best interests of my country in mind. For a couple years, probably. I've heard stories of this happening before, it's not a *total* surprise. Except for the fact that it's happening to me."

"They're approving your mission with full deniability," Pai said. "Of course."

Dayang thumbed through the sheaf again, made a clicking noise with her tongue, and then stowed the documents in her pack. "I'll have time to navel-gaze about it on the boat," she said. "Let's get going."

The process of purchasing a boat, it quickly became clear, was a deeply boring and drawn-out thing. Even with Pai using her staff to bludgeon through some of the red tape it took the better part of two hours.

Sanyago found this an uncomfortable amount of time to sit and think thoughts about what other people might know about him, and how, and what it all meant. What they thought it meant. What he thought it meant.

What the Divine thought.

He just didn't know, it all felt like an infinitely tangled knot. He supposed it was good to get started on it now.

On the bright side, the skimmer itself was a fascinating distraction. About five meters long, constructed of wood and aluminum, the sleek vessel sat light on the water and heavy in the Holy Fathom. This was, he gathered, due mostly to enchantments that channeled water along grooves in the underside to propel the vessel. He boarded, feeling the eager smile on his face. The two Staffguard were already comfortably seated on one of the benches. Pai seemed calm, Ceraen apprehensive.

Laris did not appear to share Sanyago's excitement. He stood on the pier, watching the boat move with the current.

"Sorry," Sanyago told him.

Laris just shrugged and sighed.

"Problem?" Dayang asked from behind him.

"Staafaen gets seasick," Sanyago said.

"Why didn't you tell me this before?"

"Wouldn't really change what we needed to do," Laris said through gritted teeth, and stepped aboard.

"I suppose not," she said. "But in the future, this is the sort of thing I need to know."

"Sorry," Laris said, taking a seat and a deep breath.

"Not a problem, so long as you keep it in mind going forward," Dayang said. "Fortunately, the boat part of this trip should take less than a day." She patted the skimmer's railing as she boarded. "These things can cover almost fifty kilometers in an hour."

"On a river, okay," Laris said. "But the Gyring Ash?"

"Perhaps forty," Pai cut in. "Sailing the Gyring Ash isn't all that slow, just very dangerous."

"You have to go slower to be safe?" Sanyago asked.

Pai shook her head. "You have to go slower because it isn't water. Faster is safer. Harder for things to catch up."

Sanyago shuddered. "Ashwights?"

"Sometimes," Dayang said, looking off into the distance. "Those are mostly in the Mire. There are worse things under the ash-river itself."

"I've read," Laris said, and Sanyago remembered him talking about it. Malformed monsters, no two alike, all sizes. Nearly impossible to study because they fell apart outside the Siinlan. Terrifying because they refused to within it.

As a precaution, they had no names.

"So...what do we do? If we run into one?" Sanyago asked, staring off to the south. Besides a hint of the Veil over the horizon, the Siinlan wasn't quite visible from the docks, which on the northern end of Acheronford. No one wanted to moor a vessel too near the Ashlit Mire.

"We try to get past it, go around it." Pai tapped her staff against the wooden deck. "If we can't manage that, we try to hurt it until we can. We pray. Failing all that, we make for the Mire and continue on foot. Some survivors have observed a reluctance to leave the Gyring Ash. What we never do is stand and fight. That will just draw more."

Sanyago nodded, and sat down. "You're going to be piloting, Ranger Pai?"

"Yes. I have training and some experience. But while we're still in water rather than ash-sludge, I'm going to show you all the basics. Just in case."

Learning to pilot was fun. For Sanyago, anyway. Laris had a hard time dealing with the helm and his nausea at the same time, Ceraen was nervous, and Dayang was just not very good at it. "It's too Goddamn big," she complained at one point, with her overcorrection in danger of tipping them all into the river. Sanyago knew what she meant, but for him that was part of the joy, the slow, delicate dance between the sleek hull and the currents and the jets of water controlled by the helm levers.

They were nearly the only boat on this stretch of river, passing only a handful of short-range ferries and supply barges. Rolling hills quickly rose up on both sides of the river as they went south, crossed and dotted with the streets and buildings of both Acheronford and its smaller Tenggaran sister-city Saidamlay.

Pai took over again as the Ashlit Mire came into view. Sanyago drew in a sharp breath and held it. It was a stark thing, forbidding, seemingly untouched by the daylight and instead substituting its own grey-green glow within a dense gnarl of embertrees. The buildings and roads along the river had thinned out and then disappeared, replaced in the distance by several layers of fortifications. They all stared, except for Dayang who just glanced over her shoulder and then went back to watching aft.

"*Porlyó*," Laris whispered.

"Yeah," Sanyago said. "And we're going in there."

Laris nodded back, nausea apparently forgotten for the moment.

The distance to the fortifications right before the Mire seemed eternal in the pulsing eddies of adrenaline that seemed to soak the whole boat. Everyone was silent. When at last they came up near the wall of the Salían-side fortifications, an amplified voice called down from the battlements.

"Skimmer! Slow and halt by the pier!"

Pai carefully pulled the helm levers into reverse, decelerating the skimmer until it was moving at only the speed of the river current, then slightly against it. As they drew up to the long wooden walkway that jutted out from the base of the wall, a small figure padded out onto it and sat on the end. It—he—was a white-and-grey Caustland Cat, looking out over the skimmer's occupants with amber eyes.

"Dayang Marchadesch," he said. "Just where do you think *you're* going?"

Dayang stood, and laughed, sounding as genuinely pleased as Sanyago had ever heard her.

"Jeims Dubwa. What, you think *you're* going to stop me?"

"Wouldn't dream of it," he replied. "I already know what you're up to and why. Word can travel fast in the Staffguard. Wish I could come with you, sounds interesting. But you know. Duty calls. Besides, you've already got a Ranger and an Auxiliary with you." He sat up straighter on his haunches and saluted Pai, who smiled and saluted back. "Still might be able to help, though."

"I would have loved to have you with us," she said simply. "And God knows you don't owe me anything. Not that I'm in a position to refuse help right now."

He laughed, a long *mrooowwwl*, and grinned. "Any just deity would know my debts better than that, and so do I. Here, don't drop this, I don't feel like swimming right now." He tossed something small and dull at the skimmer, trailing a short length of chain as it arced through the air. She lunged and caught it, then held it up, dangling it from one of the big dark chainlinks.

"Thanks," she said. "What is it?"

Sanyago stepped in for a closer look as well. It appeared to be a marbled, irregular lump of grey and blood-red...*something*, perhaps the size of a large human fist.

"Well, to start, it's a loan, not a gift. So you're not allowed to die and lose it. And you have to come back and visit so you can return it."

"Okay," Dayang said, smiling. "I'll do my very best on both fronts."

"Good!" Jeims said. "It's a fused Exotic Containment Canister from the *Earthseed*. I called in some serious favors to get my hands on it, but if I can get it back into the Special Equipment vault within a few weeks I might not end up owing a thousand more. So seriously. Don't die."

"Your concern is as heartwarming as ever, Mr. Dubwa," Dayang said. "And thank you. I mean it, even if you still haven't gotten round to telling me what it actually *is* or what it's for."

"It was one of the key components used to cut a path between the gravity wells of Sol and Farrod," he said. "Part of the 'Dark Energy Gravity Well Access Ring' situated at the *Earthseed's* leading edge. It was *meant* to open up a way to Ra, and whatever went wrong fused it into the lump you're holding. Maybe a dozen out of the original eighty-one have been recovered over the last three centuries. As to what it's used for? It appears to generate a field that degrades the coherence of whatever inexplicable energies drive the Gyring Ash."

Dayang frowned. "It doesn't register in the Fathom at all."

"Nope." Jeims shrugged, dipping his head down between his shoulders. "Neither do Ashwights, or...any of the things below the surface of the Gyring Ash. We only figured out what it does—well, really just *one* thing that it does—by experimentation. Probably hired some adventurer to try the mad errand of carrying it through the Siinlan. I say 'probably' because all that sort of thing is classified and I don't have need-to-know."

"So it will help us kill ashwights?" Laris asked, standing a bit unsteadily to address the Gatoparlo.

"You look terrible," Jeims said conversationally. "Should bring some ginger root to chew next time. But no, not really. It doesn't seem to resonate very strongly out in the Mire, just on the Gyring Ash itself. What you do with it is attach it to the prow of a skimmer and then, if things get really desperate, have everyone lie down on the deck before ramming right through whatever might be in your way."

"Why is it," Pai said, "that I've never heard of this, and a junior Auxiliary like yourself not only knows about it, but managed to acquire one?"

Jeims shrugged, dipping his head below his shoulders. "I've always had a strong interest in Starfall and the Siinlan. Took the right courses, pestered the right researchers. That's how I knew. It's not precisely a secret, you understand. They just don't want risk-taking Rangers and military officers seeing this as a way to safely navigate the Gyring Ash. There is no way to safely navigate the Gyring Ash. But, if you're determined to do it anyway...it might increase your chances."

"So you're not sure it will work?" Pai asked as she looped the artifact's chain around the prow railings and secured it to itself with a carabiner, letting the lump dangle slightly off the front.

Jeims unfolded a paw and scratched behind one twitching ear. "I'm confident it has the properties I described. Whether that means it will 'work,' meaning you'll survive an attempt to use it, that I absolutely cannot guarantee. Please be careful."

Dayang laughed, at once grim and full of genuine amusement. "You know, Jeims, it's a lovely irony that *you* were the one who taught me the Gentic word 'hypocrisy.' If only I'd known, back when I was just a wide-eyed girl taking lessons from some strange foreigner."

Jeims wrinkled his nose and stuck out his tongue. "Wide-eyed girl? That's not a Dayang *I* ever met. Now, get on up out of that skimmer and come share a meal with me. I know, I know, you're in a hurry. Twenty minutes. This is probably the safest place to tie up a watercraft on the whole southern end of the Mindao, and eating our food now means your rations will last at least another meal. You know I'm right. Besides, I have more to tell you."

Dayang glanced back at the rest of the group. Sanyago frowned, but then shrugged in spite of himself. They were in a hurry, yes, but if the Gatoparlo really did have more information for them they might as well listen while eating. Staafaen just nodded, and Taanixh Pai responded by snatching the strange stone off the prow before standing up. Ceraen followed.

"Safe place or not, I'm not about to just leave this dangling over the water," Pai said.

"Probably best," Dayang said, and stepped off the boat onto the pier. Then she knelt down in front of Jeims, who came up on his hind legs to hug her. She gave him a brief, fierce squeeze; he responded with a theatrical cough, followed by a long strange *mrrooowwwll*. Laughter, Sanyago supposed, judging by his expression and the way Dayang laughed along with him.

"Goddamn," Jeims said, as the rest of the group disembarked onto the pier, "It's like being caught in a scrap-metal avalanche. I don't know how you go clanking around in all that." He turned and started off toward a metal-bound door in the fortification wall. "This way."

"Not my fault if you can't handle my brilliant fashion choices," Dayang said, following him through the door.

Sanyago entered just after her, curious to see what the inside of a Salian fortress might look like. Mostly disappointing, as it turned out, all utilitarian stone closing in on a cramped hallway that led into a square room with tables and chairs. The space looked as though it could accommodate a couple dozen people eating there at once, though their little group were the only people present.

"It's leftovers," Jeims said cheerfully, jumping up onto a stool behind the serving counter. "But recent leftovers, and not bad for institutional food. Or so I'm told. I don't usually eat the stuff prepared for humans."

Sanyago frowned at the spread, wrinkling his nose. He had no way of knowing what would be Ragado or Silado here, but he thought a couple of the dishes maybe contained some kind of meat. Difficult to say for sure since that was something he'd only ever seen in pictures...that he could remember, anyway.

Jeims spotted his expression and smiled. "No worries, it's almost all vegetarian stuff, and therefore halal as well." He cocked his head in Dayang's direction. "I did learn *some* things in Kualabu, you know. This one's beef, but I don't have any way to check if it was ritually slaughtered. And this fish stew is supposed to be pretty good. Should be something here for everyone."

Laris stepped forward slightly, half-raised his hand. "Which one is your favorite?"

Jeims laughed, *mrrooowwwll*. "None of them. I'm an obligate carnivore, I mostly just eat raw meat. Cooked is okay for a change of pace now and then, but they set aside some of the fish they catch here for me and the other Pircaats, leave it raw. I'll have that."

Laris nodded slowly, face showing that same mix of pleased and disappointed he always wore when learning something new he thought he should already have known.

They each grabbed a plate and started filling them. Sanyago found a few mostly-familiar dishes, put a bit of each on his plate, and dug in with gusto—hard not to after all those days of dry rations. He also took an interest in what everyone else was eating, which he wasn't quite sure constituted good manners or not but his curiosity was just too much too resist.

Jeims was indeed making a meal solely of raw fish, scarfing down largish chunks of pale flesh without even chewing. Weird. Sanyago did his best not to stare. Dayang had piled a plate with some sort of small flatbread and was using it to scoop fish stew into her mouth, helmet sat on the table beside the bowl. Pai had a plate of strangely-shaped pasta in some kind of pinkish sauce, topped with grated cheese and washed down with an enormous glass of milk. Ceraen had piled her plate with a pretty good assortment of foods, but at least half of it was taken up by what Jeims had said was beef.

Sanyago looked away from that, too, not wanting to make faces at a new...what, friend? Comrade, at the very least, given what they'd all been through together. And then he glanced aside at Laris, who was sitting right next to him, but after that glass of beer—*beer!*—Sanyago had been afraid of what he might put on his plate, so he just...hadn't looked until now. But no, it was just bread and cheese and roasted vegetables. Laris saw him looking, gave him a sidelong smile and a raised eyebrow. It didn't really show any annoyance, that smile, just a sort of gentle sardonic jab.

I guess maybe I had that smile that coming, Divine knows what sort of judgey face I might have been wearing and Laris doesn't really deserve that, least of all from me.

"So," Jeims said once everyone seemed about halfway through their meals, "now that we all have a bit of food in the belly, let's talk. I know I've already warned you to be careful and talked about how dangerous the Gyring Ash and Siinlan in general are and blah blah blah, and of course that's true, we all know it, I won't pretend I'm not worried about you. But."

Dayang leaned back in her chair, cocked her head at the Caustland Cat, didn't say anything. Sanyago was suddenly very aware of the bit of squash he was chewing, and just how slowly he was chewing it while he listened.

Jeims stood up on his hind legs, front paws on the edge of the table, tail lashing the back of his chair in erratic patterns. "But. People are a special kind of dangerous. You all know that too, or you should. I think you'll make it to the ruins okay, not saying it'll be easy but you'll make it. What you'll find there, that I'm not so sure about, and I don't think you should be either. Mind..."

He lowered his head a bit closer to the table, lowered his voice as well, looked round at the little group, "...I'm not just talking about all the bad shit these Carvers are into. From what I've gathered, I don't think they've had time to get into *too* much of that kind of trouble. I don't think that's the kind of danger you're going to face. What I *do* think you may be facing is a woman named Lidia Almeida. High Winnow of the Carvers. Former Somonei. We think she's been one of the main driving forces behind all this crowshit, and we have good reason to believe that she left Earthmarch for the Borih'Sath ruins days ago. It's unlikely you'll beat her there."

Former Somonei. Not a surprise, really, but still a shock. Sanyago wasn't sure how much of it might show in his face, so he asked the first question he could bring to mind. "'High Winnow?' What's a 'winnow,' exactly?"

Laris answered before Jeims could. "It means to blow air through grain in order to remove the chaff."

Blank looks from everyone but Ceraen. Laris ducked his head apologetically and continued. "That's the part that's not edible, like a kind of husk. It's an old word, so is 'winnow,' but it still shows up in Gentic versions of the Star Sutra, talking about how the Divine will divide the Silado grain from the Ragado chaff."

"Star Sutra?" Ceraen said. "That's the Michyero version of the Christian New Testament, right?"

"Yeah, I suppose so," Laris said. "I haven't read the Christian version. I wanted to, it seemed like it was important, I mean for history and culture if nothing else. But it wasn't allowed. The Presilyo taught that the Star Sutra version given by Eusébio Inoue was the perfected version of that book, so no reason to read the older corrupted one." He shrugged. It said a lot, that shrug, and Sanyago winced a little, but really there was no one here to care about possible Laris-heresy except...him. And he wasn't sure how ready he was to think about that.

Ceraen pushed her empty plate to one side and leaned forward, lacing her long dark fingers together under her chin. "I know my Bible pretty damn well, my parents made sure of that, and I still read it from time to time. 'High Winnow?' That's bad news. You know what happens to the 'chaff' in the verses that title is referencing, after it gets winnowed out from the wheat? It's burned. With 'unquenchable fire.' And in the minds of fanatics like this, the 'chaff' is everyone who's not them. It's us. It's our families and all our friends."

"That sounds about right," Jeims said. "The fanaticism, I mean, I'm definitely no authority on holy scripture of any kind."

Dayang snorted at that, and Jeims threw a balled-up napkin at her before continuing. "Besides being fanatical, it seems this Lidia is a very very dangerous fighter. The Salían government keeps dossiers on all Somonei it knows about. I'm sure that's not a surprise..." he shot a small smile in Laris and Sanyago's direction, "...if you really think about it. Especially high-ranking veteran Somonei. They don't always stay Somonei forever."

So he knew they were Somonei, plain robes or no. Sanyago supposed that would have been part of whatever information the Caustland Cat had been given, and wondered just how far it would propagate. He supposed there was nothing that could be done, and there were other things to worry about.

Laris tilted himself forward with a frown. "So it will be like the Return of the Apostates? The attack on the Presilyo a few years back, I mean, facing a bunch of former Somonei she's recruited?"

Jeims shook his head. "Not so far as we can tell, those were pretty much all killed or captured during the attack. Even if she's recruited any more since then, she's probably using them to train the Promiseguard back in Earthmarch. And again we don't think the Carvers have been at the Tenggaran site long enough for there to be anyone...changed...yet. Although you can't ever be sure of that kind of thing. In any case, be careful. Lidia's plenty dangerous no matter who or...what...might be with her."

"We will be," Dayang said. "And I think we're all done eating, so thank you. For the warning, and the food."

Jeims nodded, and jumped down off his chair. "No worries. Let's see you off."

They followed him back out to the skiff, and boarded it while the Caustland Cat watched from the pier. Once they were settled, he stood up on all fours and stretched. "I won't keep you longer. It's good to see you again, Dayang. And for what it's worth, I think if anyone's suited for a mad expedition like this, it's you."

"Good to see you too, Jeims," she said. "And thank you. Again. For everything."

He smiled, flicked his tail. "Good luck," he said, and turned to pad back into the fortifications.

Pai started the skiff forward, looking at Dayang over her shoulder. "You never said you had a friend in the Staffguard."

"Yeah, well, I would have back at the tavern if my story hadn't been cut short by that message. Anyway, now you've met Jeims Dubwa." She paused. "I need a minute," she said, and turned to look out over the back of the skimmer. *Where no one can see her face.*

Sanyago stepped forward, reached out a tentative hand, then thought better of it. Then told his thoughts they could go hang, and moved forward next to her to rest his hand on her armored shoulder. He didn't say anything.

She turned to look at him, and her big dark eyes were watery and far away. "What?" she asked.

"I don't know what it's like to be you," he said quietly. "I've only known the Presilyo—my whole life, what I can remember up until a couple weeks ago, it's been there. But I know a little about what it means to miss people you've left behind, even if it hasn't been that long for me." Not long, but it hurt. Everyone he'd ever known except for Laris, with Hyon-seok an especially raw, aching absence.

She looked at him a long time, then she smiled, very slightly.

"Thank you," she said back, just as quietly. "It is hard. We'll both get through it, but it is hard." She closed her eyes, opened them, turned back toward the front of the skimmer.

"Yeah," he said, and took his hand off her shoulder. They stood looking forward together. Now that they were passing the long-anticipated fortifications, the Mire loomed up closer with terrifying speed. Sanyago stared as the hilly dirt banks of the river became weird formations of hardened ash which themselves gave way to burbling sludge under tangles of embertrees.

"Why doesn't the Mire-sludge leak into the river?" he asked.

"It hardens on contact with water," Ceraen answered.

"Huh," Sanyago said. He thought a moment. "Is that also how the river crosses the Gyring Ash?"

Ceraen shook her head. "Whatever force drives the Gyring Ash is a powerful one. The river doesn't move it at all. Some of the water flows over the top, but most of it is forced under. Makes it dangerous to cross even in a skimmer, since there's a slow but strong sideways undercurrent trying to tip your boat, and if you fall out you can be pushed down into the ash-sludge."

"Oh," Sanyago said. "So we should be glad Ranger Pai knows what she's doing."

"Definitely," Ceraen said, "but we're not trying to cross, just move from one to the other, and that's a lot easier. We'll simply hug the left bank and turn directly onto the Gyring Ash. There will only be a moment of conflicting currents to deal with. From what I understand, it's a bit trickier to turn left than right since we'll be going counter-clockwise against the flow. Nothing Taniixh and this skimmer can't handle, though."

"Okay," Sanyago said, and fell silent with the rest, watching the embertrees pass by on either side. The sun sparkled merrily off the river-water but was utterly shunned by the grey-green gloom of the Ashlit Mire, making him feel like he was travelling a ribbon of sunlight stretched through some twilight nightmare.

A few times he thought he saw something move in the sludge, but couldn't be sure. He didn't like the arrhythmic *chur, chur-chur* sounds the Mire made with its slow insistent flows and eddies round embertrees and undergrowth. It seemed to drown out the comforting rush of the Mindao somehow.

The minutes stretched out uncounted.

"There," Pai said, voice tight, pointing ahead. "Everyone hold on, I'm going to take this turn as fast as I dare. We don't want to lose too much speed."

"The Gyring Ash," Dayang said grimly. "God help us."

It was at once smaller and slower and much more terrifying than he had expected. The dark-ash flow seemed to sequester all available light under its surface, which parted here and there for a glimpse of pallid green glare. The whole thing hummed with an immense energy that he felt, not through the Holy Fathom, but the entire delicate network of his veins and nerves.

Sanyago closed his eyes in meditation, and prayed.

Please Divine let us come through this, we are still on Your errand after all.

When he opened them again, Pai was already starting the turn. He gripped the railing on one side and his seat on the other, felt the hard tilt, the shudder of the wood and aluminum frame under buttocks and feet. On his left, Laris threw up over the side. There was a terrifying lurch and a snarled curse in what must be Pai's native Manhc. Then a correction, and they were back on an even keel moving smoothly through the thrumming sludge of the Gyring Ash.

This is it, Sanyago thought, and felt the weird deformed-heart resonance under the deck, watched the inner edges of the Mire go by, tried not to look too directly at the flashes of silver-green that broke the soot-colored surface. *Now we find out just how bad it's going to be.*

But nothing happened for the first three hours.

Chapter 31

The Black Fence is harmless. We put it there, after all. It's what it wa<crossed out so violently the paper is torn>g that's the real d<obscured by bloodstain>ion.

- Caeviin Yorvalds, Head Geomancer of the Nowhere Project, notebook, final page

The Siinlan, Southeast Quadrant, 355 SE

Ashwight ashwight ashwight. Ashwight ashwight ashwight.

Juliaen couldn't quiet the mantra in her head, any more than she could steady her shaking limbs. The ninja had been terrifying, sure, but they had also been human, and the whole ordeal had happened so fast she hadn't really been able to follow it, up to the moment she lost her awareness of the mortal world. But the ashwights...she'd seen every profane detail as they lurched and bobbed from every direction, watched what passed for internal anatomy spill and splatter before being slowly absorbed by the mire-muck.

She'd set one of them on fire, and watched it burn. Heard its parody of a scream.

Smelled it.

She'd lost count of how many they had killed. Lidia had done most of it, dancing from form to misshapen form in lethal rhythm. The monsters fell and choked and cried and burbled, heads crushed, torsos caved in, innards turned to mush that spouted out from almost-mouths as they fell back into the sludge.

And they'd kept coming.

Without Lidia they would all simply have died, she knew that. Juliaen herself had managed to deal with exactly one of the horrors. Maicl had held his own, and she had praised him for it later; the surviving Promiseguard had done themselves proud, but without the former Somonei stepping grimly between killing blows, sheer numbers would have dragged them all down into the ashy muck.

Juliaen gripped the gumchitin rim of the strange Praedhc boat and stared down the barely-perceptible curve of the Gyring Ash. Or maybe she was just imagining that tiny nudge to the right by the time the flow hit the horizon. She wished she could focus on that for the few hours until the trip was done, or that she could close her eyes, find her center, but…

…but…

…but when they disembarked they would have to cross the Ashlit Mire again, the inner ring this time…

…but the image of the ashwight that nearly managed to grab her head would not leave her retinas…

…but they had already been forced to steer between towering jointed extremities that combed and curled toward them like a seven-fingered hand…

…and there could be worse to come.

That was worst of all, the "and," the maybe, and she knew she should not wrack her mind over what may or not be, a future that was not real because it was not now, but the risk and the hanging horror of it was a part of the now and she wanted to scream but instead she gripped the boat and waited and watched as was her duty. Until the end.

And it did end. They reached the spot where they would cross. They left the boats to be consumed by…something…beneath the Gyring Ash. They trudged through the Ashlit Mire. Again.

This time they met with no ashwights, only the maddening, unknowable not-rhythms of the mire-sludge. By the time they stepped onto solid ground a few kilometers south of Kualabu, Juliaen wanted to jam fingers in both ears and hum a thousand hymns. She settled for simply falling asleep.

She felt different in the morning. Not better, not really. Saner, more put-together, but that only let other, less visceral fears tug at her mind from the outskirts where they'd been waiting.

"Do you think that convert Shuvelao managed his mission?" she asked Lidia as they spooned porridge into mess kit bowls. "What could the Salíans or the Presileros figure out if he didn't?"

"There's no sense worrying about that, Juliaen," she replied, blowing on her portion and then inhaling the scent of cooked grain and brown sugar. "We'll be there soon enough and then know for ourselves if there's been any reaction from our enemies."

For the hundredth time Juliaen wished they could just pass a simple question or two ahead to the site and get an answer in return, but there were too many adventurers combing the ruins who might overhear even the most carefully-sent echogram. And adventurers by nature liked to ask questions and poke their noses places, especially when they smelled anything powerful and ancient and Praedhc.

So she nodded, and took a brief moment for prayer, and they set off.

When the ruins came into view, Juliaen did her best not to gape. She'd been prepared for disappointment, knowing that however majestic the city had been pre-Starfall it would be a carbon-lacquered pile of rubble now. And it was...but it was a massive, confounding, tantalizing pile of rubble, full of almost tangible secrets, shattered pieces both large and small suggestive of spectacular fallen grandeur.

Divine judgement has its own sort of terrible beauty, she thought, and shuddered. *What sort will I help bring?*

They picked their way through the treacherous, blackened devastation, careful to avoid any too-even paths that might be more heavily traveled. They'd all changed into the sort of outfits Lidia said Salían adventurers might wear, but hoped that wouldn't matter. No one would recount a group they hadn't seen.

When they reached the site without encountering a soul, Juliaen prayed her thanks. Finally the Divine had seen fit to bless them with one easy part in their journey.

The two Promiseguard on watch bowed at their approach, but their faces were grave. By the time Juliaen was near enough to speak, a third had emerged from the ruin. He bowed as well, his expression no less solemn than the first two.

"High Winnow. Ashtiller. It's an honor to have you here." He looked their little group over, clearly counting, and asked the obvious question with nothing but a look.

"Ambush. Ninja, just as we were coming out onto the surface. They knew about our expedition. I pray no one has discovered yours?"

His expression did not change.

"Two of our number chased off an intruder and never returned. We had to wait and then muster a substantial force to go after them, in case we were being lured into a trap. We found this message by their corpses."

He held up an echoframe. Juliaen peered into its illusory depths, and gasped. Two bodies, one relatively whole, one with its face in horrific tatters. Written near their heads in glowing quadruple strokes was a single line of blocky Gentic.

"YIIS IIZ FOR Y MRDRD CIIDS QU CARMIIC XIITSTEINS"
Lidia took in a breath through her teeth, then let it out in a long growl. "Presilero hirelings. Mercenaries of the mercenaries. We will *deal* with them."

Transcript, Partial

Time and Place of Meeting
Free District, The Sovereign Nations, 355 SE

Attending, Representing
Amrozi Samudra, Sharaf Al-Rusul Nation
Walaes Jaacsn, Wordswill Nation
Siamak Mousavi, Mahdi Nation
Shyam Thakur, Newcaste Nation
Juan Carlos Hidalgo, Opus Terrae Nation
Zhu Jianping, Huayi Nation

Surviving Fragment

(unknown): ...see how we could fully trust her.

Walaes Jackson: Of course we can't trust her. That's not really the question, though, is it?

Zhu Jianping: I would say that the set of possible questions here is near-infinite. And I can't see that there could be any good answers for most of them.

Shyam Thakur: I thought we had made it clear, Ambassador Zhu, that all your questions will be answered. We just need a modicum of patience.

Zhu Jianping: I wasn't implying that my questions might not have answers, Mr. Thakur. I was suggesting that most of them would turn out to have sinister ones. Allow me again to voice my concern, and that of my Compact, that no good is likely to come out of this meeting.

Shyam Thakur: Noted, Madame Ambassador.

Walaes Jaacsn: With all due respect, Ms. Zhu, why then are you here at all?

Zhu Jianping: Professionally? Obligation. Personally? Mitigation. Philosophically? Perhaps a larger measure of hope than is wise.

Shyam Thakur: Madame Ambassador, it was our expectation that every representative be here in good faith.

Zhu Jianping: Good faith! I'm sorry, Mr. Thakur, which of my intentions might I have failed to make clear? Which of them, in your opinion, are of dubious sincerity? I'm aware you do not like my stated reasons for being here, but that does not in any way suggest a lack of "good faith."

Siamak Mousavi: I believe, Madame Ambassador, that my Hindu colleague is referring to the way in which you seem to have arrived at this meeting with your mind already made up.

Zhu Jianping: And I'm damned well surprised that any of you arrived still giving this mad proposal even the slightest consideration. Your minds should have been made up the moment you heard the proposal.

Siamak Mousavi: There's no need for profanity, Madame Ambassador. This is a professional gathering.

Zhu Jianping: The Hell there isn't. Tell me, Mr. Mousavi, do you really think your One True God would be more offended by my choice of words than by what that Michyero madwoman is proposing we do? What she's already done herself?

Amrozi Samudra: It might be wise for a total infidel such as yourself to keep her mouth shut on matters of religion, Ms. Zhu.

Zhu Jianping: (After a moment of laughter) You are wrong on multiple fronts, Mr. Samudra. Most of my Nation may hold to no particular religion, but in our Compact a person's positions on matters of faith are not...shall we say...violently mandatory the way they are in yours.

Amrozi Samudra: It is our sovereign right to punish apostates and...

Zhu Jianping: ...and I am a Christian, Mr. Samudra. One of the, as your own scriptures assert, People of the Book? Which you would know, if you had given this meeting serious consideration beyond your Nation's eager greed to carve up portions of Tenggara and Auraramad and...how did you put it? "Punish apostates." Because you think you know their religion better than they do.

Walaes Jaacsn: Ladies and gentlemen, we are getting off track here. Ms. Zhu, your personal religious beliefs are not pertinent to the discussion at hand.

Zhu Jianping: Don't be disingenuous, Mr. Jaacsn, God frowns on liars.

Walaes Jaacsn: Excuse me, Madame Ambassador?

Zhu Jianping: I mean you don't consider me a "real" Christian at all, or you'd not dare be so dismissive. You care very much about "personal religious beliefs." And tell me, besides frowning on your dishonesty, exactly what do you think Jesus would say about this proposed course of action, hmm? But I suppose you have some elaborate theological justification.

Juan Carlos Hidalgo: (overlapping) Ms. Zhu, that is—

Zhu Jianping: —A justification, Mr. Hidalgo, not unlike the ones Old World Conquistadores used as license to rape and murder and enslave your own ancestors. Is that not so?

Juan Carlos Hidalgo: Those Old World Christians may have been overzealous, but they saved my pagan ancestors from Hell, Madame Ambassador. And perhaps they don't teach it in whatever...unorthodox...version of the faith you practice, but Hell is eternal.

Zhu Jianping: Is it? I expect we're about to find out, for a given definition of Hell anyway. Ironic, really, since you seem to think the concept can be used as an excuse for nearly any atrocity you think might "save souls."

Shyam Thakur: That's quite enough. Ms. Zhu, I believe it has become clear that you have come here merely to spar and antagonize. I move that Ambassador Zhu Jianping be ejected from this meeting.

Amrozi Samudra: Seconded. All in favor of ejecting the Huayi Nation ambassador? Show of hands.

Shyam Thakur: It's unanimous. Madame Ambassador, if you'd be so kind as to see yourself out.

Zhu Jianping: With pleasure, Mr. Thakur. A few parting words as I leave. We are well aware of the reason we were invited to send a representative to this meeting when the other Compacts were not, and that reason is real enough: we do want to liberate the people of Zhon Han. An end to that regime would be a blessing from Heaven...but nothing is worth the price you're contemplating. "For what shall it profit a man, if he shall gain the whole world, and lose his own soul?"

Walaes Jaacsn: We're all hoping to *save* souls, Ms. Zhu. Almost anything is worth that price.

Zhu Jianping: So very sure you have the keys to salvation, Mr. Jaacsn. And you, Mr. Samruda, Mr. Mousavi? Whatever happened to "no compulsion in religion?"

Siamak Mousavi: As my Shi'a colleague pointed out earlier, we wish to correct apostates, not impose our will on those not of our faith.

Zhu Jianping: You'd impose it on each other if you could, Shi'a on Sunni, Sunni on Shi'a— yes, yes, I'm going. I hope to God at least one of you finds some scrap of conscience underneath all that self-serving hypocritical zealo—

(words cut off by closing door)

Shyam Thakur: Thank you for helping the Ambassador find her way out, Sergeant. So. Now that the time for hysterics has passed, let's have a proper discussion on the Carver proposals. Shall we begin with the likely risks and benefits of the, ah, "shock troop" provisions?

Walaes Jaacsn: Well, I think the risks are obvious enough, but with proper mitigation it might be

End of Fragment

Chapter 32

Here is the trouble with having blood on your hands: it doesn't mean anything. I get blood on my hands every time I have a nosebleed. A physician gets blood on her hands from saving a life. Blood's just a fluid, nothing all that special about it. It isn't terribly relevant to identity either, for all the talk about bloodlines and being thicker than water. A flake of dead skin is every bit as much "you" as a drop of blood, and they're both easily replaced.

So forget about blood, it washes off. Worry about having lives *on your hands. Worry about the spatter of inflicted suffering. Those are the things that can't be taken back, can't be remedied. Justified, perhaps, but you'll never lose the stain.*

- Deiviid Castnr, *On the Boundaries of Peace*, 43 SE

The Siinlan, Southeast Quadrant, 355 SE

"There it is!" Dayang yelled, and ran forward, jumping over seats and gear and Sanyago, who had the presence of mind to duck down as she vaulted him. She twisted her hips to slide around Pai's seat at the helm, then went down on one knee at the very front of the boat, gripping her shield as tightly as she had ever done. And she stared at the thing that had risen from the Gyring Ash.

It was immense, it had to be: even just the parts they could see were huge. Something like a mouth in the center, surfacing at irregular intervals, and two long...tubes to either side. Not tentacles, she didn't think, not that Dayang had ever actually seen a tentacle outside drawings. These were more like...flexible tree trunks, flailing slowly over the sludge, easily ten meters long. And they *spun,* a continuous rapid roll along their entire length, covered in vicious thornlike spikes that curved forward into the motion.

It was colored like spoiled rice porridge, and dripped a pale liquid streaked with black.

"No way around!" Pai said. "Stay standing up until it's just about to pass over, we don't want it pressing down onto the boat!"

Then the massive appendage swung toward them as the skimmer sped forward and everything happened at once. Dayang angled her shield, bottom point against the prow, and wove what she hoped would be the strongest barrier-spell of her life. The thing loomed up as a churning thousand-toothed wall and she prayed and the

impact was

COLOSSAL.

She roared, and the implacable field surrounding the artifact rippled through whatever substance passed for the thing's flesh. Spikes tore at her shield and at her spell, flew off as their integrity decayed. The sheer bulk of the thing blotted out the sky, its weight relentless.

The boat slowed, the appendage rose, and Dayang stood, turned to see it pass over the boat. She prayed. They might clear it...no.

"Hold on!" she screamed, and dropped again to grab the railing. The thing came down on the stern, pushing the whole rear of the boat into the sludge and slamming Dayang upward. She jammed her armored elbow down on her mace to keep it from flying off her belt, pulled herself back down to the deck. Chunks of aluminum and wood splintered away as the thing ground down.

Shit. This is it. We go down right here.

Staafaen stood, putting him centimeters from the rolling mass, braced a foot against the back of a seat, and struck out with a cry and a roiling concentration of force within the Fathom. His palm slammed into a bare patch Dayang's shield had stripped of its tearing spikes, and the entire boat jolted forward in reaction though the thing itself barely moved.

"Turn right!" Dayang yelled, and Pai did, accelerating just ahead of the thing's ponderous sweep. Its central mouth pushed up into the air, gnashing in eerie near-silence, no sound on the air beyond the wet smacking sounds as it opened and closed. Everyone seemed to be holding their breath, only to let it out all at once as the boat passed out of reach.

"Thank God," Ceraen said, then coughed, choked, and vomited over the side.

"Al-hamdulillah," Dayang agreed. "How bad is the damage?"

"Sanyago, take the helm," Pai ordered. Her voice was calm, but her face was grim and drained, mahogany gone to ash. Sanyago scrambled up without a word, and Pai made her way aft to examine the shredded stern.

"Well, it's not going to sink," she said. "Not on the Gyring Ash, anyway. And it still has propulsion. Might have some trouble on rough waters. I'm afraid that's most of your investment gone, Dayang."

"It was really the Tentera Wira's investment anyway." Dayang said. "I've seen the military waste money on infinitely stupider shit."

Pai laughed. "Haven't we all. Now, time to make a choice. If we run into another one, do we try our luck at getting past again, or do we head straight for the Mire and go the rest of the way on foot?"

"How far out are we?"

"About halfway. Well, we would be with an undamaged boat. Our new top speed is maybe two-thirds what it was before."

Dayang sighed. Huffed, really, short and sharp, making her shoulders sag before squaring again on her next breath. "Halfway. Not good enough. We run into another one in the next couple hours, we get past it. We learn from our mistakes, we learn from experience, we do better. Now that I understand more about the artifact Jeims gave us, I think we should have rammed the thing dead-center rather than try to go under one of its...arms or whatever those were."

Pai shuddered, but didn't argue. "Okay. I hope that's a lesson we don't end up needing."

They didn't, at least not that day. The hours kept on, and so did the skimmer

They disembarked the skimmer at a spot east and just south of Kualabu, and Dayang wondered at how mad it was to feel such heavy relief at so unpleasant a prospect as trudging through the Ashlit Mire.

And it was unpleasant. The sludge made the going a literal drag, and threatened to fill every crevice and joint of her armor, somehow resistant to the enchantments that kept out more mundane sorts of soilage. Dayang had to shore them up with her own Fathom-reserves, which took a small but steady toll on top of the sheer physical exertion. She was used to that sort of toil, though. Her thoughts were what really wore at her, thoughts of Kualabu on the opposite shore, the flimsiness of wooden walls, fear for family and friends barely sheltered behind them. And the more immediate fear of what might ambush them from under the muck at any moment.

Step, drag, step. Almost no sound beyond their own, just the unknowable nearly-rhythms of the Mire, *chur-chur, chur, chur-chur-chur,* and no light at all from above, just the soft glow of the embertree bark and the now-and-then glimpse of grey-green light the ash-sludge depths.

It went on. It went on.

It went on.

Mercifully, they met no ashwights. By the time they finally saw solid ground she felt it was only simple stubbornness that kept her moving forward, though she knew she could summon up enough of a second wind for a fight if she absolutely had to.

"Laris?" Sanyago said behind her, sounding every bit as tired as she felt.

"Yes, brother?" Staafaen's voice didn't betray quite the same level of exhaustion, but was still a very long way from energetic cheer.

"I take it back. Wanting to see the Siinlan for myself instead of on a map, I mean." He fell silent for a moment. "Okay, not quite. Maybe just wishing for a shorter tour."

Staafaen laughed. "Too late for that. Now you can just wish for some sleep."

"We'll have to reach the outer ruins before we can set up camp," Dayang said. "Not a good idea to sleep in sight of the Mire."

"All the way to the horizon?" Sanyago said, his tone more resigned than upset. "That's almost five kilometers."

"No. There are ruined walls we can set up camp behind. Two kilometers, at the most."

Dayang had seen the ruins plenty of times before, from a distance anyway. Up close they were much more imposing, blocky and blackened and stretching out and up the farther she looked, but she was too tired to be properly impressed. She assigned Staafaen the first watch as he seemed the least tired, set her tent up against the wall, and slept.

"We made it," Sanyago said as he nibbled dried fruit and iron-fortified hardtack, leaning back against the crumbling, carbon-smeared wall. "We're here. This is it."

Dayang nodded and stared off to the north, adjusting the fine plating that protected her fingers. She'd spent what felt like half the morning cleaning green-grey sludge off the deep red of her armor. "This is it. Welcome to Tenggara."

He grinned, light brown eyes crinkling at the edges. "You know, it's funny. I spent my entire life just a river's breadth from this country, and never set foot on it til now."

"Did they teach you any Basa at the monastery?"

He shook his head, watching the other three have a breakfast conversation of their own, keeping Taanixh Pai company on watch. "I'm not much good at languages, I was happy just to learn Gentic well. Staafaen, though, he learned Common. Can read and write it okay too. Maybe more than okay, he tends to hold himself to a pretty high standard."

"I took Common in secondary school as well," Dayang said. It seemed like a lifetime ago. "I should brush up on it. Maybe once this is all over I'll head back to University." She frowned to herself. "No, probably not. I can't imagine sitting through years of classes on a campus at this point in my life."

"Your Gentic is really good," Sanyago said. "Did they teach you that in school too?"

"Everyone has to learn Gentic," Dayang said. "At least in the public schools I went to. But most people don't learn it all that well. I had private tutors."

"Oh." Sanyago said. He paused, looked slightly embarrassed. "What does that mean?"

She blinked, feeling a sudden sense of just how removed the young monk was from everyday life in the countries he'd grown up between but never really been part of. "It means my father paid someone to teach me extra lessons, one-on-one, outside the public school."

"Public school is free, right?"

"Well, sort of. Paid for by taxes. The government wants educated citizens. Or at least that's what the politicians say."

"Oh." Another pause. "Did the Tentera Wira give you that armor? Are you going to have to give it back?"

Dayang felt a sudden defensiveness, as she often did when the subject of her training and equipment came up with someone new—someone who might resent the sheer privilege it represented, the extent of which she hadn't fully realized herself before she'd gone off to enlist. But Sanyago probably lacked enough social context to even realize resentment might be an option. *I never really told him Hang Che was hired by Father, either. Does he think that was included in public education as well? Maybe.*

"No," she said. "Which reminds me of something that may not have been clear about in the story I told you before. My Wira—ah, Haeliiy— training also came from private lessons. My father paid for them." She grimaced, thinking of Hang Che still running free in Kualabu just north of where she stood. "He also gave me the armor and mace for my seventeenth birthday. Well, mostly. My brother Pandikar carved the mace haft, he's a mage-artisan."

"For your birthday? Why?"

She shrugged. "He said I was ready for it. And he had this iron determination to have at least one of his children know how to defend themselves. He always told me that Solace is a dangerous world and needed more decent people who could deal with it."

Sanyago took a moment to take that in. "He sounds like a good man. You're lucky."

Ah. Having a father. Having parents at all, really. Not something she normally thought of as a privilege, which she supposed was a privilege in itself.

"He is," she said softly. "I hope you can all meet him, when we're done with this. It's not exactly a long trip from here."

Sanyago nodded. "So is that a tradition, in Tenggara? To get the things you'll need as an adult on your seventeenth birthday?"

She was staring now, and she shouldn't be, especially now that Ceraen had walked over to listen. "Um," she said. "People give gifts generally, for birthdays. Especially parents to their children."

Sanyago took a moment to process this. "I don't know when my birthday is," he said. "I don't think the man who left me at the Presilyo told them. They just had a guess, but they lied about it. To Laris too...Staafaen, I mean. Told me I was a year older than I am, and him a year younger. So they could put us in the same class."

Ceraen made an incredulous noise in her throat. "I swear, every time you two talk about the Presilyo you come up with something even more messed-up to say. They lied about your ages to manipulate you? How old are you, then?"

Sanyago shrugged. "Sixteen, seventeen, something like that. I'm pretty sure Staafaen is eighteen. I think his birthday is sometime in September, I think he remembers that much. But he doesn't like to talk about it."

Now it was Ceraen who stared. "*Jesus* you're young. And they've already got you fighting and killing? Christ."

Sanyago only shrugged again. "It's what we were raised for."

Neither Dayang nor Ceraen had an answer for that, not right away.

"Let's get going," Dayang said. "We're as ready as we'll ever be. We'll start at the eastern edge of the bearing line and follow it west. Keep an eye out for anything and anyone that might help us narrow the search."

They struck camp with swift nervous energy. It took Dayang longer to take down and stow her tiny one-soldier tent than it did Ceraen and Pai to make their own shared pup tent disappear into their packs. Something to be said for teamwork, she supposed, that and the fact that she knew she wasn't especially quick at this sort of task; it was one of those soldierly skills that lingered on that irritating edge of military life she only barely had patience for.

Staafaen and Sanyago, of course, had nothing to strike and instead stood together a few meters away, speaking together with their heads bowed, well out of earshot. Dayang wondered what they were saying, but kept her peace and concentrated as best she could on the straps and stakes and fabric of her tent.

She looked up as Ceraen and Pai approached.

"Need help?" Pai asked, leaning slightly sideways on her staff. "Not fair, having to do everything alone." She paused, frowned, looked aside. "I'm sorry, that was insensitive. I know you must be missing your squad terribly and there hasn't been time to mourn."

Dayang shook her head. "That's kind of you, and I'll be okay, or at least okay enough. Honestly, what I feel most guilty about? I didn't know them all that well. Especially not the way soldiers often do, and that's my fault, I went to fairly great lengths to be assigned to that mission. They'd just lost their old sergeant when he was promoted, and more or less just slotted me in and sent us off. They deserved to be with a leader who knew them better."

Pai stepped forward, put a hand gently on Dayang's shoulder, which she didn't mind, even managed a small smile for the older woman. "Dayang. Maybe cliché, but you know, I was there for the whole thing so I think I get to say it: you did the best you could. And they were lucky to have someone who had previous experience with all this madness. Given what that traitor Shuvelao was up to, it could have been much worse but I'm not sure it could have gone better."

"Hmmm." Dayang wanted to laugh, but knew there would be too much bitterness in it. "I don't think so. I knew something might be not-right with them from the beginning, but I still let them come with us. Even after confronting them."

The corner of Pai's perpetual near-smile twitched upward. "Really? Dayang, think it through. If you hadn't let them come with us, they could have simply gone in behind us. Who knows what kind of damage Augusto, Niceto, whoever he was, could have manipulated his comrades into doing?"

"I would have had them escorted back to the surface." Dayang said, but she could hear the uncertainty in her own voice. It promised a kind of relief, and she wasn't sure she wanted to reach out and grasp that just yet, felt it wasn't deserved, it was too soon, there was death and horror and failure still to be felt.

"And?" Pai said. "You think they wouldn't have found a way around that? Talked the Salíans into it, maybe? Besides, that last fight with the...you know, I'm not sure we could have gotten through that without them. We were ready for something like that, but...I don't know that we were ready enough."

"Hmmm," Dayang said again. "Maybe. Though I don't think Niceto was really doing anything but keeping himself alive during that particular battle."

"That's still one more target for them, and the other three were fighting plenty. I do believe the boys about the other Shuvelao. I don't think he was in on it. And speaking of the boys...now we have them with us. They're young, but they're also clearly the cream of their particular Somonei crop. Don't underestimate how important that may be."

Ceraen bent down to help hold the bag so the rolled-up tent would go in more easily, taking in a deep breath before speaking. "God, those two. I mean sure we need all the help we can get, but...going into what looks like may be a serious fight with a couple of traumatized kids? Part of me kind of wants to just give them both a hug and send them off to learn about normal life for a year or three. Get them some decent counseling, let them watch a few echoplays, read some books, maybe take a visit to the Deisiindr."

Pai moved her head from side to side in that oddly fascinating way Dayang had seen in a few other people of Nainadion extraction. "I don't disagree in principle, but I also think they're old enough, and gods know have been through enough, to have the right to their own decisions. They've chosen to come with us. We're not kidnapping them, or trying to control them with guilt and obligation the way the Presilyo would. How old were you when you left home, Dayang?"

She sighed. "About their age, as you damn well know. And yes, I'd fought before too. But a lot of that choice was more or less made for me, as you also damn well know."

"Well," Paid said. "No one ever makes their own choices completely, you know? We all make what we can of what we're given. No different for them. And they may be traumatized, but that's pretty well a given for anyone who does real fighting, yes? At least we know they can handle it. We're doing something that has to be done, and someone has got to do it. They've volunteered. They're not going in blind."

Ceraen ran her foot over the sooty soil that had been disturbed by Dayang's tent. "And we're absolutely sure we can trust them? I hate to even bring that up after all we've been through together...all *they've* been through...but it might be more than just our lives on the line." She frowned, stepped back, gave Dayang an apologetic almost-smile. "I suppose I don't have to tell *you* that. I'm sorry. This whole situation just sucks."

Pai gave a slow nod. "Yes, it does suck. But also yes, I think we can trust them. That fight between them and Niceto, that was real, I'm sure of it as I am of anything. Maybe they don't know where they stand, exactly, now that their mentors are gone, maybe it will take them a few years, gods know it would me, before they have that all down. But in this thing, this mad mission we have to finish, I'm sure as I can be they will stand with us. Fight with us."

Dayang thought about that as she tightened and double-checked the straps of her pack. "It's going to have to be good enough. But for what it's worth, I agree with you. I spoke with Sanyago while we were both on watch. He seems as sincere as anyone I've ever met. Not that I don't think he's capable of deceit, I'm guessing anyone growing up the way those two did would have to learn to lie plenty well. But I don't think he was lying to me. That level of naiveté seems like it would be spectacularly difficult to fake and...I don't know. I just feel sure, or sure enough."

"Well then," Paid said, and that crooked smile spread out fully over her warm, weathered face. "I guess the 'sure enoughs' have it. We'd better get going. Too much time deciding and decisions will be made for us, yes?"

Dayang sighed, and hefted her pack. "Yeah. God willing, they haven't been already. Staafaen! Sanyago! We're ready. It's time. Here's how we'll go."

They kept silence as they moved out, Pai scouting a few meters ahead, Dayang leading a diamond formation with Ceraen and Sanyago behind to either side and Staafaen at the rear. It was too much silence. Nothing moved in the ruins, at least above-ground, and nothing growing could break through the heavy layer of carbon.

Where could such a heavy coat of the stuff have come from? The Earthseed was big but was scattered pretty evenly except for a few large chunks...and the Siinlan.

She got at least a partial answer when something crunched under her boot and she looked to see that it was a blackened human skull. And now that she had seen it, she saw more, every sort of bone, large and small. Human, dog, a few strange remnants of Abwaild monsters.

But mostly human. And as they left the outskirts, the sheer scale of the city that had once been here started to dawn on her, the height of the buildings, rivaling pictures she'd seen of Old Earth's great mechanized cities.

How many millions lived here?

She'd have to ask Ceraen. Later. She didn't want to know right now.

Maybe the better question is how many died?

But that was a stupid question, because the answer was all of them.

You know exactly what you're walking on. Exactly what you slept on, last night.

She wished she could talk, break sound discipline. Or that they'd encounter something besides ruins and more ruins, however interesting or evocative parts of them might be. Because she had enough evocation in her head, right now.

But she couldn't, and they didn't, not for kilometer after kilometer.

They reached their destination at the eastern edge, and turned to follow the bearing that pointed back toward that awful chamber back in Salía, that place of happening for all those things she wasn't sure she'd ever get fully settled in her mind.

Black carbon. Blue sky. Yellow sun. Skulls unseen by internal consensus. Massive broken shapes of human purpose and hopes made moot. All the way to the horizon, where the horizon could be seen.

Pai signaled a halt. The rest of the group stopped just behind her. She beckoned them closer.

"Group up ahead and to the right," she whispered. "Four, all Haeliiy. Almost certainly not Promiseguard, two of them are a Pircaat and a Cropr."

"Did they spot you?" Dayang whispered back.

"Maybe," Pai said. "I think we should talk to them. They had the look of people who have been out on their current expedition for some time."

Dayang nodded. "Sanyago, you go out ahead. Start the conversation."

Sanyago blinked. "Me? Why?"

"Because you're charming and not very threatening," she whispered.

He seemed to weigh whether to be pleased or insulted, then just shrugged, stood up straight, and started walking. They followed.

Sanyago stopped suddenly, shook his head. "Look, we just came to talk. Yeah, we're here in the ruins looking for a fight, but I don't think it's with you."

Dayang reached for her mace, sensing them now on all four sides. Sanyago turned with his strange, effortless speed and laid a gentle hand on her forearm.

"Please?" he said, and his light brown eyes were smiling. Dayang frowned, but let her hand drift away from the weapon.

"What do you want to talk about?" A silky voice, feline and female, Fathom-scattered so it was impossible to pinpoint.

"People with no business in these ruins," Sanyago said. "Politics rather than profit, dressed up in holy robes. Sound familiar? If not, we'd be happy to be on our way. We don't want a fight, it wouldn't do any of us any good in the end." His posture remained relaxed, hand kept ready but not still away from his sword. The Fathom was weighted but calm in his presence.

"Alright," came another voice, a man this time, and all four of the group came as well, out from behind walls and rubble and crevices no human could ever hope to navigate.

"Hi then," said the voice again. Its owner was human, medium-sized, not yet nearing middle age, armed with a longsword and wearing practical, nondescript chainmail armor. He smiled, closed-mouth, only just touching the hazel eyes set in his russet-brown face. Another man came to stand beside him, big, pale, blue-eyed, wearing a two-handed sword on his back and spikes on the plates of his armor.

"I'm Zeivier," said the smaller man, and gestured beside him. "This is Maacs." A pure-white female Lingmao circled round Dayang's group to sit next to Maacs, inclining her head. "That's Aanh, and this..." he cocked his head toward the Caustland Crow landing on Maacs' shoulder, "...is Pitr."

"Sanyago. Nice to meet you all. The tall one is my brother Staafaen. Ranger Pai, with the staff, Dayang Marchadesch, with the shield, and Ceraen Wiilqaems, our Praedhc scholar." He bowed slightly, still smiling.

"Nice to meet you too, I'm sure," Zeivier said. "We're the Knights of the Round Dollar. We're here for the same reasons most parties are. You, though, you sound like you're on a mission." He stood looking at them a moment. "We might be able to help, but we don't work for free. Give me a moment to confer with my colleagues?"

"Of course," Sanyago said with a broad smile. The Knights huddled, put up the expected eavesdropping ward, and after a few minutes seemed to have come to some agreement.

"Okay," Zeivier said. "Just to be absolutely sure we're all on the same page. You're talking about the Carver bastards holed up in one of the larger ruins, right?"

Sanyago, to his credit, didn't miss a beat on hearing this. "That's them. You've run into them before?"

"Killed a couple of 'em," Maacs said. "Aanh here has a thing about Carvers. The Presilyo atrocity offended her on a personal level."

"Killing children," Aanh said, and hissed. "Unacceptable behavior, no matter the fight. God knows I'm no pacifist, but I wouldn't hurt a kid."

"I...okay," Sanyago said, missing several beats now.

Aanh cocked her head, then padded forward. Sanyago held his ground, looking unsure. She came right up to him, stretched up on her hind legs, big paws on his chest, looking straight into his eyes. The Fathom was quiet, and nothing about her seemed threatening at the moment, but Sanyago seemed utterly frozen. It occurred to Dayang that he'd probably never been this close to a Lingmao in his life.

Staafaen walked up beside Sanyago, caught Aanh's attention. "We were there," he said quietly. "We saw it. Sanyago had to fight one of the attackers when he was just a kid. He doesn't like to talk about it. Please let it be."

Aanh's big blue eyes went wide and somehow soft, ears dropping, and she patted Sanyago's chest gently with a paw before returning to all fours and sitting herself down about a meter away. "I'm sorry," she said.

Pitr ruffled his wings. "Left the Presilyo when you came of age? Those aren't the blue robes of a working Somonei."

"Not exactly," Sanyago said, visibly recovering. "That's a long story we don't have time for. What's your proposal?"

Zeivier took in a deep breath and let it out all at once. "Right. Business. Pretty simple. You're welcome to whatever little artifact it is they went through all this trouble to locate. I assume you'll grab it and leave. We want the right to the rest of the site's loot, once the Carvers have been cleaned out."

"Wait," Dayang said, frowning and stepping forward. " 'Little' artifact? Let's make sure we're talking about the same thing. We think they're looking for a site as much as an object. Pedestal, in a niche, two sort of doorways on the walls? Deep under the site?"

Pitr cawed out a laugh and shook his head. "I got a good look at the binding they followed from out in Earthmarch to find the thing. Since they took possession, they've been trying all sorts of Fathom-assays on it, makes it pretty easy to track now that I know the signature. It's small enough for someone to wave around. Not deep, either, they have it just below ground level."

Dayang looked at the others, and they looked at her. Ceraen spoke up. "Wait...shit. I think I might know what it is. The pedestal had a hole in the top, remember? The site wasn't fully active, it only connected to itself, so there must be something to..." her eyes went wide, dark face draining grey. "We have to go. If they've found some sort of key we can't let them take it back to Earthmarch."

"That urgent, huh?" Maacs said, and pulled the big sword off his back. "Well, it happens. Tell you what. They only have one way in and out, far as we can tell. We'll attack the outer guards, lure out a few more, meanwhile you slip in past the fight, find what you're looking for. No one'll get out past us. We're good at that."

This is happening much too fast, but then I guess it always does, Dayang thought. *Just one last thing before it all goes to madness.* "Give us a moment to confer, now? We'll be quick."

Maacs grunted and rested the big sword on his shoulder. Zeivier made a "go on" gesture with his fingers.

"Time to go on gut feeling," Dayang told the others as they gathered. "Do you trust them?"

"Yes," Sanyago said. "I think they're genuine."

"More than I ever trusted the Shuvelao," Staafaen said.

"They seem like the usual plunder-hungry grave-robbing adventurer bastards," Pai said. "And they're not hiding it. So I say we take their deal."

"I sort of like them," Ceraen said. "What the Hell. We don't know how much time we've got and this is our best option."

"I agree," Dayang said. She waved off the eavesdropping ward. "We're in. Let's go."

The site was only a few minutes' walk to the west—they hadn't been lying about keeping close tabs—and so there wasn't time to do anything but prepare themselves on the way. So they did, careful mantles woven through the Fathom, limbs stretched, weapons checked. Dayang prayed, feeling the spike of adrenaline, calming muscles that wanted to spasm and shake with over-readiness.

She caught bits of prayers from the others as well...what sounded like very old English from Ceraen, invoking Jesus, Ambérico from Sanyago, from which she only managed to pick out the word "Divino"; Pai recited a Manhc mantra toward...some god, she presumed, or even gods plural, which rubbed up uncomfortably against some very emphatic bits of Dayang's own religious education but Hell, that was God's business in the end, not hers.

Nothing at all from Staafaen, but he certainly seemed to be concentrating on *something.* And Dayang didn't know all that much about the specifics of Triune Path worship anyway.

Ready ready ready here it comes and waits for no one at all.

They rounded the corner of a blocky ruin, and Dayang caught just a glimpse before it began: an excavated doorway, surrounded by rubble, flanked by two men dressed in drab expedition clothes and armed with spears.

Zeivier and Maacs made no attempt at stealth, simply charging in at the guards, who barely had time to yell before they were cut down. Dayang held her group back as five more Carvers emerged, one of whom was immediately mauled when Aanh came out of the shadows right on top of him. Two more engaged Zeivier and Maacs, who drew them away from the entrance. Another pair were hit by a dive-bombing Pitr, talons bearing lightning, and chased after him as he flew away.

"NOW!" Dayang cried, and they charged in past the fray toward the entrance. One of the pair chasing Pitr caught on and tried to intercept them, but Dayang shoved him brutally aside with her shield and felt rather than saw the rending in the Fathom as Aanh clawed him to death.

Voices up ahead, speaking Gentic. "What's going on outside? Protect the Ashtiller!"

They burst into a large room. A low table, covered in papers, and also a rough-hewn stand, cradling a strange pale scepter. Three more Carvers in soot-colored robes, spears ready. Two tall women by the table, both unarmed, in plain but heavily-imbued clothing. One, pale, blond and blue-eyed, just looked at the intruders in blank surprise. The other—tan, dark-haired and fierce, launched herself at Dayang with almost no hesitation.

She had just enough time to raise her shield. The woman's fist crashed into it, sending shockwaves through bone and Fathom. Dayang swung her mace but the woman caught the haft and kicked Dayang in the stomach. Heartvein plates flared a tangled red, and Dayang stumbled back, barely managing to keep a grip on her mace. The woman only let go when Staafaen attacked from the side with a harsh cry.

Sanyago had already killed one of the Carver guards, dancing past spear-thrusts to put his sword right through her ribs. Pai was engaged with the other two, staff spinning, fending off both spears at once. Ceraen stood off to the side, hurling glowing greenish bolts at Pai's opponents.

"Maicl!" the dark-haired woman cried. "Take Juliaen and go!"

Another Carver entered from a side chamber, grabbing the blond woman by the arm and pulling her toward the exit as Staafaen was thrown aside, hitting a wall with a heavy thud. Ceraen attacked the newcomer with another silver-green shaft of light. He screamed in defiance as it tore a hole in his dark robes, and struck out rapidly with his halberd, forcing her to parry with her nightstick and retreat.

"Lidia!" the blond woman called.

"Juliaen! Take it and go!' Lidia replied, dodging one of Sanyago's rapid sword-thrusts and striking out with a foot. Sanyago spun away and threw fire at her with his left hand, which she deflected with her palm before coming after Dayang again at an angle meant to force her away from the entrance. Dayang held her ground at first, but this Lidia was the most dangerous human opponent she had ever fought, every blow carrying immense weight through the Fathom, every movement quick and sure, taking advantage of even the tiniest imperfection in Dayang's defense. And defense was all she could manage.

Dayang fell back. It was that or be beaten to death in short order. Lidia advanced, but was forced to deal with Staafaen again. He was faring better now, anticipating her blows, managing precise counters of his own, though still not able to land any attacks. The Carver dragging Juliaen had to pull her back toward the center of the room. She'd snatched the strange scepter off the table, a thin rod with a bulbous top.

"I'm leaving the other way!" Juliaen said, and now she pulled her own bodyguard toward an exit near the back.

"Stop her!" Dayang barked, and found the right angle to slam Lidia in the back with her shield. The woman staggered forward into Staafaen and they went down in a rolling grapple. Sanyago and Pai tried to intercept the fleeing Juliaen, but another four Carvers ran in from side passages, leaving them to contend with a pair of opponents each. Juliaen and her bodyguard went through the threshold and disappeared round a turn.

Lidia leapt off Staafaen and ran to cover Juliaen's exit. Sanyago attempted to intercept her by himself and was knocked aside by a vicious backhand.

Pai knocked one Carver senseless with a rapid spin of her staff, parried the other's spear. Ceraen threw a tangled hindering spell at Lidia's back, but the woman leapt to let it pass under her, reached the exit, and turned around, breathing hard. Dayang hurried forward, jumping up onto the table rather than go around. Sanyago killed again. Pai dispatched another Carver.

Lidia roared, and the Fathom pulsed out hard, knocking them all back.

"I am the High Winnow of the true Triune Path," she growled, Fathom-amplified to rumble the air. Five more Carvers streamed in from all sides. "You will go no further. The Divine demands it."

It became an utter melee. Dayang spared only the smallest thought to wonder just how many Carvers were in this place. She struck, dodged, parried. Blades glanced off her shield and armor at precisely presented angles. Blood dripped off her mace as a woman collapsed with a caved-in skull. Dayang had never killed a person before, not with her own hands and weapon. There would be time to think about that later.

It went on for what felt like an hour, but must have been minutes at the most. She lost track of how many more Carvers they killed. Ten? Twelve? Lidia sent Staafaen stumbling backward with a precise hip-kick. Sanyago moved in to attack in his stead, alone. He went down almost immediately, resilience spent, one rib cracked by a powerful palm-heel blow. Dayang growled. *Dammit, I tried to tell him about fighting alone, hope this kind of painful lesson works better.* She swatted a Carver spear aside with her shield.

Staafaen re-engaged Lidia with a hoarse cry of anger and frustration, but was still overmatched—though she couldn't seem to land any attack on him either, every strike and combination anticipated and countered. Dayang crushed a Carver's rib-cage almost to his spine

oh God the smell oh God the look in his eyes the more than just blood no not now later

and moved to help, but couldn't find a good angle of attack with Lidia standing in the exit threshold.

But Pai could. As Ceraen fended off one more Carver, the Staffguard ranger shifted her staff and fired arrow after arrow, carefully aimed at nearly point-blank range. Lidia managed to dodge and deflect, until she didn't. One hit. Two hits. A third managed to dig slightly into her side.

Sanyago stood, wincing, and flicked a heavy dart out at her just as Staafaen parried a blow. She had to cut her counterattack short in order to pluck it from the air.

On seeing her distraction and depleted resilience Staafaen roared, reached out, grabbed her behind the neck with his left hand and slammed his right fist just below her ribs. The Fathom crackled with the shattering force of the blow.

Lidia fell to her knees, coughed, tried to breathe, coughed again. Blood. More blood. She tried to speak, but died instead.

Staafaen staggered back, hand to his forehead, then simply collapsed down onto his ass. Sanyago rushed to help him, but Staafaen shook his head. "No. Go catch her. I saw...I see everything. Her whole life. I need...I need a moment. Go."

Dayang looked at him, then at the exit. Understanding could come later. "Sanyago, stay with him. We'll go."

Staafaen looked like he might want to argue, but she didn't care. She beckoned Pai and Ceraen, and they ran.

The corridor became a staircase, spiraling down. This site had apparently decided to take the direct route rather than rely on natural Abwaild corridors. Or maybe the other had stairs once, and they'd collapsed. Either way, they managed in minutes a depth that had taken hours back at the Salían site, and soon were standing in a familiar four-sided chamber. Niche at the back, pedestal in its center, strange colorless spaces left and right.

Empty.

"Oh no," Ceraen said. "You feel that?"

Dayang did. Of course she did. Just an echo now, but a strong one, stretching far away, out of the Caustlands maybe. No, almost certainly. God, it felt awful, like a long queasy string. "She used it. That's what the scepter was for, to open the connection. She went through. Took it with her. And she didn't hesitate. We weren't even close to catching her."

Ceraen nodded slowly. "If she's still alive...if she's still the same...if she made it...this is..."

"God DAMN it," Dayang growled. "Whatever happened, the artifact's gone, and we can't follow. Not that I'd be willing to try. That's an insane risk."

"At least we stopped them using this place for now," Pai said. "Dayang, that's not a small victory. You can't always win them all at once. In fact you almost never can."

Dayang sighed. Huffed, really, squaring her shoulders before letting out all her breath. Then she straightened up again. "Okay. Nothing we can do right now. Let's go collect the boys, make sure Staafaen is okay. We've all earned some rest. And we have a lot to talk about."

She stared at the chamber a moment longer, shuddered, then turned and began the suddenly very long trudge up the staircase. When they got back to the room with the table, Staafaen was seated at it, head in his hands, staring at nothing. Sanyago stood behind him, hand on his shoulder, looking concerned.

"She got away," Dayang said, almost a sigh. "Through the doorway.

She used that scepter she took off the table to open it up somehow. We never had a chance of stopping her, not with Lidia covering her exit."

Sanyago turned, frowning. "That's not good," he said flatly. His gaze swept the room, still a chaos of blood and Carver corpses. It was beginning to stink, too, sweat and shit and copper, mixed with the strange scorched scents of recent Fathom-clashes.

Dayang tried not to look too closely, especially at the bodies she'd been personally responsible for. "It wasn't for nothing, not by a long way. Whatever they had planned for this place, it's not going to happen now. And that Lidia woman is gone, that's a huge blow for them. She was...formidable." *Took all of us to take her down, and even then maybe we were lucky.* The thought made her wince, remembering that kick to the stomach, the punch she'd thought might shatter her shield, all the other blows she'd barely managed to avoid or deflect.

"I saw her," Staafaen spoke up from his chair. "I saw her whole life." He paused, then lifted his head from his hands. "No, that's not quite true. I saw the parts that mattered to her most. I think. But I knew her. Know her, now. I know her, and I killed her." His steel-grey stare was frighteningly blank.

"What did she want, exactly?" Dayang asked gently. She didn't want to think too hard about knowing someone you had killed.

Five. You killed five Carvers today. Five you can never take back, no matter how much it needed doing.

"I don't know. It wasn't like that. I just got...moments. I mean, I saw some of how she came to hate the Presilyo. Things she was angry about, things she carried guilt for. I'm still sorting through all of it. You know that thing they say about how your whole life is supposed to flash before your eyes when you die? I guess hers did, and I saw it. But I don't know how useful any of it really was. I'm just trying to..." he let in a low catching breath, and dropped his head back into his hands.

Sanyago looked at her, squeezed Staafaen's shoulder, shook his head. She remembered the two women standing behind her when Ceraen spoke.

"We'll leave him be, Sanyago." She gestured at the papers on the table, now in serious disarray from the battle. "We've got more than enough information to sort through for now. I'll bet at least some of it will turn out plenty useful."

"Where are those adventurers at?" Pai asked.

"They're guarding the entrance against any patrols that might come back," Sanyago said.

"How do you know?"

Sanyago laughed. It didn't hold much humor. "Because they fought one while you were down there. Three more dead Carvers, far as I could tell from the aftershocks in the Holy Fathom."

"We should call them in," Dayang said. "I doubt there's more than one patrol out at a time, and even if there is it wouldn't stand much chance if it came back now."

"Agreed," Pai said, and strode out the door. Ceraen sat down and began sorting through papers. *Her way of distracting herself, I guess,* Dayang thought.

She walked around the table to stand by the door and wait, but Pai walked through it almost immediately, followed by all four of the 'Knights of the Round Dollar.' Zeivier's eyes widened as he looked round the room. The rest of them went straight for the bodies, and Dayang suppressed a grimace of distaste. *The spoils are no uglier than the battle, and we're the ones who fought that. Part of the price for their help, anyway. Still though. Looting the dead, I don't know.*

"Looks like you had one Hell of a fight," Zeivier said. "And you're all still standing. That's always a good day."

Sanyago glared at him. Zeivier raised his eyebrows. "My apologies, I suppose. Is your friend there hurt?"

"Not exactly," Sanyago said. "He's not...really used to this yet. Neither of us are." *And there's no need to tell them more than that. Glad he's showing some discretion.*

Zeivier's expression softened. "Right, of course. You're very young. I remember my first real fight too. It does get easier. I don't know if that's a consolation or not."

Maacs strode over, carrying a bag that clanked with coins and trinkets. "It probably isn't. Not everyone's cut out for this kind of life, Zeivier," he said, and leaned in to kiss the smaller man lightly on the lips. Sanyago stared. *Shock? No, not if half the stories I've heard about goings-on in monasteries are true. Something else.*

She had seen such things herself, a few times from adventurers in Kualabu, plenty of times in the Army—and here and there in the town itself. A few were even open about it; not all of Kualabu's residents were

Muslim, and the government was secular at least in theory, there were civil laws against it. Still highly forbidden according to most scholars of the religious law, of course...but so was plenty of what she'd got up to herself, with men. Not the time to worry about that now.

"No," she said, stepping around to the table to lean back against it, and incidentally block their view of the still-staring Sanyago. "I don't suppose they are. I do want to thank you for your help. It could have gone much worse."

Zeivier cocked his head. "To be honest, Sergeant Marchadesch, I'm not sure how it could have gone much better. What happened?"

"One of them got away. With what we're pretty sure was the object they were searching for."

Zeivier frowned, looking back at the entrance. "Got away how? Is there a secret tunnel we didn't know about?"

"Sort of. Worse than that, really. I'll let our Praedhc scholar explain."

Ceraen looked up from the papers she was sorting, a grim expression on her face. "I'm afraid I've got worse than that, even. From what I can tell here, the tests they were running? They found another sort of resonance in the scepter. I don't think they understood it, but it's probably only a matter of time since they've still got the damned thing."

"What do you mean, another sort of resonance?" Dayang asked slowly.

"One I've only seen from the researchers of the Nowhere Watch," Ceraen said.

Pai turned sharply and leaned over the table, eyes wide, features drained; mahogany gone to ash. "The Black Fence?"

Ceraen shook her head. "No. Sorry, I have to say it. Not from the Black Fence itself. From behind it."

Chapter 33

Yet man is born unto trouble, as the sparks fly upward.

- *Hebrew Ketuvim,* Job 5:7
  King James Translation, 1611 CE

Borih'Sath Ruin-Sprawl, Tenggara, The Caustlands, 355 SE

Laris Lozada sat on the floor by a low table as people moved and spoke around him, seeing to themselves, dealing with the dead. His brother, new friends, even newer friends, almost strangers, barely known.

Lidia Almeida sat with him. He had only a hazy view of her, and anyway she was no ghost, not present in that sense, but who she *had* been was lodged into his mind, splintered into him with the aftermath of his killing blow. He saw her only as she had seen herself, and then only dimly, because it was not all of her.

Still it was enough. Maybe too much. Certainly more than he wanted, *any* of it was more than he wanted, nothing he could ever have expected. With that man, all those years before, the killer-of-children Laris had managed to impale on his own intentions, with him it had been nothing like this. Because Laris hadn't killed him, not really, only held up a sort of...mirror.

Lidia, though. He'd killed her, no mistake, no ambiguity, had felt it, stood there still caught in the dancing web of her intentions, in-tune, enmeshed, while her mind slipped away because the organs his fist-in-Fathom had crushed could no longer sustain her, had pooled away all the necessary blood.

He didn't want to think about that, but felt he should; he had done it, after all, taken a life, moved with clear intent—and for that matter didn't regret it in the end, or at least in any end so far, however much he might abhor its reality. To look away from what was, to set it aside, that shouldn't be done, reality was a thing to be faced, understood, studied and thought upon. He hated when the teachers and priests at the Presilyo did that, tried to twist themselves around hard fact, pass by the observable with eyes averted, he always had. He wouldn't do it himself.

But maybe he shouldn't look too close, too long, not right now, not so soon. He would grant himself that, would remember some things Father Kuwat had said, in those hard days and months and years after Laris had left another person dead on the ground, another person who would have killed him and who was very far gone but still, still...and this was not where his mind should be, where it had been going; Father Kuwat had talked about Laris being kind to himself, letting himself feel, seeing that as okay, but also letting go, not to clutch what he felt too close as though it were a price to be paid or a burden only he could, only he *must,* bear.

So he wouldn't dwell on her death, not for now, not more than he already had. Instead he would dwell on who she had been, because it was important, could mean the difference in so much, and also because here she was, sitting with him, shattered into a thousand of her most important pieces within his mind.

The pieces were in something like order, or maybe he just sorted them that way without thinking:

Staring up at the stern-faced nun and felt such an immensity of fear and grief and confusion that she could not even let it out in the form of tears. "This will be your home now," the woman said, but home felt like it could never be a possibility again.

Another novice, sprawled in the manicured sand, looking up at her. Lidia felt her own arm, still extended from the blow, the power of mastering what she had learned.

Her first glimpse of the monks, the stirrings that had caused, the dreams at night, the vague guilt connected to reluctant teachings given by red-faced nuns and priestesses.

The shy, handsome face of the first boy she ever kissed, the thrill and fear of the forbidden, the smell of nervous sweat and sawdust, trysting at night in a Presilyo building undergoing renovations during the day.

Graduation. Pride, and burning nerves, and the great open-air stretch of Divine-knows-what stretching along her future.

War. And death. And skirmish, and killing. Blood on the hands, cleaned off the boots, all a blur, much it pressed down, shunted aside, never looked at directly, ancient ancient avoided anguishes. Monsters and women and men snuffed out by one of the most talented Somonei of her generation.

Heartbreak. Personal, spiritual. Political, even, though that word buzzed around the corners of consciousness, never quite let fully into any inner space. The accumulated weight of ten thousand disappointments and disillusionments.

The face of her favorite teacher, weeping, looking away, head and shoulders shaking, unable to face the decision her beloved pupil had made. The wrenching force of each step away from the Presilyo, that final time, pulling away everything she had been, had known, doing it anyway, step and tear and step and tear, all of it gone, leaving her bleeding and new.

Standing on the doorstep of her new family's home, the Carvers that would now take her in, shivering in a way she hadn't done since the preparing for her very first battles.

Pride in her new and rising place, gratitude for the opportunity to serve. Secret shameful joy in the power and respect it brought.

Horror and disgust held in as she stood before fellow former Somonei so far gone into…but they must…but they could still…

Kneeling over a woman, the spreading stain of her blood in the carpet, feeling every gushing drop somewhere deep.

Standing in front of a cell, a tall woman behind bars, pale hands clasped in front of her. Blue eyes that burned, blond hair bound carelessly back.

ABOMINATIONS UPON THE ABOMINABLE. Here, Laris could only glimpse, and he recoiled, and wavered where he sat, and hoped no one saw.

Shadowed figures attacking from trees, battle, death, but not hers.

A woman clad in heartvein armor, features vague behind a translucent faceplate. A mace, a shield. Victory, but not enough, so many foes so fast.

A tall young man, features grave, grey eyes flashing out from dark skin. Victory again, then standstill, frustration, too many, too many, no, no, Juliaen is gone thank the Divine but so is my, my, my all of it, I cannot take

a monstrous blow
no breath
no speech
PAIN
that face, those eyes, looking down, hand on her shoulder
cannot
but
relief and

and

release

Laris bent forward, coughing, gasping, grabbed at the edge of the table, surged to his feet. The others turned to stare.

"I saw…so much," he rasped. "But the worst of it, that I could only glimpse."

They went on staring.

"I think we've stopped them for now," he said. Sanyago came over, helped steady him. Laris breathed in deep.

"We've stopped them for now," he said, more confidence this time, regaining some of his calm. "I think it will take them a while to recover, move forward. But they will. And meanwhile…we're going to have a lot to do. I don't think…"

He sighed, took in another deep breath, aware of all their eyes, watching him, nervous from it, grateful for it. "I don't think this is anywhere near the end of it."

After

Piolo Marchadesch heard the door chime and stood up to stretch, setting aside his magazine and mug of tea. Khadija looked up from her own reading and cocked an eyebrow. "Expecting someone this late?"

He grunted. "No. Bad news, I'm guessing. Don't wait up for me if I'm not back right away."

She made a small noise of assent, already re-absorbed in her book.

He descended the stairs, thinking thoughts of lost inventory and deals gone bust. He avoided looking at the family echoframes in the hall and entry, not wanting to pile old worries on top of his current ones. "Be right there," he called once the front door came in view.

God willing the Surabaru caravan made it safe, some of those guards weren't quite—

He opened the door, and stared. He saw two young men in plain robes, one small and brown, one tall and black. Two women behind them, one with a long staff, but now he was only really seeing the figure in front. Almost exactly his height, clad in heartvein plate, helmet under one arm. She smiled, crinkling the corners of large dark eyes.

"Hello Father."

Glossary

Abwaild
(*AB-wild)* Term describing everything outside the Caustlands, apart from the territory of the Sovereign Nations to the northeast. Inhabited by the Praedhc (also called Pelos, Antepas, Tuzhu, and Dezya in various other Fallen languages.)

Abwarren
The extensive system of tunnels and caverns beneath the surface of Solace.

Aldonza
Capital city of Salía, one of the six Caustland States.

Ambérico
One of the two major languages of Salía, the other being Gentic.

Antepas
Ambérico term for the Praedhc (see also Pelos, Antepas, Tuzhu, Dezya)

Ashlit Mire
The embertree bog that lines the inner and outer banks of the Gyring Ash. Part of the Siinlan.

Auraramad
The northernmost Caustland State. Very linguistically diverse, though FusHa is the most widely spoken language. Contains the Zulanar mountain range, which has some Praedhc tribes on its northern slopes.

Basa
A family of languages spoken mainly in Tenggara. While there is a "Standard Basa" in widespread use, the individual "native" dialects vary in their mutual intelligibility.

Basa Mala
One of the major Basa dialects.

Basa Taga
Another of the Basa dialects.

The Black Fence
A ring of giant obsidian shards in Salía. Guarded by the Nowhere Watch.

Carvers
Dissident sect of the Triune Path. One of the Sovereign Nation Compacts. Term themselves the "only true Michyeros."

The Caustlands
The circular territory where most of the Fallen reside. Its borders are defined by the Siinlan, through which the Gyring Ash flows. Contains the six Caustland States (Tenggara, Salía, Nainadion, Auraramad, Zhon Han, and the United Admiralty) whose own boundaries are defined by five major rivers along with the Wave-Rest Berm (which forms a smaller circle in the center of the Caustlands.)

Cenicebu
Capital city of Tenggara, one of the six Caustland States.

Common
Primary language Zhon Han, central of the six Caustland States. Also highly influential in Tenggara.

Cropr
Gentic term for a Caustland Crow. See also Corvaso.

The Deisiindr
(*DEI-sin-der*) Independent city-state located within the borders of Tenggara.

Eychi
Ambérico term for a person who uses the Fathom for martial purposes. See also Haeliiy, Wira, Xiake.

Fallen

Term used to describe the peoples, flora, and fauna of the Caustlands and Sovereign Nations.

The Fathom

Commonly conceived as a "layer" situated beneath ordinary reality, though this is a massive oversimplification. Consciously accessible with training.

Gatoparlo

Ambérico term for a Caustland Cat. See also Pircaat, Lingmao.

Gentic

The de facto lingua franca of the Caustlands, with a great many native speakers in Salía.

The Gyring Ash

Strange sludge-river that flows clockwise around the edge of the Caustlands, through the middle of the Siinlan. Surrounded on both banks by the Ashlit Mire.

Haeliiy

(*HELL-lith*) Gentic term for a person who uses the Fathom for martial purposes. See also Wira, Eychis, Xiake.

Lingmao

Term in Common for a Caustland Cat. Also used as a loanword in Basa. See also Pircaat, Gatoparlo.

Manhc

(*MAN-uk*) Most widely-spoken language in Nainadion.

Michyero

Follower of the Triune Path faith.

Nikoka

Protectorate of Tenggara, located on its northeast border.

The Nowhere Watch
Special detachment of the Salían Army, tasked with guarding the Black Fence and dealing with other similar concerns.

Pelos
Basa term for the Praedhc. See also Antepas, Dezya, Tuzhu.

Pircaat
(*PIER-kat*) Gentic term for a Caustland Cat. See also Lingmao, Gatoparlo.

Praedhc
(*PRED-uk*) Gentic term for the peoples who inhabit the Abwaild. See also Antepas, Dezya, Pelos, Tuzhu.

The Presilyo Ri'Granha
Home of the Somonei warrior monks and nuns, run by the Triune Path religious sect.

Ragado
Forbidden according to the Triune Path.

Salía
Southwestern Caustland State. Very diverse, but its most widely-spoken languages are Gentic and Ambérico. Contains the Black Fence. Capital is Aldonza.

Saepi
(*SEP-ee)* Gentic term for a person or thing related to the Sovereign Nations, e.g. "Saepi woman" or "Saepi territory."

Silado
Permitted within the Triune Path.

Somonei
Warrior monks and nuns of the Triune Path. Based out of the Presilyo Ri'Granha, an island monastery within the Mindao River that runs between Salía and Tenggara.

The Sovereign Nations
A confederation of Fallen separatist groups located outside the Caustlands, northeast across the Siinlan from the United Admiralty.

Tenggara
Southeastern Caustland State. The various dialects of Basa are its predominant languages. The Deisiindr, a large independent city-state, is located within its borders. Has a protectorate called Nikoka along the eastern part of its border with the United Admiralty. Capital city is Cenicebu.

The Triune Path
Minority religious faith. Adherents are called "Michyeros." Found mostly in Salía, Tenggara, and Zhon Han. Its dissident Carver sect forms one of the Sovereign Nations.

The United Admiralty
Easternmost Caustland State. Is bordered by the Sovereign Nations on the other side of the Siinlan. Official State Language is Qhziic.

Wira
Basa term for a person who uses the Fathom for martial purposes. See also Haeliiy, Eychi, Xiake.

Xiake
Term in Common for a person who uses the Fathom for martial purposes. See also Eychi, Haeliiy, Wira.

Zhon Han
Central Caustland State. Border defined by the Wave-Rest Berm, a huge circular ridge. The five major Caustland rivers meet around the island on which the capital city Wu Jian is located.

ABOUT THE AUTHOR

Sterling Magleby lives in Salt Lake City, Utah with his wife Carolina. Besides the obvious reading and writing, he enjoys gaming, learning, languages, and large quantities of tea.

Made in the USA
Monee, IL
06 July 2020